PRAISE FOR PHILIPPA GREGORY:

'A master storyteller . . . Gregory captures the intrigue and suspense of life at the Tudor court in vivid detail' *Daily Express*

'A cleverly wrought political novel. In introducing Parr to a new audience, Gregory has done the first lady of English letters something of a favour' *Sunday Telegraph*

'Gregory dramatizes the story of a reluctant royal wife negotiating the anxious, dangerous years of her marriage . . . written with her usual authority and capacity for great drama' *Sunday Times*

'The contemporary mistress of historical crime' **Kate Mosse**

'Popular historical fiction at its finest, immaculately researched and superbly told' *The Times*

'Philippa Gregory has another hit on her hands with this gripping page-turner. Her novel simplifies and humanises the complex politics of the period' *Sunday Times*

'Popular history at its best' *Daily Mail*

'History comes gloriously alive as Elizabeth Woodville seduces and marries Yorkist King Edward IV' *Daily Mirror*

'Philippa Gregory is truly the mistress of the historical novel. It would be hard to make history more entertaining, lively or engaging' *Sunday Express*

*By the same author*

*History*

The Women of the Cousins' War: The Duchess, The Queen and the King's Mother

*The Plantagenet and Tudor Novels*

The Lady of the Rivers
The Red Queen
The White Queen
The Kingmaker's Daughter
The White Princess
The Constant Princess
The King's Curse
The Other Boleyn Girl
The Boleyn Inheritance
The Taming of the Queen
The Queen's Fool
The Virgin's Lover
The Other Queen

*Order of Darkness Series*

Changeling
Stormbringers
Fools' Gold

*The Wideacre Trilogy*

Wideacre
The Favoured Child
Meridon

*The Tradescants*

Earthly Joys
Virgin Earth

*Modern Novels*

Alice Hartley's Happiness
Perfectly Correct
The Little House
Zelda's Cut

*Short Stories*

Bread and Chocolate

*Other Historical Novels*

The Wise Woman
Fallen Skies
A Respectable Trade

# THREE SISTERS, THREE QUEENS

PHILIPPA GREGORY

SIMON & SCHUSTER

London · New York · Sydney · Toronto · New Delhi

A CBS COMPANY

First published in Great Britain by Simon & Schuster UK Ltd, 2016
This edition published by Simon & Schuster UK Ltd, 2017
A CBS COMPANY



5 7 9 10 8 6 4

Simon & Schuster UK Ltd
1st Floor
222 Gray's Inn Road
London WC1X 8HB

www.simonandschuster.co.uk

Simon & Schuster Australia, Sydney
Simon & Schuster India, New Delhi

A CIP catalogue record for this book
is available from the British Library

B Format ISBN: 978-1-4711-3303-9
A Format ISBN: 978-1-4711-5946-6
eBook ISBN: 978-1-4711-3304-6



Typeset in Plantin by M Rules
Printed and bound by CPI Group (UK) Ltd, Croydon, CR0 4YY

Simon & Schuster UK Ltd are committed to sourcing paper
that is made from wood grown in sustainable forests and support the Forest
Stewardship Council, the leading international forest certification organisation.
Our books displaying the FSC logo are printed on FSC certified paper.

For Anthony

# THE HOUSE OF TUDOR IN 1501

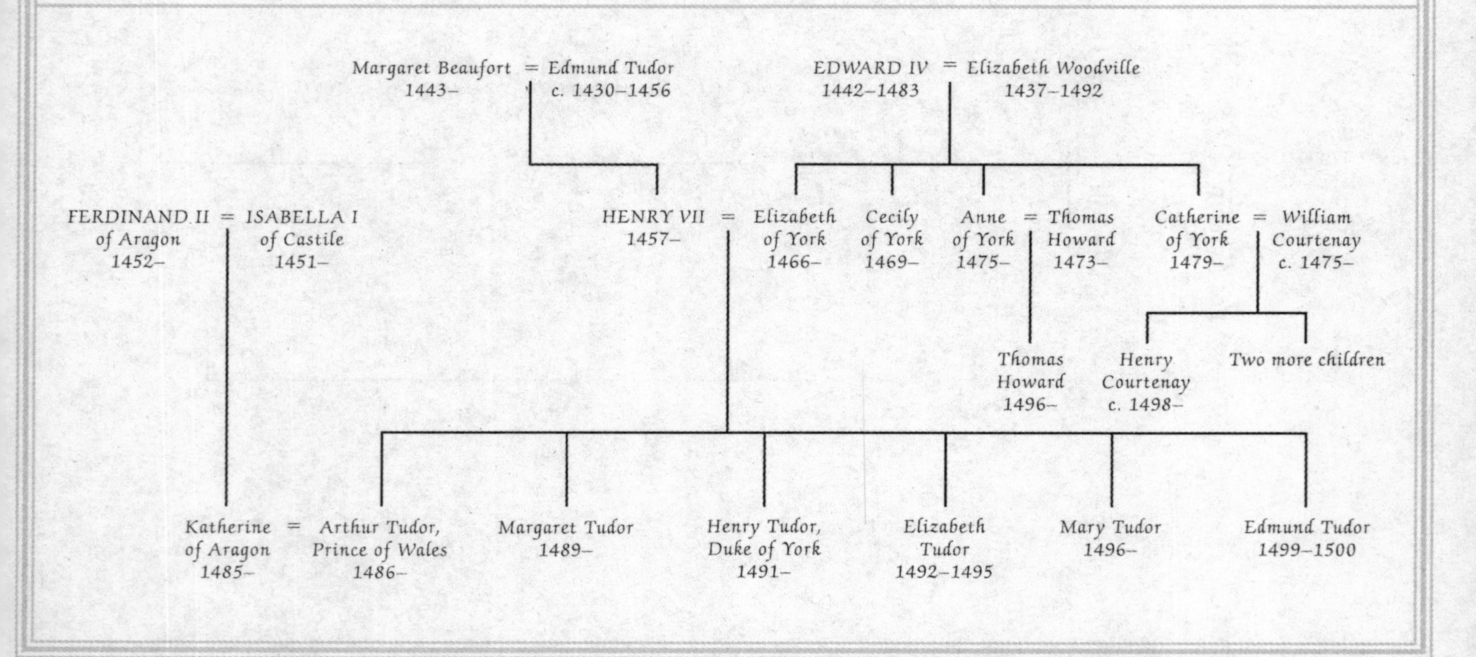

# The House of Stewart in 1501

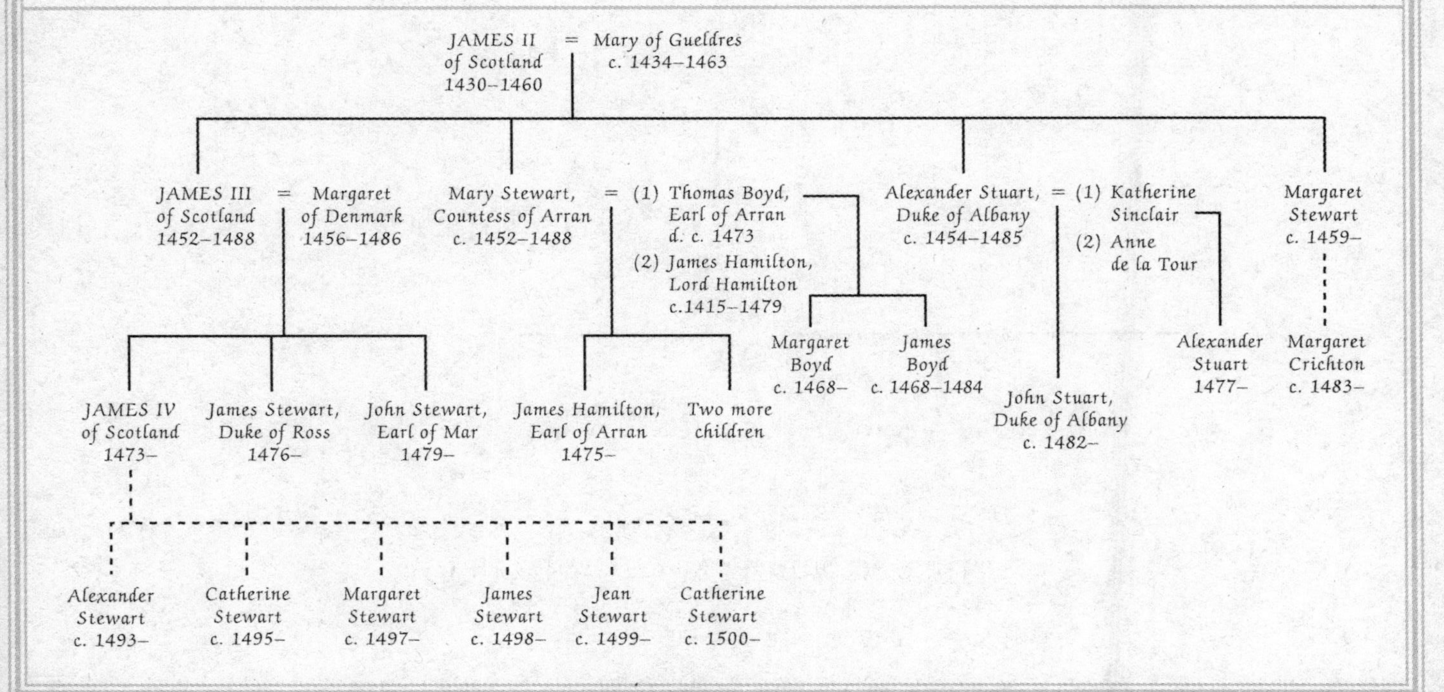

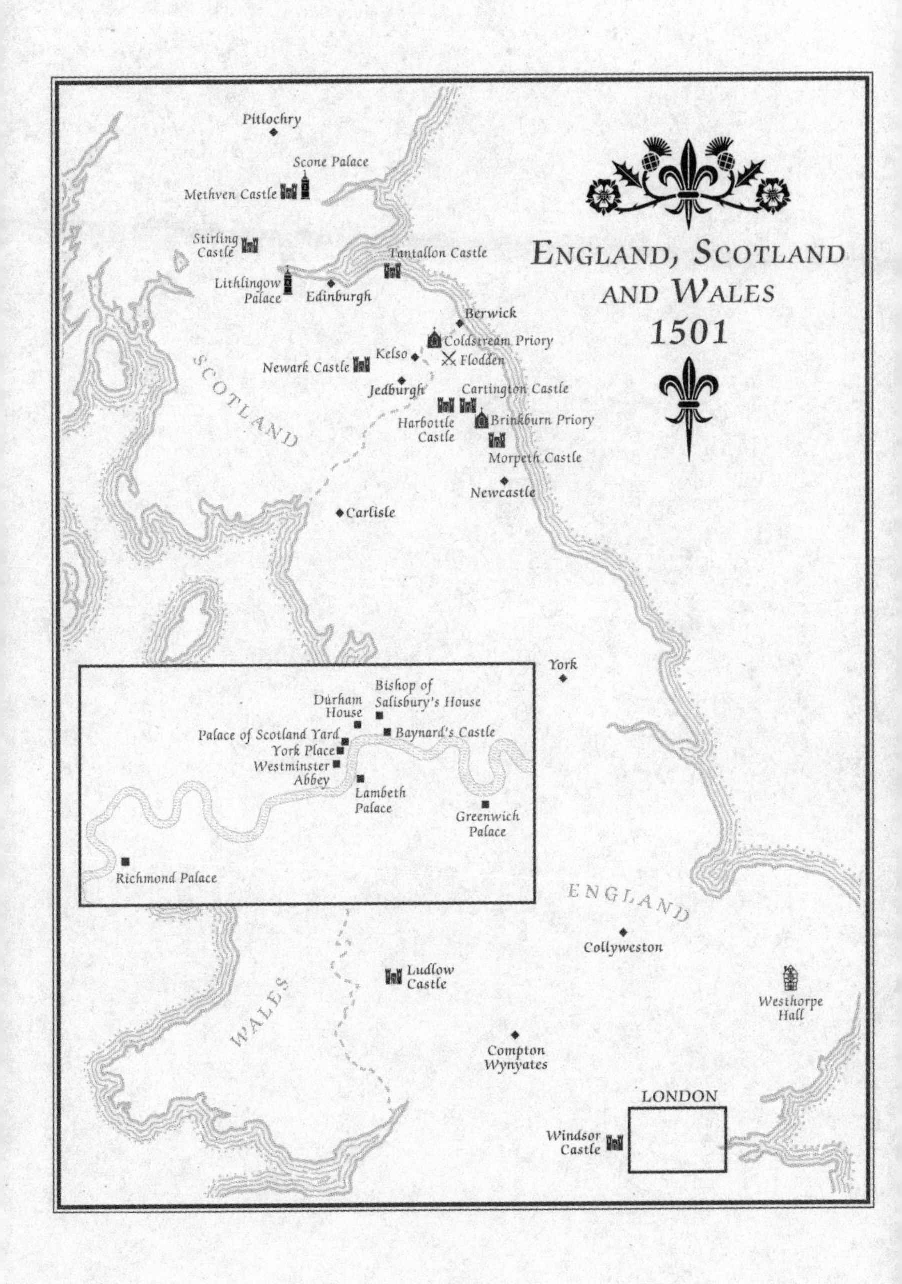
England, Scotland and Wales
1501
Pitlochry
Scone Palace
Methven Castle
Stirling Castle
Tantallon Castle
Lithlingow Palace
Edinburgh
Berwick
Coldstream Priory
Kelso
Flodden
Newark Castle
Scotland
Jedburgh
Cartington Castle
Harbottle Castle
Brinkburn Priory
Morpeth Castle
Newcastle
Carlisle
York
Bishop of Salisbury's House
Durham House
Palace of Scotland Yard
Baynard's Castle
York Place
Westminster Abbey
Lambeth Palace
Greenwich Palace
Richmond Palace
England
Collyweston
Ludlow Castle
Westhorpe Hall
Wales
Compton Wynyates
London
Windsor Castle

# BAYNARD'S CASTLE, LONDON, ENGLAND, NOVEMBER 1501

I am to wear white and green, as a Tudor princess. Really, I think of myself as the one and only Tudor princess, for my sister, Mary, is too young to do more than be brought in by her nurse at supper time, and taken out again. I make sure Mary's nursemaids are quite clear that she is to be shown to our new sister-in-law, and then go. There is no profit in letting her sit up at the table, or gorge on crystallised plums. Rich things make her sick and if she gets tired she will bawl. She is only five years old, far too young for state occasions. Unlike me; I am all but twelve. I have to play my part in the wedding; it would not be complete without me. My lady grandmother, the king's mother, said so herself.

Then she said something that I couldn't quite hear, but I know that the Scots lords will be watching me to see if I look strong and grown-up enough to be married at once. I am sure I am. Everyone says that I am a bonny girl, stocky as a Welsh pony, healthy as a milkmaid, fair, like my younger brother Harry, with big blue eyes.

'You'll be next,' she says to me with a smile. 'They say that one wedding begets another.'

'I won't have to travel as far as Princess Katherine,' I say. 'I'll come home on visits.'

'You will.' My lady grandmother's promise makes it a certainty. 'You are marrying our neighbour, and you will make him our good friend and ally.'

Princess Katherine had to come all the way from Spain, miles and miles away. Since we are quarrelling with France, she had to come by sea, and there were terrible storms and she was nearly wrecked. When I go to Scotland to marry the king, it will be a great procession from Westminster to Edinburgh of nearly four hundred miles. I shan't go by sea, I won't arrive sick and sopping wet, and I will come and go from my new home to London whenever I like. But Princess Katherine will never see her home again. They say she was crying when she first met my brother. I think that is ridiculous. And babyish as Mary.

'Shall I dance at the wedding?' I ask.

'You and Harry shall dance together,' my lady grandmother rules. 'After the Spanish princess and her ladies have shown us a Spanish dance. You can show her what an English princess can do.' She smiles slyly. 'We shall see who is best.'

'Me,' I pray. Out loud I say: 'A basse danse?' It is a slow grand grown-up dance which I do very well, actually more walking than dancing.

'A galliard.'

I don't argue; nobody argues with my lady grandmother. She decides what happens in every royal household, in every palace and castle; my lady mother the queen just agrees.

'We'll have to rehearse,' I say. I can make Harry practise by promising him that everyone will be watching. He loves to be the centre of attention and is always winning races and competing at archery and doing tricks on his pony. He is as tall as me, though he is only ten years old, so we look well together if he doesn't play the fool. I want to show the Spanish princess that I am just as good as the daughter of Castile and Aragon. My mother and father are a Plantagenet and a Tudor. Those are grand enough names for anyone. Katherine needn't think that we are grateful for her coming. I, for one, don't particularly want another princess at court.

It is my lady mother who insists that Katherine visit us at Baynard's Castle before the wedding, and she is accompanied by her own court, who have come all the way from Spain – at our expense, as my father remarks. They enter through the double doors like an invading army, their clothes, their speech, their headdresses completely unlike ours and, at the centre of it all, beautifully gowned, is the girl that they call the 'Infanta'. This too is ridiculous, as she is fifteen and a princess, and I think that they are calling her 'Baby'. I glance across at Harry to see if he will giggle if I make a face and say 'Ba-aby', which is how we tease Mary, but he is not looking at me. He is looking at her with goggle-eyes, as if he is seeing a new horse, or a piece of Italian armour, or something that he has set his heart on. I see his expression, and I realise that he is trying to fall in love with her, like a knight with a damsel in a story. Harry loves stories and ballads about impossible ladies in towers, or tied to rocks, or lost in woods, and somehow Katherine impressed him when he met her before her entry into London. Perhaps it was her ornate veiled litter, perhaps it was her learning, for she speaks three languages. I am so annoyed – I wish he was close enough for me to pinch him. This is exactly why no-one younger than me should play a part in royal occasions.

She is not particularly beautiful. She is three years older than me but I am as tall as her. She has light brown hair with a copper tinge to it, only a little darker than mine. This is, of course, irritating: who wants to be compared to a sister-in-law? But I can hardly see it, for she wears a high headpiece and a thick concealing veil. She has blue eyes like mine too, but very fair eyebrows and lashes; obviously, she's not allowed to colour them in like I do. She has pale creamy skin, which I suppose is admirable. She is tiny: tiny waist pinched in by tight lacing so she can hardly breathe, tiny feet with the most ridiculous shoes I have ever seen, gold-embroidered toes and gold laces. I don't think that my lady grandmother would let me wear gold laces. It would be vanity and worldly show. I am sure that the Spanish are very worldly. I am sure that she is.

I make certain that my thoughts don't show on my face as I examine her. I think she is lucky to come here, lucky to be chosen by my father to marry my elder brother Arthur, lucky to have a sister-in-law like me, a mother-in-law like my mother and – more than anything else – a grandmother-in-law like Lady Margaret Beaufort, who will make very sure that Katherine does not exceed her place which has been appointed by God.

She curtseys and kisses my lady mother and, after her, my lady grandmother. This is how it should be; but she will soon learn that she had better please my lady grandmother before anybody. Then my lady mother nods to me and I step forward, and the Spanish princess and I curtsey together at the same time, to exactly the same depth, and she steps forward and we kiss on one cheek and then the other. Her cheeks are warm and I see that she is blushing, her eyes filling with tears as if she is missing her real sisters. I show her my stern look, just like my father when someone is asking him for money. I am not going to fall in love with her for her blue eyes and pretty ways. She need not imagine she is going to come into our English court and make us look fat and stupid.

She is not at all rebuffed; she looks right back at me. Born and raised in a competitive court with three sisters, she understands rivalry. Worse, she looks at me as if she finds my stern look to be not at all chilling, perhaps even a little comical. That is when I know that this is not a young woman like my ladies-in-waiting who has to be pleasant to me whatever I do, or like Mary, who has to do whatever I say. This young woman is an equal, she will consider me, she might even be critical. I say in French: 'You are welcome to England,' and she replies in stilted English: 'I am pleased to greet my sister.'

My lady mother lays herself out to be kind to this, her first, daughter-in-law. They talk together in Latin and I cannot follow what they are saying so I sit beside my mother and look at

Katherine's shoes with the gold laces. My mother calls for music, and Harry and I start a round, an English country song. We are very tuneful and the court takes up the chorus and it goes round and round until people start to giggle and lose their places. But Katherine does not laugh. She looks as if she is never silly and merry like Harry and me. She is overly formal, of course, being Spanish. But I note how she sits – very still, and with her hands folded in her lap as if she were sitting for a portrait – and I think: actually, that looks rather queenly. I think I will learn to sit like that.

My sister Mary is brought in to make her curtsey, and Katherine makes herself ridiculous by going down on her knees so their faces are level and she can hear her childish whisper. Of course Mary cannot understand a word of either Latin or Spanish, but she puts her arms around Katherine's neck and kisses her and calls her 'Thithter'.

'I am your sister,' I correct her, giving her little hand a firm tug. 'This lady is your sister-in-law. Can you say sister-in-law?'

Of course, she can't. She lisps, and everyone laughs again and says how charming, and I say: 'Lady Mother, shouldn't Mary be in bed?' Then everyone realises how late it is and we all go out with bobbing torches to see Katherine leave, as if she were a queen crowned and not merely the youngest daughter of the King and Queen of Spain, and very lucky to marry into our family: the Tudors.

She kisses everyone goodnight and when it is my turn, she puts her warm cheek to mine and says: 'Goodnight, Sister' in that stupid accent, in her patronising way. She draws back and sees my cross face and she gives a little ripple of laughter. 'Oho!' she says, and pats my cheek as if my bad temper does not trouble her. This is a real princess, as naturally royal as my mother; this is the girl who will be Queen of England; and so I don't resent the pat, more like a caress. I find that I like her and dislike her, all together, all at once.

'I hope you will be kind to Katherine,' my mother says to me as we come out of her private chapel after Prime the next morning.

'Not if she thinks she's going to come here and lord it over all of us,' I say briskly. 'Not if she thinks she is going to act as if she is doing us a favour. Did you see her shoelaces?'

My mother laughs with genuine amusement. 'No, Margaret. I did not see her shoelaces, nor did I ask you for your opinion of her. I told you of my hope: that you will be kind to her.'

'Of course,' I say, looking down at my missal with the jewelled cover. 'I hope that I am gracious to everyone.'

'She is far from her home and accustomed to a big family,' my mother says. 'She will certainly need a friend, and you might enjoy the company of an older girl. I had lots of sisters at home when I was growing up, and I value them, more and more every year. You too might find that your women friends are your truest friends, your sisters are the keepers of your memories and hopes for the future.'

'She and Arthur will stay here?' I ask. 'They will live with us?'

My mother rests her hand on my shoulder. 'I wish they could stay; but your father thinks they should go to Arthur's principality and live at Ludlow.'

'What does my lady grandmother think?'

My mother gives a little shrug. That means it has been decided. 'She says the Prince of Wales must govern Wales.'

'You'll still have me at home.' I put my hand over hers to keep her beside me. 'I'll still be here.'

'I count on you,' she says reassuringly.

I have only one moment alone with my brother Arthur before the wedding. He walks with me in the long gallery. Below, we can hear the musicians striking up another dance, and the buzz of people drinking and chattering and laughing. 'You don't have to bow so low to her,' I say abruptly. 'Her father and mother are new-come to their thrones just like our father. She has nothing to be so very proud of. They're no better than us. They're not an ancient line.'

He flushes. 'You think her proud?'

'Without reason.' I heard my grandmother say exactly this to my lady mother so I know it is right.

But Arthur argues. 'Her parents conquered Spain and took it back from the Moors. They are the greatest crusaders in the world. Her mother is a queen militant. They have extraordinary wealth and own half of the unmapped world. Some grounds for pride there, surely?'

'There's that, I suppose,' I say begrudgingly. 'But we are Tudors.'

'We are,' he agrees with a little laugh. 'But that doesn't impress everyone.'

'Of course it does,' I say. 'Especially now . . .'

Neither of us says any more; we are both aware that there are many heirs to the English throne, dozens of Plantagenet boys, our mother's kinsmen, still living at our court, or run away to exile. Father has killed my mother's cousins in battles, and destroyed more than one pretender: he executed our cousin Edward two years ago.

'Do you think her proud?' he challenges me. 'Has she been rude to you?'

I spread my hands in the gesture of surrender that my mother makes when she is told that my lady grandmother has overruled her. 'Oh, she doesn't bother to talk to me, she has no interest in a mere sister. She is too busy being charming, especially to Father. Anyway, she can hardly speak English.'

'Isn't she just shy? I know that I am.'

'Why would she be shy? She's going to be married, isn't she? She's going to be Queen of England, isn't she? She's going to be your wife. Why would she be anything but completely delighted with herself?'

Arthur laughs and hugs me. 'D'you think that there is nothing better in the world but to be Queen of England?'

'Nothing,' I say simply. 'She should realise it and be grateful.'

'But you will be Queen of Scotland,' he points out. 'That's grand too. You have that to look forward to.'

'I do, and I certainly won't ever be anxious and homesick or lonely.'

'King James will be a lucky man to have such a contented bride.'

That is the closest I get to warning him that Katherine of Aragon is looking down her long Spanish nose at us. But I nickname her Katherine of Arrogant and Mary hears me say it, since she is everywhere, always eavesdropping on her elders and betters. She catches it up, and it makes me laugh every time I hear her and see my mother's quick frown and quiet correction.

The wedding passes off very brilliantly, arranged by my lady grandmother, of course, to show the world just how wealthy and grand we are now. Father has spent a fortune on a week of jousting and celebration and feasting, the fountains flow with wine, they roast oxen in Smithfield Market, and the people tear up the wedding carpet so that they can all have a little piece of Tudor glory on their sideboards. This is my first chance to see a royal wedding and I inspect the bride from the top of her beautiful white lace headdress, which they call a mantilla, to the heels of her embroidered shoes.

She looks pretty, I cannot deny that, but there is no cause for everyone to behave as if she is a miracle of beauty. Her long hair is the colour of gold and brass, and falls around her shoulders nearly to her waist. She is as dainty as a little picture, which makes me feel awkward, as if my feet and hands are too big. It would be petty and a sin to think badly of her because of this, but I admit to myself that it will be better for everyone when she conceives a son and a Tudor heir, disappears into confinement for months, and comes out fat.

As soon as the feast is over, the double doors at the end of the hall open and a great float comes in, pulled by dancers in Tudor green. It is a huge castle, beautifully decorated with eight ladies inside, the principal dancer dressed as a Spanish princess, and on each turret there is a boy from the chapel choir singing her praises. It is followed by a float dressed as a sailing ship with billowing sails of peach silk, manned by eight knights. The ship docks at the castle but the ladies refuse to dance, so the knights attack the castle with pretend jousting until the ladies throw them paper flowers and then step down. The castle and the ship are hauled away and they all dance together. Katherine of Arrogant claps her hands and bows her thanks to my father the king for the elaborate compliment. I am so furious that I wasn't given a part in this that I cannot bring myself to smile. I catch her looking at me, and I feel certain she is taunting me with the honour that my father is doing her. She is the centre of everything, it's quite sickening in the middle of dinner.

Then it is Arthur's turn. He dances with one of my mother's ladies, and then Harry and I take to the floor for our galliard. It is a fast, bright dance with music as tempting as a village jig. The musicians take it at a quick pace and Harry and I are excellent partners, well-matched and well-trained. Neither of us misses a step, nobody could do it better. But in one part when I am circling, arms outstretched, dancing a little step on the spot, my feet and ankles shown by my swirling gown, and all eyes are on me – at that exact moment – Harry chooses to step to one side and throw off his bulky jacket and then spring back to my side in his billowing linen shirt. Father and Mother applaud and he looks flushed and so boyishly handsome that everyone cheers him. I keep smiling, but I am completely furious, and when we hold hands in the dance, I pinch his palm as hard as I can.

Of course, I am not at all surprised by this scene-stealing; I half-expected him to do something to draw all eyes to him. It's been killing him all day to have to play second son to Arthur. He escorted Katherine up the aisle of the abbey, but had to hand her over at the top and step back and be quite forgotten. Now, following Arthur's restrained dance, he gets his chance to shine.

If I could stamp on his toe I would, but I catch Arthur's eye and he gives me a broad wink. We are both thinking the same thing: Harry is always indulged and everyone but Mother and Father can see what we see: a boy spoiled beyond enduring.

The dance comes to an end and Harry and I bow together, hand in hand, making a pretty picture as we always do. I glance across at the Scots lords, who are watching me intently. They, at least, have no interest in Harry. One of them, James Hamilton, is the King of Scotland's own kinsman. He will be glad to see that I will be a merry queen; his cousin, King James, likes dancing and feasting and will meet his match in me. I see the lords exchange a few quick words and I feel certain that they will agree the next wedding, my wedding, will be soon. And Harry will not be dancing at that and stealing the show, for I will not allow it, and Katherine will have to wear her hair hidden under her hood and it will be me who stands and welcomes the ship with peach silk sails and all the dancers.

Neither Harry nor I are allowed to stay to the end of the feast, the escorting of the princess to bed, and the prayers over the wedding bed. I think it is very wrong and bad-mannered to treat us like children. My grandmother sends us to our rooms and though I glance over to my mother, expecting her to say that Harry must go but I can stay up longer, she is blandly looking aside. Always, it is my grandmother's word that is law: she is the hanging judge, my mother only grants the occasional rare royal pardon. So we make our bows and curtseys to the king and to my mother and to my lady grandmother, and to darling Arthur and Katherine of Arrogant, and then we have to go, dawdling as slowly as we dare, from the bright rooms where the white wax candles are burning down as if they cost no more than tallow, and the musicians are playing as if they are going to go on all night.

'I am going to have a wedding just like this,' Harry says as we go up the stairs.

'Not for years yet,' I say to irritate him. 'But I shall be married very soon.'

When I get to my room I kneel at my prie-dieu and, though I had intended to pray for Arthur's long life and happiness, and remind God of His special debt to the Tudors, I find I can only pray that the Scottish ambassadors tell the king to send for me at once, for I want a marriage feast as grand as this one, and a wardrobe of clothes as good as Katherine of Arrogant's, and shoes – I will have hundreds and hundreds of pairs of shoes, I swear it, and every one of them will have embroidered toes and gold laces.

## RICHMOND PALACE, ENGLAND, JANUARY 1502

My prayer is answered, for God always listens to the prayers of the Tudors, and the King of Scotland orders his ambassadors to negotiate with my father's advisors. They agree a price for my dowry, for my servants, for my allowance, for the lands that will become my own in Scotland, and all through the Christmas feast the letters come and go between Scotland Yard and Richmond Palace until my lady grandmother comes to me and says: 'Princess Margaret, I am pleased to say that it is the will of God that you are to be married.'

I rise up from my dutiful curtsey and look as maidenly and surprised as I can. But since I had been told this very morning that my lady grandmother and mother would see me before dinner, and that I was to wear my best gown as befits a great occasion, I am not too amazed. Really, they are quite ridiculous.

'I am?' I say sweetly.

'Yes,' my mother says. She entered the room ahead of my grandmother but somehow managed to be second with the announcement. 'You are to marry King James of Scotland.'

'Is it my father's wish?' I say, as my lady governess has taught me.

'It is,' my lady grandmother speaks out of turn. 'My son, the king, has made an agreement. There is to be a lasting peace between ourselves and Scotland; your marriage will seal it. But I have requested that you stay with us, here in England, until you are a woman grown.'

'What?' I am absolutely horrified that my grandmother is going to spoil everything, as she always does. 'But when will I go? I have to go now!'

'When you are fourteen years old,' my lady grandmother rules, and when my mother seems about to say something, she raises her hand and goes on: 'I know – no-one knows better than I – that an early marriage is very dangerous for a young woman. And the Scots king is not . . . He cannot be trusted not to . . . We felt that the King of Scots might . . .'

For once, she seems to be lost for words. This has never happened before in the history of England that runs from Arthur of the Britons to my lady grandmother in a completely unbroken line. My lady grandmother has never failed to finish a sentence; no-one has ever interrupted her.

'But when am I to marry? And where?' I ask, thinking of St Paul's Cathedral carpeted with red, and thousands of people crowding to see me, and a crown on my head and a cloth of gold train from my shoulders, and gold shoes and jewels, and jousts in my honour, and a masque, and the pretend sailing ship with peach sails and everyone admiring me.

'This very month!' my mother says triumphantly. 'The king will send his representative and you will be betrothed by proxy.'

'A proxy? Not the king himself? Not in St Paul's?' I ask. This sounds as if it is hardly worth doing at all. Not to leave for two years? That's a lifetime to me now. Not in St Paul's Cathedral like Katherine of Arrogant? Why would she get a better wedding than me? No king? Just some old lord?

'In the chapel here,' my mother says, as if the whole point of marriage is not about crowds of thousands and fountains running with wine and everyone watching you.

'But there will be another grand service at Edinburgh when you get there,' my lady grandmother reassures me. 'When you are fourteen.' She turns to my mother and remarks: 'And they will carry all the expense.'

'But I don't want to wait, I don't need to wait!'

She smiles but shakes her head. 'We have decided,' she says. She means that she has decided, and there is no point in anyone else having a different opinion.

'But you'll be called Queen of Scotland.' My mother knows exactly how to console me for my disappointment. 'You'll be called Queen of Scotland this year, as soon as you are betrothed, and then you will take precedence over every lady at court except me.'

I steal a look at my lady grandmother's flinty face. I will go before her; she won't like that. Just as I expected, her lips are moving silently. She will be praying that I do not become overly grand, that I do not suffer from the sin of pride. She will be thinking of ways to keep me in a state of grace as a miserable sinner and a granddaughter sworn in obedience to her. She will be thinking how she can be sure that I am a humble handmaiden serving my family, and not an upstart princess – no! a queen! – filled with self-importance. But I am absolutely determined to be a queen full of self-importance and I am going to have the most beautiful clothes and shoes like Katherine of Arrogant.

'Oh, I don't care about that, all I care about is being called to the state of matrimony by God, and serving the interests of my family,' I say cleverly, and my lady grandmother smiles, truly pleased with me for the first time this afternoon.

I know someone else who will care about me walking before everyone, the equal of my mother. I know who will care so much that it will all but kill him. My brother Harry, a little peacock of vanity, a little mountebank of false pride, is going to be sick as a sinner with the Sweat when I tell him. I go to find him at the stables, coming in from a lesson of riding at the quintain. He is allowed to ride at the target with a padded lance, and the target is padded too. Everyone wants Harry to be fearless and skilled, but nobody dares to teach him properly. He's always begging for someone to ride against, but nobody can bear to let him take any risks. He is a Tudor prince, one of only two. We Tudors are unlucky with boys, my mother's side of the family has too many. My father was an only child and had only three sons, and lost one of them. Neither he nor my grandmother can bear to let Harry experience any danger. Even worse than that, my lady mother cannot say no to him. So he is a completely spoiled second son. Nobody would treat him like this if he were going to be king one day; they are making a tyrant. But it doesn't matter because he's going into the Church and will probably be pope. I swear he'll be a really ridiculous pope.

'What do you want?' he asks disagreeably, leading his horse into the huge yard. I know at once that his lesson has gone badly. Usually he is sunny and smiling; usually he rides extraordinarily well. He is good at all sports, and fiercely clever in the schoolroom too. He is princely in every way, which will make my news so particularly galling to him.

'Did you fall off?'

'Of course not. Stupid horse cast a shoe; she's got to be shod. I hardly rode at all. It was a complete waste of time. The groom should be turned away. What are you doing here?'

'Oh, I just came to tell you that I am to be betrothed.'

'Finally agreed, did they?' He throws his reins to a groom and slaps his hands together to warm his fingers. 'It's taken forever. I must say, they don't seem very anxious to have you. When d'you go?'

'I don't go,' I tell him. He will have been looking forward to being the only young Tudor for the great moments of court, with Arthur gone to Ludlow and Mary still in the nursery, he will have hoped that all eyes would be on him.

'I don't go for years yet,' I say. 'So if you were hoping for that, you will be disappointed.'

'Then you won't be married,' he says simply. 'It will all fall through. He's not going to marry you to leave you in England. He wants a wife in his freezing cold castles, not one in London buying clothes. He wants to shut you up in confinement and get an heir. What else? Do you think he wanted you for your beauty? For your grace and height?' He laughs rudely, ignoring my flush of irritation at the jibe at my looks.

'I will be married now,' I say, nettled. 'You wait and see. I will be married now and I will go to Scotland when I am fourteen, and in the meantime I will be called the Queen of Scotland and live here at court. I will have bigger rooms, my own ladies-in-waiting, and I will take precedence over everyone but my lady mother the queen, and the king my father.' I wait to make sure he fully understands what I am saying, what glories are opening up for me, how he will be thoroughly overshadowed.

'I'll walk before you,' I emphasise. 'Whether I grow any taller or not. Whether you think me beautiful or not. I will precede you. And you will have to bow to me, as to a queen.'

His cheeks flame scarlet, as if they have been slapped. His little rosebud mouth drops open, showing his perfectly white teeth. His blue eyes stare.

'I will never bow to you.'

'Absolutely you will.'

'You will not queen it over me. I am the prince. I am the Duke of York!'

'A duke,' I say as if I am hearing his title for the first time. 'Yes. Very good. A royal duke, very grand. But I shall be a queen.'

I am amazed to see he actually trembles with rage. Tears come to his eyes. 'You shall not! You shall not! You're not even married!'

'I shall be,' I say. 'I will have a proxy marriage and I shall have all the jewels and the title.'

'Not the jewels!' he howls like a baited wolf. 'Not the title.'

'Queen of Scotland!' I taunt him. 'Queen of Scotland! And you're not even Prince of Wales.'

He lets out a bellow of rage and dives away from me, through a little door to the palace. I can hear him screaming with temper as he bounds up the stairs. He will be running to our mother – I can hear his riding boots clattering down the gallery. He will be running to fling himself into her rooms and cry into her lap and beg her not to let me take precedence over him, not to let me be queen when he is nothing but a second son and a duke, begging her to put me in a place below him, to reduce me to the lesser importance of being a girl, to drag me down from being a queen.

I don't run after him; I don't even follow him; I let him go. There is nothing my mother could do if she wanted – my lady grandmother has decided it all. I am to be betrothed and to live at court for two dizzy beautiful years, a queen where I was only a princess, preceding everyone but my royal parents, draped in cloth of gold and drowned in jewels. And I really think that the shock to Harry's vanity will kill him. I cast down my eyes as my grandmother does when she has got her own way and is giving the credit to God, and I smile with her quiet satisfaction. I should think my little brother will cry himself sick.

## GREENWICH PALACE, ENGLAND, SPRING 1502

I write to my brother the Prince of Wales, to tell him of my proxy wedding and to ask him when he is going to come back home. I tell him that the day was a great state occasion, the signing of the treaty, a wedding mass, and then an exchange of vows in my mother's great chamber before hundreds of admiring people. I wore white, I tell him, with cloth of gold sleeves and white leather shoes with gold laces. My husband's kinsman, James Hamilton, was kind to me, he was at my side all day. Then I dined at the same table as my mother and we ate from the same plate because we are both queens.

I remind him, rather plaintively, that they are planning that I shall go to Scotland the summer before I turn fourteen, and I want to see him before I leave. Surely he wants to see me before I go to be Queen of Scotland in person as well as in name? Surely he will want to see my new gowns? I am making a list of everything I shall need and I will have to have a baggage train of a hundred carts. Also, I think but don't tell him, now I outrank his wife and she can follow behind me and see how she likes it now that I am the newly-made queen and she still a mere princess. If she comes to court she will find that she has to curtsey to me, and follow me when we go in to dinner. There will be no more carefully judged equal curtseys; she has to sink down as low as a princess goes to a queen. I long to see her do that to me. I really wish he would bring her just so that I could see her pride humbled.

I tell him that Harry cannot recover from the shock that I go before him on every state occasion, that I am served on bended knee, that I am a queen as great as our lady mother. I tell Arthur that we all miss him at court, though Christmas was merry. I tell him my father is spending a small fortune on the clothes that I shall take to Scotland, while making a note of every penny. I have to have everything new, red bed curtains made of sarsenet, everything embroidered with gold thread. Even so, they think it will all be ready by next summer and I will set off as soon as the King of Scotland confirms the marriage by transferring my dower lands to me. But Arthur must come home to say goodbye. Arthur must come home to see me leave. If not – when will I see him again? 'I miss you,' I write.

I send my letter to Ludlow in a bundle with my mother and lady grandmother's letters. The messenger will take days to get to Arthur's court. The roads to the west are crumbling and in disrepair; my father says there is no money to spend on them. The messenger will have to lead his own change of horses for fear that there are none available for hire on the way. He will have to spend the nights in abbeys and monasteries along the route, or if he finds himself snowed in or benighted he will have to beg for hospitality in a manor or farmhouse. Everyone is obliged to assist the king's messenger; but if the road is a quagmire, or a bridge swept away by a flood, there is little anyone can do but advise him to take the long way round, and find his way as best he can.

So I don't expect a swift reply and I don't think much of it when, early one morning in April, walking to my room with a candle after attending Prime with my lady grandmother, I see a king's messenger step from a barge, and walk quickly across the quay and through the private door to the royal quarters. He looks exhausted, leaning against the carved column as he says something quietly to a yeoman of the guard that leads the man to throw down his pike and gallop indoors.

I guess that he's going to my father the king's private rooms so I leave my post at the window and walk along the gallery to see what is so urgent that the messenger has arrived at first light and the guards are downing their arms and running. But even before I get to the door, I can see the yeoman and two or three of my father's counsellors going quickly down the privy stairs to the courtyard below. Curiously, I watch as they huddle together, and then someone breaks away, runs up the stairs, and goes to the chapel to fetch my father's confessor. The priest comes hurrying out. Now, I step forward. 'What's the matter?' I ask.

Friar Peter's face is sallow as if all the blood has gone from his cheeks, as if he has turned to parchment. 'Forgive me, Your Grace,' he says with a little bow. 'I am on your father's business and can't stop.'

And with that he walks past me! Scuttles past me! As if I am not Queen of Scotland and taking up my throne next summer! I wait for a moment, wondering if it would be too undignified to run after him and insist that he waits until dismissed; but then I hear him returning, coming up the stairs so slowly that I don't understand why he rushed down. Now, there is no hurry; he is dragging his feet, looking as if he wishes he were not going towards my father's rooms at all. The advisors trail behind him, looking as sick as if they are poisoned. He sees me waiting; but it is as if he does not see me, for he does not bow – he does not even acknowledge me. He walks past me as if his eyes are fixed on a ghost and he cannot see mere mortals, not even royals.

That's when I know for sure. I think I knew before. I think I knew as soon as I saw the messenger slumped against the column, as if he wished he had died before bringing this news to us. I step before the priest, and I say: 'It's Arthur, isn't it?'

My beloved brother's name makes him see me but he says only, 'Go to your lady mother,' as if he can give me orders, and he turns away and slips into my father's rooms, without knocking, without announcement, one hand on the door, the other clutching the crucifix which hangs from his belt, as if it might give him strength.

I go, not because I have to do as my father's confessor tells me, for I am a queen now and I have to obey only my parents and my husband; but because I am afraid that they will come to my mother and tell her something terrible. I almost think that I will bar her door so that they cannot come in. If we don't know, perhaps it hasn't happened. If nobody tells us that there is something terribly wrong with Arthur then perhaps he is still well in Ludlow, hunting, enjoying the spring weather, travelling into Wales to show the people their prince, learning how to rule his principality. Perhaps he is happy with Katherine of Arrogant; I would be glad even if she was the cause of his happiness. Perhaps she is with child and they have brought us good news. I would even like good news of her. I keep thinking of all the wonderful news that the messenger might have brought, in such a hurry. I keep thinking that Arthur is such a darling, beloved of everyone, so dear to me, that nothing can have gone wrong. The news cannot be bad.

My mother is still in bed, her bedroom fire just flickering into life. Her lady is bringing gowns for her to choose for the day, the heavy headdresses are laid out on the table. She looks up as I dawdle into her bedroom. I think I should say something, but I don't know what.

'You're up early, Margaret,' she remarks.

'I went to Prime with my lady grandmother.'

'Is she joining us for breakfast?'

'Yes.' And I think: my lady grandmother will know what to do when the confessor comes in with his face the colour of a manuscript and grief written all over it.

'Is everything all right, little queen?' she asks me tenderly.

I can't bear to answer her. I take a seat at the window and look out at the garden, and listen for the footsteps that soon come heavily along the corridor. Then, at last, after what seems like a long long time, I hear the outer doors to her presence chamber open, the sound of footsteps, the inner doors to the privy chamber open and then finally, unstoppably, the door to her bedroom is opened, and my father's confessor comes into my mother's rooms, his head bowed as low as the poorest drudge pulling a plough. I jump to my feet when he comes in, and I put out my hand as if I can stop him from speaking. I say suddenly: 'No! No!', but he says quietly, 'Your Grace, the king bids you come to his rooms at once.'

Terribly, my mother turns to me. 'What is it? You know, don't you?'

Terribly, I reply: 'It's Arthur. He's dead.'

They say that he died of the Sweat – and this only makes it worse for us Tudors. The disease came in from the gaols of France with my father's convict army. Wherever he marched, from Wales, through Bosworth to London, people died in an instant. England had never known such a disease. My father won the battle against Richard III with his sickly force, but he had to delay his coronation because of the horror that they brought with them. They called it the Tudor curse and said that the reign that had begun in sweat would end in tears. And now here we are, not anywhere near the end of our reign, but deep in sweat and tears, and the curse of the invading army has fallen on my innocent brother.

My father and my mother take the loss of their elder son very hard. They don't just lose their boy – and he was not yet sixteen – they lose their heir, the boy they trained to be the next king, the Tudor who was to come to the throne with acclaim, a Tudor that the people wanted, not one that was forced on them. My father had to fight for his throne and then defend it. He has to defend it still, even now, against the older royal family who would take it if they could, the Plantagenet cousins who are in open enmity in Europe, or those who stay uncertainly at court. Arthur was going to be the first Tudor that all of England welcomed to the throne, the son of both the old royal family and the new. They called him the sweet briar, the Tudor rose, the bush that was the union of two roses, the Lancaster red and the York white.

This is the end of my childhood. Arthur was my brother, my darling, my friend. I looked up to him as my senior, I acknowledged him as my prince, I thought I would see him come to the throne as king. I imagined him ruling in England and I as Queen of Scotland with a Treaty of Perpetual Peace and a regular exchange of visits and letters, loving each other as brother and sister and neighbouring monarchs. And now that he is dead I realise how bitterly I resent the days that we did not spend together, the months when he was with Katherine in the Welsh Marches and I did not see him, nor write often enough. I think of the days of our childhood when we were taught by different tutors, when they kept us apart so that I might learn needlework and he Greek, and how few days I had with him, my brother. I don't know how I can bear it without him. We were four Tudor children, and now we are only three, and the firstborn and the finest has gone.

I am walking down the gallery away from my mother's rooms when I see Harry, his face all puffed and his eyes red from crying, coming the opposite way. When he sees me his little mouth goes downturned as if he is about to wail, and all my anger and my grief turns on him, this worthless boy, this brat, who presumes to cry as if he were the only person in the world to lose a brother.

'Shut up,' I say fiercely. 'What have you got to cry about?'

'My brother!' he gulps. 'Our brother, Margaret.'

'You weren't fit to polish his boots.' I am choking with resentment. 'You weren't fit to groom his horse. There will never be another like him. There will never be another prince like him.'

Amazingly, this stops his tears. He goes white and almost stern. His head rears up, his shoulders go back, he sticks out his thin little-boy chest, he plants his fists on his hips, he almost manages to swagger. 'There will be another prince like him,' he swears. 'Better than him. Me. I am the new Prince of Wales and I shall be King of England in his place, and you can get used to it.'

## WINDSOR CASTLE, ENGLAND, SUMMER 1502

We do get used to it. That's the difference between being royal and being a commoner of no importance. We can grieve and pray and break our hearts on the inside, but on the outside we still have to make the court the centre of beauty and fashion and art, my father still has to pass laws and meet with the Privy Council and guard against rebels and the constant threat of the French, and we still have to have a Prince of Wales, even though the true prince, the beloved Prince Arthur, will never take his seat next to the throne again. Harry is the Prince of Wales now and, as he predicted, I get used to it.

But they won't send him to Ludlow. This makes me angrier than anything; but since we are royal I can say nothing. Darling Arthur had to go to Ludlow to rule his principality, to learn the business of being king, to prepare him for the greatness that was to be his; but now that they have lost him they won't let Harry out of their sight. My mother wants her last surviving son at home. My father is fearful that he might lose his only heir. And my grandmother advises my father that between the two of them they can teach Harry everything he needs to know to be a king, and that they had better keep him at court. Precious Harry does not have to go far away, nor marry a strange princess. No veiled beauty is going to be brought in to lord it over all of us. Harry can be under his grandmother's eye, under her wing, under her thumb as if they would keep him a spoiled baby forever.

Katherine of Arrogant – not arrogant at all now, but white-faced and thin and pale – comes back from Ludlow in a closed litter. My lady mother is absurdly indulgent to her, though she has done nothing for our family at all but steal Arthur away from us for the last months of his life. Mother weeps over her, and holds her hand, walks with her and they pray together. She invites her to visit so we have her black silks and velvets, her incredibly rich black mantilla, her stupid silent Spanish presence, sweeping up and down the galleries all the time, and my lady mother orders that we all say nothing that might upset her.

But really, whatever would upset her? She pretends to understand neither English nor French as I speak it; and I am not going to attempt a conversation in Latin. Even if I wanted to pour out my grief and jealousy, I would not be able to find words that she would understand. When I speak to her in French, she looks completely blank; and when I am sitting next to her at dinner I turn my shoulder to show that I have nothing to say to her. She went to Ludlow with the most beautiful, kind, loving prince the world has ever known and she failed to keep him, so now he is dead and she is marooned in England – and I am supposed not to upset her? Should not my lady mother consider that perhaps she upsets me?

She is living, at enormous expense, at Durham House in the Strand. I suppose they will send her home to Spain, but my father is unwilling to pay her jointure as a widow when he still has not received her full dowry as a bride. The wasted wedding alone cost thousands: the castle with the dancers, the peach silk sails of the masquing boat! The treasure house of England is always empty. We live very grandly, as a royal family should do, but my father pays out a fortune on spies and couriers to watch the courts of Europe for fear of our Plantagenet cousins in exile plotting to return and seize our throne. Guarding the kingdom by bribing friends and spying on enemies is terribly costly; my father and lady grandmother invent fees and taxes all the time to raise the money they need. I don't believe that my father can find the money to send Katherine home to the land of Arrogance, so he keeps her here, saying that she will be comforted by her late husband's family, while he deals with her tight-fisted father to make an agreement to send her home to Spain and turn a profit.

She is supposed to be in mourning, living in seclusion, but she is always here. I come into the nursery one afternoon to find the room in uproar, and she is at the very centre of it, playing at jousting with my sister, Mary. They have lined up cushions to serve as the tilt rail that divides one horse from the other, and they are running either side of the tilt and hitting each other with cushions as they pass. Mary, who has developed little unconvincing sobs every time that Arthur is named in our memorial prayers in chapel, is now romping and laughing, and her cap has fallen off, her mass of golden curls is tumbled down, and her gown is tucked into her waistband so that she can run as if she were a milkmaid chasing cows. Katherine, no longer the silent, dark-gowned widow, has her black dress bunched in one hand so that she can paw the ground with her expensive black leather shoe, and canter down her side of the list and bump my little sister on her head with a cushion. The ladies of the nursery, far from calling for decorum, are placing bets and laughing and cheering them on.

I march in and I snap as if I were my lady grandmother: 'What is this?'

It's all I say; but I swear that Katherine understands. The laughter dies in her eyes and she turns to face me, a little shrug suggesting that there is nothing very serious here, just playing in the nursery with my sister. 'Nothing. This is nothing,' she says in English, her Spanish accent strong.

I see that she understands English perfectly, just as I had always thought.

'These are not the days for silly games,' I say slowly and loudly.

Again that little foreign roll of the shoulders. I think with a pang of pain that perhaps Arthur found that little gesture charming. 'We are in mourning,' I say sternly, letting myself look around the room, resting my eyes on every downcast face, just as my lady grandmother does when she scolds the entire court. 'We are not playing silly games like idiots on the village green.'

I doubt that she understands 'idiots on the village green', but no-one could misunderstand my tone of contempt. Her colour rises as she pulls herself up to her greatest height. She is not tall; but now she seems to be above me. Her dark blue eyes look into mine and I stare back at her, daring her to argue with me.

'I was playing with your sister,' she says in her low voice. 'She needs a happy time. Arthur did not want . . .'

I can't bear her to say his name, this girl who came from Spain and took him away from court and watched him die. How dare she so casually say 'Arthur' to me – who cannot speak his name for grief?

'His Grace would want his sister to behave as a Princess of England,' I spit out, more like my grandmother than ever. Mary lets out a wail and runs to one of the ladies to cry in her lap. I ignore her completely. 'The court is in full mourning, there are to be no loud games, or dances, or heathen pursuits.' I look Katherine up and down with disdain. 'I am surprised at you, Dowager Princess. I shall be sorry to tell my lady grandmother that you were forgetful of your place.'

I think I have shamed her in front of everyone, and I turn to the door glowing with triumph. But just as I am about to go out she says quietly and simply, 'No, it is you who are wrong, Sister. Prince Arthur asked me to play with Princess Mary, and to walk and talk with you. He knew that he was dying, and he asked me to comfort you all.'

I spin round and I fly at her and pull her arm, drawing her away from the others, so that no-one else can hear. 'He knew? Did he give you a message for me?'

In that moment I am certain he has sent me words of farewell.

Arthur loved me, I loved him, we were everything to each other. He would have sent a private goodbye just for me. 'What did he tell you to tell me? What did he say?'

Her eyes slide away from mine and I think: there is something here that she is not telling me. I don't trust her. I press her close to me as if I were embracing her.

'I am sorry, Margaret. I am so sorry,' she says, detaching herself from my hard grip. 'He said nothing more than that he hoped no-one would grieve for him and that I would comfort his sisters.'

'And you?' I say. 'Did he command you not to grieve for him?'

Her eyelids lower; now I know there is some secret here. 'We spoke privately before he died,' is all she says.

'About what?' I ask rudely.

She looks up suddenly and her eyes are blazing dark blue with passion. 'I gave him my word,' she flares out. 'He asked for a promise and I gave it.'

'What did you promise?'

The fair eyelashes shield her eyes again; once more she looks down, keeping her secret, keeping my brother's last words from me.

'*Non possum dicere*,' she says.

'What?' I give her arm a little shake as if she were Mary and I might slap her. 'Speak in English, stupid!'

Again she gives me that burning look. 'I may not say,' she says. 'But I assure you that I am guided by his last wishes. I will always be guided by his wishes. I have sworn.'

I feel completely blocked by her determination. I can't persuade her and I can't bully her. 'Anyway, you shouldn't be running about and making a noise,' I say spitefully. 'My lady grandmother won't like it, and my lady mother is resting. You have probably disturbed her already.'

'She is with child?' the young woman asks me quietly. Really, it is none of her business. And besides, my mother would not have had to conceive another child if Arthur had not died. It is practically Katherine's fault that my mother is exhausted and facing another confinement.

'Yes,' I say pompously. 'As you should be. We sent a litter to Ludlow to bring you home so you did not have to ride because we thought that you would be with child. We were being considerate to you, but it seems that there was no need for our courtesy.'

'Alas, it never happened for us,' she says sadly, and I am so furious that I go out of the room slamming the door, before I have time to wonder just what she means by that. 'Alas, it never happened for us'?

What never happened?

## WESTMINSTER ABBEY, LONDON, ENGLAND, FEBRUARY 1503

I think this must be the most miserable day of my life. I had thought that nothing would be worse than the loss of Arthur but now, only a year later, I have lost my mother, in childbed – trying to give my father and the country a son to replace the one we have lost. As if any child could ever replace Arthur! It was an insult to him to even think it, it was madness for her to attempt it. She wanted to console my father, to do the duty of a good queen to provide two heirs, and then she had a hard pregnancy and nothing to show at the end of it but a girl; so it was not worth the effort, anyway. I am in a rage of grief, furious with her, with my father, with God Himself, for the way that one terrible loss has turned into three: first Arthur and then my mother, and then her baby. And yet we still have Katherine of Arrogant. Why would we lose those three and keep her?

The funeral is a triumph of my lady grandmother's ability to put on a grand show. She has always said that the royal family have to blaze before the people like saints in an altarpiece, and my mother's death is an opportunity to remind the country that she was a Plantagenet princess who married a Tudor king. She did what the country should have done: submit to the Tudors and learn to love them. My mother's coffin is draped in black with cloth of gold forming a cross on the hearse. They make a beautiful effigy of her for the top of the coffin and my little sister Mary thinks it is her real mother, just sleeping, and that she will wake up soon and everything will be as it was. This fails to move me to tears, though it makes Princess Katherine bow her head and take Mary's hand in her own. I think it is just part of the whole irritating stupidity of my family and the way that, except for my lady grandmother, we can never be anything but ridiculous. Now my father has disappeared, refusing to rule, refusing to eat, refusing to see any of us, even me. This is all so miserable that I can barely speak for bad temper and grief.

It should be me, as Queen of Scotland, who takes over my mother's rooms and the running of the court. I should have the best rooms and her ladies should serve me. But it is all done wrong: her household is turned away without my being consulted, and her ladies go back to live with their families in their London houses, in rooms at court or on their country estates. Although I am now the most important Tudor lady, and the only queen in England, I keep my old rooms. I don't even have new mourning clothes but I have to wear the same things from when Arthur died. I keep expecting to see her, I keep listening for her voice. One day I find I am going to her rooms to see her, and then I remember that they are closed up and empty. It is strange that someone who was so quiet and discreet, who was always happy to step back and hold her peace, should leave such an aching silence when she is gone. But it is so.

My lady grandmother tells me that the death of my mother is God's way of showing me that in every joy there is sorrow, and that titles and worldly show are passing pleasures. I don't doubt that God speaks directly to my lady grandmother for she is always so certain about everything and her confessor, Bishop Fisher, is the holiest man I know. But God does not succeed in teaching me to disdain worldly show; on the contrary, the death of my mother, coming so soon after the loss of my brother, makes me long for the safety of wealth and my own crown more than ever before. I feel as if everyone I love best has gone from the world and no-one can be trusted. The only reliable thing in this world is a throne and a fortune. The only thing I have left is my new title. The only things I trust are my jewel box, the wardrobe for my wedding, and the enormous fortune that will come to me on marriage.

I am to leave England in the summer; the plans are unchanged and I am glad of it, as there is nothing to keep me here. King James of Scotland is as good as his word on the marriage treaty and I will have a fortune in rents – six thousand pounds a year from the lands he has given me, as well as one thousand Scots pounds a year for my allowance. He will pay the wages of my twenty-four English servants and the expenses of my court. If he should be so unfortunate as to die – and this is possible as he is so very old – then I will be a wealthy widow: I will have Newark Castle and Ettrick Forest, and much, much more. This is something I can count on: this fortune and my crown. Everything else, even my mother's love, can vanish overnight. I know this now.

But I am surprised to feel that I don't want to leave home without making friends with my brother Harry, and I go to look for him. He is in my lady grandmother's rooms, reading to her from a Latin psalter. I can hear his clear boy's voice and his beautiful pronunciation through her door, and he does not stop as the doors are swung open by the guard, though he glances up and sees me. The two of them are framed by the carved stone arch of the window, as if posing for a painting about Youth and Age. They are both beautifully dressed in black velvet; a shaft of sunlight illuminates Harry's golden head like a halo. My grandmother is wearing a severe white headdress, a wimple like a nun's. They should both stop and bow, but my lady grand-mother gives a nod of her head and gestures that Harry shall go on, as if his words are more important than my precedence. I look at them with exhausted resentment. They are both so lean and tall and beautiful and I am so dumpy and ruffled and hot. They look completely royal, enormously spiritual, and I look overdressed.

I curtsey to my grandmother in silence and sit on a cushion on the window seat that raises me slightly higher than her, while Harry finishes reading. It takes forever before she says: 'That was beautiful, Your Grace, my dear boy, thank you.' And he bows and closes the book and hands it back to her and says: 'It is I that should thank you for putting such words of wisdom, so beautifully illustrated, into my hands.'

Then they look at each other with mutual admiration and she goes to her small privy chapel to pray, her ladies follow her to kneel at the back, and Harry and I are alone.

'Harry, I am sorry that I said that, when Arthur died,' I stumble bluntly.

Graciously, he raises his head. Harry loves an apology.

'I was so unhappy,' I add. 'I didn't know what I was saying.'

'And then it got worse.' His moment of pride is gone. I can almost smell his misery – the misery of a boy, not yet a man, who has lost his mother, the only person who truly loved him.

Awkwardly, I get to my feet and stretch my arms out to him, and hold him. It is almost like holding Arthur, he is so tall and strong. 'My brother,' I say, trying out the words; I have never felt tenderly towards Harry before. 'My brother,' I repeat.

'My sister,' he says.

We hold each other in silence for a moment and I think: this is comforting. This is my brother – strong as a colt and lonely, as I am. I can, perhaps, trust him. He can trust me.

'You know, I am going to be King of England one day,' he says, his face pressed against my shoulder.

'Not for years yet,' I say consolingly. 'Father will come back to court and it will be like it was.'

'And I am to marry Katherine,' he says shyly. He releases me. 'She was never truly married to Arthur – she is to marry me.'

I am so stunned that I just gape silently, breathless with surprise. Harry sees the blankness of my face and gives a little embarrassed laugh. 'Not at once, of course. We will wait until I am fourteen. But we will be betrothed at once.'

'Not again!' bursts out of me, as I think of the gold laces and the extravagant wedding.

'It's agreed.'

'But she's Arthur's widow,' I say.

'Not really,' he says awkwardly.

'What do you mean?' Then, in an instant, all at once I know. I think of Katherine of Arrogant saying, 'Alas, it never happened for us', and my wondering what she meant by that, and why she should say such a thing.

'Alas,' I say, watching him narrowly. 'It never happened for them.'

'No,' he says, relieved. I could bet that he even recognises the words. 'No, alas, it didn't.'

'Is this her plan?' I demand furiously. 'Is this how she gets to stay here, forever? Is this how she gets to be Princess of Wales and then become Queen of England even though her husband died? Because she has set her heart on this? She was never in love with Arthur, it was always for the throne.'

'It's father's plan,' Harry says innocently. 'It was agreed before Lady Mother's . . . Lady Mother's death.'

'No, it will be her plan,' I am certain. 'She promised Arthur something before he died. I think it was this.'

Harry smiles like a glowing angel. 'Then I have my brother's blessing,' he says. He raises his head, like when he was reading the Latin psalm, and he repeats from memory. '"If brethren dwell together, and one of them dieth without children, the wife of the deceased shall not marry to another: but his brother shall take her, and raise up seed for his brother."'

'Is that the Bible?' I ask, feeling my ignorance, but thinking it remarkable that God should plan this convenient arrangement for the expensive widow. This way we get her dowry, and don't pay her widow's jointure. How mysterious are the ways of the Lord! How nice for her and how cheap for my father!

'Deuteronomy,' says my brother the scholar. 'It is God's will that I marry Katherine.'

Harry goes for his riding lesson and I remain seated in my lady grandmother's rooms till she comes out of her private chapel followed by her ladies-in-waiting, and I see that behind her, Princess Katherine is holding Mary's hand. Apparently, Katherine often prays with my sister in the privy chapel. I quickly take in her hood, her gown, her shoes, and I note that she has nothing new. The skirts of her gown look new, but actually they have been turned inside out; her shoes are worn. Katherine of Arrogant is having to pinch pennies, her parents are sending her no funds until the betrothal is confirmed, and my father is not paying her jointure since she will no longer be a widow. I cannot help but be pleased to see that the cost of her ambition is falling on her.

My lady grandmother sees me and beckons me into her chapel as the others leave, and we are alone in the shadowy room that always smells lingeringly of incense and books.

'Have you ever spoken privately with the Dowager Princess of Wales?' she asks me.

'Not much,' I say. I don't know what answer she wants to hear. But I can tell by the grim lines grooved around her mouth that she is very displeased with somebody. I only hope it's not me.

'Did she tell you anything of our beloved son Arthur?'

I note that my grandmother now refers to Arthur as our beloved son, as if my mother had never been at all. 'She once said that he asked her to comfort us in our loss,' I reply.

'Not that,' the old lady snaps. 'Not that. Did she say anything about her marriage, before he was ill?'

'Alas, it never happened for us,' I think to myself. Aloud, I say: 'No. She hardly speaks to me.'

I see my grandmother's face fold up into an expression of deep displeasure. Something has occurred that she dislikes – someone will be sorry for that. She puts a bony hand over mine, a deep, rich ruby glowing on her finger, the band clipping my knuckle. 'You ask her,' she orders. 'Ask her for advice. You are a young woman, about to be married. Ask her for the advice of a mother. What takes place in the marriage bed. Whether she was afraid, or in pain on her wedding night.'

I am quite shocked. I am a royal bride. I am not supposed to know anything. I am not supposed to ask.

She makes a little impatient noise in the back of her throat. 'Ask her,' she says. 'And then come and tell me exactly what she says.'

'But why?' I say, bemused. 'Why am I to ask her? It was more than a year ago.'

The face she turns to me is bleached with fury. I have never seen her like this before. 'She is saying they never bedded,' she hisses. 'Age sixteen and near six months married, and now she says they never bedded? Put to bed before the whole court and rising up smiling in the morning with not a word against it? And now she says that she is a virgin untouched.'

'But why should she say such a thing?'

'Her mother!' my lady grandmother exclaims as if the words are an insult. 'Her clever, wicked mother, Isabella of Castile, will have told her to deny Arthur so that she can marry without a dispensation, so she can be a virgin bride.'

Now she can't sit still, she is so enraged. She gets up from her prie-dieu and strides about the small space, her black skirts swishing the rushes on the floor back and forth so they release the perfume of bedstraw, meadowsweet and lavender in dusty clouds. 'Virgin bride? A viper bride! I know what they are thinking, I know what they are planning. But I will see her dead before she takes my son's throne.'

I am frightened. I crouch down on my footstool like a fat duckling in the nest when a sleek raptor flies over. My grandmother suddenly stops, puts her hands on my shoulder like a stooping peregrine. Her grip is as hard as a claw. I look up waveringly.

'You don't want her to marry Harry?' I whisper. 'I don't either.' I try a sycophantic smile. 'I don't like her. I don't want her to marry my brother.'

'Your father,' she says, and it is as if she shatters into a thousand sharp pieces of jealousy and grief. 'I am certain that she wants to seduce and marry your father! She has set her sights on my son! My boy, my precious boy! But she will never do it. I will never allow it.'

## DURHAM HOUSE, LONDON, ENGLAND, MARCH 1503

Unwilling and uncertain, I obey my grandmother and go to visit my sister-in-law, Katherine. I find her seated in her privy chamber hunched over a small fire. She is wrapped in a dark shawl and wearing a black gown, in double mourning, as we all are, but she looks up and springs to her feet when she sees me and her smile is bright.

'How lovely to see you. Did you bring Mary?'

'No,' I say, irritated. 'Why should I bring her?'

She laughs at my bad temper. 'No, no, I am so pleased you came alone, now we can be cosy.' She nods at the servant who has shown me into the room. 'You can put on another log,' she says, as if firewood should be used carefully. She turns to me: 'Will you have a glass of small ale?'

I accept a glass and then I have to laugh when I see her sip hers and put it aside. 'You still don't like it?'

She shakes her head and laughs. 'I don't think I ever will.'

'What did you drink in Spain?'

'Oh, we had clean water,' she says. 'We had fruit juices, and sherbets, light wines and ice from the ice houses.'

'Ice? Water?'

She shrugs, with that little gesture, as if she wants to forget the luxuries of her home at the Alhambra Palace. 'All sorts of things,' she says. 'They don't matter now.'

'I would think you would want to go home,' I say, raising the subject in obedience to my grandmother.

'Would you?' she asks, as if she is interested in my opinion. 'Would you want to go home and leave your husband's country if you were widowed?'

I have not thought of it. 'I suppose so.'

'I don't. England is my home now. And I am Dowager Princess of Wales.'

'You won't ever be queen,' I say bluntly.

'I will, if I marry your brother,' she says.

'You won't marry my father?'

'No. What an idea!'

We are both silent. 'My lady grandmother thought that was your intention,' I say awkwardly.

She looks sideways at me as if she is about to laugh. 'Did she send you here to stop me?'

I can't help but giggle. 'Not exactly, but, you know . . .'

'To spy on me,' she says agreeably.

'She can't bear the thought of him remarrying,' I say. 'Actually, neither can I.'

She puts her arm around my shoulders. Her hair smells of roses. 'Of course not,' she says. 'I have no intention, and my mother would never allow it.'

'But they don't insist you go home?'

She looks into the fire, and I am able to study her exquisite profile. I would think she could marry anyone she chose.

'I expect them to work out the dowry payments and betroth me to Harry,' she says.

'But if they don't?' I press her. 'If my lady grandmother wants Harry for another princess?'

She turns and looks me directly in the eye, her beautiful face open to my scrutiny. 'Margaret, I pray that this never happens to you. To love and to lose a husband is a terrible grief. But the only comfort I have is that I will do what my parents require, what Arthur wanted, and what God Himself has set as my destiny. I will be Queen of England. I have been called Princess of Wales since I was a baby in the nursery, I learned it as I learned my name. I won't change my name now.'

I am stunned by her certainty. 'I hope it never happens to me too. But if it did – I wouldn't stay in Scotland. I'd come home to England.'

'You can't do what you want when you are a princess,' she says simply. 'You have to obey God and the king and queen, your mother and father. You're not free, Margaret. You're not like a ploughman's daughter. You are doing the work of God, you are going to be mother to a king, you are one below the angels, you have a destiny.'

I look around the bare room, and I notice for the first time that one or two of the tapestries are missing from the walls, and that there are gaps in the collection of silver plate on the sideboard. 'Do you have enough money?' I ask her diffidently. 'Enough for your household.'

She shakes her head without shame. 'No,' she says. 'My father will not send me an allowance, he says I am the responsibility of the king, and your father will not pay me my widow's dower until all my bridal money has been paid to him. I am between two millstones and they are grinding me down.'

'But what will you do?'

She smiles at me as if she is quite unafraid. 'I'll endure. I will outlast them both. Because I know my destiny is to be Queen of England.'

'I wish I were like you,' I say honestly. 'I am certain of nothing.'

'You will be. When you are tested, you will be certain too. We are princesses, we were born to be queens, we are sisters.'

I ride away from the house on my expensive palfrey with my fur cape buttoned up to my nose, and I think I will report to my grandmother that Katherine of Arrogant is as proud and as beautiful as ever, but that she does not intend to marry my father. I will not tell her that the princess reminded me, in her stubborn determination, of my lady grandmother herself. If it comes to a battle of wills they will be well matched – but, actually, I would put my money on Katherine.

I will not tell my grandmother either that, for the first time, I like Katherine. I cannot help but think she will make a wonderful Queen of England.

## THE BISHOP OF SALISBURY'S HOUSE, LONDON, ENGLAND, JUNE 1503

I don't know what my grandmother says to her son my father; but he comes out of his mourning, there is an exchange of letters with Spain, and never another word about his courting Katherine. Instead, he pursues the marriage contract that is going to save him so much money with as much enthusiasm as Katherine's mother in faraway Spain. Together they instruct the Pope to send a dispensation so that a brother- and sister-in-law can marry, and Katherine of Arrogant dresses in virginal white and spreads her bronze hair over her shoulders for yet another grand wedding occasion.

At least this is not in the abbey, and we don't spend a fortune on it. This is a betrothal, not a wedding – a promise to marry when Harry is fourteen. She walks into the bishop's chapel as smiling and as queenly as she was just nineteen months ago, and she takes Harry's hand as if she is glad to promise herself to a boy five years her junior. It is as if Arthur, their wedding and their bedding never happened. Now she is Harry's bride and she will be known as the Princess of Wales once again. Her serene dismissal, 'Alas, it never happened for us', seems to be the last word that anyone will ever say about it.

My lady grandmother is there too. She does not smile on the match, but she does not oppose it. For me, it is just another event in this world that means nothing. A mother can die, a brother can die, and a woman can deny her husband and retain her title. The only person who makes any sense to me is Katherine herself. She knows who she was born to be; I wish I had her certainty. When she follows me out of the chapel I know that I am trying to hold my head as she does – as if I were wearing a crown already.

## RICHMOND PALACE, ENGLAND, JUNE 1503

I go to the nursery to say goodbye to my sister, Mary, and who should I find but Katherine, teaching her to play the lute as if we don't employ a music master, as if Katherine has nothing better to do. I don't trouble to conceal my irritation. 'I have come to say goodbye to my sister,' I say as a broad hint to Katherine that she might leave us alone.

'And here are both your sisters!'

'I have to say goodbye to Mary.' I ignore Katherine and guide Mary to the seat in the oriel window and pull her down to sit beside me. Katherine stands before us and listens. Good, I think, now you can see that I too have a sense of my destiny.

'I am going to Scotland to my husband; I am going to be a great queen,' I inform Mary. 'I will own a fortune, a queen's fortune. I will write to you and you must reply. You must write properly, not a silly scribble. And I will tell you how I get on as queen in my own court.'

She is seven years old, no longer a baby, but her face puckers up and she reaches out her arms to me. I receive the full sobbing weight of her on my lap. 'Don't cry,' I say. 'Don't cry, Mary. I will come back on visits. Perhaps you will come to visit me.'

She only sobs more passionately and I meet Katherine's concerned gaze over her heaving shoulder. 'I thought she would be glad for me,' I say. 'I thought I should tell her – you know – that a princess is not like a ploughman's daughter.'

'It is hard for her to lose a sister,' she says with ready sympathy. 'And she has just lost a mother and a brother.'

'I have too!' I point out.

The older girl smiles and puts her hand gently on my shoulder. 'It's hard for us all.'

'It wasn't very hard for you.'

I see the shadow pass over her face. 'It is,' she says shortly. She kneels beside the two of us and puts her arm around my sister's thin shaking shoulders. 'Little Princess Mary,' she says sweetly. 'One sister is leaving you, but one has arrived. I am here. And we will all write to each other, and we will always be friends. And one day, you will go to a beautiful country and be married, and we will always remember our royal sisters.'

Mary raises her tearstained face and reaches out for Katherine's neck so she is holding us both. It is almost as if we are welded together by sisterly love. I can't pull away, and I find that I don't want to. I put my arms around Katherine and Mary and our three golden heads come together as if we were swearing an oath.

'Friends forever and ever,' Mary says solemnly.

'We are the Tudor sisters,' Katherine says, though obviously she's not.

'Two princesses and one queen,' I say.

Katherine smiles at me, her face close to mine, her eyes shining. 'I am sure we will all be queens one day,' she says.

## ON PROGRESS, RICHMOND TO COLLYWESTON, ENGLAND, JUNE 1503

Our journey is unbelievably grand, something between a masque and a hunt. First, at the head, free of the dust and setting our own pace, comes my father the king and me: Queen of Scots. He rides behind his royal standard, I behind mine. I change my riding outfits and they are brushed clean every time we stop, sometimes three times a day. I wear Tudor green, dark crimson, a yellow so dark that it is like orange, and a pale blue. My father tends to wear black – always dark colours – but his hat, his gloves and his waistcoat gleam with jewels, and his shoulders are loaded with chains of gold. Our horses are the best that can be had. I have a palfrey, a lady's horse that has been trained with crowds and fireworks to make sure that nothing startles her, and my groom leads a spare horse. I ride astride, on a thickly padded saddle so that we can go many miles every day, or I can ride behind my master of horse on a pillion saddle embroidered with the emblem of Scotland: the thistle. If I am tired, I have a litter carried by mules, and I can get inside, draw the curtains and sleep while it gently rocks me.

Behind us come the courtiers, as if they were out for a day of pleasure, with the long sleeves of the ladies rippling as we canter, and the cloaks of the gentlemen billowing like standards. The gentlemen of my father's rooms and my ladies mingle without ceremony, and there is continual laughter and flirtation. Behind them come the mounted guard, though England is supposed to be at peace. My father is perenially suspicious, always afraid that the foolish, wicked people still hold their loyalty to the old royal family. Behind the mounted guard comes the wagon with the hawks and falcons, their leather curtains tied tightly against the dust, and all the birds standing on their travelling perches, their little heads crowned with leather hoods, blinded to all the noise and confusion so they are not frightened.

Around them, baying and yelping, are the big hounds – the wolfhounds and the deerhounds with the huntsmen and the whippers-in riding alongside and keeping them under control. Every now and then one of the dogs gets a scent and gives tongue and all the others are desperate to give chase and follow; but we cannot stop to hunt if we are riding towards a feast or a celebration or a formal welcome. Some days we hunt before breakfast, and sometimes in the cool of the evening, and then the dogs can take a scent and make a run, and the court will spur on their horses, scrambling over ditches and riding through strange woods, laughing and cheering. If we make a kill we present the meat at the next halt to our overnight host.

Ahead of us, starting half a day before we mount, goes the baggage train. First out: half a dozen carts that carry my clothes; one, specially guarded, carries my jewels. The steward of my household and his servants either sit beside the drivers or ride alongside, to make sure that nothing goes missing and nothing is lost. The wagons are strapped with oilskins dyed in the Tudor colours of green and white and sealed with my royal seal. My ladies each have their own wardrobe cart, displaying their own shields, and when the wagons rumble, one after another, it looks like a moving tree of shields from a tournament, as if the Knights of the Round Table had decided to invade the north, all at once.

My father is not amusing company on this great journey. He is unhappy at the state of the roads, and the cost of the travel. He is missing my mother, I suppose, but this does not show itself as grief but in continual complaint: 'If Her Grace were here she would do that' or 'I never had to order that, it is the queen's work'. My mother was so beloved, and her family were so accustomed to rule, having been on the throne for generations, that she always used to guide him in the great public occasions, and everyone felt easier when she was at the head of a procession. I begin to think that it would have been thoroughly good for Katherine of Arrogant to have been forced to marry my father: serving him would have humbled her far more than marrying Harry will ever do. She is going to lord it over Harry, I know, but my father would have set her to work.

He is glad when we get to my lady grandmother's house at Collyweston because here everything is commanded by her to the highest standard, and here he can rest and do nothing. I think he may be ill; certainly, he seems tired, and my lady his mother fusses around him with all sorts of potions of her own mixing and strengthening drinks. Here we will part – he will go back to London and I will go on northward to Scotland. I will not see him again until I come back to England for a visit.

I wonder if my father is distressed at my leaving and hiding it under ill temper, but truly, I think he will feel my loss no more than I feel his. We have never been close; he has never made much of me. I am his daughter, but I resemble the smiling tall blondes of my mother's family. I am not a precious little doll-faced princess like Mary. I have inherited his temper, but his mother has made sure that I keep it hidden. I have his courage – he spent his life in exile and then came to England against all odds – I think I can be brave too. I have my mother's hopefulness; my father thinks the worst of everyone and plans to catch them out. Anyone seeing us side by side – he so spare and dark and I round-faced and broad-shouldered – would never take us for father and elder daughter, no wonder we feel no sense of kinship.

I kneel for his blessing as my train of courtiers waits in the sunshine and my grandmother inspects me for flaws, and when I rise up he kisses me on both cheeks. 'You know what you have to do,' he says shortly. 'Make sure that husband of yours keeps the peace. England will never be safe if Scotland is an enemy and always stirring up the Northern lands. It's called the Treaty of Perpetual Peace for a reason. You are there to make sure that it is perpetual.'

'I'll do what I can, Sire.'

'Never forget you're an English princess,' he says. 'If anything happens to Harry, which God forbid, you will be mother to the next King of England.'

'The grandest thing in the world,' my grandmother adds. She and her son exchange a warm glance. 'Serve God,' she says to me. 'And remember your patron saint and mine, the Blessed Margaret.'

I bow my head at the name of the woman who was saved from being eaten by a dragon when her crucifix scratched his belly and he vomited her up.

'Let her life be an example for you,' my lady grandmother urges.

I put my hand on the crucifix at my throat to indicate that, should I be swallowed by a dragon between here and Edinburgh, I am fully prepared.

'God bless you,' she says. Her old face is set firm; there is no danger of her weeping at our parting. I may be her favourite granddaughter, but neither Mary nor I can compare to her passion for her son and grandson. She is founding a dynasty: she only needs boys.

She kisses me, and holds me close for a moment. 'Try to have a son,' she whispers. 'Nothing else matters but your son on the throne.'

It is a cold farewell to a motherless girl but before I can answer, my master of horse steps forward and lifts me onto my palfrey, the trumpeters blast out a salute, and everyone knows we are ready to leave. The king's court waves, my lady grandmother's household cheers, and I lead out my court, flying my standard, on the great north road to Edinburgh.

## ON PROGRESS, YORK TO EDINBURGH, JULY 1503

I head for the borderlands of England and Scotland with little regret for what I am leaving behind. So much of my childhood has already gone. In the past year I have lost my adored brother and then my mother, and a little newborn sister with her. But I find that I don't miss them so much, in this new life that I am entering. Oddly, it is Katherine that I miss as I travel north. I want to tell her about the magnificent greetings that welcome me to every town, and I want to ask about the awkwardness of a long ride and needing the garderobe. I copy her beautiful way of holding her head, I even practise her little roll of the shoulders. I try to say 'ridiculous' with a Spanish accent. I think that she will be Queen of England and I will be Queen of Scotland and people will compare us one with another, and that I will learn to be as elegant as she is.

I have daily opportunities for practising her poise, for I am beginning to discover that one of the greatest features of being royal is being able to think quietly about interesting things while people pray for you or talk at you, or even sing anthems about you. It would be rude to yawn when someone is thanking God for your arrival, so I have learned the trick of drifting off without falling asleep. I sit like Katherine, with my back very straight and my head raised high to lengthen my neck. Most often I lift my gown a tiny fraction of an inch and look at my shoes. I have ordered slippers with the toes embroidered in fanciful designs so that these pious meditations can be yet more interesting.

I look at my toes a lot at every long boring stopping point, while noblemen make speeches at me, all the way northward. My father has ordered that my journey shall be a magnificent procession, and my part in it is to look beautiful in a series of wonderful gowns, and to cast down my eyes in modesty when people thank God for the coming of the Tudors and, in particular, for my passing through their plague-infested, dirty little town. That's when I look at my toes and think that soon I will be in my own country, Scotland. And then I will be queen. And then I shall be the one to decide where I go, and how long the speeches will take.

I am amazed by the countryside as we ride north. It is almost as if the sky opens up over us, like the lid off a chest. Suddenly the horizon gets further and further away, receding as we climb up and down rolling green hills and see more and more hills ahead of us, as if all of England is billowing under our feet. Above us arches the great northern sky. The air is watery and clear, as if we were submerged. I feel as if we are tiny people, a little train of shrimps crawling along a huge world, and the buzzards that wheel above us, and the occasional eagle even higher than they, see rightly that we are specks on the side of giant rolling hills.

I had no idea it was so far to go, no idea that so much of Northern England is empty of all people: not hedged, not ditched, not farmed, nor worked at all. It is just empty country, wasteland, not even mapped.

Of course, there are people who scrape a living from this

untouched landscape. Every now and then we see in the distance a rough stone tower and sometimes we hear the ringing of a warning bell when their watchmen have seen us. These are the wild Northern men who ride these lands, stealing each other's crops and horses, rounding up each other's cattle, scraping a living from their tenants and then robbing others. We don't go near their outposts and we are too numerous and too well armed for them to attack us; but the leader of my escort, Thomas Howard Earl of Surrey, grinds his old yellow teeth at the very thought of them. He has fought up and down this country and burned out these poor forts to punish these people for their wildness, for their poverty, for their hatred of everything Southern and wealthy and easy.

It is he who prevents me ordering matters as I would like, for everything is commanded by him and his equally disagreeable wife, Agnes. For some reason my father likes and trusts Thomas Howard, and has appointed him to the task of conveying me to Edinburgh, and keeping me to the behaviour suitable for a Queen of Scotland. I should think that by now I could be trusted without a Howard at my elbow to give me advice. He's also here as a spy, since he has fought against the Scots more than once, and he meets with the Northern lords in a little huddle at every town where we halt, to learn of the mood of the Scots border lords, and whether any more of them can be bribed to take our side. He promises our lords that they shall have weapons and money to maintain the defences of England against Scotland, though the mere fact that I am here will bring a perpetual peace.

Howard does not seem to understand what a change in the world has been made by my marriage to the King of Scotland. He treats me with every outward respect, doffs his hat, bows his knee, accepts dishes from my table, but there is something about his manner that I don't like. It is as if he does not realise the God-given nature of kingship. It is as if he thinks that he saw my father stumble through the mud of Bosworth Field to pick up his crown, and that he might one day drop it again.

Howard fought against us then, but he persuaded my father that this was commendable loyalty, not treason. He says he was loyal to the crown on that day, he is loyal to the crown now. If the coronet of England were on the head of a baboon from Afric he would be loyal to it then. It is the crown, and the wealth that flows from it, that inspires Howard loyalty. I don't believe he loves my father and me at all. If he was not such a brilliant general I don't think I would have to put up with his company. If my mother were alive she would have appointed one of her family. If my brother were alive then my lady grandmother would not be tied at court to guard the only heir we have left. But everything has gone wrong since Katherine came to court and took Arthur away, and these Howards are just an example of how my interests do not come first as they should.

My dislike of them grows at every stop, where they watch how I listen to loyal addresses and prompt me when I am to speak in reply, though I know perfectly well that I have to be admiring in York, and enchanted in Berwick, our northernmost town, a little jewel of a castle set in a bend of the river near to the sea. I don't have to be told to admire the fortifications; I can see how welcoming Berwick is to me, I know how safe I feel inside these great walls. But Thomas Howard practically dictates the speech of thanks I make to the captain of the castle. He prides himself on his knowledge of tradition. By some means or another he is descended from Edward I and this means that he thinks he can speak to me about sitting straighter in the saddle and not looking around for the dishes coming into the hall when the speeches go on and on before dinner.

By the time we reach the Scots border, just two hours' ride from Berwick, I am completely sick of the two Howards, and I resolve that the first thing I shall do when I set up my court is send them home with a note to my father to say that they lack the skills that I require in my courtiers. They may be good enough for him, but not for me. They can serve in Katherine's court and she can see what joy Thomas Howard brings her. She can see if she likes knowing that he is so loyal to the crown that he does not care whose head it is on. His grimly ambitious presence can remind her that she too married one Prince of Wales but is now determined to be the wife of another; it is always the crown for the Howards and the crown for Katherine.

But none of this matters when we finally cross the border and are in Scotland at last, and the lady of Dalkeith Castle, the Countess of Morton, whispers to me: 'The king is coming!'

It has been such a long journey that I had almost forgotten that at the end of it is this: the throne of Scotland, the thistle crown, but also a man, a real man, not just one who sends gifts and flowery compliments through ambassadors – but a real man who is on his way to see me.

The arrangement was that he would meet me as I entered Edinburgh, but there is a stupid tradition that the bridegroom – like a fairy-tale prince – is supposed to be unable to contain his impatience, and rides out early, like a 'parfit gentil knight' in a romance, to meet his bride. This reminds me of Arthur again, who rode in the rain to Dogmersfield to meet a reluctant Katherine, and makes me want to laugh and cry at the same time, remembering the poor reception that he got, and his embarrassment. But it shows at least that the King of Scots knows how things should be done, and is demonstrating a flattering interest in me.

We all get into a panic of readiness and even my chief lady-in-waiting Agnes Howard shows a little excitement when she comes to my room. I am dressed in a gown of deep green with cloth of gold sleeves and my best pearls, and we all sit as if we were posing for an artist, listening to music and trying to look as if we are not waiting. Thomas Howard comes in and looks around the room as if he were placing sentries. He leans over my shoulder and whispers in my ear that I should look as if I am completely surprised by the arrival of the king. I should not look like I am waiting. I tell him that I know this, and then we all wait. Hours go by before finally there is a clatter at the gate, and a shout of acclaim, a rattle at the main door, quick steps in noisy riding boots up the stairs, then the sentries throw open the door and in he comes: my husband.

I nearly scream at the sight of him. He has the most enormous ridiculous beard, as red as a fox, almost the size of a fox. I jump to my feet and I let out a little gasp. Agnes Howard gives me a sharp look and if she were nearer I think she would have pinched me to remind me of my manners. But it doesn't matter, for the king is taking me by the hand and bowing, apologising for startling me. He takes my wide-eyed, jaw-dropped gape as a compliment at his unexpected arrival, and he laughs at himself for being a troubadour of love, then he greets all my ladies with a smiling confidence, bows over Agnes Howard's hand and greets Thomas Howard as if they will be the best of friends and he has quite forgotten that Thomas has invaded Scotland twice already.

He is beautifully dressed, like a European prince, in red velvet edged with cloth of gold, and he remarks that we have both chosen velvet. The jacket is cut like a riding jacket but the material is priceless, and instead of a crossbow over his back, as if he were hunting, he is carrying a lyre. I say, a little faintly, that he is a troubadour indeed if he carries his lyre everywhere, and he tells me that he loves music, and poetry and dance, and that he hopes I do too.

I say that I do and he urges me to dance. Agnes Howard stands up with me and the musicians play a pavane, which I know I perform very gracefully. They serve supper and we sit beside each other and now, while he talks to Thomas Howard, I am able to look at him properly.

He is a handsome man. He is very old of course, being thirty, but he has none of the stiffness or solemnity of an old man. He has a beautiful face: high-arched eyebrows and warm intelligent eyes. All the quickness of his thoughts and the intensity of his feeling seem to shine out of his dark eyes and his mouth is strongly shaped and, for some reason, it makes me think of kissing. Except for the beard, of course. There is no getting away from the beard. I doubt there is any way to get past the beard. At least he is combed and washed and scented; it is not a beard that might have a mouse nesting in it. But I would have preferred him clean-shaven and I cannot help but wonder if I can mention this. Surely it is bad enough for me to have to marry a man who is old enough to be my father, and with a smaller kingdom than my home, without him bringing a fox's brush to bed with him?

He leaves at dusk and I remark to Agnes Howard that perhaps

she might tell her husband that I would prefer the king clean-shaven. Typically, she tells him at once as if my preferences are ridiculous, and so before I go to bed I have a lecture from them both that I am fortunate to become a queen, and that no husband, especially an ordained king, is going to take advice on his appearance from a young woman.

'Man is made in the image of God; no woman, who was made after God had completed his finest creation, is fit to criticise,' Thomas Howard tells me as if he were pope.

'Oh, amen,' I say sulkily.

In the next four days before the wedding my new husband comes to visit every day, but mostly he talks to Thomas Howard rather than to me. The old man has fought the Scots up and down the borders, but instead of being enemies for life, as anyone would expect, they are inseparable, sharing stories of campaigns and battles. My betrothed, who should be courting me, reruns old wars with my escort, and Thomas Howard, who should be attending to my comfort, forgets I am there and tells the king of his long years of campaigning. They are never happier than when they are drawing a map of ground where they have fought, or when James the king is describing the weaponry he is designing and having built for his castles. Both of them behave, as soldiers together always do, as if women are completely irrelevant to the work of the world, as if the only interesting work is invading someone else's lands and killing him. Even when I am seated with my ladies and the king comes in with Thomas, he wastes only a few moments on being charming to me, and then asks Thomas if he has seen the new guns, the Dardanelles gun, the new light cannon, if he knows of the famous Scottish cannon Monns, the largest in Europe – which was given to James' grandfather by the Duke of Burgundy. It is most irritating. I am sure that Katherine would not stand for it.

The day of our entry into Edinburgh is my last day as a Tudor princess before I am crowned in my new kingdom, and the king takes me up behind him on his horse, as if I were a simple lady and he my master of horse, or as if he had captured me and was bringing me home. We enter Edinburgh with me seated behind him, pressed against his back, my arms wrapped around his waist, like a peasant girl coming home from a fair. It pleases everyone. They like the romance of the picture that we make, like a woodcut of a knight and a rescued lady; they like an English princess being brought into their capital city like a trophy. They are an informal, affectionate people, these Scots. I can't understand a single word that anyone says, but the beaming faces and the kissed waving hands and the cheers show their delight at the sight of the handsome wild-looking king with his long red hair and beard, and the golden princess seated behind him on his horse.

The city is walled with fine gates, and behind them the houses are a mixture of shanties and hovels, some good-sized ones with plastered walls under thick thatched roofs, and a few newly built of stone. There is a castle perched on the very top of an incredibly steep hill at one end of the city, sheer cliffs all around it and only a narrow road to the summit; but there is a new-built palace in the valley at the other end, and outside the tight fortified walls of the town are high hills and forests. Running steeply downhill from castle to palace is a broad cobbled road, a mile long, and the best houses of the tradesmen and guildsmen front this street and their upper storeys jut over it. Behind them are pretty courtyards and the dark wynds that lead to inner hidden houses and big gardens, orchards, enclosures, and more houses behind them with secret alleyways that run down the hill.

At every street corner there is a tableau or a masque, with angels, goddesses and saints praying for love and fertility for me. It is a pretty little city, built as high as it is broad, the castle standing like a mountain above it, the turrets scraping the sky, the flags fluttering among the clouds. It is a jumble of a city, being rebuilt from hovels to houses, from wood to stone, grey slate roofs replacing thatch. But every window, whether open to the cold air, shuttered or glazed, shows a standard, or colours, and between the overhanging balconies they have strung scarves and chains of flowers. Every poky little doorway is crammed with the family clustered together to wave at me, and where the stone houses have an oriel window or an upper storey and a balcony children are leaning out to cheer. The noise of all the people crammed into the little streets and the shouting as our guard push their way through is overwhelming. Ahead and behind us there must be at least a thousand horses with Scots and English lords intermingled to show the new unity that I have brought to Scotland, and we all wind our way through the narrow cobbled streets and then down the hill to the palace of Holyroodhouse.

## HOLYROODHOUSE PALACE, EDINBURGH, SCOTLAND, AUGUST 1503

Next day my ladies wake me in the cool light of a blue sky at six in the morning. I attend Lauds in my private chapel and then I take breakfast in my presence chamber with only my ladies attending. Nobody eats very much, we are all too excited, and I am ready to be sick at the very taste of the bread roll and small ale. I go back to my bedroom where a huge bath has been rolled in, filled with steaming water, and my wedding gown is laid out on the bed. My ladies wash and dress me as if I were a wooden poppet, and then they comb my hair so that it is smooth and curling and spread out over my shoulders. It is my best feature, this wealth of fair hair, and we all pause to admire it and tie in extra ribbons. Then, suddenly, there is no time and we have to hurry. I keep remembering a dozen things that I want, and a dozen things that I was going to do. Already I have on my wedding shoes, with embroidered toes and golden laces, quite as fine as Katherine of Arrogant's, and Agnes Howard is ready to walk behind me, and the ladies all line up behind her, and I have to go.

Down the stone stairs, into the bright sunshine I glide to where the great door of the neighbouring abbey is thrown open for me, and then into the abbey, which is crowded with lords and their ladies dressed in their robes, the air scented with incense, and ringing with the music of the choir. I remember walking up the aisle towards James at the top, and the blaze of gold from the reliquaries on the altar and the heat from the thousands of candles and the high vaulting of the ceiling. I remember the magnificent stone window over the altar, storeys high, blazing with colour from the stained glass – and then ... I don't remember another thing.

I think it is as grand as Arthur's wedding. It's not St Paul's, of course, but I wear a gown as good as Katherine's was on that day. The king at my side is a blaze of jewels, and he is a full king whereas Katherine married only a prince. And I am crowned. She was never crowned, of course, she was a mere princess, and is now even less than that. But I have a double ceremony: I am married and then I am crowned queen. It is so grand and it takes so long that I am in a daze. I have ridden so far, hundreds and hundreds of miles, all the way from Richmond, and been seen by so many people. I have been waiting for this day for years; my father had it planned for most of my life, it is my lady grandmother's great triumph. I should feel wildly excited, but it is too thrilling to take in. I am only thirteen. I feel like my little sister Mary when she is allowed to stay up too late at a feast. I am dazzled by my own glory and I pass through everything – the wedding Mass, the coronation and the loyal oaths, the feast, the masquing, the last service at the chapel and then the procession to bed – as if I were dreaming. The king's arm is around my waist all the day – if it were not for him I think I would fall. The day goes on forever, and then he goes to confess and pray in his rooms as my ladies take me and put me to bed.

Agnes Howard supervises them as they unlace my sleeves and put them away in lavender bags, untie my gown and help me out of the tight stomacher. I am to wear my finest linen robe, trimmed with French lace, and over it I have a satin gown for the night. They lie me on the bed, propped against the pillows, arrange my gown around my feet and pull and tweak at my sleeves as if I were a wax effigy, like my mother on her coffin. Agnes Howard twists my fair hair into curls and spreads it around my shoulders, pinching my cheeks to make them blush.

'How do I look?' I ask her. 'Hand me a mirror.'

'You look well,' she says with a little smile. 'A beautiful bride.'

'Like Katherine?'

'Yes,' she says.

'Like my mother?' I gaze at my round childish face in the looking glass.

She studies me with critical, measuring eyes. 'No,' she says. 'Not really. For she was the most beautiful of all the Queens of England.'

'More beautiful than my sister, then?' I say, trying to find some measure to give me confidence to face my husband this night.

Again, the level, judging look. 'No,' she says reluctantly. 'But you should never compare yourself with her. Mary is going to be exceptional.'

I give a little irritated exclamation and push the looking glass back at her.

'Be at peace,' she recommends. 'You're the most beautiful Queen of Scotland. Let that be enough for you. And your husband is clearly pleased with you.'

'I wonder he could see me through the beard,' I say crossly. 'I wonder he can see anything.'

'He can see you,' she advises me. 'There's not much that he misses.'

The lords of his court escort him to the bedroom door, singing bawdy songs and making jokes, but he does not allow them into our chamber. When he enters he says goodnight to the ladies so that everyone leaves us and has to abandon the hope that they might watch the bedding. I realise that he does this not out of any shyness, because he has no shyness, but out of kindness to me. There is really no need. I am not a child, I am a princess; I have been born and bred for this. I have lived all my life in the glare of a court. I know that everyone always knows everything about me and constantly compares me to other princesses. I am never judged for myself, I was always viewed as one of four Tudor children, and now I am weighed as one of three royal sisters. It's never fair.

James undresses himself, like a common man, throwing off his fine long gown so he stands before me in his nightshirt, and then pulls that over his head. I hear a chink like a heavy necklace as his nakedness is revealed to me inch by inch as the nightshirt is stripped off. Strong legs covered in thick, dark hair, a mass of dark hair at his crotch and his pizzle standing up awkwardly like a stallion's, the dark line of hair over his flat belly, and then—

'What's that?' I ask as I see a circlet of metal rings around his waist. It was this that made the little revealing chink.

'That's my manhood,' he says, deliberately misunderstanding me. 'I won't hurt you, I will be gentle.'

'Not that,' I say. I was raised at court but I have been around stables and farm animals for all my life. 'I know all about that. What is that around your waist?'

He touches the belt lightly with his finger. 'Oh, this.'

I can see now that it has rubbed him raw. It is barbed and it grazes his skin every time he makes a move. The skin is rough and scarred around his waist; he must have worn this for years. He has been in constant irritating discomfort for years as every movement he makes scratches his skin.

'This is a cilice,' he says. 'You must have seen one before. You who knows so much of the world that you see your husband's cock on your wedding night, and already you know all about it?'

I giggle a little. 'I didn't mean that. But what is the cilice for?'

'It's to remind me of my sin,' he says. 'When I was young, about your age, I did something very stupid, something very wrong. I did something that will send me to hell. I wear it to remind me that I am stupid and that I am a sinner.'

'If you were my age then nobody can blame you,' I assure him. 'You can just confess. Confess and be given a penance.'

'I can't be forgiven just because I was young,' he says. 'And don't you think that either. You can't be forgiven because you are young or because you are royal or in your case because you are a woman and your mind is less steady than a man's. You are a queen; you have to hold yourself to the highest of standards. You have to be wise, you have to be faithful, your word has to be your bond, you have to answer to God, not to a priest who might absolve you. No-one can absolve you for stupidity and sin if you are royal. You have to make sure that you never commit stupidity or sin.'

I look at him, a little aghast, as he towers above me in my bridal chamber, his pizzle standing up and ready, a great chain cutting into his waist, stern as a judge.

'Do you have to wear it now?' I ask. 'I mean, now?'

He gives a little laugh. 'No,' he says, and he bends his head, unlinks it and removes it. He comes to the bed and gets in beside me.

'It must be better to take it off,' I say, guiding him to the thought that he might lay it aside forever.

'There is no reason that you should be scratched for my sins,' he says gently. 'I will take it off when I am with you. There is no reason that this should hurt you at all.'

It does not hurt because he is gentle and quick and he keeps his weight off me – he is not clumsy like a stallion in the field but deft and neat. There is something very pleasant about being stroked all over, like a cat on someone's lap, and his hands go everywhere on me, behind my ears and in my hair and down my back and between my legs, as if there was nowhere that he could not turn my skin into silk and then into cream. It has been a long day and I feel dizzy and sleepy and there is no pain at all, more a rather surprising intrusion, and then a sort of warm stirring, and just when it starts to get heavy and pushing, and too much, it is finished and I am left feeling nothing but warm and petted.

'That's it?' I ask, surprised, when he gives a sigh and then comes carefully away and lies back on the pillow.

'That's it,' he says. 'Or at any rate, that's it for tonight.'

'I thought it hurt and there was blood,' I say.

'There is a little blood,' he says. 'Enough to show on the bed sheets in the morning. Enough for Lady Agnes to report to your grandmother; but it should not hurt. It should be a pleasure, even for a woman. Some physicians think there has to be pleasure to make a child, but I doubt that myself.'

He gets out of bed and picks up his chain belt again.

'Do you have to put that on?'

'I do.' He clips it on and I see his little grimace as the metal scratches against his sore skin.

'What did you do that was so very bad?' I ask, as if he might tell me a story before I go to sleep.

'I led rebel lords against my father the king,' he answers, but he is not smiling and this is not a pleasant story at all. 'I was fifteen. I thought he was going to murder me and put my brother in my place. I listened to the lords and I led their army in a treasonous rebellion. I thought that we would capture him and he would rule with better advisors. But when he saw me he did not advance; he would not march against his own son. He was more faithful a father to me than I was a son to him, and so the rebels and I won the battle, and he ran away, and they caught and killed him.'

'What?' I am jolted from sleep by the horror of this story.

'Yes.'

'You rebelled against your father and killed him?' This is a sin against order, against God and against his father. 'You killed your own father?'

His shadow on the wall behind him leaps as my bedside candle gutters. 'God forgive me, yes,' he says quietly. 'And so there is a curse on me as a rebel, a usurper and a man who killed my own king: a son who killed his own father. I am a regicide and a patricide. And I wear this so I never forget to suspect the motives of my allies, and when I make war I always think who may be killed by accident. I am deep in sin. I will never be able to expiate it.'

The bed ropes creak as he gets into bed beside me, this king-killer, this murderer. 'Can you not go on pilgrimage?' I ask faintly. 'Can you not go on crusade? Can the Holy Father not dispense for your sin?'

'I hope to do so,' he says quietly. 'This country has never been peaceful enough for me to safely leave, but I would like to go on crusade. I hope to go to Jerusalem one day – that would wash my soul clean.'

'I didn't know,' I say quietly. 'I didn't know anything about this.'

He shrugs and pulls the covers up over his belly, spreading himself out in the bed, feet to both corners, arms folded across his broad chest, as if all the bed is his and I must fit into one corner, or mould myself around him.

'Your own father led a rebellion against a crowned ordained king,' he says, as if it is not the most terrible thing to do. 'And he married your mother against her will, and he killed her kinsmen, young men of royal blood. To take the throne and to hold it, you sometimes have to do terrible things.'

I let out a little squeak of protest. 'No, he did not! Not any of those things, or at any rate, not like that!'

'Sin is sin,' the murderer tells me, and then he goes to sleep.

The next morning is the best day of my life. It is a tradition that the Scots kings give their brides their dower lands the morning after the wedding, and I go into James' privy chamber where he and I sit either side of a heavy table as he signs over the deeds of one enormous forest and one great castle after another until I know that I am indeed as wealthy as any queen. I am happy and the court is happy for me. They too have gleaned gifts at my harvest. James Hamilton, who negotiated the marriage treaty, is to be Earl of Arran, a title created for him in reward for his work and to acknowledge his kinship to the king. All my ladies receive gifts, all the Scots lords are given money and some of them get titles.

Then the king turns to me, and says with a slight smile: 'I am informed that you don't like my beard, Your Grace. This too can be at your command. Behold, I am a willing Samson. I will be shorn for love.'

He has surprised me. 'You will?' I say. 'Who told you? I never said anything about it.'

'You would rather I kept it long?' He strokes the great bush of it from his chin to his belly.

'No! No!' I shake my head and this makes him laugh again.

He turns and nods to one of his companions and the man opens the door to the presence chamber. All the people outside peep in to see what their betters are doing, as a servant comes in with a bowl and a jug, linen, and a great pair of golden scissors.

At once my ladies laugh and clap their hands, but I feel awkward and I am glad when the door is shut and the petitioners and visitors can't see us. 'I don't know what you mean to do. Can't we send for a barber?'

'You do it,' he says teasingly. 'You don't want my beard, you take it off. Or are you afraid?'

'I'm not afraid,' I say boldly.

'I think you are,' he says, his smile gleaming through the fox brush. 'But Lady Agnes will help you.'

I glance at her in case this is not allowed, but she is smiling and laughing.

'May I?' I say doubtfully.

'If Samson comes to be shorn, who shall refuse him?' Agnes Howard says. 'But we don't want to cut off your strength, Your Grace. We would not hurt you for the world.'

'You shall make me as handsome as an English courtier,' he assures her. 'If Her Grace the little Queen of Scots does not want a handsome Highland beard in her bed, she need not endure one. She has to have me, wild enough for any woman – she need not have a great beard as well.'

He sits down on a stool, tucks the napkin around his neck and presents the scissors to me. I take them and make a nervous snip. A whole clump of red pelt falls into his lap. Aghast, I stop, but the king laughs and says: 'Bravo, Bravo, Queen Margaret! Go to it!' And I make another snip and then another until it is all off. He is still thickly bearded, but the cascade of hair that tumbled over his chest is now lying on the floor.

'Now, Lady Agnes,' he says, 'I swear that you know how to shave a man. Show Her Grace how it is done and make sure that you don't cut my poor throat.'

'Should we not send for a barber?' she asks, just as I did.

He laughs. 'Oh, give me a noble shearing,' he says, and Lady Agnes sends for hot water and a razor and the finest soap and sets about him while I watch and the king laughs at my appalled expression.

At the end she wraps him in warm linen and he pats his newly bared face gently and then unwraps for me.

'What do you think?' he asks. 'Do I please you now, Your Grace?'

His lower face is white-skinned, far paler than the rest, as it has been shaded from the sun and wind by his beard while his cheeks and his brow are deeply tanned, and he has white smile-lines around his eyes. He looks odd, but his chin is strong and slightly dimpled and his mouth is sensual, the lips full and shapely.

'You do,' I say, for I can hardly say anything else.

He gives me a warm kiss on the mouth, and Agnes Howard claps her hands as if all the credit is due to her.

'Wait till they see me,' he says. 'My loyal lords will know that I am wedded and bedded to an English princess indeed, for I have become so very English and smart.'

We stay in Holyroodhouse Palace until the autumn and there are constant jousts and celebrations. The French knight Antoine d'Arcy, the Sieur de la Bastie, is a great favourite, and swears that he would be my chevalier were he not already promised to Anne of Brittany. I pretend to be offended, but then he tells me that in honour of her he wears armour and trappings of pure white, and nothing suits him better. He really cannot switch to green. This makes me laugh and I agree that he has to be 'the white knight' for the rest of his life, but that I will know and he will know that his heart is mine. This is very pretty nonsense, especially from a young man so dazzlingly good-looking, and it is part of the work of being a beautiful queen.

## ON PROGRESS, SCOTLAND, AUTUMN 1503

When it gets a little colder and the leaves start to crisp and change colour, my husband takes me on a progress to see some of the lands that are mine as queen. I think of my lady grandmother's keen stewardship of her lands and her quiet avarice in adding to her landholding, and I look around me as I ride westwards out of the city, along the raised tracks that weave through the marshy lands at the edge of a great river, the Forth, and hope that my land is being profitably managed.

The trees grow down to the water's edge and rain their leaves on us as if we were in a parade and people were throwing flowers. The woods are all the colours of bronze and gold, red and brown, and the higher slopes of the hills are ablaze with the red of rowan trees. The few villages along the way are surrounded by a patchwork of little fields and all the hedgerows are bright with hips and hawthorn berries, and in the thicker clumps there is the fat gleam of sloes as black as jet. Above our heads the geese flying south cross the sky in huge processions, one behind the other, and we often hear the loud creak of great wings as flights of swans go south away from the cold weather of the north. Every morning and every dusk we see herds of deer disappearing through the trees, moving so silently that the hounds cannot see them, and at night sometimes we hear wolves.

We travel agreeably together. James loves music and I play for him and the court musicians come with us. He has a passion for poetry and writing, and his court carries its own makar – a poet who travels with us everywhere like a cook, as if you might need poetry like dinner when you stop for the evening. To my surprise, James does need poetry like this; he wants it like wine before dinner, and he has an appetite for talk about books and philosophy. He expects me to learn their language, for unless I do I will never appreciate the beauty of the poems in the evening. He says they cannot be translated, you have to hear them as they were first sung. He says that they speak of the people and the land and they cannot be translated into English. 'The English don't think like us,' he says. 'They don't love the land and the people the way a Scot does.'

When I protest, he tells me that further north the people only speak their own language called Erse and really, I should learn that too. The people of the islands far out in the cold north seas speak a language halfway to Danish and had to be forced to recognise his rule, thinking that they were a people and a kingdom all of their own. 'And what is beyond them?' I ask.

'Far, far away, a land of whiteness,' he says. 'Where they have no night and day but whole seasons of darkness and then months of white light, and the land is only ice.'

James has a profound interest in the workings of things, and wherever we go he is off to bell towers to see the mechanisms of clocks, or to water mills to see a new way of loading wheat into the grinding stones. In one little village they have a wind pump to get the water out of the ditches and he spends half the day with the Dutchman who built it, going up and down the sluices and up and down the stairs to the sails until he understands completely how it works. I can share some of his interests; but often I find him totally incomprehensible. He is fascinated by the workings of the human form, even the dirty bodies of poor people, and he will talk with doctors about the air that we breathe and if the same comes out as goes in, and where it goes and what it does, or how the blood will spurt from the neck but ooze from the arm and why that might be? He has no shame and he has no sense of disgust. When I say that I don't want to know why the veins in my wrist are blue but the blood that spills out of them is red, he says: 'But Margaret, this is the stuff of life, this is the work of God. You must want to understand it all.'

When we approach Stirling, riding up and up the winding streets of the little town that clings to the side of the hill, he warns me that he keeps a philosopher, who has one of the towers as his private domain and is studying the nature of being itself. He has a forge and a distilling urn, and I must not be troubled by the noise of hammering or the strange smell of the smoke.

'But what is he doing there?' I ask, disturbed. 'What do you hope to find?'

'If we were to be blessed, then we would find the fifth element,' he answers. 'There is fire, water, earth and air, and there is something else, the very essence of life. All these things have to be present for life, and we know that they live inside us, but there must be another element, unseen but felt, that animates us. If I could find that, I could make the philosopher's stone and I would have power over life itself.'

'There are philosophers all over the world looking for the secret to eternal life and the stone that turns base matter into gold,' I remark. 'And yet you hope that it will be you who finds it, before anyone else?'

'We are getting closer every day,' he assures me. 'And he is also studying how birds fly, so that we might fly too.'

The castle guns salute us with a roar as they see our standard coming up the lane that winds to and fro up the steep hill, and the drawbridge crashes down and the portcullis rattles up. The huge stone walls are unbroken except for the gate that faces us.

I can see – running away to the right and to the left – how the walls climb up along the cliff face, higher and higher until they are a narrow rim over the sheer drop below them, part of the cliff itself.

'The best of my castles,' James says with satisfaction. 'Only a fool says that a fortress cannot be taken – but this one, Margaret, this is the brooch that pins the Highlands and the Lowlands together, this is the one that I would back against any other in Christendom. It is set so high that you can see for miles in every direction from the turrets, and no enemy can make the climb to the foot of the walls unseen, let alone scale them. They are built on solid rock, no-one could mine them. I could hold this castle with twenty men against an army of thousands. Make sure you tell that to your father, when you write. He has nothing as secure as this, nothing as beautiful as this.'

'But he does not need one, for there is a perpetual peace now, thank God,' I say as if by rote. And then, in quite a different voice, I ask: 'And who are these?'

As we ride through the thick main gate, as deep as a tunnel, I can see the great courtyard ahead, built on the slant of the hill. The servants are lining up and dropping to their knees and suddenly, summoned by the cannon blast, half a dozen children of all ages, dressed as richly as little lords and ladies, are running down the steps from the highest side of the building and bounding into the courtyard as if delighted to see us, dipping into a bow or a curtsey like a loyal mob. They tumble towards James as he leaps from the saddle and hugs them all in a wide embrace, muttering name after name and blessing them in Erse, so I don't understand a word that is said.

My master of horse lifts me down from the saddle and sets me on my feet. I use his arm to steady myself as I turn to my husband. 'Who are these?' I ask him again.

He is on his knees on the wet cobblestones so that he can kiss the smallest child and he takes a baby from its nurse as he gets up. His eyes are alight with love – I have never seen him like this before. The other little ones scamper around him, pulling at his riding jacket, and the oldest boy stands proudly beside the king as if he is of such importance that he should be presented to me, as if he expects that I shall be glad to meet him.

'Who are these?'

James beams at this beautiful surprise. 'These are my children!' he announces, his wide-armed gesture taking in the six little heads and the one in his arms. 'My little bairns.' He turns to them. 'My little lords, ladies, this is the new Queen of Scotland, my wife. This is my Queen Margaret, who has come all the way from England to do me the honour of being my wife and your good mother.'

They all bow or curtsey with a trained grace. I incline my head but am completely lost as to what I should do. Wildly, I wonder if he was married before and nobody told me? Surely he cannot have a secret wife, the mother to all these children, hidden away here, in my castle. What should I do? If she were faced with these terrible circumstances, what would Katherine do?

'Do they have a mother?' I ask.

'Several,' James says cheerfully.

The eldest boy bows to me but I do not acknowledge him. I do not smile on the little bowed heads and, gently, James hands the baby back to her nurse. One of the Stirling ladies, seeing my frosty face, takes the hand of the toddler and shepherds the children towards the open doorway to the tower.

'Mothers,' the king shows no trace of awkwardness. 'One, God bless her, Margaret Drummond, is dead. My dear friend Marion will not come to court again. Janet lives elsewhere, and Isabel too. They need not trouble you, you need not concern yourself with them. They will not be your friends or ladies-in-waiting.'

Not trouble me? Four mistresses? Four mistresses and only one of them thankfully dead? As if I will not be wondering about them and comparing myself to them every moment for the rest of my life. As if I will not be looking into the pretty faces of the little girls and wondering if they take after their mothers. As if I will not be thinking every time that James leaves court that he is visiting one of this pack of fertile women, or mourning the one who is mercifully gone.

'These will be half-brothers and -sisters to our own child when he comes,' the king says pleasantly. 'Aren't they like a band of little angels? I thought you would be pleased to meet them.'

'No,' is all that I am able to say. 'I am not.'

## STIRLING CASTLE, SCOTLAND, AUTUMN 1503

I write to my lady grandmother that my husband is mired in sin. I spend hours on my knees in the chapel puzzling over what I can tell her to ensure that she is as outraged as I am. I am very careful what I say about the certainty of his damnation because I don't want to mention his rebellion and the death of his father. Rebellion is an awkward topic for us Tudors since we took the throne from the Plantagenets and they were ordained kings and every Englishman had sworn fealty to them. I am pretty sure that my lady grandmother crafted the rebellion against King Richard after swearing an unbreakable oath of loyalty to him. Certainly she was the great friend of his wife and carried her train at her coronation.

So I don't speak of my husband's rebellion against his father, but I stress to my lady grandmother that he is deep in sin and I am surprised and unhappy to encounter these bastard children. I don't know what to make of the oldest boy, Alexander, who is placed next to his father at dinner, where they sit as family in descending order from ten-year-old Alexander right down to the baby on her nurse's lap, who bangs on the table with her own silver spoon – with a thistle on the handle! The royal emblem! James behaves as if I should be happy to have them all at the royal table, as if these handsome children are a credit to us both.

This is a sin, I write. And also, it is an insult to me, the queen. If my father knew anything of them before my marriage he should have ruled that these children could not stay in my castle. They should live far away from my dower lands. Surely I cannot be expected to house them? Really, they should never have been born. But I don't know what I can do to dismiss them.

At least I can keep them out of my rooms. Their nursery and schoolroom are in one tower, the philosopher – as if it were not bad enough that I have to house him – is in the other. I have the queen's interconnected rooms, presence chamber, privy chamber and bedchamber, the most beautiful that I have ever seen. I make it clear to my ladies and to the king's steward that only my ladies are to attend my rooms. There are to be no 'bairns' of any age or description, regardless of their parentage, running in and out as if I wanted their company.

I have to know more and I have to know what I can do. While I wait for advice from my lady grandmother I consult my lady-in-waiting Lady Katherine Huntly. She is from the Gordon clan and is a kinswoman to my husband. She can speak Erse as he does – as they all do – and she knows these people; she probably knows the mothers of the children. I suppose that half of them are related to her. This is not a nobility, it is a tribe – and these are little bastard savages.

I wait till my musicians are playing and we are seated at our sewing. We are working on an altar cloth that shows Saint Margaret as she confronts the dragon. I think that I too am forced to confront a dragon of sin, and Katherine can tell me how to defeat it.

'Lady Katherine, you may sit beside me,' I say, and she comes and takes a stool beside me and starts to work on my corner of the embroidery.

'You can leave that,' I say and, pleasant as ever, she puts it down and unthreads her needle and stores it safely in its silver case.

'I wanted to talk to you about the king,' I say.

She turns her calm face to listen.

'About these children.'

She is silent.

'These very many children.'

She nods.

'They have to go!' I exclaim suddenly.

She looks at me consideringly. 'Your Grace, this is a matter for the king and yourself.'

'Yes, but I don't know anything about them. I don't know what is usual. I can't command him.'

'No, you cannot command him. But I think that you could ask.'

'Who are they anyway?'

She thinks for a moment. 'Are you sure that you want to know?'

Tightly, I nod, and she looks at me with a gentle sympathy. 'As you wish, Your Grace. The king is a man of little more than thirty years, remember. He has been King of Scotland since he was a boy. He came to his throne in violence, and he is a man of high passions and power, a lusty man of appetites. Of course he has fathered children. He is unusual only in that he keeps them together in his finest castle, and loves them so dearly. Most men have children outside their marriage and leave them to be raised by their mothers, or sometimes they are farmed out and neglected. The king should perhaps be honoured for recognising his own.'

'No, he shouldn't be,' I say flatly. 'My father has only us. He never took a mistress.'

She looks down at her hands as if she knows better. I have always hated that about Katherine Huntly; she always looks as if she is carrying a secret.

'Your father was very blessed in his wife, your mother,' she says. 'Perhaps King James will never take another mistress, now that he has you.'

I feel a rush of anger at the thought of anyone in my place, anyone preferred to me. I don't even like the thought of anyone making comparisons between me and another girl. Part of my relief in leaving England was that no-one could again look from dainty Katherine to me, that no-one can compare me to my sister Mary. I hate being compared – and now I discover my husband has half a dozen lovers. 'Who was this Marion Boyd, the mother of Alexander, the oldest boy, who is allowed to be so forward?' I ask.

Her raised eyebrows ask me am I sure that I want to know all this?

'Who is she? Is she dead too?'

'No, Your Grace. She is a kinswoman of the Earl of Angus. A very important family, the Douglas clan, you know.'

'Was she my husband's mistress for long?'

Katherine considers. 'I believe so. Alexander Stewart is a little more than ten years old is he not?'

'How would I know?' I demand sharply. 'I don't look at him.'

'Yes,' she says and stops speaking.

'Go on,' I say crossly. 'Is he the only bastard the king has got on her?'

'No, she had three children by the king, a boy died. But her daughter Catherine is here with her older brother.'

'The little girl with fair hair? About six years old?'

'No, that's Margaret, she is the daughter of Margaret Drummond.'

'Margaret!' I exclaim. 'He gave his bastard my name?'

She bows her head and is silent. My ladies glance across at her as if they are sorry she is trapped in the window bay with me. I am known for my temper and none of them ever want to tell me bad news.

'He gave them all his name,' she says quietly. 'They are all called Stewart.'

'Why don't they take the husbands' names, if they are all cuckolds' brats?' I am furious now. 'Why doesn't the king demand that the husbands house their wives and children all together? Keep these women in their place at home?'

She says nothing.

'But he called one James. Which one is James?'

'He is the son of Janet Kennedy,' she says quietly.

'Janet Kennedy?' I recognise the name. 'And where is she? Not here?'

'Oh no,' Katherine says quickly, as if that would be impossible. 'She lives at Darnaway Castle, far away. You will never meet her.'

I can be glad of this, at least. 'The king does not see her any more?'

Katherine picks up the corner of the tapestry as if she wishes she were working on it. 'I don't know, Your Grace.'

'So he does see her?'

'I could not say.'

'And what about the others?' I continue with my interrogation.

'The others?'

'All the other children. By Saint Margaret there must be half a dozen of them!'

She ticks them off on her fingers: 'There are Alexander and Catherine the children of Marion Boyd, and Margaret the daughter of Margaret Drummond, and Janet Kennedy's boy James, and the three youngest who are still so small that they usually live with their mother Isabel Stewart, not here at court: Jean, Catherine, and Janet.'

'How many are there altogether?'

I can see her calculating. 'There are seven of them here. There may be more of course, unacknowledged.'

I look at her blankly. 'I won't have any of them under the same roof as me,' I say. 'Do you understand me? You'll have to tell him.'

'I?' She shakes her head, perfectly calm. 'I could not tell the King of Scotland that his children are not welcome here in Stirling Castle, Your Grace.'

'Well, my chamberlain will have to do it. Or my confessor, or someone has to tell him. I won't bear it.'

Lady Huntly does not flinch at my raised voice. 'You will have to tell him yourself, Your Grace,' she says respectfully. 'He's your husband. But if I were you—'

'You could not be me,' I say flatly. 'I am a Tudor princess, the oldest Tudor princess. There is no-one like me.'

'If I were so blessed as to be in your position,' she corrects herself smoothly.

'You were the wife of a pretender,' I say meanly. 'Obviously, you did not achieve my position.'

She bows her head. 'I merely say that if I were a new wife of a great king I would ask it of him as a favour, not demand it as a right. He is kind to you, and he loves his children very deeply. He is capable of great love and affection. You could ask it as a favour. Although . . .'

'Although what?' I snap.

'He will be saddened,' she says. 'He loves his children.'

A Tudor does not ask for favours. As a Tudor princess I expect my due. Katherine of Arrogant did not share Ludlow Castle with anyone but our Plantagenet cousin Margaret Pole and her husband, Arthur's guardian. Nobody would have asked such a thing of her. When my little sister, Princess Mary, is married – probably to a Spanish prince – she will go to her new country with honour. She will not meet bastards or half-bloods or whores. I shall not be treated less well than these princesses, who are inferior to me either by birth or age.

I wait till the next day when we have observed Mass in the chapel, and before we leave the hallowed ground I put a hand on my husband's arm to hold him at the chancel steps and say:

'My lord husband, I do not think it right that your bastard children should be housed in my castle. This is my dower castle, my own property, and I don't want them here.'

He takes my hand and he holds it, looking into my eyes as if we were plighting our troth before the altar. 'Little wife, these are the children of my begetting and of my heart. I was hoping that you might be kind to them and that you might give them the company of a little brother.'

'My son will be born in wedlock to two royal parents,' I say stiffly. 'He will not share a nursery with bastards. He will be raised with noble companions.'

'Margaret,' he says even more softly, 'these little bairns take nothing from you; their mothers are not your rivals. You are queen above all others, my one and only wife. Your son when he comes will be a prince of Scotland, and heir to England. They can live here and be no trouble to you. We will only be here a few times in the year; you will barely see them. It will be nothing to you; but I will know that they are in the safest place in the country.'

I don't smile, though he is swinging my hand gently. I don't melt, though his touch is warm. I have seen my father terrorised by the sons and cousins and bastards of my grandfather. The Plantagenets are named for a weed that grows unstoppably and, through them, we Tudors are entwined with children of the blood and children of half-blood, boys who claim kinship and boys who are ghosts, boys who are no kin at all. I won't have my castle filled with boys from nowhere. My father put the neck of his wife's cousin under the axe, so that there should be no doubt about who was the son and heir to the English throne. Katherine's parents demanded that he was dead before she came to England from Spain. I won't have less than her. I won't allow rival heirs to my son before he is even born. I won't have rivals to me.

'No,' I say flatly, though my pulse is drumming in my ears and I am afraid of defying him.

He bows his head for a moment and I think that I have won, but then I see that he is silent, not humbled at all, but mastering himself and curbing his anger. When he looks up again his eyes are very cold. 'Very well,' he says. 'But this is small of you, Your Grace. Small and mean, and – worst of all – stupid.'

'Don't you dare.' I drag my hand from his and I round on him with a blaze of temper, but he just bows his head slightly to me, and makes a deep obeisance to the altar and walks away just as I am about to treat him to the full blast of a Tudor rage. He goes as if he has no interest in my tantrum and leaves me shaking with fury but with nothing to say and no-one to hear.

I write again to my lady grandmother. How dare he call me stupid? How dare he – with a castle full of bastards, and the murder of his own father on his conscience – dream of calling me stupid? Who is more stupid? A Tudor princess who defends her rights as queen? Or a man who meets with philosophers by day and whores by night?

## EDINBURGH CASTLE, SCOTLAND, WINTER 1503

My grandmother's reply to my first letter passes my angry second letter on the way. The messengers cross, not even seeing the other on the arduous road, and when hers arrives we are back in Edinburgh for my fourteenth birthday and the celebrations for Christmas. The seal has been broken on her letter. It is not damaged, it has been deliberately cut, and from this I know that my husband has read her answer to me and has probably already read my complaints of him.

My lady grandmother writes:

*Richmond Palace,*
*Christmastide 1503*
*To Margaret, Queen of Scotland,*

*Greetings, my daughter Margaret,*

*I was sorry to read that you are disturbed by the presence of your husband's bastards in your castle, and I urge you to pray to God that he amend his ways. He is your husband set above you by God and the laws of both our countries and you can do nothing but, by patient example and calling on the help of Our Lady, guide him to better behaviour in the future. Remember that your marriage vows to him promise your obedience. He did not promise that to you.*

*The children should be raised as the lords and ladies they are, and you will find an advantage in having a royal family that you can command. Always remember that you are in a country that is uncertain in its temper and with lords of sinfully great independence of spirit. Anyone who might be your friend and be loyal to you and yours should be kept close. These children can be encouraged and persuaded and bribed to be the friends of your prince when he is born. Nothing is more important than his safety and future. You have seen how I befriend and patronise my kinsmen, for this very reason: that my son shall have friends throughout the land who can be called on in time of need. I even married a great lord to give my son a powerful ally. Everything you do must be directed to ensuring your son gets to his throne and stays there. The bastard children must be raised to help you in this.*

*You will want to have news of our court. The king, my son, is not well and this grieves me and causes me great concern. I do what I can for his health and I take many of the burdens of government from his shoulders. Katherine of Aragon is no trouble to the court at all and we rarely see her. She is trying to live on her own, in her own house, and from what I hear she is hard-pressed to make ends meet. We owe her nothing, and we give her next to nothing. We will not release her to Spain until they have paid us the final sum of her dowry, and they will not receive her until we have paid her widow's dower. Princess Mary is growing in grace and obedience and we plan a great marriage for her, trusting to the will of God and the establishment of His peace.*

*I remain high in the favour of God as manifested by His many blessings on me and by my devotion to prayer and good works. Please make sure that you are obedient and agreeable*

*to your husband. You should be making a son of your own, not worrying about his bastards. And make sure that you befriend them now, that you may use them in the future.*
*Margaret R*

She signs herself 'Margaret R', which might mean Margaret Richmond – her title – or might mean Margaret Regina. She has never told anyone, but invented the signature without consulting anybody, in silence, as she does so much else. This is not from modesty but from a tendency to stealth. She makes friends and allies quietly, not for love of them but against the day when she may need them. She married two husbands for what they could do for her son. She oppressed my mother with rarely a word spoken, and she has stifled history about what she did during the reign of Richard. I wish I were as wise as she, I wish I were as cunning. But I am a Tudor princess and I was born proud. Surely I should not wish myself otherwise?

At any rate, the main thing is that I will get my own way. The two boys who carry the name of Stewart will be sent to college in Italy, an honour that I think they could not have expected. The other children are to be housed elsewhere in Scotland, I don't even know where, and I certainly will not ask.

I am sorry if Katherine is being kept short of money, sorry to think of her struggling to manage a large household in a big house in London without any help from my grandmother or my father; but I cannot help but be pleased that she has not taken my place at court, that she is not the favoured daughter, attending all the celebrations, seated next to her betrothed, my brother Harry, dancing with him. I love her so much better when I know that she is not usurping my place.

The most troubling thing for me in this letter is the news that my sister, Mary, is to make some great match in Europe. I am struck at once by anxiety that they don't pair her with some old man, or some cruel young tyrant. She is a little beauty: as engaging as a kitten, as exquisite as a carved angel. They must not sell her to the highest bidder, or throw her into the bear pit of some hard-faced court. She is trusting and vulnerable; she has no mother, and I am filled with anxiety and passionate protectiveness for my little sister. I want them to match her with someone kind and loving. Kind and loving, and – in truth – unimportant. For I can't bear her to marry a great king. I don't want her to rise beyond her station. This would be wrong. I am the elder sister and I should be senior to her, in greatness as well as in years. Surely this is clear to everyone? Surely my lady grandmother, with her wisdom in strategy and her love of fortune and title, will remember that I, her namesake, cannot be overtaken, must never be overtaken by my little sister?

## EDINBURGH CASTLE, SCOTLAND, SPRING 1504

In January, just at the end of the Christmas feast, they bring us the news that James' younger brother, the Duke of Ross, has died. This should be a sad event for my husband, though nothing compared with the loss of Arthur for me; but he hides his grief so well that I think he feels none.

'He was a trouble to me as well as a brother,' he explains, and he takes my hand under his arm as we walk down the gallery, past the dark gloomy pictures of the many other Jameses, as the courtiers chatter among themselves and secretly watch us.

'Brothers are like that,' I agree, thinking of Harry. 'Sisters, too.'

'I feared that my father preferred him to me, and part of my quarrel with my father was that he was going to put my brother in my place, name him as heir and put him on the throne.'

'That's a sin,' I say sanctimoniously. 'The elder child should be honoured before the others. God has chosen the order of the family, and it should not be overthrown.'

'Spoken like an older sister!' he says, with his quick rueful smile.

'It's just the truth,' I say, on my dignity. 'It was very wrong at home when they let Mary put herself forward, and even worse when Katherine of Aragon tried to take precedence over me when she was a Tudor princess by marriage and I was a true-born one. God has put everyone in their station in life and they should stay there.'

'Well, my brother's death leaves me with another difficulty. I am sorry if you dislike this, but I will have to name my heir,' he says, without preamble, direct as ever.

'Why?' I ask.

'My dear, I know you are not yet fifteen; but think like a queen! My brother was my heir, of course, and now that he is dead, I have none.'

'You will name an heir?' I ask. At once I am breathless with hope.

'I have to.'

'Will you name me?' I ask.

The crack of laughter that he cannot contain makes everyone turn and look at us. 'Oh! God bless you! No!' he says. 'It can't be you, my dear. You would be running to the border in your petticoat in a month! In a day! The only reason that we are safe on our throne is because I go constantly – constantly – from one end of the country to the other, forcing my will on those lords who would have their own way, begging the friendship of others, pacifying those who are angry by nature, soothing those who are aggrieved. I am building ships! I am forging guns! Only a peace-loving man with an army behind him can keep this country together: only a wise man with an unbeatable army. No woman could do it. I am making this into a country of peace and prosperity after years of struggle. God guard us against a ruling queen. That would ruin everything.'

I am so offended that I can hardly speak. 'As you wish, Your Grace,' I say, very cold, and dignified. 'I am sorry that you think so little of me.'

'Not of you, sweetheart,' he says, and he squeezes my hand

under his elbow. 'No woman can rule. And you have not been taught statecraft, you love the title of queen but you don't understand that it is a constant labour.'

'You speak as if you were a blacksmith,' I say stiffly.

'I am,' he says. 'I am forging a kingdom from a country of clans. I am bringing them into one body. Even now, I have to fight to keep the loyalty of the Isles, I have to watch the borders, I even have to demand the ownership of the debatable lands. Your father had to do the same when he took his throne, and his task was even harder, for everyone knew him as nothing more than the exiled Earl of Richmond. At least I was born and bred a king. Your father struggles with his lords and so do I. I have to teach them loyalty and fidelity and constancy.' He looks at me, smiling. 'I have to teach you, too.'

'But who will you name as your heir?' I ask. My belly plunges in fright as I suddenly think that he might honour my brother Harry. I could not bear for Harry to have a title that bettered mine, and how terrible it would be if it were given to him by my own husband. 'Not Harry?'

'Harry? No,' he says. 'Don't you listen at all? The Scots lords would never accept an English king. We have to have our own. The next in line after me is John Stuart, the Duke of Albany, my cousin.'

I blink. This is worse than Harry. 'I don't even know who you mean. Who is he?'

'You've not met him. He lives in France, he was raised there, and he was no favourite of my father's. But, like it or not, he will be my heir until you give me a son. In the meantime, I will make my son James legitimate. I wish to God that you would learn to love my bastards. If you would bring up James as your own I would name him as my heir. At least I can publicly acknowledge him.'

This is a worse humiliation for me than if he had chosen Harry. 'Who doesn't know about him already? Everyone knows about all of them! You can't foist a bastard on me! You would not dishonour the throne.'

'It's no dishonour,' he says. 'He's been known as mine since he was made, and all the others who came before and after him. I mean no offence to you, little wife, but until we have a son together I want a boy to bear my name and my blessing. I am going to legitimise James.'

'Which one is he?' I ask coldly. 'For there were so many tumbling out of the walls of Stirling that I could not tell one apart from the other.'

'James is Janet Kennedy's boy. I think you observed him well enough to demand his absence. Alexander and his half-brother James will study in Italy and their sister Catherine will live in Edinburgh Castle. I will have my children around me, my dear. So far, you have given me none to put in their place.'

I pull my hand from his arm. 'I will never see one of your bastard children at my dinner table or even near the throne,' I say furiously. 'And I will not dine tonight. I am unwell. You can go to dinner without me.'

He does not even blink. 'Very well,' he says. 'I will come to your room after dinner. I will spend the night with you.'

The words 'You will not' are on the tip of my tongue but the set of his mouth warns me not to defy him.

'Very well,' I say, sweeping him a curtsey, and as he walks away, calling to his lords that he is *sterving* for his dinner, I whisper 'Peasant' at his broad back, but not so loud that he can hear.

I do not dare show my bad temper to my husband but I have no restraint before my ladies, and I cuff the dogs and whip my horses, they all have to bear it without complaint. James nominates his boy Alexander to the see of St Andrews, his late brother's benefice, and collects the massive fees. The ten-year-old is sent to Italy to study with no less a scholar than Erasmus. Erasmus! Who visited my brother Harry and was impressed by his learning. Thomas More brought him. That

Erasmus! For a pair of little Scots bastards! The philosopher visited the royal English court and came to us in our nursery at Eltham and exchanged poetry with my brother Harry. We were suitable pupils for such a great man. But James is blind to rank and blind to merit. He insists that his bastards go to Padua to study and nothing will persuade him that this is to raise them too high.

I know he is mistaken. For all that he calls me unfit to rule, I know some things. I have seen my father haunted by boys, Plantagenet boys; one even called himself a Plantagenet prince. My father paid a fortune on spies to find him, and then bribes to all the liars in Flanders to say that they knew him as a boatman's son in Tournai. I saw the struggle that my father had to be rid of him when he was captured. I saw him lingering at our court, half prince and half pretender. The only thing to do with a rival is to put him to death, at once. Now James is educating two boys to be the rivals to my son, even saying he will name the oldest as his heir. I know that this is folly. Every prince, every princess, wants to be the only one.

## HOLYROODHOUSE PALACE, EDINBURGH, SCOTLAND, SPRING 1506

The king showers me with gifts for my sixteenth birthday, for Christmas, for New Year's Day, and for the pleasure of giving me gold and jewels. The Christmas feast was more playful and joyous than any I have ever seen. James' alchemist John Damien came from Stirling to act as master of the revels and we had disguisings and dancing, fireworks, masques, and surprises every day. The old wizard changed wine to the colour of ink, he made flames burn green. Every day we had a new poem, every day a new song, the court was merry and the king was open-handed with his friends, and loving to me.

The only shadow at all is that we have been wedded and bedded for nearly three years and still there is no sign of a child. There is no fault in the king; there is no 'Alas, it never happened for us' in my marriage. He comes to me without fail every night that is not forbidden by the Church, especially in the days before my course, until it comes and disappoints me again. I think that he keeps account of my times and is most attentive when he is likely to succeed, perhaps he and his alchemist judge it by the moon or draw up charts. I don't know, I don't ask. How would I know what he reads in his books of Greek, with their horrid pictures of flayed bodies, and distilling goblets, and snakes?

In my package of letters from England I get a note from my sister Mary, boasting about the wonderful time she has had this spring. Isabella of Castile has died and the heirs of Spain, Philip and his wife Juana, were sailing home to their country but were blown onto the coast at Dorset, and my father and all the court invited them to stay at Windsor and then Richmond. Katherine was dragged out of obscurity and pushed to the fore to greet her sister Juana, and Mary partnered her in dances and singing and riding out with the visitors, for archery – where they won – and hunting – where they caught everything but unicorns. There were masques, celebrations ... the list goes on and on as Mary details the parties and even the clothes she wore. I am amazed that my lady grandmother lets her put herself forward like this, but in her letter she says that they are considering Charles of Castile as a match for her, and then I understand they have set her out, like a tray of pies, to tempt the buyer. Of course Katherine was part of the team of hucksters that brought these fresh wares to market. I am surprised that she should lower herself to dance at my father's bidding when he has done nothing for her. I think she should have more pride. I would have had more pride. And, clearly, the attention to Mary was ridiculous.

*Everyone was so kind to me, and they say that I must learn Spanish!* Mary writes, her letters looping across the page and then getting cramped and small at the corners. *Think if I should marry Charles and be the Holy Roman Empress! Think how lovely that would be! And we should all three of us be queens.*

This is such a foolish plan that it makes me laugh and laugh and quite restores my sisterly affection. Charles of Castile is a baby of six years old. Mary will find herself betrothed and stuck in England for eight years at least unless they take her to live with them in Castile as nursemaid to her baby-husband. Of course, he will have a great title; but there is no certainty that he will live to see it, and she will have a lifetime to wait before she can call herself queen.

*Katherine and I are much together as she has come to live at court,* Mary writes, misunderstanding as usual that this is a massive snub to Katherine, who has clearly failed to keep her own house, and now has to live at my father's board as a hanger-on.

> *Our father stopped her allowance and dismissed her duenna for poor advice. I am so glad! I love having her at court, even though she finds it hard to make ends meet and cannot dine every day when she has no suitable clothes. She is terribly shabby, as her father will not send her money; but my lady grandmother says that I cannot give her anything and she says that she does not mind.*

I wonder why my father and my lady grandmother are driving Katherine to such straits. I suppose they are still punishing her for sharp practice with her dowry. So I send her my love, and I congratulate Mary on her brilliant prospects, giggling as I write. I say that I am happy for her, that it is a fine thing to be a queen in a fair country. I say that I am happy with my husband the king, a fine man, a grown man, a real man, and that I wish her every happiness too, when her bridegroom is grown also – a decade from now. Poor Mary! Foolish Mary! She is so dazzled by his title that she has not realised she will not marry for years, and nobody knows when Katherine will get Harry. Yes, my two sisters, my rivals, may be betrothed to the greatest matches in Europe, but Katherine cannot afford a gown to dance with her bridegroom and Mary's betrothed can barely sit on his own little pony. I can hardly sign my name for laughing at the foolish pride of the two of them, my silly sisters.

And then in the summer my joy is complete. I write a proud letter to England to announce to my lady grandmother, to them all, that, finally, I am with child.

## HOLYROODHOUSE PALACE, EDINBURGH, SCOTLAND, MARCH 1507

There is no doubt in my mind who is now the foremost of the three princesses, my sister-in-law Katherine of Aragon, my sister Mary, or myself: it is obviously me. Katherine failed to conceive a child with Arthur and then told everyone, 'Alas, it never happened for us', and now her marriage is never mentioned and she is a poor relation, an unwanted hanger-on. People may praise Mary's beauty and her talents, but her betrothal to Charles of Castile is still only a plan, and he is nothing more than a child himself. His father has died so he is now heir to the Holy Roman Emperor. But still, he is a little boy and she won't be able to marry or present the Habsburgs with a son any time in the next eight years. But I have conceived, carried and birthed a boy. It nearly cost me my life. I was deathly ill, everyone thought that they would lose me. But my husband went on pilgrimage, on foot for hundreds of miles, at least a hundred, to St Ninian at Whithorn and at the very moment that he knelt before the altar, I recovered. It is a miracle, a son and heir for Scotland, and a message from God that he blesses my queenship and our marriage.

Our child is an heir for England too. If anything were to happen to Harry (which God forbid, of course) it is my baby who would be heir to the throne of England through me. Katherine and Mary cannot dream of that for themselves, whereas I could be My Lady the King's Mother, and as great as our grandmother, who runs the English court through her son and has done so ever since he came to the throne, married or widowed.

We hold a magnificent joust to celebrate the birth and the undeniable champion is a mystery knight called 'the wild man'. He jousts with the white knight – the Sieur de la Bastie, the handsome French-born knight who fought before me at my wedding. Once again, Antoine delights the crowd and all the ladies with his ice-white armour and the white scarf streaming on his lance. He and James have a bet about the proper treatment of a charger's feet, and James loses and gives the chevalier a cask of wine to wash his horse's hooves. The greatest joust of the tournament is when the white knight comes against the wild man. There's a wonderful series of broken lances and then we all scream with excitement when the wild man challenger takes off his helmet and throws down his disguise – and it is my husband, who has fought all comers and defeated everyone! He is delighted with himself, with me, and with our son, who is named James, Prince of Scotland and the Isles and Duke of Rothesay, so Marion Boyd's Alexander can step back into half-bred obscurity and play at being archbishop and the bastard James can settle for being an earl.

Everything should be perfect since our marriage is visibly blessed by God, except that my husband doubts, or says that he doubts, my father's good faith. Scottish reivers raid the lands of the English farmers, stealing sheep and cows and sometimes robbing travellers, and my father rightly complains that this is a breach of the Treaty of Perpetual Peace. James counters with my father's treatment of Scots merchant shipping, and both of them endlessly write claim and counter-claim about the unreliable justice and constant warring of the borderlands.

My father expected my marriage to bring a peace that would last forever between England and Scotland, but I don't know how I am supposed to bring it about. James is not a boy to become besotted with an older experienced king, as Mary tells me Harry was with Philip of Castile. James is a grown man, an older man, who will not submit himself to the authority of my father. He would never dream of asking for my advice, and when I offer it – even though I am a princess of England – he takes no notice. I say with great dignity that as a princess of England, Queen of Scotland, and mother of the next King of Scotland, I have thoughts on this, and many matters, and I expect them to be regarded.

And he bows low and says: 'God save the queen!'

## HOLYROODHOUSE PALACE, EDINBURGH, SCOTLAND, CHRISTMAS 1507

I am with child again by Christmas and it is only this triumph that helps me to be serene, as serene as a madonna, when I hear the news that Mary my sister is officially betrothed to Charles of Castile. She is to have a dowry of 250,000 golden crowns, and his grandfather the emperor sent her a ruby so big that some fool wrote a poem about it. She was betrothed by proxy and made a speech in perfect French, and she takes the title Princess of Castile.

She writes to me herself to boast of her triumph, in a letter so ill-written and spelled so wildly that I take nearly an hour to understand it.

*I will be married when the prince is fourteen, seven years from now, and I don't mind waiting at all, though it is a lifetime, because I am to stay at home and learn Spanish. It's a tremendously difficult language but Katherine says that she will teach me, I think I should pay her for being my tutor as she lives very humbly at court, her parents don't support her and we won't pay her widow's dower until they have paid her dowry. But I am not allowed to see her very often or give her anything.*

*I am to have a very grand wedding but, until then, I will stay at home. I shall have my title at once, I have it now! I am Princess of Castile and they are sewing my coronet onto all my things. I shall precede my lady grandmother and of course Katherine on every occasion – you can imagine how my lady grandmother likes that! She gave me a tremendous talk about false pride and told me to look at Katherine who is a dowager princess and yet is humbled to dust every day. When you come on a visit you can see my ruby. It is the biggest stone I have ever seen in my life, you could drown a cat with it.*

*My love, Mary*

It is hardly worth the effort of spelling out this combination of triumphing over her sister-in-law and bragging of her own wealth, but I do not let it disturb me. My comfort is that I am a queen, and will continue to outrank her for years; but it is very hard to remember to be as serene as a madonna when she sends me the poem about her ruby, and a drawing of my father and my brother Prince Harry witnessing her triumph, standing on a dais under an awning of cloth of gold. The English ambassador told James that everyone ate off gold plate. Gold plate for Mary! The idea is quite ridiculous.

## STIRLING CASTLE, SCOTLAND, SPRING 1508

I think that this has always been an unlucky castle for me. I had my first quarrel with my husband here, and though I emptied it of his bastards, I often think of the children whose home it was, and the alchemist in his tower. I feel as if I miss them every time I enter under the heavy portcullis and climb up the sloping courtyard.

And it is here that the worst thing happens. The worst thing that can possibly happen. My baby, James, Prince James of Scotland and the Isles, Duke of Rothesay, dies in his sleep, in his royal cradle. Nobody knows why; nobody knows if he could have been saved. I am no longer the mother of the next King of Scotland. My belly is full with the next child; but I have an empty cradle, and I think I will never stop crying.

My husband comes to me and I am reminded of the to and fro between my mother and father's rooms when Arthur died, so I look up when James comes in, and I think he is going to comfort me.

'I am so very unhappy,' I sob at him. 'I wish I was dead myself.'

'Out,' he says shortly to my ladies, and they melt as if they are breath on cold air. 'I have to ask you to be brave as I need to know something.' He is frowning, just as he is when he listens to someone explaining something mechanical, as if I am a puzzle to be solved, not a wife to be comforted with gifts.

'What?' I say, catching my breath.

'Do you think it possible that you are cursed?'

I sit up in my bed, my sobs silenced, and I stare at him, wordless.

'Your father had three sons and two of them are dead. Your brother never got a bairn, though he died at fifteen. You were barren for nearly three years and now our son has died. It's a reasonable question.'

I wail out loud, and pitch into my pillow, both furious and heartbroken. This is typical of him, like his interest in what makes the teeth rot in a beggar's head. He is fascinated by everything, however disgusting. I don't know why Arthur died of the Sweat that spared Katherine. How should I know? I don't even think of Edmund, my little brother who died before he was weaned. I don't know why Arthur did not have a child with Katherine, I don't like to think what she meant by: 'Alas, it never happened for us' and I am not going to discuss it now, when I am heartbroken and people should be comforting me, and diverting me, not coming into my room and asking me terrible questions in a cold voice.

'Because Prince Richard himself told me that the Tudors were cursed,' he goes on.

I clap my hands over my ears as if to ensure that I am deaf to these blasphemies. It is incredible to me that a husband so kind, so gentle, should come to me at this time, at the very pinnacle of my grief, and say things that are like the bad spells of his alchemist, which will translate life to death, gold to dross, everything into dark matter.

'Margaret, I need you to answer me,' he says, not raising his voice, as if he knows that I can hear everything through my fists, through my pillow.

'You mean Perkin Warbeck, I suppose,' I say, sullenly lifting my face.

'We all know that was not his name,' he says, as if it is a simple fact. 'We all know that is the name that your father pinned on him. But he was Prince Richard, and your uncle. He was one of the two boy princes that Richard III put in the Tower of London, that your father says were happily never seen again. I know it. Richard came here to me before we invaded England. He was my dearest friend; we lived together as brother kings. I gave him my cousin in marriage, your lady-in-waiting Katherine Huntly. I rode out to battle at his side. And he told me that whoever tried to kill him and his brother Edward was cursed.'

'You don't know he was a prince at all,' is all I can stammer. 'Nobody knows that. My lady grandmother will not allow anyone to say it. It's treason to say it. And Katherine Huntly never, ever speaks of her husband.'

'I do know it. He told me himself.'

'Well, you shouldn't tell me!' I burst out.

'No,' he concedes. 'Except, I have to know. Richard said that there was a curse placed on the head of whoever killed his brother, the young king. The witch put it on – your mother's mother, the white-witch queen, Elizabeth Woodville. She swore that whoever had taken the young king to his death would lose his son, and his son's son, over and over till the line ended with a barren girl.'

I put my hand over my proud belly. I am not a barren girl. 'I am with child,' I say defiantly.

'We have just lost our son,' he says, his voice curt and quiet. 'And so I am forced to ask you. Do you think we have lost our son because there is a curse on you Tudors?'

'No,' I say furiously. 'I think we lost him because your stinking country is dirty and cold, and half the children born will die of cold because they cannot breathe in smoky rooms and they cannot go outside in the killing cold air. It is your filthy country, it is your stupid midwives, it is your sickly wet nurses with their thin milk. It is not my curse.'

He nods as if this is interesting information. 'But my other children live,' he observes. 'In this filthy country with stupid midwives and sickly wet nurses and thin milk.'

'Not all of them. And anyway, I am carrying one. I am not a barren girl.'

He nods again, as if this is a true observation that he might jot in his notebook and discuss with his alchemist. 'You are. I wish you good health. Try not to grieve too much for this one that is lost. You will endanger the one that you carry. And our boy is in heaven. We must know that he is innocent. He was baptised, he was christened. He may have been half yours, from the line of a usurper who killed children, and half mine, son of a regicide and patricide; we are a sinful pair of parents. But he was baptised against sin so we must pray that he is in heaven now.'

'I wish that I was in heaven with him!' I shout at him.

'With the sins of your family, how could you be?' he asks, and he leaves me. Just like that. Without even bowing.

*Dear Katherine, I have lost my boy and my husband is most unkind to me. He has said the most dreadful things. The only thing that comforts me is that I am with child and hope that we will have another boy. Mary tells me that you are living*

*very poorly and that there are no plans for your wedding to my brother. I am sorry for you. Now I have been brought very low myself, I understand better. I understand how unhappy you must be, and I think of you all the time. Who ever thought that anything could go so wrong for us who must be the favourites of God? Do you think there is any reason? There could not be a curse, of course? I will pray for you, Margaret the Queen.*

## HOLYROODHOUSE PALACE, EDINBURGH, SCOTLAND, SPRING 1508

James rides with me from Stirling Castle to Holyroodhouse while the hilltops are white with snow and the road along the side of the grey river is hard with frost. I have a new steady horse that carries me and my neat round belly safely. We say nothing more about the child we have lost, hoping for the one that is coming this summer.

As soon as we get to Edinburgh, James goes off to the port of Leith where he is building ships and testing cannon. He wants to build another great port, away from the sandbanks. I say that I don't know why he would want so many ships; my father also rules a country surrounded by seas and he does not have a fleet at his command. James smiles and chucks me under the chin as if I were an ignorant little sailmaker in one of his lofts, and says that perhaps he has a fancy to rule the seas and how shall I like to be queen of all the oceans?

So he is not at court when an emissary comes from my father, a watchful clerk by the name of Thomas Wolsey, who wants to see James about keeping the peace. This makes it particularly awkward for me to say that the king is not at court but testing the firing of new, bigger guns, and overseeing the building of warships.

But this Wolsey will not be denied, for Scotland has breached the alliance and he has a commission to make sure that James intends to keep the peace. It is all the fault of the bastard boys – causing trouble for me yet again. James Hamilton, the new-made Earl of Arran, who was ennobled on my wedding day, escorted the two of them to Erasmus in Italy and came home through England without a safe conduct and got himself arrested. Once again, we see the evil consequences of my husband's ridiculous attention to his bastards; now it has caused real trouble.

I may not understand everything, though everyone is always trying to explain to me the endless terms and clauses of the treaty, but even I can see what Thomas Wolsey is talking about as we wait for James to return from Leith. Wolsey says that France is trying to get my husband to renew their traditional alliance, and my father is trying to get him to keep to the Treaty of Perpetual Peace. Since our marriage was part of the treaty my husband should respect it as he does our marriage. He married a princess of England, so he should be at peace forever: that is what perpetual means. He should not make an alliance with France, and he does not need guns and a fleet of ships and the biggest cannon in the world.

Thomas Wolsey must explain this to my husband, so I send for him at once and tell him he must come home. Wolsey talks and talks and talks to me in the hope that I will persuade my husband to brush off the French, and confirm the alliance with England. But my husband is elusive and when he finally returns to court and I manage to speak to him alone he pats me on the cheek and says: 'What's my motto? What will be our son's motto?'

'"In My Defence",' I say sullenly.

'Exactly,' he says. 'I live my life, I make my alliances, I do everything every day in defence of my kingdom; and not even you, peerless princess that you are, will persuade me to endanger my country by insulting the French.'

'The French are no use to us,' I tell him. 'The only alliance we need is with England.'

'I am sure you are right, my royal wife,' he says. 'And if England becomes a more helpful neighbour than it is at the moment, then our alliance will long continue.'

'I hope you don't forget that I was born an English princess before I was a Scots queen,' I say to him.

He slaps my bottom gently as if I were one of his sluts. 'I never forget your importance,' he says, smiling. 'I would never dare.'

'So what will you say to Thomas Wolsey?' I persist.

'I will meet with him, I will talk to him for hours,' he promises. 'And at the end I will tell him what I intend to do, what I have always intended to do: to keep the peace with England and keep my friendship with France. Why would I befriend one and not the other? When each is as bad as the other? When all they both want is to swallow me up? And the only reason they care about us at all is to endanger the other.'

Wolsey has brought me a letter from Katherine and while he and James are locked in argument, I read it on my own, in my rooms. She is sympathetic, speaking kindly of the many women who lose a child, especially a first child, and urges me to rest and stay hopeful that God will give me a son and heir. *I know of no reason that you should not be fertile and happy*, she writes emphatically. *I know of nothing against the Tudors*. I take it in the spirit that it is meant – kindly sisterhood – and, anyway, I don't want to think about curses and deaths in childbirth.

*As for me*, she ends the letter, as if her situation is of little importance,

> *matters do not go well. My father will not send the rest of my dowry until I am married to the prince, your father will not pay my widow's jointure until he has my dowry. I am a pawn between two great kings, and I have no money and little company, for though I live at court I am no favourite, and often overlooked. I see your brother so seldom that I wonder if he even remembers we are betrothed; I fear that he has been advised against me. I see your sister, Mary, only when your father wants to impress the Spanish ambassador. She is growing in beauty and she is so sweet I cannot tell you! She is my only friend at court. I started to teach her Spanish but she is not allowed to come to me often. I am trapped in London, in poverty, and neither a widow nor a bride.*

*Could you, do you think, speak of me to your lady grandmother who could at least see that my servants are paid? She could loan me gowns from the royal wardrobe. Without gowns I cannot go to dinner and I have to go to bed hungry if the kitchens forget to send anything to my room. Would you help me? I don't know what to do, and the men who should advise me are determined to use me to their own ends.*

## HOLYROODHOUSE PALACE, EDINBURGH, SCOTLAND, JULY 1508

I go into the dark stuffy rooms of my confinement for the weeks of isolation and silence. I swear to myself that I am not going to think of what my husband said about a curse, that I am not going to consider his accusations – they are ridiculous, he is ridiculous. Everyone knows that it was the tyrant Richard III who killed the princes in the Tower so that he could seize his nephew's throne. Everyone knows that my father came and saved England from this monster. We Tudors are blessed for this; there is no curse.

The battle at Bosworth shows that God favoured the Tudors. My mother married Henry Tudor though she was a Plantagenet herself, the red rose enclosed the white and made the Tudor rose, they conceived Arthur, they had me. This is proof, plain simple proof, of a line that is blessed by God, unstained by sin, free from any curse. It should be enough for anyone; it is certainly enough for me who was raised by my lady grandmother to have a horror of any superstition and heresy, who knows, as she knows, that the Tudors are the favourites of God and the chosen royal line of England. It is God who has called me to my great station, for I am His favourite and hers.

It is enough for me to think also of Katherine who is arrogant no more, but a princess begging to be married to our family, and assuring me that there can be no shadow cast over us. I think of her, reduced to poverty and loneliness in the small rooms allocated to hangers-on at court, while I am in the best rooms in the finest palace of my capital city, and I feel very sweet and tender to her. I write a sympathetic reply:

> *My dear sister, of course I will write to my lady grandmother and to my father too, I shall do what I can for you. Who would have thought that you would have come to England so grandly – I remember I was so entranced by your gold laces! – and now find yourself reduced so low? I pity you with all my heart and I shall pray for your safe return to Spain if matters cannot be settled in England. Your sister, Margaret the Queen.*

I have the pyx in my rooms ready for my time, and my confessor and the good canons of Holyrood Abbey praying for me at all hours. I have no fear, despite what my husband says. I think to myself, scornfully, that he is a man who wears a hair shirt, who belts himself with a cilice, who killed his own father, an ordained king; of course he sees curses and doom everywhere. Really, he should go to Jerusalem as soon as possible. How else can he regain God's favour if not with a crusade? His sins are not ordinary errors that you can wash away with a few Hail Marys from an absent-minded priest. He is not like me, who was born for greatness with God's blessing.

I am not afraid of this birth and it is an easy one. The baby is a great disappointment as it is a princess but I think I will call her Margaret and ask my lady grandmother to be her godmother and come to her baptism. The baby goes to the wet nurse's breast quietly enough but she does not suckle well and I see the woman exchange a glance with one of the rockers as if she is uneasy. They don't say anything to me and I let them wash me and bind my private parts with moss and herbs, and I go to sleep. When I wake up she is dead.

This time my husband speaks to me kindly. He comes into my confinement chamber though no man is supposed to enter – even the priest prayed with me from the other side of a veiled screen. But James comes in quietly, waving the women aside as they flap and scold him, and he holds my hand as I lie in the bed, even though I have not yet been churched and am still unclean. I am not crying; it is strange that he does not remark on my silence. I don't feel like crying, I feel like going to sleep. I wish I could sleep and never wake up again.

'My poor love,' he says.

'I am sorry.' I can hardly speak, but I owe him the apology. There must be something wrong with me, to have two babies die one after the other. And now Katherine and Mary in England will hear of my loss and I am sure Katherine will think that there is something wrong with me, something wrong with the Tudors, and 'Alas, it never happened for any of us'. Mary is too young and stupid to know that to lose a child is the worst thing a queen can do, but Katherine will be quick to compare me to her fertile mother and her symbol of the pomegranate and press her own case to be married to Harry.

'It's nothing but bad luck,' James says, as if he has never heard of a curse and never spoken of it to me. 'But the main thing is that we know we can make children and that you can carry them. That's the greatest challenge, believe me, sweetheart. The next one will live, I am certain of it.'

'A boy,' I say quietly.

'I will pray,' he says. 'I will make a pilgrimage. And you will rest and get well and strong and when we are old and surrounded by grandchildren and great-grandchildren we will pray for the souls of these little ones. We will remember them only in our prayers, we will forget this sorrow. It will all be well, Margaret.'

'You said about a curse . . .' I begin.

He makes a little gesture of dismissal. 'I spoke from anger

and grief and fear. I was wrong to speak so to you. You are too young and you were raised to think yourself above fault. Life will teach you differently. You don't need me to humble you. I would be a poor husband if I were to try to hurry you into the wisdom of despair.'

'I am no fool,' I say with dignity.

He bows his head. 'That's good, for I certainly am,' he says.

I think I will write to my sister Mary, since she is now betrothed to the heir of the greatest of the Christian kings, and warn her not to be overproud, for it may be that she marries a great man but cannot give him an heir. Every report from England goes on and on that she is growing more and more beautiful, but that does not mean she will be fertile or able to raise a strong baby. I think she should know that my grief may be hers; she need not be certain that she will get off scot-free. I think I will tell her it may be that the Tudors are not so high and mighty and blessed by God. I think I will tell her that she may not have as great a destiny as everyone confidently predicts, she should not think that she will be spared just because she has always been everyone's pet, and always the prettiest child.

But then, something stops me. It's odd that I should have a pen and paper before me and find that I don't want to caution her. I don't want to cast a shadow over her. Of course the thought of her dancing around Richmond Palace, queening it at Greenwich, being the centre of fashion and beauty and extravagance at a wealthy court, grates on me, but I don't want to be the one to tell her that our family may not be as blessed as we imagined. We may not always be lucky. There may be some shadow that hangs over our name: we may have to pay for the death of Edward of Warwick; for the hanging of the boy we called Perkin Warbeck, whoever he was. Without doubt, it was us who won the greatest benefit from the disappearance of the two Plantagenet princes from the Tower. We may have done nothing but we gained the most.

So I write instead to my lady grandmother and tell her of my disappointment and sorrow, and I ask her – for perhaps she knows – if there is any reason why God would turn His face from me and not bless me with a son? Why would a Tudor princess not be able to get and keep a boy? I don't say anything about a curse on the Tudors, or about Katherine in poverty at court – for why would she listen to me? – but I ask her if she knows of any reason that our line should not be strong. I do wonder what she will reply. I wonder if she will tell me the truth.

## STIRLING CASTLE, SCOTLAND, EASTER 1509

We come to Stirling for Easter, in the bitter cold, the horses labouring through drifts of snow, and the carts with the goods bogged down, arriving days late, so my walls are bare of tapestries. I have no curtains around my bed, I have to sleep in coarse linen and there are no crests embroidered on my pillows.

My husband laughs and says that I have been spoiled by the balmy weather of England, but I still cannot believe that it can be so cold and so dark at this time of the year. I long for the sight of green springing grass and the lilt of birdsong in the early morning. I say that I will stay in bed until it is light, and if that proves to be midday then so be it.

He swears that I shall stay in bed and that he himself will bring the wood for my fireplace and mull me a mug of ale at my bedside fire for my breakfast. He is merry and kind to me and I am with child again, warmed with hope and confidence: this time I will be lucky, I think. I have suffered enough.

I think he has come to read to me again, and I hope that it is not Erse poetry, when he enters my rooms one afternoon with a paper in his hand. I can understand it now, but the poems are very long. He does not sit in his usual chair at the fireplace but on the side of my bed, and his face is very grave as he looks around for Eleanor Verney, my senior lady-in-waiting, and makes a little gesture with his hand to tell her to stay with us. I know at once that it is bad news from England.

'Is it my lady grandmother?' I ask.

'No,' he says. 'You are going to have to be brave, my dear. It is your father. God rest his soul, he has gone from us.'

'My father is dead?'

He nods.

'Then Harry is king?' I whisper disbelievingly.

'He will be King Henry VIII.'

'It's not possible.'

He gives me a wry smile. 'I was afraid you would be very grieved.'

'Oh I am, I am,' I assure him, feeling nothing. 'It's a shock, and yet I knew he was unwell. My lady grandmother always said that he was unwell.'

'It will make a great difference to the country,' he says. 'Your brother is quite unknown, quite untried. Your father gave him no power; he didn't teach him the ways of governing.'

'It was always meant to be Arthur.'

'Not for years.'

I can feel the tears welling up now. 'I am an orphan,' I say piteously.

He sits beside me and puts his arm around me. 'You have a family here,' he says. 'And if Harry will keep the peace as he should, then perhaps you can visit him when he comes to his throne.'

'I should like that,' I concede.

'If he will keep the peace. What d'you think he will do? He is sworn by the Treaty of Perpetual Peace to respect our borders and our sovereignty. Your father and I were quarrelling over raiders and pirates, and he tried to forbid me a friendship with France. Do you think Harry can be persuaded that peace is in the interests of us all? Do you think he will be an easier neighbour than your father? Do you have any influence over him?'

'Oh, I am sure I can persuade him. I am sure I can explain. I could travel to London and tell him.'

'When you have been brought to bed and risen up again with a bonny boy. You shall be an ambassador then. There can be no travelling until you are both well and strong.'

'Oh yes, but then . . .' I think of how wonderful it will be to return to England with my younger brother as King of England, with My Lady the King's Mother diminished and renamed as My Lady the King's Grandmother, and Mary a mere princess, whereas I will be a queen with a prince in the cradle who has brought peace to two countries. I shall have a baggage train that goes on for miles. They will see the jewels that James has given me; they will admire my gowns.

'And you have an inheritance,' my husband remarks.

'I have?'

'Yes. I don't know exactly what you will have; but he died immensely rich. It will be a substantial sum.'

'Am I to have it all myself?' I ask. 'It's not to go to you?'

He bows his head. 'You are to keep it all, my little miser. It is to come to you entire.'

I feel the tears come again. 'It will be a comfort. In my loss. In my great loss.'

'Oh, and you will never believe this,' my husband says, gently wiping my tears away with the heel of his hand. 'Your brother's first action is to punish his father's advisors who were overtaxing the people.'

'Oh, yes?' I have no interest in taxation.

'And his second is to announce his marriage to the dowager princess. He is going to marry Katherine of Aragon at last. She has been on his doorstep for seven years; but they will be married within days. They are probably married already; the roads are so bad that this letter is days old.'

I can feel something like dread. 'No. Surely not. Not her. You must have got it wrong. Let me see the letter.'

He hands it over. It is a formal announcement from the herald. It tells simply of my father's death and the declaration for Harry. I look at his title as if I still cannot believe it. Then comes the announcement that Harry is to be married to the dowager princess. It is in black and white, in ornate handwritten script. There are seals on the bottom: there can be no doubt.

'She will be Queen of England,' I say. At once my sympathy for her lonely years on the fringes of court, ignored by everyone, trying to survive by selling her plate, completely deserts me. I cannot remember my pity for my poor widowed sister. Instead I think that she has played a monstrous gamble and it has paid off. She staked her health and her safety and she has won. She gambled that she would endure longer than my father. She defeated him by outliving him; she practically wished him dead. 'That false girl has won.'

James laughs with genuine amusement at the contempt in my voice. 'I thought that you loved her?'

'I do!' I say, but the flood of jealousy rushes over me. 'I did. I just naturally love her more when she is poor and unhappy than when she is triumphing over me.'

'No, why? She has waited long enough for her reward. She has earned it. They say she was all but starving towards the end.'

'You don't understand. She failed Arthur and I thought that my father would punish her by never letting her marry Harry, nor go back to Spain. Katherine is years older than Harry. The match is quite unsuitable.'

'Only five years.'

'She's his brother's widow!'

'They have a dispensation from the Pope.'

'She is not . . .' I clench my hands into fists; I cannot explain to him. 'You don't know her. She is ambitious – it is the throne that she wants, not Harry. My lady grandmother does not . . . I do not . . . She is proud. She is not fit. She will never fill my mother's shoes.'

Gently he takes my hands. 'Harry will have to take your father's place, she will have to take your mother's place. Not in your heart, of course. But on the throne. England has to have a king and queen and it will be Harry and Katherine of Aragon. God bless them and keep them.'

'Amen,' I say sulkily, but I cannot mean it, and I do not mean it.

## STIRLING CASTLE, SCOTLAND, SUMMER 1509

As the snow clings onto the peaks of our high Scots hills, and the cool winds strip the blossom from the fruit trees, I think of the two of them in England in this, Harry's first miraculous summer, glorying in the titles they won by mischance: king and queen, beneficiaries of the deaths of their betters. I think of Katherine, saying it was her destiny, and waiting and biding her time. I think of her saying that she would outlast my father, and now she has done so. I think that there is no true love there, only ambition and vanity. Harry has stolen his brother's wife, Katherine has captured the heir of England. I think they are despicable, both of them, and that there is no true grief when a younger boy wears his dead brother's shoes and a widow throws off mourning.

And then another messenger comes from England with urgent news. My lady grandmother has died. They say that she overate at the coronation feast – soothing her grief with roasted cygnet; but I think that perhaps she had nothing to live for, once she saw her grandson to the throne and knew that her great work for the Tudors – both public and secret – was done, knowing we will have and keep the throne forever. I try to feel a sense of loss for the grandmother who ruled me so strictly, but my mind keeps returning to the thought that with the old lady gone, Katherine will be unchallenged mistress of the court and there will be no-one to rule over her. Not even my mother was allowed in the queen's rooms – they were always reserved for My Lady the King's Mother. But Katherine will do better than my mother: she will be a queen without a mother-in-law overshadowing her, free to do whatever she wants. Certainly, Harry won't know how to manage her. She will behave as if she were a queen in her own right, just like her unwomanly mother, Isabella of Spain. She will be triumphant, leaping from poverty to queenship on Harry's whim. She will think herself the victor of everything, she will think herself the favourite of God Himself. Her mother called herself a '*conquistadora*'; Katherine has been raised to ride roughshod over everyone.

I write to Mary:

*I am sure that the coronation and the wedding was very grand and I am sure that you enjoyed it; but you must be a good sister to Katherine and remind her to be grateful to Harry for raising her to this great position, when she had sunk so very low. Our brother has been generous to recognise his betrothal to her when he was not bound to do so. You should caution her against pride and greed in her new position. Of course, I rejoice in her extraordinary rise to power but we would not be good sisters if we did not warn her against the sin of ambition, and rivalry with us who are Tudors born.*

## HOLYROODHOUSE PALACE, EDINBURGH, SCOTLAND, AUTUMN 1509

James has ambassadors at Harry's new court and they report that, just as I feared, the young couple are spending lavishly on clothes, celebrations, jousts and music. There is dancing every night and apparently Henry composes songs for his own choristers, and poetry. My pregnancy is not an easy one, and the nausea that comes with my condition is worsened, I swear, by the reports of Katherine dancing in gowns of cloth of gold, the curtains in her box at the joust sewn all over with little gold letters of K and H, her pomegranate crest carved on every stone boss, her barge with silk curtains, her fantastic horses, her beautiful wardrobe, her greedy purchases of jewels.

I am so avid for reports of the most extravagantly beautiful court in Europe that people think I love to hear of my brother's happiness. I show them a weak smile, I say 'yes'. All this is troubling enough, but news of my sister Mary's wealth and freedom is even worse for me. She will be completely unsupervised – for Katherine will never command her – and Harry will just drown her in jewels and fine gowns to show her off. Everyone tells me she is the most beautiful princess in all of Europe. Harry will use her as a puppet to show the crown jewels; he will have her portrait painted and send it all round Christendom to flaunt how beautiful she is. I imagine bets are already being taken on the likelihood of her jilting Charles of Castile and marrying another applicant, if they can find anyone grander. I really don't think I can bear to see another picture of another betrothal. I can't bear to get another letter from Mary boasting of her betrothal gifts – that ruby! And they will not make her return it, I am sure.

Katherine herself writes to me. It is her first letter adorned with the royal seal on the bottom. I find it unspeakably irritating:

*We have always been sisters and now I am your sister and a sister-queen. Your brother and I have mourned your dear father and your good grandmother and we are very happy together. We should be so glad if you could make a visit to court next summer when the roads are good.*

*You will want to have news of your little sister. She lives with us at court and I think every day she grows more beautiful. I am so happy that she is betrothed to my family and so when she leaves us she will go to my former home and I know how they will delight in her fair skin and golden hair and the beauty of her sweet nature. She shares my wardrobe and my jewels and sometimes we dance together in the evenings, and people exclaim at the picture that we make: they call us Grace and Beauty – so silly. She will write to you next. I am trying to keep her to her studies – but you know how playful and naughty she is.*

*I hope soon that you two will be royal aunts to a little prince. Yes, I am with child! I will be so glad to give your brother a son and heir. How blessed we are! I pray for you daily, and I know that you think of me and our sister, Mary, and my dear husband, your brother the king. I know that you must feel, as we all do, that our dark years are behind us and we three must pray for our blessings to continue. God bless you, Sister.*

*Katherine*

I grit my teeth. I write in reply. I say how pleased I am for her. I explain that I am sick in the mornings but some people say that this proves it is to be a boy. I say that they give me broth of beef. I am not afraid of childbirth, having faced it before, and also I am so young, only nineteen. It is so much safer to have babies when you are a young mother, everyone says so. And how is Katherine feeling? How is she at the age of twenty-three? Carrying her first child at twenty-three?

She does not reply to this, and first I laugh up my sleeve at the thought of taunting her with her age, and reminding her of the long years when she was waiting as a widow, the years when she should have been married to Harry and conceiving a child, and then – when her silence continues – I take offence, thinking that she believes herself too grand to be obliged to reply promptly. Also, she said that Mary would write to me and she does the child no favours if she allows her to be negligent and lazy. She should remember that I am her sister-in-law, and a queen in my own right. She should remember that my friendship is valuable, the perpetual peace is of my making, we are royal neighbours and my husband is a great king. Certainly, she should reply promptly to me when I have taken the trouble to write to her.

In October, not having had a single word from either of my so-called sisters, I write from my childbed to tell them that I have birthed a boy. I know that I write as if it is my triumph. I cannot moderate my tone – but it *is* my triumph. I have given my lusty husband a boy and whatever Katherine achieves in her future confinement, I have already done this, and I have done it before her, and they can know that in London. I have given my husband a son and an heir, and this boy is the son and the heir of England too – until Katherine does her duty as I have done mine. Until then, it is I who have the heir to the crowns of Scotland and England in my golden cradle, it is I who have the first Tudor of the third royal generation. We are no dynasty without grandchildren to follow my father, we are nothing without sons, and it is I – not Mary and not Katherine – who has a Tudor prince in my nursery tonight.

## HOLYROODHOUSE PALACE, EDINBURGH, SCOTLAND, CHRISTMAS 1509

We celebrate Christmas in the grandest way that Scotland can afford, with masques and disguisings, dances and feasts, and John Damien the alchemist builds a machine that can fly around the room like a captive bird, which makes people scream with fright. James gives me a chain of gold, and jewels for my hair, and tells me that I am the finest queen that Scotland has ever had. I look well, I know. My gowns are too tight and they have let out the seams and lace me loosely, but James says that I am bonny and blithe, as a wife should be, and that he has no objection to a warm armful.

# HOLYROODHOUSE PALACE, EDINBURGH, SCOTLAND, SPRING 1510

James and I are so happy that not even the return of the two bastards from Padua causes trouble between us. Alexander, who was named as Archbishop of St Andrews, and his half-brother James Earl of Moray come to pay their respects and I greet them with cool courtesy. I show them both the legitimate son of their father, and I tell them this is Arthur, Prince of Scotland and the Isles, and Duke of Rothesay. Both boys kneel to the little crib and swear fealty and Alexander blinks his short-sighted eyes behind his round glasses perched on his nose, and says doubtfully, 'He's very small for such a big title,' which makes me laugh.

I don't even object when my husband names Alexander as Lord Chancellor. 'I need someone I can completely trust,' he says.

'He's little more than a boy,' I say irritably.

'We grow up early in Scotland.'

'Well, as long as he knows that all his learning has been for the benefit of his half-brother,' I say.

'I am sure that Desiderius Erasmus never forgot it for a moment,' James says with his wry smile.

To my surprise, Katherine finally replies to my letter, writing in her own hand, with her pomegranate seal. It is a private letter to say that she is so sad and so ashamed, she has lost the baby she was carrying, and though it would have been a girl, she feels that she has failed to produce the one thing that Harry lacks, the one thing they need to make their joy complete.

She shocks me out of my righteous offence. She makes me stop and think of my little girl that died, and my son before her.

I think how cruel I was to taunt her with being a mother for the first time at twenty-three. It was a poor joke when she read it and lost her baby. I am filled with remorse and I am ashamed that I let my rivalry with Katherine spill over into spite. I take her letter in my hand, and I go to chapel and pray for the little soul of the lost baby. I pray for Katherine's sorrow, I pray for my brother's disappointment and for the throne of England. I pray that a Tudor son and heir will come to them, to the young woman who has been my sister for eight years, whom I have loved and envied turn and turn about, but who has been in my heart and prayers for so long.

And then I bow my head lower and whisper to Saint Margaret who was swallowed by a dragon and must have known, as I know, the secret leap of joy of being rescued from the worst thing that can happen. Margaret came out of the dragon's belly unscathed, and I came through labour and childbirth with a son and heir – the only Tudor son and heir. I would never wish ill to Katherine, nor to Harry or Mary – indeed, I truly pity her loss – but my son, Arthur, is heir to Scotland and England and will be so, until she has a boy. Her son, when he comes, will displace mine. Who could blame me for a little secret joy that I have a son and she does not?

The ambassador to England writes to say that although Katherine lost one child, a girl, she was – praise God – carrying twins and she still has a baby.

'That's unusual,' my husband remarks to me as he reads the letter aloud by the fireside in my bedroom after all my ladies have been sent away. 'She's lucky.'

I feel a rush of understandable irritation at the thought of Katherine keeping a boy in her belly when I have been on my knees praying for her to find comfort in her loss. How ridiculous that she should write me such a tragic letter when she was still carrying a child. What a fuss she makes over nothing!

'What d'you mean, unusual?' I ask stiffly, irritated that my husband takes such an interest in the work of physicians, reading their horrid books himself and looking at disgusting drawings of diseased hearts and swollen entrails.

'It's surprising that she did not lose both children when she lost one,' he says, rereading the letter. 'God bless her, I hope it is the case; but it is very unusual to lose one twin and keep the other. I wonder how she knows. It's a great pity that she cannot be examined by a physician. It may be only that her courses have not returned, but that she is not with child.'

I clap my hands over my ears. 'You cannot speak of the Queen of England's courses!' I protest.

He laughs at me, pulling my hands away. 'I know you think that, but she is a woman like any other.'

'I would never admit a physician, even if I was dying in childbirth!' I swear. 'How should a man come near a queen at such a time? My own grandmother specifically wrote that the queen shall go into confinement and be served only by women, in darkness in one shuttered and locked room. She cannot even see the priest who comes to give her the Mass – he has to pass the Host through a screen.'

'But what if a woman in confinement needs a physician's knowledge?' my husband counters. 'What if something goes wrong? Didn't your grandmother nearly die in childbirth herself? Wouldn't it have been better for her if she had a physician to advise her?'

'How should a man know anything about such things?'

'Oh, Margaret, don't be a fool! These are not mysteries. The cow is in calf, the pig is in farrow. Do you think a queen births a child unlike any other female beast?'

I give a little scream. 'I won't hear this. It is heresy. Or treason. Or both.'

He pulls my hands down from my appalled face, and kisses each palm gently. 'You need not hear any of it,' he says. 'I'm not like the soothsayers at the mercat cross. I can know something without shouting about it.'

'At any rate, she must be the most lucky woman in the world,' I say resentfully. 'To have everyone's sympathy for losing a daughter and then carry a twin son.'

'Perhaps she is,' he concedes. 'I certainly hope so.' He turns away from me and strips off his shirt. The cilice at his waist makes a little chinking noise.

'Oh, take that horrid thing off,' I say.

He looks at me. 'As you wish,' he says. 'Anything to please the second luckiest woman in the world – if she can be pleased being, as she is, forever in second place, a second-rate queen, in a second-rate kingdom, waiting for her newborn boy to be forced into second place.'

'I didn't mean that,' I protest.

He takes me in his arms and does not trouble himself to answer.

## LINLITHGOW PALACE, SCOTLAND, SUMMER 1510

In May, when we are at our lakeside palace, I get a short hand-written letter from Katherine saying that, after all, there does not seem to be another baby. She writes in a tiny crabbed hand, as if she wishes she were not writing at all.

*I have begged my father not to reproach me. I did nothing that was careless or wrong. They told me that I had lost a baby but kept her twin, and I did not know that there was nothing there until my belly went down again as if from a bloat, and my courses started. How should I know? Nobody told me. How should I know?*

She says that her husband has been kindness itself, but that she cannot stop herself crying all the time. I push the letter away and I cannot bring myself to reply for irritation at them both. The idea of Harry being kind to his wife – my little brother who never had a thought in his head but for himself! – and the idea of Katherine of Arrogant humbling herself to apologise for something that she could not help sends me into a little fury. The idea of her unable to stop crying fills me with disdain. How would I be if I could not stop crying when I lost a child? I would never have made another. Why should Katherine revel in grief and publish it to the world? Should she not show queenly courage, as I did?

I have to concede, also, that my husband may have been right about her seeing a physician. How could people have told her that she was with child when she had just miscarried a baby? How could the wise women be so foolish? How could she have been so stupid as to listen?

I suppose it is just everyone trying to please Harry as usual. People cannot bear to tell him bad news, as he has no tolerance for anything that denies his own will. Just like my lady grandmother, he has an idea of how things should be, and he will not listen when someone says that the world is not like that. He has always been completely spoiled. I suppose that when they told him Katherine had lost a baby girl, he looked at them as if such a disappointment was simply impossible, and then they all felt they must assure him that she was still pregnant, probably with a boy. Now that lie has been revealed and Katherine will feel worse than ever. But who is to blame?

I go to the royal nursery and see my own baby, the heir of Scotland and England, plump and strong, in the arms of his rocker. 'He is well?' I ask. They smile and tell me he is very well, eating well and growing daily.

I go back to my rooms and write to Katherine:

*Praise God, my son is strong and very healthy. We are blessed indeed to have him. I am so sorry to hear of your mistake. I pray for you in your sorrow and your embarrassment.*

'Don't write that,' my husband says, looking over my shoulder and rudely reading my private letter.

I scatter it with sand to dry the ink, and I wave it in the air so he cannot read my sympathetic words. 'It's just a sisterly letter,' I say.

'Don't send it. She has enough trouble without you adding your sympathy to her burdens.'

'Sympathy is hardly a burden.'

'It's one of the worst.'

'Anyway, what is a woman like her troubled with?' I demand. 'She has everything that she ever dreamed of but a child, and surely one will come.'

I see him look away as if he has a secret. 'James! Tell me! What have you heard?'

He pulls forward a stool and sits on it, smiling up at me. 'You must not rejoice in the misfortune of others,' he instructs me.

I cannot hide my smile. 'You know that I would not be so unkind. Is it Katherine's misfortune?'

'You will rewrite the letter.'

'I will. If you will tell me what you know.'

'Well, for all his gentle upbringing, your sainted brother Harry is no better than a mere sinner like me,' he says. 'For all that you reproach me for the bairns and send them away from their little nursery, your brother Harry is no better a husband than I; he is no better than the rest of us. While his wife was in confinement he was caught in bed with one of her ladies-in-waiting.'

'Oh! No! Which one? Who?' I gasp. 'Actually in bed with her?'

'Anne Hastings,' he says. 'So now there is a great row between her brother the Duke of Buckingham, the whole Stafford family, and the king.'

I sigh as if he has just given me a rich gift. 'How very dreadful,' I say delightedly. 'How unfortunate. I am very shocked.'

'And the Staffords are very great,' he reminds me. 'And of royal blood from Edward III. They won't like to be held up for shame, nor to have Henry dallying with one of theirs. He's a fool to make enemies of his lords.'

'I suppose you never do.'

'I don't,' he says with quiet pride. 'If I make an enemy then I kill him or imprison him, I don't upset him and let him go off to his own lands to cause trouble against me. I know what I have to do to hold this kingdom together. Your brother is new to the throne and careless.'

'Anne Hastings,' I say lingeringly. 'Katherine's own lady-in-waiting. She must be absolutely furious. She must be spitting with rage. She must be sick with disappointment. After her great wedding! After her marriage for love! All those ridiculous madrigals!'

He lifts a finger as if to warn me. 'Never again scold me for having a mistress,' he says. 'You always say that your father never looked at another woman and that your brother married for love. Now you see. It is perfectly normal for a man to take a mistress, especially when his wife is confined. It is perfectly normal for a king to have his pick of the court. Never reproach me again.'

'It is neither normal nor moral,' I retort. 'It is against the laws of God and of man.' I can't maintain my grandmother's tone. 'Oh, James, tell me more! Is Katherine going to have to keep Lady Anne as her lady-in-waiting? Is she going to have to turn a blind eye to it all? Will Harry keep Anne as his whore?' I gasp. 'He'll never set her up as his mistress, like a French king, will he? He'll never let her run his court and send Katherine away?'

'I don't know,' he says, chucking me under the chin. 'What a very vulgar child you are to want to know all the details! Shall I tell my ambassador to report at once?'

'Oh yes,' I say. 'I want to know everything!'

## EDINBURGH CASTLE, SCOTLAND, SUMMER 1510

But the next news we have from England is not amusing scandal but good news: the best. Katherine is with child again. I cross myself when they tell me, for I am worried about my son, Arthur. Katherine and I have been so turn and turn about for good fortune – my betrothal coinciding with her widowhood, the death of my father meant her marriage and coronation – that I fear that the birth of an heir to the Tudor throne in England will be the death of the present heir in Scotland.

James does not laugh at my fears, but sends for his best physician to come to Edinburgh Castle, and go to the nursery where everyone is on tiptoe around the rocker who strips the little linen shirt off my son and swears that he is getting hotter and hotter every hour, that he is burning up.

He is only nine months old, he is tiny. It does not seem as if there is enough baby to fight the fever that makes his skin so hot to the touch and makes his eyes sink into his face. They soak his sheets in cold water, they close the shutters against the sun, but they cannot make the fever break. And though they cup him, draining blood from his rosy little heel, and purge him so that he vomits and cries in pain, nothing makes him better. While I am kneeling on the floor beside his chief nursemaid, watching her pat his sweating skin with a cool towel, he closes his eyes and he stops crying. He turns his head away as if he just wants to sleep and then he is still, and she says, her voice filled with horror: 'He's gone.'

*Dear Sister, I am so unhappy at his loss. I cannot write more. Pray for his little soul and pray for me, your sister, in this time of my trouble. I have been guilty of pride and envy but surely this terrible blow cannot be to teach me humility? I am so sorry if I have ever sinned against you. I pray you to forgive me for anything that I have ever said or done against you. Forgive my unkind and unsisterly thoughts that I have never even voiced. Give Mary my love, I miss you both so much. I am brought so very low. I have never known pain like this. Margaret.*

## HOLYROODHOUSE PALACE, EDINBURGH, SCOTLAND, SPRING 1511

Katherine goes into confinement in January and they send us the news of the triumphant birth on vellum that has been illustrated with Tudor roses and Spanish pomegranates. The letters are illuminated with gold leaf. They obviously had it drawn up for weeks; they had monks hand-painting the borders for months. They must have been very certain of the blessing of God to have such work done, with such brash confidence, on the chancy outcome of childbed. They bring me the letter as I lie on my bed in the afternoon. I find that I cannot stop crying. I trace the words with my fingertip; their joy seems very far away. I don't know how they dare.

But their hubris goes unpunished, as God smiles on the Tudors. Katherine has a boy. They call him Henry – of course. I think bitterly that it is as if my brother Arthur never was, as if my brother has forgotten that the name of Arthur was to be given to the firstborn Tudor boy, and the name Henry allocated to the second son. But of course Henry thinks of himself as the first son, and proudly gives his name to his boy. So there is no Arthur Tudor at all. Not my brother; not my son.

Katherine does not write of her triumph directly to me. She leaves me to be informed as if I should be grateful to be treated as any other European monarch, as if her good luck does not make me feel worse about the loss of my little boy. She did not even reply to my letter that told her of my grief. All I receive is this gold-enamelled boast.

Our ambassador sends us news of the magnificent tournament and feast that they hold to celebrate the birth of a son for Henry and an heir for his throne. The fountains of London flow with wine, so that everyone can drink the health of the new baby. They roast oxen at Smithfield so everyone can share in the royal joy. At the joust – they hold an enormous joust, of course, which goes on for days – for the first time ever, Henry allows himself to fight all comers. He risks himself as if he is a man at last. With a son and heir in the cradle, he can take challenges. He wins convincingly, beating everyone, as if he and Katherine and their son are untouchable.

'Smile,' my husband commands me as we go in to dinner. 'It is ungracious to begrudge another man the birth of his child.'

'I am in grief for my own loss,' I say in a sharp undertone. 'You ask me to forget my sorrow; but I wasn't even thinking about them.'

'You're deep in envy,' he says. 'A different thing altogether. And I won't have a spiteful, envious wife. I will give you another child, don't doubt it. Be hopeful for the next birth and smile. Or you can't come in to dinner at all.'

I give him a cold look but I smile as he commands me, and when he raises a cup to toast the Queen of England and her bonny son, I raise my glass and drink as if I can be happy for her, as if the taste of the best wine is not bitter in my mouth.

But Katherine's triumph is cruelly brief. In March we get the news from London that her baby Henry, the over-celebrated, over-praised new baby, has died. He was not even two months old.

My husband comes to me as I am on my knees in the chapel at Holyroodhouse praying for his little soul. He kneels beside me and is silent for a moment in prayer. He moves and I hear the little chink of his cilice under his shirt.

'And do you think now that your brother cannot have a healthy child?' he asks me, in a completely ordinary tone, as if it is a matter of interest, as if he might be asking me if my horse is going well.

I shift uneasily on the embroidered hassock. 'I don't know anything about it,' I say, determinedly ignorant.

He pulls me from my knees to sit on the altar steps, as if the house of God is our own and we can sit here and chat as if we were in my bedchamber. He is always shamefully informal, and I would rise up and go away but he has tight hold of both my hands. 'You do,' he says. 'I know you wrote and asked your grandmother if there was anything to fear.'

'She said nothing,' I say stoutly. 'And my mother never said anything about a curse to me.'

'That doesn't prove that there was none,' he says. 'No-one would speak of it to you, who must be so hurt by it.'

'Why would it hurt me?' I ask, though I don't want to hear the answer he is going to give.

'If the curse says that the Tudors cannot get a boy and their line will end with a barren girl, then it is you who will be unable to carry a child,' he says gently, as if he is telling me of a death in the family. I realise that he is. He is telling me of several deaths, and more to come. 'Neither you, nor Katherine of Aragon, nor your sister Princess Mary, will get a healthy boy. You will all fall under the curse. None of you will be able to birth a prince, or raise him, and the Tudor crown will go onto the head of a girl and she will die childless too.'

I am gripping his hands as tightly as he is holding mine now. 'That is a terrible, terrible thing to say,' I whisper.

His face is gaunt. 'I know it. We have to expiate our sins,' he says. 'I, for killing my father; you, for your father's sin against your cousins. I have to go on crusade. I can think of no other way that we might save ourselves.'

I drop my head into my hands. 'I don't understand!'

He pulls my hands from my face so that I have to face him, his anguished mouth, his eyes filled with tears. 'You do,' he says. 'I know you do.'

## LINLITHGOW PALACE, SCOTLAND, SPRING 1512

The king cannot possibly go on crusade without an heir to succeed him. Even his religious advisors know that, but as I am with child again, and getting near my time, he goes on constant pilgrimages to holy shrines in his own country, dispensing justice and praying for mercy for himself at the same time. He has done all he can to prepare for a crusade as soon as a son is born to us; so we, a little country, have one of the greatest fleets in Europe. He has ideas about the way ships can be used in battle – no-one has ever waged a sea battle as my husband thinks it should be done. He designs a mighty, beautiful ship, the *Great Michael*; and he oversees the building of it himself, stripped down to his shirt, working alongside the artisans: the blacksmiths and the carpenters, the shipwrights and the sailmakers. He tries, constantly, to persuade the Pope to make an alliance with the King of France, Louis XII, so that all the princes of Europe can unite in one powerful attack against the infidels who have captured the holy places and defiled the birthplace of Christ.

But the Pope has other plans and makes an alliance between Spain and the Venetians, and then my foolish young brother – completely under the sway of his Spanish wife, Katherine of Arrogant – joins what they are calling the Holy League, which will break the unity of the Christian kings. She makes Harry serve his Spanish father-in-law and drags him into war against France, just as James was hoping that all of Europe would go on crusade.

Everything that James hoped for is overthrown, Europe is divided again, and all so that my brother can pursue his dream of winning Aquitaine back for England, as if he were the heroic

Henry V and not a king from a quite different family in a quite different time. I blame Harry for vanity and a foolish young man's lust for war, but I know that he is under the influence of Katherine and I think of her as absolutely wicked to lead Harry – and England – into a war that we cannot possibly win, which will plunge all of Christendom into an internal battle when we should be fighting the infidel.

How is my husband going to organise his crusade if the Christian kings are fighting among themselves? But all that Katherine thinks of is pleasing her father and giving him an English army for his use. My brother is completely ruled by his cunning wife. I see again the boy who was my mother's pet, a slave to our grandmother. Once again, he has found a woman who will tell him what to think. She should be ashamed of herself – rescued from poverty by the King of England, but encouraging him to endanger himself. She is thinking only of her own importance. Her mother was a queen who ruled in her own right; Katherine wants to do the same. She hopes to be a royal partner, a queen who is equal to a king. She wants to send Harry to war on a wild goose chase and be regent in his place. I know her. I know her secret ambition is to be like her mother: the greatest woman in Christendom. That is why she married Arthur, so that she could rule England through him. This is why she married Harry, and now she is getting her way.

I think I will write to Katherine and tell her how wrong she is to advise Harry to go to war in alliance with his father-in-law. But before I start my letter, a messenger comes from England with a package for me. When I open it I find inside, carefully wrapped in silk and parchment, a sacred relic: the holy girdle of the Virgin Herself, and a short letter from Katherine.

*Dear Sister,*

*Knowing that your time is at hand I send you this, the most precious thing that I own, that helped me both in my time and in my loss. It is the sacred girdle of Our Lady, which she wore when she gave birth to Our Lord. It comes to you with Her*

*sanctity and my deep affection and hopes for you and your new child. I pray that it is a strong boy. God bless you,*
*Katherine*

My justifiable irritation with Katherine's meddling with the governance of England melts away as I hold in my hands this most sacred relic. I know her devotion – this will be more to her than all the silver in Spain. She could not give me anything more precious, and if it grants me a safe delivery of a healthy son, she has given me my heart's desire.

*Dearest Sister, I give you deepest thanks for the loan of this precious girdle. You could not give me a greater gift. I am fearful as I approach my time, we seem to be so unlucky with our babies. My husband has a painfully uneasy conscience and is afraid that his sins fall on me and our unborn children.*

*This is why the girdle will comfort me as I go into confinement and bear me up in my time, and bring, I hope, an heir safely into my arms and to his throne. God grant us all forgiveness for our sins and let His mercy fall on us. God bless you for giving me this, you are a true sister. Ask Mary to pray for me too as I know that you do. Margaret.*

Louis of France, alarmed by the allies massing against him, promises my husband that he shall have anything he wants if he will keep the 'Auld Alliance' between France and Scotland. I am preparing to go into confinement when James comes to find me in the tiny room at the top of the tower, looking out over the water meadows and the loch.

'I thought I would find you here,' he says. 'I am surprised you can make it up these steep stairs with that good belly on you.'

'I am breathing the air and taking the sun before I have to go into confinement,' I say.

He sits beside me. There is barely room for the two of us on the circular stone bench that lines the round room, but the unglazed windows show the countryside all around the castle and the swallows weave around this highest point. I can see for miles and miles in every direction and the huge sky arches over the tower as if it were the highest point in the world.

'I will work for peace while you are bringing us joy,' James says. He takes my hand and holds it to his chest, against his heart. 'And when you next come up here we will carry our boy and let him see his kingdom.'

We get to our feet and step outside the little room, leaning on the parapet and looking down at the loch below where it ripples with the wind, blue under a blue sky. 'If I am in alliance with the French, your brother will not invade them. He will not dare, for fear that I might invade the Northern lands while he is away.'

'You can't do that! Our marriage sealed the Treaty of Perpetual Peace.'

'I won't do that, but your brother is young and foolish and needs to fear a danger near home to keep him from seeking other dangers far away.'

'It's her,' I say miserably. 'It's her. She wants him in alliance with her father, and her father is the most untrustworthy man in Christendom. My own father never liked him.'

James laughs shortly. 'You're right about that,' he says. 'But you go to your work and be sure that I am keeping this country and even England safe for the boy that you may give us. Who knows? He might be heir to both kingdoms.'

I find my mouth trembles a little as I try to ask him if he has given up thoughts of a curse. 'You don't think . . . ?'

He knows at once what I mean, and with a quick gesture he draws me to his side and kisses my downturned head. 'Hush,' he urges me. 'I have the whole of the Church in Scotland in my keeping, and they are every one of them praying for you, for your boy, and for us. Go with a glad heart, Margaret, and do your work. Come on, I'll take you down to it.'

He goes before me down the tight curves of the winding stone stair and makes me walk with one hand on his shoulder so that I cannot stumble. We enter my presence chamber and all of my household is waiting to say farewell and wish me well. The two bastards, James and Alexander, kneel to me and wish me good health. At the doorway of my bedchamber, shrouded in darkness, my chamberlain gives me a cup of ale and my husband gives me a kiss on the mouth.

'God speed, my love,' he says. 'Be of good heart. I will be waiting out here for news.'

I try to smile but I go into the darkened room with my head down, and my shoulders hunched. I am afraid; I am afraid that my family is under a curse for what we did to get the throne of England, and that the curse will fall on me and the baby that I have got to bring into the world.

I have a boy. Perhaps it is the blessing of the Virgin's girdle, which we tie around my straining belly, perhaps it is the prayers of we three sister-queens; but I, Margaret, Queen of Scotland and Princess of England, have a strong, healthy boy. As soon as James is told he goes silently through the crowded presence chamber to the chapel and down on his knees in thanks for our good health, and puts his forehead to the stone floor to pray that it continues. Then he rises up and comes to the screen in my privy chamber.

'Go away,' I say. 'You know you're not allowed here.'

'Let me see him. Let me see you.'

I rise up from my great state bed, for the little one I used in child-birth is cleared away, and now I rest under curtains of cloth of gold and sleep on pillows under a headboard carved and gilded with the thistle and the rose. I beckon the rocker to bring the baby to the screen and I stand beside her, in my beautifully embroidered robe, and spread the lace on the baby's gown for his father to admire. James' dark intent face is bent to his small son; he does not notice the Mechlin lace at all, though it cost a small fortune. The baby is asleep, his dark eyelashes laid on pale cheeks. He is tiny. I had forgotten how tiny a newborn baby is. He would fit into one of his father's broad hands; he is like a little pearl in a sea of the finest silk.

'He is well.' James says it like a command.

'He is.'

'We will name him James.'

I bow my head.

'And you are in no pain?'

I think I would have died after my first birth if James had not interceded with the saint. This time too was a hard birth but the most sacred girdle of Our Lady helped me in my ordeal. I will never forget that Katherine shared it with me, that she thought of me and trusted me with her greatest treasure to help me to this joy. 'There is pain, but the relic eased the worst of it.'

He crosses himself. 'I shall stay up all night praying; but you must drink some birth ale and sleep.'

I nod.

'And when he is christened we will have days of jousting and feasting to celebrate his birth.'

'A joust as good as . . . ?'

He knows I am thinking of the tournament they had at Westminster when Harry's son Henry was born. 'Better,' he says. 'And I will get them to send your inheritance from England so you can wear your jewels. So sleep well, and get well soon, my dear.'

I go back to my bed. I take one fold of the curtain in my hand so that I can feel the threads of gold and I close my eyes and imagine the jewels of my inheritance as I go to sleep.

## HOLYROODHOUSE PALACE, EDINBURGH, SCOTLAND, AUTUMN 1512

I am too ill for a great celebration of our son and heir. In any case, James is desperately trying to keep the peace between the kings of Christendom who have all forgotten their duty to God. It is impossible for him to call the monarchs of Europe to a crusade if they insist on quarrelling among themselves. The worst offender, obviously, is Katherine of Aragon's father, Ferdinand.

I write to Katherine, as a sister and a sister-queen, asking her to influence Henry for peace. It is not easy for me to write her a long letter in my own hand as I am with child again and terribly tired this time. The baby sits heavily and low and I suffer from aches in my back and shooting pains in my belly. But James insists that I appeal to Katherine, telling me that we have to persuade my brother and his wife not to destroy the peace of Christendom, that Harry should be going to the Holy Land with James and not invading France with Ferdinand. 'Tell her that I am afraid of sin,' he urges me. 'Tell her everything. Tell her you are with child again and that I have to go on crusade to fulfil my promise, to keep you safe.'

Nobody cares for peace as my husband does. Nobody else has his driving desire to go on crusade. The sorrowful thing is that he cannot even tell them why he wants to go on crusade so badly. He cannot trust his brother kings with the story of his sin, or his fears of a curse on the Tudors.

When I lose my baby, a little girl who comes before her time in November too small to live, I share his urgency. He is right, I know it. I am convinced that there is sin to be expiated and none of us – not me, nor Katherine, nor even my little sister, Mary – will be able to feel safe in the future of our children until Jerusalem is back in Christian hands, the curse is lifted from the Tudor line, and James is forgiven his sins.

## STIRLING CASTLE, SCOTLAND, SPRING 1513

But nothing will stop my brother from invading France. He will not even cancel his plans for fear of a war with my husband on his Northern border. I am insulted at the suggestion that the perpetual peace created in honour of my marriage could be broken; Harry just sends an emissary to my husband to order James not to invade England while Harry is hell-bent on invading France.

There is no point in sending a man to speak so to us. James would never stoop to act against the rules of chivalry, he would never take up arms first, but he is in alliance with the French and they have promised to pay him the cost of any punitive raid and, even more, to finance an entire crusade when they have finished with Harry. My brother is a fool to make war on the French – of course the first thing that they are going to do is suborn his neighbours to rise up against him. Why can he not see that the future of these islands is to live in peace, one with another? My baby son is his heir! Is he going to risk war with his heir's father? Is he going to make war on his own sister's country and on her husband?

James spends all of Lent in the monastery. Unlike my brother – who is so ostentatious in his theology studies – or Katherine, his wife, always draped in crucifixes, my husband is a genuinely spiritual man. So Doctor Nicholas West, hailed as a peacemaker and a cunning diplomat, makes the long journey from London and finds that my devout husband is missing, and he has to deal with me instead.

All dinner, which is lean fare, for this is the very last day of Lent, he speaks of how wonderfully tall Harry has grown and how handsome he has become. He almost makes the slip of saying that he takes after our mother's family, the famously beautiful Plantagenets, but he manages to stop himself in time and refer to Tudor physique. This is ridiculous, as my father and grandmother were both dark and spare, mean with their smiles and hopelessly lacking in charm. Katherine, too, is apparently beyond beautiful and now she is blooming. I wonder if she is with child again, but I cannot ask Doctor West. Privately, I wonder if she will carry any baby to full term? Doctor West tells me that everyone praises her beauty and her health, her certain fertility. I nod; they always do. It means nothing.

Doctor West boasts that Henry is taking an interest in governing, as if this should not be his principal duty. I roll my eyes and don't say that my husband lives for his country. He too is a composer and poet and a great prince, but he does not waste his time like my brother does. Then Doctor West praises the ships that Harry is building. Now I do interrupt, and I tell him about those my husband has designed and planned, and that the *Great Michael* is the biggest ship at sea.

I am afraid that we bicker then, a little, as if he thinks I am boasting of the greatness of my own country of Scotland. As it is Lent and there is no music or dancing I tell him that we are a devout court and that we go to chapel after dinner, and we part company with very little joy.

It is no better when we have the feast of Easter, though it is good to be able to eat meat again. And on the second day of Eastertide we almost come to blows as Doctor West tells me bluntly that Harry is depending upon me to honour my birthright as an English princess by ensuring that James keeps the peace.

'You owe him this loyalty,' he says pompously. 'You owe the love of a sister to him and to your sister-queen.'

'And what about what England owes me?' I demand. 'Have you brought my jewels? My inheritance?'

He looks a little embarrassed. 'These are matters of state,' he says. 'Not for discussion between me and a royal lady.'

'These are personal matters,' I correct him. 'My father left me an inheritance, and my lady grandmother left me jewels of equal value to those that she gave to Katherine and Mary. Have they had theirs? For I have had nothing from England though I have reminded my brother and my husband has written to his ambassador. These are mine by right. They cannot be withheld.'

Doctor West shifts in his chair as if he has a little tiara pricking him in his pockets. 'You will have them,' he assures me. 'There can be no doubt of that.'

'I have no doubt of that,' I say. 'For they are mine, left to me by my beloved father and my grandmother. My own brother would not stoop to withhold them, and defy the wishes of his own father, of his own grandmother! If he has given Katherine and Mary their inheritance then I should have mine.'

'No, he does not withhold it,' Doctor West stutters. He has flushed red with embarrassment and he is looking around as if someone might come and help him out of this trap. He can look all he likes; this is a Scots court and the English are not and never have been great favourites. They make an exception for me because James shows that he loves me and I have given them a Scots prince.

'Then why have you not brought it?'

'You will receive all your inheritance when the king is assured that your husband will keep the peace.'

'But he does keep the peace!' I burst out. 'He has been working for peace all this time while the rest of them have been arming for war.'

'He is arming ...' Doctor West interrupts, 'his weapons, his huge guns ...'

At once I see that this is a spy as well as an emissary, and I am sorry that I boasted about *Great Michael.*

'Will I not get my jewels without my husband's assurance of peace?'

'No,' he says, finally finding his voice. 'His Grace your brother commands me to say that if your husband makes war on him he will not only keep your jewels, but he will take from your husband the best towns that he has.'

I jump to my feet, my hand closing on my goblet, really thinking that I will fling my wine into Doctor West's startled face, when the door behind the high table opens and James emerges, composed and smiling as ever, returned from the monastery, shining from his bath, and perfectly informed of this conversation. I would guess that he has probably been quietly listening at the door for all of this time.

Down goes Doctor West on his knee, as James greets me sweetly with a kiss and with a little gift of a golden brooch. I make much of it. Doctor West can see that I have many jewels already, I don't need anything from Harry; but I will never consent to Katherine flaunting herself in my grandmother's jewels. She probably has taken my legacy as well as her own. I go to whisper in James' ear that the emissary is part spy and part enemy and he puts me gently to one side. He knows this already. He knows everything.

Not one word can Doctor West get from him that evening nor for the remaining days of Easter week. James has returned from his vigil to enjoy himself. The best of the meats and the finest of the wines are brought to him, and he begs me and my ladies to dance. I pass Doctor West with a scornful turn of my head, as if to say: See here! This, my husband, is a king! Not some fool who steals someone else's jewels, and goes to war against a mighty power like France as his father-in-law bids him. This is a king and I am his chosen wife, and Harry can keep his stupid jewels. My husband will give me more, I have no need of them, and Scotland has no need of the friendship of England; they need not threaten us with taking our towns because we can just as easily take theirs. And we will do so if we so decide. And the French will pay for our army and pay our navy. So Harry had better think of that before he threatens us. And Katherine need not think that because we are sisters she can ride roughshod over me and my rights. She may call herself my dear sister but that does not earn her my inheritance. She may not wear my mother's jewels.

# HOLYROODHOUSE PALACE, EDINBURGH, SCOTLAND, SUMMER 1513

Harry does not think of anything but invading France. James begs him to reconsider, reminds him that both French and English lords will die on the battlefield and that they – and the kings – should only give up their lives for the glory of God, to recapture the Holy Land. He writes with patience, as an older, wiser man to a foolish young one, and he gets no reply. Harry – stupid, strutting Harry – is going to go to war, just as when he was little he had to ride at the quintain or write the best poem, or learn the new dance. Harry has found an audience, and the great stage of Europe, and he is going to make sure that everyone watches him. Harry wins uncritical admiration from his own wife and he will do anything to please her and her wicked father.

And then he threatens us through the Church. He gets Doctor West to warn James that if he breaks the Treaty of Perpetual Peace he will be excommunicated by the Pope, and go to hell. This! To a man who wants only to go on crusade, who wears a hair shirt for the forty days of Lent and a cilice around his waist all the time. A man so conscious of his sin and so fearful before God that he goes on pilgrimage four times a year and never sees me into confinement without praying all night. It is a wicked threat, struck at the darkest of James' fears, and I know at once where it has come from. It is Katherine who has told Harry that James is so fearful for my safety. It is Katherine who has told him that James is driven by guilt. It is Katherine who has told of the terrors that my husband confided in me that I trusted to her. She has taken my confidences, my sisterly confidences, and used them against my husband, against us. This is such a betrayal I can hardly bear to think of it.

I run to James' rooms, furious that Katherine has broken my trust, and I find my husband, smiling and happy, at his working table with tiny screws of brass and rings all around him, and comical spectacles pinched on his nose, assembling an instrument that he says can be used to tell a sailor at sea which direction is north.

'Look at this, Margaret,' he says. 'I have taken it apart and now I am putting it back together. Have you ever seen a more tiny compass? Isn't it a beautiful thing? Venetian, of course; I think we could make them ourselves for our ships.'

'James, they are saying that they will have you excommunicated!'

He smiles and waves the threat aside. 'They can threaten,' he says. 'They can even buy the Pope against me. But God and I know that I would be halfway to Jerusalem by now if your brother was not swelled up like a pig's bladder by false pride. I won't be troubled by a boy who goes to war at the bidding of his wife. I won't be frightened by the cursing of a pope who has been bought by him.'

'It's all her fault,' I say eagerly. 'Just as I have been a peacemaker, she has been an agent of war.'

James looks at me over his spectacles; but he is not listening. 'I am sure you are right.'

*Sister Katherine,*

*Forgive me for my bluntness, I speak as the Northern people do, without concealment and clever turns of phrase. If you persist in advising Harry to support your father in his quarrel with France then you will act against the interests of England. France has long been a true friend to the Scots, and we will support them if we have to. Please don't let your father put such a rift between James and Harry, your husband and mine, England and Scotland, and between my brother and me. It is unsisterly and un-English.*

*Also, I don't have the jewels that my grandmother left*

*me, nor my inheritance from my father. These are objects of great importance to me for my love for the giver – the value means nothing. Has Mary got hers? Do you have yours? Can it be possible that my brother is withholding my inheritance? I cannot believe that he would do such a thing nor that you would permit it. In particular there is a garnet brooch that belonged to my grandmother and that I know she meant for me. Mary can hardly want it, now she has the largest ruby in the world. I demand that it is sent to me. I insist upon it.*

*Please be a true sister to me, and a true queen to England, and prevent war and deliver my inheritance. I pray that you see the path of duty in this. I think that God's will is clear.*

*Margaret*

She does not even reply. She persists in encouraging war with France and I don't even know if Mary has had her jewels. Only when our ambassador tells us that the invading army has actually left England for France do I understand why Katherine has behaved so badly; only now do I see her reward.

Henry sets sail, and leaves Katherine in command of England. All of England! Given to the woman who once could not afford fresh apples from Kent. He names her as regent. I cannot believe it, even though I predicted that she wanted this, she would be like this. I am so furious with her that I raise no objection when James tells me that he is honour-bound by his alliance with France. He will invade the Northern lands of England.

'I shall probably have to face your old friend Thomas Howard,' James says when he comes into my rooms to lead me and my ladies in to dinner. I can tell from the smell of gunpowder in his hair that he has been at the powder mill.

'He was no friend of mine,' I reply. 'It was you he talked to all the time. He was overproud, I was delighted when he went home.'

'Well, now he has been left to guard England,' James says. 'Your brother has taken his best men and all his army to France and left no-one but old Howard and his son and the queen to defend England. I will meet him on the field of battle once again.'

'Will he be short of men? Has Harry taken everyone?'

James takes my hand and comes close, so that no-one can hear but me.

'He has enough, but if the clans will come out for me then I will have more. And they will come out for me, for I have been a true king to them and an honourable leader and never led them astray.'

Ahead of us, in the great hall, I can hear the rumble of voices and the scrape of the benches on the floor as people take their seats. I can hear the ripple of music and the slow chant of the choir from the gallery.

'I won't fail them,' James says quietly. 'I am the true-born King of Scots and the English are led by a man new-come to his throne and terribly inexperienced. I have served them for years and they have served me, and the English king is just a boy.'

He glances at me and says the thing that he knows I will want to hear the most: 'And I have a queen, a young woman but a great queen, at my side, and he has nothing but a Spanish princess, the widow of his brother, the cat's paw of her father. How can we fail?'

'And Thomas Howard is so very old,' I say. 'Surely his fighting years are over?'

James frowns. 'He is out of favour with your brother the king,' he says thoughtfully. 'And he has lost a son, who drowned at sea and lost Harry's ships. Your brother blames the Howards for failing him, he has turned against them. Howard is the only earl not taken to France in Henry's great army. I think he will fight like a cornered rat when he faces me. He knows it is his last chance to win back the king's favour. He will be a desperate man – I don't mind admitting that I would rather not face a man who has nothing to lose.'

'Perhaps you had better not fight?' I suggest nervously. 'Perhaps we had better not invade England?'

'This is our chance,' my husband rules. 'And we haven't had a better chance for decades.' He smiles, knowing how to tempt me.

'Your sister-in-law and your greatest rival is the English regent. Don't you want me to march against her army? Don't you want to see her completely defeated?'

## LINLITHGOW PALACE, SCOTLAND, SUMMER 1513

We visit Linlithgow to see James, our son. The ride is beautiful in the warm summer weather. We go cross-country until we reach the broad banks of the Forth and the water meadows that stretch for miles. As it is midsummer the milkmaids go out every morning and evening and call the cows who are hock-deep in lush grass, and at dinner we eat possets and milk puddings, creamy toppings and the rich cheese of the area.

We approach the castle up the sloping ride from the loch and as we enter through the broad gateway, I can see my son James in the arms of his wet nurse in the pretty inner courtyard. Thank God he is growing and strong, past the dangerous date of his first birthday, settled with his Irish nurse, giggly and waving his little clenched fists at his father, screaming with delight when he is pursued, toddling off on fat little feet.

We have easy days at this most comfortable palace. I take the baby down to the loch every day and sometimes we take a boat out, and I let him paddle his toes in the water. The lake is teeming with fish: trout and even salmon. His father wades into the cold deeps with a rod and line and promises me that I will have salmon for my dinner. The gillies go out with him and together they bring back a string of fish, scales like silver, too heavy for one man to carry.

In the evenings I summon James to drink wine with me at the top of the tower on the queen's side, where the stairs go up and up and at the very head there is the tiny room, roofed against the rain, which looks all over Lothian. When the sun sets I can see the sky all around me as if I am an eagle in an eyrie, the clouds like lace lying over silk. When it rains or when the clouds roll down from the hills I can see huge rainbows, arching up as if they are pointing the way to heaven.

'I knew you would like this,' James says with satisfaction. 'When I planned it and had it built for you I imagined you, like this, at the very top of your own palace, looking around. Tell me it is as fine as Greenwich!'

'Oh, it's so different,' I caution him. 'Greenwich is a palace set flat on a tidal river, built for peace. Here you have a palace but still you have a hill and a moat and a drawbridge. Greenwich has a long marble quay before it, modelled after the Venetians, where anyone may land, and doors stand open all the summer. This is more like a castle than a palace.'

I see the disappointment in his face. 'But there is no comparison,' I reassure him. 'Here we have the most beautiful rooms which lead into one another, the most beautiful great hall. People all around are amazed by it. And here I can ride out around the loch, sail in a boat – look at the quay you have built for the royal sailing boat! And if I want to hunt there is a park filled with game for me. It is a beautiful palace, perhaps the loveliest in Scotland. And this, at the top of the tower you built for me, is the prettiest room I have ever been in.'

'I am glad that you have come to love it.'

'I have. Nobody could fail to love it.'

'That's good, because here I have to leave you. I have to go to Edinburgh tomorrow,' James says, as if it is nothing but an errand to fetch something. 'And then I will meet with my lords and march on England.'

I feel a sick heave in my belly. 'What? So soon? Do you mean to go to war?'

'As I must.'

'But the peace . . .'

'Has to be broken.'

'The treaty . . .'

'It's void. Henry voided it whenever he arrested my men on the seas, and whenever he let his Northern lords raid our lands. If my fleet had caught him as he sailed for France we would have been at war already. As it is, they will wait off the French coast and catch him on his return. In the meantime, we will strike hard and quickly into England.'

I put my hands over my eyes. I am an English princess. I came here to prevent this. 'Husband, is there no way that you can find peace?'

'No. Your brother wants a fight. He is a young man, and a fool, and I can lead this campaign, paid for by the French, to regain our lands, and establish ourselves as a mighty neighbour.'

'I am so afraid for you.'

'Thank you. I imagine you are afraid for yourself.'

'That too,' I say honestly. 'And for our boy.'

'I have provided for him.' He speaks as if this is merely careful housekeeping, not a preparation for his death. 'His tutor will be William Elphinstone, the Bishop of Aberdeen.'

'You don't even like him!'

'He's the best we have. I don't need him always to agree with me. Actually, I won't be here to disagree.'

'Don't say such a thing! And don't leave me here. I don't want to wait here for you.' I gesture to the little tower, to the room like a beacon at the top. 'I don't want to stand here and look for you.'

He ducks his head as if this is a reproach. 'I pray that when you look, you see me return, standard flying in triumph. And if not, my little sweetheart, then you must manage without me.'

'How will I manage without you?'

'I have appointed my son's tutor, I have nominated a council of lords.'

'But what about me?' I hear my voice: it is the whimper of the Tudor child, always wondering who comes first.

'I have made you Regent of Scotland.'

I am stunned. 'As good as her.'

He smiles wryly. 'Yes, as good as her. I knew that would be

your first thought. I think of you as highly as Harry thinks of Katherine. But this is not just to make you feel equal to your sister-in-law, Margaret. It is because I think that you can rule this kingdom and raise our son, and keep Scotland safe. I think you can do it. You will have to be cleverer than your brother – but I think you are cleverer than your brother. You will have to become a woman like your grandmother was – devoted only to her child, determined to see him as king. I think you can do that. Don't let anything distract you, not vanity or lust or greed. Take my advice on this and you will be a good woman, indeed a great woman.'

His approval is like a breath of sunny air blowing across the loch.

'But perhaps I won't have to?' I say, quailing.

'I surely hope you won't have to.'

We are silent for a moment looking down at the clean waters of the loch and the people boating for pleasure, and those swimming off the shore. Some girls have kilted up their skirts and are paddling, screaming when one of them splashes. Everyone looks so carefree, as if nothing bad could ever happen.

'I don't know that I can do it,' I say miserably. 'If you don't come back from the battle, I don't know that I can do it.'

He chucks his hand under my chin and raises my face so that I have to meet his eyes. I have always hated how he does this, when I am forced to look into his own face, as if I were some milkmaid in the dairy and he the all-powerful master. 'Nobody knows they can do it,' he rules. 'When they killed my father and I was the one who gave the order and I became king I was sure that I could not do it. But I did it. I learned to do it. I studied to do it. Be the woman you were born to be and you will see my children on the thrones of Scotland and England. Be a fool and you will lose everything. I think your brother is a fool and will lose everything that he prizes by running after the things that he cannot have. You might have the wisdom to keep what you have. He will always choose to satisfy his own whims rather than being a true king. You must be a queen and not a fool like him.'

## LINLITHGOW PALACE, SCOTLAND, AUGUST 1513

I dream terrible dreams: of James sinking beneath the waves and pearls bubbling from his drowning mouth; of walking on a seashore and calling to him, pearls crunching under my feet; of sitting before a mirror and watching him fasten a magnificent necklace of diamonds about my neck which melts into dripping pearls as he ties it. I wake in tears and I say to him: 'You will die, I know you will die, and I will never wear diamonds again. I will have to wear pearls for mourning, nothing but pearls, and I will be alone with my son and how will I ever bring him safely to the throne?'

'Hush,' he says gently. 'Nothing can stop it going forward.'

He bids me a formal farewell, as if we are a king and queen of a romance. He bows before me and I put my hand on his stubborn red head and give him my blessing. He rises up and kisses my hand. I give him a silk handkerchief embroidered with my initials and he tucks it inside his jacket, as if it were a favour and he was only going jousting. He wears his finest jacket of crimson red embroidered with his name on the collar in gold thread and with his crest of thistles all over the front. I embroidered it myself, it looks very fine. He turns from me and vaults into the saddle of his warhorse, vaults like a boy as if to show me that he is as young and lusty as my brother. He raises his hand and his personal guard close up behind him and then they move off. The hooves are like thunder, hundreds of big horses moving like one great beast. The dust rises in a cloud. I gesture for the nursemaid to take our boy inside; but I stand and watch till the men are out of sight.

Then we have to wait. I find I keep hoping for a last-minute change of plans. I am a symbol of the perpetual peace; I cannot make myself understand that the peace is broken. They bring me news almost daily. James takes Norham Castle, and then Wark, Etal Castle and others. These are no petty victories; these are great fortresses, engraved on the hearts of the border men, and we are moving the border, pushing it further and further south, towards Newcastle. We are taking English castles, we are taking English land. The area that they call the 'debatable lands' will be debated no more; it will become Scotland. This is becoming a great expedition: no mere raid, this is a victorious invasion.

Each time the messenger draws close to the castle on the loch, the king's standard rippling before him, a guard thundering behind him, we become more confident. As we foresaw, Thomas Howard brings all the forces that he can muster, but Thomas Howard is under-provisioned and fearful. He has no reserves, he has no local support. His own English border lords rob his wagon train and steal his horses. His allies are uncertain, and begrudge sending servants to fight at the border when they have already paid fees for a war in France. Harry has taken the flower of his nobility to France to make war for his father-in-law, to oblige his wife. He has left England woefully unprotected. He is a fool. We can win this war against an absent king and half-hearted defenders.

Then James sends a short message to say that they will come to open battle. He will take possession of Branxton Hill. He has outmanoeuvred Howard who should, if he had any sense, withdraw to Newcastle. Howard's soldiers are hungry, thirsty, stealing their own rations, and the borderers – wild men, English and Scots – set upon stragglers, kill them, and strip them naked. James' army, well fed and well armed, is established on the high ground of Flodden Edge. The English will have to fight uphill against Scots gunners.

I wait for news. A battle must have been joined. Thomas Howard dare not go back to London to face Katherine without a battle to report. If he returns defeated, then the Howard family will be ruined. He has everything to lose. His reputation and the friendship of his king hang in the balance; I know how doggedly, how bitterly he will pursue his only course. But James need not fight, James could withdraw. He and his army could melt away back across our border, and boast of another successful raid on England that frightened them to death in the Northern counties and showed Harry that he cannot treat us with contempt.

I am sure that is what James will do – it is how the Scots have always tormented the English – but then a message comes and tells us that battle has been joined. Half a day later someone comes from Edinburgh with news that we have won the day, and the Scots are marching south. They may march as far as London! What is to stop them if they have defeated the English army? Then another report comes from a runaway soldier that there was a terrible battle, but when he fled it was going against us.

It pours with rain, a wall of water that holds us in the castle as if the sky has decided that no news shall come through. Every morning I wake to the patter of raindrops against the window and hear the gurgle of rainwater in the cisterns and the rush from the stone-carved gargoyle faces splashing down their streams into the stone courtyard. I think of my husband outside in the wind and the storm; I think of his archers with wet bowstrings, his gunners with damp powder. I swear that no-one is to believe anything, they are not even to speak, until we hear from James himself. I have to be, as he called on me to be, a true queen, a Queen of Scots, a gallant heart and a proud one. But then they tell me that a messenger has come from the lords' council in Edinburgh, with definite news, and he is waiting in my presence chamber.

I find my heart is thudding fast and I feel sick, as if I am with child again. I put my hand to my throat and feel my pulse race. Everyone who has any business to be in my rooms and anyone who has any excuse to attend has crowded into the great chamber. I walk slowly from the chapel, where I was praying for James to come home, defeated or victorious – I find I don't care as long as he comes home. The guards throw open the doors and the babble of speculation goes instantly silent as I walk through the massed crowd of strange faces and mount the steps to my throne, turn and stand before them, looking calmly around me. I think, irrelevantly, God help me, I am only twenty-three years old. Someone else should be here listening to this, someone who knows what to do. Katherine would know how to stand, how to listen, how to respond. I feel as if I am like my little sister, Mary – too young to be part of important times.

The messenger is standing before me in James' livery, his writ from the lords' council in his hand. 'What news?' I say, and I try to speak steadily. 'Good news, I hope?'

The man is filthy from his ride from Edinburgh, muddy and wet from fording rivers, soaked from his head to his dirty boots. They will have told him to let nothing delay him and to report only to me. He kneels and I realise at once from the anguish in his face that there is no point in my saying 'Good news, I hope?' in my stupid little-girl voice. It is not good news and I know it.

'Speak,' I say quietly.

'Defeated,' he chokes, as if he is ready to take my place and weep.

'The king?'

'Dead.'

I sway but the carver of my household holds me upright, as if I have to hear this news on my feet, though my husband is face down in the mud.

'You're sure?' I say, thinking of my little son, nearly a year and a half old, and now a fatherless boy; thinking of the baby that I may be carrying. 'You're certain? The Privy Council have confirmed it – there is no doubt?'

'I was there,' he says. 'I saw it.'

'Tell me what you saw.'

'It will be a miracle if anyone survived,' he says bleakly. 'We went down among them in a charge, and they had billhooks to our pikes and they sheared heads off like they were hedge-trimming. Our gunners didn't have the range, so though the English were bombarded the cannon fired over their heads, they were still in their ranks, unbroken and unhurt. We thought they would all be smashed up but they were fresh. The king led a mighty charge of horse and foot, and the clansmen were all behind him. Nobody failed him – I can't say a word against any house – they were all there; but the ground gave way under our feet. It looked sound when we viewed it from the top of the hill; but it was treacherous, a green, weedy marsh. We got bogged down and sank, and couldn't get up, and they let us struggle towards them. They stood in their ranks as we came on, going slower and slower, and then they ripped off heads and ripped out bellies and pulled down horses.'

My ladies gather around me murmuring horrified questions, whispering names. They will have lost sons and husbands, and fathers and brothers.

'How many lost?' I ask.

'Dead,' he insists. 'They're dead. About ten thousand.'

Ten thousand men! I feel myself reel again. 'Ten thousand?' I repeat. 'It's not possible. The whole army was thirty thousand. They cannot have killed a third of the Scots army.'

'Yes they can. Because they killed those who surrendered,' he says bitterly. 'They killed the dying. They killed the wounded where they lay on the field of battle. They chased after those who had thrown down their weapons and had turned for home. They declared they would take no prisoners and they did not. It was brutal and evil and long-drawn-out. I have never seen the like of it. You would think yourself somewhere barbaric, like Spain. You would think yourself on a crusade among pagans. It was conquistador killing. There were men screaming for their lives and crying out as the billhooks went in their faces all the long afternoon, all the long night. There were wounded men only silenced when someone cut their throat.'

'The king?' I whisper. James cannot have died on a hedging tool. Not James, not with his love of chivalry and the honourable ritual of the joust. He cannot have died bogged down in his beautiful armour with some English peasant's axe in his face.

'He fought his way through to Thomas Howard himself – it was nearly a single combat, just as he had challenged. But a bill-hook smashed his head to a pulp just as he reached the English standard, and an arrow opened his side.'

I bow my head. I cannot believe this, and I don't know what I should say or do. Although I warned him, although I dreamed of widow's pearls, I never really thought that he would not come home. He always comes home. Again and again he goes off to his mistresses or off to see his children, a pilgrimage, a progress to give judgement, riding off to see a cannon out of the forge or the launch of a ship; but he always comes home. He swore to me that he would never leave me. He knows I am too young to be left alone.

'Where is his body?' I ask.

We will have to have a grand funeral; I will have to arrange it. My boy James will have to be declared king; he will have to be taken to Scone Abbey for a great coronation. I don't know how to do it without my husband, who has always done everything for me, everything for his country.

'Where is his body? It must lie in state in the chapel. They must bring it to Edinburgh.'

He shall lie in state in the chapel at Holyroodhouse, where we married, where he crowned me queen; and the country – every-one, even his bastards and their mothers – will come and pay their respects to the greatest King of Scotland since Malcolm, since Robert de Brus. The chieftains shall come in their tartans and the lords will come and their standards will fly over the coffin, and the swell of a Scots lament will sound out for their great king, and we will all always remember him. We will bury him in a coffin of Scots pine under a pall of black velvet with a cross of gold thread, we will fly the flag of a crusader, for he would have been a crusader, the bells will toll for every one of his forty years. The cannon that he commissioned will roar as if they too are heartbroken. We will honour our king, we will never forget him.

The messenger sinks to his knees as if the weight of his words is too much for him to bear. He looks up at me and his white face is agonised beneath the dirt.

'They took his body,' he says. 'The English. They took his precious body, out of the mud, broken and bleeding as he was. And they sent him to London for her.'

'What?'

'The English queen, Katherine, said she wanted his body as a trophy. So they turned him over in the mud and took his breastplate and his coat, his beautiful coat, they stripped it off him, and his gloves, and his boots and his spurs. So he was barefoot, like a dead beggar. They took his sword, they levered off the crown from his helmet. They stripped him like he was a spoil of war. They threw all his things in a box, and they put his body on a cart and they have taken it away to Berwick.'

My knees give way then and someone helps me down to sit on a stool.

'My husband?'

'Dragged from the battlefield like a carcass on a wagon. The English queen wanted his dead body for a trophy, and now she has him.'

I will never forgive her this. I will never forget this. In France, Harry wins a battle at somewhere called Thérouanne, and in reply to his triumph Katherine writes to him that she has won a battle just as good as his. She boasts that she wanted to send him my husband's severed head but that her English advisors prevented her. She wanted to pickle James in brine and send him as a gift. But Thomas Howard had already had the body encased in lead and sent on a wagon to London. Deprived of her corpse, Katherine sends instead the royal standard, and James' own coat. His red coat, with the gold thread, that I embroidered myself. Now it is stained with his blood, and dirty with the mud of the battlefield, and stinking of smoke. His brains were spilled on the embossed collar where I had sewn golden thistles. But she sends it to Harry, triumphantly, as if such a thing can be a gift, as if such a thing should be anywhere but reverently buried in the king's own chapel.

She is a barbarian, worse than a barbarian. This is the body of her brother-in-law, the sacred body of a king. This is the widow who saw her own husband taken out in the most solemn procession to be buried, travelling in the night with burning torches, a woman who wore black and begged me to be kind to her in her grief – but when I am widowed, she has my husband's body tumbled into a cart and brought like a butcher's carcass to Smithfield. What savages are these? Only a brute would not return a king's body to his people for an honourable burial. Only a beast would feed off it, as she wants to do. I will never forgive her this. I will never forget it. She is no sister to me, she is a harpy – a monster who tears at flesh.

I will never speak of it either. I cannot put it out of my mind. But they must never know how I hate them for this and how I will never forgive her. I am going to make peace with this thief, with this grave robber. I am going to have to claim sisterhood with this wolf that feasts off the dead. I am going to have to send ambassadors and write letters and perhaps even meet the man who was once my brother and the vulture that is his wife. If I am to be queen and get my son on the throne, I am going to need their support and their help. I am going to beg for it and never let them see the contempt in my eyes. I am going to have to be what my husband commanded me to be: a great woman and not a silly girl. But she is a demon, a woman who besmirches the honour of her place, who has smeared my mother's throne with blood. She is a woman who wants to be equal to a king, a woman who sat beside my brother's deathbed, and ordered the killing of my husband. She is a Lilith. I hate her.

We have to get my baby James to Stirling Castle – the fortress that his father promised me was the safest in the kingdom. He will have to be crowned there. I dare not take him further north to Scone Abbey; the danger is too great. Thomas Howard, no great friend before and my deadly enemy now, is almost certain to follow up his victory by invading my poor country. With all our cannons on our ships at sea or stuck in the mud of Flodden, how can we defend our capital city? What will prevent Thomas Howard's victorious army from marching on to my palace at Linlithgow? Or coming further north to Stirling? Thomas Howard – who knows the traditions of Scotland as well as I do – may be coming now, as fast as he can, on a forced march to snatch my little King of Scotland before he is crowned.

We set out before dawn the next day, while the moon is low and only a line of grey, like tailor's chalk on mourning cloth, marks the sky in the east. Ahead of us goes the royal standard and the guards shoulder to shoulder around it. In the centre rides my husband's makar, the poet Davy Lyndsay, on a strong horse with James, not yet two years old, on the saddle bow before him. A standard bearer rides beside them with the prince's own coat of arms rippling over their heads. Nobody can attack us and leave the prince down on the ground with a spear through his heart and then pretend that they did not know who it was. James sits up straight, confident in Davy's grip. They have ridden together dozens of times, but never before pursued by an enemy at break-neck speed. Davy sees my white face and gives me his lopsided smile.

I ride just behind them, certain now that I am with child, my belly tight with the baby that James has left me, my eyes on the son that I have to guard. I don't think of anything; I just watch my son, and the windswept road ahead of us. If I took a moment to think, then I would pull up my horse and lean forward on his neck and cry for fear, like a girl. I dare not think. I can only ride and hope that we get to Stirling before the English come after us.

As soon as we are north of Linlithgow the open countryside gets wilder and bigger and the skies get higher. The rounded hills of Lothian, great bowls of valleys and wide ranges of uplands, become grander still as we go north into Stirlingshire. As the sun comes up and we ride onward we enter the thick forests of the valley floors. There is just a trace of the road through the forest, skirting a boggy patch, winding around a long-fallen tree, disappearing altogether where a stream has burst its banks and swept the track away. We have to keep the rising sun behind us but we can hardly see it through the thickness of the canopy. We ride blind, hoping that we are going west. James knew the way very well. He made this journey often, riding between Linlithgow and Stirling and then onward to the north to keep the peace and sit in judgement. But James will never ride in these high hills again. I don't think of this. I look to his son and see that he has fallen asleep in the saddle, in Davy's careful grip. I won't think that my son's father will never ride with him like this, that his father will never ride again.

No-one has planted these woods, no-one manages them. No-one fells them, not for firewood or charcoal, not for beams for the shipyards or houses. There are no shipyards or houses anywhere near, there are no charcoal burners' cottages, there are no woodsmen making a living from little shanties. There are not even poachers for there is scant game, nor brigands: for there are not enough people for them to prey on, there are so few travellers. The woods are empty of anyone but elusive deer and the beasts that we cannot see: foxes, boar and wolves. The guards close up, riding knee to knee around Davy Lyndsay and my precious boy, and they lower the royal standard and hold it like a lance, so that it does not catch on the low, sweeping boughs of trees.

This is not like England, not even like the great royal parks of England where no-one is allowed to cut trees or hunt game.

These are thick forests like the ones before the making of man, and we are like ghosts riding silently through them. We don't belong here. These trees are older than the time of Christ; these are not Christian forests, they are the land of the little people, the old people that James used to tell me about in stories.

I shiver in the cool gloom, though the sun is high in the sky outside. We cannot feel the heat, we cannot even see the noonday light. The trees and even the air seem to press against us.

It is a relief when the land starts to rise up and we can see a little brightness ahead as the forest grows thinner and there are shrubs and plants at the side of the track, growing towards the light, and then we are going through glades of silver birches and slowly, almost leaf by leaf, we leave the shadows. Now we can see the sky, and we are climbing higher and higher and come out on the flank of a hill that still stretches high above us. The horses blow out and we lean forward as they lower their heads and start to climb up and up, following the faintest of tracks that skirts the cliffs, which fall away on the far side, and takes us over the rounded top. But all we can see are more hills, stretching on and onward before us, as if they were towering waves in an unending sea, before we have to wind down again to the valley floor, now going north, always looking behind us for any sign of the glint of sun on metal, or the distant rumble of Howard's army.

We ride all day, stopping before noon for something to eat, and then riding on all of the afternoon. As the sun begins to sink towards the top of the hills and the shadows lengthen over the track, almost obscuring it so that we begin to fear we will lose the way, James cries in a little whiney voice that he is tired, and Davy reaches into his pocket for a piece of bread and gives him a flask filled with milk. James eats, held steady on the saddle, and then leans back against his guardian and sleeps as we keep the steady pace.

Still we go north, now with the setting sun on our left, and I say softly to Davy, 'Is it much further? It will be dark within a few hours.'

'We'll be in before dark, God willing,' he says. 'And if they are following us, they won't dare to come on in the dark. They'll camp for the night. They'll be afraid of ambush and they don't know the country at all. They can't find their way in the dark.'

I nod. I am aching in every bone in my body and fearful for the new baby that I am carying.

'You'll have a grand dinner and a good night in a soft bed,' Davy says quietly to me. 'Behind strong walls.'

I nod; but I think, what if he is wrong and darkness falls and we are still travelling? Will we have to camp out and sleep on the cold hillside? Or what if we have missed the road and gone past the town? What if we are riding onward and onward north, and Stirling is now behind us and we won't know till tomorrow morning? Then I think: I had better not think like this or I will break down and not be able to ride at all. I have to think, for now and for always, of only one thing at a time, the next thing that I have to do. I have to see these small tasks laid out like matched pearls strung on a necklace with a knot between each one – and not worry that they are the symbols of mourning, as I knew when I dreamed that my husband, my charming, playful husband, tied a string of diamonds around my neck and I watched them melt and drip into widow's pearls.

Finally, we see a few lights, high up on a hill above us.

'That's Stirling now, Your Grace,' the standard bearer reins back to tell me, and the horses prick their ears and go forward more briskly, as if they know there are stables with hay and water waiting for them.

I think – pray God there is no trap. Pray God that Thomas Howard has not done a forced march around us and we are not coming in towards him, expecting refuge but finding a battle. There is no way to tell what is hiding in the shadowy hedges at the side of the road as we wind our way towards the little town. The curfew has been sounded and the town gates are bolted shut.

My trumpeters sound the royal salute, then we have to wait while the royal burghers rush to the gate and the town guard fling themselves at the bolts and then the great gates creak open, and we can ride inside.

The burghers come towards me, uncovering their heads, some of them shrugging on their jackets and wiping their mouths, called from their dinner. 'Your Grace,' they say and they kneel before me as if I am a triumphant Queen of Scots with a victorious husband at war.

Wearily, I make a gesture that tells them everything: the defeat, the death of James, the end of everything. 'This is your king,' I say, showing them the little boy, fast asleep in his guardian's arms on the big horse. 'King James V.'

They understand at once that his father is dead. Heavily, they drop to their knees on the cold cobbles. They bow their heads; I see one man put his hands over his eyes to hide that he is weeping, and another buries his face in his bonnet.

We are the first people of authority in Stirling since the battle. Nobody has heard anything but rumours, no soldiers have yet made it back to their homes. The deserters who left before the outcome are certain to have kept their cowardice quiet, and few have got so far north. So now the people come into the streets, their doors banging behind, or they throw open their overhanging windows, hoping that this is a victory progress and that I have come to tell them the king is halfway to London, his army richer every day. Then they see my downturned face and note that I don't wave or smile, and they stop cheering and fall silent. Someone calls out with sudden sharp urgency:

'The king?'

Everyone looks at me; but I can't say anything. I can't pull up my horse and make a grand speech in which I declare that defeat does not mean despair, death is not the end of everything, Scotland has a great future. It would not be true. We are despairing, it is the end of everything, and I cannot see how to make a future.

I raise my voice. 'The king is dead. God save the king.'

Slowly, understanding spreads through the silenced crowd. Men pull off their hats, women put their hands to their eyes. 'God save the king,' they whisper back to me, as if they cannot bear to say the words. 'God save the king.'

They have lost one of the greatest warrior-kings that Scotland has ever had. They have lost a musician, a physician, an engineer, an educator, a gunner, a poet, a shipwright, a deeply convinced Christian anxious about his own soul and theirs. They have lost a great prince, a man among men. His coat and banners have been sent to France, his body is rumbling south, a trophy wrapped in lead in a wagon. In his place, all I can offer them is a baby-king, a helpless baby-king, with Scotland's greatest enemy on our doorstep. They kiss their hands blow the kisses to me as if to say: God bless you. God help you. And I look back at them grimly and think: I can't do this.

## STIRLING CASTLE, SCOTLAND, SEPTEMBER 1513

I move into my beautiful rooms in Stirling Castle and I send to the families of the great lords to come to crown James. Very many of them fail to reply; more than half of them are dead. In all of the kingdom there are only fifteen lords left alive. We have lost half a generation of men. But they send the sons who were too young to fight, and the old fathers who are mourning their heirs. They come from all the corners of the kingdom to swear loyalty to the new king.

He is not yet two years old, only a baby, but destiny has laid a heavy hand on my son James. He sits in the lap of his governess and she opens his shift of linen under the cloth of gold gown, and the bishops anoint his little chest with holy oil. He makes a little noise of surprise and looks towards me: 'Mama?' I nod that he is to stay still and not cry. They put his tiny hand on the barrel of the sceptre and the little fingers close on it, as if he will hold on to power, and they elevate the crown over his head. His eyes look up wonderingly as the trumpets blast, his lip trembles at the noise and he turns his head away.

'God save the king!' the bishops cry out; but there is no triumphant shout from the congregation of lords in reply.

They should shout in answer, something has gone terribly wrong. I am aghast at the silence behind me – what can it mean? Do they not accept him? Are they refusing to swear allegiance? Have they secretly decided to surrender to the English and stand dumb at the oath for James? Fearfully, I turn to look behind me at the crowded chapel where the lords are ranged in their clans and families in complete silence. Their faces are pale as they raise them to where the bishops have shouted their oath of loyalty. Then, one by one, each man's lips form the reply, 'God save the king!' but they have lost their voices. It is not a loyal shout but a whisper of grief; the lords are hoarse with sorrow. At the back of the church someone sobs and these strong, battle-hardened men drop their heads to rub the tears from their eyes.

'God save the king,' they say quietly, one after another, with voices straining to speak. 'God bless him,' they say, and someone adds: 'God take him to His own.' So I know they are thinking not of my little son and the terrible burden we are laying on him today, but of James the dead king, my husband, and his body stolen far away.

I write to my brother Harry, who is joyously celebrating his triumphs in France. I dip the nib of my pen in honey and I beg him to recall Thomas Howard to London and not order him to invade deep into Scotland. I say that my son is young and tender and Scotland has been knocked into despair. I beg him to remember that I am his sister, that our father would have wanted him to protect me in this difficult situation and not make it worse for me. I say that I am the symbol of peace between England and Scotland, and that I wish we were at peace now.

I grit my teeth and take a second sheet of paper to write to Katherine, who is Regent of England and the sole author of my disaster. I wish I could write the truth: that I hate her, I blame her for the death of my brother Arthur, I believe she tried to seduce my father, I know that she captured my little brother and has turned him against me. I blame her for the war between England and France, between England and Scotland, and, most of all, for the death of my husband. She is the enemy to my peace, and to my country.

*Dearest, dearest Sister . . .*

A guard opens the door of my privy chamber and one of my ladies comes in and leans over my chair to whisper in my ear. 'There is a man come to see you, one of the late king's servants. He has come from Berwick.'

Her voice chokes when she has to say 'late king'. Nobody can say his name.

I put my lying letter to one side. 'Send him in.'

Someone has given the man a plaid to throw over his shoulder for warmth but his padded jacket shows he was one of James' guard. He kneels before me, his bonnet clutched in one dirty hand. I see that his other hand is strapped to his side, a stained bandage at the shoulder. Someone nearly cut off his arm. He is lucky to be alive.

I wait.

'Your Grace, I have to tell you something.'

I glance at the letter to Katherine:

*Dearest, dearest Sister . . .*

This is her doing.

'The body they sent to England was not the king,' the man says bluntly, and at once he has my full attention.

'What?'

'I was the king's groom. I followed the English back to Berwick. I thought I should wash the body and prepare it for the coffin.' He swallows on a dry throat as if he is trying to choke down tears. 'He was my lord. It was my last duty.'

'And?'

'They let me see the body but they would not let me wash him. They wanted him dirty and bloody. And there was no coffin. They were rolling the body in lead so they could take it to London.' He pauses. 'In the heat,' he explains. 'The body in the heat . . . the flies . . . they had to . . .'

'I understand. Go on.'

'I saw the body as they got the lead ready to roll him up. It wasn't him.'

Wearily, I look at the man. I don't think he is lying; but equally this cannot be the truth. 'Why don't you think it was him?'

'It didn't look like him.'

'Wasn't his head smashed by a billhook?' I ask harshly. 'Wasn't his face cut off?'

'Yes. But it wasn't that. There was no cilice.'

'What?'

'The body they rolled in lead and shipped to England had no cilice around the waist.'

This is incomprehensible. James would never have taken off the cilice before battle. Surely nobody could be so wicked as to cut it off for a trophy? Can he have escaped from the battle? Can someone have stolen his body from Katherine? My thoughts are whirling but nothing helps me. I look down at my begging letter to the sister-in-law I despise. 'What difference does it make to me?' I ask despairingly. 'If he was coming home he would be here by now. If he wasn't dead he would still be fighting. It makes no difference at all.'

We convene a council of the lords that have survived and they recognise me as regent according to the king's will. I am to rule with their advice. I am to have my son in my keeping. I am to have a council of lords to assist me. Head of them will be the Earl of Angus, whom they call 'Bell the Cat' from an old triumph. He stands before me now with his face grooved with grief. Two of his sons rode with my husband at Flodden, and they won't come home either. I know that he is untrustworthy. He has sided with England and Scotland one after the other through a long life of border warfare, and James once imprisoned him over a woman, the mother of one of the bastards. But he looks at me and his dark eyes are sharp. 'You can trust me,' he says.

I can tell by the glances between the lords that they can hardly believe themselves, sitting in unity under the command of an English woman. I can hardly believe it myself. But everything is unexpected, everything is wrong. There is not a man at the table who has not lost a beloved son or brother or father or friend. We have all lost our king, and we still don't know what can be saved.

We agree to reinforce Stirling. This will be the new centre of government, the focus of our defence. We agree to build a new wall at Edinburgh Castle, but we know that if Howard comes with his army in force, the castle will fall. I tell them that I have written to my brother and sister-in-law to beg for peace and they greet this news with unfriendly silence. 'We have to make peace with them,' I say. 'Whatever we feel.'

I tell them that my brother Henry, King of England, has commanded me to send my baby into his keeping in London to be raised as King of Scotland far from his home. He says I must not let the lords of Scotland lay hands on my little boy and take him off to the Isles where he will be 'in danger and hard for the king to attain'. They laugh shortly at that, though there is little real mirth among us all. We agree, without discussion, that James V, the new King of Scotland, will stay in his country and with his mother. Katherine has stolen the body of the father; she is not getting the son as well.

The law of the land has ceased to run. There are too many fatherless sons and they are not being given their inheritance. There are too many widows with no-one to protect them. The borderlands are in a constant state of warfare, as the Warden of the Marches, Thomas Lord Dacre, under Katherine's orders, rides out every day to burn crops, destroy homes and keep the debatable lands in a state of constant danger and distress. No man trusts his neighbour. They arm against one another. Without my husband James to hold the kingdom together it is breaking down into lordships and tribal lands, warring against each other.

We pass laws, we issue commands. Soldiers returning from Flodden must be supported, but they must not steal and rape. Orphans must be provided for. But there are not enough lords to enforce the laws and the good men who rode with them are dead.

It is a dark council. But I have one piece of good news for them. 'I must inform you, my lords, that I am with child,' I say quietly, my eyes on the table. Of course this should be done by an announcement by herald, from a queen to her royal husband: but nothing is as it should be.

There is an embarrassed murmur of sympathy and congratulation from the lords but old Bell the Cat does not respond as a lord but as a father. He puts his hand over mine, though he should not touch a royal person, and he looks at me with rough sympathy. 'God bless you, poor little bairn,' he says shockingly. 'And God bless you that James has left us something to remember him by. And are you due in the spring?'

I gasp at his familiarity, and the three ladies seated behind my chair rise to their feet and come forward as if to shield me from rudeness. Someone's head goes up and someone says a short angry word, but then I see that there are tears in the earl's eyes and I realise that he is not thinking of me as a queen, or an untouchable English princess, but like one of his own, one of the many Scots widows who will have children in the cradle and babies in the womb and no husband coming home to help them ever again.

## STIRLING CASTLE, SCOTLAND, CHRISTMAS 1513

We have a quiet Christmas. I have no money to spend on feasting and dances, and no-one is in the mood for a celebration. The court is in mourning, still shocked by the loss of so many men. There is no handsome king to call for music or wine, and there is no money to pay for either.

The old advisor the Earl of Angus retires to his castle, perched on a cliff at Tantallon, and dies at Whithorn to the sound of calling gulls. The title goes to his grandson, a young man in my household who serves as my carver, and I have lost another experienced man. My council is divided between those who would like to make peace with England, our dangerous neighbour, and those who will never forgive the English for our losses and long to take French money to make war on them for our revenge.

But we have one visitor who makes the arduous journey north from London, travelling slowly through the mud and the ice, struggling through the snowdrifts, rising late in the dark mornings, having to find shelter in the dark afternoons. Friar Bonaventure Langley brings me the condolences of my sister-in-law, as if all my troubles were not made by her. Incredibly, Katherine, knowing that I am widowed, knowing that I am with child, knowing that I am alone in a dangerous kingdom with a little boy in my keeping, knowing that I am penniless and heart-broken, thinks that the most helpful thing she can do is to send me a confessor.

Gently, he takes my hands; kindly, he signs the cross over my bowed head. I kiss the crucifix he offers me as he helps me to rise, and then he says: 'Can you assure me, daughter, that he really is dead? There is a fearsome rumour in England and abroad that the King of Scots is alive. The queen must know – she has promised her husband that she will discover the truth.'

I feel a wave of nausea and bile rises into my mouth. I put my hand to my face and swallow it down like grief. 'She sent you all this way to ask me this? In the steps of the army who killed him?'

'She promised the King of England that it was done. She has a body. She has to know for sure that it is the right body.'

What a ghoul this woman is.

'He's dead,' I say bitterly. 'Oh, reassure her. Set her loving heart at rest. She has not boasted to her husband without reason. She didn't steal the wrong corpse. She killed my husband and half the nobility of Scotland. He's dead all right. She can set her tender heart at peace. Make sure you thank her for her kind inquiry.'

## STIRLING CASTLE, SCOTLAND, SPRING 1514

In the cold dark months of the new year, as my belly broadens, I grow more and more weary of the lords of my council, more and more tired of their suspicion of me, confined to my rooms by the darkness and storms of snow before I am confined by childbirth. I write to my sisters – for who else do I have in all the world? – weeping a little with self-pity, in case this is the last they ever hear of me:

*Dear Sisters, Katherine and Mary,*

*I am writing to you as I go into confinement, conscious that life is uncertain and children are born into sorrow. If I should not survive this, then I beg the two of you to take care of my boy and my new baby if it lives. There is no-one here that I can trust more than the two of you, who, I know, love me and mine, whatever has passed between our countries.*

*Mary, as my younger sister, I require you to ensure that my son is raised as a King of Scotland and that he is kept safe from his enemies. Katherine, as my sister twice over, I require you to ensure that my son inherits the kingdom his father left him and whatever else is his by right.*

*If I live, I shall hope to serve the two of you as a dear sister and trusted ally. And if I live, I hope to receive my lady grandmother's jewels and the rest of my inheritance.*

*God bless you both,*
*Your sister,*
*Margaret*

With no father to pray for my baby's safety, with no king to go on pilgrimage or promise a crusade, it is a long, painful birthing and no sign of any help from God; but at the end of it I have a boy, another boy for the Stewart house, and I name him Alexander. Last time, James insisted on coming to see me, breaking all the rules of the confinement chamber. Last time he took me to his bed the moment that I was churched, ignoring feast days and fast days and the commands of the Church, desperate to give me another child before he had to leave for war. But this time no husband comes to the screen in the confinement room, no impatient father demands to see his son. This time I lie alone at night, the baby in the nursery next door, listening to the quiet squeak of the rocking chair of the night nurse. This time I lean back on cool pillows and know there will be no tap at the door and no bobbing candle as the king comes to visit. This time I am alone, I am very alone. I really cannot bear to be so alone.

I write to my brother Harry who has returned in triumph from France to find that Katherine, his wife, can kill a king and steal his body but not bring a healthy child to full term. Apparently she lost a son while Harry was away at war. I am sorry for her, but I am not surprised. I don't see how any woman who could send the bloodstained coat of a kinsman as a symbol of triumph could be woman enough to bear a child. How can Katherine be in a state of grace? How can God forgive her for her savagery? Surely He must love the widow more than the murderer. No wonder that He gives me a strong boy and Katherine gets a dead child. What else does she deserve? I hope she never gets a baby. I hope she fails to give Harry a live boy since she revelled in giving him a dead king.

My sister, Mary, writes me a letter of congratulations. She spends but a moment of her misspelled criss-crossed letter on the birth of my child, she is so full of her own news. Charles Brandon – Henry's great friend and companion – has been made master of horse, Charles Brandon rode with Harry to France and never left his side through danger and battle, and was so engaging to the Archduchess Margaret at Flanders that everyone says he will marry her. They say that this is a disgrace for such a noble lady but Mary does not think so.

*Do you think so? Do you not think it would be a wonderful thing to marry for love? If you were Archduchess Margaret would you be able to resist him? For he is the most handsome man in England and the bravest and the best jouster.*

*I am very glad to know that you have had a son, your letter made my cry so much that Charles Brandon said that my tears were like sapphires in a river and that a brave knight would want to drink from such a stream.*

I reply briefly to her:

*Of course, the archduchess, like all noble ladies, must marry for the benefit of her family and the safety of her country to the choice of her father or guardian. And anyway, I believe that Charles Brandon is betrothed already?*

Then I take up a page and write to Katherine. I spend some time on the letter: it is a masterpiece of spite. I say that I am grieved, deeply grieved, that she has lost yet another child. I wish she too had the happiness of a newborn son, another son. I tell her that he is to be called Alexander and he will carry the traditional title of the second son of Scotland: Duke of Ross. I remark (in case it has slipped her murderer's mind), that this is all I have left of my husband.

*It was a long birth but he is a strong baby. His little brother, our king, is well also. I am so glad to have two sons, my two little heirs. I do hope that you, Queen of England and trusted advisor to the king, will work for peace between our two kingdoms for the sake of myself – the king's sister – and my two little boys – his nephews and heirs.*

I am not surprised that she does not have the gall to reply to this, but Harry sends a message to me by the Warden of the Marches, Thomas Lord Dacre, the man who bundled the body of the King of Scots onto a cart as the spoils of war, the man who is destroying the peace of the kingdom, gnawing on the border castles like a dog on a bone. My brother gives me a warning that the French are going to send John Stuart Duke of Albany, my husband's French-born cousin – apparently to help me, but actually to rule Scotland in my place. Henry demands that I refuse entry to the Duke of Albany, and ensure that he gains no power.

'How?' I ask John Drummond, the justice-general, a great Scots lord, who has brought this letter from Edinburgh and is seated beside me at dinner. 'How exactly does he think I am to do this?'

The young Earl of Angus carves a pheasant for us with nonchalant skill and places a beautiful slice of meat before me, his queen, and before his grandfather. John Drummond smiles at me. 'That's not a question he has to answer. He only has to give the command. That's the joy of being a king.'

'It's not the joy of being a queen,' I retort. 'I cannot collect my rents and my tenants refuse to pay. Half my stewards and servants are dead anyway. I cannot send a guard to collect my money as I cannot pay the guard; and without money and a great household I cannot command the country.'

'You will have to sell the king's ship,' Drummond says.

I sigh at the thought of the *Great Michael* going to the French. 'I have done so already.'

'And if the Crown has no money then you must secure the treasury,' he says quietly. 'For yourself. The little king's household has to be guarded.'

I flush. This is theft – royal theft – but it is theft all the same. 'I have done so,' I say. 'I keep the keys, nobody can draw any gold without my consent.'

His slow smile acknowledges that I have acted rightly, if not legally. 'What about the lords who agreed to rule with you? Do they have keys?'

'There's only one key, not six.'

Again I see the little gleam at my ruthlessness. 'Aye, well, that was well done. We can explain it when the council find out.'

'They won't like it. They don't like being ruled by a woman.'

He pauses for a moment. 'Perhaps you would be well advised to take another husband?'

'My Lord Drummond – I have not yet been a year widowed. I have just come out from confinement. My husband appointed me regent and told me that I should rule Scotland alone.'

'But he wasn't to know the difficulties you would face in council. I don't think anyone could have imagined it. God knows, it is a different country without him.'

'There's the emperor,' I remark, thinking of the great men of Europe who are seeking a wife. 'Not that I can marry for a year. And the King of France has just lost his wife.'

'So you have been thinking? Fool that I am! Of course you have.'

'I had no-one to talk to in confinement, and I have long dark nights alone. Of course I consider my future. I know that I will be expected to marry again.'

'You will, and your brother will want to advise you. He'll want you to marry for the advantage of England. He won't want the little King of Scotland to have a stepfather who is his enemy. He would forbid you to marry the King of France, for instance.'

'If my sister Mary married Charles of Castile, and I married Louis of France, then I would be the greater queen,' I remark. 'And if I were to be Queen of France then I would be the equal of Katherine.'

'Superseding your sisters is not important. What matters more is that Scotland has a powerful ally, not which of you has the bigger crown.'

'I know, I know,' I say a little irritably. 'But if you had seen Katherine of Aragon when she married my brother Prince Arthur, you would understand that I never want to come second to her—' I break off, remembering the bloodstained coat. 'Now more than ever.'

'Aye, I understand it well enough. But think again, Your Grace. If you married one of these distant kings you'd have to go and live in Burgundy or in France, and the council would keep your boys in Scotland. On the other hand, if you married a Scots nobleman, then you'd still be Queen of Scots, you'd still be regent, you'd still have your title and your fortune, you'd live with your sons, and yet you'd have someone to keep you warm at night and safe in your castles.' He pauses, looking at my thoughtful face. 'And you'd be his master,' he adds. 'You'd be his wife, but you'd still be his queen.'

I look down the dining hall at my court, the mixture of the wild and the cultured. The highlanders who cut their meat with their daggers and eat it off the points of their knives, the young men who have been raised in France and use the new forks and have napkins tossed over their shoulders to wipe their fingertips. Those who eat at the trestle tables from a common bowl, arguing in broad Erse, and the lords from the distant islands and mountains who come to court very seldom and sit with their households, proudly ignoring each other, speaking their own incomprehensible language.

'Yes, but there's no-one,' I say desolately to myself. 'There is no-one I can trust.'

John Drummond is right to think ahead. Almost as soon as I am out of confinement the marriage proposals arrive. God forgive me, I find it hard to hide my delight at the thought of the courts of Europe gossiping about my future and seeing me, once again, as a prize. Once again I am a trophy to be won, not a wife tucked away in the ownership of a king, of interest only when I am with child. I am a princess and I must choose a husband – who is it going to be? Katherine may wear the crown of England (though she has no baby in the cradle and I have two), Mary may have been drenched in jewels and betrothed to Charles of Castile, but I am free to choose either Maximilian, the Holy Roman Emperor, or Louis, the King of France. These are the wealthiest and most important men in Christendom. I feel my ambition rise. Graciously, I receive emissaries from both courts. It is clear that both great kings would be glad to marry me, both of them would endow me with a fortune, and make me queen of huge lands and wealthy beautiful courts. One of them would make me an empress.

This is not a personal matter, it is a decision about a dynasty. My brother will have to negotiate the terms and advise me; I will have to consider very carefully what is best for my country of Scotland, my home of England and my future. My Scots advisors will have a say in my decision too, since I am regent, and my choice will affect the country, taking us into alliances, making new enemies. If I choose well, Scotland could be enriched by my new husband, and guarded by him. If I choose badly I will give them a tyrant, my son an evil guardian, and myself a lifetime of unhappiness. There is no more important decision. Divorce is unthinkable, and anyway unattainable. Whoever I choose, I will have him till death.

Suddenly, I am high in Harry's favour. He remembers that he has a sister now that I am a player in the continual struggle for power in Europe. My throne is the gateway to England – whoever marries me is married to England's dangerous neighbour. My country is poor, but powerfully fortified and learned. My fortune is not great, but I am fertile, and I am young and in the flush of beauty. Harry is very warm and friendly, happy to advise, writing to me through Lord Dacre, recommending him as a good neighbour and reliable advisor, urgent that I must consider what is best for my sons and for myself. Harry thinks that an alliance with the emperor would be the best. Of course he does, he is married to the emperor's kinswoman and desperate to go to war with France again.

I shall decide for myself, I say, looking at Harry's letter, written in a perfect clerk's hand by one of his secretaries. Obviously, he has dictated it while busy with something else. But at the end he has scrawled his good wishes and signed his own name. Katherine has written an affectionate note in the margin.

*I should be so happy to call you cousin by marriage as well as sister, and I know that my uncle Maximilian would keep you safe and prosperous. I do hope that you don't think of France, my dear. I hear that Louis the king is very old and diseased and vicious in his habits, and we would never see you. It would be very dreadful if yet another husband of yours were to make war on England, when you think of the last outcome.*

I read and reread this odd mixture of affection, threat, and spite where she warns me against marrying the King of France, and even dares to threaten me with another husband's death.

Mary encloses a page of news of her studies in Spanish and her music and her new gowns. I see, with a little added bitterness, how much more attentive they are now that I have such prospects. If I become empress I will be more important than my brother, and I will never again write him a letter in my own hand. As empress I shall outrank Katherine, as empress I shall outrank Mary, whose boy husband – the emperor's grandson – will not inherit until the emperor dies.

This gives me pause; there will be a great pleasure in taking a throne seated beside a man who outranks my sisters' husbands – but when he dies I will be widowed again. He is fifty-five years old now – how much longer can he live? I don't want to be widowed again and worse, worst of all, I would be Dowager Empress and Mary, my little sister, would step up into my place and inherit my crown while I would have to step back and watch her do it. I know I couldn't bear that.

I do want a great husband, but I want a friend and a lover, a companion and a comrade. I hate sleeping alone, I hate dining in front of the whole court without a husband at my side. My only comfort at the great dinners when I am seated alone before the whole court is my carver, Archibald Douglas, the only man allowed to be at my table. The haunches of meat are put beside me on the high table and he carves my portion and slices for the rest of the lords, and he smiles at me and talks to me quietly so that I don't feel so lonely.

I really can't marry Louis of France, I think. He is nearly as old as Maximilian, almost decrepit, and he is quite vile. He divorced his first wife, declaring her to be too malformed to allow lovemaking, then he forced his second wife to marry him and still could make nothing but dead boys and two girls. Marriage to him would put me at the head of a great power, a Scots ally to be sure, but constantly at war with England. I don't want to be in a country facing an English army ever again. Also, I cannot believe that we would have a healthy child. He is certain to die and leave me a widow again so I lose the crown almost as soon as I win it. Besides, the man is a monster.

It is a choice between two evils. The only handsome young king in Europe is my brother and Katherine showed me that you have to snatch a husband young. I will take a risk whatever I choose. I order my court to Perth for the summer and promise myself that when I am among the green hills and far away from Katherine's malevolent letters, I will decide what I should do.

## METHVEN CASTLE, PERTH, SCOTLAND, JUNE 1514

'Oh, marry neither,' Archibald Douglas says, laughing. He has come on a picnic to carve the cold venison, but is serving also as the groom of the ewery, handing me the linen and the wine. I am revelling in the fact that we are a family at play, practically alone – this attentive young man, and my children and their nurses. James is running around on the grass, his arms windmilling, his nurse chasing him till he drops down laughing so much that he cannot stand. His Lord Chamberlain Davy Lyndsay is calling 'Run, laddie! Run!' as the baby, Alexander, sleeps in his crib in the shade of the trees, his rocker beside him, his wet nurse dozing on a pillow in the shade.

'No, I have to marry,' I say. 'It's lovely now, with the children here and the court at play in summertime, and it feels as if there is nothing to worry about and it will be summer forever. But you know what it will be like when the autumn comes and the winter follows: the lords will plot together and against each other, and the French will try to make war on England through us, and my brother will make demands that I cannot meet, and the cursed Lord Dacre will raid the border and the people will starve and riot.' My voice is trembling at the end of this list. 'I can't face it. I can't face another winter alone.'

Archibald's quick sympathy shines in his face. 'I would lay down my life for you. We all would,' he says. 'All the border lords are my friends. Just say the word and we will put down the reivers, summon the council, insist that they work together. You know I am from a great family, one of the greatest. I have influence. My grandfather John Drummond is clan chieftain of the Drummonds, my late grandfather was Bell the Cat, my father died at Flodden so now I am head of the Douglas house. These are the mightiest families in Scotland. Say the word and we will protect you.'

'I know you would,' I say. 'And when it is summer and all the lords are at court and happy to be here, or safely on their own lands, and the hunting is good and there is dancing every night, I think that I am safe and will be safe forever. But I have to prepare. I have to find someone to face this beside me.'

He hands me some fruit and a glass of wine. He has such a fluid grace that when he does some small act of service he makes it look as if it is a move in a dance. He never drops or spills anything or swears at his own clumsiness, and he's always so beautifully dressed. Among the Scots lords who please themselves, ride hard, fight hard and don't always trouble to bathe, he is always beautifully barbered and shaved, his hands are always clean and he smells of clean linen and a musky scent that is all his own. Lord knows he is handsome – half the ladies of my court are in love with him – but he wears his fresh good looks as if they were a jacket he has had forever; he does not know how well he looks. He is betrothed to a girl who lives near his home, one of these Scots family betrothals from the cradle, I suppose. But he does not act like a man betrothed. John Drummond parades his handsome grandson like a prize cock, with his long legs, his slim, lithe strength, the broadness of his shoulders and that surprisingly dainty Celtic face, hair the colour of autumn leaves, dark eyes and a fascinating smile.

'Janet Stewart of Traquair is a lucky girl,' I say, referring to the young woman he will marry.

He bows his head and flushes. But his eyes come up and meet mine. 'It is I who am lucky,' he says. 'For I am promised to one of the prettiest girls in Scotland, but I serve the most beautiful queen.'

'Oh, there can be no comparison between us,' I say instantly. 'I am a mother of two and an old widow of twenty-four.'

'Not old,' he says. 'I'm the same age as you. And widowed like you. And I am Earl of Angus, the head of a great family, the leader of a great house. I know what it feels like to have everyone look to you.'

'Janet Stewart is a young girl, is she not, a maid?'

'She's nearly thirteen.'

'Oh! A child,' I say disdainfully. 'I didn't know. Everyone spoke of her prettiness; I thought she was a young woman. I am surprised that you didn't want a woman of your own age.'

'She is my little sweetheart. We have been promised since she was in her cradle. I have watched her grow and never seen a fault in her. I will marry her when she comes of age. But you are my queen, now and forever.'

I lean towards him just a little. 'So will you not leave me, Archibald, when you marry your child bride?'

'Call me Ard,' he whispers. 'My lovers call me Ard.'

He loves me. I know that he does. I know that his pulse is racing like mine and that he feels the same dizzy elation that I do. I want a man to love me, I need a man to love me, and the young Earl of Angus – Ard, as I secretly name him to myself – clearly does so. And he will never leave me, he will always be in my service, at my side at dinner, riding with me when the court goes out, playing so sweetly with my little boy, admiring my baby. Of course, I will have to marry a great man, the King of France or the emperor, for the sake of my country and my own fortune, but I will always keep Ard at my side. He will be my knight errant, my chevalier. I will be like the lady in the fables, in troubadour songs: adored and forever unattainable. And I really think he shall not marry Janet Stewart of Traquair. I really think that I will allow myself to forbid the wedding, even if the little girl cries into her pillow for a month. I can do this. I am queen; I can do it without explanation.

I receive a letter from my sister, Mary, eighteen years old this year and still at home, unmarried. She writes news of the court on their summer progress. They are all well, the Sweat has not come to court, and they are travelling informally in the South of England, sometimes going by barge on the river with musicians accompanying them so that people crowd to the banks to cheer and to wave and to throw rushes and flowers as they go by. Sometimes they go on horseback, with the royal standards ahead, and at every town a delegation comes out to praise Henry for his military might, his victories against France and Scotland, and to give him purses of gold.

*I have a wardrobe filled with new gowns paid for by the Spanish, they say that nothing is too good for the bride of Castile. They have demanded yet another portrait and the artist swears that I am the most beautiful princess in Christendom!*

She says that she is to marry little Charles next year and already they are planning an enormous series of feasts and jousts to celebrate her departure to Spain. Charles Brandon is certain to joust and certain to triumph. Henry has made him a duke, an honour quite beyond anyone's imagining. Some people think he has been elevated so far above his station so that he can propose marriage to the Archduchess Margaret, but Mary knows better. She tells me so, her handwriting sprawling, misspelled in her excitement, with added scribbled remarks in the margin.

*He is not in love with Archduchess Margaret though she adores him; he tells me he is not in love with her at all, he has no eyes for her. He says he has lost his heart to quite another.*

Mary believes that he has been given ducal honours – the greatest honour in the kingdom, short only of royal status – because Harry loves him so much.

*Now he is acknowledged as one of the truly great men of England, honoured as he should be. He is Harry's best friend, he loves him like a brother.*

This gives me pause. Harry had a brother, a finer young man than Charles Brandon can ever be. Can he have forgotten Arthur? Can Mary have forgotten who Harry's real brother was? Can she use the word 'brother' to me and not know who it means? Have they forgotten Arthur, and me as well?

*Without doubt he is the most handsome man at court, everyone admires him. I will tell you a secret, Margaret, but you must not breathe a word of it. He has asked to carry my favour at my wedding joust! It will be the finest joust in Christendom and he is certain to win. He says he will wear it next to his heart and he would happily die with it there!*

At the end of her letter she remembers that I am a widow with two babies, fighting to rule a difficult country, and that all her talk of gowns and love affairs may grate on me, so she adopts a more personal note. She has studied to be charming, she knows well enough how to be endearing:

*I am so sorry that you cannot be with us. I should have so loved you to be here. I want to show you my jewels and my gowns. I wish you could come. It won't be the same without you, Katherine says so too.*

Brandon is not the only scoundrel dragged into the nobility in this prodigal scattering of titles. Thomas Howard, the victor of Flodden, finally regains the title he lost at Bosworth – he is to be Duke of Norfolk and his son will be named Earl of Surrey as a reward for the billhook that smashed my husband's crowned head, for the arrow that pierced his anointed side. Perhaps he gets his title for the bloodstained jacket that he sent to France? Perhaps for the corpse in lead, which remains, unburied, somewhere in London?

Apparently, my brother thinks that he should reward a murderer before burying his victim, and Thomas Howard wears ducal strawberry leaves while my husband is stored – half-forgotten – uncoffined, waiting for the moment when the Pope says that his poor body, excommunicated at Harry's request, shall be forgiven and his soul may start its journey to heaven.

Mary does not describe Norfolk's honours, but I know that his ducal crest is a lion: the lion of Scotland, James' lion, with an arrow through its jaw to represent the billhook cutting off my husband's face, the arrow in his side. Noble indeed, a beautiful crest to choose. I hope my brother does not rue the day that he honours a king-killer.

I hold Mary's silly vain letter on my lap and I note her facile regrets that I cannot come to her wedding. But I think: perhaps I could attend? I could take a small court, a small guard in new livery. I could make it a state visit: the queen travelling in grandeur, and then I could visit towns, and people could come out and recite poems to me. I think Ard could ride at my side and make me laugh and see how people in England love me, their first and best Tudor princess. I would like him to see me in England, to see the welcome that they would give me, that I am a great woman in England, a princess in my own right. And on the journey he would lift me down from the saddle and hold me close every day. Nobody would notice that moment. He would stand beside me while I dined every night, and we would dance together. I would have new gowns and my portrait painted, and perhaps I would have him painted beside me, as a favoured member of my household. Mary is so spoiled and stupid that she does not invite me, merely assuming that I cannot come; but perhaps I will come – and surprise them all.

It is a daydream – as false and beguiling as Ard's whispered promises of love. I don't have the money to make a great trip to London, I don't have the gowns to outshine my little sister, I don't have better jewels than the Queen of England, I don't even have the royal jewels that my father left me – and they have not invited me to attend.

Mary says that Katherine is travelling on the summer progress in a litter and at once I turn the page and read it again. Yes, she clearly says it. I know there can be only one reason that Katherine would be in a litter and not on horseback trying to keep up with Harry: she must be with child and praying with all her heart that this time she can keep the baby.

I put the letter in my empty jewel box, and look out of the small arched window at the rolling hills that go on and on to the horizon beyond. It is so unlike the rich low-lying meadows of the Thames valley. Here there is no succession of beautiful houses and rich abbeys surrounded with bobbing apple trees heavy with new fruit. There are no walled parks, or smooth greens for bowling. There is just the wide arching sky over the climbing hills and the steep ridges and cliffs, the darkness of the ancient mountain forests with the eagles soaring above them.

I have been happy this summer with my boys, revelling in the respectful adoration of Ard, and with the country at peace. But my joy falls away from me at this one piece of news. I imagine Katherine riding in a silk-curtained litter, Queen of England, expecting another baby, and I think: she will be ahead of me forever. Forever she will be at peace when I am troubled. She has a husband who protects her, who is victorious when he goes to war. She has a litter to ride in and a country where she is safe. Now she is with child and if she has a boy then she has an heir to the throne of England and my own prince will only ever inherit Scotland and that is a hard kingdom to hold.

I think: I am always going to be in second place to her. I can't bear for her to be Queen of England with a Prince of Wales in the cradle, while I endure my life, half-forgotten in a distant poor kingdom. And in that minute, I think defiantly: well then! I shall defy her mealy-mouthed good wishes, her sisterly hints. I shall marry Louis of France and I will have an ally for my country who is strong enough and rich enough to defeat England if it comes to war again. I will be Queen of France and Scotland with two strong boys in Scotland and perhaps more to come, and that is better than being Queen of England, clinging to the sides of a litter and hoping not to miscarry your future.

I write privately to the Scots ambassador in France. I tell him that I have made my choice and he can communicate it to the old king that I called a monster. He can tell him that I am prepared to marry. Louis of France shall make a formal public proposal and I will give him my hand. I will marry him, whatever old beast that he is, and I will be Queen of France, England's enemy, and Katherine's superior.

## METHVEN CASTLE, PERTH, SCOTLAND, JULY 1514

A terrible thing has happened to me, and I cannot comprehend it. I cannot understand the falseness of my sister, my own sister! I cannot believe the duplicity of my own brother. I feel as if I never knew either of them, as if they have betrayed me in some wicked concordance of their own. It is disreputable, it is to brand themselves publicly as liars. They are beneath contempt. They seek to destroy me and my prospects. First they widowed and now they ruin me.

Mary has repudiated her marriage contract with Charles of Castile. Repudiated it! As if it never was! As if she can give her word and accept the jewels and go through with the vows and stand under the canopy of cloth of gold – for I have not forgotten the canopy of cloth of gold, I have not forgotten the woodcut that was printed and went all around the kingdom, everywhere. She did all of that, and now she says that she did not. She did not promise, it will not happen. Mary is not going to marry Charles of Castile.

How is anyone to trust the word of a princess if Mary can be betrothed for years – not for a little while, but for years, with gifts coming every month – and then withdraw her promise, retract her betrothal and repudiate such a monarch? What of the wardrobe of gowns? The biggest ruby in the world? The grandson of the emperor is suddenly not good enough for her? How high is my sister going to aim? Is this not sinful vanity? Is this not the very sin that my lady grandmother warned her about when she was a little girl in the nursery? Surely someone should tell Mary that she cannot give her word and then break it: the word of a princess should be solid gold.

I am horrified. I am furious. My ladies gather around me and ask if I am ill, for I have blanched white and then blushed feverishly red. I brush them aside. I cannot tell them what is the matter. Nobody must ever know the terrible blow that has fallen on me: for it is the worst thing. The worst thing in the world. Unbelievably, she is going to marry Louis of France.

The very moment that I had decided to accept his proposal, for such politic reasons, for such queenly reasons, Mary has pushed in first and is going to marry him instead of me. In my place! And how could he make a proposal to her when he was in the middle of an offer for me? Is it not dishonourable of him? Everyone says he is a byword for dishonour and oath-breaking, but nobody warned me that he might throw me over for my little sister. And what of Harry, who knew that Louis had proposed to me, and that I was considering his offer? Should Harry not say: 'How dare you make a proposal to a great queen, and at the same time court her younger sister?' This is double-dealing by Louis – but by Harry and Mary too!

Why should Mary even consider him? Is he not old enough to be her grandfather? Her great-grandfather? Is he not riddled with the pox and a danger to any wife? Did he not drive one wife into a nunnery and the other into an early grave? Why would Mary accept? Why would Harry desire it? Why would Katherine consent? For sure, this will be Harry's doing: Harry and Katherine's. God knows it will be they who pull the strings, as if Mary were a little marionette in a morality play. How Harry could do this to his sister is beyond me. Louis is his enemy! The enemy that he marched against only last year. The lifelong enemy of his Spanish wife and all her family!

There is dealing here that is so double and re-doubled that I cannot begin to understand it. But one thing is clear – Katherine's father has changed his mind about France and so his daughter obeys him and marries off her little sister to a monster, humiliating me in the process, leaving me husbandless and helpless in Scotland – a consequence that no-one has considered.

If that were all it would be bad enough, but there is more, and it is worse. Our ambassador in France reports that Harry is negotiating with the French and demanding they accept his ownership of the French towns he has conquered, and pay him a massive fee. If Louis marries Mary, he must pay one and a half million crowns. It is a fortune, it is a ransom for a princess beyond imagining. It shows the world how highly Harry prizes his beautiful little sister, and what Louis will pay for her. But if Louis chooses to marry me, he gets me at a discount. If he marries me he only has to pay England one hundred thousand crowns.

I see it. I see what he thinks of me, what they all think of me. I see how I am valued. Harry has told everyone how I am valued. I am publicly shamed. I see that Mary's hand is worth one and a half million crowns and the handing over of French towns; but I am priced for a quick sale. Harry has told the world that he thinks she is worth fifteen of me. Louis has confirmed that he will pay almost anything to marry her. I have never been so cruelly insulted in all my life.

I march up and down my presence chamber at Methven, passing the open window without a glance at the warm summer landscape, my gown swishing around like the twitching tail of an angry cat at every turn. One of my ladies runs to my side but I brush her away. Nobody must know of my boiling rage of hurt and wounded vanity. I have to be sly and secret when I am screaming with rage and hurt inside.

I can't bear it. To think that I had told Louis that I would be his wife, to think that I had decided to sacrifice myself to be Queen of France, and now it will be Mary! I stop in horror at another thought: how humiliated I should be if I had told my council of lords that I was accepting Louis, if the world knew that I had agreed – and then everyone saw him choose Mary! I can't bear that anyone should know it was my intention; I can't bear that anyone should even guess it. I should marry my farrier at once so that everyone can see I had no thoughts of Louis. I should marry the emperor. I have to make sure that no-one will ever say that the disgusting, dangerous King of France could have married me, but decided against it. That horrid old man proposed to me and proposed to Mary and then decided that he preferred Mary! My little sister! A foolish child with nothing in her favour but a pretty face! Worth more than ten of me at my brother's own estimate. What does that say about Harry and how he prizes me?

John Drummond and his grandson, my carver Archibald, come in without announcement, as I am pounding up and down the length of my presence chamber, my ladies pressed back against the walls, keeping out of my way. Clearly, one of my ladies, terrified of my temper, slipped away to fetch John Drummond. He takes one look at me and nods to my ladies, who whisk out of the room as if only these two men are strong enough to hear my whispered curses, my hissing rage.

'What's to do, Your Grace?' John Drummond says gently. 'I take it that there is bad news from England?'

'They dare …' I break off. 'They shame themselves …' I choke. 'And I …'

I whirl around and I see the tiniest of hand gestures from the older man to the younger, as a shepherd will make to a working dog, a mere movement of a fingertip to tell the dog to curve around the flock and move it smoothly towards the pen. Ard steps forward, his handsome face filled with sympathy.

'What have they done to you?' he asks intensely. 'Who has distressed you like this?'

'My brother!' For a moment rage fights with self-pity and then I pitch towards him and find myself held in his arms, his strong arms around me, and I am crying into the beautiful velvet of his jacket as he sways with me, holding me as if I were a hurt child, stroking my hair, and whispering soothing words.

'Ard, Ard, they have shamed me and thrown me down, and they always, always do. They have made me look a fool and feel a fool and set themselves up above me, and they always do this. And I hoped that I would be safe and that I would be a queen for Scotland and that I would have help . . .'

'My dear, my love, my queen,' he says, and it is like a song as sweet as any from the Isles. He rocks me in his arms, swaying from side to side like a balladeer. 'My love, my sweet, my beloved.'

'Am I?' I say. 'Oh, that they should do this, in concert, against me!'

Behind me, I hear the door gently close as John Drummond takes himself silently out of the room. I hardly hear the key turn as he locks us in, safe from interruption. Ard rocks me in his arms, kisses my wet eyelashes, my closed eyelids, my trembling mouth, kisses my neck, my breasts, and then gently leans me back on the window seat. His warm mouth is on mine and I taste the sweetness of his tongue, and shiver at his touch, and then, almost amazed at myself, feel myself lean back and pull up my beautiful gown, and whisper 'Archibald,' as he takes me, and owns me, and I hear my own sobs of temper turn into repeated gasps and then a cry of joy, and I don't care any more about my selfish brother, or my vain sister, or Louis of France, or anyone at all.

## KINNOULL PARISH CHURCH, PERTH, SCOTLAND, AUGUST 1514

We have to marry, at once. Of course we do. We have to marry at once, because urgent desire has taken hold of me and for the first time in my life I could sing and dance and laugh for the power of it. This is my summer: I have never before had a summer when I felt myself to be a woman, when I felt the blood in my veins and the warmth of my skin. I am in love with myself, my smooth young body, the fullness of my breasts, the warm wetness of my secret parts. This is my moment: I have never been beloved by a man who wants me for myself, and not as the emblem of a treaty between two countries. This is the man I have chosen: this fascinating, engaging, charming, delightful man who gives me such pleasure that I cannot bear to be parted from him, night or day.

As soon as I wake in the morning, tingling with lust, I want to see him at once. The court has learned that now we go to chapel very early and that he must be standing beside the royal chair so that I can see him, even if we cannot speak. As the priest celebrates the Mass before us I close my eyes as if in prayer but actually I am already dreaming of how he will kiss me and how he will touch me the moment that we are alone. I feel as if I am running a fever, I am so hot with desire. At breakfast, he must stand beside me to carve the ham and cold beef and now I eat slice after slice for the pleasure of having him lean towards me and slide the meat onto my plate. Sometimes his arm just brushes my shoulder and I look up at him and see his eyes on my mouth as if he too is longing for a kiss. When we ride out his horse must pace beside mine, and I want to talk only to him. Anyone else who approaches us is an interruption, and I can't wait for them to leave. We ride our horses shoulder to shoulder, so close that our knees gently brush one against the other, and he can reach over and pat my gloved hand on the reins. I dance only with him; I cannot bear to see him partner anyone else. When the pattern of the dance turns him towards another woman and he takes her hand I feel an instant dislike for her and wonder that she can bear to attend my court and push herself forward. I have no interest in the affairs of state, I don't even look for letters from Lord Dacre, lecturing me about what would be best for England. I have no interest in Katherine and her pregnancy, Mary and her betrothal. Especially, I don't want to hear about Mary and her double-dealing betrothal to

Louis of France. They are far away and they don't care about me – why should I trouble myself about them? I forget my council, my country, I am even neglectful of my little boys in this burning constant urgent need to be with him – just to be with him.

This is love, and I am fascinated by it. I never knew that it felt like this, I never expected to feel this at all. I reread my romances to see if this is what the troubadours are talking about, and I command the musicians to sing songs of love and longing. I wonder if this is what Harry felt for Katherine – can he possibly have felt like this? Was it this uncritical desire that made him overlook everything about her that grates on me? I wonder if my silly little sister Mary is in this urgent fever for Charles Brandon? Can Mary, young as she is, fool as she is, long for Charles Brandon as I long for Ard? If she does, then I really pity her – not because I have the better man (though I do), but because she is faced with renunciation and loneliness whereas I, in blessed freedom, can marry the man that I love. I could not let him go. If she feels as I do, she will not be able to let Charles Brandon go, and to marry the King of France will break her heart. Thank God, I do not have to walk that terrible path.

Instead, Archibald's cousin the Dean of Dunblane meets us at dawn and opens the door to his chapel. I walk down the little aisle in my green gown, with my hair spread loose over my shoulders as if I were a virgin bride. Why should I not? This is just as Katherine did at her second wedding. A choirboy sings a psalm, his voice achingly sweet as the sun comes through the arched windows and falls on our feet as if to say that the path before us will be warm and golden. I laugh when I find that Ard has no ring, and I take one of my own off my right hand and he gives it back to me, putting it on my wedding finger. I don't even think of Charles of Castile and the ruby. The dean celebrates Mass, and we share the bread, the wine, the holiness of the moment, and then we quietly leave the chapel, and I feel filled with thankfulness that he is free and I am free, that we are young and beautiful, that we are healthy and God has blessed us with desire for each other, and that is now a holy desire. I think we will be happy, deeply happy forever, and I will never envy anyone again, for I have married a young man who could have courted any woman in the world and won her favour, but he fell in love with me. He chose me for myself, he loves me for myself, not for my name or my title or my inheritance. I think he is the first person in the world to love me for myself since I lost my brother Arthur.

'God bless you,' says Archibald's uncle Gavin Douglas, the Dean of St Giles, Edinburgh, and one of the greatest makars of my first husband's court. 'I would write a poem but I don't think I could capture the joy in your face. I only wish you could have been married in a great ceremony and blessed by a bishop.'

I give him my hand and he bows over it and kisses it reverently.

'You bless me, Uncle,' I say impulsively, bowing my head, and he makes the sign of the cross over me. 'There!' I say triumphantly. 'And so I *have* been blessed by a bishop, because I will make you Archbishop of St Andrews.'

He bows again, hiding his delight. 'I am honoured, Your Grace. I will serve you, your new husband, and God.'

Archibald and I ride back to the castle and go at once to my rooms, bold as a pair of young lovers who now have nothing to hide. I am still in my first year of mourning, Ard has broken his betrothal to Janet Stewart. But it means nothing. Nothing can stand in our way. We are married, I have his ring on my finger and I may well have his child in my belly. We walk hand in hand past my astonished ladies and we close my bedroom door in their aghast faces. It is done. I have married the man I love, and Katherine of Aragon, who had to wait for years before Harry would condescend to marry her, and my sister Mary, who will be tied to a rotting lecher, can envy me from this day forward. Everything is changed. They will envy me.

## HOLYROODHOUSE PALACE, EDINBURGH, SCOTLAND, AUGUST 1514

My council of lords dares to tell me that I have forfeited the regency. They dare to tell Archibald that they will summon him on a charge of marrying me without their consent. They even dare to say that Gavin Douglas shall not be a bishop and that I cannot make him Archbishop of St Andrews, since another bishop is already nominated. As if the Church places are not in my keeping! As if I have not asked Harry to support the Douglas claim! I am regent and can marry and honour whomever I wish! The council summon me – the regent! regent! – to meet with them; and Archibald and I storm south to Edinburgh filled with rage and determination that no-one shall ever question me or my rights.

We wait for the council in the throne room. Deliberately, I stand before the throne with my handsome husband on my right and his grandfather John Drummond on my left. They can see the power that I have to support me now: Clan Douglas on one side, Clan Drummond on the other. But they are mutinous. They send the herald Sir William Comyn, Lyon King of Arms, to announce that they are rejecting me as regent and taking my sons away from my keeping. At the first moment that he is announced with the weighty respect commanded by all heralds, and he comes in, his standard above him, I feel a sudden pang of dread. I am in far more trouble than I dreamed possible. I knew that the council would not like my marriage, but I did not think that they would turn on me. I did not think that they would take my title, my sons, everything. I thought this was my triumph; now, suddenly, it is my ruin.

The herald addresses me: 'My lady Dowager Queen, mother to His Grace our king . . .'

There! It is said. He should be addressing me as queen regent but he denies me. Archibald's grandfather, blazing with rage, steps forward and punches him full in the mouth before he can say another treasonous word.

It is the most terrible act. A herald's body has to be sacred. He is the untouchable go-between from one warring party to another. Chivalry itself defends him. Sir William stumbles and nearly goes down but one of the lords catches and steadies him as Archibald cries out: 'No, sir! No! Not a herald!'

The herald is terribly shaken. They help him to his feet and he confronts Lord Drummond. 'This is dishonourable,' he chokes. 'Shame on you!'

Archibald leaps in to support his grandfather, as if he is going to push the Lord Lyon down again. 'You don't cry shame on us!'

I scream, 'Archibald, no!' and grab him by the arm. Lord Drummond yells 'Angus!' like a battle cry, and flings open the door to my inner chamber and the three of us scramble from the room, leaving the lords and the herald and the Lord Chancellor completely aghast. We pitch into my private room and I fall into Ard's arms and the two of us cling to each other, crying and laughing at the same time at the terrible thing that has just happened, at the truly terrible thing that his grandfather has just done.

'His face!' Archibald still whoops with laughter, but I am steadying and it does not seem so funny any more. I turn and see the black anger in John Drummond, as he flexes his hand where he hit the Lord Lyon. Ard is still laughing.

'My lord,' I say cautiously.

Drummond looks at me. 'They will arrest me for that,' he says. 'My temper got the better of me.'

'When you hit him!' Archibald crows.

'Hush,' his grandfather says irritably. 'That was wrong of me. It's no laughing matter.'

Ard tries to look serious but an irrepressible giggle bursts out of him. I am not laughing now. I am afraid. The lords will raise this as a serious complaint against us, and I will have to write to Harry with some kind of account of this that smooths the roughness over, and makes us look less like rash fools, brawling in our very first council, as my lords turn against me and defy my authority.

My young husband and I attend the council meeting like two children called before angry guardians, and then there is a meeting of the parliament. Everyone is furious, the lords are angry and divided, the parliament of lesser men is outraged at my behaviour. They were already furious with Ard for aspiring to marry me, and disgusted with me for marrying him, but now they are filled with complaints about the history of the Douglas clan.

Old legends that I never heard before are invoked against my young husband as if centuries-old crimes are all his fault. I am as calm and as thoughtful as I can be, meeting many of them individually, trying to explain to them that Archibald will be a force for unity in this troubled country, that he will help me be a good queen for all the clans. We will not favour Clan Douglas; the throne has not been captured by Clan Drummond. But they swear that the Douglas family has made attempts on the throne before, that my own husband the late king made it his life's work to keep them humble. They say things about the family and about John Drummond that I cannot believe. They say he sold his own daughter to my royal husband. They tell me that Archibald's other grandfather, Bell the Cat, fought James for the favours of Janet Kennedy and James threw him into prison indefinitely, only releasing him because he needed his sons to lead their men at Flodden.

'Don't say that,' I interrupt. I can't bear to think of Archibald's bright young honour sullied with any of these old lusts. Ard and

I are a groom and bride new-come to each other, fresh to happiness. We have no connection with my husband's lovers, nothing to do with the messy feuds and quarrels of the Scots lords. We are young and clean; this is old, dirty history. 'The Earl of Angus is devoted to me. Nothing that his grandfather or his father did matters now.'

They disagree. They say he is the head of the Red Douglases, a family even worse than the Black Douglases, and that they have been a danger to the throne from the time of James II.

'This is ancient, ancient history,' I say. 'Who cares about all this now?'

But they are determined never to forget old injuries. Nobody is newborn in Scotland; everyone is an heir to injustice, plotting revenge. When I say that Ard will sit beside me and share the regency, they swear this will never happen. Despite all that I say, though I remind them of their oaths of loyalty to me, to my son, they will not hear another thing but declare they will send for the Duke of Albany to take my place and be governor.

This is the French-raised duke, an heir to the Scottish throne, the very man that my brother Harry said I should keep out of Scotland. 'He may not come,' I tell them.

'We forbid it,' Ard says.

Lord Hume declares that I have lost the regency by losing my widowhood. The Earl of Arran says that as a Hamilton he should have a higher place in government than a Douglas. Ard says simply in my ear, 'We're not safe here, we must go back to Stirling,' and I cannot control my delight at the thought of running away from all this anger and unhappiness. So that very night we take our horses and a small guard and we get away from my capital city as if we were a pair of vagabonds and not the ruling regent and her consort – or co-regent as I swear Ard shall be when we return.

## STIRLING CASTLE, SCOTLAND, AUTUMN 1514

My sister Mary writes her last letter from England, her last letter as an English princess. She says that when she next writes it will be as a French queen. I grit my teeth at this and remind myself that at least I have chosen my husband and I could not be happier. Really, I could not be happier. I have married for love and I care nothing for the disapproval of the council.

As I read her letter, my natural envy – eighteen wagons sealed with the royal French fleur-de-lys, a more elegant symbol than my Scots thistle – fades away and I start to feel sorry for my little sister. In some parts the letters are smudged into illegibility and I think that she was crying as she wrote and her tears blotted her words. She tells me that she is in love, deeply and truly in love, with a gentleman, a nobleman, the most handsome in the court, probably in the world. She has struck a bargain with Harry, one that she swears he must honour. They have agreed that when the King of France dies she shall be free to marry the man of her choice. Coyly, she does not say who it is, but judging from her childish infatuation for Charles Brandon I guess it must be the newly-made duke.

*Will you support me? Oh, Margaret, will you be a good sister to me? Will you remind Harry of his solemn promise? The day must come that I am a widow, for the old king cannot live long, I am sure that he cannot. Will you help me to follow your example and marry once for the benefit of my family, and the second time for love?*

Her hand wobbly with emotion, she writes that she cannot bear to go to France and marry the old French king without being certain that she has to endure only a short while, that she will one day be happy.

*I could not do this without hope of the future. I hear that your husband the Earl of Angus is young and handsome – I am so glad of this for you, dear Margaret. Will you be a true sister to me, and help me to be as happy as you are, with the man that I love?*

I think: how ridiculous she is – there is no comparison. Ard is the great love of my life, from the noblest family in Scotland. He was raised to lead one of the greatest houses, his kinsmen are members of the lords' council, his grandfather was Lord Justice, his father died nobly at Flodden, he has royal blood. Charles Brandon is an adventurer who was married for money and then betrothed for profit. He kidnapped a wife and she died in childbirth. He married an old lady for her fortune and abandoned her. He has wended his way upwards by charm, sporting skill, and by being one of Harry's uncritical cronies. My Archibald is a nobleman, Brandon a stable boy.

But I reply to her kindly, my silly little sister, smiling as I write. I say that I am sending her a book of hours as a wedding gift and that she should pray and think on God's will; He will take her husband in His own good time. If that day comes I will gladly remind our brother that she wishes to choose her next husband, and I think, but I do not say, that she is a fool to hope to ruin herself, demean herself for love. I say that she must do her best as a Queen of France and as the wife of Louis – I think of him as the old lecher but I do not say that either. I write that I hope she is able to give him a child, though my lip curls even as I write it. How shall such a diseased old man get a son? I say that I hope that she will find happiness in her new country with her husband and I mean it – this is my dear little sister, as pretty as a doll and as brainless. From my pinnacle of experience and happiness I promise to pray for her. I am afraid of what he will do to her, I am afraid for her. I will pray, as she will, that the old monster dies quickly and sets her free.

Finding a messenger to take my letter and smuggling him out of the sally port at night is like getting a spy out of a castle under siege. The lords of the council have come in force and are barracked in the houses of the town at the foot of the hill. We keep the portcullis down and the gate closed and nobody comes in or goes out without Ard's express permission. It is his clan who man the lookouts and guard me. I love their fierce undying loyalty to him; they served his grandfather, they served his father, now he has only to call for them and they are his. This is strange and moving for me, for I belong to a family new-come to the throne. We have no-one sworn to our service through centuries.

'This is what it is to be a Scots lord,' Archibald tells me. 'I am born and bred here and so are my men. I cannot help myself but I must lead them. They cannot help themselves but they must follow me. We are kin, we are sworn to one another, we are of the clan.'

'It's wonderful,' I say. 'It is the greatest of loves.'

Of course people say that this proves I am not a queen for Scotland, I am not queen for every lord, raising my son to be a king for every man. They say it shows I am in the Douglas camp but what else can I do? The parliament have fulfilled their threats, denied my regency and sent for the Duke of Albany to come from France. All very well for the French king to write to me with such careful courtesy and promise that he will not send Albany to Scotland unless I ask for him, the Scots lords are demanding him to replace me.

The Lord Chancellor, James Beaton, comes to see me, bearing the seal that stamps every law. I say that he should leave it with me; he says that he is to hold it. Laws must be made when the king commands parliament, not when a woman, a mere mother of a king, takes some whim into her head. I am beyond fury that he should speak to me like this. I exchange a glance with Archibald and I see him go white around the mouth.

'You dare insult me,' I say. 'I am regent. Don't forget who makes the laws in this land.'

'Don't forget who holds the seal,' he says. 'I am Lord Chancellor.'

Like a boastful fool he holds it up in my face. It is a big silver thing, the size of a dinner plate, carved and grooved to be filled with the hot wax. He holds it before me as if it were a looking glass and I see my furious face distorted in the carving.

'That's easily mended,' Archibald says and, like a child, snatches it from the Lord Chancellor's hand and darts to the other side of the room.

I breathe 'Archibald!' in absolute horror, and his grandfather shouts: 'Angus! No!' But before anyone can say anything he has dashed from the room, the great seal of Scotland in his hands, as if he were rushing a trencher to a table. The Lord Chancellor looks at me, his mouth agape, as if he is gasping for air like a landed carp.

I can say nothing. It is so funny and so naughty, so powerful and yet so childish. I exchange one horrified glance with Archibald's grandfather and then I take up my skirts and I swirl from the room before anyone can say anything to me. I burst into my privy chamber and find Ard dancing around, waving the seal over his head, a beam of triumph on his face. I cannot scold him.

'We'll have to give it back,' I say.

'Never!' he shouts like a pirate in a play.

'We will, and we will be in terrible trouble.'

'What can they do? What dare they to do to us?'

'They have stopped all my rents, I have no money; they can demand that Albany comes; they can insist that my son goes into their keeping . . .' I volunteer the list. 'That's just the start of it.'

'They can do nothing,' he declares. 'You are Queen of Scotland, I am your husband. You are the mother of the king. They can come on their knees to you. They are nothing but rebels and traitors, and now we have the great seal we can pass any law that we want.'

I long for him to be right, and his grandfather and all his

kinsmen, both Drummonds and Douglases, agree with him. They say we can defy the lords who disagree with us. When we take this bold position of power other lords come over to our side. Lord Dacre says that the lords who oppose me and would send for the French heir, Albany, are my enemies, pure and simple, and that I must use the power of the Douglas clan to impose my will on them. England will support me if I make war on them. Archibald says we have to appoint our own government, and so I name his uncle, Bishop Gavin Douglas, as a rival Lord Chancellor and summon a parliament – a rival parliament – to meet under our command at Perth.

I think this may be a great gamble, a powerful, courageous gamble. For the very lords who have sworn to reduce me are obliged to send me a message from the Duke of Albany, who has ruined their treasonous game by the chivalrous fairness of his response. He will only agree to come to Scotland as an advisor; he will not be my enemy, he will not usurp my son's power. He will not come at their bidding but only at mine.

But what am I to do with the lords? They are rebelling against me and I have no money for an army and no men to muster. It is all very well for Ard to say that we shall set a siege and they will never take Stirling. It is no life for us to be cooped up in a castle while the parliament are sending to France for their preferred regent. I write to Harry and say however busy he is with Mary and her beautiful gowns, her magnificent betrothal and her wonderful voyage to France, he must send me an army for I am besieged by my own people. I say that I am in Stirling for my own safety, but now I find I cannot leave. I am imprisoned in my own castle, and the only one who can rescue me is Harry.

Harry sends me messages through Lord Dacre, Warden of the Marches, who I must now consider a true ally and a friend. Clearly, Harry will not help me as he should. He tells me that he cannot send an army to Scotland for me and my husband the co-regent, because he has just heard that we attacked the Lord Lyon King of Arms and snatched the seal from the Lord Chancellor. Harry says that I am not safe in Scotland and that I must get myself and my sons out of the power of these rebel lords. He tells me that I must flee to Lord Dacre, who will bring me to London. He promises that my boys will be raised as English princes and James will be named as his heir. But I have to get out of Stirling and cross the border to England before Albany arrives and imprisons me. Harry says that he has done his very best with his new brother-in-law, the French king, to ensure that Albany will not come – but if the Scots lords have turned against me and invited him, what can anyone do?

I take the letter to Archibald. 'He won't send an army,' I say shortly. 'He says we must escape to England. Ard, what shall we do?'

He looks sick with fear, my brave young husband is afraid for the first time in his life. I feel a powerful wave of tenderness towards him. He was counting on my brother to support us with an army. 'I don't know,' he says. 'I don't know.'

## STIRLING CASTLE, SCOTLAND, WINTER 1514

Mary is crowned Queen of France in November, and I hear that her husband gives her a massive jewel every morning. Her coronation robe was gold brocade, she processed through Paris in an open carriage under arches of lilies of France and roses for Tudor England. The king has gout and can barely stand; but everyone praises the composure and beauty of his bride. He sends Harry a gift of harness, thanking him for sending such a mount. Those are his very words. They make me feel quite sick when our ambassador tells me; this is what it is to be a princess married for her country. We cannot all have the happiness that I have won with Archibald.

He gives me such joy! Even though we are entrapped by our own strategy, locked up in our own castle, it does not feel like defeat while Ard is with me. I long for the nights when he comes to my room – and he comes every night through feast day and fast, and he laughs with me and says he will have to confess lust, passion, love and even idolatry. These are the words he says as he kisses my eyelids, the achingly hard tips of my breasts, my belly button, even my hidden sex. He loves me without hesitation, as if I am his kingdom and he is coming into his own. And I, sprawled like a whore, longing for his touch, let him say and do whatever he would like, as long as his mouth is against mine. I have become shameless, I am entranced. I had no idea that pleasure was like this, that a man could inspire such sensuality that I am hardly conscious, hardly queen, hardly a mother. I am all nerves and yearning. All day I am damp with desire. I cannot wait for night-time and his quiet closing of my bedroom door. I cannot wait for his smile that tells me that he will come to me later. I cannot bear dawn, when we have to get up and go to chapel and put on our daytime faces and pretend that we are not wholly absorbed, wholly obsessed, with each other.

During the day I have to be queen, I have to guard like a captain and plan like a Lord Chancellor. The news is bad. Although I gave Archibald's cousin Gavin Douglas the archbishopric of St Andrews, the Scots council opposed him, and, even though Harry supported my choice, the Pope denied the appointment. The Scots lords sent their army to the castle of St Andrews, and Gavin Douglas is besieged there, just as we are held in Stirling. It was a bad gift that I gave him as his reward on my wedding day.

Then I have Christmas letters. A long one from Mary telling me of her extraordinary jewels and the glamour of the French court. They have lavished wealth on her wedding and her marriage is a dazzling success. Charles Brandon carried her colours in the wedding joust and gossip says that her husband's heir, Francis, has fallen in love with her, just as much as the old king Louis. She says it is true; I can almost see her simper.

*It is embarrassing, he is so wildly in love with me, he says he would die for love of me. My husband the king says that I must send him away, and that he is jealous.*

She writes a long inventory of what Louis has given her and how many people said that she was as beautiful as a painting, how the rich clothes suit her and how the king insists that she receive every honour. Her coronation as queen, the wealth of Paris, her ladies, her amusements . . . she goes on and on, and I turn over two or three pages barely reading the words:

*You would be amazed if you could see how I am revered. The French are so silly, they say that I am beautiful as a saint, and the king says that he will have a dozen portraits painted of me but nothing will capture my looks. He says that no country in Christendom has a queen to match me, none is better loved, that every queen is jealous of me.*

No, I am not jealous, I think to myself. Don't count me among the women who wish they had your looks, your jewels, your gowns. I am going to win my country by my merits as a governor, not by being the most beautiful woman. I am a queen regnant, not a pretty doll.

Then I look at the brief note I have from Katherine.

*I am sorry to have to tell you that I have lost another child. He came too early and though we thought we might have saved him, he slid away from us. He was a boy. This is my fourth dead child. God have mercy on me and spare me another day like this. Pray for me, Margaret, I beg you, and for his poor little soul. I don't know that I can bear another loss. I don't know how to bear this one, after all the others.*

I sit by the fire with the letters in my lap, my constant awareness of the rise and fall of these two women stilled for once, my envy at bay. I don't think I can judge which of us is in the best position: myself married for love but under siege from my own people; Mary sold into a beautiful slavery, as much a whore as any in the bath houses of Southwark; Katherine bowing her head against the most terrible ill luck, breaking her heart every year with another loss.

A fourth dead baby? Is this possible without a curse? Would God send four tragedies to a queen that He loved? Does God refuse to raise another Tudor boy to the throne of England? Is He showing us this? Or is it Katherine who is cursed? For insisting on the death of my cousin Warwick and the boy we called Perkin, for killing my husband, an ordained monarch?

Ard comes into the room and I know that my face lights up when I see him. 'Are you sitting in half-darkness?' he asks, smiling. 'I think we can still afford candles!' And he goes quickly and gracefully round the room, lighting the expensive wax candles one after another as if he were still my carver and devoted to my service and I were still the most beautiful queen.

## STIRLING CASTLE, SCOTLAND, JANUARY 1515

It was no joyful Christmas for us as newly-weds for we were surrounded by an army led by the Earl of Arran, James Hamilton, who chose me to be his king's wife, danced at my proxy wedding and received his title when I was crowned. Now we are enemies and he has to set a siege against me in midwinter, constantly undermined by Albany, who refuses to come from France unless his ancestral home is guaranteed for him, and his title, and his lands.

'Can they not see that he will fleece them like sheep?' I demand of Archibald. He shakes his head. He is playing with

James, setting up a line of nodding toys for him to move the first so that they all tumble down. They do this over and over again, while I sit at the table and read impossible demands from the lords' council and want to scream at the distracting chatter between the two of them, and then the clatter of the toys as they fall.

There is the noise of marching feet, and a quick exchange of passwords. I jump up, always afraid now. I thought that the Douglas family would own me and keep me safe, but all I find is that their enemies are added to mine. A messenger comes in with a packet of letters.

'Will you read these?' I ask Archibald.

'If you wish,' he says unwillingly. 'But shouldn't it be you? They're from your brother. Shall James and I go and play in the nursery tower?'

'For God's sake, open them,' John Drummond says grimly from the shadowy corner. He has been quiet for so long that I thought he was asleep, lulled by James and Archibald's repetitive game. 'Open them and see the news. God knows it can't get worse.'

This is no way for a lord to speak to a co-regent, but I try to nod cheerfully, and I sit on the floor beside James. 'I will play with you while your lord father reads the letters,' I say.

'No,' he whines at once, and I look around for Davy Lyndsay to take him away. I can't set up the little game to James' liking and he starts to whimper in disappointment and asks for Ard to come back and play.

'Here, see this,' says Davy, and shows him some hand-carved skittles and a little round ball.

'Oh, go and play with that,' I say impatiently.

'Good God,' Archibald says, reading the messages. 'Louis of France has died. Weakened and died.'

'Poison?' John Drummond asks.

'They're saying exhaustion,' Archibald says, reading intently, a quiver of laughter in his voice. 'Because of his beautiful young wife. The King of England writes that Francis will take the throne, and he is no friend to England. Your brother says we cannot let Albany come, he will deliver the keys of the North of England to the French.'

He reads slowly, his smooth brow furrowed. 'Your brother says he will do what he can to delay Albany. But you have to reverse the council's decision and forbid him to come.'

'How?' I say flatly. 'I have spent all the gold and goods in the treasury on this siege. There is no money, and no army and no power. Your men slip away every day, we can't hold out.'

'Write and tell your brother,' Drummond recommends. 'Tell the king that you will do his bidding but if he does not want a French governor for Scotland then he has to send us money. We will hold the country independent, or as an English fief – we don't care which – but he has to send us the money. Look! This is the best thing that could happen for us. Now he needs us. Make it clear that he has to pay us to hold Scotland for him. We can name our price.'

'But what about Mary?' I ask, as I take my place and pick up my pen to write my begging letter. 'What does he say about her?'

'He says nothing.' Archibald looks through the secretary's careful handwriting. 'Oh, he says that he is sending the Duke of Suffolk, Charles Brandon, to France to bring her home, if she is not carrying the French king's child.'

'He's sending Brandon?' I can hardly believe my brother's folly. He might as well give his little sister to this nobody as throw them together in the first month of her widowhood. Who did he imagine that Mary wanted when she forged the agreement that she should be free to choose a second husband? He cannot have been thinking at all.

## STIRLING CASTLE, SCOTLAND, APRIL 1515

It takes weeks and weeks before I hear that Harry has been fooled by our pretty sister, and she has danced her way into disgrace. Her letter comes to me by a merchant who had it from one of his customers in Paris, knowing he was bringing goods to Scotland. It is travel-stained but the seal is unbroken.

She writes:

*The most terrible thing, and the most wonderful thing. I know that you will support me, for you promised that you would. I have to call on you as a sister. I do. I demand your support as my sister. I call on Harry as my brother too, but he is furious. Katherine won't even write to me. Would you tell her that I could do nothing else? That it is my turn for love. Would you persuade her? She will listen to you and then she can talk Harry round.*

*I love him so much, Maggie, that I could not say no. Actually, to tell you the truth, he could not say no, for I cried and begged him and he was so loving that he lifted me up and swore that he would marry me, whatever happened.*

*So we are married – oh! me and Charles Brandon – married and nobody can do anything about it, and I could not be happier, I have loved him, I think, all my life. Of course everyone is completely furious with us both; but what were we to do? I could not leave my home again, and be married to a stranger. Harry promised me that my second marriage should be my choice, so why should I not hold him to it? Katherine chose in her second marriage, you did. Why not me too? But everyone is very angry.*

*The Privy Council say that Charles will have to be charged with treason! But I know we will be forgiven if you and Katherine ask. Do write to Harry and beg him to forgive me. All I want is to be happy. You and Katherine are happy. Why should I not be?*

It is so childish and so selfish that I have no reply for her. Then I reflect, I have my own troubles, and I am not so sure now that a queen is right to marry for love. I think it is dangerous to make a prince from a commoner, even for love. I think that it would not hurt Brandon to spend a few months in the Tower for his presumption. In the end I write to Katherine:

*Dear Sister,*

*I hear that Mary is fearful of losing our brother's favour because of her marriage. I believe he told her she might take a second husband of her own choosing, and now it is done. She is so young, and she had no-one in France to advise her. I hope you will urge Harry to be kind to her, though, God knows, she has no troubles as grave as mine. When you speak with Harry I beg you to remind him that I cannot hold this country and keep the French out without his help. When is he going to send men and money?*

## HOLYROODHOUSE PALACE, EDINBURGH, SCOTLAND, SUMMER 1515

Finally freed from the siege but only so that I may greet my enemies like a queen, I am dressed in robes of state, every inch a Tudor princess and Queen Regent of Scotland. Archibald, beside me, is dazzlingly handsome, tall, with red-brown hair and piercing eyes, looking, at this moment, stern and noble: even regal. We have had our official wedding before the lords, and, standing side by side, so close that our fingers brush, we draw courage from each other. We wait for the arrival of the Duke of Albany from France, who is coming to take up his place, despite my objections, as Governor of Scotland.

My brother Harry swore that he would not renew the treaty of peace with France unless the French kept Albany at home. But he signed it and Albany was allowed to go on his way. The peace that Mary's marriage made is renewed, despite her remarriage. The peace that I made is forgotten.

It is an insult to me that Albany should be invited over my head, but this is what love has cost me. The parliament deny the brilliance of my husband, deny the greatness of his family. Archibald is at the centre of a storm of jealousy; I know that they have nothing against him but envy.

Behind us are the great representatives of his family, the Douglas clan and the Drummonds. Beside my husband stands his grandfather Lord John, and his uncle the bishop Gavin Douglas, my nominee for St Andrews and Dunkeld. I am, as I have always longed to be, surrounded and supported by a family who love and prize me. They do not compare me with another woman; my place among them is unique. I am their kinswoman and their queen, as outstanding among them as my grandmother was to her wide family of cousins. All wealth and patronage flow from me, all the power is mine. They don't compare me to another woman because they cannot; there is simply no-one like me. I am their heart, I am their head, these are my people.

But today I am diminished. All the patronage and power was mine, but here comes the Duke of Albany to take my place at the head of the table of the lords' council, to draw the country closer to France. He would not even be here if my brother's fleet had been able to catch him at sea. It was Harry's intention to capture or perhaps even sink the duke's ship. In the great North Sea they sighted him and missed him, and now here he is, fresh from his landing at Dumbarton with a train of a thousand – a thousand men! As if he were king already.

He enters the room with a flourish, and my decision to dislike him melts away. He is dressed very beautifully in velvets and silks, but not like a king, as he wears no ermine trim. His hands sparkle with jewels and there is a great diamond in his hat, but he is not a walking jewel chest like my brother. He perfectly judges his bow to me, respectful to a queen regent and Tudor princess, but as from a kinsman – not a servant. I curtsey to him and when I rise up we kiss each other to acknowledge the family connection. He smells beautifully of orange flower water and clean linen. He is as immaculate as a princess on her wedding day, and I am seized at once with admiration and envy. This is a Frenchman of the highest breeding, a real nobleman. He makes the rest of my council look like Lowland beggars.

Behind him, bowing with a warm smile on his handsome face, is my chevalier, the Sieur de la Bastie, the white knight who jousted before me when I was a bride, and when I was a new mother. He bows very low and then he takes my hand and kisses it. It is as if I were a girl again and he promising to ride in the joust for me. If de la Bastie is with Albany, I feel I can trust both noblemen. I introduce him to Archibald and I see, with my anxious attention, Albany's small sideways glance at me, as if to confirm that I did indeed choose this willowy youth as my second husband – I, who had been married to such a great king.

We walk aside from everyone to exchange a few words. I gesture that Archibald shall walk with us, but Albany takes my arm and walks close to me so that Ard has to tag along behind and does not hear and cannot comment. 'Your Grace, your councillors advise me that matters have come to a pretty pass here,' he says, smiling. 'I hope to help you set things to rights.'

'I have to protect the inheritance of my sons,' I say. 'I swore to their father, your cousin, that his son would inherit his throne and continue his work of making this a wealthy and cultured country.'

'You are a scholar like your husband?' he asks me with sudden interest.

'No,' I admit. 'But I have continued my husband's work endowing schools and universities. We are the first country in Europe to provide schooling for the sons of our free-holders. We are proud of our learning in Scotland.'

'It's a remarkable achievement,' he says. 'And I am proud to help you with it. Can we agree that Scotland must continue to find its own way – we cannot bow to English influence?'

'I am an English princess but a Scots queen,' I say. 'Scotland must be free.'

'Then your husband's uncle, Gavin Douglas, must give up his claim to St Andrews,' he says quietly. 'And also Dunkeld. We all know that he got them only because his nephew married you.'

I give a little gasp. 'I don't agree at all.'

'And your husband's grandfather will have to answer for his assault on the Lyon Herald,' he goes on, his voice low and patient. 'You cannot allow your new kinsmen any special favours – it destroys your reputation as a just queen.'

'He barely touched him!' I protest. 'Perhaps his sleeve swept his face.'

He looks at me ruefully, his blue eyes smiling. His charm is completely self-aware; he is so beautifully mannered. 'You had better think about this, Your Grace,' he says. 'I cannot keep you in your place and restore your dower rents and get the government to pay you what they owe, and honour you as they should, if you do not make your new kinsmen behave as they should.'

'I must have my rents. I am practically penniless.'

'You shall have them. But your kinsmen must obey the law.'

'I am queen regent!' I exclaim.

He nods. I see now that he has an air of superiority, as if he had foreseen this conversation and prepared for it. 'You are,' he says. 'But – I am sorry to say – your young husband is neither royal nor courtly, and his family are known rogues.'

I am so furious, so insulted, and also – to tell the truth – so afraid, that I call Bishop Gavin Douglas and Lord John Drummond and Archibald into my privy chamber and send my ladies away so that we can whisper together.

'I don't think we should have insisted that you were made bishop,' I confess to Gavin. 'And we shouldn't have bribed you into Dunkeld.'

'I was the best choice,' he says, quite unrepentant.

'You may be, but the parliament don't like the Drummonds and Douglases getting everything.'

'It's not unreasonable,' Lord Drummond says, his hand on my husband's shoulder. 'We are the natural rulers.'

'And we're not getting everything,' Gavin adds, as if he hopes for more.

Archibald nods. 'You are queen regent: the right to make Church appointments is in your hands. You cannot be commanded by others. And of course you favour my family. Who else should you favour? Who else has shown you any support?'

'You shouldn't have struck the Lyon Herald.' I find the courage to confront John Drummond, though I quail beneath his sharp look. 'I am sorry, my lord, but the duke says you will have to answer for it. I didn't know what to reply.'

'You were there, you know it was nothing.'

'I know that you struck him.'

'You should have denied it,' he says simply.

'I have denied it! But clearly the herald has made a complaint and it is his word against yours.'

'His word against *yours*,' he emphasises. 'You will continue to deny it. Nobody can challenge the word of a queen.'

'But they do challenge it!' I wail, really afraid now. 'I won't get my dower rents if Albany does not think I am being a good queen. And he will take my boys into his keeping! He will take them away from me.' I put my hand over my belly. 'You know I am with child. I dare not go into confinement and leave all this mess. Who will look after—' I break off. I nearly said, who will look after Archibald? 'Who will look after my sons?' I correct myself.

'We will,' Lord Drummond says. 'Their Douglas and Drummond kinsmen, their stepfather Archibald. And that fool Albany has made his first mistake. He insulted Lord Hume at the first moment of their meeting, so he has lost his greatest ally. Hume has come over to our side, and he will bring in the Bothwells. Soon, the lords on our side will outnumber those that called for Albany and we can throw him out of the country and send him back to France.'

This is good news, but the favour of the lords gives me neither money nor power until they vote for me in parliament. Until then, Albany has a thousand men in his train, ten thousand to follow them, French backing; and I have only the Douglas men but no money to pay them. I don't even have money for the household; I cannot even feed my servants.

'Hadn't you better go to your brother?' Archibald asks. 'As Lord Dacre suggested? As your brother invites you? We have lost the first round here. Hadn't you better go to England and get an army and money?'

I turn a burning look on him. 'To England? And leave you? Do you want to be rid of me now?'

'My love! Of course not!' He catches up my hand and kisses it. 'But think of your boys. Should you not take them to King Henry? He has invited you: go to him for your own safety. You could come back home when it is safe.'

'Go to my brother like a beggar? And walk behind Katherine like a pauper?'

He does not understand the importance of precedence. 'It's all going wrong here,' he says, as simple as a boy. 'The country is splitting into clan against clan, as it used to be. You have not kept the lords in unity as your husband did. What can you do but go back to your brother? Even if you are nothing more than a dowager queen, a woman who once was queen? As long as you are safe. As long as the boys are safe. What does it matter if you walk behind the Queen of England, as long as you are safe?'

'I am damned if she eats humble pie!' His grandfather rounds on him, and makes my heart leap with pride. 'Why should she? When she has everything to play for here? And where would you go? Are you sick of the fight? When you tell her to run away, where would you go? Back to Janet Stewart?'

I never thought I would hear her name again. I look from my angry councillor to my white-faced husband. 'What? What is this? Who speaks of Janet Stewart?'

Archibald shakes his head. 'It's nothing,' he says. 'I was thinking only of your safety. There is no need for this.' He scowls at his grandfather. 'Does this help us?' he demands quietly. 'All quarrelling among ourselves? Are you helping me?'

'We'll go back to Stirling,' I say suddenly. I cannot bear this. 'And you will come with me, Archibald. We'll set the castle for a siege again. We'll protect my sons and I'll have my baby there.' I glare at him. 'Our baby,' I remind him. 'Yours and mine, our first child together. There will be no talk of going to England. There will be no thought of our parting. We are married in the sight of God, once privately and once before the congregation, and we will never be parted.'

He kneels at my feet and takes my hand and crushes it to his lips. 'My queen,' he says.

I bend over his bowed head and kiss the nape of his neck. His soft curly hair is warm beneath my lips; he smells clean, like a boy. He is mine and I will never leave him. 'And there will be no talk of Janet Stewart of Traquair,' I whisper. 'Never another word.'

There is a thunderous knocking on the door, we start apart and all look at one another. The door is swung open by my guards, and there are Albany's men, his captain of the guard wearing his sword in the French fashion, and in his hand he has warrants of arrest, the ribbons trailing from the seals.

'What are you doing here?' I demand. I am proud that my voice does not tremble. I sound outraged because I am outraged.

'I have a warrant of arrest for John Lord Drummond, for striking the Lyon Herald, and for Gavin Douglas, wrongly named bishop, for fraudulently taking the see of Dunkeld.'

'You can't,' I say. 'I forbid it. I, the queen, forbid it.'

'The regent commanded it,' the captain explains as the guard comes into the room and leads them away, closing the door quietly behind them, leaving Archibald and me quite alone, with no-one to support us. Ard raises his hand as if to protest and the captain gives him a steady look. 'This is the law,' he says. 'These men have broken the law. They are to be tried and sentenced. This is by order of the duke regent.'

Next day, I demand to see the Duke of Albany in person. I call for my horse and, sitting pillion for comfort, I ride up the Via Regis from Holyroodhouse Palace to the castle at the very top of the hill. Everyone cheers me as I go by, for I am still beloved in my capital city and the people remember when I rode in, seated behind my husband the king.

I smile and I wave, and I hope that the so-called duke regent is hearing the cheers as I come to the crest of the hill and over the drawbridge and into the castle. He will learn that he cannot act against me and mine.

I am admitted at once and I go from the great chamber through into the privy chamber, and there is Albany himself, as smart and perfumed as always. He bows very low to me, as he should, and I am gracious to him and we agree that we shall both sit. They bring us chairs, and mine is a little higher, and I sit and do not sigh with exhaustion though my back aches, nor do I lean back and clasp my round belly. I sit with my hands held in my lap, as upright as Katherine of Arrogant, and I say:

'All the charges against Gavin Douglas are false and he must be released at once.'

'The charges?' Albany repeats, as if it has slipped his mind that he has arrested my husband's uncle.

'I understand that he is charged with colluding and conspiring with England against the interests of Scotland,' I say boldly. 'And I am here to tell you that he did not do so, and would not do so. You have my word.'

He flushes and I think, triumphantly, that I have out-bluffed him, and that he will have to release Gavin, and how pleased Archibald will be. Ard was in a panic after his uncle's arrest, doubting my judgement, anxious to hurry us back to Stirling, fearful that we have made terrible mistakes, in terror for his grandfather. Now he will see that I am indeed the great queen he fell in love with, and I can still command.

But Albany's blush is not for himself: it is embarrassment for me. He shakes his head, looking away, and then he rises to his feet and goes to a table in the corner of the room and picks up some papers. 'There are letters,' he says reluctantly. 'Letters from Gavin Douglas to your brother the king through Lord Dacre, who is such an enemy to our peace. They show that your husband's uncle asked the English to support his bid for the sees of St Andrews and Dunkeld, and that they did so. They show that he paid for the Church appointment. He is corrupt, and your brother favoured him at your request.'

'I . . .' Now I am lost for words and I can feel the rising heat in my face as he confronts me with Gavin Douglas's crimes. 'But this is not against the interests of Scotland . . .' I am floundering.

'It is plotting with a foreign power,' he says simply. 'It is treason. I also have letters that passed between your brother, King of England, and you,' he continues very quietly. 'You invited him to make false proposals of peace to the Scots parliament, while you secretly asked him to invade. You asked him – Scotland's enemy – to invade your own country. You sent letters in secret, you used a code. The letters show that you are betraying your country to the English.'

I cannot meet his reproachful brown eyes. 'I asked my own brother for help. There is nothing wrong with that.'

'You advised him how to trick your own lords.'

'My people are rebelling against me. I cannot trust the lords . . .'

'I am sorry, Your Grace, but I know that you are plotting against Scotland. I know that you plan to run away to England, that Lord Dacre is ready to take you to your brother.'

I am so mortified that I feel tears coming into my eyes and I let them rise and fall. I put my hand to my hot forehead while with the other I clasp my belly. 'I am alone!' I whisper. 'A royal widow! I have to protect the king's sons, I have to have the help of my family. I have to be able to write to my brother. I have to be able to write to my sisters, my dear sisters.' I glance up from under my wet eyelashes to see if he is moved.

He goes to take my hand, but he checks himself.

'Pardon Gavin Douglas,' I beg him. 'And Lord Drummond. All they have done has been in my defence. You don't know what the lords are like! They will turn on you too.'

He is beautifully mannered: he begs me not to cry and from inside his silk jacket he produces his own handkerchief, also silk, embroidered by his wife, a French heiress, with her crest and initials. Who carries a handkerchief in Scotland? They wouldn't even know what one was.

I hold it to my eyes. It has the lightest of perfumes. I peep at him over it. 'My lord?' I ask. I think I have won him over.

He bows low but he speaks coldly: 'Alas, Your Grace, I cannot oblige you in this,' and then he goes from the room.

Goes from the room! Without being dismissed! Without a word more! And I am left with tears on my cheeks, having to get up and ride back to Archibald and tell him that his grandfather and his uncle will stay imprisoned, and that Albany knows what we are plotting, and so we are lost. I cannot force this duke to do anything. He is all but incorruptible. I have nothing to show for this but the knowledge that they know our plans before we do, and a silk handkerchief.

But then – just as I knew they would – the lords turn against the Duke of Albany. Perversely, in a fit of temper at foreign manners and French etiquette, the parliament orders that Lord

Drummond is to be freed in the autumn. He may have been in the wrong to strike the Lyon Herald, but he is a Scots lord, and if anyone can be in the wrong in Edinburgh with everyone's blessing, it is a Scots lord. They only obey the rules that they admire, and they are not going to be taught manners by a French-raised newcomer.

I write to my brother that now is our chance. The lords have had their moment of love for Albany, now they want to return to their true king. If Harry will help me, I can buy some of them, hire others, and persuade the rest. But he must be aware that I am surrounded by enemies. If they make me write to him against my will I will sign my letter with the signature of our grandmother, Margaret R; if I am writing my own mind I will sign Margaret. He must watch for this, he must conspire with me, he must send me soldiers at once. We have everything to play for now, we Tudors. We are about to win.

## STIRLING CASTLE, SCOTLAND, SUMMER 1515

The duke regent, Albany, may have been bested by the parliament, but they agree with him that my son the king is not safe in my keeping. He is going to come for my son. Both my sons. He won't take James without my baby Alexander. Both my children are to be taken from me and I have no power to resist.

Albany may be a great courtier, but I am a great queen. I allow the parliament to come to the drawbridge at Stirling Castle and I stand in the great gateway holding my eldest little boy by the hand. We look both pathetic and indomitable. I have taught James to hold up his head and not to say a word, not to scuff his feet or gaze about. It is as well that I have coached him in the ways of majesty, for outside the castle walls is the whole of the town, come as if to a fair, to see what will happen when the French duke brings the newly appointed royal guardians to take the little king away from his mother.

It's as good as a play for them, and I make sure that we look like the heroine and her child in a play. Behind me, my hundred-strong household servants and guards stand to attention, in complete silence, their faces grave. My handsome young husband waits with his hand on his sword as if he would challenge anyone to single combat if they dare to come against me.

Little James is perfect. I have dressed him in green and white to remind everyone that he is a Tudor prince, but on his back he carries his father's lyre. It's a beautiful touch. I am wearing white, widow white, and a cloth of gold train and a heavy gable hood in gold like a crown. My belly is broad, as if to remind everyone that I gave King James sons and heirs. Beside me the nursemaid holds the baby Alexander in his white lawn gown with a perfectly white lace shawl gathered around him. Here is the widowed queen – we say it just by standing here. Here is the King of Scotland, here is his brother, the Duke of Ross. We are dressed in white like the heavenly host. Who is going to dare to part us? Who would bring us down to earth?

People roar with approval at the sight of the three of us. We are royal Stewarts, we are beloved. Nobody can hear anything over the shouts. The people are mad for the sight of their little king and his mother dressed like a martyr, pale as a widow, her belly large with another Scot.

The delegates from parliament come forward and I call out: 'Stay and declare the cause of your coming!'

I see the grimace from the councillor in front. This is not going to look well, given the mood of the crowd, and he is wishing himself elsewhere, doubting that he can do this at all. In a voice so low that the crowd shout out, 'Sing up!' and 'What does he say?' and 'Only villains whisper!' he tells me quietly that they have come for the king. He must live in the care of his new guardians who have been appointed by the Duke of Albany and the council.

I make a little gesture with my hand and the portcullis slams down before us, the delegation shut out, my household and myself safely within. James jumps at the rattle of the chain and the scream of the metal coming down and the crash of the teeth on stone, and I pinch his little hand to remind him not to cry. The people roar with approval and I raise my voice and shout to them that I am my son's guardian, and his mother, that I will consider the recommendations of parliament, but my son is my son, he will always be my son and I must always be with him.

The roar of approval is an endorsement. I let the adulation wash over me, restore me, and then I meet the eyes of the parliamentary delegation through the stout portcullis with bold triumph. I have won this match, they have lost. I smile at them and turn and lead my son and household back inside. Archibald follows.

I try to hold that moment of triumph. I try to remember the deep bellow of the crowd and my knowledge that the people of Scotland love me. I try to remember the endearing touch of James' little hand in mine, knowing that I have a son, knowing that my son is a king. What greater joy can a woman have than this? I have achieved what it took my grandmother a hard lifetime to achieve, and I am still only twenty-five. I have a royal family, and I have a husband who risks everything to be with me.

I am clinging to the love that the Scots had for my husband, have for my son, surely have for me. I am clinging to my love for Ard – I cannot consider what it has cost me – when I get a letter from England with Mary's scrawl over the front and her seal on the flap. She is using the royal seal of France; she will forever call herself the Queen of France, I know it.

*Dear Sister, dearest Sister, I am so happy, this must be my greatest day. I have married my beloved Charles, for the second time, in England, and Harry and Katherine came to the wedding and rejoiced in my happiness. We have a terrible debt to pay, we will never have any money, we will have to live on prayer like Franciscans, but at least I have got my way. Even queens can marry where they love. Katherine did, you did, I have. Why should I not choose my happiness when she and you did? And everyone who says that I am a fool can ask themselves – who married the greatest king in Christendom and then married for love? Me!*

There is more. It goes on and on. She predicts that Harry will be unable to be angry for long. He has fined them into poverty, they will never be out of debt to him, but he loves his friend Charles and he adores her . . . and so on, and so on, criss-cross over the page, with foolish exclamations about her happiness added in the margins.

At the very end she says that she must surely be forgiven the debt because Harry is in the greatest of spirits about Katherine's pregnancy. They are certain this time the baby will go to full term, and all the physicians say that she is carrying him well.

I hold the letter in my lap and look out of the window. I remind myself that I have two sons in the nursery, and I am carrying another child. I have not married a nobody that I am trying to foist on my family and drag into the nobility. My son with Ard will not be a prince, but he will be born an earl in his own right. What was Charles Brandon's family a generation ago? How will Mary bear it when the first flush has worn off and she sees a man whose entire reputation rests on her? Does she think that the joy of the first year lasts forever?

I have a young husband, a handsome husband from a great family, and he loves me, only me, while Katherine has to look the other way from Harry's infidelities and pretend not to mind. I am a queen just as good as her, and better than her – far better – I have a son who is king. She gives birth to nothing but dead babies or babies who die after birth; she must be wretched. She should be wretched. When I think what she has done to me I know that she should be wretched forever.

But it is no comfort to think of her hunched over her swelling belly and praying that this time God grants her a live child, hoping that Harry won't be unfaithful during the months of her confinement. Although I feel sour and envious, I find I get no pleasure in imagining her being wretched. For despite listing my blessings – my handsome husband, my two boys, the baby in my belly – I feel rather wretched too.

We wait to hear what the response will be from the Duke of Albany, and the council of lords. Archibald rides out with James every day, teaching him how to sit on his pony and raise a hand to take a salute. He talks to him of battles. I don't like them to go far afield, as I am afraid that the council may grow impatient and kidnap our little king. I am uneasy, nervous in my pregnancy. I think that I am allowing myself to be frightened of shadows. Then sometimes I think that I have much to fear.

I have the vivid dreams of pregnancy. I start to think of Albany with dread, as if he were the devil himself and not a careful, courteous politician. I think he will take James by force. I think he will take Ard from me. I think of him stripping John Lord Drummond of his wealth, for nothing more than being a good advisor to me, a tender grandfather. Although they have promised to release him from imprisonment, they have ruined him, taking his estates and his castles. Ard has lost his inheritance and now we have no money at all. Bishop Gavin Douglas is imprisoned with no hope of release, and my secret letters to Harry have been read by everyone. Everyone knows that I was plotting to bring the English down on my own country, that my husband and his family were profiting from my treason. George

Douglas, Ard's younger brother, has fled to England, marking the whole family as traitors. I feel as if I have lost all my friends, I feel as if Ard has lost his family for me, and yet still my brother sends neither money nor help. Still Katherine does not advise him that they should compensate me – yet who brought me into this danger but her?

I know that the Duke of Albany will not wait forever, and at the end of July he sends for James, my son. The council is determined that I hand over the little king to his new guardians.

Again, I speak through the portcullis, but this time there are no cheering spectators. I say that Stirling is my own castle, my husband the king gave it to me himself. I say that my son is in my own keeping, my royal husband made me his protector. I say I will not hand him over. I will not surrender the keys of the castle.

They call on Archibald, who is standing silently behind me, and they order him to advise me. Confidently, I turn and smile, but Archibald astounds me. Then and there, in the courtyard of Stirling Castle, where he used to count himself lucky if I let him lift me into the saddle, he says that his advice to me as my husband has always been that I should obey the governor, the Duke of Albany, who has been appointed by the parliament as regent. He says that this is the will of the lords of Scotland and we should all obey the earthly powers. I am completely silent, my eyes blazing at his pale face as he betrays me completely, politely, and in public. I say nothing at all until we have gone inside the castle and the door is closed on my privy chamber and we are alone. Then he stands with his hands behind his back, his head down, his face sulky as a child's, waiting for the scolding that he knows is coming.

'How could you? How could you?'

He looks tired. He looks pale, like a boy who has been forced to take on troubles beyond his years. 'So that they don't charge me with treason like my grandfather,' he says.

'How could you betray me? You owe me everything. I have done everything for you. You are nothing more than Charles

Brandon is to my sister. We both have honoured husbands far below us, men who would be nothing without us.'

He shakes his head and it only makes me angrier.

'I will never forgive this,' I rail at him. 'I have lost my throne for love of you. If I had not married you I would still be queen regent. All this is your fault, and yet when they call on you, you answer obediently! But you are not free to answer to them, you are bound to me! You are my husband, I am queen regent. You should not even speak when they address you!'

'I answer fair so that I keep my lands and goods,' he says slowly. There is no rage in his voice; unlike me, he speaks slowly and steadily. 'I keep my castles and my tenants. I am going now, to raise troops to defend you. We have no-one here in Stirling; we have no money to pay an army. But if I can get home and raise my tenantry and call on my friends and borrow money, then I can come back and get you out of here.'

'You are defending me?' My rage turns to astonishment. I feel the pulse of a complete change of heart.

'Of course. Of course.'

I grab his hands, tears pouring down my face, as anguished as I was angry. 'You swear it? You're not just leaving me? You're not just saving your own skin and leaving me here?'

'Of course not.' He kisses my hands, he kisses my tear-stained face. 'What do you take me for? Of course I am going to raise an army to save you. I am your husband, I know what I must do.'

'I thought you had betrayed me. Before them all! I thought that you had gone over to their side and left me.'

'I knew you would. But you had to believe it, and they had to believe it, so that I can serve you.'

'Oh, Archibald, stay with me.'

'No, I shall go and get my men so I can save you. I shall go to my home.'

'And you won't see her?' The words slip out before I can stop myself.

At once the tender look falls from his face and he looks as old as his grandfather and weary. 'I will have to see her if I am trying to raise troops from her lands. She is a sweet loyal girl and has never failed in kindness towards me. Even now, she would do anything for me. I will have to meet with her family to plead your cause. But I am not leaving you for her. I don't forget I am married to you. I know my duty, even though it is not what I thought it would be.'

'We will be happy again,' I promise him as if he is a child, like James, desperate to restore the love to his eyes. 'Your duties will be merry again. We will break out of this, Harry will send an army. We will have our child and you will be glad. I will give you a son, I know I will. I will give you the next Earl of Angus. You will like that. And we will take power.'

He shows me a weary smile. 'I am sure. I will go now and make all the speed I can to come back to you.'

'You will come back? You won't run away to England like your brother George?'

He shakes his head. 'I have given the word of a Douglas.'

I wait in the castle alone. Albany's retinue and the lords who support him have invested the town of Stirling, and the castle is under siege. I have to guard my sons and defy the parliament, the lords and the governor. I write to Harry. I tell him that I am alone, surrounded by my own parliament. They insist on taking my boys, his own nephews, his heirs. If he does not come to rescue me I cannot predict what will happen. I get no reply. Lord Dacre advises me in a secret letter that Harry and the new French king, Francis, have agreed together not to meddle in the affairs of Scotland. I know what this means: Harry has abandoned my cause; my brother has betrayed me.

I am sick at the thought of Harry agreeing to leave me to chance, but then I realise that the treaty cuts both ways. Albany, too, has no patron as he tries to rule Scotland; he will get no help from France. He and I are equally isolated, equally alone. He is camped in the town of Stirling, I am stuck in the castle. He has no king supporting his attempt to be governor, I have no brother helping me to be queen regent. I have no sisters pressing my case. We are to fight it out, like cocks in a ring, until one rips out the throat of the other.

I wait for Archibald to come back, but he does not. I play with the boys, I rest in the afternoon, I rack my brains to think who might come to rescue me since Harry has betrayed me and Archibald does not come; and I know that there is no-one.

At the end of the week I can delay no longer and I agree to hand over the boys to the lords of my choosing. I nominate my husband the Earl of Angus and our friend Lord Hume. Albany does not even pretend to consider my proposals. He merely demands that I send out my boys. I answer him by keeping the drawbridge up and arming the guns. I know that we are moving towards a battle, I know that this can end only one way. I cannot win. I send a note to my husband by one of his menservants.

'If you don't come I will lose my sons. Save me.'

I send the same letter to Harry.

Neither of them answers.

We are short of bread; we are short of the flour to make bread. The well is deep, there is always reliable water, so we will never go thirsty. But we are short of meat, and cheese. There are hens and cows inside the castle, grazing on the green, but we are short of hay. I order the horses to be driven out of the little gate, where Albany's soldiers catch them and shout ironic thanks for the gift; but still we have only enough hay for a few weeks. When we kill the animals for meat we will have no milk or eggs. My sons need fresh food – they are children, they should not be starved in a siege. I don't know what I can do.

I am sitting in my nightgown and robe, my hand on my swollen belly where the new baby is moving, when the doorway in my private chamber opens a crack. A lady-in-waiting gasps and points, her other hand over her mouth. 'Your Grace?'

I get to my feet, my knees trembling. I am half-expecting the Duke of Albany himself, entering through a secret door, having taken the castle by stealth, but instead it is Archibald.

'You've come! You've come.'

He tumbles into the room and catches me up and covers my face with kisses. 'I promised. Did I not?'

'You did. My God! Thank heavens you have come! I have been so frightened. How many men do you have?'

'Not enough,' says his brother, coming through the door behind him. 'Only sixty.'

'Oh, George! You've come back. I thought you were gone to England forever.'

He bows his dark head over my hand. 'Just to gather news and get help,' he says. 'Just to serve my brother and you.' His smile is quick.

I flush at the thought of the Douglas loyalty. They are sworn to death for their family, and now I am one of them.

'There are six hundred traitors out there,' Archibald says. 'I couldn't find men who would fight for us. I have only my own tenants and some of Lord Hume's. I never thought Albany could muster such force.'

'My cause is just! I am queen regent.'

'I know.' George rubs his hand over his young face. 'But the common men won't turn out against the governor, and I couldn't get any help in England.'

'What can we do?'

'Come away,' Archibald urges me. 'Come at once and bring the boys, and we'll get away to England. Lord Dacre says we'll be safe the moment we cross the border, and we can all go to London.'

'It's not safe,' I say instantly.

'Safer than here,' George says.

Archibald nods. 'You can't hold the siege here.'

'My brother will send help if he knows how desperate we are.'

'I've tried,' George says. 'I've spoke to Dacre and to the other Northern lords. They don't want war. Your sister, Princess Mary, has brought a peace treaty home from France and your brother won't break it.'

'And I am to be grateful to her! Don't they think of us?'

'You shouldn't be grateful for anything,' Archibald corrects me. 'You have nothing to thank Henry for. She has come home from France in triumph, married to the man she loves, and is received at court and forgiven. But you – who have done exactly as she has done – are trapped here and I with you, and they have forgotten all about us. You must write to him! You must tell him he cannot betray us.'

'But not now,' George cuts in. 'The time for writing is over. Alexander Hume is at the gate with the horses. Come now, Your Grace, and bring your boys with you.'

'I don't dare.' I give a little moan. 'What if they catch us? They'll know that I am running to Harry and they'll imprison me so I can't get to England. They'll take my sons away from me forever, and you – I give a little sob – 'Ard, they will behead you for treason.'

'Come on,' he says. 'I'll take the risk.'

'No,' I say, suddenly deciding. 'I won't put you in mortal danger. I can't bear that. I can't lose you. You go, hide somewhere. I'll get out of here. I'll get nearer to the border as soon as I can. Come for me, when it is safer.'

'I'll stay with the queen and guard her here,' George says boldly to his brother. 'You raise men, Archibald, and get a message to Dacre. Tell him that she will come to England. Tell him to meet us.'

'Yes,' I say. 'But don't be captured, Archibald. They won't dare to do anything to me or my boy James, but they will behead you for sure. Go now. Go, my love.'

I bundle him out of the door, exchanging one passionate kiss as he leaves. George goes out of the chamber to the guardroom. When the door is shut and bolted behind them, I find that the rapid thudding in my ears slows. I put my back to the door and lean against it. My feet hurt, my husband has gone, my baby is heavy in my womb, and I am all alone, once again.

I have taken to walking on the castle walls in the evening. Sometimes James comes with me, his Lord Chamberlain, Davy Lyndsay, beside him. I think the exercise is good for me and for the baby that lies so heavily in my belly. I walk the perimeter of the castle from one tower to another, watching the road that winds up through the trees from the little town below, as the sky grows darker. Looking at the rolling hills towards the green south, the road that would take me to freedom is a green track down from our cliff top, through the town, past the fields and then disappearing into the darkness of the forest. Something catches my eye: a plume of dust and a glint of metal.

God be thanked! I am saved – it is Harry's army. It is Harry's triumphant army. He has come himself and marched north, taken Edinburgh and come onward to take Albany from the rear and free me, and the Scots lords will see that if they defy a princess of England then revenge is swift. I could cheer at that little spark of metal among the trees, the English army coming for an English princess with perhaps my brother at the head, like a true chevalier.

I squint and cup my hands over my eyes to concentrate my gaze on the standards. I think I can see the Tudor rose, my rose. I think I can see the Beaufort portcullis, my lady grandmother's flag. I think I can see the red cross on the white ground of Saint George.

'Look!' I say to Davy, a little laugh in my voice. 'What can you see? What's that on the Edinburgh road?'

Davy Lyndsay gets up on the sentry step and looks where I am pointing. He steps down in silence and his face is white. Behind him George Douglas is standing in the lee of one of the towers. 'Look, George!' I call to him, and I point to where the cloud of dust hides the marching men and the horses, the wagons coming behind them. I rub my eyes with both fists, hoping that I am mistaken, hoping that the evening sun is playing tricks, but now I can see perfectly well. These are not the beloved standards of my country coming up the Edinburgh road to the very walls of the castle. It is not an army for our relief. Now I can even hear the rumble of the wheels of the heavy wagons and the lowing of the oxen as they heave the weight. It is my husband James' artillery, which he designed and cast. It was his great pride. At the front of the train of wagons is the greatest cannon of all, the greatest cannon in Europe, the one that he said was the end of chivalry and the beginning of a new warfare, called Monns. James said that no castle could withstand her massive power. The Duke of Albany has brought my husband's cannon to use against me with seven thousand men in support, and this is the end of my defiance and the end of my hope, and we will have to surrender before he pounds down the walls of my castle and turns Stirling to dust. I turn to George Douglas.

'I'll have to surrender,' I say. 'Tell Ard.'

Grimly, he nods. 'I'll go now.'

## EDINBURGH CASTLE, SCOTLAND, AUGUST 1515

I am a prisoner of my own people. My son the king, the true King of Scotland, and his brother, the next heir, are held in Stirling Castle, honoured as guests, but really prisoners of the false duke who holds the keys. I, the queen regent, am held in Edinburgh Castle as if I were a criminal, as if I were a prisoner awaiting trial, awaiting execution.

God knows what is going to become of us. George Douglas

disappeared before the cannons were even brought before the castle. So much for him guarding me so that his brother could get to safety – at the first sight of Monns he was gone. The other servants melted away. I don't know where Archibald is, I don't know why Harry does not demand of the French king that Albany return my castle to me. I took my little boy James down the stair to surrender the castle at the front gate, and, like the little king he is, he did not waver. He is only three years old but he is princely. My little son held the keys to Stirling Castle and gave them to this French puppet, without a moment's trembling.

A true man, a true chevalier, would never have parted a mother from her boys and turned her out of her own home. But Albany put me in the charge of lords faithful to his own rule, and sent me back to Edinburgh Castle. My boys he returned to their nursery at Stirling. Davy Lyndsay went with them, with a little bow to me, as if to say that wherever James goes, his faithful guardian will go too. Albany took his army onward, hunting my innocent husband and his family. He says he will see the rule of law running from sea to sea in Scotland. He says he has been made governor by the council of lords and is going to rule justly. He is not the man to do it. There was one man who could do it; but he is gone, and Katherine of Aragon holds his body, half-forgotten, encased in lead, somewhere in a box in London.

I get urgent letters from Dacre and swift scribbled notes from Archibald, urging me to get away at the first opportunity. Now we see how far Albany will go, how terribly he will act. I know that I am not safe in his keeping, and I am near to my time. I cannot go into confinement as a prisoner. If I die in childbed then I will leave two orphans in the care of my enemy.

I send a message to Albany that I want to go to Linlithgow Palace for my lying-in and he makes me sign a letter to Harry to tell him that I am going into confinement and that I am happy leaving my sons in the hands of their cousin. Lies. I am desperate with worry and I sign my name 'Margaret R', as our grandmother used to sign hers – the sign to Harry that I am under duress, but I don't even know if he will remember this code. I don't even know if spies will intercept my letter and copy it wrongly to him. I don't know that Lord Dacre will tell him the terrible danger that we are in. I don't know where my husband is tonight.

That night, feverish with the weight of the baby on my belly, I turn restlessly from one side to the other and feel the baby shift and grind on my bones, as if I am breaking open like a walnut in the crackers. I think that nowhere is safe. Nowhere is safe for me if my brother will not protect me as he should. Nowhere is safe if my sisters don't advocate for me. And I don't even know if they are praying for me as sisters should. They have sent no Virgin's girdle, no good wishes. I don't even know if they are thinking of me at all.

As soon as I am dressed for the journey I sink into a chair, turn to my lady-in-waiting and say, 'I am ill, I am sick. Tell the duke that I need to see my husband.'

She hesitates.

'It is a matter of life and death,' I say. 'Tell the duke that I fear I am failing fast.'

That frightens her. She scuttles down the stairs like a mouse with a broom behind it, hurrying into the castle to find the duke's many French servants and make them understand that the queen regent is causing trouble . . . again. As we descend the stairs I put out both my hands to my ladies and they guide me down to the stable yard where my litter is waiting for me. On the turn of the stair I am faint and have to stop. I cannot stand, and have to rest on the windowsill. By the time we are in the stable yard, filled with my enormous baggage train and my waiting retinue, Albany has arrived and is bowing before me.

'I am sorry, my lord,' I say weakly. 'I cannot greet you as I should. I have to make such a long journey, and then I will take to my bed.'

'Please . . .' He almost dances on the spot, he is so filled with courteous chagrin. 'Is there anything I can do? Can I fetch anything? Physicians?'

I stagger a little. 'I fear . . .' I say. 'I fear that my child may come early. This is a dangerous time. I have been forced to travel at the most dangerous time. My life . . .'

He blanches at the thought that his tyranny over me might lead me to lose a child, perhaps to my death. He is under instruction from the French king to rule Scotland but not to make matters any worse between Scotland and England. If he kills me, then my sisters will be forced to complain, Harry will take action, realising that he has been wickedly, shamefully remiss. If I die then the world will blame Albany; and those who have not prized me in life will be anguished with grief at my death.

I double up. 'The pain!' I gasp.

My ladies rush towards me, and I let them help me into the litter, put a warm brick under my feet, an earthenware bottle filled with hot water against my straining belly. 'My husband,' I whisper. 'I must see Archibald once more. I cannot go into confinement without his blessing.'

I see Albany stop and turn again. He has been pursuing Archibald with a charge of treason, determined to see him on the scaffold.

'You have to pardon him,' I pant. 'I have to see him. I have to say farewell. What if I never come out of confinement? What if I never see him again?'

Albany does not want to be remembered as the governor who drove the queen to death while he was chasing her young husband through the borderlands, up hill and down dale in country where no stranger could ever overtake a Scot. 'It was treason!' he says feebly. 'He was guilty of treason. He was ordered to join with the other lords.'

'How could he besiege his own wife? It made no sense to ask it of him!' I snap, for a moment forgetting my part, and then I recoil and clutch my back. 'Aah – something is wrong. Where are the midwives?'

'I'll pardon him, and send him to you at Linlithgow,' Albany assures me. Like any man he is desperate to be away from a woman suffering with mysterious pains. 'I will send out a message and tell him he is free to come to you. Take care, my lady. Take care, Your Grace. Should you really be travelling? Should you not stay here?'

'I insist,' I say weakly. 'I have to have my baby at Linlithgow with my husband at my side.'

'I will make sure of it,' he promises me.

I nod, I don't even thank him, as the faintness sweeps over me as I lean back in the arms of my ladies. They lay me down on the goose-down pillows, they flutter around the litter, and I wave them away and command them to drop the curtains. When the litter is shielded by the thick curtains of cloth of gold and they are mounting their horses to escort me, and Albany is gone, I sit up and hug myself, and have to put my hands over my mouth to muffle my joyous laughter.

## LINLITHGOW PALACE, SCOTLAND, SEPTEMBER 1515

I am seated in a chair at the fireside, in a loose silver night robe. My hair is combed out and spread over my shoulders like a golden veil. When the captain of Albany's troop brings my husband into the room I raise my eyes and make a little gesture as if to show that I cannot rise, as Archibald, tanned and smiling after weeks of hard riding, runs to fling himself at my feet and bends his smooth fox head into my lap.

'Your Grace,' he says, muffled. 'My wife, my beloved.'

'I'll leave you,' the captain says, anxious to be out of the perfumed room. 'My lord – you are on parole. I will report to the

Duke of Albany in Edinburgh that you are safely here and on your honour to stay here within the palace walls.'

My husband turns his head and smiles at our enemy. 'Thank him for this,' he says. 'I am grateful. Whatever happens in the future, he has behaved with the courtesy of a lord of chivalry.'

The captain puffs up a little, and bows and goes out.

Silently, Archibald tiptoes across the room and locks the door behind him. He turns back to me. 'Ready?' His dark eyes are sparkling with excitement.

'Ready,' I say. I throw off the billowing night robe, underneath I am wearing my riding gown. Archibald himself kneels at my feet and helps me into my riding boots. My lady-in-waiting hands me a dark cape and I draw the hood over my head.

'You have everything?'

'Tom, my groom, has my jewels and what money I have to hand,' I say. 'The luggage train will come after.'

He nods. 'You know the stair?'

I lead him through the adjoining door to the little chapel. Behind the altar is a hidden doorway, used only by the visiting priests. It opens without a creak and I take a candle from the altar and lead him down the winding steps. The door at the bottom is unbolted, Archibald pulls it open and there, waiting for us, are George Douglas and a couple of servants and men-at-arms.

'Can you ride?' George asks, eyeing my swollen belly.

'I have to,' I say simply. 'I will tell you if I have to stop.'

They have a pillion saddle on Archibald's horse and a man-at-arms lifts me up behind him. My maid and my lady-in-waiting go on their own horses and the grooms lead a couple of spares.

'Not too fast,' I say to Archibald.

'We have to get away,' he reminds me. 'We have to meet with Alexander Hume and his guard, and ride to my castle before they know you are gone.'

I wrap my arms around him and I put my belly against his back. My baby's father is going to save us. He has rescued us from an unjust imprisonment. We are free.

# TANTALLON CASTLE, FIRTH OF FORTH, SCOTLAND, SEPTEMBER 1515

We ride all night through country that I sense, but cannot see. There are wide skies above, and a rolling landscape around us. I hear owls, and once a white-faced ghost of a barn owl lifts off the hedge before us, making the horse shy, and I grip onto Ard in fright. For most of the journey I can hear the sea, which grows louder and louder, and then I hear the piercing cry of seagulls.

It is dawn before we come to Tantallon Castle, Ard's own fortress, his family home, and I gasp when there is a gap in the trees and I see it for the first time. It is a formidable hulk of a building, beautifully designed with proud turrets each capped with a conical roof. It is faced with grey limestone but here and there the stone has been battered away by hard weather, and the plum colour of the local stone makes the castle gleam as warm as sunrise.

It faces the North Sea, where the sun is showing long brilliant rays across the rolling waves. The sound of the sea roars on, as loud as our hoofbeats; the smell of the sea makes me lift my head, and breathe the salt air. The seagulls cry, whirling in the dawn light, and beyond the castle I see the Bass Rock: a great dome of rock like a mountain, blazing white in the morning light, with a cloud of seabirds around its cliffs and a little fort perched facing the land. Castle and island face each other, equally impregnable. Round the castle there is a constant swirl of house martins, and now I hear their screaming cries.

'We can't stay here long,' Angus says. 'It's too small, there's no comfort for you, and it can't withstand a siege.'

'Surely it could hold out forever!'

He shakes his head. 'Not if Albany brings up cannon. We know he has Monns. If we set a siege we can't get out again, and he could wait us out. This is a good castle for short battles, for defence and attack. But we can't wait for your brother. Are you sure he will come?'

'He will not forget me,' I say awkwardly. 'My sisters will tell him . . .'

'Will he send Lord Dacre?'

'I promise you, Harry loves me. His wife will tell him; the Dowager Queen of France will speak for me. He will not forget a Tudor princess. He will act now I have escaped. He will come for me, or I will go to him.'

'I certainly hope so,' Archibald says unpleasantly. 'For if he does not rescue you, I don't know what we're going to do. Or where we will go next.'

'Next?' I ask. 'But I need to rest, Archibald. I need to be somewhere safe to have my child.' The excitement of the escape has worn off and I am anxious about my boys, left in Albany's keeping in Stirling. Someone will tell my son that his mother has run away and left him and his brother to their enemies.

'You can rest here,' he says begrudgingly. 'We will tell Lord Dacre that you have escaped, as he demanded. We are near to the border. He must come for you.'

We ride down a narrow track and cross a massive ditch, deep enough to lose a regiment of cavalry. They would go down and never ride up again. There is an open field and then the castle moat crossed by a wooden bridge to the gatehouse.

The guards recognise my husband and I have a flush of pride that the drawbridge falls down and the portcullis rattles up without a word being spoken. Ard rides into his own, like the lord that he is.

Inside the curtain walls it is a jumble like a poor village. The farmers and the peasants and serfs who live outside the castle have learned, in the way that these people always learn, that Archibald has ridden against the governor in the service of his wife, the queen regent. They may not understand what this means but they know that trouble is coming their way. Everyone who lives within a score of miles in any direction has piled inside the castle walls, and they have brought their livestock too. I see what Archibald means, that such a great castle cannot withstand a siege. The people will eat up everything in days.

'They shouldn't be here,' I say to Ard, quietly against his back. 'You'll have to send them away.'

'These are my people,' he says grandly. 'Of course they come to me when we are in danger. My danger is their danger. They want to share it.'

Ard jumps off the horse and turns to lift me down. I am cramped from sitting behind him for so long, and weary and hungry.

'The best rooms are not very comfortable,' he warns me. 'But your ladies shall take you up.'

I cannot think why he would bring me somewhere that is neither defensible nor comfortable, but I go up to my rooms without a word of complaint. He is right. Inside the cold walls it is damp and bleak. The fire lit in my bedchamber steadily emits smoke which finds its way out, upwards and through the arrow-slit windows, and when I go to look out towards the sea I shiver in the cold mist that slides in over the sill. Though I try to be glad that there will be no attacking my tower from the land, I cannot help but long for the luxury that I left behind in Linlithgow.

'Fetch a warming pan, I'll go to bed,' I decide. But then there is a long discussion about where the warming pan might be, and whether a brick would do as well, and that the sheets, which are rough and coarse, are not really damp. I am so tired that I lie on the bed and wrap myself in my travelling cloak while they puzzle how to make the room comfortable and what they have that is fit for me to eat.

All my royal furniture and linen is left behind in Linlithgow. It won't get here for days. I don't have more than one change of clothes. I understand that we could not travel with my wagons with all my treasures, but this is not good enough. I cannot be neglected. I doze for a little while but I wake when Ard comes quietly to my bedside.

'What now?'

He bites his lip, he looks intensely anxious. 'A message from Albany. He knows you're here. We'll have to go to the Humes' castle, Blackadder. It's properly garrisoned and guarded, and they have promised to defend you. They've got nothing left to lose – they're declared as traitors already. And they are well paid.'

'Paid?' I demand. 'Not by me!'

'Dacre,' he says shortly. 'He pays all the border lords.'

'But what for?' It is Dacre who has advised me into this danger. I have trusted him with everything.

'He pays the lords to keep the borders in continual uproar,' Archibald says, 'so that he can invade and claim to be keeping the peace. So that he can raid like a reiver himself, stir up trouble and steal cattle. So that he can have some lords obliged to England for money or support, and so that your brother can argue in the courts of Europe that the Scots are ungovernable. So we all look like lawless fools.'

'He is my brother's chief advisor!' I protest. 'He serves me. He is loyal to me, I know this. He advises me, he cares for my safety.'

'Doesn't stop him being an enemy to the Scots,' Archibald says stonily. 'Anyway, he has paid the Humes enough to keep them on your side. We can go there.'

'What about my goods and my gowns and my jewels? My wagons are all coming here?'

'They can be safely stored here till you send for them.'

'Can't we stay here and parley with Albany?' I ask weakly.

'He'll have my head,' Ard says grimly. 'I broke my parole for you, remember.'

I shudder. 'We'll go at once.'

We leave at first light and I climb wearily onto the horse behind him. The touch of his jacket against my cheek comforts me like an embrace. The scent of him, the glimpse of his profile when he looks back and smiles at me and says, 'Are you all right?' – all these things make me feel treasured and protected by him.

I push disloyal thoughts to the back of my mind. I will not think that we are going to William Hume because Ard does not know what else to do, and, even worse, that if Dacre has been paying the border lords to rebel, was he paying my husband, too? Was he paying the Douglases before I married Ard? Did I marry Dacre's spy?

There is no road, there is no lane. There is a track wide enough for a single man riding alone from village to village; but little more than that, and some of the way we ride across fields, the crop standing in stooks. We know the direction only by keeping the sea cliffs on our left and our faces to the south. The skies arch above us, it is enormous countryside, and when I look up I can see the fields rolling away to the distant horizon, to the distant hills. Archibald knows the land for miles all around his castle and after that we take up a lad from every village we pass to guide us to the next.

I go into a daze of tiredness and pain, and I fall asleep against my husband's back, clinging to him and moaning a little at a new ominous pain in my hip, like something grinding into the very bone.

I wake to see a horseman coming towards us, his mount muddied to the shoulders and sweat creaming his withers and neck. 'Who is it?' I demand fearfully.

'One of mine,' Archibald reassures me, and jumps down from the saddle and goes to talk with him.

When he comes back to me his young face is grim. 'We can't stay at Blackadder Castle,' he says flatly. 'Albany has raised a troop and is coming down the road from Edinburgh for you. We're going to have to head for the border.' He pauses. 'Dacre was right, we should have gone to England straight away. Albany has sworn he will recapture you and he is mustering an army.'

'An army?' I say, and my voice trembles. 'He is leading an army after me?'

'Forty thousand men,' Archibald says tightly. 'We can do nothing against such a force. Blackadder wouldn't hold, we're safe nowhere but over the border.'

'Forty thousand?' I repeat in a shriek. 'Forty thousand? Why would he send so many? Why would he come himself? If he just agreed to my demands I would return to my sons in peace!'

'We're past that,' Archibald says bluntly. 'That's what the forty thousand shows. It's war. It's not you and him trying to come to agreement – it's not a private quarrel – you have split the nation. The army of the governor will set siege to the Lord Chamberlain's castle if you are inside.' He turns to his horse and rests his head against its neck as if he would weep. 'It's the very thing that your husband prevented. It's the very thing he never wanted: Scotland divided on itself, a war of brother against brother; and I have helped to bring it about. I have led you into danger, I have left your sons in danger, and I have set the stage for a whole new battle.'

'It's not our fault,' I say stoutly. I snap my fingers for a groom to lift me down from the saddle, ignoring the shooting pain that goes from hip to toes, clinging to the footrest of the saddle with my hands so that my knees do not give way beneath me. 'If they had accepted my rule—'

'It is our fault,' he insists. 'If you had been more amenable to Albany when he came, or if you had been fairer to the Scots lords, if we had waited before marrying, if we had asked for their consent . . .'

'Why should I ask for consent?' I demand furiously. 'My sister, Mary, married who she pleased and my brother forgave her in a moment. Why should Mary marry the man she loves and you – my own husband! – tell me that I should be bound where she is free, that I should be less of a princess than her! That I should be a lonely widow but she can celebrate her second wedding the moment she steps out of her widow's confinement? How can you tell me that Mary can be happy and I cannot?'

'Nobody but you cares about Mary!' he shouts at me, before everyone. Everyone turns around to look at us. My ladies, white-faced, know that a Tudor princess, a queen regent, cannot be abused. But Archibald is furious. 'Not about Mary and not whether you get the things she has, not about Katherine. It's not about the rivalry of three foolish women! This is about Scotland – my God – it's about your late husband's wishes, about his wisdom. And I have not been guided by him, but by you, and by the enemies of Scotland. And we have all been advised by the man who took your husband's body off the battlefield as a trophy. Yes! It was Dacre who did that! No need to look as if you did not know! And now he tells me to bring you to England as if you were another royal corpse! And I know that you will never get back to Scotland if I do. You will never get back to Scotland. We will never bring the king's body home. Your son will never get to the throne. He is advising me to destroy the royal family and my country, and he is our only advisor!'

'And what is he paying you?' I spit. 'What are you getting? What is Alexander Hume getting? What is your brother George getting? What are the Douglases getting from Lord Dacre? What did he pay you to conspire against my husband the king?'

There is a terrible silence.

His face is white. 'You insult my honour,' he says, suddenly quiet, and I have a pang of fear. We have never quarrelled like this before. I have never seen him beside himself with anger, and then suddenly grow icy like this. We have quarrelled like lovers, hot words forgotten in hot kisses. But this is something new and terrible. 'I will take you to safety in England, and then I will leave you. If you think I am a traitor to you I can serve you no longer.'

'Archibald!'

He cannot choose to leave me. I am queen regent: he has to wait until he is dismissed. But he bows very low and he gestures to the groom to lift me back up on the horse. 'Mount up,' he says. 'We're going to Berwick.'

My face pressed to his unyielding back, I cry silently. I feel my big belly heaving with my sobs and I think this child is having the worst preparation for the world possible. Surely he will never survive this. Then I think that I will never survive this, and then I think I hope that I don't. Archibald can struggle with his honour and his conscience, and my brother can be merry with his wife and my sister, and everyone can forget that I ever lived and tried to do the right thing for my two countries and my two sons while they all squander a fortune and throw away political advantage to satisfy their own desires. I sniffle a little with jealousy and self-pity as it starts to rain, and I fall asleep, my cheek against my husband's back, my hood shrouding my face and my shoulders getting steadily more damp.

I wake when they stop to water the horses and for everyone to eat. The sky is a beautiful hazy dark blue; clouds like grey gauze laid over blue satin define the horizon. Archibald lifts me down from the horse and helps me to a seat on the ground where someone has spread a rug. My lady brings me wine, a little bread, some meat, my maid kneels before me to hold the cup. I do not dare to tell anyone how very ill I feel.

The countryside is wild and open – it is wasteland, nobody lives here, nobody farms, nobody even hunts here. These are the open lands of the border where it is too wild to live and unsafe for any house less than a fortified tower. I have a sense of huge over-arching skies and our little procession crawling like ants across a massive plain. At least nobody will find us, I think. There is so much wild land and so few roads, nobody will be able to guess where we are.

I eat some bread, I drink some wine and water. My ladies press me to have more but the pain in my belly is so intense that I think I will vomit if I eat more than a mouthful.

Archibald comes over while they are urging me to drink some small ale.

'We have to go on,' he says bluntly.

'My leg hurts,' I say. 'I don't think I can get back onto the saddle.'

'I am sorry, but you have no choice. We have to get to England. Albany will know that we are heading for Berwick. We've got about six miles still to go; we're halfway there. We have to get over the border. Lord Dacre says that we must make sure there is no shot exchanged between Albany and ourselves. King Henry's orders. A single shot would mean war between England and Scotland. And France would send an army to support Scotland. He says we must not be the cause of breaking the peace.'

'I don't care,' I say stubbornly. 'Let Albany come! Let us make a stand and start a war. It can serve Harry right for not coming earlier.'

'D'you know where you are?' Archibald asks me. His young voice is taunting, as if he were bullying another child in the schoolroom. 'Do you know where you are, when you talk about starting a war?'

I shake my head.

My lady-in-waiting bends down to whisper in my ear. 'We are on the route your husband the king took when he marched south to Flodden, Your Grace. My own husband died on the way, and is buried near here.'

Archibald sees my aghast face and laughs harshly. 'There will be no war for you,' he says. 'We would all be dead before Henry's army took one step out of London. The cannon would plough these fields again, before your brother even called his parliament. You forget what a great general your husband was – he said that his cannon would mean the end of the old warfare, the end of all chivalry, and he was right. We have to live in the world that he foresaw. Now get up. We have to go.'

I cry out and cling to Archibald when they lift me onto the pillion saddle behind him. I think that my hip must have broken, the pain is so intense. It is like a sword thrust every time I move, and I am jolted at every pace as the horse starts to plod south again.

'We're going to Berwick Castle.' Archibald tightens my hands around his waist and pats them gently, reassuringly. He is kind again, now that we are on the move. Resentfully, I think that he can be loving only when we are on the road. It is when we halt that he is so afraid that he hides it in anger. 'We're going to England and we'll be there in about two hours.'

'I can't ride for two hours,' I whisper. 'I can't.'

He puts his hand inside his jacket and hands me back a horn flask. 'Take a sip,' he says. 'Only a sip. It's *uisge beatha* – whisky.'

The smell is like a potion from James' old alchemist. 'Ugh,' I say.

He gives a little grunt of irritation. 'It'll ease the pain,' he says. 'And your temper,' he adds in an undertone.

I take a sip and it burns my throat, but then the burning spreads to my belly and all through my body. 'It helps,' I say.

'Be brave,' Archibald recommends. 'We're going to get to safety tonight. To England.'

## BERWICK CASTLE, ENGLAND, SEPTEMBER 1515

The town is closed; the curfew is dusk to dawn. Alexander Hume goes to the gate in the curtain wall and hammers on the door. There is a bell rope beside it and he pulls on it. A great bell tolls over our heads, and I can see lights coming on in the guardroom. A hatch in the great door opens, and a dark face peers out.

'Who goes there?'

'The Queen Regent of Scotland and the Earl of Angus, her husband, demand admittance,' Alexander bellows.

I sit a little straighter in the saddle, expecting the bolts to shoot back and the huge gate to open. This is a fortified town, an English town. I have come home, I have come to my own country. I remember Berwick: the town square, and the castle with its own portcullis and drawbridge. I remember the welcome they gave me when I rested here on my way to Scotland. I am thinking of dinner and the merciful release from pain when I can get into bed.

'Who?'

'The Queen Regent of Scotland and the Earl of Angus, her husband, demand admittance. Send for the governor to welcome them at once.'

There is a scuffling from behind the gate but still the bolts are not opened. Archibald glances over my shoulder. 'We couldn't send ahead,' he says.

Obviously, we should have done that to say that we were coming, and he did not think to do so, and now we have this cold welcome, and a delay until they open up, and I have longer to wait before I can be comfortable.

There are lights at the hatch and someone glares out at us and then at last the gate opens but it does not swing back to admit us. A man comes out with two guards on either side of him, a cape thrown over his nightgown. He stares at me for a moment and then he bows very low. 'Your Grace, forgive me.'

'Anything! If you will let me in and give me a bed for the night,' I say, trying to keep the fury out of my voice. 'I am very tired and I am with child and we have come all the way from Scotland. I expected a better welcome to my own country than this.'

He bows his head and then looks at Archibald. 'Do you have papers of safe conduct?' he asks.

Obviously, we don't. We don't have food or my jewels or my wardrobe or my shoes. We don't have my horses or my hawks or my furniture. We don't have my tapestries or my silver plate. We don't have my books or my musicians or my secretary. We don't have the late King James' lute. We don't have a safe conduct because we are seeking safety.

'This is the queen regent!' Archibald shouts. 'She doesn't need a safe conduct to get into her own brother's castle! You should be on your knees welcoming her in. She is carrying my child! She is the mother of the King of Scotland. Open the gates or by God I will—'

He breaks off. He does not say what he will do. Of course, this just reminds everyone that there is nothing he can do. We are a party of a dozen people and three of us are ladies and one of us is eight months pregnant. What are we going to do if the governor refuses us entry?

'Sir Anthony,' George Douglas says pleasantly, 'out of chivalry, out of loyalty, you must admit the king's sister in the middle of the night when she is flying from Scots traitors.'

'I can't,' he says miserably. He bows low to me. 'I am commanded, absolutely commanded by the king himself, to admit no-one from Scotland without a safe conduct from the king himself. Without a signed and sealed safe conduct, my gates must be kept closed.'

'To the king's sister?' I repeat.

He bows in silence and I think, this is what sisterhood with those two women has brought me: nothing.

'What are we to do?' Archibald goes from rage to helplessness. 'We have to get her somewhere safe. She is less than a month from her time. We have to get somewhere safe!'

'What about Coldstream Priory?' Sir Anthony says, eager to move us on. 'The abbess will admit her, and from there you can send for help from London.'

'She has to come in here!' Archibald rages again. 'I insist!'

'How far is it to Coldstream?' I ask shortly.

'Only about four hours,' the governor replies. 'Three,' he says when he sees my face.

George throws his reins to one of the servants and comes to Archibald and myself. 'He won't let us in; he can't,' he says. 'We waste time and we lose our dignity begging here. Coldstream is our best chance. We're in England now, we should be safe. Albany probably won't cross the border. Let's force this fool to give us food and we'll go down the road and get a bed for the night in an abbey or a house or somewhere, and go on to Coldstream in the morning.'

'I'm so tired,' I say quietly. 'I don't think I can.'

'We'll stop as soon as we can,' George promises me.

'I tell you, I can't,' I say, my voice catching on a sob.

'You've got to,' Archibald replies. 'You should not have left Linlithgow if you were not prepared to run to England.'

## COLDSTREAM PRIORY, ENGLAND, SEPTEMBER 1515

This time my husband thinks far enough ahead to send one of the servants to warn the priory that we are coming, and as we plod towards them the gates are flung open and I can see the nuns coming down the lane to greet me.

The prioress herself stands by my horse when Archibald lifts me down from the saddle, and she exclaims at my agony, at my huge belly, and summons three nuns forward to help me walk. My legs won't support me, there is something terribly wrong with my hip. They send for a chair and the lay sisters carry me into the abbey.

The guesthouse is large and comfortable and there is a big bed with good linen and curtains. My ladies strip off my filthy clothes and I get into bed in my dirty linen. 'Leave me,' I say. 'I have to sleep.'

They don't wake me until it is afternoon and then they bring me a bowl of gruel and tell me that dinner will be served whenever I wish it. I can come to the guest hall and dine with the prioress or I can have it in my rooms, just as I prefer. 'Where is Archibald?' I ask. 'Where is he dining?'

Ard is housed in the pilgrim-house, at a distance from the abbey buildings with his brother and the menservants, but he can visit me in the guesthouse if I wish.

'He must come at once,' I say. 'And I will take my dinner in the hall. Make sure that I have a suitable chair.'

'There's no cloth of estate,' my lady-in-waiting reminds me. 'And Alice has brushed your gown but it's not really clean. The prioress has loaned you some linen.'

This silences me. I am not myself unless I am seated beneath a cloth of estate, in beautiful clothes, dining like a queen. All my life I have been on the top table, beside the throne. What will I become, if I am as poor as Katherine once was?

'I'll eat here,' I say sulkily. 'And you will have to get me new clothes.'

I don't discuss with her how, in the middle of the borders, she is to get me new clothes, and she is too wise in the ways of royals to ask me how I think this will happen. She goes to order my dinner and to fetch Archibald and I think, just for a moment, how I made this journey twelve years ago, and came into Berwick and there was a loyal speech, thanking God that I, the senior Tudor princess, had honoured the little town with my presence.

Archibald comes in looking boyish and fresh. Breakfast and a wash have restored him to health and energy. He is not bowed down by pregnancy and crippled with pain. A young man can endure much and rise up full of life and joy; but a young woman – and I am still a young woman – has to struggle.

'My poor love,' he says as he kneels to me.

He has borrowed some clean linen and his hair, damp from a bath, is curly and glossy as a ram's fleece. He gleams with vitality.

'There is nowhere for me to dine,' I say miserably. 'And I have no clothes.'

'Couldn't you borrow a gown from the prioress?' he asks.

'She's a very cultured and thoughtful lady. She has beautiful linen, I am sure.'

'I cannot dress as a nun,' I say shortly. 'I cannot wear another woman's linen, however much she has impressed you. I have to dress as a queen.'

'Yes,' he says vaguely. 'Perhaps we can write to Albany and demand that he sends your clothes. Perhaps your wagons are already at Tantallon and they can send them on?'

'We can write to Albany? He can know where we are?'

'You're safe now, in England. You can start to negotiate, I suppose. Indeed, we will have to tell him what we expect.'

'I can?' I have a sudden gleam of hope. I had felt that we were running like criminals from an army of forty thousand Scots who were determined to capture Archibald and try him for treason, determined to imprison me so that I would die in captivity. But now we are safe, now I am home in England, everything is changed.

'I have saved you,' Archibald says. 'I did. It's quite incredible. It's like a romance, it's like a fairy tale. That journey! Good God, the ride that went on and on! And now we are here, and we have won.'

'Get me some paper and a pen from the lady abbess. I will write at once,' I declare.

I inform the duke, in the frostiest letter, that I am safe in England. I don't say where, for I am still frightened at the thought of his army. I say that I will return on a number of conditions. I don't stint myself: I want my lands back and my dower rents, the full restitution of my fortune, my jewels and especially my clothes. I want a pardon for Archibald and for everyone who has defended me, regardless of whether or not they are facing criminal charges. I want free access to my sons and the right to appoint their governors, tutors and household. I want, in fact, everything that I had that Albany took from me, but I don't object to him keeping the title of governor as long as he works alongside me (I mean beneath me) for the good of Scotland, as clearly the parliament intended that he should.

I rest. I eat well. I sleep at night without troubling dreams. The pain goes from my hip and I feel the baby squirm and turn so I know he is well and strong too. I talk at length with the prioress, Isabella Hoppringle, who is a thoughtful and astute lady of letters. She advises me to wait to hear from Lord Dacre what I should do next, and that I should put no trust in Albany. She tells me that Lord Dacre will save me. Airily I tell her that I am in control of my own life, winning the war of words with the duke. I show her the letters that pass and repass between us, when he offers me one thing and I demand another. I think that I am playing this hand well. The queen counts high in this game, and I am dealing the best cards to myself.

I am winning. By getting to safety I have restored my power, I am a force to be reckoned with. The Duke of Albany appoints the French ambassador to negotiate between us and he will come to me at Coldstream, carrying all the compliments and courtesies of the duke and of parliament. He will bring me proposals that have been forced through parliament by the duke, anxious that I shall return to my place. The last thing Albany wants is to drag France into war with England over Scotland. Indeed, he is specifically commanded by his king not to allow matters to worsen. He was to bring peace and order to Scotland and now everybody blames him for bringing anarchy and the risk of war. To turn a queen from her own castle is to threaten every monarch in Christendom. Nobody will support him. So I am to have my children at my side, I am to stay wherever I like, I am to have my fortune restored to me, my husband will be pardoned. The ambassador will arrive at midday, and his name on the agreement will make it binding on both sides. I am not winning; I have won.

I walk in the garden with Isabella, the prioress, and I say to her what a joy it will be to go back to Edinburgh and to see my boys again, and how I never thought that I would long to take my place as Queen Regent of Scots, but that now I do. I tell her that my sister, foolishly, without producing an heir for the throne of France, left her new home, married a commoner and returned to England, and now it will be as if she never went away. The French will forget her in a sennight. She will have to return her jewels. Of course, she may have the pleasures of the English court and the prestige of being the king's sister – these are trivial pleasures for a foolish girl – but a woman called by God to do her duty by her husband's country should stay there, serving the country and serving God, as I do. I declare that to be the mother of a king is the greatest calling that a woman could have. I have become as great as my lady grandmother, who bore a king and saw him to the throne. She had God's hand over her every action and so do I. I am closer to God than a prioress. I have a vocation and a duty. I am that great woman. I will serve Scotland and God.

It's very pleasant to stroll around the herb garden with the prioress, our skirts swishing against the end-of-summer lavender, releasing the sharp smell on the heady air. As we walk she picks a sprig of mint and sniffs it, I brush my hands over a bush of rosemary. There is rue growing, and the daisy flowers of camomile, the bright little faces of johnny jump-up and the scented leaves of lemon balm. 'I wonder that you trust him,' she says casually.

'What?'

'Albany,' she says. 'The Sieur d'Albany.' She says it like a French name, the very accent of deceit. 'He has tricked you and betrayed you every single time he has made an agreement with you from his first coming to Scotland. Surely he is false to you? He brought the cannon against you in Stirling; he shamed you before your son. He took the keys of the castle out of your little boy's hand. He separated you from your two boys. Would you really put yourself in his power again?'

'He's a duke,' I say. 'And a man of great courtesy. And now he acknowledges that I am queen. I have his word in writing.'

She makes a little face and shrugs her shoulders. 'He's a Frenchman,' she says dismissively. 'Or as good as. Married a

Frenchwoman for her money. Sworn to the French king. False as a Frenchman; and dishonest as a Scot. Between him and your parliament I fear they will destroy you.'

I am horrified. 'You surely cannot think that!'

'Ever since he came to Scotland he has been your undoing!' she exclaims. 'Why are you here if not driven into exile? Did you choose to leave Stirling? Was it your free choice to leave Edinburgh? Did you not run from Linlithgow in fear of your life? Did you not ride from Tantallon in only the clothes you stood up in?'

I think for a moment that she seems remarkably well informed for a prioress in a border abbey; but perhaps she has been talking to George.

'If I were you I would return to Edinburgh only at the head of an army,' she remarks. 'I would do as Lord Dacre advises, and go to his grand house at Morpeth, and muster your forces there.'

I laugh uncertainly. 'You make me sound like Katherine and her warlike mother.'

'I am sure you will prove as brave as she. I would have sworn that you were her equal.'

'Oh, I am, certainly I am. Katherine is no braver than I am. I know her, and I know this for a fact.'

'And I am sure that you have a husband as brave as Ferdinand of Spain.'

'Archibald is worth ten of him.'

'Then why should you not reconquer Scotland as Isabella and Ferdinand did Spain? And then you won't have to argue and bow down to the duke. You will just send him back to France.' She pauses. 'Or behead him, as you think fit. If you were ruling queen and not a mere regent, you could do whatever you pleased.'

There is a loud banging on the outer door. I look up in alarm. 'Could that be the French ambassador early? Isabella, you will have to show him into the guesthouse hall and make him wait while I dress. I have to sign the agreement with him.'

She waits as a nun from the gatehouse comes through the garden, bobs a curtsey to me and whispers. Isabella laughs and takes my hand. 'You are lucky,' she says. 'Great men and women are always lucky, and you have all the luck of a queen in the special keeping of God. That is Lord Dacre, at the door, a day ahead of the French liar, bringing you a safe conduct so that you can go anywhere in England. He can take you to London right now.'

I gasp, my hand closing on a leafy bush of rue so the sharp scent fills the air. 'To London?'

'Lord Dacre has come!' she says, as delighted as if it were her own triumph. 'And you are free!'

I can hardly believe that he has come, with a troop of horse, with a safe conduct, ready to escort me south at once. I kiss Isabella as if she were a sister, and we mount up gladly. I have a little stabbing pain as I sit in the saddle behind my husband, but I can see my future unrolling ahead of me. Isabella is right: I can persuade Harry to do his duty by me, I will return to Scotland at the head of an army and enter Edinburgh in triumph. I can bring up my boys to be the sons their father would have wanted, heirs to the throne of Scotland and even England.

I am in the saddle before I remember: 'Oh, but Lord Dacre, the Duke of Albany is sending the French ambassador with proposals. Shouldn't I wait for him and give him an answer? What if he is offering me the regency? What if he will give me everything I demand?'

'He can send it to you at Morpeth, my castle. He can meet with us at Morpeth,' the old guardian of the borders replies to me. 'Better that he discuss with you what terms he will offer when you are behind strong walls in an English castle that will never fall to siege, than when you are in one gown in a priory in the borders, surrounded by the dead of Flodden.'

'But if he is coming, with a capitulation?' I press my case.

'Would you want him to see you like this?' the old lord asks. 'So very travel-stained? So very shabby? And – forgive me, Your

Grace – but your belly is so big. Shouldn't you be in confinement? Do you really want to see the French ambassador in this condition? Don't you think he will tell everyone that you were near your time and riding pillion around the borders like a poor woman?'

I am mortified. If I had my linen from Edinburgh or my furniture from Linlithgow I could meet him, and dare him to glance at my swelling belly. But Lord Dacre is right: I can have no confidence in myself looking like this. When I am washed and dressed I will meet him. He can come to me when I am seated under a cloth of estate in a great castle. Right now, I am dressed as poor as Katherine of Arrogant when my lady grandmother was reducing her to nothing.

'God bless you!' Isabella calls. 'And bring you to your own again.'

We go out like English lords, not as we came in, like Scots criminals. Lord Dacre's standard goes before us, the royal standard of England before that, and my standards as Queen Regent of Scotland at the very head. He has had this all prepared; I think he may have been prepared for months. He knew that I would come to England before I did.

'I do think that we should have waited, out of courtesy to the French ambassador,' I say to his lordship, who reins in his horse so that he can fall back and talk to me, seated on my pillion saddle behind my husband. Lord Dacre hardly troubles to acknowledge Archibald, I could be riding behind my groom. In his turn, Archibald is sullen as a boy.

'Oh, why not set off for London, for a comfortable confinement and then Christmas there?' Dacre asks.

'Because I think the ambassador was authorised to offer me everything that I wanted,' I say. 'The letters from the duke made it clear that he had spoken to parliament and forced them to agree to all my demands.'

Dacre shakes his head. 'He's false,' he says simply. 'And he's weak. He is lying to you. He was not coming to meet with you, he was coming to delay you, and to keep you here, right on the borders, in a house that cannot be defended, while the duke gets his army on the road. They would have made you wait here, writing and talking to the French ambassador, while they marched through the borders and snatched you, and even your husband. Your Grace, they would have imprisoned you, perhaps in a nunnery, perhaps in a tower at Glamis, miles away where we could never have reached you. And you, my lord, alas, you would have been hanged like a common criminal on Coldstream priory gates.'

I can feel Archibald stiffen in the saddle. 'Good that we left then,' he says. 'I saved her from Linlithgow, I took her to Berwick and Coldstream, and now I have saved her from capture here.'

'You have indeed,' Dacre says, like a man praising a child. 'All of England will know what you have done for us.'

'At risk,' Archibald insists. 'At enormous risk, and no payment.'

'You will be rewarded,' Dacre says smoothly.

Archibald ducks his head. 'Everyone else is. How much does the prioress get?'

His lordship gives a little chuckle, but does not answer. 'And here, we have to part,' he says firmly. 'I have no safe conduct for you, my lord. I cannot take you into England or admit you to my castle at Morpeth. It was all done in such a rush that you, your noble brother, and the lords Hume, were not listed. I can take Her Grace, but that is all.'

'But Archibald has to come with me,' I say, hardly understanding what Lord Dacre is saying. One moment all of England is in Archibald's debt. The next moment he cannot enter the country. 'He is my husband. A safe conduct for me must mean a safe conduct for him.'

Dacre shouts to his troop, who halt as he pulls up his horse at the crossroads. 'We have to get you to my castle as soon as we can,' he says. 'You should be in confinement within the week. But you, my lord, must grant me your patience. I will send to

London for your safe conduct and that of your brother, and then you can join us at Morpeth. It's just a little delay.'

'I would rather come with you now,' Archibald says. He glances up the road that leads back to Scotland and I guess that he is imagining an army of forty thousand around the next bend.

'And so you shall,' Dacre assures him. 'But you would not want me to delay in getting Her Grace to safety? When you can so easily find a refuge, keep out of sight, live off your wits, till I send for you to escort Her Grace your wife to London. I know that the king is eager to greet you, his new brother-in-law. What a hero you will be if you get yourself out of Scotland, on your own skills, not riding on a pillion saddle with your wife.'

'Of course,' Archibald stammers. 'But I thought that I would come with you to Morpeth.'

'No safe conduct,' Lord Dacre repeats regretfully. 'Will you step down from the saddle, my lord? I have fresh horses for you and your brother, and a purse of gold in the saddlebag that I don't want any groom to get his hands on.'

Archibald pulls up our horse, and boyishly swings his leg over its neck, jumping down to the ground. He turns and takes my hands where I sit, sideways on the horse, without a rider before me, my face in a grimace of pain.

'Is it your wish?' he asks me urgently. 'Shall I leave you here now, in Lord Dacre's safekeeping, and come to you again at Morpeth Castle when I have my own safe conduct?'

I turn to Lord Dacre. 'Can't he come with us?' I ask.

'Alas, no,' he says.

So he leaves me. I have to be glad that he will find safety. Everyone knows where to find him if he is with me. I cannot bear to endanger him. But he, his brother George, and

Alexander Hume ride off at high speed on fresh horses, and I see them, bent over the horses' necks, racing each other, as if they were boys with nothing to worry about. I have a moment when I think that he is free now, a young man with everything to play for and danger to avoid, and he is free of me. He rides like a young man born to be in the saddle. He is a border lord. He was born to danger and chance and midnight raids. He is out of sight in a moment and I think perhaps I am out of mind before then.

I turn a cold, closed face towards Lord Dacre, who was supposed to be my saviour but who has brought me nothing but heartache. 'I am having birth pains,' I tell him. 'I'm going to have the baby. You have to find me somewhere to give birth.'

Even then there is no easy road to a comfortable refuge. We ride all day, and I cling to a stranger in the saddle before me, but nothing can ease the jolting of the horse as it goes on and onward. The country becomes steeper, the valleys are rich and green and cold under the shade of the thick forests, and I look around us and fear that there are Scots lords waiting for us in an ambush. The road winds through the trees and comes out of the woods into high moorland; as far as the eye can see there is nothing but an unending pelt of weeds and heather and shrubs and reeds. The track is hard to detect: it is almost nothing through the heather and the grasses. It twists and turns up and up and up, and then when we are at the peak there is nothing to see but more hills and more sky and the track looping its way down to the river valley again. The rivers are broad, winding through lush floodplains. If there were men and women to farm these valley floors they would be fertile; but I see no-one. Anyone who lives in these bare open lands has learned the trick of lying low like a leveret when someone passes by. Or else they scuttle away into the occasional stone towers that glower over the landscape. Nobody will greet anyone on the road. There are no travellers, and there is no road. I think that I have done little good for my kingdom since I have not made the peace run here. There is a warm sun; but I feel cold in my very belly.

On we go, and I beckon Lord Dacre to ride alongside me.

'How far?' I say through my teeth.

'Not long now.'

'An hour?'

'Maybe more.'

I take a breath. It might be half a day more. I have learned on this long ride that his lordship feels no obligation to accuracy.

'I tell you the truth, I cannot do it.'

'I know you are tired . . .'

'You know nothing. I am telling you. I cannot go on.'

'Your Grace, my house is at your command, it is comfortable and—'

'Do I have to write you a letter in code? I am going to have my baby. I cannot wait. I have to get into a house. My time has come.'

Of course, he reminds me that I am not due till next month, and I tell him that a woman knows, and that a woman with two strong sons and several losses certainly knows, and we pull up the horses and squabble away, standing on the road, till a cold east wind whips up some rain, and I say: 'Am I to have this baby in a ditch?' Only then does he give up the idea of Morpeth and says that we will turn aside off the road and go to his little castle of Harbottle.

'Is it near?' I demand.

'Quite near,' he says, and from that I know that I have hours of pain ahead of me.

I rest my head on the groom's broad back and I feel the

horse go down into the valleys and up into the hills, and from time to time I look to left and right and I see the trees and then the high lands. I see a buzzard circling over a wood. I see a fox slink into the bracken at the side of the track and his red back makes me think of Ard and I wonder where he is right now. Then we pass through a little village that is nothing more than a series of tumbledown shacks with children playing in the dust who run inside when they see us, and Lord Dacre says: 'Here we are.'

The track to the castle rises steeply from the village, and as we climb upwards the drawbridge bangs down, and the portcullis rattles up. The horse bows its head and climbs and climbs. The castle is on a little cliff above the village and around me are other empty peaks. We go through a stone gateway and we are inside the curtain wall, and then the groom jumps down from the horse and I let his lordship lift me down and I cling to him as my legs are weak beneath me and he leads me through the guardhouse and into the keep.

## HARBOTTLE CASTLE, ENGLAND, OCTOBER 1515

I rest, I sleep. I wake and I eat. The food is not good but at least there is a rope bed, not a heap of straw tied up in sacking; but there is no good linen and no bed curtains to keep out the draughts and only one small pillow. It is the bedroom of the commander of the castle and I must say that the posting will not make him soft. The mattress is stuffed with lumps of rock from the feel of it – no bird can have had feathers like this – and it has fleas or lice, or at any rate something that bites. I have red weals all over my skin. But at least I am off the horse, and after a few days the pains subside and I think perhaps my baby may not come too early, but at any rate if he comes now it will be under a roof like a Christian and not in a hedgerow like a beast.

I don't fret about Archibald, living wild in the debatable lands between Scotland and England, with no permit to enter one country, an outlaw in the other. I don't even think about my son James, with Davy Lyndsay at Stirling Castle, no doubt asking for me, learning that the path to the throne is lonely and hard. I don't think about his little brother, Alexander, my baby, my pet. I don't think about Katherine, pregnant once again, hoping for a boy for England. I don't think about Mary, pregnant too, according to Lord Dacre – though what does it matter really? At the very best all she can have is Charles Brandon's son, heir to his father's debt and his mother's folly. I am the only queen likely to have a living son and I should be exultant, but I am so tired that I think that we are truly sisters at last, sisters in suffering and sisters in disappointment.

My pains come to nothing, I fall into a dull passivity, like a cow with a stuck calf inside her. There is nothing I can do to bring it on, and nothing I can do to hold it safe. I am afraid that the constant riding of the last few days has shaken him loose. I am afraid that he will die inside me, and then they will have to cut me open and I will certainly die too. I think this is my Flodden, this is my battle against an enemy and I am almost certain to lose. I have to be desperately courageous and know that my duty has brought me here, and anyway, there is no way to escape.

When I try to get out of bed – for I need to urinate all the time, and they have no garderobe here but just a bucket under the bed – I realise that I have become paralysed. These are not labour pains, they are some deep disease of the bones. I need a physician, not a wise woman. I tell Lord Dacre that I must see the French ambassador now, that I have no choice: I must make peace with the Duke of Albany because I am likely to die. He has to send me physicians from Edinburgh. 'Send for the French ambassador,' I say. 'He can follow us here. You can give him safe conduct.'

'I don't know where he is. He may still be at Berwick.'

'He was at Berwick?'

He realises that he has let this slip.

'He came to Berwick?'

'If you remember, we had to leave. What if his men had arrested your husband? You wouldn't want to risk the earl's arrest?'

Of course, Ard's safety comes before everything, but if I had only seen the French ambassador, and he had been able to make an agreement with me, then I might not have been forced here, to this miserable fort, to suffer this pain without a physician or a wise woman or a herbalist I can trust.

'Send for him!' I command. 'If he and I can make an agreement he can send me physicians from Edinburgh.'

'Not yet, Your Grace,' he replies carefully. 'We don't want to jeopardise your husband's courage, his great endeavour.'

'Why, what is he doing?' I ask. 'I thought he was hiding out till he can join us?'

Lord Dacre smiles, his old eyes twinkling. 'I think you will find that a brave young lord like him can do better than that!'

'He is rescuing my sons,' I say, without a moment's doubt, and the lord gives me a broad wink.

'He is, God speed him,' he says. 'How will it be when you are both safe behind the walls of Morpeth Castle and your sons with you?'

'He will bring them to England?'

'There is nowhere else for them. You will all be together again.'

I don't answer. He is right. Every step that I have taken, every choice that I have made, seems to lead me onward to places where I don't want to be, to more choices that I don't want to make.

'I'll see,' I say. I think of my lady grandmother, who never told anyone what she was thinking nor what she might do. 'I will decide when I have given birth to my child.'

'I have sent for physicians from Berwick,' he says. 'If we could only get to Morpeth I could house you more comfortably. My wife is there, and her ladies. They would care for you and you would have rooms to your liking.'

'I know,' I say. 'But it can't be done. I can't even walk, I couldn't ride.' A sudden pain like a sword thrust to the belly makes me hold myself and gasp.

Dacre gets to his feet. 'Is it now?'

I nod. 'It's now. I think it is really coming now.'

It takes days for the baby to come. Two days and three long nights of pain and drink and sleep and waking again to pain, hobbling up and down the room and groaning on the bed, before they give me a squalling bundle in a wrapping of linen cloths and say: 'A girl. A girl, Your Grace.'

I am so exhausted that I don't even care that it is not a boy. I am so glad that it is over and that I have a live child for all my labours that I lift my tearstained face to look at her and see a perfect little tiny baby, as neat and as complete as the bud of a rose, as sweet as a subtlety, an angel made of marchpane. I can't speak for pain and exhaustion. I think, if I die from giving birth to her, at least I have seen her, and Archibald will have a child from me.

'What will you call her?' someone asks.

'Margaret,' I say. 'Margaret Douglas. A little Scots lady, even if her mother is dead.'

I really think that I will die. My pains go on even though the baby is born, the bleeding goes on, and nothing the midwives can do will stop it. They are frightened. They are poor, ignorant women who have made a little money from attending the births of their neighbours; usually they are paid in eggs. They have never been in the castle before, they have never swaddled a baby in good linen. They do all that they can, but nobody can help me as I slide into a fever and don't know where I am, and I call for James, my husband

James, not to go to the battle and not to give me pearls for mourning. I dream that he is nearby, and that Katherine has the wrong corpse. I dream that he is living wild like an animal in these wild lands and that he will come to me at the moment of my death.

I have long painful days, half-drunk on rough ale mixed with *uisge beatha*. I drift in and out of consciousness, and see daylight and then the flickering lights of wax candles, and then the cold light of dawn. I hear, as if from far away, a thin cry and the sound of someone walking up and down and hushing a wailing child.

A girl is not much use to me. Archibald will not come out of hiding to see a girl. The Douglases don't need a girl, they need the next head of the clan. But I am glad that she is alive. I was afraid that riding when I was so near to my time had killed her. And I am glad I am alive, though I still cannot sit or stand without pain, and my leg seems to be in a palsy.

I raise my head. 'Write to my brother,' I say. 'Tell him that I have another healthy child and that I am hoping he will be her godfather. Tell him that she needs an uncle to defend her.'

I lie back and drift away as I watch them swaddle her and bind her to the board. They have not been able to find a wet nurse, and they can't even ride out to the distant villages, the roads are so dangerous with reivers and brigands and armed men. They are feeding her with sops – bread dipped in watered milk squeezed into her mouth. 'Oh, I'll feed her,' I say irritably, and then I whimper with a new pain as I put her to my breast.

She feeds a little and then they take her away and say that I can rest at last. I lie on the thin pillow, it is damp with my sweat, but there is no change of linen for the bed. They bind my bleeding parts with moss and then at last they sit quietly and I hear the rocker tap her foot up and down on the pedal of the cradle and all the other noises die away as the rest of them go to eat or to sleep.

The candlelight flickers and gutters, the fire dies down in the grate. I cannot believe that I, a Tudor princess, should be trapped here, in little more than a border tower, watching the shadows jump on the mudplaster ceiling and hearing the rats scratching on the floor. I close my eyes. I cannot understand how I can have been born so high and fallen so low. There is a cold draught through the shutters that makes the candle flames flare up and die down. There is no glass in the windows to keep out the cold. I can hear the night-time noises of these hills, the persistent hooting of an owl, the sharp bark of a dog fox, and somewhere, miles away, the howl of a wolf.

## HARBOTTLE CASTLE, ENGLAND, NOVEMBER 1515

A month later and my baby is thriving. We have found her a wet nurse and my birth pains have ceased. Lord Dacre comes to the door of the castle commander's bedroom and asks if he may be admitted. Nothing is as it should be. I was churched in my bed, the baby christened in the tiny chapel. Her godfather named as Thomas Wolsey in his absence, with no time for his consent. We are like reivers ourselves, camped on the wild lands of the border. I say that he can come in. There is no point in trying to live to the standards of my lady grandmother's book of the household when we are little better than outlaws.

He takes in my pale face, the poverty of the furnishings. 'Your Grace, I was hoping that you might be well enough to make the journey to Morpeth Castle where my wife can care for you.'

I shake my head. 'I don't think I can go. There is something wrong with my bones. I am recovered from the birth but I am strangely lame. I cannot walk. I cannot even sit up. The Berwick physicians have never seen anything like it.'

'We could take you in slow stages.'

'I can't do it,' I repeat.

One of the ladies who has been found to serve me steps forward and curtseys to the English lord. 'She can't get out of her bed,' she says bluntly. 'Her pain is quite terrible.'

He looks at me. 'It is so bad?'

'It is.'

He hesitates. 'Your brother has sent you wagonloads of goods for your comfort at Morpeth Castle,' he remarks. 'And Queen Katherine has sent you some beautiful gowns.'

I feel desire clutch me like hunger. 'Katherine has sent me gowns?'

'And yards of rich cloth, yards and yards of it.'

'I must see them. Can you bring them here?'

'I would be robbed on the road,' he says. 'But I can take you to them. If you could find the courage, Your Grace.'

The thought of Morpeth and wagonloads of goods, clean linen and decent wine, and my gowns – new gowns – gives me courage.

'I have commanded physicians to come to Morpeth and see you there,' he says. 'Your brother is determined that you shall be well again. And then you can go to London in the New Year.'

'London,' I repeat wistfully.

'Yes indeed,' he says. 'And half of Europe is up in arms at the way that you have been treated. People are calling for war on France, and war on the duke. You are their heroine. If only you were able to rise up you could claim your throne.'

'How ever can I get to Morpeth?'

'My men can carry your bed.'

My lady-in-waiting billows forward. 'Her Grace cannot be carried in her bed by common soldiers.'

Lord Dacre turns his weather-beaten hard face to me. 'What d'you think? It's that, or hold your Christmas feast garrisoned here, and we could be attacked at any time.'

'I'll do it,' I say. 'How many gowns has she sent?'

They tie me into the bed for fear of an accident, and I grip the rope as they manhandle it down the three steps from the chamber to the great hall below. I hide my face in the pillow to silence my moans; at every jolt I feel as if I have been stabbed with a burning poker in my hip. I have never known such agony, I am certain that my back is broken.

Once in the great hall the men gather around my bed and run long poles underneath it as they might carry a coffin. There are six on each side and they go carefully, in step, out of the hall, across the drawbridge and down the long winding ride that leads up the steep slopes of the castle. Before us go the guards, Dacre riding among them, my baby held in the arms of my maid-in-waiting, riding pillion.

The ragged inhabitants, and the poor people who live in shanties against the castle walls hoping for some protection from the weather and the reivers, stand amazed as I go by, swaying like some icon being paraded on a feast day around the borders of a parish. I would feel foolish if I were not completely absorbed by the pain. I lie back on my pillow, and I see the snow clouds thickening in the skies above me and I draw on every scrap of Tudor courage that I have, and pray that this nightmare journey of swaying, jolting steps does not outlast me, and that I don't break down before we have reached the end of it.

## CARTINGTON CASTLE, ENGLAND, NOVEMBER 1515

It is hours before we arrive at another poor fort, perched on a hill overlooking a burn with a jumble of rough shacks against the walls and a stone-walled keep inside. They carry my bed into the great hall and set it down there. The men are exhausted and cannot face heaving the bed up the narrow stairs, while I can't bear to go further.

Here we rest for five days. I am in a daze of pain; every time I shift in the bed I can feel my bones grinding and I scream with the agony. When they lift me for the pot they have to give me a gulp of spirits before I can bear to be moved. I eat lying down and they spoon broth into my mouth.

On the morning of the fifth day I know that we have to go on.

'Not far,' Lord Dacre says comfortably.

'How long?' I ask. I wish that I did not sound fearful, but I know that I do.

'About three hours,' he says. 'And they'll carry you better now that they have learned to match their pace.'

I grit my teeth so as not to complain but I know that they will jolt me every step of the five miles. We leave the castle without regret but they stumble a little on the potholes and slip in the ruts of the road and I cannot muffle my cry.

'Not far,' Thomas Dacre says staunchly.

## BRINKBURN PRIORY, ENGLAND, NOVEMBER 1515

The priory is a poor, small little place with half a dozen monks who are supposed to be Augustinians but keep up a half-hearted practice. They have a stone wall around their buildings and a great bell to sound the alarm, but they are rarely robbed as the local people know that there is not much here to take, and, besides, it is helpful to them all if the monks are there, feeding the poor, housing travellers, and nursing the sick.

They are flustered by my arrival and the prior suggests that my bed be put in the hall of the little guesthouse. They can barely get it through the door and, when it is in, it completely fills the space of the cell-like chamber. But the floor is swept and clean, and when they bring me something to eat it is well-stewed mutton and I am glad of it. They serve a thin red wine and the prior himself comes to bless the food and pray for my recovery. I see from his anxious face that I look desperately sick and when he says that they will pray for my health and for the life of my baby I whisper: 'Please do.'

I rest for another two days and then Dacre's men take up the poles again, and, with my bed swaying and jolting between them, we set off again. This is the longest journey that we have made; it will take all day, from dawn to dusk, before we get to Morpeth. At midday, Dacre orders a halt and the soldiers make a circle around us, with their halberds facing outward, while I and my ladies eat some bread and drink some ale, and then the men stand and eat, watching the road behind us and the way that we have to go, always ready for a raid, fearful of any passing band of brigands. Lord Dacre's face is set in a grimace of constant resentment.

I think of Archibald telling me that Lord Dacre has paid brigands to ride this border and make it unsafe, stir it up so that it is impossible for a Scots king to govern. I wonder how he is feeling now, unsafe in a desert of his own making, knowing that the men he has paid to be lawless may turn on him.

The sun is setting when I see the massive gatehouse of Morpeth Castle and Lord Dacre reins back his horse and says: 'Here, Your Grace. You will be safe here.'

I cry with relief as we go under the huge gateway. It is a triumph to get here, I am safe at last. But I tell no-one, as they hurry to greet me, that I wish with all my heart this was Windsor Castle and not Morpeth, and that the gate was opening and my two sisters were coming out to welcome me.

## MORPETH CASTLE, ENGLAND, CHRISTMAS 1515

There are gifts waiting for me at Morpeth, as Thomas Dacre promised. Lady Dacre has had them spread out in the great hall so that I can see everything Harry and Katherine have given me; so that everyone can see how my brother treasures me. There are gowns of gold cloth, and gowns of tinsel, there are sleeves of ermine and great bolts of red and purple velvet for me to have made up as I wish. There are headdresses in beaten gold as befits a queen of my importance, there are cloaks, and satin shoes with gold heels. There are heaps of embroidered linen and capes lined with fur. There are bonnets of velvet with brooches of gold. There are perfumed leather gloves and patterned stockings. Finally, there are the jewels of my inheritance, my lady grandmother's garnets, her crucifix with pearls, my mother's diamond necklace and a gold chain. There is everything that a queen should have, and Katherine has chosen it and sent it all to me, to show my brother's gratitude for my courage in the service of England.

There are letters waiting for me with the gifts. These bring me no joy. Katherine is in her most triumphant mood; I feel that she is taunting me with my losses as she celebrates. She is carrying her child so high, she is certain it is a boy. This baby is stronger, she is sure.

*We were all so grieved when we heard that you have had to flee your country.*

I grit my teeth at this, since if Harry had supported me, if Katherine had told him to save me, I would have kept my throne.

*And so shocked that you left your sons behind.*

What does she think I could do? Does she forget that they are fatherless and by her order?

I don't look far for the reason that she did not insist I was rescued. Why would she save my son and heir, when she is hoping to have one of her own? Her anxiety for me must be a lie. It is to Katherine's advantage if I am in danger and my sons imprisoned. I know this; her loving words don't convince me otherwise.

*And, my dear, you must be so lonely and afraid without your husband.*

This from the woman who ordered my widowhood! I could laugh if I were not so bitter.

*I hope you enjoy your gifts – we so want you to have a merry Christmas after the year that you have endured, and come to us as soon as you can.*

I make sure that my contempt does not show on my face. Katherine, from her big-bellied greatness, endows me with her sympathy. Yes, she is riding high now, and I am brought as low as can be. I cannot even stand without crutches. But I will recover and, no matter how she is feeling now, there is no certainty in childbirth, she cannot be sure of having a healthy son. She need not crow over me. I may yet win back my kingdom and I still have two royal boys in the nursery and all she has is an empty cradle. She can send me gowns, she can send me furs, she can send me – finally! – my inheritance, but these are all nothing but my due. I am still a queen and a regent, and I am My Lady the King's Mother.

My sister Mary writes too. She has convinced herself that the baby she is carrying will be a boy. But really, who cares about the baby who will be the heir of the Duke of Suffolk? Mary is inferior to me, her children come after mine, and I have two strong handsome boys: she will never get her son on the throne of England.

Mary's letter is filled with news of the court and their autumn doings. Henry has built and equipped a great ship, the greatest galley in Europe, and everyone calls her the *Princess Mary* in a ridiculous compliment to my little sister. Mary writes that they all had the greatest of fun, that Harry took her on board, that he was dressed in a sailor suit of cloth of gold, that he took the wheel and Mary called time for the rowers and banged on the drum like the hortator, that they went faster than the wind, faster than a sailing ship could travel. There are pages and pages of this boasting and a few more pages as to how blessed she is with a loyal husband, which I take as a taunt for having to part from Ard, and how happy they are preparing their country house together, which I understand is her telling me that she knows I could not stay at Tantallon. I hand the whole bundle of letters to the groom of the chamber who is throwing logs on the fire. 'Burn this,' I say.

He takes it as if it might scorch him. 'Is it secrets?' he asks, awed.

'Sinful vanity,' I say, as irritable as my lady grandmother would have been.

I lie in the great bedchamber, the best room of the house. Lord Dacre and his wife, Elizabeth, have hastily vacated it for me and there are royal hangings on the wall from London, and a cloth of estate over the chair by the fireside. Massive stone carvings, showing the arms of the Greystokes, which Lord Dacre gained from his heiress wife, boast of their importance. But they have to sleep in a lesser chamber while I am here.

They put on a great Christmas feast in the massive old hall in my honour. There has never been a queen in residence at Christmas before, and the steward and the servants and the master of horse have excelled themselves in preparing the castle for the season. Dacre has appointed a witty actor to be master of the feast and every day there is a concert of music, or singing, dancing, a play or an entertainment, a hunt, a race, a challenge. The bleak countryside all around has been stripped of food and provisions so that the castle may feast. Even the woods have their greenery hacked down and carried in so that there are boughs over every door, a Yule log in every fireplace, and the sweet smell of evergreen hanging in the air. The castle is bright in the deep darkness of the North of England, burning like a brand in the night of the North. Travellers from miles away can see the lighted windows as priceless candles are set in every sconce and every fireplace is hot.

Half the nobility of Scotland and all of the North of England come to pay their respects to me and to celebrate the season which is such a promising one for them. They are all determined that England shall make war on the Duke of Albany's Scotland. They all hope to gain Scottish lands, to steal Scottish goods. The simmering unrest that Thomas Dacre has kept stoked through two reigns is coming to the boil as he declares to every visitor that the King of England will not tolerate such an insult to his sister, that he is certain to invade, that my suffering makes his cause just and (though he never says this) Dacre himself can find his greatest happiness in going to war again.

I cannot receive anyone, though the Dacres make over their great presence chamber to me, and Lord Dacre says that he himself will carry me in his chair. He says he will pad it with cushions and hang the cloth of estate over it and it will be my throne. But I cannot bear even to be lifted from the bed; my leg is swollen so that it is nearly as big as my body. I see only those people whom I admit to my bedchamber, but I can't leave my bed for them. I have become a cripple, as weak as one of the beggars at the mercat cross who has to be pushed around on a little cart and carried to the steps in the morning.

So Lady Bothwell and Lady Musgrove make their visit to my bedroom to sit with me, and Lady Dacre comes to my chamber a dozen times a day to see if I need anything. I receive Lord Hume, who has been loyal to my cause though it has cost him his lands and his safety, and together we discuss how I shall return and how I shall get my sons back. He looks a little askance as if there is something wrong when I speak of them.

'My boys must live with me,' I say. 'I don't intend to put them into the keeping of my brother or his wife. They shall come to me.'

'Of course, of course,' he says with the sudden anxious soothing of a married man who knows that a woman should not be crossed when she is in pain. 'We will talk about it more when you are better. And besides, I have some news for you that will be the best physic in the world.'

I can hear the tramp of booted feet along the gallery outside my chamber. 'I cannot have visitors,' I start.

'You will welcome this one,' he says confidently, and he throws open the door to my bedchamber and the guard outside steps back . . . and Archibald, my husband, comes in.

I bounce up in bed and I cry out in pain at the same moment as he flings himself across the room. 'My love, my love,' he whispers into my hair. He kisses my face, he embraces me tightly, and then gently holds me away from him so that he can see the tears streaming from my eyes as I say, 'Archibald, oh, Ard! I never thought that I would see you again. And our little girl! You must see her.'

Lady Bothwell has already sent someone running to the nursery and now the chief nurse comes with little Margaret in her arms. Ard holds her at arm's length, looks into her sleeping face, shakes his head in awe at her. 'She is so small!' he marvels. 'She is so perfect.'

'I thought we would lose her, and that I would die!'

Carefully, he restores her to her nurse and turns back to me. 'It must have been terrible for you. So many times I have wished that I was with you.'

'I knew you couldn't be. You couldn't risk being in England without a safe conduct!' At once the thought strikes me. 'Ard, my love, are you safe now?'

'Your brother the king has sent a safe conduct for me and for Lord Hume, and for my brother. We are all to go to London in honour, as soon as you are well enough to travel.'

'I will be well soon,' I promise him. 'The pain has been terrible. Not even Lord Dacre's best physician from Newcastle knows what is wrong with my leg. But resting in bed is easing the pain, and I am sure the swelling is going down. I will be well enough to go to London, I swear I will, if you can come with me.'

They dine on cygnet and heron, venison and wild boar. They bring the best dishes to my room and Ard sits with me and feeds me from his own spoon. He keeps me company through the twelve days of Christmas and through the cold days, and together we listen to the merriment from the hall, he on a humble stool at my side, for I cannot bear anyone sitting on the bed and making the feather mattress dip. I lie propped low on only one beautifully embroidered pillow, so that my legs and back are still.

'I am no wife to you,' I say fretfully. I cannot hold him, I cannot lie with him, I cannot even stand beside him. In a few months I have become an old lady and he is far stronger and more handsome than when he was the young man appointed to be my carver. He has been hardened and toughened by his winter on the run; he has had to command men, face danger, defy the Regent of Scotland. He is more lithe than ever, quick on his feet, alert to any danger. And I am tired and in pain, fat from pregnancy, unable even to move from my bed without crying out.

'It was being my wife that has brought you to this,' he says. 'If you had stayed a widow queen, you would still be in Stirling Castle.'

He is speaking soothingly, almost by rote, but suddenly the enormity of what he has said makes him fall silent and look at me. He swallows, as if he has never before felt the despair of these words on his tongue. 'I have been your ruin.'

Bleakly, I look back at him. 'And I yours.'

It is true. He has lost his castle Tantallon, his beautiful family home, which stood so proudly, so inviolate on the cliff. He has lost his land, and all the people who were his men and had belonged to his clan for generations have lost their leader and the head of their house. He is a named outlaw, he owns nothing but what he stands up in, he is a landless man, a man without followers: in Scotland that is as good as being a beggar. He is completely identified with the English cause: in Scotland that is as good as being a named traitor; and he is a named traitor.

'I have no regrets,' he says. He is lying. He must have, he does have. So do I.

'If Harry sends his army . . .'

He nods. Of course. Of course, it is what we always say to each other. If Harry sent his army then the world could change again in a moment. We must become warmongers like Thomas Dacre, wishing a merciless invasion on Scotland. We must argue for revenge, we must demand a fleet. If my brother will be a brother to me, if Katherine will advise him as a sister should do, then I will be queen regent again. It all depends on Harry. It all depends on my sister-in-law his wife.

'There is something I have to tell you,' Ard says, picking his words with care. 'They did not tell you before, because they feared for your health.'

I feel my belly plummet as if I am falling. I am wildly, suddenly afraid. 'What is it? Tell me quickly. Is it Mary, my little sister? She's not dead in childbirth? God forbid it. It's not her?'

He shakes his head.

'Katherine has lost her baby,' I say with certainty.

'No, it is your son.'

I knew it. I knew as soon as I saw the gravity on his face. 'Is he dead?'

He nods.

I put my hand over my face as if to blot out his sympathy. Beneath my fingers my tears run sideways from my eyes and into my ears. I cannot raise my head to mop my face dry. I cannot cry out at this new pain, having screamed so much at the pain in my joints. 'God take him to His own,' I whisper. 'God bless and keep him.'

I think, naturally enough, even in the first shock, that at least I had two princes. If one is gone there is still a son and heir. I still have another. I still have an heir for Scotland, an heir for England. I am still the only one of the three queens to have a son. Even if one is dead, even if I have lost my boy, my heir, I still have my especial treasure; I still have my baby.

'Don't you want to know which one is dead?' Archibald asks awkwardly.

I had assumed it was the king. That would be the worst thing. If the crowned king is dead then what is there to prevent a usurpation but one little baby alone? 'Is it not James?'

'No. It was Alexander.'

'Oh God, no!' Now I wail. Alexander is my darling, my pretty boy, my baby boy. This is the baby that James left me with. Not even the new baby, Margaret, has replaced him in my heart. 'It can't be Alexander! He is so bonny and strong.'

Archibald nods, his face pale. 'I am so sorry.'

'How did he die?'

Ard shrugs. He is a young man. He does not know how babies die. 'He was sick, and then he weakened. My dear, I am so sorry.'

'I should have been there!'

'I know. You should have been. But he had good nursing, and he did not suffer . . .'

'My boy! Alexander! My little boy. This is the third boy that I have lost. My third boy!'

'I'll leave you to the care of your ladies,' Archibald says

formally. He does not know what to say or what to do. He is always having to comfort me. Nothing has ever gone right for us. Now he is bound to a crippled woman screaming for the loss of her son. He gets to his feet, bows to me, and goes from the room.

'My baby, my little boy!'

I swear that the Duke of Albany shall pay for this. However Alexander died, it is the duke who is to blame for it. I should never have been forced away from the boys at Stirling Castle. I should never have been separated from him. My own sister, Mary, a royal widow just like me, married a man in secret, and was allowed to leave her country with full honour. Why should I be an exile and my husband with a price on his head, and my son dead? Always, always, I am not granted my due as the senior Tudor princess. Thomas Lord Dacre agrees completely with me and together we compile eight pages of charges against the duke to send to London. Dacre adds every instance when the Scots have been allowed to invade English Northern lands, everything they have stolen, every cottage they have burned, every traveller they have robbed. We will destroy the duke; we will persuade Harry to invade. If it causes war with France it is a small price to pay for the revenge that a queen should exact for the death of her son.

The false duke writes to me, sympathises with my loss, congratulates me on the birth of my daughter and says that he hopes we can come to an agreement. He is sending an emissary to Harry. He hopes we can come to peace.

'Never,' I say flatly to Dacre. 'I shall tell him what he has to do before I will consider a peace treaty. He is to release Gavin Douglas, he is to forgive Lord Drummond, he is to lift the outlawry from my husband, he is to send me my jewels and he is to restore my husband's lands and wealth to him.'

'He can't do all that,' Dacre says, looking worried.

'He has to,' I say. 'I will write to him myself.'

The old border lord looks cautious. 'Better not to negotiate with him while he is sending a man to your brother. Better let the two men agree together.'

'Not at all,' I say fiercely. 'I am queen regent, not anyone else. I shall tell him my demands, and he will meet them.'

I write also to my sister the Queen of England, Katherine, who seems to have held this child in her belly for all this long time, and tell her that I am praying for her as she nears her time, and ask her to write to me at once, as soon as her baby is born, a little cousin to my Margaret. I think of my two sisters, nearing their time, lapped in luxury, advised by physicians, with gold cradles ready for their babies, and I think that it is the unfairness that hurts me the most. They have no idea of the pain that I suffered; they will suffer nothing like it. They have no idea of the danger I was in. They are sisters together; I am like a changeling, forever excluded.

Albany writes to me promising peace, promising agreement, but at the same time his emissaries write to my brother. Perhaps he is trying for a peace, trying to speak to Harry and agree with me, but I would rather that he deal with me direct. I cannot allow Harry to agree with Albany keeping charge of my son the king. I cannot impress on Harry the importance of my jewels. Everyone thinks that I am thinking of trivial things, women's things. But I know that Albany treats me with contempt, treats my allies with contempt. Nobody but me seems to understand that the men who fought for me have to be rescued from Albany's imprisonment. Gavin Douglas is still imprisoned. He must be released and given the see that I said he should have. These are not things that can be lightly traded; they are, like my jewels, my possessions. Anyone who takes them from me is a thief.

Sometimes I think that I should creep back into Stirling Castle and raise a siege again, just so that I can be with my boy. Sometimes I think that I should go to Edinburgh and negotiate with the duke in person. But then Dacre comes to my chamber with letters from London when I am seated before the fire.

'Give them to me!' I say delightedly.

'There is one here from the queen,' he says, indicating her royal crest.

I show an excited and happy face, and put out my hand, eagerly breaking the seal to read. I make sure that I give Dacre not a clue that I am filled with dread, certain that she has given birth to a healthy boy at last, after so many attempts. If she has got a boy then my son has lost his inheritance of the English throne, and there is no reason for Harry to rescue him. I put my hand over my eyes as if to shield my face from the heat of the fire. That would be the worst loss of this year of losses.

And then I see that Katherine has not done her duty. God has not blessed her. Thank God, she has failed again, and her heart will be breaking. Tucked down at the bottom of the page, almost scribbled out by her signature, is the news that makes me smile.

'She's had a girl,' I say flatly.

'God forgive her. What a pity,' Dacre says, heartfelt, as every Englishman will say. 'God save her. What a disappointment.'

I think, I have given birth to four royal sons and I still have one left. And all Katherine has is a girl. 'She is going to call her Mary. Princess Mary.'

'After her aunt, the dowager queen?' Dacre asks cheerfully.

'I doubt that,' I snap. 'Not since she came home in disgrace married without permission. It will be Mary for Our Lady, as Katherine will want the Queen of Heaven's protection on this little child, after all her previous sorrows. We must pray that the little one lives; none of the others have.'

'I hear they are very close, Princess Mary and the queen,' Dacre perseveres.

'Not particularly,' I say. 'Duchess of Suffolk, she is now.'

'And here is a letter from your brother's steward,' Dacre says. 'And he has written to me.'

'You may read yours here,' I say, and we break the seals and read together.

It is the letter we have both been waiting for. Harry's master of horse writes to say that he has commissioned a special litter to come for me from London with a guard of honour, extra horses, wagons for my goods, and soldiers to keep me safe through the wild Northern lands. Harry himself has scrawled a note at the side of the careful script to say that I must come at once.

'What about Archibald?' I demand, smiling at my husband as he comes into my room.

He stands behind my chair and I feel his hand rest gently on my shoulder. I straighten up in pride and ignore the twinge in my hip bone. I know we are a handsome young couple. I see Dacre take in Archibald's strength and my determination.

Dacre smiles. 'I am pleased to be able to tell you that your brother the king has sent a safe conduct for His Grace, your husband. You are to go to London together and the two of you will live there as queen regent and consort. He will be accorded all appropriate honours and you will take precedence before everyone but the queen. You will go before your sister the Dowager Queen Mary and her husband.'

'You shall see what I have tried to describe to you,' I promise Ard. 'You shall see me at my home, in the castles that were my childhood homes. I shall present you to my brother, the king. We will follow him and Katherine in to dinner and then everyone else, *everyone*, will come behind us. You will be the greatest man in England after the king and I will be the greatest woman after Katherine.'

He comes around to my side and he goes down on one knee. He turns his handsome face up to me and I cannot stop myself from putting my hand to his smooth shaved cheek. My God, this is a handsome man. I feel myself yearn for him. It has been so many days that I have had to lie flat as a corpse in a bed while he sat beside me, not daring to touch me for the pain that it would cause. I want to be his wife again, I want to be his lover. I want to be his queen and walk proudly at his side.

'My lady wife, Your Grace, I cannot come,' he says simply.

Dacre and I exchange shocked looks over his head.

'What?'

'I cannot come to London.'

'But you have to,' I say flatly.

'If I go with you, as a Scots outlaw, all the lands will be taken from my kinsmen and my castles will be destroyed,' he says bluntly. 'Everything that my father left me, everything that my grandfather owns, will be torn down. My clan will be leaderless, my people will die of starvation. I will have abandoned my birthright, and everyone will know that I left them for the comfort of being your husband in London when I should have been fighting for my home. They will think that I ran away to safety and left them to disaster.'

'You can't stay here and fight,' Dacre says. 'The king himself is trying to get a peace. You can't stir up trouble now.'

'Are you a gentle dove now, your lordship?' Archibald says bitingly. 'I never thought to hear you say that a Scot should not be fighting other Scots.' He turns his attention to me, as if Dacre is too despicable to answer. 'My love, my queen, I can't leave those who have risked everything for your cause. Lord Hume will lose his lands too. Albany has already threatened his wife and his mother with imprisonment. We can't run away and leave our families behind.'

'But I am your wife! This is your family!'

'It would be dishonourable to run away.'

'Your duty is with me!'

'My duty is in Scotland,' he says. 'Your brother will guard you and keep you in England. But no-one will guard and keep my people if I abandon them.'

'Think it over,' Dacre recommends. 'Don't be too hasty, my

lord. You might be a long time, hiding in the hills. The king may get a peace with France that doesn't restore you. If you're not in London, they may forget all about you.' He looks at me. 'It is the way of great men, sorry though I am to say it. If your husband is not there he may be forgotten.'

This is a sneer against my husband and against me. Dacre is always my brother's man first and my servant second. I know very well they will not remember Archibald – they barely remember me. Who would know better than I that a princess passes over the Scots border and disappears from memory? Who would know better than I that they only fight for you when it has all become such a disaster that they can overlook it no longer? I am not Mary, who can come and go without losing her brother's attention, behave disobediently, disloyally, and be welcomed home with celebrations. I am not Katherine who can fail to give him a son year after year and still be the wife of his choice and the queen of the court. I am Margaret, Queen of Scotland, and they forget me altogether until the extremity of my danger threatens them.

'He will come with me to London!' I say hotly. 'They will see us together. They will remember us then!'

Dacre turns to my husband with a small smile, and waits for his reply. I remember that this man has had years pitting one Scot against another, one Englishman against another, Scots against English, English against Scots. Now he is setting a wife against her husband. Dacre is a border man in every sense. He will think that he knows men like Archibald inside out, that he has paid them to dance to his piping. He has always thought him bought, easily turned, easily betrayed.

'I can't come,' Ard says flatly. 'Remembered or forgotten, I can't come.'

We leave without him. I am only twenty-six years old, and yet I seem to have spent my life leaving the people that I love and losing those who should guard me. We leave my son Alexander in the cold ground of Scotland, for Albany buried my boy in December, before I even knew that he was dead. We leave my surviving son the king, a child of four years old, in the keeping of his tutors. I pray that Davy Lyndsay is at his side, for who else is there who can give him comfort? We take Margaret with us, and her wet nurse and her rockers and her endless entourage. We travel as lightly as we can and yet there is a long train of wagons with my goods, and Dacre's goods, and the men-at-arms that guard them, and the lords who accompany us – glad of the chance to get to London after years on the border. We take half of Northumberland with us, but we leave without my husband.

He kisses my hand, my wet eyes, my lips, my hands again, before I leave. He swears that he loves me more now than when he was my pretty carver, my knight, my friend. He says that he cannot abandon his friends and his allies, his men, his lowly tenants who know nothing of king or regent or queen regent, but will follow him wherever he leads them. He cannot leave his castle, that great fort overlooking the sighing sea and the crying gulls. He tells me that we will be together again some day. We will be happy again, some day.

'I will come back,' I promise him. 'I will come back to you and you will wait for me. I will command Harry to make peace with the French and with the Scots lords and they will allow me to come home and I will be queen regent, as I was, and you will be my consort.'

His loving gaze is as clear and as true as when he was my young carver. 'Come back to me, and I will hold my castles and my lands and my power. Come back to Scotland and I will welcome your return as queen. Come back soon.'

# ON THE ROAD SOUTH, ENGLAND, SPRING 1516

It is a long journey but there are signs of my returning power. The further we go, by slow, painful stages, the grander becomes our procession. I enter York in state and process through the city which remembers my entrance as a princess all those years ago. Every day we add more followers. I appoint new people in my household, and I am surrounded by hangers-on and petitioners. Dacre says that he cannot house and feed so many on the road, and I shrug and say that I have always been beloved in England; he should have listened to me when I told him that the people would flock to be with me.

I receive letters from London: from Katherine, saying that her new baby is thriving and strong, and from my sister, Mary, who has given birth to a boy. It is hard to be glad for her. This is not a boy who will be a stepping stone to greatness for his mother, my little sister. This is not a boy who is going to take up a great place in the world. His parents are all but bankrupt since they have to pay the royal exchequer a massive fine for their marriage. The boy's very title was only a reward to his father for being an amusing friend; Brandon has no talent or breeding or merit. They are calling the little mite Henry in an attempt to win my brother's favour. I expect they will ask Thomas Wolsey, that rising star, to be godfather, as he is to my baby. They will have to do something to turn their fortune around. So I cannot celebrate the birth of this boy, who will be nothing but a cost to the family.

But I am glad that Mary is out of danger. I always thought that she would be fertile and strong. All of our mother's family are prolific breeders. The Plantagenets flower like the weed of their name. I was certain she would not be weakly like Katherine. I am delighted that she is up and well, and that she will be able to greet me when we get to London. The thought of seeing her again, even seeing Katherine, becomes more and more exciting as we get closer to the capital city. It has been thirteen years of exile. I never really thought that I would get home again. I never thought that I would sleep under an English roof with the Tudor standard flying over my head again. There were times when I never thought to see any of them, ever again.

And I don't forget, not even in my joy at my return, that my misfortune has come about because Henry broke my treaty and insisted on war with Scotland, and because Katherine commanded the Howards to lead a brutal army, ordered to spare no-one. For all that the Howards' new standard flaunts emblems of my husband's defeat, they were not the ones who decided to take no prisoners. That was Katherine: ruthless and bloodthirsty as her mother, who took a Christian sword through Spain. For all that she sends me loving letters now, and promises that we shall fall into each other's arms on meeting, I don't forget that she ordered my husband's naked body to be pickled in a jar and sent as a trophy of war to my brother. A woman who can think of that is not a woman that I can ever call my sister. I don't even know where James' poor body is buried in England. I don't even know where his bloodstained jacket is – in some cupboard somewhere, I suppose. There is bad blood between Katherine and me. She has been generous and kind to me since my terrible downfall, and I have profited from her uneasy conscience; but she was the cause and reason for that downfall and I don't forgive or forget.

The day that we are about to leave York there is a tap at the door of my privy chamber and it swings open, without my consent. I look up to see who comes in without announcement to the private rooms of the Dowager Queen of Scotland, and there before me, bonnet in his hand, smiling and heartbreakingly handsome, is my husband, Archibald.

I get to my feet – I can stand now without pain – I reach for him and he is across the room and on his knees at my feet in a moment. 'Go,' I whisper to my ladies, and they scurry out of the room and close the door behind them as he rises up and wraps me in a tight, hot embrace. He kisses my wet eyelids, my lips, my throat, his hands are warm through my tight stomacher. He bends his head and kisses the top of my breasts, and I feel him untie my laces.

'Come,' is all I say, and I lead him into my bedroom and let him strip me as if I were a peasant girl in a hay barn, push my rich skirts and my fine lace-trimmed linen to one side and enter me with as much desire as when we were first married and thought we would rule Scotland together.

It is blissful. We lie together in a tumble of clothes and bedding as the sun shines in through the window and I hear the church bells of York toll one after another for the afternoon service of None. 'My love,' I say sleepily.

'My queen,' he replies.

I take his tanned smiling face in my hands and I kiss him on the lips. 'You came to me,' I say. 'I thought I had lost you forever.'

'I couldn't let you go like that,' he says. 'I couldn't let you go without knowing that my love is with you, as faithful as I always am, as much in love with you as I ever have been.'

'I am so glad,' I say quietly. I rest my head on his shoulder and I feel, through the thin linen of his shirt, the beat of his steady heart.

'And you are treated well?' he murmurs. 'I see you have beautiful gowns and ladies in attendance and a fine household around you?'

'I am cared for like the Tudor princess I was born to be, and the Scots queen I am,' I say. 'Dacre is a most loyal servant.'

'As he should be,' Ard says irritably. 'And has he given you money from your brother?'

'I am rich again,' I confirm. 'And everyone tells me that I will get my jewels and goods back from Albany. You need not fear for me, my darling. I am well provisioned.'

'Thank God,' he says. 'And when do they plan that you shall come back to Scotland?'

'Nobody knows yet. They will have to deal with Albany. But Harry says he will speak with nobody until he has first heard from me. And Dacre and I have compiled a great book of my grievances. Albany shall answer for them, the Scots lords who supported him shall answer for them. You and I will be avenged.'

There is a knock at the door and a voice says: 'Your Grace, will you be dining in the hall?'

I turn with a lazy smile to Ard. 'Everyone will know that we have been to bed in the afternoon,' I say.

'We are husband and wife,' he says. 'They can know that. I can tell them that I will sleep in your bed tonight, if they want to know.'

I chuckle. 'In my bed every night all the way to London.'

A little shadow crosses his face. 'Ah, love. Don't let's speak of it.'

'What?' I ask with sudden alarm. I call out to the lady-in-waiting. 'Yes! Yes! Come and dress me in a little while.'

'I can't come to London,' Ard says. 'Nothing has changed for me in Scotland though you are wealthy and well guarded now. But I am still an outlaw. I am still running and hiding for my life in the hills.'

'But you will stay with me now. You too will be wealthy and well guarded.'

'I cannot,' he says gently. 'My people still need me. I must lead them and protect them against your enemies.'

'You came just to say goodbye?'

'I couldn't stay away,' he whispers. 'Forgive me. Did I do wrong?'

'No, no, I would rather see you for a moment than not at all. But Ard, are you sure you cannot come?'

'My castle and my lands and my tenants will all be in danger if I don't go back. You will forgive me?'

'Oh yes! Oh yes! I would forgive you anything; but I can't bear you to leave me.'

He gets up from the bed and pulls on his leather riding breeches. They are worn soft and pliable from hard rides in all weathers.

'But you are not going now?'

'I will stay to dinner, if I may. I have had few good dinners in the last few weeks. And I will sleep in your bed tonight. I have had no soft pillows and no tender loving. And I will leave at dawn. It is my duty.'

'At dawn?' I repeat, feeling my lips tremble.

'I am afraid I must.'

I love him for his pride and for his sense of honour. I get up at dawn with him and watch him dress in his old worn breeches. 'Here!' I say. 'At least take these shirts.' I give him half a dozen fine linen shirts, beautifully hand-sewn and trimmed with lace.

'Where did you get these?' he demands, drawing one over his lean back.

'I commandeered them from Lord Dacre,' I confess. 'He was most unwilling but he can get more made for himself, and you should have nothing but the best.'

He laughs shortly and pulls on his old riding boots. 'Do you get enough to eat?' I demand. 'Where do you sleep?'

'I stay with other outlaws in their castles and forts all along the border,' he answers. 'Sometimes I sleep rough, under the sky, but usually I know a friend, someone loyal to your cause, who will take the risk of having me under their roof. Sometimes I even get back near to Tantallon, where everyone would risk their lives to give me a bed for the night.'

I know that Janet Stewart would open the doors of Traquair to him. But I won't mention her name.

'Do you need money?' I ask eagerly.

'Money would help,' he says wryly. 'I have to buy arms and clothes and food for those who ride with me, and I like to pay for my hospitality, especially when the people are poor.'

I go to my chest. 'Here,' I say. 'Dacre gave me this from my brother, for my benevolences on the way. He can give me more. Take it all.'

He weighs the purse in his hand. 'Gold?'

'Yes,' I say. 'And take this too.'

I open my treasure box and take out a long chain of gold links. 'You can break it up and sell it as you need,' I say. 'Take it, wear it around your neck and keep it safe.'

'This is worth a fortune,' he protests.

'You are worth a fortune to me,' I assure him. 'Take it. And take these too.'

I find a handful of heavy gold coins at the bottom of the box.

'This is too much,' he says, but he lets me press the gold into his hands. 'My wife, you are good to me.'

'I would do so much more for you if I could,' I swear. 'When I come home to Scotland you will have half the kingdom for your own. Ard, keep safe. Be true to me.'

He bends his knee and bows his head for my blessing, then he rises up and takes me in his arms. I close my eyes, inhaling the smell of him, adoring him. I would give him the rings off my fingers, I would give him the jewels from my hair, I would promise him the world.

'Come back to me,' I whisper.

'Of course,' he says.

## COMPTON WYNYATES, ENGLAND, MAY 1516

I am waiting in the home of my brother's good friend and servant Sir William Compton, in my best gown of purple velvet with cloth of gold lining. My brother the king is coming to accompany me into the city. We will make a great show for all the people – we Tudors know that we have to make a great show – and my authority with the Scots will be greater when they hear that the king himself rode at my side to bring me home again. It has been thirteen years since I saw him, a boastful vain little boy, and in that time we have lost our father and our grandmother, he has become king, I have become a queen, and we have both had and lost children. Everyone tells me that he has grown to be extraordinarily handsome and I am torn between excitement and nerves as I stand by the window in Sir William's beautiful presence chamber and hear the rattle of the guards' weapons outside the double doors and the tramp of many feet. Then finally the doors swing open and Harry comes in.

He is changed so much. I left a boy and here is a man. He's very tall, taller than Archibald, a head taller than me, and the first thing I see, and recoil to see it, is a thick bronze beard beautifully combed and trimmed. It makes him look like a fully-grown man, far from the memory I carried of my light-footed, fair-skinned little brother.

'Harry,' I say uncertainly. Then I remember that this is the King of England and I drop into a curtsey: 'Your Grace.'

'Margaret,' he says warmly. 'Sister,' and he raises me up and kisses me on both cheeks.

His piercing eyes are a bright blue, his features regular and strong. He smiles and shows white even teeth. He is a stunningly handsome man. No wonder that the courts of Europe call him the handsomest prince in Christendom. I think for a swift, spiteful moment that Katherine of Aragon is lucky that she caught him when she did – at the very moment of his coming to the throne. Any woman in the world would be glad to marry my brother now; no wonder Katherine is on constant watch over her ladies-in-waiting.

'I would have known you anywhere,' he says.

I flush with pleasure. I know that I look well. The pain has gone from my legs and I can stand and walk without a limp. I have lost all the weight that I gained before the birth of Margaret, and I am beautifully dressed, thanks to Katherine.

'Anywhere!' he goes on. 'You are as beautiful as our lady mother.'

I give him a little mock-curtsey. 'I am glad you find me so,' I say.

He offers me his arm and we walk a little way down the room, head to head so that no-one else can hear us.

'I do, Margaret. I am proud to be a man with two beautiful sisters.'

Mary; already. He has hardly greeted me and already we have to speak of Mary.

'But what of her little namesake?' I demand. 'How is your daughter? Is she strong and well?'

'She is.' He beams at me. 'Of course we wanted a boy first, but there is no doubt that she will have a little brother at her side soon. And you are older sister to a king, you can tell her how to go on.'

I was not. I was younger sister to Arthur, my brother who should have been king. But I smile and say: 'And Her Grace the queen? Is she well also?'

'She has returned to court,' he says. 'And you will sit with her at the great joust we have planned this month. The biggest event we have ever planned – to celebrate your coming, and the birth of my daughter, and Mary's son.'

Mary; again. 'I must show you Margaret, your niece.' I nod to her nursemaid, who brings her forward with a low curtsey for Harry to see. She is a plump little thing, brown-haired and brown-eyed, and she waves her hands and beams at Harry as if she knows that his favour will make her fortune.

'As lovely as her mama,' Harry says fondly, tapping her little fist with his finger. 'And as sweet-tempered, I am sure.'

'She is a very good baby,' I say. 'She had a hard enough time of it.'

'Good God, what you have suffered!'

I rest my head gently against his shoulder. 'I have suffered,' I agree. 'But I know that you will make it all right again.'

'I swear that I will,' he promises me. 'And you shall go back to Scotland as queen regent. Nobody shall mistreat you again. The very idea!' He seems to swell inside his beautiful green velvet jacket – the huge shoulders get even broader. 'And where is your husband? I expected him to be here with you.'

He knows, of course; Dacre will have reported everything as soon as it happened. 'He had to stay to protect his people,' I say. 'He was heartbroken, he wanted to be with me; we wanted to be together. Especially, he wanted to come to meet you. But he felt that those lords who had supported me, and the poor people who had suffered for keeping me, would be in danger of Albany's revenge if he were not there to protect them. He is a man of great honour.'

I find that I am talking too much, too fast, trying to convey to Harry the danger and the difficulty of Scotland. He cannot know, safe behind the walls of secure castles in a peaceful land, what it is like trying to rule a country where everything is by agreement, and even the will of the king has to be accepted by his people. 'Archibald has stayed in Scotland. To do his duty. He felt that he should.'

My brother looks at me and suddenly there is a hard calculation behind his smile. 'Done like a Scot,' is all he says, and I think his voice rings with contempt for a man who could leave his wife in danger. 'Done like a Scot.'

## BAYNARD'S CASTLE, LONDON, ENGLAND, MAY 1516

Katherine sent me a white palfrey for my state entry into London. She sent me headdresses of gold in the heavy gable style that she prefers. She sent me gowns, and rich materials for more gowns. I think it is she who gave the orders for the great wooden furniture to be installed in every room of the castle, and for fresh rushes with meadowsweet and lavender to be scattered on every floor. She certainly appointed the heads of my household so that it can run as a great palace, and her steward bought the food in the larders. The king pays for my household servants: my carver Sir Thomas Boleyn, my chaplain, all the yeomen of my household – ushers, cellarers and guards – and for the ladies who attend me. Katherine has loaned me jewels to add to the inheritance which she finally sent to Morpeth, and I have furs from the royal wardrobe and sleeves lined with royal ermine.

And then, finally, she comes herself. One of her ladies, the wife of Sir Thomas Parr, comes in the morning to tell me that the queen will give herself the pleasure of calling on me in the afternoon, if I wish. I say that this will be a pleasure for me, but my assent is nothing but a formality as Maud Parr and I both know. Katherine can come whether it is convenient or not. She is Queen of England; she can do anything she wishes. I grit my teeth when I think that she will come and go as she pleases and I owe her thanks for the attention.

I hear her guard of honour accompanying her down Dower Gate and I hear the cheers that follow her. The English love the Spanish princess who waited and waited for the day when she would finally be queen. I cannot see her from my window, though I press my face against the glass. I have to sit on my throne in my presence chamber to wait for her to arrive.

They throw open the doors. I rise to my feet and advance to greet her, for however I remember her from our girlhood – pale, sorrowful, poor – she is Queen of England now and I am the exiled Queen of Scotland and it is me waiting for my luck to change, not her. I curtsey to her, she curtseys to me, then she opens her arms and we hug. I am surprised by her warmth. She pats my face and says that I have grown into beauty, what lovely hair I have. How well the gown suits me.

I give her one searching glance, and I could laugh aloud. She has run to fat after five pregnancies, her skin has gone dull and sallow. Her beautiful golden hair is hidden under an unflattering hood, she is loaded with chains around her neck, reaching to her broad waist, a crucifix resting at her throat; her little plump hands have rings on every finger. I note with unworthy triumph that she looks all of her thirty years, she looks tired and disappointed, but I am still a young woman with everything to hope for.

She says at once, 'Don't let's talk here among everyone. Can we go to your privy chamber?' and I hear once again that familiar, irritating Spanish accent, which she has ostentatiously retained, thinking it makes her special, after fourteen years of speaking English.

'Of course,' I say, and even though I live here, I have to step back and show her into the room that leads off the presence chamber, just before my private rooms.

Informally, she takes a seat in the window and beckons me to join her, seated beside her at the same height, as if we are equals. Her ladies and mine sit on stools out of earshot, though they are all dying to know how we will make friends, when everyone knows there is so much between us, and so much of it bad.

'You are looking so well,' she says warmly. 'In such good looks! After all that you have endured.'

'And you too,' I lie. When I last saw her she was a young widow, hoping against all the evidence that my father would let her marry Harry, fragile in black, dainty as a doll. Now, she has achieved her heart's desire, and found it lacking. They married for love – passionate boyish love on his part – but they have had five pregnancies and only one healthy child, and she is a girl. Harry takes a lover every time Katherine is pregnant, and she is pregnant almost every year. They are not the golden couple of her dreams. I expect she thought that she would be like her mother and father, equally proud, equally beautiful, equally powerful, in love forever.

It has not turned out like that. Harry has grown taller and more handsome, wealthier and more kingly than she could have hoped, and he casts a great shadow over her – over everyone. She is tired, she aches with mysterious pains. She fears that

God does not favour their marriage, and she spends half the day on her knees asking Him what is His will. She has none of the radiant confidence of her mother, the crusader. Now she comes to befriend me but even here she brings guilt. She has blood on her hands: her army killed my husband, and I do not forget it.

'I hope that you can stay with us for a long time,' she says. 'It would be such a pleasure to have both the king's sisters at court.'

'Both of us? Is Mary here very much?' I ask. 'I didn't think she could afford to live at court.'

Katherine flushes. 'She comes often,' she says with dignity. 'As my guest. We have become very good friends. I know that she is longing to see you.'

'I don't know how long I can stay, I will have to go home as soon as the Scots lords have agreed to my rule,' I say. 'It is my duty. I cannot walk away from my husband's country.'

'Yes, you have been called to a great office,' she says, 'in a country that I know is not easy to rule. I was so sorry for the death of your husband the king.'

For a moment I cannot speak. I cannot even glare at her. I cannot imagine how she dares to talk of his death as if it were a distant event, beyond anyone's control.

'The fortunes of war,' she says.

'An unusually cruel war,' I remark. 'I have never heard before of English troops being ordered to take no prisoners.'

She has the decency to look abashed. 'These border wars are always cruel,' she says. 'As when neighbours fight. Lord Dacre tells me—'

'It was he who found my husband's body.'

'So sad,' she whispers. 'I am so sorry.' She turns her face and, hidden by the enormous headdress, wipes her eyes. 'Forgive me. I have recently lost my father and I—'

'They told me that after Flodden you were triumphant,' I interrupt, suddenly finding the courage to speak out.

She bows her head but she does not shrink from the truth. 'I was. Of course I was glad to keep England safe while the king was far away, and fighting himself. It was my duty as his queen.

They said that the King of Scots was planning to march on London. You would not believe how afraid we all were of his coming. Of course I was glad that we won. But I was very sorry for you.'

'You sent his coat to Harry. His bloodstained coat.'

There is a long silence. Then she gets to her feet with a dignity I have never seen in her before. 'I did,' she says quietly. Behind her, all her ladies rise too, and mine. They cannot be seated when the Queen of England stands, but nobody knows what to do. Awkwardly, I stand too. Are they leaving already? Is the queen offended? Have I dared to quarrel with the Queen of England while I perch in a house that she has loaned me, the first decent roof I have had over my head in months?

'I did,' she says quietly. 'So that the King of England, fighting for his country, should know that his Northern border was safe. So that he should know that I had done my duty to him, my husband, even though it cost you your husband. So that he should know that English soldiers had triumphed. Because I was glad that we had triumphed. I am sorry for this, my dear sister, but this is the world that we live in. My first duty is always to my husband; God has put us together, no man can put us asunder. Even the love that I bear for you and yours cannot come between me and my husband the king.'

She is so dignified that I feel foolish and rude beside her poise. I never thought I would see Katherine rise to her queenship like this. I remember snubbing her when she was a poor hanger-on at court, I never knew that she had this righteous pride in her. Now I see that she is truly a queen, and has been a queen for seven years, while I have lost my throne and married a lord, who does not even live with me.

'I see,' I say weakly. 'I understand.'

She hesitates, as if she sees herself for the first time, on her dignity, on her feet, ready to walk out of my chamber. 'May I sit down again?' she asks with a little smile.

It is gracious of her, as she does not have to ask.

'Please.' We sit together.

'We buried him with honour,' she says quietly. 'In the Church of the Observant Friars. You can visit his grave.'

'I didn't know.' I choke on a sob. I am more embarrassed than anything else. 'I didn't even know that.'

'Of course,' she said. 'And I had Masses said for him. I am sorry. It must have been a terrible time for you. And then you had worse times to follow your grief.'

'They say that it is not his body,' I whisper. 'They say that he was seen after the battle. That the body you brought to England did not wear the cilice.'

'People always make up stories,' she replies, steady as a rock. 'But we buried him as a king with honour, Your Grace.'

I cannot bully her, and I cannot shake her. 'You can call me Margaret,' I say. 'You always used to.'

'And you can call me Katherine,' she says. 'And perhaps we can be friends as well as sisters. Perhaps you can forgive me.'

'I thank you for the gowns, and for everything,' I say awkwardly. 'I was glad to get my inheritance.'

She puts her hand over my own. 'All this is no more than you should have,' she says gently. 'You should have your throne again, and the wealth of Scotland. My husband the king has sworn that you will have all that is yours again, and he will make sure that it is so, and I will speak in your favour.'

'I am grateful,' I say, though it costs me to say such a thing to her.

Her palm is warm, the rings are heavy on her little fingers. 'We were not good sisters to each other before,' she says quietly. 'I was very afraid that I would never be married to your brother, and I was homesick, and terribly poor. You don't know what I went through in the years that I waited. I was never happy after your mother died. When she had gone it was as if I lost my only friend in the family.'

'My grandmother . . .' I begin.

She shrugs her shoulders. Rubies gleam at her throat. 'My Lady the King's Mother never cared for me,' she says shortly. 'She would have sent me home if she could have done so. She tried to say—' She breaks off. 'Oh! All sorts of things. She tried to prevent my marriage to the prince. She advised him against me. But when he came to the throne he took me, despite everything.'

'She was always ambitious for him,' I say quietly. And she was right, I think to myself – he could have done better than a widow who cannot bear a son.

'So I understand what it is to be far from home, and to think that no-one cares for you, that you are in danger and no-one will help you. I was very, very sorry when I learned that you were widowed and had lost the guardianship of your son. I swore then that I would do what I could to help you, and to be a good sister to you. We are both Tudors. We should help each other.'

'I always thought you looked down on me,' I confess. 'You always seemed so very grand.'

Her ripple of laughter makes her ladies look up and smile. 'I ate day-old fish that we bought cheap from the market,' she says. 'I pawned my plate to pay my household. I was a princess in rags.'

I clasp her hand in my own. 'I too have been a princess in rags,' I say quietly.

'I know,' she says. 'That is why I have urged Harry to send an army to put you back on your throne.'

'Will he listen to you?' I ask curiously, thinking of how James would chuck me under the chin and go and fulfil his own plans, ignoring anything I said. 'Does he take your advice?'

A shadow crosses her face. 'He used to,' she says. 'But Thomas Wolsey has grown very great recently. You know that he advises the king on everything? He is Lord Chancellor, he is very able, a very able man. But he thinks only of how to do what the king wishes. He doesn't consider God's will as well as the king's desire. Indeed, it has become very rare for anyone to advise the king against his desire.'

'He is the king,' I say flatly. Really, I don't understand her at all; why should anyone advise him against his wishes?

'But not infallible,' she says with a ghost of a smile.

'Is Thomas Wolsey in favour of my return to Scotland? He

must want the best for my daughter, as her godfather?'

She hesitates. 'I think he has greater plans for you than just your return,' she says. 'He knows that the Scots must accept you and that your boy must be in your keeping, but I think he hopes . . .'

'He hopes what?' I ask.

She bows her head for a moment as if in prayer, as if she has to think what she says next: 'I believe that he hopes that your present marriage can be annulled and you shall marry the emperor.'

I am so shocked that I say nothing. I just look at her, my mouth agape.

'What?' I say, when I find my voice. 'What?'

She nods. 'I thought you did not know of this. Thomas Wolsey is playing for high stakes in Europe. He would be very pleased to have an ally bound by marriage to England, to hold against France. Especially now that he is trying to get the French out of Scotland.'

'But I am married already! What is he thinking of?'

'The Lord Chancellor thinks that your marriage could be annulled,' she says quietly. 'And then Harry observed that your husband did not accompany you, though he had a safe conduct. Harry thought that you might be estranged. He thought that you might welcome a separation.'

'Archibald has duties in Scotland! I told the king myself. He is obliged, by his honour . . .'

'You would be empress,' she remarks.

That silences me again. As the wife of the Holy Roman Emperor I would be queen of enormous lands, half of Europe. I would outrank Katherine. Indeed I would be married to her kinsman. Mary, the wife of a nonentity like Charles Brandon, would be nothing beside me, she would have to serve me on bended knee. I would never see either of them again, and I would be wealthier than my brother Harry. This is the destiny that slipped away from me when I considered the emperor and the King of France as husbands, and then found that the King of France had jilted me for my little sister. When I married Archibald I lost my chance of being one of the great rulers of Europe. Now, once again, the possibility of greatness opens before me.

'How could it be done?'

Katherine is no longer smiling. She withdraws her hands from mine as if the touch of an unfaithful wife might contaminate her. 'I am sure that if you consent, the Lord Chancellor will find a way,' she says coolly. 'I have performed my task in asking you if you would consider it. The king says that Scotland was under excommunication when you married the Earl of Angus. The Lord Chancellor argues that no marriage during that time could be valid. And also, your husband was betrothed to marry another woman, was he not? The Lord Chancellor will argue that it was a full marriage, not merely a betrothal. That your husband was married to Janet Stewart, a marriage that took place before yours, and while Scotland was in communion with Rome. His marriage to her predates yours, and yours was not valid.'

'He was not. He never sees her!' I say fiercely. 'He does not care for her. He married me. He was free to marry me. He is faithful to me.'

Katherine looks at me and I see that it is not just the loss of her four babies that has put the darkness in her gaze. She has been disappointed by Harry too.

'It doesn't matter if a husband is faithful or not,' she says quietly. 'It doesn't matter if he loves you or another. What matters is that you swore to be together before God. The priest was a witness to your vows but you made them to God. A marriage cannot be dissolved because great men wish that a woman is free. A marriage cannot be dissolved because a husband has been so foolish and so weak as to fall in love with another woman. A genuine marriage, made before God, cannot be dissolved, ever.' Her gaze drifts from me to her companions, her ladies-in-waiting, chattering together, whiling away the time until they can go back to Greenwich Palace and dine with the men. One or more of them will have caught the eye of the king, one or more will already have been in his bed, one or more will be hoping.

'I know that,' I say. 'I know that nothing matters more than the marriage vows. Archibald and I made those vows. He is my husband and will be until death.'

She bows her head. 'That's what I believe to be true,' she says quietly. 'If Harry asks me for my opinion I will tell him that you are married in the sight of God and that neither the Lord Chancellor nor the Holy Roman Emperor nor the King of England himself can change that.'

## GREENWICH PALACE, ENGLAND, MAY 1516

The joust to celebrate my arrival in England is to take place at Greenwich, and I travel in the queen's barge downriver to the most beautiful of all our London palaces. I so wish that Archibald was with me to hear how the people of Greenwich cheer as our barges go by, to hear the sound of the musicians playing and the roar of the cannons welcoming me home again.

The new Tudor baby, Princess Mary, is in the arms of her nurse, on our barge. Katherine keeps her close and watches her all the time. My little Margaret, just a few months older, is so much brighter and more alert; her colour is rosy and she looks around her and smiles when she sees me or her nursemaid. But to see Katherine or Henry dote on their baby you would think that no other child had ever been born.

Privately, I swear to myself that my Margaret will be acknowledged as the prettier girl. I will see that she is dressed to perfection; I will ensure that she marries well. She may not be a princess, and her father could not give her a crown, but she is every inch royal and she is half a Tudor. Who knows what the future will be for these two babies? I swear that my child will never suffer for the comparison. Nobody is going to send her to a foreign country and then fail to support her. Nobody is going to praise Mary over her. Nobody is going to neglect her and praise the other to her little face.

I cannot say that I am neglected now. I am dressed beautifully from the royal wardrobe, in cloth of gold gowns, and though I follow the Queen of England, everyone else follows me. I am addressed as Queen Regent of Scotland, and Thomas Wolsey pays my debts from the royal treasury without hesitation or query. As I follow Katherine off the royal barge and smile at the royal household drawn up on either side of the carpet that leads us to the wide open doors of the royal palace, I have no complaints. I might wish that Archibald were here to see me, in the place of greatest honour, I might wish that everyone could see my handsome husband, that he might ride in the joust, but I myself am where I should be. It's all that I've always wanted.

'We'll go to the wardrobe rooms,' Katherine rules. She smiles at me. 'I hope that Mary will be there already, choosing her gown.'

At last I am to see her again. Mary, my darling little sister, has come from her country house for my joust. Charles Brandon is to do what he does best – perhaps his only skill other than whoring and spending money; he and Harry will take on all comers.

'She's here already?' I am so impatient to see her, and I also hope that we get there before she has chosen the best of the gowns for herself. I hope that Katherine has ordered the groom of the wardrobe to make sure that we three queens have gowns of equal quality. It would spoil everything if Mary's is French cut or more richly embroidered, or more fashionable. She has become used to the very best; but she should not be allowed to outshine the queen. It is a disservice to all the royal ladies if Mary is encouraged to exceed her situation. She may be Dowager Queen of France but she is married to a commoner, not a nobleman like Archibald. I don't want her to stand out, or put herself forward. I don't want people to shout her name and throw flowers and encourage her to show off before everyone, just as she did when we were little girls.

The yeomen of the guard, standing either side of the door,

salute us and swing the doors open to the shaded rooms where the royal gowns of state hang in great linen pouches, lavender heads stuffed into sleeves to ward off moths, gorse prickles at the wainscoting to deter rats. In the half-light of the shuttered room I see the little elfin face under the elegant French hood and I have the illusion that my sister is unchanged from the girl that I left behind thirteen years ago, my little pet, my little sister, my little pretty doll.

At once I forget everything about her getting the best gown, everything about her being overdressed, everything about precedence. 'Oh, Mary,' I say simply. I stretch out my arms and she falls into them and clings to me.

'Oh, Margaret! Oh, my dear! Oh, Maggie! And I was so sorry about your boy Alexander!'

I gasp at his name. Nobody has spoken of him since I left Morpeth. No-one has even mentioned him. They have all offered me condolences for the death of the king, but no-one has spoken of my child. It is as if Alexander never was. And all at once I am crying for him, my lost little boy; and Mary – a little girl no longer, but a woman who has known loneliness and heartbreak like me – embraces me, unpins my hood, pulls my head to her shoulder and rocks with me, whispering like a mother soothing a hurt child. 'Hush,' she says. 'Ah, Maggie. Hush. God bless him, God bless him in heaven.'

Katherine comes closer. 'It's her son,' Mary says over my shoulder. 'She's crying for Alexander.'

'God bless and keep him and take him to His own,' Katherine says instantly, and I feel her arm around my shoulder as she and Mary and I hold each other, our heads pressed together, and I remember that Katherine, too, has lost a boy, more than one. Katherine's losses are never mentioned either. She too has buried little coffins and is required to forget them. Nothing in the world is worse than the death of a child, and we share that too, in a sisterhood of loss.

We three stand together, clinging to each other in silence in the darkened room, for a long time, and then the storm of grief passes me, and I glance up and say: 'I must look a fright.' I know that my hair is all tumbled and my nose will be red. My face and neck will be flushed and blotchy and my eyelids swollen. Katherine looks ten years older, ugly from grief. Two tears balance like pearls on Mary's thick eyelashes, her rosy lips tremble, and there is a flush like a sunrise in her cheeks. 'Me too,' she smiles.

The jousting arena at Greenwich is as fine as any in Europe. The queen's box is set opposite the king's, and my sisters and I, with our ladies, sit in the centre of the stand, curtains billowing in the warm winds, facing the tilt rail. Harry and his friends are never in their box, of course; they are challengers, not spectators. There are long rippling flags flying all around the arena. The ground is sifted sand, white as snow. The seats in the stands are packed with people in their very best clothes. Only the nobility and their favourites are invited – you cannot buy a ticket, this is a diversion for the very cream of the country. The merchants of London and the country people come to this great spectacle, wait behind the half-walls of the arena and jostle one another for room. The younger ones, the bolder ones, climb the sides to get a better view and are cuffed and pushed down when they bob up alongside the nobility. Everyone laughs as they tumble down.

The poorer people cannot even get into the palace, but they line the riverbank where they can watch the ceaseless coming and going of the barges of the noble houses, bringing the guests. They stand along the lane that runs from the gates of the walled palace to Greenwich and the docks. This is where the horses are brought in, and they see the magnificent saddles and the beautiful jousting costumes as the big chargers, sidling and snorting, come down the road ridden by the squires, or led by the grooms.

The smell of a tournament is instantly recognisable. There is a hint of woodsmoke from where the people are frying bacon on little fires, to eat when the joust is over, and the tang of the black smoke from the forge where horses are being quickly re-shod and the sharp ends of lances hammered down to make them blunt. Everywhere, there is the smell of the horses, a mixture of sweat and dung and excitement like a hunt or a race, and over it all the perfume of the flower garlands that hang around the boxes. The orchards have been stripped of apple blossom for our pleasure; the costly pink and white flowers have made the queen's box into a bower. At every corner the buds of early roses are in posies that we will throw to the bravest challenger. Over all the blossoms, threaded through them, are the starry flowers of honeysuckle in rose pink and yellow and cream, with their haunting heady scent, as sweet as honey. The queen and I and all the ladies have bathed in rosewater and our linen has been sprinkled with lavender water. The bees buzz into the royal box, dazed by perfume, as if they were in an orchard.

I have a sudden memory, unexpected as summer lightning, of my husband James the king in his strength and beauty when he rode as the wild man in green, and the Sieur de la Bastie was all in white, and I was the queen of the joust that celebrated the birth of my first son, when I thought that I would be happy and triumphant and the first in the land forever.

'What is it?' Mary asks me gently.

I shake away the flood of grief. 'Nothing. Nothing.'

Everyone is waiting for the entry of the king into the arena. The sand is raked flat, as if a retreating sea has lapped it clean; the squires in their bright liveries stand at every doorway. There is a buzz of excitement and laughter that becomes louder and louder and louder until there is a sudden blast of trumpets and a gasp, then silence as the great doors roll open, and Harry rides into the arena.

I see him as others see him, not as my little brother, but as a great king and a magnificent man. He is on a huge warhorse, a black brute of an animal, broad at the shoulder, powerful in the haunches. Harry has ordered it to be shod with silver and the nails sparkle on the black hooves. His saddle and bridle, the breastplate and the stirrup leathers, are a gorgeous deep blue, the best leather dyed as dark as indigo, and the shine on the horse's black coat is as bright as if it has been polished. It is wearing a trapper of cloth of gold, set with golden bells that tinkle at each great bouncing stride. Harry himself is wearing deep blue velvet embroidered all over with golden thread in bursts of honeysuckle flowers, so that he sparkles as he rides the full circle of the arena, one hand holding his magnificent horse on a tight blue rein, the other holding his tall lance, couched in gold-inlaid leather at his dark blue leather boot.

Like a warm summer breeze, the crowd sighs in awe at this appearance: a knight from a storybook, a god from a tapestry. Harry is so tall, so handsome, his horse is so toweringly big, his velvets so deep and iridescent, he is more like a portrait of a king, a great king, than the real presence. But then he halts the great horse at the queen's box and pulls off his hat, set with sapphires, and his bright smile at Katherine tells us all that this is a man, the most handsome man in England, the most loving husband in the world.

Everyone cheers. Even the people outside the arena, on the banks of the river, on the roads leading to the port, hear the deep-throated roar of approval and they cheer too. Harry glows like an actor welcomed to the stage, and then turns and beckons his companions.

There are four challengers, dressed to match the king, Charles Brandon among them, his handsome face turning this way and that to acknowledge the applause. Behind them come eighteen knights, also in blue velvet on their great horses, behind them their attendants on foot, wearing satin of so deep a blue that it shines with colour, and after them all the grooms and the knights, the trumpeters, the saddlers, the servants, the water-carriers, the runners of errands, dozens and dozens of them, all in blue damask.

They all draw up before the royal box and Katherine, in her blue gown which suddenly looks dull and dowdy beside the blaze of peacock blue from her husband's livery, stands to take the salute from the challengers.

'Let the tournament begin!' bellows the herald. There is a blast of sound from the trumpets so all the warhorses sidle and trample in their excitement and Harry rides slowly towards his end of the list while his squire waits with his helmet and gold-inlaid gauntlets.

When he is ready, strapped into his beautiful suit of armour, helmet on his head, visor lowered, horse sidling slightly from nerves on one side of the brightly painted tilt rail, his opponent waiting at the other end, on the opposite side, Katherine rises to her feet, holding her white napkin in her bare hand. Her glove is tucked inside Harry's breastplate, over his heart. He is meticulous in these chivalric signs of devotion. She holds the napkin high, and then she lets it fall.

The minute it is released Harry has spurred his horse and the beast leaps from its powerful haunches and thunders down the long list. His opponent starts at the same time and the lances thunder closer and closer. Harry's reach is longer, his stance low in the saddle but thrusting forward. There is a terrific clang of noise as his lance crashes against his opponent's breastplate, and Harry wrenches it back, so that he does not overbalance and come down. A few seconds later and the opponent's lance, off balance and reeling from the impact, has struck him a glancing blow on the shoulder. But Harry is already riding by, regaining his balance, heaving the long lance back towards him as his opponent rocks in the saddle, grabs the pommel and horse's neck with his mailed hand, is falling, is going, and reels backwards off his horse, flung to the ground with the ringing crash of metal armour. The horse bucks, its trappings flapping, its reins trailing; the knight lies still, obviously winded, perhaps worse. Grooms in their blue damask catch the horse, squires in their blue satin run to the knight. They open his visor, his head lolls.

'Is his neck broken?' my little sister asks anxiously.

'No,' I say, as I always used to say to her when she was a little princess, afraid for every horse, for every knight. 'He's probably just shaken.'

The physician comes running, and the barber surgeon. The hurdle comes, carried by four squires. Carefully they lift the knight on. Harry, down from his horse, his helmet under his arms, goes stiff-legged in his armour to see his opponent. Smiling, he says a few words to the fallen knight. We see them touch gauntlets as if shaking hands.

'There,' I tell Mary. 'He's fine.'

There is a roar as they carry him out of the arena and Harry turns all around the circle, taking in the applause, his bright smile gleaming, his red hair dark with sweat. He puts his mailed fist to his breastplate as he bows to Katherine and then he walks off. He passes Charles Brandon, high on a bay charger, who acknowledges his king with a comradely salute and a bow of his head as he trots around the arena and stops before our box to salute his queen, me, and then his wife.

'Does he not have your glove?' I ask Mary, seeing that she is wearing a pair.

She makes a little face. 'He forgot,' she says. 'And I didn't feel like running after him to remind him.'

'He doesn't carry your favour?'

'I can't afford to throw away a pair of gloves every time he jousts,' she says in an irritable undertone. 'The king pays for his armour and trappings, the wardrobe gives me a gown. But my gloves and my linen I have to find myself, and we are as poor as mice, Maggie. Really we are.'

I don't say anything but I squeeze her hand. That a Tudor princess should be brought so low as to worry about the price of a pair of gloves is quite shocking. Harry should be generous to Mary; he should be generous to me. Our father would have paid my debts earlier; he would not have fined Mary for marrying the man of her choice. Harry should remember that we are all Tudors, even though he is the only surviving boy. We are all heirs of England.

All day fresh incomers ride against the challengers, and the sand is churned and dirty, and the beautiful harness and livery are torn and dulled by the time the sun starts to set over the arena and the king's team are declared the victors, and the greatest of them is Harry.

Katherine stands in the box as he comes and bows before her, and I think that she looks like our mother did when she was weary but making the effort to respond to Harry's constant need for praise. She smiles as warmly as our mother did, handing down the prize of a gold belt of sapphires, giving a fortune to the young man who already owns everything. She clasps her hands together as if she is overwhelmed by joy at his victory, and then, when she has done everything he could hope for, she turns and we follow her back into the palace for the lengthy tournament dinner. There will be speeches, there will be masques, there will be dancing late into the night. I see her sideways glance at her baby, Mary, who has been brought to the box to witness her father's triumph and to be shown to the cheering crowd, and I know that she would far rather be in the nursery watching her baby feed, and going to bed herself.

I have no sympathy for her. She is Queen of England, the wealthiest woman in England, the greatest woman in the kingdom. Her husband has just beaten all comers. I would expect her to be beside herself with joy. Lord knows, if I were in her place, I would be.

I am to meet with the Scots lords who have come to England to persuade Harry to peace. They will ask him to keep me in exile, they will ask him to allow the Duke of Albany to rule my country, they will remind him that my husband is an outlaw and suggest that he should stay that way, to be hunted like a beast till they catch and kill him. They must be sick with anxiety, for I am a Tudor princess again, in prime place in my brother's fickle attention. He will not even see them.

'They shall attend you before me,' Harry promises me at dinner at Greenwich Palace. I am seated on his left side, Katherine is on his right, my sister is beside me, exquisite in a gown of the palest yellow, her thick blonde hair hidden by a pale yellow hood studded with diamonds, undoubtedly the most beautiful of the three of us – but she is two seats away from the throne, not adjacent as I am. 'You shall state your demands. They shall make their explanations to you.'

'And will you see them after?' I ask.

He nods. 'You can tell me what they have said to you. We'll talk with Wolsey. We'll bring them to heel, Margaret, never doubt it.'

'When will they come?' I am not nervous; I know that I can persuade them. I know that I can be a good queen regent. Scotland is a mass of warring loyalties; but so is England, so is France. Any throne attracts rivals – James taught me that – and now I am ready to learn his lessons and be the great Queen of Scotland that he said I should be.

'In a few days' time. But I want you to move house. Guess where.'

For a moment I wonder if I am to go into one of the royal palaces, and for a moment I hope for Richmond. But then I know where I should be. 'The Palace of Scotland,' I say.

Harry laughs at my quickness and clinks his golden goblet against mine. 'You're right,' he says. 'I want them to see you in the London palace of the kings of Scotland. It can remind them that you own it as much as Edinburgh Castle.'

## THE PALACE OF SCOTLAND, LONDON, ENGLAND, AUTUMN 1516

They have sent the Bishop of Galloway and the Commendator of Dryburgh. Monsieur du Plains comes too, to represent the French interest and to persuade us all to a compromise that leaves the duke as regent. They have half a dozen clerks as well and a couple of minor lords. I receive them in the throne room. The palace is terribly dilapidated; nobody has used it since the visit of the Scottish lords for my proxy wedding and that was thirteen years ago. But the fresh rushes hide the worn stones and the old floorboards, and Katherine has loaned tapestries to keep out the draughts from the doors where the timbers have shrunk. The building itself is imposing and Harry's groom of the household has given me massive oak furniture, including a throne inlaid with silver. As always, the appearance of royalty matters more than the reality. Nobody approaching the throne room of the Palace of Scotland could doubt for a moment that I am a great queen.

I sit on my throne beneath a cloth of estate as they come in, as still as if I were the Spanish princess, on her best, most formal manners, all those years ago, and I let them bow to me, without rising from my chair.

I speak with a balance of majesty and diplomacy. I have thought long and hard what agreement I will make. I cannot be impulsive and angry about my son, James, my husband, or the deep terrible loss of Alexander. I have to win them over. I have to make them want me to return.

I see them warm to me. I have the Tudor charm – we all have it, Mary and Harry and I – we all know that we do – and I am patronisingly pleasant as I listen to them, and pretend an interest in their views. I play them, as my lady grandmother used to play the great men of England: asking them for their opinions, consulting them as experts, feigning deference, while all the time she had her own plan. And all the while, they are standing before me, and I am seated under a cloth of gold, the cloth of estate of majesty. The duke that they call regent may rule them but he does not sit under cloth of gold, his sleeves are not trimmed with the white ermine of royalty.

I speak to them frankly. I say that I must have my goods returned to me. There were gowns and jewels sent to Archibald's castle at Tantallon, my summer wardrobe in Linlithgow – I expect them to be sent to me here in London. The regent owes me the rents on all my lands in Scotland: my dower lands, which were given to me by my husband the King of Scotland himself. Albany cannot say that he is ruling a country at peace, and then pretend that rents cannot be collected. And it must be me who appoints my son's tutors. I have to hear from James, my son. I have to be free to return to Scotland and he must live with me.

My husband and his grandfather and all his family must be pardoned, they must be free to live with me.

The Scots suggest quietly, politely, that I cannot return and expect to rule. I tell them that is exactly what I do expect. They were wrong to put Albany in my place; they have obeyed the French king, not me, their true queen. Look at their ally of France, advancing unstoppably across Europe! I give Monsieur du Plains a little smile as if to say that I perfectly understand his interests, he does not fool me. Who can doubt that France hopes to hold Scotland by this transparent device? If Scotland continues to side with the French spy Albany, with his French wife and loyalties, they will lead the kingdom of Scotland into war with England. My brother will not tolerate the French army on his doorstep. He insists on my safe return. Do they really want another war with England? Have they so many sons that they want to lose another generation at another Flodden? When we are still grieving for the last one?

Monsieur du Plains protests quietly at this, saying that France has no intention of capturing Scotland by deceit, that the duke is a Scot, heir to the throne after my son, not a Frenchman. I smile beyond him to the commendator and the bishop. My smile says – we know, we three Scots, that he is lying. And they smile back at me. We know, we three Scots.

## LAMBETH PALACE, LONDON, ENGLAND, AUTUMN 1516

I ride to Lambeth Palace on the white palfrey that Katherine has given me, to meet with Thomas Wolsey and my brother Harry. They are in Harry's privy chamber with only half a dozen companions and three or four servants. I note with one swift glance that no-one stands closer to the king than his new friend, Wolsey, the son of an Ipswich butcher. The smooth-spoken commoner must pinch himself every morning to be sure that he is not dreaming. It is extraordinary that a man from such humble beginnings should have the ear of the king. Surely no-one has ever risen so high from so low before? But this is the England that Harry and Katherine are making: one where ability matters more than breeding, and what you do matters more than who you are. For someone like me, who is completely defined by my birth, this is an uneasy prospect. It feels wrong. No king from my mother's side of the family would ever have made a butcher's boy Lord Chancellor, and I know – as if she were speaking to me from beyond the grave – that my lady grandmother would never have allowed it.

I make sure that none of this shows in my face as I greet my brother with warm courtesy and give my hand to his advisor as if I am pleased to see him there.

'How were they?' Harry asks briskly.

Clearly, Thomas Wolsey already knows who 'they' are and is to be part of this conversation.

'They will return my jewels,' I say with quiet pride. 'They admit they were wrong to seize them. They have them safe, all accounted for, and they will send everything to me. My dresses too.'

Wolsey smiles at me. 'You are an able diplomat, Your Grace.'

I really think I am. I incline my head. 'And they agree that my rents shall be paid. I think I am owed a fortune, perhaps as much as fourteen thousand pounds.'

Harry gives a low whistle. 'They say they will pay them?'

'They have promised.'

'And what do they say about the Duke of Albany?' Wolsey asks. 'Now that we have settled the question of the gowns?'

I incline my head as the butcher's son dares to remark on my conversation with my ambassadors. 'They insist he remains as regent; but I was very clear to them that this is to deliver Scotland into the power of the French.'

Harry nods.

'I made sure that they know you will not tolerate it.'

'You did well,' he says. 'I will not.'

'And so we are to meet again, when they bring my jewels.'

'I will talk with them in the meantime,' Wolsey remarks. 'But I doubt I will make more ground than Her Grace has done. What a queen regent you are: two of your aims gained at one meeting!'

'I must have my son restored to me,' I say.

'Your son is safe,' Wolsey says gently. 'But there is bad news from Scotland about Alexander Hume and his brother William.'

I wait. Alexander Hume is a turncoat of ridiculous pride. He changed sides against Albany and in my favour because he feared that Albany had made a joke about his little stature. He has all the fiery pride of a short man. But once he had joined my side he was a staunch servant. He rescued me from Linlithgow, and he rode with us from Scotland. He kept Archibald company and we would not have been so brave without his courage. But I know he is terribly unreliable.

'Has he changed sides?' I ask suspiciously.

'He won't be changing again,' Wolsey says with vulgar humour. 'He gave himself up to Albany for a pardon, but then he broke his parole and he has been executed for treason. He's dead, Your Grace.'

I give a little gasp and I stagger. 'Good God. He was executed after a pardon? No-one will ever trust Albany again!'

'No.' Wolsey has the impertinence to correct me. 'Nobody would ever trust a Hume again. It was he who broke his word. He received a pardon, he swore allegiance, then he rebelled again. He deserved to die. Nobody could argue in his defence.'

I would argue it. I don't think any promise to Albany needs to be honoured. But I am not going to disagree with my brother's favoured advisor, who, in my opinion, should not even be speaking unless invited.

Wolsey nods at Harry, as if to cue him to a speech. 'It means that the queen regent has lost the support of a powerful family,' he says, as if thinking aloud. 'If only we could get her another ally. A great ally, who would frighten the French. Perhaps the emperor?'

Harry takes my hand and tucks it under his arm. He guides me away from them all: Thomas Wolsey, the courtiers, the servants. There is a long gallery that leads from the privy chamber to the privy stairs and we walk, side by side, our paces matching.

'The emperor would be glad to offer marriage to you,' Harry says frankly. 'And with him as your husband you could dictate your terms to the Scots. With him as your husband, and me as your brother, you would be the most powerful woman in Europe.'

I feel a little flare of ambition at the thought of it. 'I am married already.'

'Wolsey thinks it could be annulled,' Harry says. 'It took place when Scotland was under a ban of excommunication: it is invalid.'

'But it is not invalid in the sight of God,' I say quietly. 'I know it, and so does He. And I would make my baby Margaret a bastard. I won't do that, any more than you would make little Mary a bastard. You couldn't do it, I know. Neither can I.'

Harry makes a grimace. 'It would give you such power,' he reminds me. 'And the husband you are defending is not at your side, and his greatest ally has been executed.'

'I can't do it,' I say. 'A marriage is a marriage. You know it cannot be set aside. You, who married for love, as I did, know what a sacred thing that is.'

'Unless God shows His will otherwise,' Harry says. 'He did so with our sister, when her husband died within weeks.'

I don't say out loud that Mary was lucky to get off so quickly, but I think it. 'If He shows His will,' I agree. 'But God has blessed my marriage with Archibald, and yours with Katherine. He has given us health and issue. I am married for life. As are you. It is till death do us part.'

'I too,' Harry says, yielding to my certainty. He is still the child of my lady grandmother's raising. He will always take a pious woman's advice. He cannot help but think that a woman who is determined is a woman who is in the right. It is the consequence of having a self-righteous grandmother. If he ever throws off this belief he will be free to think anything. 'But you will consider it, Margaret? For your husband has all but abandoned you, and who knows where he is now? He could be dead. It could be God's will that your marriage is already over.'

'He has not abandoned me,' I say. 'I know exactly where he is now. And I married him for richer or for poorer, I cannot desert him now that he is an outlaw, fighting for what is his own, fighting in my cause.'

'If he is an outlaw still,' Harry suggests. 'If he did not surrender with Hume, and make his peace with Albany and abandon your cause.'

'He would never do that,' I maintain. 'And I know where my honour and my love lies.' There is something about talking with Harry that always tempts me to speak as if in a masque. He is always rather staged. He never speaks without an eye to his effect. He never walks without an eye to his appearance. His natural pomposity is choreographed.

Now, he kisses me on both cheeks. 'God bless you for your honour,' he says gently. 'I wish that both my sisters had been so careful of their reputations.'

And there's a snub for you, little Mary, I think, as I smile under his praise.

## THE PALACE OF SCOTLAND, LONDON, ENGLAND, AUTUMN 1516

But I don't overlook Henry's hints. I write to Lord Dacre to ask him for news of Archibald, and of all those who support me in Scotland. I tell him I know all about Hume; he need not shrink from the truth. I know the worst. But even with that assurance, he does not reply and I take it that he either knows nothing, or does not want to tell me. I meet again with the Scots ambassadors and I cannot tell from their quiet courtesy whether my husband is on my side or has turned his collar and joined theirs. In the end I have to ask Thomas Wolsey to come to me.

I show him his god-daughter, my darling little Meg, and she smiles at him, just as she should. I serve the sweet pastries that he likes with a glass of malmsey wine. Then, when he is flattered and fed, I ask him for a loan. The Scots have sent my jewels and my gowns from my palaces, but no rent money. Thomas Wolsey is obliging – why should he not be? As Lord Chancellor he has control of the royal treasury and is amassing a fortune on his own account. His fat little fingers are loaded with jewels. He lends me money that will be repaid when my rents are paid. Dacre will collect them at the border and send Wolsey his share.

He congratulates me on the agreement I have made with the Scots. 'You can go home in safety, you can rule as co-regent,' he says. 'They promise to pay your dower and consult you. This is a triumph, Your Grace. I am impressed.'

I smile. 'Thank you. I am glad that I have been able to achieve so much. But I really wanted to ask you about the Earl of Angus,' I say.

I am hesitant to say his name. Nor do I want to say 'my husband' to this plump clerk whose eyes are so bright, whose wit is so sharp but who knows nothing about living hard, of the hazard and luck of being on the border.

He says nothing, he merely bows.

'I wanted to ask if you know where he is,' I say. 'I am concerned . . . after what you told me of Alexander Hume. They were all riding together, the Humes and my husband.'

He knows something. I swear that he has known for weeks.

'Indeed yes, I think that the earl, your husband, surrendered at the same time as the Humes, Alexander and William,' he says evenly. 'We think the three of them surrendered to Albany the regent and took the pardon. Your husband has given up.'

For a moment, I simply cannot hear him. 'Given up? Given himself up?'

'I only just learned it myself. It is a blow,' Wolsey says, quiet as a priest in confession.

It is a lie. It must be a lie. 'He can't have done,' I say hotly. 'He hasn't written to me. He wouldn't have done such a thing without telling me. He wouldn't have surrendered without winning me the right to see my son. He wouldn't just give up.'

'I think he has got his own lands back,' Wolsey says gently. 'He has traded your cause for his own. He has Tantallon Castle back in his keeping. I know it was important to him and to his – clan, do they call themselves? – that he recover his own. And his own fortune, of course.'

'What about my own?' I demand, suddenly furious with this soft-skinned man who tells me such terrible news in a softly confiding voice. 'This is my husband! He should be fighting for me! He did not come with me to England so that he could continue the fight. He should be fighting for me now!'

Wolsey spreads his fingers, heavy with diamond rings. 'Perhaps he did not come to England so that he could regain his castles and lands. And he has done that. It is, for him, a victory.'

I am so furious that I can hardly speak. 'It is no victory for me,' I say, choked.

His round face is tender. 'No,' he says. 'You have been overlooked again.'

I could cry that he names this grief so exactly. This is always what happens to me, over and over again. I have been put into second place. My needs have been neglected; where I should be first, I have been put aside. My own husband befriends my enemy rather than fighting for my cause. He has betrayed me.

'I can't believe it,' I mutter. I turn away from Wolsey so that he cannot see my face, twisted with anger. I am torn between fury and despair. I cannot believe that Archibald would surrender without telling me. I cannot believe he would ride to Edinburgh and not to London. I cannot believe that he would get his lands back, and leave me with nothing.

'The wife of the emperor would be the greatest woman in Europe,' Wolsey says silkily. 'You would be first. You would be able to command everyone in Scotland.'

Even in my distress, I don't forget my marriage vows. 'Archibald may have neglected his duty to me, but I do not neglect mine to him,' I say. 'We were married in the sight of God and nothing can change that.'

'If you're sure,' Thomas Wolsey says.

## LAMBETH PALACE, ENGLAND, AUTUMN 1516

I surprise myself by not collapsing into tears. I find I want to talk to someone who will understand how I feel – not someone whose softly-spoken advice only makes me feel worse. I call for my horse and for my grooms of the stable. I put on my best riding cape and my gown trimmed with marten, and I ride to Greenwich. I don't go to the king's presence chamber to see my brother, I take the stairs to the queen's side, and the chief of my ladies asks the head of Katherine's household if she will see me. He shows me in at once, and I find her ladies sitting quietly in her presence chamber, and the door to her privy chamber closed.

'You may go in,' he says quietly. 'Her Grace is at prayer.'

I enter quietly, closing the door behind me on all of them, and I see her through the open door to the private chapel that she has made adjoining her privy chamber. I stand in the doorway and watch as the priest makes the sign of the cross over her bowed head and crosses himself, and she rises from the luxurious prie-dieu, speaks a few words to him, and comes out, her face smiling and serene.

She lights up with genuine pleasure when she sees me. 'I was just praying for you, and here you are,' she exclaims. She puts her hand out to me. 'I heard the news from Scotland. You must be glad at least that your husband is alive and restored to his own.'

'I can't be,' I say, with sudden honesty. 'I know that I should be. I know that I should be glad for him. And I am glad that he has not been killed. I have been in a constant terror that there would be an accident, or a raid, or a fight . . . But I can't be happy that he has agreed with Albany and left me here.' I swallow a gulp of tears. 'I know I should be glad for his safety. But I can't.'

She draws me to the fireside and we sit together on stools of equal height. 'It is hard,' she agrees. 'You must feel quite abandoned by him.'

'I do!' I trust her with the painful truth. 'I left him behind because he wanted to fight for me and would not come to England with our cause in so bad a state. It broke my heart to leave him, and he was so loving, he followed me to York and swore that he would fight for me to the death, and now I find that he has made an agreement with our enemy and is snug in his own little castle! Katherine – it must have been he who sent on my gowns!'

She looks down, she purses her lips. 'I know. It is hard when you think someone is very good, very great, and they disappoint you. But perhaps it will be for the best. When you go back to Scotland you will have his castles to live in, he will have a fortune to support you. He will be on the council and can speak for you. You will be the wife of a great Scots lord and not an outlaw.'

'Have you been disappointed?' I ask so quietly that I wonder if she can hear me.

She turns her honest blue eyes on me. 'Yes,' she says shortly. 'You will have heard of some of my troubles. I think that everyone knows that Henry took a lover in the very first year of our marriage, when I was confined with our first child. Since then, there have been others, always another. There is one now.'

'One of your ladies?' I dare to ask.

She nods. 'That makes it twice as bad,' she says. 'It feels like a double betrayal. I thought of her as my friend, I thought of her tenderly.'

I can hardly breathe, I want to know so much which one it is. I don't think I can ask. There is something about Katherine, something forbidding, even sitting on a stool before a fire, side by side with her sister.

'But it's not serious,' I state. 'It's an amusement, for a young man, as all these young men do. Harry is gallant, he likes to play at chivalrous love.'

'It is not serious to him perhaps,' she says with quiet dignity.

'But it is serious to me; and of course it is serious to her. I say nothing about it, and I treat her as kindly as I have always done. But it troubles me. On the nights that he does not come to my bed, I wonder if he is with her. And of course,' her voice quavers, just a little, 'I am afraid.'

'Afraid?' I would not have thought she was ever afraid. She sits so straight, she looks out of the window to the sunlit river as if she would know all the secrets of the world and is afraid of nothing. 'I never think of you as fearful, I think of you as indomitable.'

She laughs at that. 'You left England before I was diminished. But you must have known I was defeated by your lady grandmother. She set out to bring me very low, and she was succesful.'

'But you recovered your place. You married Harry.'

She gives a little shrug. 'Yes, I thought I had won him and I would keep him forever. The girl – it is Bessie Blount, you know, the pretty girl, the fair one, very musical, very charming . . .'

'Oh,' I say, thinking of that blonde head bent over a lute and that sweet clear voice.

'She is young and, I expect, fertile. If he were to get a child on her . . .' Katherine breaks off and I see that her eyes are filled with tears. She blinks them away as if they mean nothing. 'If she were to give him a son before I do, then I think my heart would break.'

'But you'll have a son next time!' I declare with false certainty. She has had four dead babies and one live little girl.

She looks at me; this is not a woman for an optimistic lie. 'If God wills,' she says. 'But I held a boy in my arms and named him Henry for his father, and then I had to bury him, and pray for his immortal soul. I don't think I could bear for Bessie to have a son from my husband.'

'Oh, but surely he'd never let her call him Henry,' I remark, as if it matters.

Katherine smiles and shakes her head. 'Ah, well. It's not happened yet. Perhaps it will never happen.'

'So she must be married off to someone,' I say. 'At least you can arrange her wedding and get her sent away from court.'

Katherine makes a little gesture with her hand. 'I don't know that it would be very fair to her, or to her husband,' she says. 'She's very young, I would not want to order her to marry a man who might resent it. He would know that she was the king's leavings. He might be cruel to her.'

I simply cannot understand why she should care about Bessie's happiness, and my bewilderment must show in my face, for Katherine laughs and pats my cheek. 'Ah, my sister,' she says. 'I was raised by a woman whose husband broke her heart over and over. I am always on the side of the woman. Even if the woman is my rival. And little Bessie is not really my rival. She is just a lover, not the first, and I doubt if she will be the last. But I am always the queen. Nobody can take that from me. He will always come back to me. I am his first, his true love. I am his wife, his only wife.'

'And I am Archibald's,' I say, comforted by her certainty. 'And you're right that I should be pleased that my husband has gained a pardon from Albany and can live in his own castle again. Of course I am glad that he is safe. I can go home to him there and perhaps my son can come to us.'

'You must miss him so much,' she says.

'I do,' I agree. But I am thinking of Archibald, and she is thinking of my son James. 'And at least he has been living on his wits in the borderlands,' I continue. 'It's hard to find somewhere safe for the night, hard to get enough to eat. There are no beautiful girls composing songs there.'

Katherine does not smile. 'I hope that he never turns from you, wherever he lives,' she says. 'It is an awful bereavement, when the man who has your love and your happiness in his keeping forgets about you.'

'Is that how it feels for you?' I ask, thinking of my wild fury with James and his open infidelities; of all the little bastards who came running towards him, and I knowing that their mothers lived conveniently nearby and that he rode out to see them on his way to holy pilgrimage.

'It makes me feel as if I am of no use,' she says quietly. 'And I don't know how to remind him that his honour and his heart are mine, sworn to me. I don't know how to recall him to do his duty before God, as I do mine. Even if we never have another child – though I pray every day that we have a son – but even if we never have another child I am his partner and his helpmeet, at his side through war and through peace. I am his wife and his queen. He cannot forget me.'

I have a moment of shame that my little brother should treat his wife so badly. 'He's a fool,' I say abruptly.

She stops me with a small gesture of her heavily ringed hand. 'I cannot allow a criticism of him,' she says. 'Not even from you. He is the king. I have promised him my love and obedience forever.'

## RICHMOND PALACE, ENGLAND, SUMMER 1517

I am to leave England again. It has been a long and beautiful year, but I always knew that I would return north on the long road to Scotland. Once again I have to say goodbye to my family and my friends, once again I have to travel that journey and hope to succeed at the end of it.

'Do you have to go?' Mary asks childishly. We are beyond the formal privy garden, strolling beside the river, and we turn to sit on a little bench under a tree, the sun warm on our backs, and watch the barges and boats bringing visitors and goods to entertain and feed the insatiable court. Mary's hand rests on her swelling belly. She is with child again. 'I so hoped you would stay.'

I don't dare to say that I was beginning to hope so too. It seems very hard that Katherine should live here, and Mary with her, and that I am the only sister who has to go far away, to such an uncertain future in a country that has been so hard-hearted to me.

'It's been like being girls again, having you home. Why don't you stay longer? Why don't you live with us and never go back at all?'

'I have to do my duty,' I say stiffly.

'But why now?' she asks lazily. 'At the start of summer, which is the best time of year.'

'It is the best time of year for me to do the journey and I have my safe conduct to Scotland.' I cannot keep the bitterness from my voice. 'My son, my five-year-old son, has sent me safe conduct.'

That catches her attention, she sits up. 'You have to have little James' permission to go to him?'

'Of course I do. He's the king, it is under his seal. It isn't him really, of course. It is Albany who has decided that I can come home. And he sends conditions: no more than twenty-four companions, no rebels at my side, and then there are conditions for seeing my son. I may not go as his tutor, not as regent. Just as his mother.'

'The French are very powerful,' she says. 'But I found them kind if you obey their rules. They love pretty things and courtesy. If you could only agree . . .'

'Of course, you would be on their side, since they pay your allowance,' I say sharply. 'Everyone knows that you have nothing to live on but your dower money from them. But they do not pay mine, they do not honour their debts to me, so you cannot expect me to jump to their piping like you and Brandon.'

She flushes a little. 'Of course I need the money,' she says. 'We are paupers, we are royal paupers. And every day there is a new masque or a new dance or a new pageant and the king insists that I lead it. If there is a joust he insists that Brandon fights in it. The horses alone are worth their weight in gold and a suit of armour costs ten times as much as a gown.' She puts her hand to her belly to comfort herself. 'Anyway, perhaps this is another boy and he will make our fortune. He will be heir to the throne after his brother and after your son James, after all.'

'Only if Katherine has no son,' I remind her smartly.

'God grant it.' She wishes her son out of the succession with complete sincerity. 'But, Maggie, I do really think that you should try to agree with France. Can't you make a better agreement with Albany? He is such a well-mannered nobleman. I liked him and his wife. And now she is ill and he is bound to want to go home to her. He might go back to France and leave Scotland to your rule? You could trust him, you could talk to him.'

'How much do they pay you for this?' I ask suddenly. 'The French? And could you tell them, when you report back to your spymaster, that I would be happy to agree with them if they would take their soldiers out of my country and see to the paying of the rents on my dower lands, just as they pay you? You have been cheaply bought; but I have a country to take care of. I come at a higher price.'

I see the flush of her temper in her cheeks. 'I am no spy. I take French money and so does half the court. There's no need to throw it in my face. And I know you've been borrowing money from Wolsey, just as we all do. You're no better than us and you have no right to scold me.'

'I certainly have,' I say. 'I am your older sister – it is my duty to tell you when you are wrong. You're as bad as a traitor – in the pay of the French. You can tell them to pay me my rents if you are so friendly with them.'

'I can't tell them,' she blazes out. 'It would do you no good if I spoke to them. You're such a fool! It's not the French who have been keeping your rents, but your own husband. You can't blame Albany for it. Your husband has been collecting your rents in your name and not passing them on to you.'

'That's a lie! A stupid lie as well as a wicked one. Archibald would never do such a thing. He's not like your husband, who married you only for your fortune and title. Archibald is a great lord in his own right, he has great lands in his own right. He wouldn't stoop to cheat me. You wouldn't know. You've never loved anyone but an adventurer. A commoner, a climber! Of course Brandon would take your lands. He lives off you and every woman he has ever married. My God! Brandon makes Wolsey look well bred.'

She leaps to her feet, her blue eyes blazing with temper. 'You think your husband doesn't cheat you? When he makes peace with Albany without you? When he lives with a woman he calls his wife? When he tells everyone you will never go back to Scotland, and he is glad of it? You dare to compare your traitor to my Charles, who has never been disloyal to Harry or faithless to me?'

I feel as if she has punched me in the belly, as if the air is knocked out of me. I double up as if I am winded. 'What? What? What are you saying?' I hear the words ringing in my ears, but I cannot understand them. 'What did you say? A wife?'

At once she is sorry. She pitches heavily on her knees beside me to peer up into my face, her own face still wet with angry tears. 'Oh, Maggie! Oh, Maggie! I am so sorry! Forgive me! I am so wicked! Oh, my dear! I should not have said. We agreed we would say nothing – and then I . . . ! It was when you spoke against Charles! But I should never have said a word!'

She is patting my gown and stroking my shoulder, and pushing my chin up so that she can look into my face. I keep my head down, my face hidden. I am speechless with humiliation.

'I am so sorry. I should not have said anything. She made me promise to say nothing.'

'Who?' I ask. I put my hands over my face so that she cannot see my burning eyes, my blanched cheeks. 'Who told you to say nothing?'

'Katherine,' she whispers.

'She says this? She told you all this? About my rents? About Archibald living with a woman?'

The golden head nods. 'But we swore that we would not tell you. She said that it would break your heart. She made me promise I would say nothing. She said that you could not bear to hear that he is unfaithful. That you must talk to him yourself. It must be between the two of you.'

'Oh, rubbish,' I say. All at once, I am completely furious at the thought of this mealy-mouthed gossip. 'She's such an old maid. As if all men don't take lovers! As if Ard was going to live like a monk for months at a time! As if a wife should care!'

'Don't you care?' my little sister asks me, aghast.

'Not at all!' I lie furiously. 'She is a nothing. She is nothing to him and so she is nothing to me. Katherine is making a fuss out of nothing because she is grieved that Harry has taken Bessie Blount for a lover and she wants the world to think that Ard is as bad as he. That it matters, for God's sake! That anyone cares!'

'Did you know about your husband's woman then?'

''Course I did,' I say. 'Half of Scotland knows of her, and her easy virtue. Half the lords have probably had her. Why should I care about a whore?'

'Because she says she is his wife,' she says softly.

'As do all whores.'

Mary wants to believe me. She has always looked up to me. She wants to take my word for this. 'Didn't he marry you for love? And it was a proper wedding? He was not married to her at all?'

'What d'you mean at all? You're such a fool. No. Never. They were betrothed when she was a child. It was never intended it should go ahead. He left her for me, for love of me, he preferred me to all the other women in Scotland. So what if he now amuses himself while I am away? As soon as I return to Scotland he will leave her again.'

'But my dear, they say that she lives in your house as his wife.'

'It means nothing to me.'

'But what if they have a child?'

'Why would I care about another bastard?' I demand, furious at the parroting of Katherine's sentimentality. 'James had dozens and our grandmother and our father sent me to marry him, knowing full well that he housed them in my dower castle. You think I care that Janet Stewart might have a baby when my husband the king had his own regiment of bastards? When he named one of them as his heir before I had my boy!'

She sits back on her heels, her eyelashes dark with tears, her forehead crumpled with a puzzled frown. 'Really? You really don't care?'

'Not at all,' I say. 'And when you find your husband has lain with some slut, you won't care either. It should make no difference to you, one way or the other.'

She puts her hand to where her pulse is beating in the little hollow at the base of her throat. 'Oh, I would care,' she says. 'I would, and Katherine does.'

'Then you're a pair of fools,' I declare. 'I am queen, I am his queen. He looks up to me and loves me as a subject and a lover and a man, my man. It doesn't matter to me if he eats his dinner off a wooden platter now and then. It does not devalue my gold plates.'

Wonderingly, she looks at me, her blue eyes wide. 'I never thought of it that way. I always thought a husband and wife should be all in all to each other. Like Brandon is to me.'

'You should rest,' I say abruptly, suddenly noticing the creamy pallor of her perfect skin. 'You're not carrying a prince, but you should still take care. You shouldn't be crying, you shouldn't be kneeling. Get up.'

I put out an unfriendly hand to her and haul her to her feet. I take her arm and lead her back through the gardens, into the cool of the garden stairs.

'You are sure he will come back to you when you get to Scotland?'

'I am his wife. Where else should he go?'

We walk for a few moments in silence.

'How do you know all this anyway?' I cannot hide my irritation that she and Katherine have been sorrowfully whispering about me. I cannot stand the thought that they have been mumbling over news from Scotland, all big-eyed and anxious.

'Thomas Wolsey told Katherine, and she told me. Thomas Wolsey knows everything that goes on in Scotland. He has spies everywhere.'

'Spying on my husband,' I remark.

'Oh, I am sure not. Not specially. Just if he is—' She breaks off before saying that they suspect him of disloyalty to my country as well as to me. She hesitates. 'May I tell Katherine that you are not concerned about this rumour? She will be so relieved.'

'Why, do you have to tell her everything? Is she your confessor now?'

'No, it's just that we always tell each other everything.'

I snort. 'That must please your husbands. Did you tell her that Harry was bedding her maid-in-waiting Bessie?'

She dawdles behind me, up the stairs. 'Yes,' she whispers. 'I tell her everything I know, even when it breaks my heart to tell her.'

'And does she tell you of your husband's flirtations?'

She puts her hand to the stone wall as her feet fail her. 'Oh! No! He has none.'

I cannot claim, even in my temper, that he does. 'None that I know of,' I say disagreeably. 'But he will have someone while you are like this, the size of a barn and unable to lie with him. Every man takes some slut when his wife goes into confinement.'

Once again the easy tears well up into her eyes. 'Don't say that! I am sure he does not. I am sure that he would not. He comes to my bed and sleeps beside me, he likes to hold me. I like to sleep in his arms. I really don't think he has a lover. I really believe he would not.'

'Oh, go and cry with Katherine,' I say, irritated beyond endurance, as we reach the top of the stairs. 'The two of you make a fine pair weeping over nothing. But keep your spiteful tongues off my husband and me.'

'We didn't gossip!' she exclaims. 'We were keeping it secret for fear that you should be distressed. I promised I would say nothing. It was very wrong of me to say anything.'

'You're so stupid,' I say, falling into nursery abuse. 'I look at you, and all I think is that it is as well you are pretty for God knows you are the stupidest girl I know. For Katherine, old and plain as she is, there is no hope at all.'

She turns her head away from this unkindness and hurries up the stairs to the queen's rooms. I turn away to my own rooms. I am cured of my longing to stay here. I want to go home to Scotland. I am sick of this household of women; I am sick of these women who call themselves my sisters but gossip about me behind my back. The English queen and the French queen, I hate them both.

I am not the only one who is sick of the French and the way that they buy the favourites at court. Mary and her husband are openly French pensioners, and half the English court is taking bribes. The French merchants and craftsmen have taken bread from honest English mouths in every trade and store in the city. I warn Harry that the French won't have to invade by coming with a fleet, they are so numerous already that you can hardly hear English spoken on a London street, it is so packed with M'sieurs and Milords.

Harry laughs – nothing can penetrate his sunny mood. He spends all his day hawking, while all the work of kingship is done by Thomas Wolsey, who brings him the documents to sign when he should be listening to Mass. Harry scrawls his signature, attending neither to God nor to his duty.

But the people of London feel as I do, that there are too many foreigners stealing a living from the trusting Englishmen. Every day there are half a dozen incidents reported of foreign tradesmen cheating, of French seductions and abductions, of good Englishmen shouldered off the highway, or pushed out of jobs. When the French are summonsed they bribe the magistrates, and walk away scot-free. The people of London become more and more angry.

The apprentices take the freedoms of Easter, when ale flows freely and everyone is exuberantly liberated from the long fast of Lent. They get stormingly drunk and arm themselves against French intruders. A powerful French-baiting sermon in Spitalfields stirs them up. The masters give the lads the day off for May Day, and they are armed with the weapons that they have to carry for the defence of the City. It all turns into a potent brew for the young men who would as soon fight as drink, and find that on this day they can do both. Bigger and bigger gangs of lads come together and roam around smashing the windows of the foreign merchants, bawling abuse at the doors of foreign lords. The Portuguese ambassador has the filth from the midden thrown at his walls and tightly closed gate, the Spanish ambassador's servants sally out for a battle, the French traders batten down their shutters and sit in darkness in the back rooms of their houses. But wherever there is a French name over a shop door, or a swinging sign in French, or anything that might be French – for the apprentice boys are not the most educated of youths – they catcall at the windows, and lever up the cobblestones, throw a hail of dirt and pebbles and bellow insults.

Even Thomas Wolsey – a man from their own class – does not escape. His beautiful new London house is ringed by a mob who shout that he shall answer to them for his attempt to distribute charity to the poor. There shall be no charity to foreigners, they warn him. They don't like him and his clever ways. Besides, if they were paid a good wage they would need no charity. Demand succeeds demand as they chant for good times to come, for justice to be restored. The Lord Chancellor, listening behind his stout doors with his enormous household armed and ready, fears that sooner or later someone is going to call for the white rose, for the Plantagenets, for my mother's defeated family, and those are the words that cannot be allowed. He sends for the king to turn out the yeomen of the guard, who are keeping a safe distance from the city at Richmond Palace.

'I shall ride against my own people,' Harry says grandly. It is late in the evening, the dark blue evening of a summer midnight. We have been dining and drinking late into the night. Katherine looks exhausted, but Mary's husband Charles Brandon and Harry are flushed with exercise and with wine and look as if they would dance till dawn. Mary, exquisite in cream and pearls, with her arms linked with the two men, looks up in concern at her brother. 'Oh, but you can't!' she says.

'They can't get out of hand,' Harry announces. He tips his head to me. 'Ask the Queen of Scots: she knows,' he says. 'She knows that you have to keep the people in their place with all the skill you have. But once they disobey, you have to smash them down. Don't you? Smash them down.'

I can't deny it, though both Mary and Katherine look to me to soothe Harry. 'When they rise up they have to be put down,' I say simply. 'Look at me – d'you think I would not be on my throne now, but for the people turning against me in their folly?'

'But that was because—' starts Mary and I see, though no-one else does, that her husband pinches her hand, to tell her to be silent. Charles Brandon is Harry's favourite friend, his companion for jousting and drinking, dancing and card-playing. And he has kept his place at the king's side, month after month, year after year, by never disagreeing with his royal friend and master. Whatever Harry says, Charles agrees. He's like one of those hinged dolls that Archibald gave to James that just nods its head: nod, nod, nod. Brandon can be nothing but agreeable to his royal master. The hinge of his neck only works one way: nod, nod, nod: 'yes, yes, yes.'

'I shall ride out,' Harry insists. He turns to the captain of the guard behind him. 'Send for the Duke of Norfolk, and his son the earl.'

'My lord—' Katherine begins. Harry has listened to her since the first days of their marriage. But he was bedding her then, besotted with her, and certain that together they would make a son and heir. Now, after all the losses, he doubts that she knows so very much. He doubts that she speaks God's truth. He doubts that he could learn anything from her. He gives a little swagger and glances round to see that Bessie Blount has noticed his courage. He interrupts Katherine: 'We ride tonight.'

Brandon knows they're in no hurry, and doesn't even bother to arm. They don't leave that night, not until late the next morning. Brandon orders his horse in its finest trappings, and rides beside Harry, but they go at a leisurely pace and while they are on their way the Howards, father and son, take the heavily armed guard through the streets and sweep them clear of the lads. The apprentice boys, some of them grown men, some of them little more than children, are sobering up and tiring, wishing that they were not so far from home, and starting to find the way back to their own districts, when they hear the ring of many hooves on cobbles and see, coming round the corner, the Duke of Norfolk at the head of his men, his visor down, a small army behind him with grim, unforgiving faces, riding them down as if they were Scots at Flodden.

The boys go under the hooves of the warhorses, like children falling beneath a plough. Norfolk takes it upon himself to be judge and jury. Dozens are killed in the first charge, forty lads are hanged, drawn and quartered for the crime of not taking to their heels fast enough, and hundreds – nobody knows how many – two hundred? three hundred? four? – are herded into every prison in the city, awaiting a mass trial and a mass execution, by the time that Harry and Brandon and half a dozen lords ride in.

The ladies of the court follow the noblemen, and a date is set within the week for the trial of all of the young men, regardless of age, or intent, or act. Mostly, they are boys in their first year of training, drawn from homes in the country, new to the City. They were excited by the sermon and fired up against the French; they were drunk on the May Day ales and free from work in a long four-year apprenticeship. Their masters laughed and told them to burn down the houses of rivals. Nobody told them to stay home. Nobody warned them what would happen – how should they know? Who would bring an army against children in their own capital city? These are boys working to learn the trades of maltsters, saddlers, butchers, smiths. Some of them have inky fingers from the presses, some of them are scalded from making candle wax. Some of them are regularly beaten by their masters, most of them are hungry. It does not matter, no individual matters at all. Henry is too great a king to worry about a little lad, to trouble himself about an orphan boy. They will be judged all together in one great trial and Thomas Wolsey, whose father was once an apprentice boy like these, opens their trial at Westminster with a long speech that reproves them for causing a breach of the peace and warns them that the penalty is death.

I think sourly that they probably know that already, as each one of them is standing with a rope around his neck, holding the spare end in his shaking hand. They are to go out of here and queue up at the public gallows that have been put up at street corners all around the city, each wearing his own halter, carrying his own rope, and wait in line to be hanged.

'We're going to have to do something,' Katherine says quietly to me. 'We cannot allow hundreds of apprentices to be killed. We will speak out.'

Mary is white. 'Can we ask for mercy?' Her belly is large before her; she has never looked more beautiful. She is like a swollen bud with a white petal face. The three of us huddle closely together, like angels conspiring to turn tyranny into mercy.

'Has Harry asked us to plead for pardon?' I question Katherine.

Her quick gesture of denial tells me everything. 'No, no, it should look like our idea. It is the queen's prerogative. He should stand for justice, we should beg him for kindness.'

'What do we do?' Mary asks.

'I am asking you to plead with me,' Katherine says.

'Of course we will,' I say, cutting off Mary's enthusiastic assent. 'It's just another dance in a new masque. We should do it beautifully. Do you know your cue?'

Mary is puzzled. 'Don't you want to save them, Maggie?' she asks me. 'See, the youngest ones are barely more than children. Think of your little boy. Don't you want them to have a royal pardon at your request?'

'Go on then,' I say. 'Let's see you beg your wonderful brother.' I turn to Katherine. 'Let us see the Queen of England begging the king for the good of the people. This is better than a play, better than a masque. Let's have a joust of pitiful tears. Which of us can be the more poignant? Which of us will do it most beautifully?'

Mary is confused by my bitter tone. 'I am sorry for the boys.'

'So am I,' I say. 'I am sorry for everyone who comes up against the Howards. They're not famous for chivalry.'

Katherine's sideways glance at me shows that the barb has hurt her. But she takes Mary's hand. 'Let's all sue for mercy,' she says.

The younger boys are dumb with terror; they don't understand what is being said. The fat Lord Chancellor in his blazing red robes is an incomprehensible figure to them, the great hall of Westminster Palace, draped with gold banners and the standards of the lords, is overwhelmingly bright, too rich for them to dare to look around. Many of them are openly crying; a couple are craning their necks to see beyond the great men and women to where the common people are standing in silence. One calls out 'Mama!' and someone slaps him.

'Don't you want to see them freed?' Mary whispers.

'I don't like masques,' I say shortly.

'This is real!' Katherine snaps at me.

'No, it's not.'

Thomas Wolsey gets down from his judgement seat and goes to where Harry is sitting on his throne, a golden cloth of estate over his head, his crown on his auburn hair, his handsome face stern. The fat fool Wolsey kneels slowly onto a huge hassock that just happens to be conveniently placed before the king. I see, behind Wolsey, equally positioned, three smaller hassocks, embroidered with gold thread. I imagine these are for us. I wait. Katherine will know what is to be done. She will have designed this with her husband. They may even have consulted a dancing master.

A sigh goes through the four hundred boys as they see Wolsey put his hands together in the sign of fealty. They realise now that the great man is pleading for their lives from the great king who still sits in silence. Some of the common people whisper 'Please!'

Some of the mothers are weeping. '*À* Tudor!' someone calls, as if to remind Harry of old loyalties.

Henry's face is as grave as a beautiful statue. He shakes his head. 'No,' he says.

A shudder goes through the hall. Do all these boys have to die? Every one of them? Even the little one who knuckles his eyes and whose grubby face is tracked with tears?

Katherine turns to Margaret Pole, who stands beside her. 'My headdress,' she whispers. Margaret Pole, my mother's cousin, who has seen this before, knows what is to be done. Mary at once copies Katherine as if she is her little mirror, removing her headdress. I turn to my ladies. 'Take off my hood,' I order. In a moment we are all bareheaded. Katherine's greying hair is spread over her shoulders; I toss my head, and my hair, a fairer shade than Harry's, falls limply down my back, Mary puts her hands to her head and sweeps back a mass of the finest blonde curls that tumble to her waist like a golden mane.

Katherine leads us forward, as the Lord Chancellor bows even lower. First Katherine, then I, then Mary, kneel before Harry and put out our hands like exquisitely gowned beggars. 'I beg for mercy,' the queen says.

'I beg for mercy,' I repeat.

'I beg for mercy,' Mary says, her voice thick with tears. Of all of us, she is probably the only one who believes in this charade. She really thinks that Harry may forgive these poor boys on our pleading.

I can hear a shuffle like quiet thunder as all the apprentices go down on their knees, and behind them the common people drop down too. Harry looks over the great hall of Westminster at all the bowed heads, he listens to the susurration of pleas, then he gets to his feet and stretches out his arms like Christ blessing the world and he says: 'Mercy.'

Everyone cries, even I cry. The apprentices pull the hangman's ropes from their necks and the guards stand aside and let them run through the crowds to their parents. People call down blessings on the king, purses filled with gold, that would have bribed the hangman to make a quick end by tugging on a lad's kicking feet to break his neck before the disembowelling, are dropped at Harry's feet and picked up by his pages. The Duke of Norfolk, Harry's executioner, is smiling as if he is delighted by forgiveness. Everyone is bowing to the throne, pulling off their caps, saying: 'God bless King Harry! God bless Queen Katherine!' Never has London loved a king more, not even one of the Plantagenet kings. Harry has spared the boys. They will live because of this great king. He is a reverse Herod, he has given life to a generation. People start to cheer, and someone starts to sing the bold tune of a Te Deum.

Katherine is flushed with delight at the success of her gesture. Margaret Pole, behind her, keeps tight hold of her gold-plated headdress – she, for one, does not trust a crowd. Harry, in a lordly gesture, stretches his hand out to Katherine and she comes to stand beside him, smiling warmly at the loyal cheers. Unbidden, Mary goes to his other side, sure of her welcome, and the radiant three beam at the crowd like a trio of angels, more beautiful, more powerful, richer than any of these people could even dream. Harry smiles at me, revelling in my admiration of the picture that the three of them make.

'This is how I rule England,' he says. 'This is kingship.'

I smile and nod; but inside I say – no, it's not.

I set off for Scotland with that picture of the three of them – the King of England and my two sisters – bright in my mind, the only bright thing in my intense inner darkness. I feel outcast from the Eden that is Tudor England, from the court of wealth and glamour where my brother play-acts the part of king, with his wife, who cannot even give him a son, as his pretend queen. My sister, without a fortune and with a nobody for a husband, leads all the dances, the most beautiful girl at the court. I think: this is all false, this is all portrait and no reality, this is all masque and no battle. They glory in themselves, in the picture that they make to people so poor that they cannot tell pretence from life. My sisters flaunt their beauty and blessings and persuade themselves that they are rightfully blessed.

But it is not like that for me. Everything I have has to be won. The people in my kingdom will not kneel to me with halters around their necks, my husband will not proudly embrace me before everyone. My sisters are not at my side. I have to go away, up the long road north. Not for Mary, the clamber into the saddle every morning, and the summoning of the courage to ride into drizzle or cold winds. Not for Katherine, the patient waiting on the back of a tired horse while my host for the night recites a long lecture of greeting. Not for Harry, the ceaseless plotting of the capture of a kingdom and the struggle for rightful power. My little girl rides in the arms of her nursemaid; she does not sleep in a gold cradle like her cousins. While I trudge northward my brother and my two sisters go on pilgrimage to Walsingham, riding a short journey in good weather, inviting the blessing of Our Lady on Katherine's empty womb: denying the omen of barrenness. I go on and on, wondering what Ard is doing. I am solitary, lonely, travelling every day, weary as a beaten dog every night.

## BERWICK CASTLE, ENGLAND, SUMMER 1517

My guards and, after them, the lords and ladies of my small household ride towards the little town of Berwick and remark on the pretty gleaming stone, the river before the castle, the sea beyond. I remember coming here and gripping Ard's hand when the captain of the castle would not admit us. Now, I smile grimly as the cannon bawl out a salute, the drawbridge rattles down, the portcullis clanks up, and the captain of the castle hurries out, his officers behind him, his lady behind them, his bonnet under his arm, his face wreathed in obsequious smiles.

I don't dismount. I let him come to my stirrup and bow his head to his knees. I let him read his speech of welcome. I don't reproach the town of Berwick for sending me out into the darkness to find refuge at Coldstream Priory, but I won't forget it either. Then, from under the shadow of the gatehouse, I see a slight, tall figure step forward. I blink. I cannot be sure what I am seeing. I rub my eyes with the backs of my hands. It cannot be him, and yet it is him. It is Archibald. My husband has come to greet me.

'My love,' is all I say. I forget in a moment everything that I have heard against him, everything that I have feared.

Quickly, he steps towards my horse and reaches up for me. I spring down into his arms and he holds me closely. My head against his shoulder, his mouth on my neck, I feel the familiar lithe hardness of him, and know, with a little delicious shudder, his strangeness. We have not been together for more than a year. I lean back in his arms to look at his face. His skin is as dark as a gypsy's from the months of living rough on the borders. There is a hardness about his profile that reminds me of the two old lords, those two great men, his grandfathers. I married a boy, but this is a man who has come to claim me. At once Harry seems soft and lazy, his court rich and overblown. My sister is a delicate doll married to a jouster, a pretend warrior. A man like my husband needs a woman like me, with courage to match his own, with ambition that runs neck and neck with his.

'I know you are well. I have heard nothing but praise for you on your journey,' he says against my hair. 'And my daughter?'

I turn and beckon her nursemaid. Margaret, russet as a Tudor, smiles and waves at the stranger as she has been trained to do. 'A princess!' her father exclaims, with real tenderness in his voice. 'My little girl.'

He tightens his arm around my waist. 'Come in. There's a feast ready for you and a celebration planned. Scotland wants its queen back. I can't wait to get you over the border.'

The captain of the castle bows again, his lady curtseys, their household snatch the hats from their heads and drop to their knees as Archibald walks past with my hand in his. I see him glance across the hundreds of people bowing as we go by and the proud curl of his smile, and I know that he will always love me better than any woman in Scotland while every man drops to his knees at the sight of me. Archibald was born to marry a queen. I am her.

He pauses before a stunningly handsome man, dressed all in white.

'You remember the Sieur de la Bastie?' Archibald says without much warmth in his voice. 'He is serving as the regent while the Duke of Albany stays in France.' His tone makes it clear that the Duke of Albany makes no difference to us, in France or in Scotland, and that I would be wise not to admire the dazzling nobleman who bends over my hand and kisses it.

'Of course I remember the chevalier. We are old friends.'

'You are welcome home, Your Grace,' he says. He straightens up and tosses his head so his mane of chestnut-brown hair falls away from his face. He smiles at me. 'I am sure that we can work together.'

## HOLYROODHOUSE PALACE, EDINBURGH, SCOTLAND, SUMMER 1517

I have every reason for confidence this summer as I come back to my country and my power. Ard has done great work in my absence. Not only did he negotiate a free pardon from the Duke of Albany, but he has recovered his lands, his wealth, and has rejoined the council, where he can choose the guardians who are appointed to my son. He has prepared the council for my return, and encouraged Albany to go home to France to his sick wife. 'I have done everything to persuade them that you as regent and an alliance with England is our future,' he says quietly in my ear as he lifts me down from the saddle in the courtyard before the palace. 'I think we can take Scotland together, my love.'

As always, as he lifts me down from my horse and holds me, I feel the warmth of his breath on my neck.

'I have to go and see my son at once,' I say unsteadily. Truth be told, I cannot even remember that I am a mother, that I am a princess. I have forgotten that I am a dowager queen with national ambitions. I would go in a moment to my bedchamber like an eager girl, and lie with him.

He smiles at me as if he knows this perfectly well. 'Go,' he says. 'And when you come back we will dine and we will go to bed. I had to wait for you for a year of absence. I can wait another hour or two.'

'Ard . . .' I whisper.

'I know,' he says. 'Be as quick as you can. I want you. I want you with a hunger.'

I give a little smothered gasp and I walk back to the wagons to see that the gifts I have brought for my boy are unpacked at once, and tell my master of horse that I will take a fresh mount up the Via Regis to the castle. The horse must have my English saddle with white damask cloth of gold that Henry commissioned for my journey; the people will watch me ride up the steep cobbled hill and I want them to see that I am returned in my power, surrounded by rich, beautiful things. The acting regent, Antoine, the Sieur de la Bastie, is as handsome and as smiling as if the hard years have never been, the same young man who rode at my wedding joust. He tells me he will come with me, appearing in the stable yard dressed in his usual dazzling white, and I say that he matches my livery. I laugh. 'You are the beauty that they call you,' I say. 'You will outshine me.'

'I am the moon to your sun,' he says with his attractive French accent. 'And I should be honoured to ride with you to your castle to visit your boy. I have had the pleasure of meeting with him often, and I tell him about jousting and what a chevalier his father was. I promised him that I would bring his mother as soon as you arrived. But say the word and I shall stay here and you go alone. Whatever you wish, Your Grace.'

'Oh, you can come,' I say as if it does not matter to me; but I am flattered that he wants to ride with me. He is a handsome man; any woman would be glad to have him at her side. Since he is regent in Albany's absence I need to befriend him. God knows, I still don't have enough friends on the council.

The horses slip a little on the cobbles and lean forward to get up the hill. Just as I expected, the people call blessings on me from their windows, and come out of the dark doorways to wave and smile. The market women stand with their baskets wedged on their jutting hips and bellow their good wishes to me in Erse and in the dialect of the borders. I can understand them; but Antoine de la Bastie laughs at the incomprehensible language and takes off his hat with the white plume and bows to one side and the other. 'I am hoping they are wishing me well,' he says to me. 'For all I know, they could be damning me to hell.'

'They are glad to see me home, at any rate,' I say. 'And no woman under ninety ever has a bad word to say against you. They call you the M'sieur of Beauty.'

'Because they can't say my title,' he laughs. 'There's only one beauty here.'

I smile. 'They admire you, but I don't think your regency is popular with the people.'

'Nobody likes to pay taxes, nobody likes to obey laws. If the Scots lords did not have a regent to command them, they would just murder each other.'

'But I should be the regent,' I say. 'My husband, your friend, left the authority to me at his death.'

'Oh yes,' he says, his accent very strong. 'But he was not to know that you would marry the first handsome boy you set eyes on! Who could have guessed such a thing?'

'Archibald is the Earl of Angus and a great lord among the lords,' I say furiously. 'No mere boy. And you should remember that you are speaking to a princess of England and a Dowager Queen of Scotland.'

He tips his head towards me as if to whisper. 'I don't forget who you are,' he says. 'I was at your wedding. I would never forget your first husband, who was a great king. But I tell you, without fear or favour, that your second husband is not his match.'

'How dare you?' I demand.

He shrugs. Someone cheers us and he flashes his brilliant smile at an upstairs window and someone throws a flower. 'Your Grace, you have been away a long time. Your handsome young carver is now serving himself.'

'What do you mean?'

'Ah, bah!' he says. 'Who am I to speak of a straying husband? You must ask him yourself whether he is in command of the lords. Ask him yourself where are your rents? And ask him yourself where he has been living while you have been in exile, and if his life was very hard? Ask him who gets the best cuts now?'

'He was in the borders,' I say firmly. 'I know all this. And his life was very hard. He was an outlaw until he could negotiate his own peace with the regent, the Duke of Albany.'

'A hero no doubt; he should have his own makar, like your first husband, to compose poems of his many victories,' and then he waves at the sentries on the wall of Edinburgh Castle to raise the portcullis and drop the drawbridge.

Nothing happens. The two of us rein in our horses and wait. My master of horse goes forward: 'Her Grace, the Dowager Queen of Scotland,' he yells.

I sit proudly in the saddle, waiting for the bridge to come crashing down and the portcullis to roll up, but still nothing happens. I am smiling, thinking of seeing my son for the first time in two years, when Antoine says: 'There is some difficulty, I think.'

From the sally port at the side of the gate the captain of the castle comes out, sweeps off his bonnet and bows low to me and then to Antoine. 'I apologise,' he says. He looks embarrassed. 'I am not allowed to open the castle to anyone without a letter of entry from the council.'

'But this is Her Grace, the king's mother,' the chevalier exclaims. 'And I, the deputy regent, at her side.'

'I know that,' the captain says, red to the ears. 'But without a letter I am not allowed to open the gates. Besides, there is plague in the city and we may not admit anyone without a letter from a physician saying they are well.'

'*Capitaine!*' Antoine shouts. 'It is I! Escorting the dowager queen. Are you closing the gate to us?'

'You can't come in without a letter.' The captain is anguished. He bows to me, he bows to the chevalier. 'Forgive me, Your Grace, there is nothing I can do.'

'This is to insult me,' I gasp. I am near to tears with fury and disappointment. 'I will have that man beheaded for this.'

'There is nothing he can do,' Antoine confirms. 'Let's go back to Holyroodhouse. I'll get that letter signed and sent to us. It's how we run Scotland now. It is all done by the clerks. It's the only way we keep the peace. The strictest of rules and everything allowed only by permits. If we did not have rules we would have unending war. It would be as bad as the borders and we would all be ruined. It is I who am to blame. I should have got a permit at once. I did not think.'

'My son will be waiting to see me! The King of Scotland! Is he to be disappointed?'

'They will tell him you came at once, they will tell him that you will come back. I will tell him when I see him after dinner this evening. And I will get the permit so that you can come tomorrow.'

'Archibald would never have let them close the door to me.'

Diplomatically, he says nothing.

Archibald is waiting for me, leaning against my throne in my presence chamber. He comes to me as I walk in and wraps me in his arms. He sees my flushed face and the tears in my eyes and at once he soothes me, whispers words of love in my ear, draws me away from all the people waiting to see me: the tenants who have come miles, the petitioners with their lawsuits, the debtors with their pledges, the endless population of people with troubles. 'Her Grace will see you tomorrow,' he announces to the room and leads me to the privy chamber, past my waiting ladies, and into my bedroom. He closes the door behind us and unties the bow of my cape.

'Ard, I . . .'

'My love.'

Carefully, he unpins my velvet riding bonnet and puts it to one side. He pulls ivory hairpins from my plaited hair and it tumbles down over my shoulders. As if he cannot stop himself, he buries his face in it and inhales the scent of me. I hesitate, shaken with desire.

'The castle was locked . . .'

'I know.'

His skilled hands unlace my gown at the back and over my shoulders, shuck me out of the stiff stomacher, untie the ribbons of my skirt, drop it to the ground.

'I could not . . .'

'The chevalier is a weak fool. I adore you.'

He peels the embroidered sleeves from my arms, lifts the hem of my beautiful fine linen petticoat, and takes it over my head. I am naked before him but for a little shift. I fold my arms over my breasts and belly. Suddenly I am terribly shy. I have not stood naked in daylight before him since the birth of our baby, and I am conscious of the fatness of my belly, the roundness of my breasts.

Gently he takes one hand and puts it on the back of his neck, as if I should pull him into a kiss. He takes the other and puts it on the front of his breeches. He is not wearing a codpiece; the hard warmth under my hand is all him, all his desire for me.

'Oh, Ard,' I whisper. Everything that has happened this morning – my disappointment in being kept from my son, the locked castle, the insinuations of the chevalier – all fades away at his touch as he presses me against him, his hands on my half-naked buttocks, pulling me closer, as his mouth comes down on mine.

An hour later, when we are stirring in the big bed, I remember. 'There are rumours against you,' I say.

'There are always rumours against great men,' he replies. He sits on the edge of my rumpled bed and pulls on his riding breeches over his lean thighs. I sit in the bed, a sheet caught up to my throat, and watch him. Even now, after an hour of lovemaking, I feel my desire rise at the sight of him. He knows this. He stands before me and lets me watch him lace the opening at the front of his breeches, drop a linen shirt over his broad, smooth chest, tie the white laces at his tanned throat.

I crawl down the bed towards him. I kneel up to put my lips to the base of his neck where I feel his pulse speed at the touch of my mouth. His hands come onto my shoulders, he presses me back towards the bed. I yield dreamily. 'We have to go to dinner,' I remind him. 'Everyone will be waiting.'

'Let them wait,' he says, and he pulls the sheet away from me.

Slowly, luxuriously, he takes a handful of my hair and kisses my neck, just below my ear. I let him trace a line of kisses down my breast.

'They tell me that you have my rents,' I say, distracted by the tide of pleasure that is rising up in me again.

'Hmm, some of them,' he says. 'The tenants have no money. There is no law in the borders. How can anyone collect rents?'

'But you have some of them?'

He stops his gentle caress. 'I do,' he says softly. 'Of course. I never stopped working for you, though you were far away. I have done all I can to collect your dues.'

'Thank you,' I say.

He slides his thigh against me. I grip his waist and pull him towards me. His riding breeches are the softest of leathers, the touch of them against my naked skin causes ripples of pleasure. 'And have you been living in my houses?'

'Yes, of course. How else could I guard your lands and collect your rents?'

He unties the laces on his breeches and I am eager for his touch. I pull the strings from the holes and feel for him.

'They will have told you about Janet Stewart,' he guesses, as my hands find him, and I give a little sigh.

'I did not believe a word,' I swear.

'It's nothing,' he promises me. He is close, he is gently entering me; I can feel that I am dissolving with desire. 'Just gossip. Believe in me now. Believe in this. Believe in us.'

With each command he thrusts gently inside me and I breathe 'Yes. Yes. Yes.'

## CRAIGMILLAR CASTLE, EDINBURGH, SCOTLAND, SUMMER 1517

My son the king is moved from the plague-struck city to Craigmillar Castle, just an hour south of Edinburgh, where the Sieur de la Bastie is living. He says that I may come and stay for as long as I wish, that I must see my son without obstacle. I would be wise to leave Edinburgh during the time of sickness. I say that Archibald will come too, and Antoine rolls his handsome brown eyes and laughs at me. 'You are a woman in love,' he says. 'And you will not be warned. So come, bring the earl. I am always delighted to see him, whoever he is married to, today.'

I pay no attention to anything but his invitation, and Ard and I ride out, with James' presents, the very next morning.

It is a tower castle built in the French style, with a handsome courtyard wall. 'A toy castle,' Archibald says scathingly. 'For a pretend chevalier.'

'Not every castle can be like Tantallon with the North Sea as its moat,' I tease him.

We ride in through the stone archway, the guards at attention on either side. They are beautifully turned out. I see new gates on the doorway and shiny new hinges. De la Bastie takes his duties as James' guardian very seriously.

He is there to greet us at the doorway of the castle and comes himself to help me down from the saddle. Ard jumps down like a boy to be at my side first; but I see neither of them – not the handsome Frenchman nor the dazzling Scot – for in the doorway is Davy Lyndsay whom I have not seen for two years and beside him, standing alone, is my little boy, five-year-old James.

'Oh, James,' I say. 'My boy, my son.'

The moment I see him, the loss of his younger brother, Alexander, strikes me again, and I can hardly stop myself from crying out. I don't want to disturb him with my tears, so I bite my lip and I go carefully towards him, as if I were approaching a little merlin, a falcon that might bate away from me. He looks up at me, with eyes as bright and as dark as a merlin. 'Lady Mother?' he asks in his clear little-boy voice.

I see that he is not sure who I am. He has been told that I will come, but he does not remember me and, in any case, I imagine I am much changed from the woman who kissed him goodbye and swore that she would come for him soon. We were in terrible danger then, I was pregnant, and I left him, certain that his crown and his blood would keep him safe, while Archibald's name and behaviour would endanger him. I left my son for love of my husband, and I don't know even now if I did the right thing.

I drop to my knees so that he and I are face to face. 'I am your mother,' I whisper. 'I love you very much. I have missed you every day. I have prayed for you every night. I have longed—' again I have to swallow a sob, '—I have longed to be with you.'

He is only five years old, but he seems far older, and reserved.

He does not seem to doubt me, but clearly he does not want declarations of love nor his mother's tears. He looks diffident, as if he would rather I was not kneeling in the yard before him, my eyes filled, my lip trembling.

'You are welcome to Craigmillar,' he says as he has been taught.

Davy Lyndsay bows low to me.

'Oh, Davy! You stayed with my son.'

'I would never leave him,' he says. He corrects himself. 'Och, no credit to me, I had nowhere else to go. Who wants a poet in these poor days? And he and I have been here and there together. We always remember you in our prayers, and we made up a song for you, didn't we, Your Grace? D'you remember our song for the English rose?'

'Did you?' I ask James; but he is silent, and it is the makar who answers.

'Aye. We'll sing it for you this evening. He's as good a musician as his father was before him.'

James smiles at the praise, looking up at his tutor. 'You said I was deaf as an adder.'

'And here is your stepfather, come to visit too!'

I think I sense a little chill. Davy Lyndsay bows to Archibald, James nods his head. But neither of them greets him with any familiarity, or warmth.

'You will have seen him often?' I ask Ard.

'Not very often,' he replies. 'He signed a warrant for my execution, remember.'

'He signed your pardon too,' Davy Lyndsay interjects.

My son the king inclines his head and does not remark on this. This is a child and yet he minds his manners, and takes care what he says. I feel a slow burn of rage that my son has never been carefree. Katherine of Aragon ordered the death of his father and so destroyed his childhood. He was a king before he was out of swaddling; she made him in her own disciplined image. She could not make her own baby, she took mine from me.

'Well, we shall see a lot of each other now,' I declare. 'I have been in England, James, and I have won a truce for Scotland. There shall be peace between our countries and peace on the borders, and I shall see you whenever we wish. I shall live with you as your mother again. Won't that be wonderful?'

'Yes,' says the little boy in his clear Scots accent. 'Whatever you wish, Lady Mother. Whatever my guardians allow.'

'They have broken his spirit,' I rage at Ard, striding up and down our room in the tower at Craigmillar. 'They have broken my heart.'

'Not at all,' he says gently. 'He has been raised carefully and well. You should be pleased that he thinks before he speaks, that he is cautious.'

'He should be running around laughing. He should be boating and playing truant, he should be out on his horse and stealing apples.'

'All at once?'

'I won't be mocked!'

'Indeed, I see you are distressed.'

'They drive me from the country, they separate me from my son, then they bring him up as quiet as a monk!'

'No, he is playful and he does chatter. I have heard him myself. But of course he is shy with you after so long. He has been waiting for your return – of course he is a little overwhelmed. We all are. You come home more beautiful than any of us remembered.'

'It's not that.' But I am mollified.

He takes my hand. 'It is, my love. Trust me, all will be well. You be as loving to him as I know you long to be, and he will be your little boy again within days. He will play with his sister, and the two of them will be as noisy and as naughty as you could wish.'

I lean towards him. 'But Ard, when I left him, he had a little brother. He had a little brother who smiled and cooed when he saw me.'

He puts his arm around my waist and presses my head against his shoulder. 'I know. But at least we still have James. And we can make another little brother for him.'

I let my face nestle against his warm neck. 'You want another child?'

'At once,' he says. 'And this one will be born at Tantallon with every delicacy and luxury you can command. I shall dress you in a cloth of gold gown with rings on every finger as you go into confinement. And I shall keep you safe in confinement for month after month. I shall have a bed carved for you enamelled with gold and you won't get up for half a year.'

I smile. 'It was so awful with baby Margaret.'

'I know. I thought I would die of fear for you. But everything will be better now.'

'There is nothing to explain or forgive?' I ask. 'I hear such gossip.'

'Who knows what people say?' He shrugs and then draws me close again. 'You should hear the things they told me about you!'

'Oh, what did they say about me?'

'That you would divorce me and marry the emperor, that your brother was determined to make the match. That Thomas Wolsey had drawn up the peace treaty that would make my poor Scotland the helpless victim of England and the empire. That they would say that our marriage had never happened.'

'I never even considered it,' I lie with my eyes on his.

'I knew you would not,' he says. 'I trusted you, whatever they said of you. I knew that we were married for life, for good or bad, forever. I heard all sorts of things about you, but I never even listened.'

'Neither did I,' I say, and feel my passion for him burn me up. I like to hear the loyalty in my voice. 'I never listened to one word that anyone ever said against you.'

In the days that follow I set myself to spend time with my son and make up for the missing months. I know it can never be done. I did not teach him to play the lute or sing the songs that Davy Lyndsay has taught him. I didn't put him on his first shaggy little highland pony, and trot alongside him, holding him steady in the saddle. I didn't take him out last winter to play in the snow, I did not build him an ice castle with a turret. He tells me all about it and I think, yes – that was when I was at Morpeth Castle, unable to get out of bed for the pain in my hip, when I thought I would die; that was when they told me that my younger son was dead. The closer he and I become, the more he tells me about his adventures while I was away, the more I remember that it was Katherine who gave orders to Thomas Howard to take no prisoners at the Battle of Flodden. The more he tells me of his life behind castle walls the more I resent the Duke of Albany taking power as regent and Katherine not insisting that my boy and I were rescued together.

I introduce him to his little half-sister Margaret and he pulls faces at her to make her laugh, and encourages her to run behind him. When she falls he flinches at her loud cry and I laugh and tell him that she has the temper of the Tudors.

Thomas Dacre, who always knows everything, writes to me that my sister, Mary, has had a pretty baby, Frances, and that she is well and returned to court. A few days later I get a letter from Mary herself, praising the baby and saying that her confinement was easy this time. She says that she misses me, that she prays I can find happiness with my husband at my home, and that we may both come to England again when it is safe for me to do so. She says that she is my little sister still, even when she is a matron with her children around her. She asks me to write to her to tell her that I am safe and well and that I have seen my son.

*I hear that your husband is with you now, and I hope that you are happy,*

she writes, as if she doubts that it can be so.

I reply cheerfully. I tell her that I have heard that Albany, the regent, is still in France and does not want to return to Scotland, and I pray that he will not. In his absence the country is at peace. I tell her that Antoine d'Arcy, the Sieur de la Bastie, is a true knight, as handsome as a woodcut in a book, and that we are happy as his guests; he is a nobleman in every way. I don't say one word about her gossip with Katherine against Archibald's good name. I ignore her concern for my happiness. She can learn from my silence to hold her tongue.

I speak to Antoine and suggest that we might share power. We might both be Regent of Scotland; we could work together. He never denies that it is possible, he always says it is essential that England keep the peace on the borders. It is from these troubled lands that all the unrest in Scotland flows. If I can persuade my brother, the king, to order Thomas Dacre to honour the peace of the borders then we can plan a future for Scotland together.

'If you will trust me?' Antoine teases me.

'If you will trust me?' I reply, and make him laugh.

He takes my hand and kisses it. 'I would trust you and your son,' he says. 'I would trust the dowager queen and the king. Nobody else. I cannot make promises to your husband or to any of the Scots lords. I don't believe a word any of them says.'

'You may not criticise him to me,' I say.

He laughs. 'I don't single him out. I say no worse than I say about any of them. All of them think of their own wealth and their own power and their own ambition before anything else. All of them are true only to their clans. None of them even knows how to serve their king. None of them has any idea of their country. Few of them think of God as anything other than an invisible tribal chief more unpredictable and dangerous than any other. They have no imagination.'

'I have no idea what you are talking about,' I say flatly.

He laughs. 'For you have no imagination either, Your Grace. You do perfectly well without it. Now tell me the scandal of the English court. I hear that your brother, the king, is in love?'

I frown. 'I won't gossip with you,' I say repressively.

'And the young lady is very, very beautiful?'

'Not particularly.'

'And very educated and musical and sweet-tempered?'

'What does it matter?'

'The king, your brother, would not consider putting his wife aside? Since God does not seem to be inclined to give them a son? His wife, the queen, would not consider withdrawing to a convent? So that he might get an heir with this beautiful young lady?'

I feel that instant unworthy flame of delight at the thought that gossip speaks of Katherine being humbled to nothing. Then, immediately, I think of how heartbroken she would be – she who cannot bear the thought of Harry even flirting with another woman. 'It would never happen,' I say. 'My brother is a great protector of the Church and of all the institutions of the Church. And my sister-in-law would never desert her duty. She will live and die Queen of England.'

'She has been a great enemy to Scotland,' he points out. 'We might do better if he listened to a new wife.'

'I know,' I say. 'It is a matter of sorrow to us both. But she is my sister. I am bound to be loyal to her.'

We plan that Ard and I should stay at Craigmillar Castle for a few weeks more and then go to my dower lands at Newark Castle. Antoine says that when we all return to Edinburgh, after the plague has passed, he will call a council of the lords and that I shall attend and address them. If I can persuade them that I should be co-regent he will be happy to share power with me. I shall have free access to my son, who is easier with me every day. I shall have a seat in the council chamber. I shall be acknowledged as dowager queen.

'And Archibald on a chair beside mine,' I say. 'Equal height.'

The chevalier makes a little gesture with his hands. 'Ah, don't ask it,' he begs. 'You love your husband, I know. But he has so many enemies! If you force him down their throats, they will be your enemies too. Be the mother of the king and the dowager queen in your public life. Be his wife in your private rooms. Be his slave there, if you wish. But don't take him into the council chamber as your equal.'

'He is my husband,' I say impressively. 'Of course he is my master. I won't keep him in my closet.'

'He was granted a pardon only by the generosity of the Duke of Albany,' de la Bastie reminds me. 'His cousin and fellow outlaw was beheaded for treason. There are many who think that Hume did only what your husband would have done, if he had the courage.' He holds up his hand as I am about to interrupt. 'Hear me out, Your Grace. Scotland will only survive as a kingdom for your son to inherit if we can keep the peace. Your husband and his family and all his affinity are enemies to that peace. They use their castles as a base for raids, they allow their tenants to steal cattle, they disrupt the markets and they rob the tenants and the poor. They collect the royal taxes but they don't remit them. And whenever they are in danger, they slip over the border to Thomas Dacre, who tells them to continue lawbreaking and pays them to do worse. You are going to have to find some way to confine your husband's ambition and his violence to your bedroom where, I suppose, you like it. The rest of us don't want him carving and dancing around us. The rest of us know that he says one thing and does another.'

'How dare you—' I start, when there is a loud knock at the door. It swings open and the captain of the castle is there, his helmet under his arm. 'Forgive me,' he says with a bow to me, and then speaks to de la Bastie. 'A message from the Tower of Langton. They are under siege from George Hume of Wedderburn and his affinity.'

De la Bastie is on his feet at once. 'The Humes again?' he says with a nod to me as if to remind me that these are Archibald's allies and kinsmen. 'How many?'

The messenger steps forward. 'Not more than five hundred,' he says. 'But they say they will burn out the tower and all who are in it.'

Antoine glances at me. 'We have to have peace,' he says. 'D'you know George Hume?'

'Kinsman to Alexander?' I ask.

'Exactly,' he says. 'An outlaw's kinsman, continuing his work. I shall arrest him. Will your husband ride with me against lawbreakers?'

I am silenced. I know Ard will never ride against his cousins, the Humes.

De la Bastie laughs. 'I thought not,' he says. 'How can he be the king's protector when he does not protect the king's peace?'

He bows to me and goes to the door, as the captain shouts orders that the guard shall be mustered to ride out.

'How long will you be?' I ask, suddenly nervous.

He looks at the messenger for the answer. 'It's a good half-day's ride,' the man says.

'Should be back by tomorrow,' he says casually. He bows to me with his hand on his heart, a gleam of his smile, and he is gone.

We expect him for dinner, but they serve and we eat without him. Archibald remarks that perhaps the famous French chevalier could not catch George Hume as easily as he expected. He says that jousting is one thing, a tournament is another, but riding hard across wild country commanding men little better than reivers takes courage that the chevalier would never have needed before.

'They are breaking the peace,' I say shortly. 'Of course he has to arrest them.'

'They are defying the regency that sent you into exile and made you a stranger to your son,' he says. 'The regency that I had to beg a pardon from before they would let me back to my own.'

'We have to have peace,' I repeat.

'Not on any terms,' my husband says. 'I wish I were with them.'

'De la Bastie thought you might ride with him!' I exclaim.

Ard laughs. 'No, he didn't, he just said that to trouble you. He knows, and I know, that there will be no peace for this country until it is ruled by you, the dowager queen, for your son the king. He knows I would fight for no regency commanded by him or the other Frenchman. I am for the queen and England.'

'What's that?' I say, starting up as I hear the portcullis chains clanking and the roller creaking as the gate is lifted. 'Is he back at last?'

Together we go down to the castle door, expecting to see de la Bastie and his guard riding in. Instead there are half a dozen men with his standard. They are carrying it lowered, as if in mourning, as if there has been a death.

'What is it?' I demand, and Ard goes down to the captain of the guard and speaks quickly to him. When he turns back to me his face in the flickering torchlight is bright.

'De la Bastie was defeated. George Hume has escaped,' he says shortly.

'Come and report to me at once,' I say to the captain of the guard. 'And bring all your men. They're not to speak to anyone. They must tell me first.' I turn into the castle and wait beside the great stone fireplace in de la Bastie's presence chamber as the guards straggle in and stand together.

The captain speaks for them all. 'It was an ambush,' he says slowly. 'There was no siege of the tower. That was a lie, a feint to draw us out.'

Behind him I can see Ard intently listening. There is no shock on his face, no unease. He might be hearing of the unfolding of a successful plan, perhaps even his own plan.

'Why?' I ask. But I know.

'We met with George Hume and his force just north of Kelso and the chevalier commanded him to come into the town and explain himself. We rode together, side by side, but just outside Langton it turned nasty. Hume drew his sword, all his men drew theirs. The chevalier shouted to us to follow him and gallop back to Duns. They were after us all the way. It wasn't a battle, it was a trap, an ambush. I thought my lord would get away. He was headed for his castle. But there is a thick part of the wood, you can't see more than three feet behind you, with a cliff to one side and a steep slope down to the river on your left.' He turns to Archibald. 'You know.'

Ard nods. He knows.

'They caught us there, forcing us off the track, driving us down the hill. There's a marsh at the bend in the river. We fought back but they had the advantage of the ground, and of surprise. More of them poured out of Duns on foot, twisting round the trees, jumping over fallen branches. Our horses struggled, many fell, we got pushed down the hill, and his lordship's horse went over the bank into the river, the Whiteadder. It's deep. Most of the other horses went in too. It was a mess: floundering and screaming and men drowning.'

I put my hand to the warm stone of the chimney breast, clinging to it as if the ground is unsafe beneath me as well. 'And then?' I hear my voice say thinly. 'And then?'

'His lordship came off his horse. His armour weighed him down, but he had one arm around his horse's neck and they were swimming together, struggling together. I thought he might get to dry land. One of the Humes – John – called out to him, he had one arm around a leaning tree, his feet on the roots, dry-shod in the marsh. He reached out to his lordship and he took his hand.'

'He saved him?' I ask incredulously.

'He drew him towards him like he was pulling him from the marsh, saving him from drowning, and then he stabbed him in the armpit, where he could get the blade in under the armour. His lordship went down and Patrick Hume drew his sword and hacked off his head.'

The other men nod, too stunned to speak.

'You saw this?' Archibald asks. 'Where were you?'

'I had fallen over a tree stump,' one man says.

'I was on my horse on the road.'

'I was fighting out of the marsh.'

'I fell from my horse. God forgive me, I lay still.'

'And what then?' I ask unsteadily.

They bow their heads, they shuffle their feet. They ran away, but they don't want to admit it.

'Did many come home?' Ard asks. 'Did the Humes not pursue you? It's not like them not to finish the task.'

They shake their heads. 'We're the only ones that got away, I think,' the captain says. 'But it was getting dark, and you could see nothing among the trees, it wasn't like a battle at all, more like a brawl. There might be others, run off home. There might be others stuck like fish in a barrel, drowned like kittens in the river.'

'Not like a joust,' Archibald says with a swift smile to me. 'And he was always so beautiful in the joust.'

## NEWARK CASTLE, SCOTLAND, SEPTEMBER 1517

We go to Newark Castle as we planned, leaving Craigmillar with the chevalier's standard at half-mast in deepest mourning. It is a miserable journey in cold driving rain. I am glad that my boy, James, does not come with us and Margaret stays behind in the nursery. But it is odd to ride into my own castle that I hardly know. I find I am looking around for any signs that another woman has lived here, but my rooms are bare and clean and the bed linen fresh and newly changed and the strewing rushes green on the floor. There is no evidence at all that anyone has used this house. I think that the chevalier must have forgotten his code of honour when he spoke against Archibald to me. And Ard is right – all great people are the subject of slander.

My son James cannot come with us because the lords of the council command that he goes back to the greater safety of Edinburgh Castle. Now, since the death of Antoine de la

Bastie, they fear their own shadows. They don't trust me not to steal him away to England, and now that the deputy regent has been murdered they fear that this is the start of an uprising against the regency.

'They suspect that your uncle Gavin Douglas will kidnap my son for me,' I say to Archibald. 'They have no faith in anyone.'

'Foolish,' he says levelly. 'Is there any charge?'

'No! It is just gossip,' I say. Something in his face makes me hesitate. 'Surely it is nothing but gossip, isn't it?' I ask him. 'Nobody would be so mad as to try to kidnap James and take him from his own country? Your uncle would not think of such a thing? Ard – you would not allow such a thing?'

'Wouldn't James be safer in England?' Archibald asks me. 'Wouldn't we all be safer over the border? If they can kill the deputy regent, your partner?'

'No! James has to stay here. How will he ever get his throne if he is in exile?'

'If he were in England, wouldn't your brother feel honour-bound to restore him? He gave you money and sent you home to rule.'

'I don't know.' I cannot promise for Harry. I have hardly heard from him since I came home. I am afraid that when I am not there before him, I slip from his mind. He is careless. He is a careless young man.

It is not just the lords' council who are fearful and shocked by the death of de la Bastie. They say that George Hume took a handful of the chevalier's beautiful long brown hair and tied his severed head to his saddlecloth like a trophy. He rode with it banging against his knees all the way to Duns and he nailed it to the mercat cross.

'This is savagery,' I say.

'It's opportunity,' Ard corrects me. He takes my hand and draws me away from the smoking fire in the centre of the great hall. It is early in the morning and the autumn light is bright and clear. If I were in England in weather like this I would go hunting. It is a perfect day, the air so cold, the ground frost-hard, the light so bright. Here, I stay indoors and look from the window, and wonder if I am safe.

'Walk with me,' Ard says, his voice warm.

I let him put my hand on his back, tucked into his belt, while he walks with his arm around my waist. He leads me away from the household preparing the hall for dinner, out of the heavy wooden doorway and down the steps to the green outside. A few steps more and we are over the drawbridge and looking down on the forest tumbling down the hill below us, the heads of the trees bronze and copper, only the pines dark deep green.

'The country is without a leader,' Ard says. 'Albany away, and never coming back, de la Bastie dead. The only person here who can take the regency is you.'

'I won't profit from his death,' I say with sudden revulsion.

'Why not? He would have done so if he had the chance. Since he is dead, you can take your rightful place.'

'They don't trust me,' I say resentfully.

'They are all in the pay of the French. But the French regent is away and the French deputy regent is dead. Now is the chance for England and for those who love the English princess.'

'Harry himself told me that we must have peace. I was married to bring peace to Scotland and I came back to try again.'

'And now we can. Before we could not, not under a foreign power. But now we can, under you with the power of England.'

The way Ard speaks is a seduction; his arm around my waist is as persuasive as his optimism. 'Think,' he whispers. 'Think of being regent again and bringing your son to the throne. We would be a royal family to match Henry and Katherine. They have a throne, but no boy to inherit. You would be queen regent, I would be your consort, and your boy would be king. We would be a ruling royal family with a young king. Think how that would be.'

I am persuaded. The very thought of ruling like a queen again is enough to tempt me. The thought of being a greater queen than Katherine is irresistible. 'How would we do it?'

He gives me a little sly smile. 'It's half done already, beloved. De la Bastie is dead, and you have me at your side.'

Scotland lies before us like a banquet ready for feasting. Thomas Dacre writes to advise that I seize my chance at the regency. He hints that my brother will ensure that the Duke of Albany never comes back to Scotland. Scotland needs a regent – it should be me.

'Accept,' Ard breathes in my ear, reading the letter over my shoulder. 'This is your victory.'

I accept. I think: these are my days, at last. This is what it is to be a queen. This is what Katherine felt when Harry named her regent. This is what I was born for, and what I knew I should be. I am a beloved wife, I am a reigning queen, I am the mother of the king. My brother and my husband have won this for me; I shall take it. My son will come into my keeping. Already my happiest days are those that we spend together and nobody could mistake the way his little face lights up when he sees me.

The lords are sick of French rulers. They would rather follow a woman than a French nobleman. They are weary of the constant jockeying for power – they want a queen who was born higher than them all. I can do what my dead husband, the king, asked of me: care for his country and his son like a clever woman, not like a fool. I can be his true widow. I can honour my marriage vows to him and all that he taught me. I can honour his memory. I can even bear to think of him as a hidden survivor of the battle, perhaps walking in the wild country, a terrible scar on his head, content to be as the dead, knowing that I have come back to his country and taken the throne again, knowing that I am doing my best, knowing that when my moment came, I did not fail him.

So I think that my first meeting with my council will be a decisive one: they will welcome my return, I will be gracious with them. I plan to remind them that I bring peace with England, and that they can serve me as dowager queen and an English princess.

I go alone, telling Ard to wait at Holyroodhouse, to come when he is invited. As soon as the lords are seated, I tell them that I will accept the regency and my husband will serve beside me as co-regent. There is instant uproar, as one man after another pounds the table and yells out his objection. I am shocked at the outburst of fury, the same old rivalry, the same rage that Archibald warned me about. Once again, Scotland tears itself apart for no reason but that they cannot work together. But then, over the general noise, a few of them make themselves heard. They make me listen. They make me understand. Slowly, I hear what they are saying. Slowly, like a growing chill, I comprehend.

They ask me – they don't tell me – they ask me what rents I received in England from my Scottish lands. I start to complain – they should know the answer to this, it was their duty to send the money – nothing! Nothing! Next to nothing! And they say: they were paid. Hear us! The rents were faithfully paid. We sent the money.

There is a silence. They look at me with contempt, at my slowness, at my stupidity. 'Paid to whom?' I say with icy majesty; but I know. Although they can see that I know, they tell me. They say that the rents were paid to Archibald, my husband, and it was he that sent nothing on to me. It was he that left me in England forced to borrow from the butcher's son, forced to have my household bills paid by my rich sister, to wear her cast-off dresses.

They ask me, where do I think that Archibald has been living since his pardon? I say that it is no business of theirs where he has been living, as long as his parole has been unbroken. I had believed till this minute that he was in Tantallon. They shake their heads at my arrogance and tell me, 'no', he has hardly been at his own castle. He has gone from one of my dower houses to another, collecting my rents, drinking out of my cellars, hunting my game, taking food from the storehouses of the peasants, employing my cooks, living like a lord.

'He has every right to live in my houses: he is my husband,' I say staunchly. 'Everything that I have is his by law.'

One of the old lords drops his head and bangs his forehead on the table with a terrible thud, as if he would knock himself senseless with frustration.

I look blankly at him; I can say nothing. I feel that I am a fool, worse than a fool: a woman who has chosen blindness and lust instead of reason.

'Exactly,' says one of them. 'He is your husband, he lives in your houses, he takes your rents, he does not send them to you.'

The old lord raises his head, a red bruise on his forehead, and looks at me. 'And who is the lady of the house?' he asks. 'Your house? Who sleeps on your fine linen, who dines at the head of your table, who tells your cooks to bring the finest of dishes for her to eat off your golden plates? Who has been wearing your jewels? Who sends for your musicians? Who rides your horses?'

'I will not listen to scandal,' I warn them. My hands are as cold as ice. All my rings turn loosely on my white fingers. 'I care nothing for gossip.'

I think: I will show them. I will be a queen like Katherine of Aragon, I won't even remark when my husband falls in love with my lady-in-waiting. Katherine's heart was broken, her trust shaken, but she never said one word of complaint to Harry. She never even frowned at Bessie Blount. I know that a husband's fidelity does not matter. I will show them queenly pride. I will show them that I care nothing for their petty worries. I am a queen. No-one can displace me. Even if someone else eats off my plates, even if someone else wears my jewels, I am still Archibald's wife, I am still dowager queen, I am still the mother of the king, the mother of Ard's daughter.

'It is his own wife that he has put in your house,' someone says from so far down the table that I understand that even the lowest of the lords knows everything. He is a man so unimportant that he is standing with the commoners at the back of the room. 'It is his own wife, whom he married long before his grandfather made him swear to you. Bonny Janet Stewart of Traquair. She has been living like his lady, as she should, as an honest wife should. And the two of them have made merry on your rents and on your cellars and in your bed. You are not his wife. You never were. You are his ambition, his clan's bloody ambition. He was married to her, years ago, not betrothed. He was married. He pretended to marry you, and you have given him everything and now you want to give him Scotland.'

'I don't believe it,' is the first thing I can say. Deny them! Deny everything! I say to myself. 'You are lying. Where did they live together? Where was all this marital joy?'

'In Newark Castle', they say, one after another. They are united in this, it has to be the truth. 'Didn't you notice the swept floor, the fresh rushes, the clean linen?'

'Janet Stewart moved out the day before you moved in and left it clean and tidy for her husband, like the good wife she is.'

'She even took your stockings to mend.'

I look from one furious frustrated man to another. There is no sympathy, just rage that I have been fooled and that I have tried to fool them in turn. I think: he chose Janet Stewart in preference to me. When I left for England he went to her. While I was struggling with the ambassadors and borrowing money from Wolsey he was happy with her, his first choice.

I don't know how I get out of the council chamber, how I get down the hill, that steep mile to Holyroodhouse. I don't know how I dismount from my horse and wave aside my ladies and get to my own bedroom and find myself terribly alone in the beautiful royal rooms.

I put myself to bed as if I am a little girl, overtired by the day. The ladies come and ask me, am I well? Shall I dine with the court? I say I am sick with women's troubles. They think I mean that I am bleeding, but I think that these are women's troubles indeed – when a woman loves a man who betrays her. Betrays her completely – in thought and word and deed. In plan and in whisper, in the day and in the night, and – worst of all – in public, before the world.

They bring me a dark sweet ale, they bring me hot mead. I don't say that I don't need this, that the women's troubles are those of jealousy, bile, envy, hate. I drink the ale, I sip the mead. I say that Archibald may not come to me, that I must be alone. I lie on my bed and I allow myself to cry. Then I sleep.

I wake in the night, thinking I am the greatest fool that ever lived and I am humbled to dust for my stupidity. I think of Katherine marrying a King of England and standing at his side, never considering her own feelings, never pursuing her own desires, but being ceaselessly, faultlessly loyal to him because she had given her word. She has constancy of purpose. She makes up her mind to something and nothing moves her. That is why she is a great woman.

I think of me, married to a king, giving him my word that I would be a good regent, and then falling in love with a handsome face, a youth that I knew to be promised to another. I think of my determination that he should like me best, even when I knew he was betrothed. I think of my delight that I took him from another – in truth – I preferred it that he was not free, I triumphed over a girl I had never even seen. I took her sweetheart from her, I stole her betrothed. Now, for the first time, I feel ashamed of this.

I feel so low that I even think that my little sister, Mary, has made more sense of her life than I have done. I have called her a fool and yet she has played her cards with more skill than me. She married a man for love and she took him with simple authority and now she is his wife. She lives with him, I know that he never looks at another woman. They are never apart. But I – I turn my face into my pillow and I muffle my groan of despair at my own folly. I go to sleep again with my head buried as if I never want to see the dawn.

In the morning when I wake, I hear that Archibald has gone hunting, but he has left me a dozen loving messages and promised to bring me a fat buck for my dinner. I suppose that he has heard what the lords said to me: this is a city of spies and gossip. I suppose that he is planning on brazening it out, or sliding his arm around my waist and seducing me into stupidity once again. From the quiet attentive service that my ladies give me as they dress me and bring my things for the day, I suppose that they know, too. I imagine everyone in Edinburgh knows that the queen has been told that her husband has stolen her fortune and was all along married to another woman – the wife of his choice. Half of them will be laughing at this humiliation to an English princess, and the other half shrugging at the folly of women of any nation. They will say that women are not fit to rule. They will say that I have proved that women are not fit to rule.

I go to Prime but I cannot hear the prayers. I go to breakfast but I cannot eat. A delegation of the lords is coming from the council and I have to receive them in the presence chamber. I dress carefully, patting rice powder onto my swollen pink eyelids, a little red ochre on my pale cheeks and lips. I choose a white gown with Tudor green sleeves, I wear my silver slippers with the gold laces. I let them enter when I am seated on my throne with my ladies around me and my household servants ranged obediently against the walls. We put on as good a show as we can; but it is an empty show, like a canvas castle in a masque. I have no power, and they know it. I have no fortune, and they know who has it. I have no husband and everyone but me has known that for months.

They bow with the appearance of respect. I note that James Hamilton Earl of Arran, who negotiated my wedding settlement to James the king and was made an earl for his trouble, is towards the back, unusually modest, and that the lord at the front has a paper in his hand, spotted with seals. Clearly, they have agreed something and are coming to me to announce it. Clearly, James Hamilton is not going to be the one who speaks first.

'My lords. I thank you for your attentiveness.' I must not sound sulky, though Our Lady knows I feel it.

They bow. Clearly, they are uncomfortable at my subdued shame.

'We have elected a new regent,' one of the lords says quietly. I see the door at the back of the presence chamber open, and Archibald comes. He stands there quietly listening, his intense gaze on me. Perhaps he thinks I have been able to force the lords to do his will. Perhaps he hopes that they are going to say his name. Perhaps he is waiting to see if I can face down the humiliation that he has caused.

The lords hand me the scroll of paper. I glance at the name of the new regent. As I guessed, it is James Hamilton Earl of Arran, grandson to James II, kinsman to my first husband the king. I look up; Archibald is watching me, prompting me to speak.

'And this is the wish of you all?' I ask.

'It is,' they say.

James Hamilton himself gives a modest little bow and starts to come forward.

'I would suggest that there are two regents, ruling together,' I say. 'Myself and the noble Earl of Arran, James Hamilton, who has always been my friend.' I completely ignore Archibald, but fix my gaze on James Hamilton's frowning face. 'I am sure that you would want to work with me, my lord? We have been friends for so long.'

He pauses. Certainly, he does not leap at the chance. 'As the council wishes,' he says unenthusiastically.

One of the older lords, a man I don't know, speaks up from the back of the room, and he doesn't mince his words. 'Not if you're the wife of a traitor and bound to obey him.'

Archibald darts forward to stand by my side. He's still dressed for hunting and although all blades are forbidden at court everyone knows that he has his hunting dagger in his boot. 'Who dares say this?' he demands. 'Who dares slander me and the queen, my wife? Who dares defy us and the English king?'

At once there is an angry swell of noise as the lords object to his tone. Ard ignores them, and turns to me. 'Propose me,' he says sharply.

'They never will . . .'

'I want to see who refuses.'

'Would you accept a regency with the Earl of Arran and the Earl of Angus?' I say, giving Archibald his full title, looking around at the furious faces.

'Never,' someone says shortly from the back, and all the lords – every single lord present – say, 'Nay.'

I turn to Archibald. 'I think you've seen well enough,' I say bitterly. 'And now James Hamilton is regent and the guardian of my boy, and I am despised.'

The lords bow again, and file out of the presence chamber. I hardly notice them go. 'See what you've done!' I say to Archibald. 'You've ruined everything!'

'It's what you've done!' he says, quick as a whip. 'It is your brother who has failed you. He is making peace with the council without consulting you. It was he who secretly agreed to Arran being regent, and you being nothing. It is he who has made you a nothing here.'

It must be a lie; Harry would not make an agreement behind my back with the council. 'He loves me,' I gasp. 'He would never abandon me. He promised . . . He sent me back here and he promised!'

'He has abandoned you,' Archibald says. 'You see the result.'

'It is you who abandoned me,' I say bitterly. 'I know all about Janet Stewart.'

'You know nothing about her,' he says coldly. 'Nothing now, and you never will. You cannot imagine her.'

'She is a whore!' I blaze at him. 'What is there to imagine in a whore?'

'I will not allow you to speak like that about her,' he says, with strange dignity. 'You are the queen. Act like one.'

'I am your wife!' I shout at him. 'I should not even hear of her.'

He bows in silence. 'You will hear nothing of her from me,' he says icily, and he walks out.

## HOLYROODHOUSE PALACE, EDINBURGH, SCOTLAND, SUMMER 1518

I receive merry news from the court in England. I wonder if they realise that it is like a physical pain to me to hear that they are well and happy and prosperous, making confident plans for the future, secure in their loves and their fortunes? I wonder if Mary ever stops to think that her breathless scribble about dresses, or the plans for a glorious betrothal of little Princess Mary to the French king's son, makes me feel miserably excluded? She writes page after page and I decipher the excited criss-crossed script and picture the plans for the masque and the dancing and the joust, the dresses that must be ordered, the shoes that must be made, the tirewomen coming and going with gold wire and woven flowers and little diamonds, Harry's laughter, Harry's joy, Harry's triumph at making peace with France and sealing it with the betrothal of his daughter, a baby of little more than two years old. At the very end of it she writes:

*And I have saved the best news of all – our dear sister Katherine is with child again, Our Lady of Walsingham has answered our prayers. God willing, the baby will be born in the Christmas season. Think what a Christmas we will have this year, with a new Tudor in the royal cradle!*

She commands me to think of their joy – she need not! I cannot stop myself thinking. I am haunted by their happiness. I know only too well what sort of a Christmas there will be at court, and I not there, and never even mentioned. While I am abandoned by my husband, shamed before my council, with my brother conspiring against me, Katherine will go into her confinement and Mary will be unchallenged queen, the leader in all the dances, the prizewinner in all the games, the mistress of the wealthiest court in Europe. Then when Katherine comes out with a baby in her arms, there will be a tremendous christening to honour the precious new child, the parties will begin all over again. If she has a boy there will be an enormous tournament and the celebrations will last for days and spread all over the kingdom. If she has a boy Harry will give her the key to the treasury of England and she can wear a new crown every day of the year, and my son will be disinherited.

I look out of my window at the driving rain, at the grey mountains, shrouded in cloud, and the grey sky above them. I can hardly believe that such a world of joy and music and happiness still exists somewhere, and that once that world was mine. I don't even begrudge their happiness without me. I cannot really blame them for forgetting about me. Myself, I can barely remember their faces.

## HOLYROODHOUSE PALACE, EDINBURGH, SCOTLAND, SPRING 1519

Christmas comes and goes and I have no news of my husband. It is hard to make merry without him carving the meat, or dancing with the ladies. Nobody speaks of him, but I hear that he is snowed-in with Janet Stewart at Newark Castle. The council do not consult me. I give no advice to Lord Dacre. It is as if I have stepped away from the regency, from my marriage, from life itself.

My poor brother has lost a child, again. All their high hopes came to nothing and I am truly sad for him, and for her too. I hear late, long after their grief; the letter from Thomas Lord Dacre comes through only when the first spring thaw clears the road from the south. Bundled in his letter comes a note from Katherine.

*God did not grant us the happiness of her birth. Blessed is His Holy Name, and who can doubt His will? She was a little girl and she came early. I hoped it would not be too early, we had physicians and midwives ready when I thought she was coming and I tried to hold her into this unsteady life ... but Our Father knew better, and I bow to His will, though I cannot understand it.*

*I know that your life is not easy but I urge you to spend your time with your son, who is such a gift from heaven to a queen and a mother. This was my sixth child and yet I have only one in the nursery, and she is not the prince that I prayed for. God's will be done, I tell myself this: God's will be done. I say the words over and over, all through the night when I cannot sleep for crying.*

*Our sister Mary is with child again, thank God, and in my own sorrow I cannot do too much for her. I can hardly bear to let her out of my sight and I pray for her safety in her ordeal that is to come. I wish I felt better able to help her, but I am weary and exhausted by disappointment. You will understand how low I feel when I tell you that my maid in-waiting, little Bessie Blount, has left court to give birth. I cannot write more. The ways of God are mysterious indeed. I hope you will pray for me that I learn to resign myself gladly to His will.*

*Oh, dear Margaret, I feel that I am ready to die with grief ...*

*Katherine*

I cannot face the spring weather with the courage that I should. Every day is Tudor green, every day the snow melts away and the sun shines a little more strongly. In front of the church the snowdrops are lifting their heads above the whiteness of the frost under the silver birch trees. The birds are starting to sing in the mornings and the smell of new buds and of the turned earth comes in through the open windows and makes me feel that renewal is possible, that I might recover from this long winter of disappointment.

The council does not let me see my son more than once a week but this much at least they allow. I send no message to Archibald, I think that I will never see him again and it is as if I am a widow. I wish I could grieve for the loss of him; once again I am a widow with no body to bury. He sends me neither messages nor money. He keeps all my rents and all my fees are paid to him. To get through these cold days I have been forced to pawn all the gifts that I brought from England. My last two gold cups I sent to Lord Dacre as a pledge for a loan. Now, as we come to the end of the winter quarter, I dismiss my household staff so that I am served by no more than a handful of people. I lend my horses to private stables, I send my ladies back to their homes. I live as if I were a private gentlewoman of scant means. The council are full of sympathy but they can do nothing. Archibald collects all my rents as my husband, and he lives like a lord in Newark Castle, with the woman who calls herself his wife. She has given birth to a child – a daughter. They live well, the castle fortified, the household staffed. They are rich, on the fees that are paid by my tenants. Undeniably, he is my husband and he has a legal right to my fortune. He is the lord and master of my houses and he can live where he pleases; his treatment of me does not amount to grounds for divorce. He is a bad husband: but the Church does not concern itself with that. He is still my husband, he still has my fortune.

The only way I could defend myself would be to declare that he is indeed Lady Janet's husband; she is the Countess of Angus, our marriage is bigamous, our daughter is a bastard, and I am an adulterous whore. The question of whether I should regard myself as a betrayed wife or a sinful adulteress wakes me in the early hours of the morning, and haunts me all the day.

I have lost my position as a wife, and also my authority as a queen. Another woman makes merry in my house and revels in the love of her husband who was once mine. I can see no-one and go nowhere; I shall become like my dead husband – a ghost that people say still lives, but one that is never seen. They will write ballads about us and say that one day we will return to bring peace to Scotland and set our boy on the throne. People will see us in mists and tell stories about us when they are drunk.

I know that I should fight this half-death, this non-life. I have to surrender all my hopes of Archibald and give him up. I must take the shame of being a whore and declare him my enemy. I must forget that I ever loved him. I must go to England and throw myself into my brother's arms, and call on him to help me get a divorce from Archibald.

Now I think wistfully: if only I had taken the advice of the good Lord Chancellor Thomas Wolsey I would be the Dowager Empress of the Holy Roman Empire, with a treasure house of jewels and a wardrobe full of gowns. No-one would be powerful enough to refuse my command that my son lives with me. I would be called 'Her Majesty' and I would create an imperial court in Scotland. I was such a fool to tell Thomas Wolsey and my brother that I would be true to Archibald. Wolsey is a papal legate now, he could win me a divorce from Archibald with one letter. I should never have spoken of vows that cannot be broken and love that cannot be denied. There is only one bond that I trust and that is between a woman and her sisters. Only the three of us are indissoluble. We never take our eyes off each other. In love and rivalry, we always think of each other.

I write to Harry. I don't speak of Archibald's infidelity; I say only that we are not together and that he has taken my rents. I say to Harry that I will come back to London to live at court, and that I will only be married again with his advice. I am saying, as clearly as can be: I will be divorced. I will be your sister again, I will be all Tudor and no Stewart. You can use me as you will, marry me to where I can serve you, as long as you keep me as you should. I don't expect to be a rival monarch, I don't expect to outshine your wife, Katherine. I see that she has done what I could not do – even my little sister, Mary, has done better than I.

The two of them married for love and kept their husbands. Once, I jealously compared myself with them and was filled with pride; now I am humbled. I write to Katherine and to Mary and I send the letters in the same package. I tell them that I am brought very low and that I want to come home.

## LINLITHGOW PALACE, SCOTLAND, SUMMER 1519

It is a long summer before I receive any reply from my brother Harry. A long summer, when my son is moved from plague-sick Edinburgh; but I am not invited to travel with him. A long summer when nobody visits me and I turn from sorrow to coldness, when I resolve that from this summer onward I shall never again be guided by passion, but only by my interests. A long summer when I see that my only friends, my only true loves, are my sisters, who know what it is to lose a child, who know what sorrow means for a woman, who write to me.

Harry is silent; I know why. He will be travelling away from the crowded, dirty city of London. He will be visiting the beautiful palaces on the Thames and then hunting around the great houses of Southern England, always delightedly welcomed, always offered the very best that the countryside can provide. He will leave Thomas Wolsey with all the work of the kingdom; he will not trouble himself to write to anyone, least of all me. He will not think of me, abandoned by my husband, unprotected by my brother, constantly trying to come to some accord with the lords of the council, constantly appealing to the absent Duke of Albany.

My sister, Mary, does not neglect me. She writes and tells me that she has given birth to another girl – the Brandons do seem to run to girls – and has called her Eleanor. For sure, they would have preferred another boy, anyone would. A second Brandon boy would have been another heir to the throne to follow my son James. Their oldest boy is one step behind mine, and my James looks more and more likely to inherit every day that goes by. If the last lost baby was Katherine's final attempt – and surely soon she must reach the end of her fertile years – then it will be my boy who takes the throne after Harry.

It is impossible not to think like this, however hard-hearted it feels. I pity Katherine very truly. I wept when I read her letter telling me of the loss of her baby, but I cannot help but know that while she has no son, my boy stands to inherit the kingdom of England and Ireland as well as Scotland. Surely Mary too must think like this? Surely Mary must wish that she had another boy? She cannot love Katherine so selflessly that she does not hope for the end of her fertile years. Can anyone love a sister so much that she puts her interests first?

But perhaps Mary is a better sister to the queen than I, for she writes very gaily that the new baby is the prettiest of children with skin like the petal of a pale rose and that they are all delighted with a daughter.

> *And something very dreadful has happened. Bessie Blount, who was such a dear little maid-in-waiting to our sister, left court without leave from the queen and simply disappeared. The young woman has had a baby and, oh Maggie, I am sorry to say – she has had a boy and it is, without doubt, Harry's son.*

I put down her letter and walk to the window and look out, not seeing the waves cresting white on the grey waters as the wind moves across the loch. I think firstly: I need not worry; this does not matter. This baby will have no place in the line of inheritance, he is a bastard and counts for nothing. But then I think more coolly that he is the first Tudor bastard that Harry has ever made, and that counts for something. That counts for a lot. Bessie has shown the world that Harry can get a boy, and if the child lives, he will show the world that Harry can get a healthy boy.

This is no small thing on its own. And – in turn – it proves that the fault with all these dead heirs lies with Katherine, and not with my handsome brother. Everyone thought this before, but nobody dared to say it. Now it is proven as the truth. She is older than he – only by a few years, to be sure; but she is thirty-three now, with a string of miscarriages and stillbirths behind her. She comes from a family that is riddled with death and sickness, and in all these years she has managed only one delicate little girl. But Harry's mistress, the lively, healthy, young Bessie, has given him a bonny boy in the fifth year of their affair. This is a triumphant proof of my brother's virility and denies, contradicts, and silences forever the belief that the Tudors are cursed for their invasion of England and for the disappearance of the princes in the Tower. Whoever it was that killed the princes and was left with a curse on their line, it is not us. For I have a strong boy, Mary has Henry Brandon, and now my brother has a fat little bastard. They are calling him Henry Fitzroy. Henry for the king and Fitzroy to indicate a royal bastard. They could not have chosen two names that would hurt Katherine more. I should think it will break her heart. Now she will know what grief is. Once she taught heartbreak to me; now Bessie Blount has taught her.

## LINLITHGOW PALACE, SCOTLAND, AUTUMN 1519

Not until the leaves are turning to bronze and gold in the woods that surround the loch do I receive a reply from my brother, wrapped and sealed by Lord Dacre, whose messengers have carried it, and whose spies will have read it. I don't care. At last, here is my safe conduct, this is my escape. I knew that my brother would respond to me and that Thomas Wolsey would find a way to make it right. I have no doubt that this is my invitation to return to London, get my accursed marriage dissolved and – if I know Thomas Wolsey – find a brilliant match. Why should he not? It was just what he was begging me to do three years ago, with my brother promising me that it would be the best choice that I ever made.

I take the letter to the little stone-walled room at the very top of the tower where I will not be disturbed and in my haste to open it I actually tear the heavy seal from the page. I see at once that it is not in Harry's scrawl. He has dictated to a clerk. I imagine him, seated behind a table, sprawled and smiling, a glass of wine in his hand, Thomas Wolsey dealing out papers for signature like a winning hand of cards, as the groom of the ewery serves him dainties to eat. Charles Brandon, my self-seeking brother-in-law, lounges nearby, other men – Thomas Howard, Thomas Boleyn – stand back against the walls, quick to laugh, swift with a word of advice, as Harry dashes off a quick letter to me, one of the many duties that he has left too long, but which really cannot be delayed longer. It is nothing to him – an invitation to me to come to London. To me it is a release from prison.

At first, I cannot understand the words on the page. I have to read and then reread them, they are so far from what I was expecting. Harry is not encouraging. Instead he chooses to be stern, as pompous as a little chorister. He speaks of the divine ordinance of inseparable matrimony, and he tells me that all disagreement between husband and wife is evil, and a sin. I turn the page to be sure that he has signed this farrago. This from a man whose bastard has broken his wife's heart!

Then I return to reading. Incredibly, he orders me to return to Archibald in thought and word and deed. We must live together as husband and wife or he will regard me as a sinner bound for hell, never more to be his sister. Archibald, his brother-in-law, has written to him, and Harry has listened to my faithless husband rather than to me. Perhaps this is the worst of all the terrible things that he says: that he has listened to Archibald and not to me. He has taken the man's word for it, and been deaf to his own sister. Helpfully, he tells me that Archibald will take me back without complaint, that only with Archibald at my side can I hope to regain my authority in Scotland. Only with Archibald at my side will he, the king, or his spymaster Lord Dacre, support me. Ignorant as ever, he explains that Archibald has authority over the lords of Scotland, only he can keep me on the throne. I drop my head in my hands: Dacre will have read this. And all his spies.

Then Harry writes more. As if it were not enough to break my heart, he writes more, turning my shock into rage. He tells me that Katherine agrees. Apparently Katherine's opinion counts heavily in all of this and she has decided that if I intend to defy God and live as a miserable sinner then I can be no sister of hers. I am not to come to England, I am not to divorce my husband, I am not to be happy. Katherine has decreed this, and so it will be. Katherine will not invite me to England: a divorced woman can never be her guest; her court could not be shamed, an adulteress could not come near her.

*For ye are yet carnal* – Harry quotes Saint Paul at me, as if I did not know by heart every word that the old woman-hater said – *for whereof is there among you envying and strife and divisions, are ye not carnal?*

I am so shocked by Harry's tone, by his intent, by his leap from younger brother to preacher, from king to pope, that I read the letter through several times in silence and then I go in silence down the steep stone stairs. One of my ladies is sitting in the window seat at the bottom. I wave away her exclamation at my white face and red eyes. 'I must pray on this,' I say quietly.

'There is an Observant Friar from London,' she warns me. 'Sent by the Queen of England to assist you. He is waiting to see you.'

Again? I can hardly believe it. Once again Katherine has sent me a confessor to advise me, just as she did after the death of

James, after her orders killed James. She knows then, she knows that she has sent me a deadly blow and she hopes to soften it. 'Who is he?'

'Father Bonaventure.'

'Ask him to wait in the chapel,' I say. 'I will come in a moment.'

More than anger at Harry's refusal to allow me to come to England, more than frustration at his misunderstanding my situation here – and how desperate for me that he does not have the wit to see the danger that I, my son and the whole country are in! – more than all of this is my despair that Katherine should conspire with him, safe in the haven of complacent matrimony, and agree that what matters most – more than I! more than their own sister! – is the will of God. That they should invoke God and His holy laws against my all-too-mortal troubles, that Katherine should not write to me as a sister to offer her help to a woman just like her, publicly humiliated, crushed by neglect, trying to hold up her head in a world that laughs behind its hand – this is the worst thing about these smug joint letters that send me a friar and not a friend, that counsel me to return to my husband and say that I cannot come to them.

How could a woman not say: yes, come, if you are unhappy and lonely? How could Katherine receive Mary who arrived without warning, married in secret to her lover, and yet reject me? How could she be so kind and warm, so hospitable and loving to me for a year and then say later: return to your husband and endure his treatment? How could she say to me: be neglected as I am, be unhappy! Endure desertion! Don't hope for better? I have no chance of better, there is no chance for you!

Katherine is my sister, my older sister-in-law. She is married to my brother, she is Queen of England. All these should be reasons for her to be kind and loving and sympathetic to me. She should understand my sense of loss, my hurt, my humiliation. She knows what it is to long for a husband, to wonder what he is doing, what his lover is doing with him. She must have visions – as I have visions, of a young and beautiful woman entwined around my husband's body, sobbing with pleasure against his naked shoulder. She should help to ease my pain in any way she can. What sort of sister says to her husband, we must teach this young woman to behave according to the Word of God, and not do what is the best for her? How can I think of her as a sister? This would be the work of the wickedest rival and enemy.

I have no hope of any influence in the council without the support of Harry. If he disowns me I am nobody, in Scotland or anywhere else in the world. If he sides with Archibald against me then I am nothing more than a deserted wife, without even my rents to call my own. If I am not an English princess then I am a ghost, like my first husband, with nowhere to live and nothing to live on. I did not dream that Harry – the little boy who would not learn his catechism – would grow so devout, would speak with God, would speak as God.

It is Katherine behind every word of this letter, Katherine behind the quotation from Saint Paul, Katherine demanding reconciliation with my husband, Katherine defining marriage as a heavenly sacrament from which there is no escape. Katherine – whose husband has christened and acknowledged a bastard son – is of course determinedly against divorce, against any divorce.

Fool that I am, I should have thought of this. Katherine is never going to let the thought of divorce get anywhere near Harry's butterfly concentration. Instead, she sends me an Observant Friar to shout at me and bring me, as one did before, to a true sense of my own misery and the belief that all the wrongs that have come to me have been brought down on me by God, and that I had better accept His will.

In the shadowy darkness of the chapel, as the sun sets over the loch outside and the priest lights candles on the altar, Father Bonaventure reproaches me for forgetting my duty as a wife and mother, for going to England and deserting my son and husband in Scotland. He suggests that it is no surprise that a nobleman like Archibald should live in my house and draw my rents in my absence. He is my husband in the eyes of God; everything that I own is his. Why should he not live at Newark Castle and hunt my game? What can I possibly say against Archibald living in our house? He is my husband, suffering my absence without complaint.

I am so humiliated at the thought of Archibald living with Lady Janet Stewart, her sitting at the foot of my table as his wife, and presenting his baby to my tenants, that I cannot even cite this against him. Kneeling beside the altar in the chapel I rest my face in my hands and I just whisper: 'But, Father, my husband has broken his marriage vows, and in public. Everyone knows. He loves me not.'

The stern friar interrupts me: 'You deserted him, Your Grace,' he says. 'You left him to go to England.'

'He said he would come too!' I gasp.

'But did he not welcome you on your return to Scotland? Did he not meet you as your husband at Berwick? Did you not openly go to the bedchamber as husband and wife? Did he not forgive you for leaving him and take you into his keeping again?'

Katherine has told him this. She has betrayed my confidences, perhaps even reading from my letter, of my bliss in his arms, of our hopes of a new baby.

'He will come here to see you,' Friar Bonaventure says. 'He has asked me to request that you receive him. The Queen of England requests that you receive him.'

'She said that herself?'

'Receive him as a husband.'

'Father, he has deserted me. Am I to live with a man who cares nothing for me?'

'God loves you,' he says. 'If you treat your husband with the love and respect that is due to him, God will kindle love for you in his heart again. Many marriages have difficult times. But it is God's will that you live together in harmony.' He hesitates. 'It is the king's will also. And the queen's sisterly advice.'

I have no choice. Katherine's sisterly advice will rule my life. I shall live as she wishes, I am to demonstrate to Harry, to the world, that marriage is indissoluble, that it lasts to death. She will have no mercy, she will make no allowances. All Tudor marriages have to last till death. I have become her example.

Father Bonaventure comes and goes, his words falling on the stony ground of my despair. Archibald does not risk a visit. But I am not spared Katherine's unending supply of spiritual advisors, for Father Bonaventure's place is taken by another. As reliable as automata, as one little figure goes by – tick-tock – another takes his place and a new Observant Friar arrives at my palace of Linlithgow, wound up and sent on his way, as soon as Katherine hears that I refused to meet Archibald, and Harry hears that I am writing to the French. Katherine is anguished about my immortal soul and determined that no marriage shall ever be escaped, Harry thinks only about his alliance with France. He does not see that if he will not support me, I have to turn again to the absent French regent and try to work with him. Now they send me Friar Henry Chadworth, minister general of the Observant Friars, a domineering, highly educated man, who has rarely spoken with a woman since his mother sent him off to the monastery.

He has no patience with any woman, none at all with me. They have tasked him to break my wilful spirit and reduce me into loving communion with God, with my husband, and with my brother's plans.

'They don't understand,' I say to Friar Chadworth, with as much patience as I can muster. 'Father, it is no good telling me to reconcile with my husband. He does not stay at home with me. He does not care for my interests or the interests of my son. He steals from me. Are you saying that I should let him take my lands?'

'These are his lands. And he is a faithful servant of the king,' Friar Chadworth says.

'He is certainly a well-paid servant of the king,' I say smartly. 'Thomas Dacre throws a fortune at him and at all the border lords who cause trouble and infect the whole of Scotland with anger and division.'

Now that I am estranged from Archibald and all the Douglases, a few of the lords of the council trust me with the truth. They show me that Thomas Dacre brings distrust and disunity to Scotland as if he is determined that we should tear ourselves apart and save him the trouble of invading.

'God made you an English princess,' Friar Chadworth says, his voice raised over mine. 'Your duty is to God and to England.'

I look at him as mutinously as if I were still a princess in the schoolroom. 'I owe a duty to me, myself,' I say. 'I want to be happy. I want to see my son grow to be a man. I want to be wife to a good man. I won't give up on these ambitions for the good of my country or the good of the Church, and I certainly won't give them up only because my sister-in-law the queen would prefer it. She wants to prove that an unfaithful husband is still married. But I don't.'

'That is a sin,' he says flatly. 'And God and the king will punish it.'

The friar gives me letters from my sisters, Mary and Katherine. Mary says that she has taken a long time to recover from the birth of little Eleanor but her husband has been attentive and the king sent his own physician. She says that she has had a little velvet cape made so that she can sit up in bed and receive well-wishers in her great bed of state. She says how funny it is that the Holy Roman Emperor Maximilian, whom I might have married, has died, and that his grandson, whom she might have married, is the new emperor. *Just think!*

she writes joyously. *You might be dowager empress now, and I your heiress. Empress! Both of us! How very funny!* Of course, there is nothing funny about this. It is the very reason that I decided against the Holy Roman Emperor and only came to my senses too late. This is not funny at all. She says that Harry is irritated that he was not offered the royal diadem of emperor and that Katherine seems very low.

> *It's not surprising. She is finding the blessing of Bessie Blount with a boy quite mystifying. We all went to Walsingham hoping that God would give a boy to Katherine; but He gave one to Bessie instead – His ways are mysterious indeed.*

Then she says that they will all go to France to celebrate a new treaty with the French next year. She says that she can hardly wait to visit France again and that it is to be a great event. Charles is to have new jousting armour, she is to have a dozen new gowns.

> *They call me* 'la reine blanche' *and say that there has never been a more beautiful Queen of France. It is so silly, but so dear of them. It is lovely to be beloved in two countries, a princess in one, a queen of another, and applauded in both!*

That's all she writes. That is all my little sister writes to me when she knows that her letter will be carried by a friar who is coming to me to urge me to act against my own interests and serve those of my country, to return me to a marriage with a man who has betrayed me; when she knows that I am alone in a difficult country, trying to see my son, trying to escape from a marriage that has become an insult to me. All she writes about are the thirty new gowns and the adorable little crown that Harry is commissioning especially for her. She remembers, almost too late to find any space on the page, that the French ladies are wearing their capes very short and their hoods pushed back on their heads. *Nobody*, she tells me, underlining it three times, *Nobody is wearing a gable hood any more at all.*

I put her letter down. She feels very far away. I am so far from her thoughts she does not even recall me while she is writing. If Harry goes to France and renews his treaty with King Francis, and persuades him never to send the Duke of Albany back to Scotland as regent, then the lords and I will struggle on, not really at peace, on the edge of rebellion for another year. I don't even know if we can manage another month. I don't know if Mary knows this, or if she is just not interested. Clearly, she does not think much about my worries. I doubt she thinks of me at all, other than as someone who might be interested in how to wear a French hood.

I open the letter from Katherine. Unlike Mary's scrawl, it is very short. She says that she sent me Friar Chadworth to tell me the will of God. She says that to even think of leaving a husband is to condemn my soul to eternal damnation. She says that she will do anything in her power to help me if I will step back from this terrible plan. She says that she and Harry were appalled to hear that I have written to the Duke of Albany for his help. She says I have held up my shame to the world, that I have no cause for divorce and no cause to even speak of such a sin. She says that she cannot bear that I should rush to hell like this. That it would be better for my son James if I had died with his father than for him to know that he has a whore for a mother.

Can she really think that I would be better dead than shamed?

I read her letter in silence and I step to the fireplace where a little fire keeps the evening chill away, and I put the letter on the flames. It flares up, the red seal twists and writhes in the heat, the ribbon makes a little popping noise, and then it is just a blanket of ash over the logs.

Can my own sister really think that I would be better dead than shamed?

Surely she can never have loved me at all if she thinks only of the Word of God and not of the words she says to me. She can never have cared for me as a true sister if she thinks of the sin of divorce and not of the sinner – me – a woman alone and unhappy. Does she not understand that I am heartbroken at the loss of my husband, publicly humiliated, fearful of sin and far from the grace of God?

I think of her watching Mary trying on crowns, the most beautiful young woman in two kingdoms, who effortlessly, constantly, casts Katherine into a shadow. I think of her knowing that Bessie's baby boy is named Henry Fitzroy, so that everyone knows the king has acknowledged him as his own. I think of how a proud woman like Katherine must feel when she is second at her own court, with no son in her belly nor in her cradle, and less and less chance with every year that goes by. And then I think – well, she need not take it out on me.

Friar Chadworth watches in silence as the letters burn. 'Well?' he asks. 'Do they persuade you to repent your sins?'

'No,' I say. 'They say nothing to comfort me, and they give me no reason to think that they will help me.'

'They will not,' he confirms. 'There will be no help for you unless you reconcile with your husband. You have no choice. I am here to tell you that you have no choice. Without your husband at your side you will get no support from England. Without support from England you will never command your council. Without your council you cannot rule your kingdom and you will never see your son again. He will be raised without a mother or a father. He will be an orphan.'

There is a long silence. I wonder that he can be so cruel.

I bow my head. 'Very well,' is all I say. 'You win.'

I cannot bear to meet with Archibald in public. I am mortified, as if it is I who has stolen and lived as an adulterous thief. I know that my ladies will think the less of me for taking him back, my son will hear of it and think that I have no pride, that I am a beaten dog. Everyone who saw us at Berwick when I was a lovesick fool will think that I am drunk on desire again. So I say that he must come to the top of the tower, where I have my little eyrie, the tiny stone-built room where – such a long time ago – James my husband said goodbye to me, and told me not to watch for him. My lady sends Archibald up the winding stairs, I can hear his boots ring on the stone, and she closes the door at the bottom, so that no-one can hear what we say to each other. She will think that she is concealing a tryst, she will think that the door will silence the noise of lovemaking.

I am so angry and so distressed that I am shaking by the time he walks around to the little doorway of the tower and ducks his head to come under the stone lintel. He kneels at my feet, drops down like a penitent pilgrim without a word. He takes my hands, he feels me tremble and exclaims at the coldness of my fingers.

'Beloved,' he says.

'You have no right!' I say, choked.

Vehemently, he shakes his head. 'No right at all.'

'You have stolen my rents!'

'God forgive me. But I have kept your lands in good heart, and protected your tenants and your good name as a landlord.'

'You put another woman in my place!'

'My love, my love, no woman could take your place. Forgive me.'

'I never will.'

He bows his head. 'You should not. I have been like a madman. You are good, you are kinder than I deserve, just to let me come to you, and beg your pardon. I would not want to die with this on my conscience. My will and my happiness have been destroyed by our troubles, both public and private. I have seen terrible things in your service, I have had to contemplate terrible crimes to bring you to your rightful place. In defending your throne I have sinned against God. It's not surprising that my will broke, my determination failed me.'

He glances up at me. 'I couldn't go on. I didn't have the strength to continue,' he says. 'For a mad month or two I thought I might escape. I thought for a moment that I could be a private man, a man with a wife and little daughter in a little house. When de la Bastie died and you failed to seize power and blamed me,

I just wanted to run away. I felt that I had failed you so badly – I had done so much and still failed. My love, my wife, I was wrong to go. I am called to greater things, I am called to be your husband. Forgive me for failing you this once. I will never fail you again.'

'You wanted to be free of all these troubles?'

He bows his head. 'It is the only time my courage has failed me. In all these five years. I could see no way to bring you to victory. It was my mistake. I thought if I could not restore your son to you, and you to your place, then I had better do nothing, go right away. I even thought that I should kill myself, that it would be better for you if I were dead.'

He feels at once the quick clutch of my hands and he raises his eyes and smiles at me. It is as if he has touched me – that smile, that sweet boyish smile, is like a caress, a deep secret pulse. He knows this. He knows I cannot bear the thought of his death. His voice is warm, confiding.

'Can you understand, you who are so brave, that I wanted to be less? Can you imagine that I might want a smaller life, an ordinary woman, a nobody in a little world? That for a moment, for just a moment, I could not be the man that I am with you, the wife of my passion?'

'You went to her from me,' I whisper. Even now, it pains me to think that he would prefer another woman.

'Oh, Margaret, have you never wished you could run away from all this and go to England? Return to your girlhood?'

'Oh yes. Yes, of course.' I don't tell him that I begged to go back and that they rejected me.

'That's what it was for me. I had a dream that I might live with the girl that I once promised to marry, in a little castle like we might have had. I thought that I should retreat from the council of lords, go far from you and the court. I felt that you didn't need me, that you would do better without me, that you might work with James Hamilton, the Earl of Arran; you might write to the Duke of Albany. I thought you would be free to speak with these great men as the great woman that you are without me holding you back, and embarrassing you. I know I am an obstacle to your regaining your son. I thought you would be better off without me. The council hates and fears me – I wanted them to be able to see you without me. I thought that the last thing, the finest and most loving thing, I could do for you would be to free you from me. I thought I should give you the excuse to deny our marriage, if you wanted to be rid of me. I thought that the best and kindest thing I could do for you would be to let you go.'

'I can't be free of you,' I say flatly. 'They won't allow it. Katherine won't allow it.'

'Neither can I,' he says. 'Not in the eyes of God, nor in my love for you. So here I am, at your feet. I am yours till death. We have been parted – not for the first time – and I have come back to you. Take me back. Take me back, beloved, or I am a dead man.'

'I have to take you back,' I say. 'My sisters insist. Harry insists.'

He bows his head and he gives a little choked sob. 'Thank God.'

'You can get up,' I say uncertainly. I don't know whether to believe him or not.

He does not get to his feet and stand before me as a suppliant. He rises up to his full height and he keeps hold of my hands and draws me up as well so that I am close to him, and the whole length of his body is against mine, and his arm is around my waist and his hand is under my chin and he is lifting my face to his and he kisses me. At once I feel desire rush through me like a new wave on an incoming tide, a mixture of relief and triumph and jealousy. I had forgotten the joy of it, the taste of him, the scent of him, and now I know it again. And I think that I have taken him from Janet Stewart; I have taken him from her for the second time. I am first with him, as I should be.

'You cannot be free of me,' he says, his mouth on mine. 'You will never be free of me. We will never be free of each other.'

## HOLYROODHOUSE PALACE, EDINBURGH, SCOTLAND, AUTUMN 1519

We make a triumphant entry into Edinburgh. Archibald's men escort me with bagpipes and drums and all the people come out of their houses and from their stables and shops and trades to watch the dowager queen and her handsome husband ride back into Holyrood. They call out that I am welcome in my capital once again, and that I must show them my boy, the little king. Some shout that Archibald is a traitor, that I have a traitor at my side. I turn my head away. There are many ways of being a loyal Scot, and Archibald's way has not been the way of the Hamiltons. Some of them lift up their purses and wave them above their heads. I flush, and glance at Archibald; his expression is furious. They mean that he takes an English pension, that he has been bought by Thomas Dacre, with Thomas Wolsey's money, to be a servant of my brother the king. They mean that he is cheaply bought and cheaply sold: an English slave and not a free Scot.

'I will have every one of them arrested,' Archibald says through his teeth.

'Don't,' I say urgently. 'Let people remember this as the day we came home and there was no trouble.'

'I will not be insulted.'

'It means nothing, nothing.'

The palace is warm and welcoming; there is a household fit for a dowager queen once more, horses in the stables and cooks in the kitchen. Archibald is paying for everything: he says I am to buy what I want. He dances me around the rooms and makes me laugh, saying I must send for the sempstresses and get new gowns for myself and for our daughter little Lady Margaret who crows and claps her hands to see her Dada again, following in his footsteps like his puppy. He says we will dine in state and everyone will come to visit us. We must appear great, we are great.

'But the cost . . .' I object.

'Leave business to me,' he says. He is lordly. 'I have your brother's trust and he has sent me money to support your claims. I have your rents, and I have my own fortune. It is all for you. You are the queen of everything you see. Especially, you are my queen, and I am still your most humble servant.' He laughs. 'You will see, when they bring your roast meat I shall carve it for you tonight.'

I cannot help but laugh with him. 'That was a long time ago.'

'It was the happiest time of my life,' he tells me. 'I fell in love with you so instantly, so deeply, and then I began to see that you might love me too. It's not a long time ago, it is just yesterday.'

I want to believe it. Of course I do. It is like a dream that he should come back to me. I think that if Katherine was right and it is God's will that a husband and wife should never be parted then his return is an act of God. Archibald and I are together again, our marriage is blessed, Scotland will come under my rule, and find peace. I don't want to wonder where his wealth comes from, I don't consider Dacre forgiving me my debts. I don't think where Janet Stewart is sleeping tonight.

I visit my son. He is shy with me; we have not lived together since Craigmillar Castle. 'They won't let me be with you,' I tell him. 'I try and try to come to you. They will not allow me.'

I cannot believe he is only seven; he is so careful as he chooses his words to reply. 'I tell them that I would like to see you, but I cannot yet command,' he says. 'But the Earl of Arran is courteous to me, and kind. He says that the Duke of Albany will return soon and then we shall have peace. He says that then you will be able to live with me as my lady mother and we will be happy.'

'No, no, Scotland must be free of the French,' I say to him earnestly. 'You are the son of an Englishwoman, you are the heir to the English throne. We don't want a French advisor. Never forget that.'

David Lyndsay, my son's constant companion and friend, steps forward and bows to me. 'His Grace is proud of his inheritance,' he says carefully. 'But he knows that his French guardians are his friends and kinsmen too.'

'Oh, Davy!' I protest. 'When James Hamilton takes a French pension and calls my husband a troublemaker! He can be no friend of ours!'

'His Grace has to be a friend to everyone,' Davy reminds me steadily. 'He cannot be seen to favour one side over another.'

The little boy is looking from one to the other of us, as if he is trying to decide who to believe, who he can trust. He is a boy who has had no boyhood, a child without a childhood. 'I wish to God your father had raised you,' I say bitterly.

He looks back, his big dark eyes luminous with tears. 'I do too,' he says.

Archibald leaves me at Holyrood and says that he has work to do on his estates.

'Oh, shall I come with you?' I ask. 'I'll ride with you. Where will we go?'

A tiny hesitation, a flick of his glance sideways, gives me a second's pause. 'Are you going hunting?' I ask. 'Archibald, where are you going?'

He comes close so that the people around us cannot hear him. 'I am meeting Thomas Dacre,' he says in my ear. 'I am about your business, my love. I will ride in the night to our meeting, get news of your brother and his plans, and come home quickly.'

'Tell Lord Dacre that we have to come to terms with the French regent,' I say. 'We cannot oppose James Hamilton as acting regent, and the Duke of Albany will come back sooner or later. We have to work with them both, we have to make me regent and get custody of James.'

'Albany will never return,' Archibald promises me. 'He will never come back. It is your brother's wish – and it is my preference – that we never see him again. Your brother has served us well. He has trapped Albany in France, he has made his exile from Scotland as part of the treaty with France, he has done so much for us! And without him, Hamilton is no more than the leader of another clan. He can call himself deputy regent – he can call himself whatever he likes! – but the French will not support Hamilton against the English. We can destroy him, as soon as we are ready.'

'No, no,' I say. 'No more fighting. We have to do all we can to hold the peace till James is old enough to take the throne. Hamilton or Albany, the regent or the deputy regent has to run the council and keep the lords at peace. I must work with them.'

'I'll tell Dacre that's what you think,' Archibald promises me. 'You know that I want Scotland kept at peace for your son. I want nothing else.'

We walk down to the stable yard with our arms around each other's waists, entwined like young lovers. I kiss him goodbye in a turn of the stair where no-one can see how he holds me, how I cling to him.

'Will you be back tomorrow night?' I ask longingly.

'The night after,' he says. 'It's not safe in the borders after dark.'

'Don't take risks. Stay another night rather than ride after sunset.'

'I'll come back safe to you.'

'Two nights,' I whisper.

'No more.'

'You do know where he is?' James Hamilton, the deputy regent, asks me. 'It is a matter of common knowledge.'

I feel cold at his tone, as if he had put an icy hand on the nape of my neck. 'What is a matter of common knowledge?' I return.

I have ridden out from Holyrood, through the Canongate, around the great looming mountain that people call Arthur's Seat, knowing that James Hamilton and the lords who favour France are hunting in the wild fields and marshes south of the city. Hamilton, the Earl of Arran, sent me a private message, telling me that he wanted to talk with me beyond the listening walls and spying windows of the city, and I need to know what he will say. I cannot help but trust him, I have known him for years. Of course, I want to hear his plans for Scotland, what the word is from France; but I don't want to hear gossip about my husband.

'Archibald is visiting his estates in the borders,' I say flatly. My horse, held too tightly as my hands grip the pommel, sidles and shifts his head. 'Our estates. He cares for my lands. He will be away for only two nights.'

'I am sorry to tell you, Your Grace, but he is lying to you again. He has gone to Lady Janet Stewart at Newark Castle,' he says bluntly. 'I thought that you did not know.'

'Certainly, it is not for you to tell me,' I say sharply. I speak very grandly but I have a sense of foreboding, almost a premonition. I don't want this old friend to tell me any more. I don't want this man who saw me as a princess at my father's court and judged me fit to marry a king to judge me now as a fool who clings to an unfaithful husband and lets him shame her before the world.

'Who else would tell you?' he asks. 'Who is on your side? All his clan are sworn to secrecy and loyal only to him. Dacre defends him because he has bought your husband lock, stock and barrel with English gold. Will your sisters not advise you?'

Unwillingly, I shake my head. 'They will not speak against lawful marriage.'

'Then you have no counsellors.'

Around us my ladies are chatting with his men. They are hunting with falcons, the sleek birds waiting on the falconers' fists to be released as soon as his lordship gives the word. The beaters will drive the game upwards, the falconers will release their birds and they will soar in the sky above us and look down. From that height, we are as nothing, a scattering of figures on a vast unmapped country.

'I have advisors,' I say coldly. 'They would warn me.'

'You have no-one. Thomas Lord Dacre is your husband's master. He won't warn you against him. He works for the King of England and not for you. They have bought your husband; they're not going to tell you that.'

This is so near to my fears that I cannot reply at first. I give a little laugh. 'If Dacre has bought him he will command him to be faithful to me and mine. James, you do wrong to warn me. Archibald and I are reconciled. There's no division between us. He will come home to me. You do wrong to speak against a husband to his wife.'

'Oh, is he your husband? I thought he was precontracted? And Dacre couldn't care less. All Dacre does is pay him to keep him on the side of the English. He doesn't care where he gets his bed and board. Thomas Dacre looks the other way when Douglas steals your rents and is unfaithful to you. Thomas Dacre may tell the king that your husband is not the best husband in Scotland, but he does not warn him that the Red Douglas clan will destroy the council of the lords. For Dacre the only thing that matters is English influence in Scotland, and he believes the safest way to secure that is to keep Archibald married to you and you in his thrall.'

'I will not be used!' I exclaim. 'I will not be abused. I am not enthralled.'

'You must judge for yourself,' he says quietly. 'But I tell you that the man you call your husband is snug in another woman's bed tonight. And he calls her his wife. He suborns the council and he courts you to serve his paymaster: England.'

'I am queen regent.'

'So take your own power. Deal with me and with the Duke of Albany, and keep that traitor out of our business.'

'What if Albany never comes back?'

'He will come back. He knows his duty is to see your son safely to the throne. It is in your interest that he returns.'

'I am an English princess. Your master the king knew it when he married me. You knew it when you came to London to see me and I was just a little girl. I was married to bring an alliance between England and Scotland. I came here to break the French alliance, not to keep it.'

'King James said that he would make you a Scot, and that your son would be a true Scot, born and bred,' Hamilton says to me gently. 'D'you think he was at peace with your kinsmen when he rode to Flodden? He knew that there is no agreeing with the English. And for all your kinship, the English have not proved so loving to you. It is not just the peace of the Scots that they destroy. Your peace and happiness do not matter to them, not to any of them.'

I run my fingers through my horse's mane. It is true what James Hamilton says. Nobody cares for my peace or happiness; not even my sisters. All they want is to ensure that I do not reflect badly on them. 'Do you swear that I would be safe if the Duke of Albany returned? Would I be able to see my son? Would I sit in council?'

'He would share the regency with you,' he assures me. 'Not with the Earl of Angus. Never with him. None of us trust him. But with you, on your own. You could have a joint regency with the duke, you could have your power back, and your son in your keeping, and the wealth and power of France behind you.'

'I'll write to him,' I decide. My mistrust of Archibald, my sense that my sisters have betrayed me for their own ends, Katherine's hardness of heart, Mary's ignorance of everything that matters – these prompt me to work for myself, against them all. 'I will write to the duke and invite him to come home.'

Of course, Thomas Dacre, with his spies everywhere, knows what I am doing the moment I do it. He writes that he knows I rode in secret to meet James Hamilton and his men. He says, anxious as Katherine about the reputation of a marriage, that I went alone, under cover of darkness, that my honour is stained. He knows for a fact that I was out at night in secret when my husband was away from home. My behaviour is shocking. He has been forced to tell my brother the king that I am now widely known to be the lover of James Hamilton, the Earl of Arran.

Defiantly, I reply, I am furious that Dacre should insult my name. Hear this! I say: I have written to the Duke of Albany and asked him to come home to Scotland and rule as regent, since the country is falling into a state of brutal savagery with one lord against another, half of them paid by England to tear Scotland apart. I say that I was forced to write by the council of the lords because neither Dacre nor my husband protects me against the council. I have to live in Scotland and come to terms with the lords and see my son. Is Dacre going to help me or not?

This is how women are treated: when they act on their own account they are named as sinners, when they enjoy success they are named as whores. Thomas Dacre never lifted a hand to help me get my rents from Archibald or make him be a good husband to me. But James Hamilton and the lords of the council have agreed that I shall have the money from my dower lands. Has Thomas Dacre ever done so much? His silence is the most eloquent reply.

Silence too from Archibald. So I know that Dacre will have told him, as well as my brother, as well as my sisters, that he thinks I have taken James Hamilton as a lover, that I am enticing the Duke of Albany back to Scotland. I don't even know where to find Archibald. I will not send a messenger to Newark Castle, I will not believe for one moment that he is there, with Janet Stewart. But if he is not there, then where is he? And why did he not come home after two nights as he promised? And why has he not sent for me?

After many nights when I sleep alone in our big bed between the cool sheets I realise that he may not come back at all. Dacre will have warned him that I know that he went to Newark Castle, Janet Stewart will have begged him to stay with her. He is a border lord accustomed to swift changes of fortune. He will not care that he is caught out. He will not care that I know where he is. He does not come back to Edinburgh and I do not look for him in the palace. I think he is like the migrating flocks of ducks that darken the sky in the autumnal days. He comes and he goes and nobody knows why. Certainly, I don't know why.

But as it starts to grow cold, and the leaves of the silver birches turn yellow and shiver in the cold winds, and the oak leaves whirl around us as we ride beside the silvery waters of the lake, I receive a travel-stained package from France and inside is a letter from the duke himself, the absent regent, and he says that he thinks he will stay away for longer still (he does not say, but I guess he is all but a prisoner of the agreement between my brother and Francis of France). In the meantime, he proposes smoothly, I should go to the council of lords as his nominated deputy. I should be regent again; I may take his place.

I cannot believe he has written so kindly. At last, someone who thinks of the good of the country; at last someone who thinks of me. Of course, it is the right solution. It is the regency that the late king wanted, it is the regency that I want. Who better to be regent than the king's mother? Anyone who had seen my lady grandmother's care of England would know that the best person to rule a country is the mother of the king. Albany makes it clear that Archibald is to have no place in the council. He makes it clear that he thinks of Archibald as Dacre's spy – his little bleached talbot, his puppy. Archibald has taken the English shilling and will never be trusted in Scotland again. Oddly enough, I – an English princess – am known to be more independent.

I will accept. It is the right solution for me even though it puts me in firm alliance with the French. But there is more. Albany offers to do me a service in return for my taking up the duties. He tells me that he is going to Rome, that he has much influence with the Vatican. As regent, all the Scots Church benefices are in his keeping. He is powerful in the Church, can meet with the Holy Father himself – and he offers to urge the matter of my divorce from Archibald. If I wish it. If I believe that my husband has deserted me for another woman and I want to be free of him.

It is as if I am at the top of my tower in my little stone lookout and finally I can breathe the clean air. I can be free. I can defy Katherine, and I can punish Archibald for his open adultery. Katherine may have to endure an unfaithful husband and pretend that his bonny boy was never born; but I do not. She can be more of a wife than I am – accepting everything that her husband does – but I can be more of a queen than she – taking my independent power. We shall see whose reputation is the greatest in the end.

Recklessly, delightedly, I rush on in my mind. Archibald can be Janet Stewart's husband; she can have him. I will not be his step to the regency, his drawbridge to my son, his entry to power. He can keep Janet Stewart and her insipid daughter, and his little life, and I will be Regent of Scotland without him. I will be Regent of Scotland with the support of the French, not the English. I will forget my hopes of my brother just as he forgets me. I will not yearn for the love of my sisters. Katherine can disown me and Mary can think only of her hoods, and if I have no sisters at all, then so be it. I am My Lady the King's Mother and regent. That is better than being a sister, that is better than being a wife.

## EDINBURGH CASTLE, SCOTLAND, SPRING 1520

Finally accepted by the lords as Regent of Scotland and head of the council, I am allowed to enter Edinburgh Castle to see my son. I can even stay in the castle if I wish. They no longer fear that I will run away with him to England: they no longer think that I will give the Douglas clan the keys to the castle. They start to trust me, they start to understand my determination to see my son become king of a country with a chance of survival. Together we are starting to agree that England is an awkward neighbour, the nearest and the most dangerous. I acknowledge to them my disappointment that the greatest English influence in Scotland is not me, working for peace, but Thomas Dacre, working for uproar. Carefully, I convince them that Archibald does not speak for me, is not my husband in anything but name, cannot be trusted with my interests. We are publicly estranged. Carefully, they tell me that he must be charged with treason, for his actions against Scotland, for his spying for my brother. I nod. They need say no more. I know that Archibald has betrayed his country as well as his wife.

'Do you consent that we issue a warrant for his arrest for treason?' they ask me.

I hesitate. The penalty for treason is death, unless a man can win a pardon. With a sudden pulse of desire I think that Ard might beg me for pardon, I might have the upper hand. I might forgive him.

'Arrest him,' I say.

To my delight, I am allowed into my son's apartments and I sit with him to hear him at his lessons and I play with him when he is at leisure. We meet early in the morning, before breakfast, on the battlements of the castle, to rehearse a comical play that Davy Lyndsay has written, in three parts. James and Davy and I have become actors in our own little masque. We are going to perform for the court at dinner time, and as the sun comes up and melts the frost on the slates of the roof, we start to rehearse.

It is based on the old fable of the fox and the grapes. One after another Davy and then James and then I sit on the battlement and recite a poem to the imaginary grapes dangling, far too high, quite unreachable, over our heads, and then invent our own reason why the grapes are not really desirable. Davy is particularly funny as he declaims that the grapes are English and come at too high a price. You have to buy the grapes but you also have to pay for the wall, the earth that the vine is growing in, the rain that fell on the vine to make it grow and the sun that shone to ripen the grapes. And then the English expect you to be grateful for the taste of them, and tip the gardener. James laughs and laughs and then does his own little play in French, when he says that the grapes are very fine, but not as fine as we might get in Bordeaux, that nothing is as good as the Bordeaux grape and that if we had any sense we would chop down the vine altogether and use the wood to make a boat to sail to Bordeaux and buy grapes there.

Now it is my turn, and I swagger along the wall in a fair mimicry of Thomas Dacre's bluster when something below catches my eye, a glint of bright metal in the spring sunlight, and I say: 'What's that?'

Davy follows my gaze, and the humour drains from his face. 'Soldiers,' he says. 'In Douglas colours.'

Without another word he turns and yells at the guard who stands on sentry duty by the portcullis. 'Are you blind?' He bellows a string of curses. 'Drop the gate!'

I clutch James' cold hand in mine as we hear the portcullis slam down, chain screaming on the wheel, and the groan and creak as the drawbridge is raised and bolted up. All around the castle we can hear the shout of trumpets as men are called to their muster stations, and the rumble as the cannons are rolled out, and the bellowed orders as men run from one post to another and everyone turns and looks down into the narrow streets.

'What's happening?' I demand of Davy Lyndsay.

'James Hamilton is arresting your husband Archibald Douglas, for treason,' he says quietly. 'Looks like he is not going quietly.'

'Archibald is in the city? I didn't know.' I glance down and see that James, my son, is watching me, his eyes narrowed, as if he would understand what he is seeing, as if he would see through me, see through the words I say to the truth. 'I didn't know,' I tell him. 'I swear I knew nothing of this. Not that the council had summoned him, not that he was here.'

'No, they wouldn't tell you,' Davy Lyndsay says. 'A wife may not keep a secret from her husband by law. If he asked you anything, you would be honour-bound to answer. They would want to spare you that – they wouldn't want you to know.'

'James Hamilton is arresting Archibald?'

'Looks as if the Douglas clan are resisting. Shall I go and discover what's amiss?'

'Go! Go!'

He is back in a moment.

'What is happening?' James asks, and I smile to hear him take command like the little king he is. Davy does not smile but answers us both, as his equal masters.

'It's as I thought. The council locked the city gates to keep Archibald and his household inside but then found they are outnumbered. There are five hundred of the Douglas clan in the city and they are armed and ready for a fight.'

Below us, I can see the Netherbow Gate closed tight, and all the houses beside it with barred doors and closed shutters. As I watch, every house down the Via Regis is hurriedly slamming doors, men and women are vanishing inside and bolting their shutters closed. The tradesmen who were bringing out their trestle tables to display their goods are quickly dismantling them, the hospitable windows and doors, open to the morning for business, are quickly secured. Everyone knows there is going to be trouble.

'The earl broke out and led his men towards the castle, as if to take it and you and the king,' Davy says, his face dark with worry.

'Shouldn't the captain of the castle take the guards into the city and keep order?' I ask Lyndsay.

He shakes his head. 'They had better stay here and guard the king.'

Again James looks at me with that dark, calculating gaze.

'Let's go indoors,' I say nervously.

'I want to see,' is the first thing that James says. 'Look.'

We can see now that as the first rays of the sunlight come over the hill there are men running silently and quickly like sleek rats, into every blind alleyway, every courtyard between the houses, every cobbled street and every wynd and back.

'Douglas men,' says Davy Lyndsay. 'Early risers. As if it was planned.'

'What's going to happen?' my son asks. He does not speak in fear but in a sort of detached curiosity. This is not how an eight-year-old boy should be. This is not a sight for him.

'We had better go inside,' I say.

'Stay,' he replies, and I, too, am fascinated by the drama that is being acted out below us.

I can see one of the guards from the city gate throw open the door of a guardhouse and bellow a warning. At once all the doors are thrown open as the Hamiltons spill out. The first man has run into a knot of fighters armed with pikes and axes. He goes down in a moment under a hail of blows, but all the men who heard his warning are struggling out of their houses, clapping on their helmets and shouting for help. There is the crack of arquebus and the scream of injury, and then we see the billow of flame and the darkness of smoke and hear more screams of people burning alive inside buildings.

'Oh, God help them!' I exclaim. 'Davy, we must send out the guard to stop this.'

He shakes his head, looking down into the town, his big face quivering with distress, his eyes filled with tears. 'There's not enough of us to stop it,' he says. 'There's just enough of us to be butchered. This is Scot against Scot and we shouldn't throw more Scots to their deaths.'

James is silently watching.

'Come away,' I say to him.

The glance he throws up at me is of burning resentment. 'These are Douglas men?' he asks me. 'Your husband's men? Killing our men? Hamilton's men?'

'This is not my doing,' I say desperately.

Down below we can see that the Douglas men have taken all

the major lanes and alleys and are waiting, like rat-catchers, for the Hamilton men to burst from the burning houses and desperately fight for their lives against an enemy better armed and better prepared than them. We see the puffs of smoke from the handguns. We can even hear the screams from the dying men. There is horrible fighting, hand-to-hand in the narrow streets with no quarter given, never a moment of mercy even when a man falls to his knees and screams his surrender. The Douglas men are drunk on a wave of violence and victory; they stab and chase and tumble over Hamiltons, running and slipping on bloody cobblestones. The whole of the Via Regis, from the castle at the head to Holyroodhouse, my home at the foot, is filled with tussling, stabbing murderers, one hand against another, and Edinburgh is a city no more, it is a shambles, a killing ground.

'Let's go to the chapel,' I burst out to Davy Lyndsay and my son. 'For God's sake, let us go and pray that this stops.' The two of them, their faces bleached, turn with me. We almost run down the steps of the walls, push past men who are aiming the cannons down the approaches from the town in case the Douglas men come up here, for us, and we fall through the tiny doorway to St Margaret's Chapel and the three of us kneel, shoulder to shoulder, before the little altar.

At once, the peace of the chapel envelops us. Distantly, outside, we can hear the sound of gunfire and screams, we can hear the sound of the fortress readying itself for attack. I put my hands together and realise that I don't know what to pray for. Outside, my husband, my former helpmeet, my lover and the father of my daughter, is fighting against the only hope for Scotland, my friend and my ally James Hamilton. A thousand of their followers are running up and down the narrow alleys, bursting out of doorways, fighting like cornered rats to get out of the traps of the dark courtyards. They have brought hand-to-hand warfare into the streets of Edinburgh; the disorder of the borders has come into the heart of the capital. This is the end of Scotland, this is the end of my hopes, this is the end of peace.

*'Ave Maria, gratia plena, Dominus tecum. Benedicta tu in*

*mulieribus, et benedictus fructus ventris tui, Iesus. Sancta Maria, Mater Dei, ora pro nobis peccatoribus, nunc, et in hora mortis nostrae*. Amen. Pray for us,' I add. 'Pray for us.'

My son raises his bowed head and looks up at me. 'He's coming, isn't he?' he asks simply. 'Archibald Douglas, your husband. When he has killed everyone out there, he will come for us.'

The fighting goes on most of the day, but James and I stay inside the little chapel praying for peace. In the afternoon the captain of the guard comes to report and I tell him to kneel beside me and tell me the news, as if the holy silence will soften the horror of his words.

'The Red Douglases have taken the city,' he says. 'There are nearly a hundred dead in the streets. They are clearing the bodies from the causeway with the plague carts. It's been a war out there while we have locked ourselves in here and done nothing.'

'You had to defend the castle and the king,' I insist.

'But the deputy regent, James Hamilton, was nearly killed,' he says. 'We didn't defend him. We didn't defend the king's peace.'

'James Hamilton has escaped?'

'He got away on a coalman's packhorse,' the captain says tightly. 'Ran from the field of battle and had to swim to safety across the loch. The archbishop, James Beaton, was dragged out from his hiding place behind the high altar in Blackfriars. They would have torn him to pieces but Gavin Douglas said it was a sin to kill a bishop.'

'My husband's uncle was there, commanding the mob?'

'He is all Douglas, and no churchman,' he says surlily.

'It was a Douglas mob?'

'It was the Red Douglases against the Hamiltons. It was a clan war in the streets of the city though one is deputy regent and the other is the representative of England.'

'But they spared Archbishop Beaton?'

'They did, and they called on all Hamiltons and their kinsmen, their affinity and their friends, to leave the city. All the Hamiltons are going now.'

'They can't go. Edinburgh cannot be in the power of one family.'

'The gates are open and the Hamiltons are leaving. The Douglas clan holds the city. Soon, your husband will order that we open the castle gates to him.'

I see my son's gaze turn on me. He has said nothing while the captain tells us this terrible news. I wonder what he is thinking behind that expressionless mask. I take his cold hand.

'Can we hold out?' I ask.

'Till when?' the captain says sharply. 'Yes, we can hold a siege, but what if he brings in the English army against us?'

'Can't we hold a siege until it is relieved?' I ask.

'Who is going to relieve the siege?' He asks the key question. 'The deputy regent has just run away disguised as a coalman and hidden himself in the marshes of the Nor' Loch. The regent is far away in France. You have no army and your brother is not going to send one against his own man – your husband. Who is going to save you and the king?'

I feel very cold. I put my hand on my son's shoulder and feel that his muscles are tight as a bowstring. 'Are you saying that we have to admit the Douglas clan to the castle?'

The captain bows, his expression grim. 'I regret that is my advice.'

'Led by my husband?'

He nods.

I look at Davy Lyndsay. 'I am not afraid,' I lie.

James sits on the throne in the presence chamber, I sit beside him as dowager queen. James Hamilton is hiding in the marshes with the coalman's horse, we have no defence against Archibald who walks into the room, drops to his knee before James, and lifts his head to wink at me.

'I've returned,' is all he says.

## LINLITHGOW PALACE, SCOTLAND, SUMMER 1520

The council of the lords is dominated by the Clan Douglas, led by my triumphant husband, Archibald. He makes it clear that he has captured the city, and captured me. He demands that we live together as a royal family, I at his side as his wife, in his bed at night, at his right hand during the day, my son and daughter in his keeping: he is their father and head of the royal household.

I won't surrender to him. I won't let him take me, like the spoils of battle. I won't allow this murderer into my bed. I won't let him touch me. I shudder with horror at the thought of him hiding his men in my city, and calling them out for massacre. I think of the people of Edinburgh, my people, washing blood from the cobbles, and I leave Edinburgh to live alone at Linlithgow.

Once again, I am parted from my son, I have to leave him behind as a prisoner at Edinburgh Castle. Once again I have no money. Archibald has my rents, he has ownership of all my lands, and the council of lords don't dare to complain. I don't expect help from Lord Dacre, who is Archibald's friend and paymaster. I don't expect help from Harry, who commanded that I should return to this husband and said that I was lucky that he received me. I have no sisters to advise me: they don't write. I am very alone. It is a cold, wet summer, there is much illness in the city of Edinburgh and even in the country people are terrified of plague. I don't write to Katherine, for what will she reply? I know what she thinks, and I know why she says it. I know she cannot hear the word 'divorce' without thinking that her own life as Harry's ageing barren wife is guttering away like a candle clock. But then, in midsummer, I get a package of letters from London.

The first is from my sister, Mary. She writes that she was ill in spring but that she was well enough, thank God, to go with the king and queen to France. She bubbles with delight, her letter filled with misspellings and blots of excitable ink. Through the scrawl I make out that the visit was to sign a great treaty to confirm the peace between England and France, and that they made a masque every day. Harry took a hundred tents, a thousand tents, to the field outside Calais and all the nobility of England took their households and their horses and their hawks and their servants and built their own summer palaces out of canvas and wood and showed off their wealth and their joy. Harry summoned a city for a summer's day and at the centre of it a fountain flowing with wine with silver cups for anyone to drink.

Mary has thirty-three gowns, she lists her shoes, she had a cloth of gold canopy held over her head when she walked out in the brilliant sunshine. She rode the most beautiful horses, everyone cheered her as she went by.

*I so wish you had come! You would have loved it so!*

I dare say that I would. It is a long long time since anyone cheered me, or the Scots had anything to cheer about. I open a small package from Katherine.

*My dear Sister,*

*The king, my husband, was much surprised to learn from His Grace King Francis of France that you have been writing to the Duc of Albany and urging his return to Scotland. I was ashamed to hear also that the duc has spoken to the Holy Father and urged that you should be released from your marriage on the grounds that King James IV was not killed at Flodden – you know this is not true. You know that I was obliged to take his body so that this lie should never be spoken. They are saying that you and the Duc of Albany are plotting his return to Scotland so that you can marry should his wife die.*

*Margaret, please! This is horrifying scandal to attach to you. Write at once to your brother and say that it is not so, and then publicly return to your husband so that there can be no doubt that you have not become the French duc's whore. God forgive you if you have forgotten what you owe to your family and your name. Write at once and assure me that you are in a state of heavenly grace and married to the good Earl of Angus. My love to your dear son – Margaret, think of him! How can he inherit the throne if there is any question of your honour? And what of your daughter? A divorce will name her as a bastard. How can you bear this? How can you be my royal sister and declare yourself as a whore?*

*Katherine*

I walk across the courtyard and go out of the little sally port to walk down the hill to the loch. The water meadows stretch before me to the side of the water, the short-legged cattle graze on the rich grass, the swallows weave in and out of them. A dozen milkmaids go past me with their buckets swinging from the yokes laid across their shoulders, carrying their milking stools in their hands. They call the cows in, and the animals lift their heads when they hear their names sung out in the high, sweet voices. James used to like to go out with the milkmaids and they would take a ladle and let him drink from the bucket. It would leave a little creamy moustache on his upper lip, and I would wipe his round face with my sleeve and kiss him.

I have not seen my boy since the battle between Angus and Hamilton that they are calling 'the cleansing of the causeway' after the scrubbing of the blood from the cobbles. I have not seen Archibald since he marched into the castle and I withdrew to Linlithgow, riding out through his army in silence. I have not seen James Hamilton since he galloped away to save his life. I have no daughter; she must live with her father. I have no son; he is all but imprisoned. I have no ally. I have no husband and now Katherine tells me I have sisters only upon impossible conditions.

Mary is not the fool that she pretends to be. She is desperate to avoid being caught in a quarrel between Katherine and me. She will write to me forever about gowns and lutes and hunting, always avoiding the knowledge that I am alone and unhappy and in danger. She won't speak for me to Harry – she is too fearful for her own status at court. She will be the very model of an English princess, a radiant beauty, a wife beyond reproach. She will not risk her position at court by saying one word in my favour.

I know that I am lost to Katherine. This is a woman who left home at fifteen and endured years of loneliness and poverty in order to marry the king and become Queen of England. She will never contemplate anything that might threaten her place. She may love me, but she cannot bear me to challenge the vows of marriage. She may love me, but her whole life depends on there being no end to marriage but death.

## STIRLING CASTLE, SCOTLAND, DECEMBER 1521

My luck changes, at last, at last.

The Duke of Albany himself walks into my chamber, handsome as ever, urbane as always, and bows over my hand with a French flourish as if he has just stepped out to order his cape to be brushed, and has been no time at all.

'Your Grace, I am at your command,' he says in his Burgundian French – the very pinnacle of elegance and charm.

I jump to my feet; I can barely breathe. 'Your Grace!'

'Your loyal servant,' he says.

'How ever did you get here? They're watching the ports!'

'The English fleet was at sea looking for me but they did not find me. Their spies were watching me in France – they saw me leave court but they did not see where I went.'

'My God, I have prayed for this,' I say frankly.

He takes both my hands and holds them warmly. 'I came as soon as I could get away. I have been begging King Francis to let me come to you for more than a year, as soon as I heard the terrible trouble that you were in,' he says. 'The deaths of the Hamiltons! Fighting in the streets of Edinburgh! You must have thought the kingdom was being destroyed before your eyes.'

'It has been terrible. Terrible. And they forced me to leave my son!'

'They will beg your forgiveness, and your son will be restored to you.'

'I will see James again?'

'You shall be his guardian, I swear it. But what of your husband? Is he your enemy? You cannot reconcile?'

'It's over between us, forever.' I realise that the duke and I are still holding hands. I flush and release him. 'You can count on me,' I promise. 'I will never return to him.'

He hesitates, before he lets me go. 'And you can depend on me,' he says.

## EDINBURGH CASTLE, SCOTLAND, SPRING 1522

We take Edinburgh Castle without a shot being fired. Archibald simply surrenders, leaving the castle and my children, and the duke has him escorted to France under guard. His uncle Gavin Douglas flees to England, to Harry, with a mouthful of lies.

The duke and I, on matching white horses, wait outside the castle while the trumpets sound from the battlements and the drawbridge is lowered. All the people of the city are on the castle hill, watching this masque of power. The constable comes out in the livery of the Stewarts – I imagine wryly that he has made a hasty change of clothes, and that Archibald's colours are kicked under his bed – and bows and presents the keys of the castle to the regent, the Duke of Albany. In a beautiful gesture Albany takes them, and turns to me. He smiles at the delight in my face, and presents them to me. As the people cheer, I touch the keys with my hand to acknowledge acceptance, and return them to him as regent, and then we all ride inside the castle.

James, my son, is in the inner keep. I jump from my horse without ceremony and go quickly towards him. I glance at Davy Lyndsay's beard – grizzled grey in the months that we have been apart – and I could curse Archibald for what we have all endured, but I can see nothing but my son's pale face and his urgent expression. I curtsey, as a subject should, and he kneels to me for a mother's blessing, as I wrap my arms around him and hold him tightly.

He feels different. He is a little taller, a little stronger since I last saw him. He is nine now, he has grown stiff and awkward. He does not yield to me, he does not lean against me. I feel as if he will never cling to me again. He has been taught to mistrust me and I see that I will have the task of teaching him to love and value me all over again. I look up to see Davy's brown eyes are filled with tears. He rubs them away with the back of his hand. 'Welcome home, Your Grace,' is all he says.

'God bless you, Davy Lyndsay,' I say to him. I rest my cheek against James' warm curls and I do indeed bless Davy Lyndsay for staying beside my son, through it all, for keeping him safe.

I am not the only Scot to rejoice in the return of the Duke of Albany. The Hamiltons know that with him returned to Scotland, and the power of the French behind him, they can recover. The Scots lords can see a way out from the tyranny of the Clan Douglas. The people of Scotland, their borderlands destroyed by Dacre's continual raids, their capital bloodstained and unruly, long for the rule of the regent who brought them peace before.

I write a gleeful taunting letter to Lord Dacre and tell him that, despite his gloomy predictions, the duke has returned to Edinburgh, peace will come to Scotland, and England will not dare to invade now that we are protected by France. I say that his good friend, my husband, seems to have abandoned his post and his family and I beg nobody will reproach me for failing to accompany him into a traitor's exile. At last we can have some happiness in Scotland again. I laugh as I write; Dacre will know that the tables are turned on him and that I am a free woman and I am in power.

I think my brother must have gone mad. I cannot believe that anyone would dare to speak of a reigning queen in the terms that they are speaking of me. I cannot believe that my brother would listen. A true brother would denounce the gossips. If his wife were a true sister to me, she would insist that they are silenced. The English blacksmiths are commanded by law to slice the tongue of anyone who slanders the royal family, but it is my own brother who writes scandal to Dacre and permits him – a border lord! – to accuse me of unspeakable crimes.

Archibald's uncle, Gavin Douglas, is an honoured guest at the court in London and has told everyone that I am the Duke of Albany's mistress. He swears that the good duke came to Scotland only to seduce me, to murder my son and put himself on the throne.

This much is madness: insane to say, worse to hear, but Gavin Douglas says even more. He claims that the duke keeps my son in poverty, stealing the red velvet and the cloth of gold sleeves for his own pages, refusing to let my son see his tutors or even eat. He says that the regent is starving the young king to death and that I am allowing it to happen, and together we will claim the throne. Worse than this – if there could be worse – he claims that the duke poisoned my poor lost boy Alexander. They say that I am bedding the murderer of my son. They say this, in the courts of Westminster and the throne room at Greenwich, and nobody – not my brother the king, not my sister-in-law, the queen, not their favourite, my own little sister, Mary – leaps up and denies it. Not even Mary cries out that it cannot be true.

How can the three of them not speak up for me? Katherine saw me just months after I had learned of the death of Alexander. She saw me unable to speak his name for grief. She and Mary both held me while I sobbed for him. How can she listen when my proclaimed enemy says that my lover murdered my son, and that I allowed it?

The two of them, my two sisters, have hurt me before, they have ignored me, they have misunderstood me. But this is greater than anything. This time they are making accusations that I would not level at a witch. I think they must have lost their minds. I think that all of them must have lost their minds and have forgotten everything that we were to each other. I said that they were no sisters to me, that I would forget them. But they have gone further than this: they have become my enemies.

## EDINBURGH CASTLE, SCOTLAND, SUMMER 1522

My brother sends a Clarenceux Herald to Edinburgh to discover the state of affairs since, apparently, I cannot be trusted to report, and my word is worthless. The great man brings grooms and servants, and his clerks carry letters from my sister, Mary, and my sister-in-law, Katherine.

'Her Grace said to give these to you privately and suggest that you read them alone,' says the herald, awkwardly. He does not know what is in them, but – like everyone in England – he knows what is being said about me.

I nod and take them away to my bedchamber. I lock the door behind me and break the seal. There are two letters. First, I read the one from Katherine, the queen.

*Dearest Sister,*

*I cannot and will not believe the things that I have heard about you. Your husband's uncle Gavin Douglas speaks of vile things. Please believe that I will not hear them said in my presence.*

*I am sorry that he has the ear of Cardinal Wolsey and of the king. There is nothing I can do about this, and I dare not try. Your brother used to listen to my advice but now he does not.*

*I am sure that you are lonely and sad. Believe me, sometimes a good wife has to suffer while her husband is in error. If Archibald returns to you from France, and his uncle swears that he will, then you must take him back. Only reuniting with your husband will silence these terrible stories. If you were only living with him now, nobody could say anything against you.*

*My dear, it is God's will that a wife has no choice but to forgive an erring husband. No choice. However much her heart may break. I do not advise this lightly. I did not learn this easily. Your sister,*

*Katherine*

Stubbornly, I screw up the letter into a ball and toss it into the red embers at the back of the fireplace. I break the seal of the Dowager Queen of France, which she still insists on using, and smooth Mary's crumpled letter on my knee. As always she writes of the court, and of the clothes and of the fashions; as always she brags of her own beauty and the masque that she led and the jewel that Henry gave her. But for once there is a different twist in this old story. Mary's pretty nose is out of joint because another girl is leading the dancing at court, and it sounds like a merry dance. At once I begin to understand the intensity of Katherine's unhappy tone. I try to decipher Mary's terrible handwriting and contain my secret squirm of shameful delight. Mary writes that yet another lady has taken Henry's eye and captured his fancy and this time it is far more public than any previous affair. He chooses her as his partner in masques, he walks with her and talks with her, rides out with her and plays cards with her. As one of Katherine's ladies-in-waiting, she is constantly in the queen's sight; she is acknowledged, not hidden. She has become the most important woman at court, favoured over the queen, and she is pretty and blooming and young. Everyone knows that she is the king's mistress and closest companion.

I should not smile. But the thought of Katherine having to eat humble pie while yet another girl delights her young husband lifts my spirits. If she had understood my pain when Archibald was unfaithful to me, I would be full of sympathy now. But then she said it was God's will that a wife should forgive.

*She is far worse than Bessie for she has no discretion at all. And of course, the girl is very beautiful, and, worst of all, Harry is quite besotted. He carried her handkerchief over his heart in a joust, he told Charles that he can't stop thinking of her. She makes it worse by running after him wherever she can, and Katherine can't send her home to her husband because she is married to young Carey and he is most helpful: a shameless cuckold. He is to receive lands and places, all for looking the other way. You would pity Katherine if you could see her. And no signs of another baby yet. It is quite miserable here. You would be sorry, I know.*

I can see her writing change as she turns the page and remembers that I have troubles of my own. *They are saying the most terrible things about you,* Mary tells me, in case this has slipped my attention.

*You must take great care that you are never alone with the Duke of Albany. Your reputation must be perfect. You owe that to us, to Katherine and to me, especially now. The three of us – you and me and Katherine – must always be above scandal and above suspicion. If Katherine is to survive Harry's folly she has to be far above it. If he is to return to her, penitent, when this is over then nobody can say anything against us Tudor sisters and our marriages. Please, Margaret, you cannot let us down. Remember that you are a Tudor princess as we are. You must be above scandal and shame. We all must.*

She finishes the letter with love to me and to my son and to Margaret with a reminder that Archibald will be coming back to Scotland to beg a pardon from Albany and that it is essential that I speak for him. *A wife's duty is to forgive,* she parrots. Then finally at the very last corner there is a tiny squeezed scatter of words.

*Oh God forgive me, I can hardly write. My son Henry has this day died of the Sweat. Pray for us.*

I go out of my room to find the Clarenceux Herald. 'My sister has lost her son?' I ask.

He is uncomfortable speaking to me, as if I might suddenly strip off my bodice and dance as naked as Salome. God knows what he has heard of me. God knows what he thinks of me.

'Alas, yes.'

'I will write to her,' I say hastily. 'You will take my letters to England when you return?'

Absurdly, he looks as if he would like to refuse. 'What is the matter?' I demand. 'Why are you looking like that?'

'I am instructed that all letters are to be left unsealed. You may write, and I am to carry them, but I am bound in honour to warn you that they are to remain open.'

'Why?'

He shuffles his feet. 'So that it is clear that you are not writing love letters,' he says.

'To whom?' I demand.

He gulps. 'Anyone.'

If this were not so terrible it would be funny. 'Good God, man, do you not know that the lord Dacre reads everything I ever write and always has done so? Spies on my very thoughts before I have them? And still has no evidence against me? Who do you imagine loves me in England, where Gavin Douglas calls me a whore to my brother's face, and nobody challenges him?'

There is a horrified silence. I realise I have spoken too wildly. I should never ever say the word 'whore'. I have to be, as Mary says so clumsily, above scandal.

'Anyway, I can carry your letters if they are unsealed,' he says weakly. 'But now I have to speak to the regent.'

'I'll come with you,' I say.

Clearly, the herald would rather have met with Albany alone, and soon I see why. He has brought a letter from Harry, which accuses Albany of seducing me, of 'damnable abusion' and of working for my divorce against my best interests and for his own ends. I am so horrified by these words from my brother to a stranger that I can hardly bear to look at Albany while the herald reads out these accusations in a quiet monotone as if he wishes we could not hear him and he did not have to say them.

Albany is white with fury. He forgets the rules of chivalry and speaks to the herald with contempt. He says that he did indeed apply to the Holy Father for my divorce for me, at my request; but that he himself is a married man and faithful to his wife. He does not look at me, and I know that with my burning face and the tears on my cheeks I look like a guilty fool. Bitingly, the duke tells the English herald that the matter of my divorce is with the Pope, and that the Holy Father will be the sole judge of it. Albany himself merely delivered the message.

'How could my brother say such things?' I whisper to the herald, who glances at me and then dips his head in a little bow.

Albany says that he finds it extraordinary that the King of England should accuse his own sister of becoming another man's concubine. The herald is crushed into silence. He mutters only that he has a letter that he must put before the Scots lords, and he leaves the room.

As I could have told him, the Scots lords have no time for a herald from England, especially one that comes to slander their regent and their dowager queen together. They scowl at him, and one of the older, angrier lords throws himself out of the council chamber, banging the door behind him. The herald, in the face of grim hostility, reads out Harry's ridiculous demands with a quiet voice, and the Scots lords reply that they are all willing to serve under the regent, Albany, until the king my son is of age, that they are happy that the regent appoints tutors and guardians from among them, according to my wishes. They regard as slanderous lies the suggestion that the regent and I are lovers. They declare that my husband and his uncle are traitors, banished from the kingdom, and that everyone knows that my son Alexander, the little Duke of Ross, died of ill health. The herald shuffles his feet and leaves. I watch his humiliation with delight.

I hope he goes back to London and tells Harry that he is a fool to speak so to the Scots. I hope he goes back to London and tells Katherine that I live apart from Archibald and I will never return to him, and I don't agree that a wife has to forgive an erring husband, I don't agree that a Tudor wife has to be above criticism. I hope he goes back to London and tells Mary that I am sorry for the death of her son but she should be glad that no-one suggests that he was murdered. I hope the herald tells her that now Archibald is exiled I have my rents and my fees again, and I am buying new gowns. I don't need any of them to support me. I have given up on all three of them.

## HOLYROODHOUSE PALACE, EDINBURGH, SCOTLAND, AUTUMN 1522

The one thing that my marriage to the King of Scotland was supposed to prevent was war between the country of my birth and the country of my marriage. I have tried to keep peace in Scotland, and peace between Scotland and England, so it is a bitter day for me when the Duke of Albany serves his French king better than his country of Scotland, when he is truer to his French paymaster than he is to me, and marches against the English. Not even the prospect of the humiliation of Lord Dacre can comfort me.

In this emergency, my brother turns to me once more, as if we have never quarrelled, and sends me secret messages, asking me what sort of force the French will bring against his men. He reminds me – as if I ever forget – that I am an English princess, bound to him and to my country by unbreakable bonds of love and loyalty. I advise him as best I can and when Albany gives up the attempt to march on England and sails for France, for more funds and men, I find I am left alone in Scotland, the regent gone, my husband exiled, my enemies defeated. Finally, I am the peace-bringer, the only leader left standing.

## STIRLING CASTLE, SCOTLAND, SPRING 1523

Amazingly, despite the odds, I find that I am a single woman, in possession of my own fortune, the only regent left in power, and the guardian of my son. I was ill over Christmas but I grow strong again as the days become lighter and then I get a letter, forwarded by Dacre, from my sister, Mary. She writes very briefly from her confinement. *God has blessed me and I have had another boy, I am calling him Henry.*

I know that this is the name of the son that she lost, I know that Mary will be thinking first, before anything else, of the little boy who died so young. But she gives him the name of the Lancaster kings, she gives him our brother's own name, our father's name. I am certain that secretly she hopes he will be King of England, Harry's heir. She must want Harry to pass over me, and my son James, and honour her boy. Charles Brandon will be hoping to get his boy on the throne, of course, and there is no-one in London who will advocate for me and my son, not my sister nor my sister-in-law.

Of course Mary will listen to scandal against me, and naturally she repeats it. It is wholly in her interest to suggest that I am no true wife, no true Tudor, no true queen. If Harry can be convinced that I am no true mother either then he will disinherit my son. Mary may urge me to a spotless life, but she knows that the real world is not an easy one for a woman with a wicked husband. I have to live as a woman alone; people are bound to gossip. But will Mary let them gossip so much that they turn against my innocent son?

I wonder what Katherine makes of this hidden jostling for

inheritance. I wonder how bitter it is for her, whose fault it is that there is no Tudor prince. I wonder if she ever wavers in her loyal love towards my sister, when Mary's marriage is blessed and she is fertile, and as soon as one Henry dies he is replaced with another? Mary goes on and on having babies, and Katherine has clearly stopped.

England is at peace with Scotland after Albany leaves, and I thought I could make them keep the peace. But Harry sends the son of the Duke of Norfolk, the murderer of Flodden, to arm the North, and there is no doubt that he plans to ruin the country that marched against him. They will do it Dacre's way – by making a desert of the borderlands. Every building they tear down, every thatch they fire, every castle they destroy. They leave not a sheaf of wheat in the field, not a stook of hay. Not an animal survives the gleaning, not a child is left standing. The poor grab what goods they have left and rush like a tumbling stream of terror north or south, wherever they think they might find help. The soldiers steal their goods and harry them on their way, the women are abused, the children screaming with terror. It is Dacre's plan to make a desert of the borders so that no army can ever cross them again, and by the start of the summer he has conquered the very land itself – nothing will grow, nothing will ripen, nothing will yield. When I came to Scotland these were fertile wastes where any man could make a living if he did not mind the empty roads and the tiny villages. Any man could seek a night's rest at any of a thousand little castles where strangers were a rarity and hospitality a law. Now the land is empty. Only the wolves run through the borders and their howls at night are like a lament for the people who once lived here, who have been wiped out by the malice of England.

# LINLITHGOW PALACE, SCOTLAND, SUMMER 1523

My son James and daughter Margaret and I have a summer together as a true royal family at the beautiful palace beside the loch where I have spent so much time – happy times and mourning times. James rides out every day, his master of horse offering him bigger and stronger horses as he grows in confidence and strength. His carver, Henry Stewart, rides with him. He's a young man in his mid-twenties and he has a natural grace and charm that James admires and that I am eager he should copy. Unusually for a Scot, Henry has light brown hair, which curls around his head and tumbles down the nape of his neck, like a statue of a Greek god. He is no pretty boy; he is hard, as all these young men are, from families accustomed to war, but he is always merry. He has the most enchanting smile and his brown eyes dance when he is laughing. Together with the other young men of the court, he teaches James all the games of mounted skill: throwing a lance, shooting an arrow from the saddle, picking up rings on his lance from the ground, and – we all laugh at this – catching a thrown handkerchief on the tip of his lance, as if a lady were offering him her favour.

'Throw for me, Lady Mother!' James demands, and I lean over the tilt yard royal box and drop a handkerchief down for him, and he spurs forward and misses it over and over again until he catches it, and his companions and I applaud.

The Scots lords beg the Duke of Albany to return, but I don't. In his absence Harry writes to me about a lasting peace treaty between England and Scotland, and peace for the borderlands. He writes a long, thoughtful letter, as if his insults had never been. He writes about the care of his nephew, my son, acknowledging that James is the heir of both England and Scotland. He writes that God has not yet blessed him and the queen with a boy, no-one can say why – God's will cannot be questioned – but it may be that one day James will be called to be king of a united island. Dizzy with ambition, I think that there will never have been a king like James since Arthur of Britain. Cardinal Wolsey writes to me with his customary respect – I can hardly believe that he dines nightly with my estranged husband's uncle and hears nothing but ill of me. Even Lord Dacre changes his tone, now I am acknowledged once again as a princess of England and Dowager Queen of Scotland – and with Albany back in France, I am the only regent.

There is no reason that my son should not be crowned king next spring, when he will be twelve. Why not? He has been raised to be king, he knows it is his destiny, he has been tutored as a king and guarded faithfully and constantly by Davy Lyndsay and served all his life on bended knee. Nobody meeting him for the first time and seeing him gracious and cautious could doubt for a moment that this is a boy coming into manhood, coming into majesty. Twelve is a good age for a boy to come into his own – old enough for a marriage, so why not old enough for a coronation? What better way to unify the kingdom than the coronation of the king?

Just as I have decided to push this through, against the lords who would rather wait, the Duke of Albany returns without warning, determined on war with England, and Norfolk's son the Earl of Surrey – a cruel commander and the son of a cruel commander – destroys the town of Jedburgh and blows up the abbey to show English power over defenceless Scots.

I write to Harry in despair. This is not the way to persuade the Scots lords to accept my son as king! If he wants to command Scotland through James and me he has to give me money to bribe the council, he has to show me as a peacemaker. If he wants to do it by force he had better bring an army to Edinburgh, and impose a rule of law; torturing the poor people of the borders does nothing but make them more furiously opposed to England and the lords more suspicious of me.

Of course, Albany has to respond to the challenge and he brings his fresh troops from France against England with heavy cannon and thousands of mercenaries. This time he brings with him a great army. I am completely torn. Of course I want to further the power and influence of Scotland, of course I am thrilled at the thought of a new border for a new king – if Albany could push the border south and take Carlisle and Newcastle into Scotland then my son would have the great inheritance that his father dreamed for him.

'And the White Rose our ally will invade from the south at the same time,' Albany promises me, confident of my support.

I put a hand on the cool stone of the chimney breast. It steadies me. The great terror of our childhood, as Tudor children, was the coming of the other – the other royal family, our mother's side of the family – the Plantagenets. Always fertile, always ambitious, my mother's many sisters and their many children were always on the edge of our kingdom looking for a chance to return. The White Rose – as they call him – is the last of the very many. Richard de la Pole, my mother's first cousin, has seen one brother after another die in battle against my father or on my father's scaffold. My father swore an oath that no-one from the old royal family would ever take back what the Tudors won at Bosworth, and I have been raised to think of any pretender as a nightmare enemy to our safety and our power.

They were the terrors of my childhood; nothing was as bad as learning that one of our cousins had disappeared from court into open enmity. I can remember even now my mother's aghast expression when she realised that yet another of her kin had turned against us. Whatever the benefits for my son, I could never join with a Plantagenet cousin against my Tudor brother. Albany cannot have known this when he sought such an ally. I cannot tolerate a Plantagenet. I cannot imagine friendship with this enemy. I could have considered an invasion of England – I would have supported it as an addition to my son's power and the breadth of his kingdom – I could tolerate an alliance with France; but never, never, never with one of my cursed cousins.

That night I betray the Duke of Albany and – called by my childhood loyalty to the Tudors – I write to my brother:

> *Albany has German mercenaries and French soldiers but he cannot keep them here in winter. If you can hold him long enough at Wark Castle then the weather will do the work for you. Defend us all against the White Rose. If Richard de la Pole comes to Scotland I will come to you and bring James. We Tudors will stand together against the White Rose forever. Your sister – M.*

## STIRLING CASTLE, SCOTLAND, AUTUMN 1523

The Duke of Albany is defeated thanks to my advice, and he and the Earl of Surrey negotiate an uneasy peace without consulting me. Neither of them trusts me with his confidence. There is not another word about me going to England, there is not another word about James taking the throne next year, not another word about him being named as the English heir. Instead Harry cuts my English allowance and throws me into debt with the French. I cannot understand why he should suddenly turn so cold, when only a few months ago I was his spy and confidante. I cannot think what I have done to offend him, I cannot imagine what is wrong; surely I have served him as no fellow monarch or sister has ever done? And then I receive a letter from my sister Mary:

*My dear Sister,*

*Katherine – our sister and queen – has asked me to tell you that your husband, Archibald Earl of Angus, has come to us from France to be welcomed by the whole court as a friend to the cardinal and a brother to the king. He intends to return to Scotland at once and Katherine and I join together in urging you to receive him kindly and live together as man and wife. He speaks so sweetly of you and his hopes for a reconciliation.*

*I am sorry to say that our brother is clearly very much in love with Mary Carey (that was Mary Boleyn) and she with him. If she were free and he were free I think he would marry her. But neither of them has that choice. The marriage vow is indissoluble. If a man can set aside his wife because he loves another woman then what would become of us all? What marriage would last beyond the first year? What does an oath before the altar mean if it can be put aside? How could anyone trust an oath of loyalty between king and subject, between master and man, if the oath of marriage is temporary? If marriage is uncertain then everything is uncertain. You cannot be the only Tudor who shows the world that our word is unreliable.*

*You have to play your part in this, you have to take your husband back and tolerate him as best you can. I beg you. We cannot live in a family in which annulment or divorce is even mentioned. We are too new to the throne for our behaviour to be questioned, for our heirs to be made bastards. Please, Margaret, take your husband back for all of our sakes and write at once and tell me that you will do so.*

*Your loving sister, Mary, Dowager Queen of France*

I take her letter with me and I walk across the steep slope of the castle yard and out through the thick gates that stand open, two French guardsmen watching the people who come and go out of the castle. I take the winding footpath through the woods, and then follow the stream as it falls down towards the village that clusters at the foot of the hill around the market cross. No-one comes with me. I am alone under the leafless branches of the trees and I scuff my boots in the dusty-smelling autumn leaves. It is a sharp, clear day, the sky as blue as the shell on a duck egg, the air cold and the sunshine bright. I think of Mary, taking her courage to the sticking point to write me a letter that she knows I will not like, I think of Katherine, bleakly cautioning her that if Harry sets his wife aside, then no woman in England is safe. I know this is true. Women in this world have no power: own nothing, not even their own bodies; hold nothing, not even their own children. A wife must live with her husband and be treated as he wishes, eat at his table, sleep in his bed. A daughter is the property of her father. A wife outside marriage is in the care of no-one. Legally she owns nothing and no-one will protect her. If a woman cannot marry knowing that she will be a wife till her dying day, then where can she find safety? If a man can put his wife aside on a whim then no woman can count on her fortune, her life, her future. If the king shows that marriage vows mean nothing, then all vows mean nothing, then all laws are nothing – we will live in a world of nothingness as if there is no law and no God.

I walk home up the steep hill with dragging feet. Even knowing all this – I cannot live with Archibald again, I cannot bear to be with the man I married for love, that I gifted with everything I owned, and who preferred someone else. I cannot return to a man with blood on his hands. But I do see what Katherine and Mary are saying – marriage vows must last forever. A royal marriage is indissoluble.

I don't reply to Mary, but I write a painful letter to Cardinal Wolsey, knowing that he will write an accurate synopsis and set it before Harry, when Harry can take the time from his love affair to listen.

*I must tell you that the French have promised me a safe haven in Paris if ever Archibald returns to Scotland. I solemnly swear that I will never live with him again, but I understand that I should not pursue my divorce. I beg you to make sure that Archibald never comes back to Scotland, that the king my brother does not grant him safe conduct, that he is advised to live in exile. The Duke of Albany is going to France soon, before the winter storms make the seas too dangerous, and in his absence I will try to see my son safely on the throne. I hope to take James away from Stirling Castle and the guards who are paid by the French. I hope to take him to Edinburgh and make him king. I believe I can do this with the lords of the council and with the help of James Hamilton, as long as the Douglas clan remain quiet and Archibald in exile. For I am not fickle, and I am not faithless, and your great friend Archibald Douglas, the Earl of Angus, is both.*

*God and Scotland would be best served if he stayed away forever. I too.*

## HOLYROODHOUSE PALACE, EDINBURGH, SCOTLAND, SUMMER 1524

I can hardly believe that I have got my way, but it seems that I am lucky again. With English gold and an English guard I snatch my son from his French guardians at Stirling Castle and bring him to Edinburgh. Triumphantly I move him into his rooms in my palace and have his bed hung with cloth of gold, and the two of us dine together under the royal cloth of estate.

The people of Edinburgh are wild to see him. We have to bar the gates of the palace to keep well-wishers out of the gardens and courtyards, and once a day my boy goes to the balcony and waves to the people who gather below. When the midday gun is fired from Edinburgh Castle my boy salutes the crowd as if it is a cannon fired for respect and not to declare noonday. All the bells of the churches ring at once and James smiles and waves as the crowd doff their caps and kiss their hands and call out blessings on him. 'And when will ye be king? When crowned?' someone shouts, and I stand behind him and smile and call out: 'Soon! Soon as we can! Soon as the lords agree!' and there is a swell of cheers.

Albany has left for France and in his absence I dominate the council. I have each lord come in, one at a time, to swear loyalty to their little king and everyone does so, except for two, and I imprison them. No longer do I hesitate, thinking that perhaps they will change their minds, perhaps I can persuade them. I have learned to be ruthless. I will take no risks. Henry Stewart, now serving as lieutenant of my son's guards, smiles at me. 'You stoop like a peregrine falcon,' he says. 'Sudden and fast.'

'I am flying high like a falcon too,' I smile.

I make the royal court in Holyrood as rich and as beautiful as when my husband James first showed it to me. Around my son I gather a community of people that I want him to study and admire: ladies-in-waiting who are beautiful and elegant, courtiers who are sporting and musical and cultivated. The finest of them all is Henry Stewart, who shines out for his good looks and keen intelligence. I promote him to the post of treasurer of James' household: he is careful with money and completely trustworthy. He is a cousin of sorts; I can see royalty in him. Even though he is young he is astute: I would take his advice before anyone in the kingdom but James Hamilton Earl of Arran, who is restored to court as my principal advisor and deputy regent.

My son is at the centre of everything, guarded and tutored like the boy he is, and yet a king at the heart of power. Of course he does and says nothing without my advice, but he understands everything – the need to keep the Scots lords on our side, our reliance on the money from England, the risk that the French may return, and yet the advantage of that ever-present danger, for it is only when Scotland is threatened that Harry remembers his sister is holding it for England and for him.

So I am pleased when Harry sends two great gentlemen from his court and they can report to him that Holyroodhouse is as great a palace as Greenwich. Archdeacon Thomas Magnus and Roger Radcliffe come with beautiful gifts for James. He is delighted. They give him a suit of cloth of gold, wonderfully tailored and with exquisite fabric, and – best of all for a twelve-year-old boy – a jewelled sword of just the right size.

'Look, Lady Mother!' He shows me the scabbard, the rubies on the hilt, he takes it with his trained skill, feels its balance, swishes it through the air.

'Take care ye don't behead me!' Davy Lyndsay warns him, and James beams at his head of household.

To me they bend the knee and present a gift. I peek inside the silk wrapping. It is a long piece of cloth, enough for two gowns or several sleeves. My favourite: cloth of gold, the cloth of kings, woven with gold thread, a treasury on a roll. 'Thank you. Please thank my brother,' I say quietly. They need not think that I am going to scream with delight or have it made into gowns and set before me so I can see it all the time and boast that it proves my brother's love for me. We are all a long, long way now from Morpeth and I am not as easily pleased as I once was.

I beckon the ambassadors to come closer and the musicians play a little louder and my ladies move away so that the men can tell me the news from London without every gossip in the Canongate knowing our business half an hour later.

'We bring a proposal that we think will make Your Grace very happy.' The archdeacon bows. 'And also private letters written for you.'

I put out my hand and they hand over the packages. 'And the proposals?'

He bows again; he smiles. Clearly, this is going to be worth hearing. Across the room I catch the eye of Henry Stewart. He gives me a naughty wink as if he understands my delight that my star is in the ascendant again, and my brother is treating me as he should, as a monarch in my own right. I long to wink back, but I turn to the ambassador and say quietly, 'Yes. The proposal?'

They draw closer, they all but whisper. I have to put my glove up to my face as if I were sniffing the scented leather in order to hide my great beam of delight. They are offering James the hand in marriage of his cousin Mary: Katherine and Harry's only daughter. They are all but confirming that he is to be named as England's heir. It is the best resolution for Harry that there could be – his true-born daughter becomes Queen of England, her place ensured by marrying her cousin, my son the King of Scotland and heir to England.

I master my expression and I look at them with pleasant indifference. 'Is the princess not betrothed to the Holy Roman Emperor?' I ask.

'At present.' The archdeacon spreads his soft white hands. 'Such arrangements are often changed.'

Such arrangements are changed at the mere whisper of my brother's volatile will. Princess Mary has already been betrothed to France as well as Spain. But if he betroths little Princess Mary to my son it will be with a contract that will hold: I will make it unbreakable.

Henry Stewart comes across the room to my side. I feel my cheeks glow. He bends close to me so that he can speak confidentially in my ear. 'Your Grace, guard yourself, I am about to give you bad news. Guard your face.'

This is so sudden and so intimate from a young man who has proved himself such a good friend that immediately I raise my gloves to my nose again and glance down, veiling my eyes to hide my alarm. 'What?' I ask tersely.

'Your husband, Archibald Douglas Earl of Angus, is in the city.'

I turn to the ambassadors, feeling, like the brush of an angel's wing, Henry Stewart's finger at the back of my shoulder, giving me strength, as if this young man is willing me not to falter.

'I hear that the Earl of Angus has returned to Scotland,' I say coolly; there is not a tremor in my voice. Henry Stewart steps back and narrows his eyes in a hidden smile at me as if I am everything that he hoped for.

The ambassadors bow their heads, and exchange embarrassed glances.

'He is,' Radcliffe finally says. 'And we hope that it is no inconvenience to Your Grace. But they failed to hold him in France, and we had no grounds to arrest him in England. Your Grace's brother the king did not wish him to disturb you, but the earl is a free man – he may come and go where he wishes. We could hardly imprison him.'

'We did not want it to trouble you . . .' the archdeacon adds.

'He will not trouble Her Grace,' Henry suddenly interrupts, forgetting the caution that he preached to me. 'Nothing should trouble her. She is dowager queen in her own kingdom, she is regent. What should trouble her here? Did you actually bring him with you? Did you travel together as friends?'

He gives me the confidence to be queenly where I feel most hurt. 'My brother should think about my rights as a queen before he considers Archibald's rights as an earl,' I say. 'His lordship forfeited any rights over me when he failed me as a husband. You can tell him that I will receive no letters from him, that he may not keep an entourage of more than forty men, and he is not to come within ten miles of the court.'

My two advisors, James Hamilton Earl of Arran and Henry Stewart, nod at this. It is only a matter of our own safety. Nobody will forget what Archibald did when he had his clan inside the city walls. James Hamilton doesn't want to go for a gallop on a coalman's pony again, and Henry Stewart has the fierce pride of a devoted young man: he would rather die than see me in danger.

I take my letters into the quiet of my chapel where I will not be disturbed, not by my son, not by my chattering daughter, not by the quiet smile of James' handsome treasurer. There is only one personal letter, from my sister Mary. Katherine is silent, and it is the missing letter from the queen that tells me as much as the three pages from my sister. The clue is on Mary's last page. She says:

*Lady Carey (who was a nicer girl when she was Mary Boleyn) has taken to her bed and had a little girl. Of course, everyone knows Harry is the father, and the Boleyn family have grants of land and titles and lord knows what else. Very good for a family from nowhere. Harry, God bless him, is delighted that another child of his making is safely born and thriving, and Charles says that we should all understand that he is a man and he has his pride. Charles says that I am a fool to be troubled by this, it is of no matter, but if you could see our sister's hurt, you would feel as I do. Charles says that no-one cares: a bastard child here or there makes no difference to anyone, but everyone knows – though no-one says – that the queen's childbearing years are over. Harry dines with her, his manners to her are quite beautiful, and sometimes he stays the night in her rooms, but it is for courtesy; she is no longer his lover, she is only his wife in name, and their lack of a son is so marked while Bessie Blount's boy grows strong and healthy and Mary Boleyn's daughter coos when she sees her father. What if he has another bastard boy? Another after that?*

*Katherine has taken to fasting and wearing a hair shirt under her beautiful gowns as if she were at fault. But she makes no complaint; she says nothing. Nothing at all. I think Harry feels awkward, and it makes him boisterous and loud and the whole court has become a little wild. Charles says I am becoming a grumpy old lady, but if you could see Katherine when she withdraws from court early to pray, while they dance till all hours, you would understand what I mean. Everyone is drinking the new baby's health as if it were a little princess born. People were discreet about Henry Fitzroy but this Boleyn bastard is openly celebrated. Everyone is aware of Henry Fitzroy growing bigger and stronger every day and served in a nursery which is as good as any of ours. Harry is king, of course, he must do as he wishes. But, oh! Maggie! if you could see Katherine you would feel as I do that our happy times are over.*

Yes, I think. And how the world turns, especially for women. The young princess from Spain who married my beautiful older brother, Arthur, entranced my father, seduced my young brother and then preached the unbending laws of marriage to me, now watches her husband walk past her to a younger woman. Now she sees a young woman go into confinement and bring out a red-headed Tudor baby. Katherine always got her own way through a combination of intense charm and fierce opinion. Katherine always had God and the law on her side. Now her charms are fading and nobody is listening to her opinion at all. All she has left is God and the law. I think we will see her cling to them.

Of course I am sorry for her, of course I know that vows must be kept, especially by kings and queens, but I also think that this is my opportunity. I have publicly declared that Archibald cannot come near the court, is banished from my presence. I will not be swayed from that. And now I think the chance has come for me to go further. I will get my son on the throne of Scotland and I will get my divorce. While Harry is falling in love with a married woman and owning his bastards he cannot forbid my freedom, he could not be such a hypocrite. Katherine's decline – sad though it is, a pity though it is – is my opportunity. The world is not as she commands. We do not have to live as she thinks is right. I shall not be sacrificed to prove her point. I will be free, whatever she thinks of me. I will dare to end my marriage vows just as my brother dares to break his.

# HOLYROODHOUSE PALACE, EDINBURGH, SCOTLAND, AUTUMN 1524

I am awakened in the darkness by the violent ringing of the church bells pounding out a jangle of tones, the tocsin, an alarm. I jump out of my bed and the lady-in-waiting who sleeps with me throws my robe around my shoulders and gasps, 'What is it? What's happening?'

I fling open the door of my privy chamber as the guards throw open the door at the other end and Henry Stewart comes running in, wearing his breeches and his boots and pulling on his shirt over his naked chest.

'Dress,' he says to me urgently. 'The Douglases have defied your ban. They have entered the city.'

'Archibald?'

'Climbed over the walls and opened the gates from the inside. There are hundreds of them. Do I have your permission to set a siege?'

'Here? We can't hold a siege here?'

'Depends how many of them there are,' he says tightly.

He turns on his heel and runs out, shouting for the guards to go to battle stations. I run back into my room and pull on a gown and push my feet in my slippers. My lady-in-waiting is plumped down on a stool, crying with fear.

'Fetch the others,' I say to her. 'Tell them to go to my presence chamber, and close the shutters on all the windows.'

'The Douglases are coming?' she quavers.

'Not if I can stop them,' I say.

I stride into my presence chamber and find Davy Lyndsay

with James. My son is pale and nervous. He tries to smile when he sees me and he bows for my blessing.

'We're holding the palace,' I say to Davy over James' bowed head. I raise James up and curtsey and kiss him. 'You be brave and make sure that you go nowhere near the windows or out on the walls. Don't be seen, don't be a target.'

'What do they want?' he asks.

'They say they want to be restored to the lords' council and not arraigned as traitors,' Lyndsay says shortly. 'They go an odd way about it.'

'Archibald's way,' I say bitterly. 'Hidden weapons, a secret army – he should be ashamed of himself. How many did he kill last time?'

The English ambassadors, half-dressed, the archdeacon bare-legged, come running in. 'Is it the French?'

'Worse,' I say bitingly. 'It's your friend Archibald Douglas, with hundreds of his men at his back and no control over them at all.'

They are literally white with fear. 'What will you do?'

'I will destroy them,' I swear.

Holyroodhouse is a palace, not a castle, but the walls are high and there are towers at every corner, and a great gate that can be barred shut. I hear the tremendous roar of the guns from the castle and I know that Henry Stewart will have ridden like a madman up the Via Regis to tell them to arm and direct their guns on whoever threatens them; the castle must not fall.

'Roll out our guns,' I say to the captain of the guard. 'They can't come here.'

We don't have gun stations like a castle, but they roll out the guns before the gate and my men stand behind them, grim-faced, cannonballs stacked behind them, ready to bombard the Via Regis, their own city. Before them, kneeling on the cobbles, are my guard with handguns and bows.

'Before God, I beg of you, don't fire on your own husband.' The archdeacon appears at my shoulder as I stand at the porter's gate, looking as anxiously as my gunners for any sign of the Douglas army on the Via Regis ahead of us. 'It would be an act of such wifely disobedience. No reconciliation would be possible, no pope could condone—'

'You get back to your lodging,' I spit at him. 'These are Scottish matters and if you had not given him safe conduct he would not be here.'

'Your Grace!'

'Go! Or I will shoot you myself!'

He falls back, stricken. He throws one aghast look up the cobbles as if he fears a horde of madmen running down in their plaids with their knives in their teeth, and he scuttles away.

I glance behind me. James is there, his English sword on his hip. 'You go to the presence chamber,' I order him. 'If it all goes wrong let them find you on the throne. If they get in, be calm and surrender to them. Davy will guide you. Don't let them touch you. They must not put a hand on you.' I turn to James Hamilton Earl of Arran. 'Guard him,' I say. 'And get horses ready in case he has to escape.'

'Where will you be?' he asks me.

I don't answer. If they get in, I will be dead. They will step over my corpse to capture my son. This is not play-acting; this is war between Archibald and me, between the Douglas clan and the regency, between the outlaws and the throne. This is our final battle, I know it.

Davy Lyndsay guides my son away. 'God bless you,' he says shortly to me. 'Where's young Harry Stewart?'

'Holding the castle for us,' I say. 'As soon as it is safe we'll get up there. Be ready.'

He nods. 'Take care, Your Grace.'

'This is to the death,' I reply.

All day we stand at the ready, hearing news of a few casualties, a little unrest, some looting, a rape. All day we hear that Clan Douglas are in every ward and alley in the town, trying to turn out the men to storm the palace and getting no help. The townspeople are afraid of the guns of the castle and of the palace and they are sick of warfare, especially fighting inside the town gate. More than anything else, they are sick of the Red Douglases. Finally, at midday, after dozens of false alarms, we hear the rush of feet and skirl of a pipe, as a force in Douglas colours runs down the street towards us, their pikes before them, their faces contorted with rage, as if they think that we might fail for fear.

'Fire!' I say.

The gunners don't wait to be told twice. The archers loose their bowstrings, the handguns crackle and then bang and the cannon roar out. Three or four men lie groaning on the cobbles. My hand is to my mouth, my ears ringing, deafened by the noise, I am blinded by the foul-smelling smoke; but I don't move from behind my guard. 'Fire!' I say again.

The Douglas affinity scatters before the second cannonade and drag their groaning wounded away, their blood smearing the stones. Now there is no-one before us but we hold our positions; the cannon are rolled back, rearmed, the handgunners blow on their glowing fuses. We glance from one to another, we are alive: we are determined, we are filled with a hard rage that anyone should dare to come against us, should threaten our king. We keep guard. I think we will be here till midnight. I don't care if we are here for days. I don't care about the suffering, I don't care about death. I am gripped with fury. If Archibald were here I would kill him myself.

The smoke starts to clear. My ears are still ringing when high above me, halfway up the steep hill, I see a man on a black horse. It is Ard. I would know him through smoke, I would know him through darkness, I would know him through the heat haze of hell itself. He is looking directly at me, and I raise my eyes and look at him.

It is as if time stands still. All I can see is the outline of the mounted figure and all I can imagine are his dark eyes, which once looked at me with such passion, and are looking at me still. He is frozen: only his horse shifts on the cobbles, held tightly by a hard hand. He is looking towards me as if he might speak, as if he might ride downhill and claim me as his own once more.

I don't drop my gaze like a modest woman. I don't blush like a woman in love. With my eyes locked on his, I say loudly, loud enough for him to hear:

'Gunners, take aim. On the horseman.'

They set their sights. They await my command to fire. My husband, my enemy, tips his bonnet to me – I can almost see his smile – and he turns his horse away and goes slowly, quite without fear, up the stony hill of the Via Regis and out of sight.

We wait, certain that Ard is regrouping, or secretly climbing the back walls of the palace to come at us from behind. We wait with our nerves raw with fear, a guard at every doorway, arrows on strings, the gunners softly blowing on glowing fuses so they stay alight. Then, at last, we hear the hour bell of St Giles tolling four o'clock, and then a high sweet bell tolling a single note over and over again, calling for peace.

'What's happening?' I demand of the captain. 'Send someone out.'

Before he can respond I see a horse riding faster than is safe, skidding and cantering on, down the steep slope from the castle. I see a glimpse of Stewart tartan over the rider's shoulder. It is Henry Stewart. Only this mad boy would ride so fast downhill on cobbles. He pulls up before the guns and jumps off his horse.

He bows to me. 'Are you unhurt?'

I nod.

'Beg to report that the Clan Douglas with Archibald Angus at their head have withdrawn from the city and the gates are shut on them,' he says.

'They're gone?'

'For now. Come with me. Let's get you and the king to the castle and safety.'

The captain shouts a message for the stables; someone runs for James. We have all been waiting all day for this moment and the horses are saddled and ready. We go up the hill at a hand gallop. The drawbridge is down, the portcullis up, the gates open, the castle welcoming, and we hammer over the bridge and inside. The gates slam behind us as we hear the creak of the drawbridge going up and the loud scream of iron on iron and the rattle of chains as the portcullis falls.

Henry Stewart turns to me. 'You're safe. God be praised, you're safe.' His voice cracks with emotion, he lifts me down from the saddle and he wraps his arms around me, as if we are lovers, as if it is natural that he should hold me, and I should rest my head on his shoulder. 'God be praised, my love, you are safe.'

He loves me. I think I have known it all along, from the first days when I noticed him among James' companions, head and shoulders above the others. I think I noticed him when I dropped the handkerchief for James and saw him cheer. When he helped James off with his armour he took my handkerchief, with the embroidered rose in the corner, and kept it. Now, more than a year later he shows me that he has it still. He knew from then, from that moment. I knew only that I liked him, that he made me laugh, that I was glad of his care for me, that I felt safe when he was with me. I had not thought of love. I was so shaken by Ard's repeated betrayals that I think I had forgotten that I might love.

I step back from his embrace at once. We have to be careful. I cannot have a word said against me while my application for a divorce is going slowly through one stage after another at Rome, while I am regent to a young king, while my brother is openly promiscuous and my sister-in-law upholds the state of marriage as if it were the only gateway to heaven.

'Don't,' I say quickly.

He releases me at once, springs backwards, his face anxious.

'Forgive me,' he says earnestly. 'It was the relief of seeing you. I have been in hell all day.'

'Forgiven,' I whisper passionately. I think of the long threat in Ard's look, I think of the acrid smoke of cannons that swirled between me and my husband. I think of the sudden passion for life that comes when death has been close, and how hatred and love are both a passion. 'Oh, God, you are forgiven. Come to me tonight.'

## HOLYROODHOUSE PALACE, EDINBURGH, SCOTLAND, SPRING 1525

Nobody can know that Henry Stewart is in love with me. Oh, Davy Lyndsay knows, for he knows everything. My ladies-in-waiting know for they see how he looks at me – he is twenty-eight, he does not know how to hide desire. James Hamilton Earl of Arran, knows, for he saw me gripped in Henry's arms in the castle keep; but nobody who might tell England knows that I have a good man to love me and I am not alone against the world any more.

I revel in his attention, it is like salve on a burn. To be loved by a man like Archibald Douglas is to be scorched, to be rejected is to be scarred. I want to heal and forget that I ever knew him. I want to rest in the adoration of Henry Stewart. I want to sleep beside him in the cool Scots nights and never dream of Archibald again.

With Henry I can be peaceful, which is just as well for I have many enemies and no allies. Archibald withdraws to Tantallon Castle and sends a stream of complaints about me to my brother Harry. He says that he has tried to reconcile with me but I am madly dangerous. He says that Harry's own ambassadors will confirm that I turned the guns on him. Harry and his mouthpiece Cardinal Wolsey urge Archibald to try, and try again. They want the Douglas clan to keep the French out. They say that he must command me, that he may force me to reconcile. Ugly advice, violent words.

They won't listen to me, they won't support me. I hear nothing from them for the whole of the Christmas season and then I get a few pretty gifts and a note from my sister Mary. She speaks of one of the best Christmases ever . . . the clothes and the dancing and the masques and the gifts . . . at the very end she tells me why the court headed by an ageing queen is making so very merry.

> *Mary Carey has a rival in her sister, Anne Boleyn – really! these Boleyn girls! She was my little maid-in-waiting in France, and she is very charming, very witty, very clever. I would never have been so kind to her if I had known what she would do with my lessons. I am sorry to say that she and her sister are turning the whole court wild with an unstoppable round of entertainments. Harry is quite dizzy between the two of them. He is cold to our sister Katherine, who cannot please him whatever she does, and distant to me. The Boleyn girls have been queens of the court this Christmas and they devise all the entertainments and games and Anne Boleyn wins them all. She makes her sister, who was so beloved, seem dull beside her, she makes me seem plain, think how she compares to poor Katherine! She is dazzling. God knows where this will end, but this is no pretty little whore; she is hungry for more.*

Nothing about me. It is as if I never commanded Holyrood and turned the cannon up the Via Regis and defied my own husband, stared him down and defeated him. Nobody knows that I have left him, I am not a deserted wife, I am mistress of my own destiny. I am the very centre of talk for the whole world but for London, where Harry has a new fancy and is making his queen unhappy. That is all that matters to London. It is against this, no doubt, that Archibald struggles to be heard. This is why

I am forgotten. I may be fighting for my son's rights, plotting to keep him safe, desperate for help from England, planning for Scotland, but all that they think about in London is Anne Boleyn's promising dark eyes and Harry's doting smile. Thank God that as I receive this letter I can rest my head on Henry Stewart's shoulder and know that someone loves me. In London they may have all but forgotten me, but now I have someone who loves me for myself.

But there is no escape from Archibald. The English ambassador insists that Clan Douglas be admitted to Edinburgh and the lords who are in English pay must be admitted to the council. In turn they promise to support me as regent, and we all agree that there shall be peace with England and a betrothal between James and his cousin Princess Mary.

'You will bring peace and an alliance with England,' Archdeacon Magnus promises me. 'You will serve both your countries. They will both be grateful to you.'

I am in a terror of being near to Archibald again. I feel as if he can cast a spell on me and I will be helpless before him. I know that I am being foolish, but I feel the helpless horror of a mouse in the yard which will freeze to watch a snake coming closer and closer, knowing that death is coming, incapable of running away.

'I don't really want to walk with Archibald in procession,' I say feebly to Henry Stewart and James Hamilton Earl of Arran. But how can I tell these two men that I am shaking at the thought of Archibald coming near me?

'He should be ashamed even to come near you,' Henry says hotly. 'Why can't we insist he stays away?'

'When was the last time you saw him?' Hamilton asks.

I shake my head to clear the vivid picture of Ard, so tall on his black horse, and the sulphurous smoke all around him. 'I don't know. I can't remember.'

'There has to be a procession,' James Hamilton says. 'You don't have to go handclasped; but you will have to walk in procession. The world has to see that you will work together with the council.'

Henry spits out an oath and goes from the fireside in my privy chamber to stand at the window and look out at the swirling snow. 'How can they ask it of you?' he demands. 'How can your brother ask it of his innocent sister?'

'They do ask it,' James Hamilton says to me, looking worried. 'You have to show that all the lords are united in the council, that the council is as one. The people have to see the council all together. But it's as bad for him: he has to kneel to you and give you an oath of fealty.'

'You should spit in his face!' Henry swears. He turns to me in sudden despair. 'You don't mean to do it? You're not going back to him?'

'No! Never! And he can't kiss me,' I say in sudden panic. 'He can't take my hands.'

'He has to swear fealty,' Hamilton repeats patiently. 'He can't hurt you. We'll all be beside you. He will kneel to you and put his hands together, you will take his hands in yours. Then he will bow and kiss your hand. That's all.'

'All!' Henry explodes. 'Everyone will think that they are husband and wife once more.'

'They won't,' I say, finding my courage at his despair. 'It means his fealty to me. It means I have won. Thirty paces – we have to take little more than thirty paces. Don't think that it means anything, don't think that I don't love you, don't think that I take him as my husband again for I swear that I do not. I never will. But I have to walk beside him, and I have to hold his hand, and we have to be dowager queen and the Earl of Angus, her husband, to lead all the lords into the council.'

'I can't bear it!' He is wild, like an angry child.

'Bear it for me,' I say steadily. 'For I have to bear it for my son James.'

At once his gaze softens. 'For James,' he says.

'I have to do this for him.'

'It's only a public oath of fealty,' James Hamilton reminds us both.

I hold myself still so I don't shiver.

I walk beside my son James dressed in cloth of gold, both of us wearing our crowns as we enter the Tollbooth at Edinburgh. Archibald leads the procession carrying the crown, James Hamilton Earl of Arran, follows him carrying the sceptre, and the Earl of Argyll comes behind him with James' ceremonial sword. Behind the three of them come James and I, walking side by side, with the cloth of estate carried over our heads. It is bitingly cold – we can see our breath in the air as we walk along – and little snowflakes swirl around us. I am paying a high price for peace between England and Scotland, a high price for the safety of my son. At dinner tonight in Holyroodhouse I will have to share a loving cup with my husband and send him the choicest dishes. He will smile and take the best cuts of meat just as he is legally collecting the rents from my lands once again. I will not look across the room at Henry Stewart where he sits, white-faced, among James' household, eating nothing.

It is this evening that the English ambassador Archdeacon Thomas Magnus gives me a letter from Katherine herself.

'She sent it to you? Why not directly to me?'

'She wanted me to give it to you on this day, the day that you and your husband led the council.'

'Oh, did the earl dictate it? Just as he decided the procession?' I ask bitterly.

The archdeacon holds it up to show me. 'Her Grace wrote it,' he says. 'See, here is her seal unbroken. I don't know what she writes to you, nor does anyone else. But she said you should have it when the Earl of Angus joined the council and swore loyalty to your son.'

'She knew it would happen?'

'She prayed for it as God's will on earth.'

I take it from him and he bows and goes from the room so I can read it alone.

*My dear Sister,*

*Harry has told me that he has commanded your husband, the earl, to support you and your son in the council of lords and that he is satisfied that the earl will honour his duty to you and his vows as your husband. I am so glad and so thankful that your troubles are at an end, your husband returned to you, your son accepted as king, and you in power as regent. Your courage has been rewarded, and I thank God for it.*

*Knowing you as I do, I have begged Harry to urge your husband to be generous to you and patient, and he has promised me that you need not return to Archibald and live as man and wife until Whitsuntide so that you have time to become accustomed to him again and perhaps so that you have time to grow in love for him who has been so true – in exile and in England – to you. I have watched him and he has convinced me that he is your true and loving husband. You have no reason not to return to him.*

*I have sworn to Harry on my own honour that the rumours we have heard about you are false. I have pledged my word that you are a good woman and that you would not make your own child a bastard nor make a mockery of your royal name by seeking a divorce, especially from a husband who is seeking your forgiveness.*

*To be a good wife is to forgive. A queen like you, like me, and like our sister Mary, is especially obliged to show the world that there is no end to marriage, no end to our forgiveness.*

*So I have agreed with Harry that you will take Archibald back as your husband at Whitsun, and I hope that you will be happy again. As I hope to be too, some day soon.*

*Your sister the queen,*
*Katherine*

I am not even angry with her for delivering me into the arms of an unfaithful traitor who brought his army against me. I think this is her master stroke.

Archibald is to live at Holyrood with our daughter, my son and I, and we are to show the world that we are a family reconciled. We are to prove to Harry that there can be no divorce, that a husband always returns to his wife, that marriage is truly till death. To the common people, coming in to see us dine seated side by side, overlooking the magnificent hall, we look like a lord and his wife and his son. The cloth of estate extends over James and me, our chairs are set a little higher than Archibald's, but it is he who sends the dishes around the hall and walks around and chats to his friends, and commands the music like a great man at his own table.

The kitchens send out feasts with many dishes, as if they revel in cooking for the lord himself again. The musicians play dance tunes and Archibald teaches everyone the new steps from London, which Anne Boleyn has made fashionable. The players perform the new masques – choosing one of the court and drawing them out to dance and play their part in the drama. Often they select Archibald and he dances at the centre of a swirling circle, his dark eyes smiling at me, a shrug of his shoulders as if to say that he does not seek this praise, it just comes to him. He is the constant centre of attention.

He is pleasant to James – not overwhelming him with attention which would make my cautious twelve-year-old son suspicious, but speaking to him of hair's-breadth escapes, battles, strategies, the wars of Christendom, the plans of the King of England and the constant adjustment and power plays of the courts of Europe. He has not wasted his time in France, nor in England. He knows all that is happening, and he tells James little stories to teach him statecraft, and claps him on the shoulder and praises his understanding. He takes him into the library, spreads out the maps on the great round table and shows him how the Habsburg family have grown great and greater, and that their lands are spreading across the face of Europe. 'This is why we have to have an alliance with England and with France,' he says. 'The Habsburgs are a monster that will gobble us up.'

He is loving and easy with Margaret and she adores him as a father miraculously restored to her. He praises her prettiness and he takes her with him everywhere, buying her ribbons for her hair every time they pass a market. To me he is as charming and as graceful as when he was my carver and could not do enough for me. He throws me a warm smile over James' head as if to praise me for raising such a boy, he laughs when I make a remark, his arm is always ready to escort me into court. When the court dances, the musicians play, the cards are set out, everything is entirely according to my wish. He knows me so well, he guesses what I want before I have time to command it. He asks after the old pain in my hip, he reminds me of our breakneck ride to safety; our history is a love story that he retells from time to time in little reminiscences, always asking me do I remember the time . . . ? Do I recall the night . . . ? Day by day he draws me to him with a gentle weave of shared interests and shared memories.

Often he turns to James and praises my courage and tells my boy that he is lucky to have a mother who is such a heroine. He tells Margaret about the dozens of gowns that my kingly brother sent me as a reward for my bravery. Always, he suggests that he himself was fighting for my cause, for James' safety. It is as if he sings a ballad of the story that we know, but it is set to a strange new tune.

Behind Archibald's cocked attentive head, I see Henry Stewart glowering but powerless. There is nothing I can do to prove to him that I am not soothed and comforted by this new gentle Archibald, for he can see – everyone can see – that I am. I have had so little affection in my life that I am hungry for attention, even from a man who has been my enemy.

I am in love with Henry Stewart, my heart leaps when he comes into court and bows to me, his tawny hair shining in the light of the candles, his hazel gaze direct and honest; but when Archibald stands behind my chair, his hand resting on my shoulder, I know that I am safe: the only man in Scotland who could challenge my power is on my side, my brother's friend and ally stands beside me, the husband that I married for love, who betrayed me so painfully, has come home.

'This is our happy ending,' he bends over me and whispers, and I cannot find the courage to contradict him.

Henry Stewart comes to my privy chamber in the hour before dinner while everyone is getting dressed. My lady comes and tells me that he is waiting and I send them away and go out to him, dressed like a queen in green velvet with silver sleeves. He bows and waits for me to sit, but I go towards him, and I look up into his sulky face and I feel a pulse of such desire that I cannot stop myself putting a hand on his chest and whispering: 'Henry?'

'I have come to ask permission to leave court,' he says stiffly.

'No!'

'You must see that I can hardly live under the same roof as you and your husband.'

'I can't bear for you to go. You can't leave me here with him!'

He clasps my hand to his beautifully embroidered jacket. 'I

don't want to go,' he says. 'You know that I don't. But I cannot live in his house as if I were his man.'

'It's my house! Your loyalty is to me!'

'If he is your husband then everything is his,' he says miserably. 'Me as well. I feel ashamed.'

'You're ashamed of me?'

'No, never. I know you have to share power with him, I know you have to have him here. I understand. It is the agreement with the English, I understand this. But I cannot do it.'

'My love, my darling, you know that my divorce will come and I will be free of him!'

'When?'

I check at his gloomy tone. 'Any day now, any day it might come.'

'Or it might never come. In the meantime I cannot wait for you in your husband's house.'

'Don't go back to Avondale.' I tighten my grip on his jacket. 'If you can't stay here, don't go back there.'

'Where else?'

'Go to Stirling,' I say rapidly. 'It's mine – nobody can deny that – go to Stirling and muster the castle guard. Check the reinforcements and make it a safe refuge for us, if it ever goes wrong here.'

I am making work for him, giving him a task that will make him feel important. 'Please,' I say. 'Though you can't protect me here, you can give me somewhere safe to go, if we ever need it. Who knows what the Douglas clan will do?'

'They will do whatever the English command,' he says drily. 'And you will too.'

'I will for now,' I agree. 'I have to, for now. But you know that I am working for my freedom and for the freedom of my son to be a true king of a free country.'

'But still you keep Douglas and his clan on your side,' he says astutely.

I hesitate before telling him the truth. My feelings are so contradictory I can hardly explain them to myself. 'I am afraid of him,' I admit. 'I know he is ruthless, I don't know how far he will go. And because of that, when he is on my side I know that I am safe.' I give an unhappy laugh. 'I have no enemy outside the castle when he is inside. When he is good to me I know that nothing can hurt me.'

'Don't you see that you must get free of him?' he demands with the impatient clarity of youth. 'You are living with him for fear.'

'My sisters insist,' I say. 'My brother insists. I am doing it for James.'

'You will not become his wife in deed as well as in name?'

He is a young man, he cannot tell when I am lying. 'Never,' I tell him, thinking that Katherine has promised just that, at Whitsun. 'Don't ever think it.'

'You don't love him?'

He does not yet know how a woman can love and fear and hate all at the same time. 'No,' I say carefully. 'It is not love like that.'

He softens, as he bends his head and kisses my clinging hands. 'Very well,' he says. 'I will go to Stirling and wait for you to send for me. You know that I only want to serve you.'

I endure the spring without my young lover, though I miss his sulky presence and jealous looks from the back of the hall. Every day I grow more anxious as Archibald's ambition becomes clearer, as he increases his influence on the council of lords, and his determination to rule Scotland becomes more obvious. His connection with England is so strong, his fortune (my fortune) is so great, his authority as a man dominates them all. He remains tender and attentive and easy with me but I am dreading Easter and then Whitsun when he will return to my bed and I can see no way to refuse him. What makes it worse is that he speaks of it as an agreement that we have both entered freely, as if we wanted to wait for the season of summer to mark our reconciliation, as if we hope for another child like a pair of pretty blackbirds nesting in an apple tree.

Katherine's plan – to give me time to become accustomed to him – has become a courtship leading, inexorably, back to our marriage.

He's too clever to say any of this openly, but he orders new hangings for my bed and new linen, and tells the sempstress that it must be ready for Whitsun. He speaks confidently of the summer and says that we will go to Linlithgow, and farther north, that we must take James around his country on a royal tour, as his father used to do. He says that he will teach Margaret to ride astride, like a boy, so that she can enjoy hunting and riding out. There is never any doubt in his voice that we will be together, man and wife, this summer and every summer thereafter.

Confidently, he applies to Cardinal Wolsey for the full use of my lands: all my rents and all my fees and all the produce will go to him as my acknowledged husband. I can get no news of the woman that he once called his wife, Janet Stewart of Traquair. I don't know if she is living at Tantallon Castle in state as its lady or in one of my properties and no-one dares to tell me. I don't even know if she is discarded and he has abandoned her and she is somewhere, perhaps Traquair House, on a knife edge of hope that he might come back to her and fear that he will. He never mentions her, and a terrible awkwardness stops my tongue too. I have lost the courage to challenge him.

By singing the song of our happiness, of our marriage against the odds, of our struggle to be together, he has painted a new picture. I can see how he must have done this so well in London, as he does it here too, in Edinburgh. He convinces my son, almost he convinces me that he and I were deeply in love, separated by accident, true through so many difficulties, and are now restored to each other. I cannot cling on to my own sense of myself. I start to think that he is right, that he loves me, that he is my only safety. His view of the world, his opinion of me, his account of our lives together, slowly overwhelms me.

One day, he even dares to say: 'The smoke of the cannons cleared and I saw you behind the guns, and I thought then – my God, that is the only woman I have ever wanted. It's always been a great passion with us, Margaret, hatred and love all at once.'

'I gave them the order to prepare to fire. I knew it was you,' I tell him.

He smiles, his confidence is quite unshaken. 'I know you did, and you saw me look at you, and you knew what I was thinking.'

I remember his silhouette on his horse, as he stood at the height of the Via Regis as if he were daring me to fire on him again.

'No, I didn't know what you were thinking,' I say stubbornly. 'All I wanted was for you to go away.'

'Oh, I'll never do that.'

He represents my brother, the great king, he has the God-given certainty of my sister-in-law, the Queen of England, he is endorsed by the power of man and of God. He has me in his thrall. I am not in love – God save me from such grief – but he dominates the court and he masters James and he lords it over me and I feel as if there is nothing that I can say or do to claim my freedom. He tells me what I think as if my own mind is subject to him. I can only wait for news from Rome that my divorce has been approved, and only then will I be able to say to him that I am free and that he is a lord of the council and nothing more to me. On that day I will be able to tell him that he is not my husband, he is not stepfather to the king. He is father to my daughter but he does not command me. He may be an ally of the King of England but he is no longer his kinsman. Every night I kneel before my crucifix and pray that the Holy Father's clerks will write at once and free me from this strange half-life where I live with a husband that I dare not defy, and long for a man that I may not even see.

It is unbearable. I have to get away this summer. I cannot ride with Archibald every day and watch him dance every night. I cannot kneel beside him in the chapel and take the Mass beside him, as if we were sharing a loving cup. I know that soon, sometime after Easter, he will come to my bedroom and my ladies will open the door and let him in, curtsey, and leave us alone together. I am so ruled by him and dominated by him and overpowered by him that I know I will not resist. Legally, I know that I cannot resist. Increasingly, I fear that I will have forgotten how to resist: I will not resist.

I must break the engagement that my brother has made for me, break the spell that Katherine has woven. The two of them decided, for their own private reasons, that Archibald and I should honour our marriage vows and reconcile. My marriage with Archibald allows Harry's passion for Mary Boleyn, for I demonstrate that no betrayal can destroy a marriage. I am to prove this. The two of them – Katherine and Harry – have worked upon the two of us to come to agreement. Harry pays for James' guard, buys the council of the lords, supports Archibald, on the condition that Archibald represents the interests of England and is true to his marriage to me, the English princess. Harry writes to me, Katherine writes to me, even my sister Mary writes to me, and they all say that my future and the future of my country and of my boy rest in the hands of my good husband. He will be true to me, I must take him back. We will be happy.

Secretly, disguising my hand and sending the letter by the back ways to the port and from there on a French merchant ship to France, I write to the absent Duke of Albany. I say that I will do anything – anything – to obtain my divorce from the Pope. I say that I know he can prevail upon the Vatican for me. I say that I will deliver the council of lords into his keeping, that I will hand over Scotland to the French, if he will only free me of Archibald and this terrible dreamy half-life that is drowning me, even as I write for help.

## SCONE PALACE, PERTH, SCOTLAND, SPRING 1525

Scone Palace is an abbot's palace set alongside the abbey buildings beside the church of Scone. It is the famous coronation place of all Scots kings, and I have loved the grey stone abbey, the palace, the little church set high on the hill above Perth, ever since I first came here with my husband James, the king. The landscape is wild here; the mountains rise up high, their lower slopes dark with forest so thick and so deep that nobody lives there and the narrow tracks are followed only by deer and wild boar. The tops of the mountains are white with snow at this time of year, though the lenten lilies are bobbing their heads along the riverbank. It is too cold to walk by the tumbling river, white with winter spate, or in the walled gardens around the monastery, where the first green buds of vegetables are showing in the dark earth beds.

Archibald does not come with us, on this unseasonal visit north, but stays at Edinburgh in council with the lords, and James and I are suddenly free. Only now that we are away from him, do I realise how he holds me in silence, how I watch him. It is as if my son and I go on tiptoes around him, as if he were a sleeping snake that might strike us. Only Margaret misses him – he is so charming and affectionate with her and she does not secretly fear him.

We go out hunting or riding every day and my master of horse leads us up through the woods and into the high bare moorland country where the wind is sharp and cold and strong. My son the king loves these highlands, which are such a large part of his kingdom. He rides out all day with just a handful of companions. They go to a tiny monastery for their breakfast, they hammer on the door of a remote farmhouse for their dinner. People are delighted to find their king among them, and James thrives on the freedom after years of being all but a prisoner in his own castles. He resembles his father: he likes to surprise his people, ride among them like a commoner, talk to them like an equal. I tell him that his father used to go by the name of the Gudeman of Ballengeich, a village near Stirling, and pretended to be a common man so that he could dance with girls and give money to beggars, and James laughs and says he will be a Gudeman too, and go by the name of 'Gudemanson'.

Henry Stewart joins us, riding at James' side, a perfect companion to a young king, speaking of chivalry and nobility and the old stories of Scotland. All day he is James' companion and friend and at night he comes quietly to my room and takes me in his arms.

'You are my love, my love,' he whispers in my ear, and I say, 'hush,' and we make love in whispers and he steals away before dawn so that when I rise for Prime, it is as if I have had a dream of a young lover, and I can hardly believe that we were together at all.

We are so happy in the north, and so remote from the troubles of Edinburgh, that I am surprised when Archdeacon Thomas Magnus is announced at dinner, newly returned from a visit to England. We dine early here, and we go to bed when the wax candles start to gutter in their candlesticks. The sky up here is as dark as black velvet, with little silver pinpricks of stars. There are no lights showing from Perth, there are no torches from the little hamlet of Scone. There is nothing but the gleam of mysterious light – not dawn and yet not starlight – where the unlit earth meets the night-black sky, and the only sound is the haunting call of the owls.

'I did not expect to see you back in Scotland so soon, archdeacon,' I say. 'You are very welcome.'

He is not particularly welcome. I know that he has been in London and will be carrying messages from England. I don't doubt that he has stopped at Edinburgh and shared all the news with Archibald, and received his instructions there. 'Is my brother the king in good health? And Her Grace the queen?'

He bows. He says quietly that he has letters for me and very grave news from London.

'My brother is well?' I ask anxiously. 'And Her Grace the queen?'

'God be praised,' he says piously. 'They are both well. But there has been a terrible battle. I regret to have to tell you that your former ally, the kingdom of France, has been defeated. The King of France himself has been captured.'

'What?' I ask blankly.

I can see – no-one could miss – his little gleam of pleasure at my shock, his knowledge that this leaves me without an ally against my brother and his man.

'King Francis has been captured and is being held by the emperor,' he says coolly. 'Your friend the Duke of Albany, commanding his troop for his master, has been completely defeated. Your brother's enemy, Richard de la Pole, the pretender to his throne, has been killed.'

'He was my enemy too,' I say stoutly. 'Our kinsman and our enemy, both. Thank God he will trouble us no more.'

'Amen to that,' says the archdeacon as if he would prefer to be the one invoking God. 'And so, you will see – a princess of your wit will quickly see – that you have no powerful friends any more but the English, that the French are destroyed and will remain destroyed for a generation, their king is in captivity, his rule broken. He was your ally but now he is a prisoner of the Habsburg Empire. Your brother's kingdom is safe from attack from the French, your own friend the Duke of Albany is humiliated and defeated.'

'I am glad of anything that makes England safe,' I reply at random, hardly knowing what I am saying. If the French are defeated and the duke humbled, then he cannot speak for me at the Vatican; he can be no help to me in Scotland. The archdeacon is right: I have lost a friend and an ally. I will be dependent on Harry and in Archibald's power forever.

'This is a shock for you,' the archdeacon says, with unconvincing sympathy. 'It is the end of France as a force. All of the Scots lords in the pay of France will find their wages stopped.' He pauses; he knows that the French send money to me. He knows that I am dependent upon them for a pension and for their guards, that half the lords are paid for their support.

'I rejoice for my brother,' I say numbly. 'I am so glad for England.'

'And for your sister the Spanish Infanta who now sees her nephew rule all of Europe,' the archdeacon prompts.

'Her too,' I say through my teeth.

'They have written to you.' He offers me the package, heavy with royal seals.

I nod to one of my ladies: 'Tell the musicians to play out here, I will go to the privy chamber to read the news from London.'

'Good news, I hope,' she says.

I nod with a confidence that I don't feel, and I let the guards close the door behind me before I go to the abbot's great chair, set on a dais overlooking the silent empty room, and sit and cut the seal.

I have never read such a letter in my life. I have known Harry to be intemperate, but never anything like this. I have known him to be angry but this is worse than anything. He writes like a man who cannot be crossed, he writes like a man who would kill someone who argued with him. He is wild with rage, his pen spills blots and spatters of ink across the page as if he was spitting with fury. He is mad with rage, quite mad with rage. He says that he knows that I was hand in glove with Albany but I should know that Albany is a broken man, utterly defeated. He says that he has captured my letter that shows that while I was pretending to be publicly reconciled with Archibald I was all along pleading for Albany to hurry my divorce through the Vatican. He says that he read with horror that I said I will do 'anything, anything' to be free. He says that he understands very well what I mean – that I was offering myself to Albany to shame myself and my family. He knows that I have been bought by the French, that I was pleading with the French duke to use his influence to set me free. He says I am false, through and through, and that he should never have listened to his wife who swore that I was a good woman and could be trusted. He says that she has no judgement, for she said that I would be reconciled with my husband. He says I have proved her to be a liar and a poor advisor, and that he will never waste his time in listening to her again, and this is my fault. He says that I am a liar and she is a fool.

He says that Katherine's nephew is the victor of Europe and that the kingdom of France is ended as swiftly as it began. He says that Princess Mary will never marry my son James, but is to be betrothed at once to the emperor and she will be the greatest empress the world has ever known. He says that when he is ready he will personally lead an army to conquer Scotland and James will be under the throne of England, as Scotland has always been. He says that I need not think that James will inherit the throne of England, for Harry has a son, a hearty strong son, a Tudor through and through, who will be made legitimate and will take the throne as Henry IX, and I need not think that James will ever see the inside of Westminster Abbey. Indeed, I need not think that he will ever see London, except perhaps to pay tribute, and nor will I ever see London again. Harry says that he warned me of this, that Katherine – the stupid woman – warned me of this. Infidelity to my husband will be met with disgrace, disloyalty to England will be met with destruction. I was warned of doom, and now I am lost.

I hold the letter before me and then I realise there is a repeated rustling sound. It is my hands trembling as I hold the letter. I drop the scrawled papers to the floor and I realise that I am shaking all over, as if I have an ague, as if I were some madwoman in a village about to fall down in a fit. I find I cannot breathe and I am so cold, as if I am shivering in an icy wind. I try to stand, but I find that my legs won't support me. I sink back onto the abbot's throne and call for help but I have no breath, I have no voice. Now there is a rattling sound of my rings clattering against the gold-inlaid wood of the throne. I clench my hands over the arms of the chair to keep them still; but my knuckles go white and still I am trembling. I think that I will have to endure this fit, this descent into madness, as I have endured other terrible shocks, other terrible losses. My brother has turned against me, my friend has been defeated, the French are destroyed, and the world is too much for me. My husband has won. I am lost.

It is growing dark before I am able to open the letter from Katherine. She writes very briefly. She sounds as if she is filled with sorrow, but I know this is Katherine triumphant.

*My husband and I are agreed that if you are determined on divorce then you are unfit to be the guardian of your son or a queen. You will have to go into exile in the keeping of your new lover – we have heard that you favour Henry Stewart. Margaret, if you deny your marriage vows, you are a nobody bound for eternal damnation, and no sister to me nor to my husband.*

*Katherine*

*Nothing can end a true marriage. You will see what I have to accept as God's will and the king's wish. But it does not end my marriage. Nothing does that. Nothing will ever do that. K.*

I have to talk with James. He is a boy of only twelve years old but he is king. He has to know that I have made such a terrible error putting him in alliance with France whose power is defeated, his betrothal has been cancelled, and I am publicly shamed. I go to his bedroom as he is saying his prayers with Davy Lyndsay, who looks curiously at my white strained face, and I know myself to be a failure as a mother, a guardian and a queen.

James kneels for my blessing and I curtsey and kiss him. Then he jumps into bed and looks at me as brightly as if he were still a little boy and I had come to tell him a bedtime story. Davy Lyndsay bows and turns as if to go, but I say:

'You can stay. This will be all over the court tomorrow. You might as well hear it from me.'

James exchanges a surprised glance with Davy and the older man steps back quietly and stands with his back to the door, as if on guard. I turn to my son. 'You will have heard of the news from Pavia? Of the decisive defeat of the French?'

James nods. 'Archdeacon Magnus told me, but I was not sure what it means to us.'

'He won't have failed to tell you that it means our ally France is weakened for years, almost destroyed. They don't even have a king any more. He has been captured and will not be returned.'

'The French will ransom him,' James asserts. 'They will buy him back.'

'If they can. But the emperor will get all he can in the way of land and cities and fees before he restores the King of France to his kingdom. He will rewrite the borders of Europe. We have lost an ally, we are without a friend. We have no choice but to make a full peace with England. If they ever choose to make war on us, we have no defender.'

James nods. 'My uncle the king was seeking peace with us anyway.'

'He was. He was seeking peace with a little country in alliance with a very great and dangerous power. But now he has nothing to fear from us.' I hesitate. 'And he is very, very angry with me.'

My boy looks up at me with his clear gaze. 'Why?'

'I have been trying to obtain an annulment of my marriage to Archibald, the Earl of Angus,' I say very quietly.

'I thought that you were reconciled,' my son says.

'Not fully. In my heart I was not.'

Even I can hear how duplicitous I sound. I glance towards Davy Lyndsay whose face is completely impassive, his eyes on his charge. 'I had written to the Duke of Albany to ask him to use his influence to speed my divorce through the Vatican,' I say. 'I hoped it would come before Whitsun. Then I would have told the earl.'

'But the duke is defeated and France has lost its king,' my son observes.

'It's worse than that. My brother the King of England has seized my letters to the duke and now he knows that I was trying to divorce my husband, and so I was breaking my agreement with England, and playing them false.' I take a shuddering breath. 'He is very angry with me. I have lost his friendship.'

James' young face is very grave. 'If the lords of the council turn against you, we are alone, Lady Mother. If you are not the wife of the Earl of Angus, nor the regent chosen by the French, nor the favoured sister of the King of England, then you have no influence.'

I nod.

'And the Earl of Angus will be offended that you were trying to divorce him behind his back while living with him as his wife.'

It sounds so much worse when it is spoken in the clear treble voice of my son.

'I know.'

'And you have played him false? You pretended that you were reconciled with him but all the while you were writing to the Vatican for your divorce?'

'Yes.'

'And were you unfaithful?' he asks coldly.

'I wanted to be free,' I mutter miserably. 'I wanted to be free of Archibald.'

'You took a lover?'

I bow my head before my son's righteous anger. 'I wanted to be free.'

'But I am not free,' my son points out. 'I am in his keeping and in the keeping of the lords of the council. If you have lost your power then my case is worse than ever. You will be in disgrace and they will have me as their prisoner. He will have me as his stepson.'

'I am so sorry . . .'

He turns a sulky face to me. 'You have done very wrong,' he says. 'You have ruined us.'

## STIRLING CASTLE, SCOTLAND, SUMMER 1525

I lose all influence over the council of the lords; Archibald will not even see me. I go to Stirling Castle and live like a widow, alone. I keep a small court, but I have hardly the money to pay them. I receive nothing from France and get only a small part of my rents and my fees from my lands – a pitiful allowance paid by Archibald from his charity. He is a wronged husband; he would be within his rights to let me starve and nobody would blame him. Henry Stewart greets me with joy, but soon learns that I am in disgrace and that we will never be married. I publicly protest that my case is still before the papal court and that my rents should be paid to me and not to Archibald, that my son should be in my keeping until we have their decision. The council of lords reply that until the marriage is ended I should live with my husband, and that I must come to Edinburgh to answer before them all. They hate me for being a woman trying to win my freedom. They know that I would have sold them all, lock, stock and barrel, to get my freedom from Archibald. They hate me for betraying them. They feel betrayed as James does – they know that I was trying to get away and leave them in Archibald's power.

I don't go to Edinburgh. Not even to see James will I return to Archibald, and in my absence they declare that I have forfeited all my authority. They say that my son shall be kept by a council of nobles, a rotating set of guardians, and Archibald takes first place. Takes it and keeps it. James is in Archibald's power and will never return to me. I don't even know if James wants to see me. He feels I have betrayed him and he will not forgive me.

Archibald takes Margaret, too. There is no protest I can

make. She is his daughter and he has evidence from the King of England that her mother is shamed. She is glad to go: she is her father's little pet, his favourite. I think I should try to persuade her to stay with me but I cannot bring myself to beg her, and I have no power to command.

I write to my brother the king to appeal to him in the name of his nephew, even if he is still angry with me. I write to Katherine and say that as a mother she must understand that I cannot bear James to be held by my enemy. Neither of them replies, but I get a letter from my sister Mary that reminds me that my troubles and sorrows mean little in London; they are all convulsed with gossip.

*Our brother has ennobled his bastard son Henry Fitzroy. The little boy is made a duke – Duke of Richmond and Duke of Somerset – and so is the greatest duke in the kingdom. He has far greater lands and fees than my husband Charles. Charles says that Harry will name Fitzroy as his heir, to inherit the throne of England.*

I can see her writing change as she realises that she is speaking to the mother of the legitimate heir.

*I am sure you will be very troubled by this, but it is only what Charles says. It may be that your boy will inherit the throne in the end. It's just that, with everyone speaking so badly of you, Harry cannot name your son as an heir. People even ask if we can be sure of James' fathering. If you are an adulteress now, might you have been so before? This is so very terrible to hear – I am sorry to repeat it. I wish you would reconcile with the Earl of Angus. Everyone thinks so highly of him. Can you not withdraw your application to the Pope? It's never going to succeed now.*

*Of course the queen is very saddened by the honouring of Henry Fitzroy, and now Mary Carey is with child again and everyone knows that it is the king's baby. Her sister Anne Boleyn is at court too and the king is every day with either one or the other of them as they vie for his attention, and Katherine feels this very much. She is living among her rivals and now she sees a bastard boy is housed in as great a palace as that given to the true princess, her daughter. Princess Mary is to go to Ludlow Castle but she is not made Princess of Wales. I cannot see why not, but Charles says that the English would never accept a woman on the throne. So nobody knows what will happen, the queen least of all.*

*It is not a happy court any more. The two Boleyn girls are quite frantic in their desire to please and entertain Harry – they sport and dance and play music and compose, they hunt and boat and flirt, but the queen seems very tired. And I am tired of it too. I am tired of all of it.*

That's all. She has no new advice for me but to return to Archibald, it is all any of them ever say. I don't think she has any thought of me. She cannot imagine my life, short of money, lonely for company, unable to see my son, deserted by my daughter, unable to enter my capital city, a queen in name but stripped of power, wealth and reputation. For Mary the world is fixed in London and the battle between two pretty Boleyn girls, a great question mark hanging over the throne of England like a sparkling cloth of estate. There is so much more to trouble me, but neither she nor my sister-in-law Katherine ever thinks of me.

## HOLYROODHOUSE PALACE, EDINBURGH, SCOTLAND, SPRING 1526

At last I am able to return to Edinburgh and see my son. For more than a year he has been in Archibald's keeping and I have been able to do nothing but write to him and send him little gifts, and beg him to remember that his mother loves him and would be with him if she could. I can't forget the coldness in his voice, the irritation in his face. He blames me for our defeat – and he is right. I blame myself.

Amazingly, it is Harry, my brother, who makes my return to court possible. Harry orders Archibald to give me my rents and my fees and not keep them for himself. Harry says that I must be allowed to see my son. Harry tells Archibald that I should have a divorce if it can indeed be proved that the marriage was invalid from the very beginning. Harry has changed his mind completely: he is turn and turn about. He has forgiven me, he wants me to be happy.

I am amazed. I cannot understand this change of heart that has brought me such opportunity. I am so encouraged and so hopeful that I write to him and to Katherine and thank them for their kindness to me, and promise them my gratitude, and my loyalty to the country of my birth. For some reason, the royal favour has returned to me, and I am restored to the family. I don't know why I am suddenly beloved again, but I am as grateful as a beaten puppy that squirms to lick the hand that held the whip. Harry has all the power, and, suddenly, he bestows his blessing on me.

It is Mary who explains:

*You will have heard that the Boleyn girl Mary Carey has given birth to a boy. The king our brother is pleased, as any man is pleased, to have a healthy son to show to the world. His second healthy bastard boy. They are calling him Henry but he will take the husband's surname of Carey. This spares the queen the humiliation of another bastard named Fitzroy, but that is all that she is spared. Everyone knows that the boy is of the king's fathering and so everyone knows that it must be the queen's fault that they only have one child, and that one a frail girl. Katherine is fasting more than ever, she hardly ever eats at dinner, and her hair shirt has scraped her skin raw on her shoulders and her hips. I really think that she will mortify her flesh to death and then Harry will be free. You would be heartbroken to see her, you who love her so well. I, her other sister, can do nothing but watch as she tortures herself. It is unbearable.*

*The Boleyn girl Mary seems to have lost the attention of our brother who is now publicly at the feet of her sister Anne Boleyn. She queens it around the court as if she were royal-born. You would not believe how this girl from next to nowhere behaves at a royal court, at our court. Not even you and I, as princesses of the blood, were ever allowed these freedoms. She takes precedence wherever she can and also where she should not, and Harry leads her in to dinner and out to dance as if she were queen. It is quite extraordinary, she walks before duchesses as if she had a right. Katherine smiles with almost saintly dignity but anyone can see that she is near to despair. I am called upon to admire and accompany the Boleyn girl and I often say that I am unwell or too tired or that I have to go home. I pretend to be sick so that I do not appear to be in her service. Truly, this is how she makes it appear. She decides to do something, and she looks at Harry, and the next moment we are all running to her bidding. It is like a terrible masque of a court, like players trying to enact royalty. There is no grace or laughter or beauty here at all any more, there is just posturing and bitter laughter, the terrible cynicism of the young and the queen's loneliness.*

*What makes it worse is that I still don't think that she is his lover. She acts the part of a frantic tormentor who will not leave him alone and yet will not submit to him. She's always touching him and touching her lips, caressing him and putting her hands on her own narrow waist, but she does not let him touch her. She seems to love him to damnation but she will not sin. And if she will not be his mistress – what is going to happen? Charles says that if Harry would just swive her it would all be over in a sennight, but Charles always does say things like that, and Mademoiselle Boleyn is not a girl to be simply taken for love.*

*You remember when we were children and Sir Thomas More brought Erasmus to visit and Harry couldn't think of anything else until he had composed a poem, and read it aloud to the great philosopher? He's like that now. He wants her to see him as exceptional. Or when he first saw our sister Katherine? He's like that again. He can't seem to be himself unless she is admiring him. He has ordered new jackets, he is writing poetry, he is striving for eminence like a boy in the grip of calf love. Katherine is fasting and praying for his soul. So am I.*

So now I know why Harry is so tolerant of me. Now I know why Katherine's rules no longer apply to us all. I taste triumph on my tongue, I dance a jig to the song in my head. At last Katherine's power over Harry is waning. He has a boy that she could not give him and he is thinking of that boy as his heir. Now another woman has given him a second boy and it is blindingly obvious that it is Katherine's fault that Harry has no legitimate son and heir to inherit our newly won Tudor crown. For years, Katherine's disappointment and sorrow have been Harry's disappointment and sorrow, her refusal to question the ways of God has been a model for him, her cleaving to the laws of unending marriage has been her only answer to their disappointment. But it is not his way any longer. Now he can see for himself that God does not intend him to die without a son and heir. Now he has a second boy in the cradle – as if God is saying to the world: Harry can get a boy, Harry shall have sons – it was Katherine all along who could not bear and birth one. This is not a sorrow from God mortifying the golden couple who seemed to have everything, this is a sorrow from God on Katherine, on her alone. Their marriage is not the spar that they must cling to in the wreckage of their hopes, it is their marriage itself that is the wreckage, Katherine's wreckage. Without her, Harry can make a son.

So I doubt very much that Katherine will command me again to return to my husband, and I doubt that my brother will insist on marriage until death. Now I understand why he has told Archibald that if there is good evidence for a divorce, then even a royal Tudor divorce may go ahead. Now I know that Harry, nominated Defender of the Faith, who swore that marriage must continue until death, does not think like this any more.

And Katherine, the sister who threatened me that I would be no sister to her, may find instead that she is no wife. And I would have to be an angel in heaven not to think that her hard-heartedness to me is justly repaid.

I am to see my son in his privy chamber, with no-one present but my former husband, Archibald, and James' trusted guardian Davy Lyndsay. I am to have no companions; I am to come alone. There is no point objecting to the presence of Archibald since he has power as great as a king himself; he rules the council, he guards James. Everything is in his gift.

I dress carefully for this meeting in a gown of Tudor green with lighter green sleeves and a necklace of emeralds, and emeralds on my hood. I wonder if James will find me much changed. I am thirty-six years old, no longer a young woman, and I am finding a few silver hairs at my temples. I pluck them out and wonder if Mary has silver among the gold yet? Sometimes I think I look as if I have had a hard life, a life of continual struggle, and then at other times I catch a glimpse of myself in a looking glass laughing and I think that I am still a beautiful woman, and if I could only marry the man that I love and see my son on the throne of Scotland then I could be a happy woman and a good wife.

The double doors of the privy chamber – once my privy

chamber – swing open, and I go in. As Archibald promised, the room is empty but for him, Davy, and my son, who is seated on the throne, his legs just reaching the floor. I forget the speech that I have prepared and I run towards him. 'James! Oh, James!' I say. Abruptly, I stop and drop into a curtsey, but he is already off the throne and tumbling down the steps and into my arms.

He is my love, he is my boy, he is different and yet completely unchanged. I hold him tightly to me and feel his warm head under my chin; he has grown since I last saw him. He has filled out too, and his arms around my waist are strong. He says, 'Lady Mother', and I hear the adorable croak of a boy whose voice is breaking. He will lose his childish treble and I will never hear it again. The thought of that makes me sob and he looks up into my face and his honest hazel eyes gaze straight at me, and I know that I have him back, just as he was. He has forgiven me, he has missed me. I am so sorry to have failed him, but I am so flooded with delight to be holding him again. He is smiling and I brush the tears from my eyes and smile back at him.

'Lady Mother . . .' is all he can say.

'I am happy . . .' I cannot finish the sentence, I cannot catch my breath. 'I am so happy, so happy.'

My delight in seeing James makes me grateful to Archibald for allowing me back to Edinburgh. Margaret is my daughter once more, she comes to my rooms every day, I supervise her education and she lives under my guidance. Archibald has complete power over the council of lords; no-one dares to oppose him. If he had wanted to ban me from the city he could have done so, and no-one would have defended me. He is generous to me – I cannot deny it. He is serving Harry, he is following the wishes of England: really, he has no choice, but still he is being kind to me.

'You cannot really have been frightened of me?' he asks in his low caressing tone. 'When I think of the queen that you were when we first met, you were frightened of nothing, and I was so lowly a server in your household, you didn't even see me. And when you faced me behind the cannon and I saw you smile through the smoke! I didn't believe it for a moment when they said that you were frightened of me. You cannot be frightened of me, Margaret.'

'I am not,' I say, instantly defiant.

'Of course not. You have been in my life like a moon on my horizon – not like an ordinary woman at all.'

'I didn't know you felt like that,' I say cautiously.

'Of course. We have been lovers, we have been husband and wife, we have been parents to a beautiful daughter, we have been either side of a cannon, but we have always been the most important person to the other. Isn't it true? Who do you think of most of the day? Who do you think of every day? Who do you think that I think of, all the time? All the time!'

'It's not the same as loving someone,' I protest. 'I won't hear any words of love. I know that you have another woman; you know that I love Henry Stewart. I will marry him if the Pope grants my divorce.'

He gives a little laugh and makes a gesture with his hand as if to say that Henry Stewart means nothing to him. 'No, God no, it's not the same as loving, it's more,' he says. 'Much more. Love comes and goes; if it lasts the length of a ballad or a story it is long enough. Everyone knows that now, the Queen of England, God bless her, among them. Love has ended for her. But belonging goes on. You are more than one of the loves of my life. I am more than a favourite. You will always be the first star at twilight for me.'

'You speak of a moon and you speak of stars,' I say a little breathlessly. 'Are you setting up as a poet?'

He gives me a slow, seductive smile. 'Because it is in the nights that I think of you. It is the nights with you that I miss the most,' he whispers.

Archibald's tenderness to me and his generosity to my son continues, for he persuades the council to declare James as king in the summer, at the age of fourteen. Now, at last, the officers who make up James' household and rule in his name are dismissed. The French guardians are gone, the lords of the council lose their posts, James and I can choose our own household and take command. Exultantly, we start to draw up lists of men that we will choose to serve us, but it does not happen as it should. Instead of letting us appoint our choices, Archibald takes all the work upon himself. He nominates his own people to the royal household and we see that James is still going to be king only in name.

All the letters go out under James' seal, but they are dictated by Archibald and copied by his clerks. All the wealth is audited and kept by Archibald's lord treasurer, guarded by the soldiers of the castle. Once again, Archibald has all the money. The royal guard answer to Archibald's captains and to Archibald himself; they are all of the Douglas clan. To the outside world James is king, but behind the high walls he is nothing more than Archibald's stepson. I am dowager queen, but first and foremost I am Archibald's wife.

I am in no doubt that Archibald means this to continue forever: James will never be allowed to take his power, I will never name my household officers, I will never be free of Archibald's rule. The Archbishop of St Andrews, James Beaton, who has been such a bitter enemy of mine in the past, is smarting from losing his office as Lord Chancellor, and he manages to meet me in the chapel at Holyroodhouse when I am praying alone, and offers me his support. He says that others will follow any lead that I give. He says that they will help me free James from his overbearing stepfather.

But first, I must get away. Every day that I sit at Archibald's table with James at my side reinforces the belief that we are reconciled. Every time he presents me with the best cut of meat or the first taste of the finest wine it looks as if he is serving his wife with love and honour. Even James glances at me as if to confirm that I am not falling under the spell of the Archibald charm. I think of the moon on the horizon and the first star at twilight and I tell James that I have to go.

He goes pale. 'And leave me here? With him? Again?'

'I have to,' I say. 'I cannot gather supporters while I am under the same roof as Archibald. He watches me day and night. And I cannot write to London for help while he pays the messenger and breaks the seal.'

'When will you come back?' my son asks coolly. I feel my heart twist with pain at the way that he hides his fear behind a clipped tone.

'I hope to come back within months, perhaps even at the head of an army,' I promise him. 'I will not be idle, you can be sure of that. I'll get you away from him, James. I will get you free.'

He looks so unhappy that I say: 'Francis of France got free, and no-one thought that he ever would.'

'You are going to raise an army?' he whispers.

'Yes.'

'You swear on your honour?'

We hold each other very tightly for a moment.

'Come back for me,' he says. 'Lady Mother, come back.'

## STIRLING CASTLE, SCOTLAND, AUTUMN 1526

I make three attempts to kidnap James from Archibald's keeping but my husband is too skilled, and his household is loyal to him and determined to keep James. A raid on his men when he and James are riding in the borders is defeated, a kidnap attempt inside Edinburgh Castle fails. But more and more of the Scots lords come to our side, repelled by Archibald's abuse of his power. Even so it is a bad day for me when Davy Lyndsay walks into my presence chamber and kneels.

'Davy?' I am on my feet in a moment, my hand on my heart. 'You here? James is ill? You've come for me?'

'I am dismissed from his service,' Davy says, very low. 'The Earl of Angus sent me away and I was not allowed to stay though I said I would lie under the same roof as him without pay, without my keep, so that he knew I was there. I said I would sleep in the stables. I said I would lie down with the hounds. But he sent me out. Your son is to have another head of his household. I am not allowed to serve him any longer.'

I am horrified. James has never been parted from Davy before. All through his life of partings and death, he has always had Davy at his side.

'He's alone? My boy?'

'He has companions.' The twist of the old man's mouth shows me that he does not think much of them.

'Who is his tutor?'

'George Douglas.' Davy names Archibald's younger brother, who cares for nothing but the triumph of Clan Douglas.

'My God, what will he teach the boy?'

'Whoring and drinking,' the old man says sourly. 'He knows nothing else.'

'My son?'

'They're spoiling him on purpose. They are taking him to the stews and getting him drunk. They laugh at him when he falls, when a whore takes him. God forgive them for what they are doing to our boy.'

My hands are over my mouth. 'I have to fetch him.'

'You must. Before God, you must.'

'And Davy, what will you do?' I ask him. This is as hard on him as it is on me. He has not been apart from James since he was born.

'If I may, I will join your household, and when you send your troop to rescue the king from the Douglas clan, you will send me too, and I can get back to my boy.'

'You – a poet – want to fight for him?'

'God knows, I would gladly die for him.'

I take both his hands in mine, and he puts his palms together in the old gesture of fealty. 'I can't bear to be without him,' he says simply. 'Let me fetch him.'

'Yes,' I say without hesitation. 'We'll get him out of there. I promise.'

I write to the lords of the council, I write to Archibald himself, I write to Harry. I write to Katherine:

> *At your insistence I have publicly lived with the Earl of Angus as his wife since his return to Scotland and though he is now in Edinburgh and I am in Stirling, we are not estranged, nor have I heard anything from the Vatican about the progress of my divorce. For all I know it will be refused and I will live and die Archibald's wife.*
>
> *But Archibald is in breach of his agreements with you and with me. He is keeping my son, your nephew the king, under close confinement. James is not allowed out without an armed guard of Douglas men, he can only hunt near to the city, and his people are not allowed to see him or petition him. I beg that you speak to my brother the king and ask him to order the Earl of Angus to set James free as he should be. I have done everything that you asked of me; James should not be punished.*

This is not as it seems – a sisterly request for help. This is a test of Katherine's power. I think she is failing. I think her influence is dwindling. If Katherine still has influence with Harry she can use it to set James free, but I believe that she has lost the great power that she used to wield over him. Harry is advised by the cardinal in matters of state, he discusses religion and philosophy with Thomas More, and he is influenced more and more by the other woman in his life. Certainly, Anne Boleyn won't be satisfied, as her sister was, with a title for her father in exchange for a bastard baby. I imagine that Anne is a young woman who will want to share Harry's power as well as his bed. This is no pretty whore, this is a new player for power. She will be uncrowned mistress of the court and the leader of reformist religious thinking. She will bring French ways into London and we will see the king with his old queen on one hand and his lady companion on the other.

My sister, Mary, confirms this. In a long letter that tells me of her health and the progress of her little boy she adds,

> *... the queen is very quiet and distant while the court becomes more and more boisterous. You would think she was ill when you see her thinness and her fever. It is as if her spirit is the only strong thing in her, burning in her eyes. She has taken to rising at night for Matins and Lauds and so of course she is exhausted in the evening, white as a ghost at dinner. I can do nothing to comfort her. Nobody can comfort her.*
>
> *Everyone is saying that the birth of the Carey bastard proves the king is fertile and he could get a son and legitimate heir if our sister were to step aside and he remarry. But how can she do this? God called her to be Queen of England and she believes that she would fail Him if she retired. Having been once married to Arthur, losing him and then winning the throne through Harry by the direct intervention of God, she cannot now abandon it. I cannot think that it is God's will, and Bishop Fisher says that there are no possible grounds for naming the marriage as invalid.*
>
> *It is terribly painful to her, and to me, that you continue with your application for your divorce at the Vatican. Since they have taken so long to reply surely it would be better to withdraw it and announce that you are reconciled with your husband? Then you could make sure that your son is treated well instead of asking us to help? If you do this all your troubles are over at once. Dear Sister, I must tell you that Katherine the queen thinks as I do. We both of us think that*

*you should return to your husband and safeguard your son. We are both certain that would be the right thing to do – we do not see that you can do anything else.*

A party of the lords who support me demands to meet James at Edinburgh Castle and Archibald takes him there in state. Publicly they ask him if he is truly free and my boy answers that no-one, not even his mother, need fear for him, and that he could not live a more pleasant and cheerful life than he does with Archibald – he calls him his good cousin.

'Can this be true?' Henry Stewart is with me, with Archbishop Beaton, and the Earl of Lennox, as one of the friendly lords comes to report. Davy Lyndsay stands in a doorway, listening like a faithful hound missing his master. 'Has Archibald turned the boy's head by giving him nothing but amusement, by allowing him to be corrupted?'

We turn to the messenger. 'The young king spoke without coercion,' the lord says. 'The Earl of Angus was with him all the time, but the boy could have spoken out, he could have taken three steps across the great hall and joined us. He did not do so. He specifically said that his mother need not fear for him.'

'But I do!' I burst out.

Henry puts a gentle hand on my shoulder. 'We all do,' he says.

There is a clatter in the presence chamber and a murmur of sound from the people waiting out there to see me. I notice Henry's hand go to where his sword would be. 'Are you expecting anyone?' he asks.

I shake my head as the guards swing open the door and a young man comes in wearing royal livery. I recognise one of James' grooms. He comes straight to my feet and kneels.

'I come from His Grace the king,' he says.

Davy Lyndsay steps forward. 'I know this lad,' he says. 'Is the king well, Alec?'

'Aye, he is in good health.'

'You may stand,' I say.

He gets to his feet and says: 'I bring a message. He didn't want to write it down. His Grace says that he was forced to speak to the lords as he did, that he is a prisoner of the Earl of Angus and that he begs you to save him. He says that you promised to come for him. He says that you must come.'

I put my hand to my heart as it thuds at the appeal from my son. The youth realises, as he speaks, that he should not address a queen like this, and his colour flames up into his face and he drops to one knee and bows his head. 'I am speaking His Grace's words,' he mutters. 'He taught them to me just like that.'

'I understand.' I touch his bowed head lightly with my hand. 'Are you to go back with an answer?'

'Yes. Nobody saw me leave and no-one knows where I am.'

'You hope,' Lennox says dourly.

The boy shows a swift brave grin. 'I hope,' he agrees.

'Tell him we will come for him,' I say. 'Tell him I will not fail him. Tell him I am putting together an army that will march against the Earl of Angus and that we will free him.'

The boy nods. 'You know that George Douglas, brother to the Earl of Angus, is now master of the king's household?'

'Master?' Davy Lyndsay asks.

There is an aghast silence. 'Then the king is in danger of his life,' the Earl of Lennox says soberly. 'There is no-one around him who loves him. There is no-one around him who would not benefit from his death.'

'Archibald wouldn't kill him,' I protest disbelievingly. 'You can't say that.'

Lennox turns on me. 'Archibald has royal blood, and he has taken all the power of the king. He has the keeping of the king and no-one can free him. What is this but the step before imprisoning the king and then declaring him sick or mad? And that is one little step before declaring him dead, and Archibald as king himself.'

I shrink back and sink into my chair. 'He would not. I know

him. He would never hurt my son. He loves him.' I nearly say: 'And he loves me.'

'Not if we stop him,' Henry Stewart says.

We muster an army, and a number of lords join us with their armed retainers. Some are Archibald's sworn enemies and would join any venture against him, some hope for the profit and opportunity of a battle, but some – a good number – want to see my son freed. We plan to attack Archibald's new ally, my former friend the turncoat, James Hamilton the Earl of Arran, at the village of Linlithgow Bridge, before Archibald can bring up his army from Edinburgh. The Earl of Arran and the Hamilton clan hold the bridge and so Lennox takes his army through the river and through boggy ground to attack their flank. They wheel to meet him and then the Douglas army comes up in a rush from the south. My lords are horrified to see the royal standard at the rear of Archibald's forces. The wicked man, my husband, has brought James to his first battle. He has brought James to watch his mother's men dying in the fight to free him.

Of course, this is not just spite, it is a brilliant tactic. He is using James just as I did when I sent him out, a boy of just three years old, to surrender the keys of Stirling Castle. This child has been hauled about like an icon before the people since he was born, and now Archibald is putting James and the royal standard at the heart of a treasonous army. Half of our men will not raise arms against the royal standard; it is like blasphemy for them. The Earl of Lennox looks around helplessly as his allies hang back, but the men at the front of both armies are bitterly engaged, shouting insults, stabbing with pikes, hacking with axes and swinging great battle swords. It is bloody and dreadful, and James, trapped at the back, can hear the cries of men mad with rage and those screaming as they go down. He thinks he sees a chance to get away and spurs his horse forward to weave through the armies, and it is then that the new master of the king's household, George Douglas, my husband's brother, snatches my boy by the arm, and holds him in a cruel grip in his metalled fist. George yells into my boy's face that he had better stay with them for the Douglas clan will never let him go.

'Bide where you are, sir, for if they get hold of one of your arms, we will pull you in pieces rather than part with you.'

James, terrorised, turns his head away from the man who sits so high on his horse and holds him so hard, but he obeys. He does not dare try to get to the Earl of Lennox any more. The struggle breaks off – it was doomed as soon as they raised the royal standard – and our men fall away and scatter. One leader fails to retreat; we have to leave the Earl of Lennox injured on the field, and when we recover his body it has been stabbed over and over again. Our forces fall back to Stirling Castle and Archibald pursues us, coming behind us on the dirty tracks as we wind through the hills and splash through the fords, and climb up and up the rocky road to the castle where we scuttle inside, raise the bridge, drop the portcullis and set the siege.

Just as James promised me, all those years ago, Stirling Castle is strong. Archibald cannot take the castle until he brings the cannons, but there is nobody to rescue us.

'We have to go,' Henry says to me and to Archbishop Beaton. 'We'll have to surrender the castle, and it will be better if he does not find us here.'

I look at him miserably. 'We surrender?'

'We lost,' he says shortly. 'You'd better go back to Linlithgow and hope that Archibald will come to terms with you. You can't stay here and wait for him to capture you.'

The archbishop does not need telling twice. He is throwing off his good cloak and his thickly padded jacket. 'I'll go out of the sally port,' he says. 'I'll get a crook off one of the shepherds and his jacket too. I won't be taken by the Douglas clan. They'll behead me like they did the chevalier. I don't want my head nailed on the mercat cross.'

I look from the man I love to the man I trust. They are both desperate to get away from my castle, to hide from my husband. They are in terror of the man who is coming for them, coming for me. I realise, once again, that no-one is going to help me. I am going to have to save myself.

I ride cross-country with just a handful of men to guard me. It rains and the torrential water blots out the signs of our passing, and muffles the sound of the horses. Archibald, riding his men hard through the storm towards Stirling Castle, does not know that I pass within a mile of him. I know his army is there, on the road, headed north, but I cannot see him nor hear the splash and clatter of his cavalry. The country is so empty and so wild that there is no-one to tell him of our hard ride over the twenty miles from Stirling to Linlithgow. No-one sees us go by, not even the rain-soaked fishermen, not even the herdboys. When the castle at Stirling lowers the drawbridge and opens the gates in a shameful surrender Archibald learns that, once again, he does not have me, he cannot hold me, I am gone.

## LINLITHGOW PALACE, SCOTLAND, AUTUMN 1526

But he knows that he has won. I don't need a letter from Cardinal Wolsey in London to tell me that open warfare against my husband is a disaster. Nobody can support a militant queen, never if she is arming against her lord and husband. But the cardinal writes very mildly; he is not so violent an advocate of Tudor marriage as he once was:

*Of course, my dear daughter in Christ, it may be that the Holy Father will find that there are grounds for an annulment, and if so, it would be my advice that you should try to agree with your husband about your lands and your daughter. He will want to rule the council of the lords and you would have to assent to his pre-eminence. We are all agreed that he is the best ruler that Scotland could have, and the safest guardian for your son. If you could only agree with the earl, you would have an honoured place at court and be able to see your son and your daughter, even if you were to marry another man in the future.*

This is such a far cry from the usual insistence from London that I must stay married or I will overthrow the Church itself that I hold it and reread it for a little while wondering what the cardinal intends from the smooth words in the clerkly hand. I decide that fathoming the cardinal is probably beyond me; but when Archibald writes pleasantly to me, as urbane and courteous as if his army had not murdered a wounded man, the Earl of Lennox, as if his brother had not laid violent hands on my son, I understand that the English policy has changed, completely changed.

Now we are to separate, but I must not overthrow Archibald. I can be free if I surrender my power. Clearly, someone in England no longer thinks that a royal divorce is anathema. Someone in London thinks that a royal divorce can take place and the husband and wife can come to terms. Someone in London believes that a royal marriage can end and the parties remarry. My guess is that someone is Anne Boleyn.

How shameful it is that the great-granddaughter of a silk merchant should be advising English policy in Scotland! Katherine abused her power and was a tyrant more than a queen, but at least she was born royal. Anne Boleyn is a commoner, her father was proud to serve me in my household, her grandparents were born lower even than those of Charles Brandon, Mary's husband. But, thanks to Harry's love for the vulgar and showy, Charles is married to my sister and Anne is advising the King of England. No wonder that my troubles with Archibald shrink by comparison. No wonder it matters less to them that I am in love with Henry Stewart – a Scots lord with royal blood. What could they say against him? What can they say against me, when the King of England chooses his friends and his whore from the dross of his country and passes them off as gold?

Archibald invites me to visit my son in Edinburgh. He says I will be an honoured guest at Holyroodhouse and I will be able to see James without witnesses, as often and for as long as I like. He says that our daughter, Margaret, is well and happy at Tantallon Castle, and will come to Edinburgh to see me, her mother. With cool courtesy, he offers me the palatial rooms that once housed the Duke of Albany: the regent's rooms. I understand from this that there is no question of us sharing a bed, and the Whitsun sheets will stay in the linen store. I understand from this that he too has heard from London that divorce is now permissible and he is to treat me with fairness and respect. I understand from this that though I lost the battle against Archibald, I may still come to terms with him. Smiling, I reply that I will be happy to see my son James, my daughter, and my dear cousin Archibald once again.

## HOLYROODHOUSE PALACE, EDINBURGH, SCOTLAND, AUTUMN 1526

The citizens of Edinburgh line the streets and cheer me as I enter the city and proceed, more like a victor than a defeated estranged wife, to Holyrood. Retainers and servants, Stewart and Douglas, bow and doff their hats to me as I dismount, and Archibald greets me as courteously as if we have never been anything but queen and head of the council. He escorts me to James' private rooms and he leaves me at the door.

'Whatever he says,' he nods at the closed door behind the grim-faced Douglas men who guard it, 'whatever he says, I would not hurt him. I have loved him like my own son. You know that.'

'Yes, I do know that,' I say grudgingly. 'But what complaint can he make of you?'

He gives me his rueful smile. 'I keep him from the throne,' he admits. 'He cannot take power. I have to rule the lords until I am certain that I and my house are safe and the kingdom in alliance with England. You know that.'

I nod. I do know that.

They swing the doors open and I go in to my son.

He jumps up from the floor where he was playing with dice, right hand against left, and he strides across the room to me. He has grown to become a young man, I see it at once. Only last year he would have bounced over the floor like a fawn. Now he comes quickly, but his shoulders are set like a man's, and he plants his feet, he does not skip. He has presence – he never had it before.

'Every time we meet, you are changed,' I mourn, scanning his face and seeing the shadow of a moustache, and the beginning of a straggly beard on his cheeks. 'A beard! You are never growing a beard?'

'You are always the same,' he says gallantly. 'Always beautiful.'

'It's been terrible,' I say bluntly. 'I tried and tried to get you away.'

'I know. I tried to come to you.' He drops his voice. 'They laid hands on me,' he says. 'They said they would tear me limb from limb. You told me never to let them touch me, but they would have dismembered me. I had no authority. They had no respect and I could not make them.'

Miserably, we look at each other. 'I've failed you,' I say. 'God forgive me, and I hope you will forgive me.'

'No,' he says quickly. He has thought about this. 'You have always tried to do the best for me, hold the power, get me to the throne. Those who have failed me are your brother the king, your husband my guardian, and the lords who have let themselves be led like sheep following a wolf. You are not at fault for these men and these fools.'

'I have no money and no army and no support from England,' I say bluntly. 'I have no plan.'

'I know,' he says, and suddenly his father's joyful smile lights up his face. 'So I thought we would just be happy together. Even if we are imprisoned. I thought that we might be happy this winter and spend Christmas the three of us, and know that every year that I grow older, every month that my beard grows in, the end of the rule of the Red Douglas comes closer. Archibald cannot hold me as his prisoner when I am a full-grown man. We will win in the end just by surviving.'

I take his hands and I kiss his cheeks where the scattering of dark hairs are as soft as his baby curls. We are the same height now, my boy is as tall as I am, and still growing. 'Very well,' I say. 'Let us send for Margaret and all be happy.'

## LINLITHGOW PALACE, SCOTLAND, SUMMER 1527

To my amazement we live together, all four of us, and we are happy. The long cold Scottish winter finally melts and then the miracle that is the Scottish spring comes slowly, slowly, first in the rain-soaked, meltwater-soaked greenness of the grass, then in the honking calls of geese flying overhead, then in the jumble and ripple of birdsong at dawn, and then finally with the lenten lilies and the buds thickening on the trees and every living thing springing into life as the sap rises so strongly that I can almost taste it on the warm air and the year turns towards summer.

Archibald rules the council. There is no doubt that all the power is centred on him, but he brings the laws and proclamations for James' signature. James signs and seals the documents as he is told to do, with a little grimace, he never speaks out against his guardian. James is delighted that I am with him again, and I appoint Davy Lyndsay to my household so James has his dearly loved companion at his side every day once again and we are not completely dominated by the Douglas clan.

The court revolves around me and my son, as it should, and we all go hunting and riding out together; we organise little jousts and competitions. When the weather grows warm we all go to Linlithgow, and there is rowing on the lake and James goes fishing for salmon. At night we hold masques and dances and James shows himself to be a good dancer and a musician. No-one raised by Davy Lyndsay could fail to be a poet, and James writes the lyrics to his own songs. A band of young noblemen gather around him. I think that some of them are bad influences, drinking too much, playing cards for high stakes, and perhaps whoring. But these are the sports of a young man and, God knows, James' father was no saint. No-one seeing James on horseback or jousting could forget his father. Everyone thinks that he must be granted his power this year or next.

We have news from England and from Europe. The troops of the emperor go on taking ground and even riot inside the gates of Rome, and sack the city. People speak as if every Christian has been killed and all the churches desecrated, as if the end of days must surely come now. The Pope himself is captured by the emperor's forces, and though I know that I should pray for him, I cannot help thinking of myself, and that this is the end of my hopes of freedom. All Church business will be overseen by the emperor, Katherine's nephew, so I don't doubt that my application for an annulment for my marriage has been lost, or burned in the wreck of the Vatican. I don't believe I will ever be divorced from Archibald, and Henry Stewart will always live outside the court and see me only when we can snatch an afternoon together, which we waste in complaints and regrets. We both think that we will never be allowed to be together, that he will be forever barred from the honour and the profit of royal service and I will never give him a half-royal heir.

My brother never writes to me now. Scotland and England have signed the peace treaty and evidently he feels that my work is done and that he has no need of my affection. Mary writes me a letter of such dizzy despair that I have to read and reread it to even understand what she is saying. God knows what is happening in London.

*The Boleyn girl has chosen to withdraw from court to her father's home at Hever Castle and Harry writes to her often, in his own hand, begging her to return. In his own hand! For some reason, she is allowed to refuse a royal command, and instead of a punishment she has been rewarded with jewels and money.*

*Maggie, I cannot tell you how demeaning it is to us all to see Harry pursuing this woman as if he were a troubadour and she a lady as grand as a queen. Katherine is completely admirable, she says nothing, she acts as if nothing is wrong, she is as tender and as loving to Harry as she has always been and she never has a cross word for anyone, not even behind closed doors, even though both the whore, the sister Mary and the mother Elizabeth Boleyn (now Lady Rochford – if you can believe it) are still serving in her rooms and she has to endure their half-apologetic, half-triumphant simpering every day. Katherine believes this will all be forgotten as other flirtations have been forgotten, and I suppose it must – for who cares for Bessie Blount now? But if you had seen the velvet that he sent her, you would be as angry as I.*

*The court is divided between the young and foolish relishing the excitement and the scandal of this courtship, and the older ones who love the queen and remember all that she has done for Harry and for England. But why is the Boleyn girl hiding at Hever? I am so afraid that she is with child. Surely we would know? Besides, she made such an icon of her virginity.*

*The Holy Father is sending a papal legate to England to reconcile Harry and our sister. Perhaps he will tell Mademoiselle Boleyn to stay at Hever. I hear that she will only come back to court if she is given her own rooms and her own attendants, as if she were a princess born. She wants a bigger household than mine. You need not wonder who is paying her bills. Nobody wonders, everyone knows, it is completely public: they are sent direct to the exchequer.*

*There is no joy at court any more but we have to attend since Charles says that he cannot lose touch with the king, and I feel I must be beside Katherine as she endures this trial. Her pain can be seen on her face – she looks like a woman with grief like a canker. No-one has told the Princess Mary, who is kept at Ludlow as much as possible, guarded by that old dragon Margaret Pole; but of course she knows, how could she not know? All of England knows. Henry Fitzroy is always at court and now he is treated like a prince. I cannot tell you how unhappy we are. Except for Harry, and Anne Boleyn of course – she is a cow in the corn.*

*We hear that you are returned to your husband and living in harmony. I am so glad for that, dear Maggie. The queen says that you give her hope: to part from him, to make war on him, and to reconcile at last. It is like a miracle.*

I may give the queen hope, but I doubt very much that anyone else thinks of me. Clearly, Harry is happy to leave Scotland to be ruled by his brother-in-law. Indeed, he nominates Archibald to be the Warden of the Marches, and puts him in charge of the peace and security of all the border regions, like asking a lion to lie down with a lamb. As my husband, Archibald, once again legally receives all the rents and fees from my lands. If he chose to leave me penniless he could do so, but he is generous to me, making sure that the council pays me an allowance as dowager queen and giving me beautiful material for Margaret's gowns. If he ever visits Janet Stewart of Traquair, tucked away in one of my many properties, then no-one mentions it to me. Anyone seeing him, respectful in chapel, courteous at dinner, playful during dancing, would think him a faithful husband and me a lucky wife.

More than that, they would think him warmly affectionate. When he comes into a room he always makes his bow to me with one hand over his heart, as if he does not forget that once he loved me. When he kisses my hand he lingers over my fingers. Sometimes when he is standing behind my chair he rests a gentle hand on my shoulder. When I am riding he is always first at my side to lift me down from the saddle and hold me, for a moment, as he sets me on my feet. He appears to all the world like a loving husband, and this must be what they hear in England, for my sister Mary writes on the turned-over corner as an afterthought:

*Do write to Katherine and tell her of your happiness – it will comfort her to know that a husband and wife can come together again after such a long time apart. She is very troubled by the many rumours that have started about her marriage to the king. If anyone asks you, Margaret, be sure that you tell them you remember perfectly well that our father decided before his death that Harry should marry Katherine, and that she and Harry received a full dispensation from the Pope. If anyone says anything about God not giving them a son, you are to say that the ways of God are mysterious indeed and that we have, thanks be, a beautiful healthy princess as our heir. Don't say a thing about Henry Fitzroy, we never mention him. I pray every day that the Boleyn woman consents to a normal love affair and proves barren. At the moment we are all waiting, like servants in a bath house, for her to name her price. Only God Himself knows what she is holding out for.*

I ought to be glad that Katherine's long rule over my brother has ended. I think I must be glad, though I don't feel it. I keep thinking: this is my moment of triumph – why do I not feel triumphant?

While she lives, cast aside by a merry young court that is dominated by Harry's new favourite, while she is neglected by the Boleyn family and their kinsmen the Howards, while she is silenced as an advisor to the cardinal and the others who do the business of the country, she cannot influence Harry against me. She cannot persuade any man of the sanctity of marriage when the king is hell-bent on seduction. A Boleyn court thinking only of pleasure, excited by temptation, breathless with scandal, is no audience for Katherine's profound thoughts on fidelity and constancy. As her influence wanes it must be my moment. But now – as bad luck would have it – is the very moment when the Pope is the emperor's prisoner, and no business is being transacted at all.

'D'you know, I think we will be together forever, like Deucalion and Pyrrha,' Archibald says, coming into my privy chamber and nodding to the ladies as if he had every right to stroll in without announcement.

I don't smile. I can't remember who Deucalion and Pyrrha are, and I am not committing myself to anything with Archibald.

'Faithful husband and wife who repopulated the earth,' he prompts. 'I think we might make a new Scotland when our boy here is old enough to rule.'

'He's old enough now,' I say unpleasantly. 'And he is my boy, not ours.'

Archibald laughs gently, puts his hand over his heart, and makes a little nod with his head. 'I am sure you are right,' he says. 'At least we have a daughter together to make us happy.'

'If we are so very happy then I am sure that Archbishop Beaton can return to court?' I ask, testing the ground.

'Och, is he tired of shepherding?' Archibald asks me with a

gleam in his eye. 'I heard that he had taken up a modest crook in place of his gold one, and left Stirling Castle in a hurry.'

I flush with annoyance. 'You know very well what happened,' I say.

He winks at me. 'I do, and yes, he can come back to court as far as I am concerned. Your son must be the one who issues the invitation, of course. Anyone else?'

'What do you mean?'

'Anyone else that you would like to restore?' he says pleasantly. 'If we are to live together, merrily and forever? Anyone else that you would like in your household? Just confirm it with James. I am happy to have any of your friends here, any of your household. As long as . . .'

'As long as what?' I demand, ready to be offended.

'As long as they understand that your reputation is not to be damaged,' he says, as pompous as a choirboy. 'While you are with me, as my wife, I would not want there to be any gossip about you. Your reputation as James' mother, as our daughter's mother and as dowager queen should be above reproach.'

'My reputation is above reproach,' I say icily.

He takes my hands as if he would console me. 'Ah, my dear, there is always gossip. I am afraid that your brother has heard from the French that you are in constant communication with the Duke of Albany.'

'I am supposed to be in constant communication with him! He is Regent of Scotland!'

'Even so. Your brother believes that you are hoping to marry him.'

'This is ridiculous!'

'And someone has told your brother that you have taken a lover, Henry Stewart.'

I don't stammer. 'I deny it completely.'

'Someone has told him that you and Henry Stewart are planning to kidnap your son and put him on the throne as a pawn of the Stewart clan.'

'Oh, who would that be?' I say bitterly. 'Who is my brother's spy, who has such detail, and is heard so sympathetically in England?'

Archibald presses my hands to his lips. 'Not me, actually. But since I know how much your family means to you, and since the king is inquiring into the validity of his own marriage – it matters all the more to him that there is no scandal about you.'

'Harry is inquiring into the validity of his own marriage?'

'Of course.'

'You believe that he means to leave Katherine?' I whisper.

'He should,' Archibald says, as if pronouncing sentence on her, a blameless woman, a woman of no power.

'I heard that a papal legate was coming to England to reconcile them?'

Archibald gives a short laugh. 'To tell her to let him go.'

I turn away from him and go to the window and look down into the gardens. The blossom is whirling down from the apple trees as if it were snow in springtime. I don't know whether I feel triumphant or bereft. It is as if the high cliff that they call Arthur's Seat has suddenly shifted and sunk; the horizon has changed completely. Katherine has dominated my life; I have envied her and loved her and been irritated by her and been nearly destroyed by her more than once. Can she suddenly disappear? Can she suddenly be unimportant?

'She will never ever agree,' I predict.

'No, but if the marriage is shown to be invalid, then it is not up to her.'

'On what possible grounds could it be invalid?'

'Because she was married to your brother Arthur,' Archibald says simply, as if it is obvious.

I remember Mary's letter, warning me what I was to say. My two sisters whispering together will have prepared a reply to every question. They don't consult me, they instruct me. 'There was a dispensation,' I say, as Mary told me to say.

'Perhaps the dispensation was not valid.'

I look blankly at him. 'What sort of argument is this? Of course a papal dispensation is valid.'

'It hardly matters now. The queen's nephew holds the Pope in his keeping. I doubt that the Holy Father will be brave enough to put shame on his gaoler's kinswoman. He will never allow your brother's divorce. He will never allow yours.'

'But this has nothing to do with me!' I exclaim.

'The Pope has his own troubles – he won't care about yours. And Harry won't want anyone to get a divorce but himself.' Archibald sums up with complete accuracy the focus of Harry's growing vanity and his habitual selfishness. 'He won't want anyone to think that a Tudor applies for an annulment for any reason but God's proven will. The last thing he wants is you – with your history of marrying for your own desire, so far from God, such a scandalous woman – applying for a divorce before him, and besmirching his own reputation. He will want everyone's behaviour to be beyond question so that he can apply for an annulment without any suggestion of his . . .' He breaks off, looking for the right word.

'His what?'

'Selfish lust.'

I look at him, shocked at his naming Harry's vice so bluntly. 'You should not say that of him, not even to me.'

'Be very sure he won't want it said of you.'

I think that Henry Stewart may as well come to court so that we can have the comfort of each other's company since we will never be free to marry, but to my surprise, it is my son James who refuses permission. He draws himself up to his full height, just a little taller than I am, and says that he cannot condone any immorality at his court.

I almost laugh in his face. 'But James!' I say, speaking to him as if he is a cross little boy. 'You may not be the judge of my friends.'

'Indeed I shall,' he says. He speaks coldly, not like my boy at all. 'Be very sure that it is my household and I will be the judge of who is here. I have one stepfather set over me, I won't have another. I thought you had enough of husbands.'

'Henry would not try to rule you!' I exclaim. 'He has always been such a friend to you. He's so charming, I like him so much, he is a pleasure to be with.'

'Those are the very reasons I would not want him here,' James says stiffly.

'He is not your stepfather; he can never be my husband.'

'This makes it worse. I would have thought that you would have seen that.'

'Son, you mistake yourself,' I say, my temper rising.

'Lady Mother, I do not.'

'I will not be ruled by anyone. Not even you, my son. I am a Tudor princess.'

'That name is becoming a byword for scandal,' James says pompously. 'Your brother's adultery is known throughout the world, your own name is slandered. I will not have my mother spoken of in every tavern.'

'How dare you? When everyone knows that you and your court gamble and fornicate, that they are a lewd company and drink to excess! How dare you reproach me? I have done nothing but marry once for love and been betrayed. Now I want to marry again. What could be wrong with that?'

He says nothing. He looks at me steadily, as his father would have done.

I turn without curtseying and I fling myself out of the room.

## STIRLING CASTLE, SCOTLAND, SUMMER 1527

I go to Stirling and at once someone tells Harry that I have been banned from my own son's court and that I am living adulterously with a lover. Someone has told him that my son pleaded with me to amend my ways and turn away from sin and that when I would not, he rightly sent me away. Harry sends me an outraged letter in which he threatens me with eternal damnation if I will not give up my adultery. He writes to James, too, and tells him that he also must reform. He must stop drinking, stop whoring, and commit himself to knightly practice and noble sports. I am baffled by this stern new morality until I get a scribbled note from Mary:

*Mademoiselle Anne will not yield to the king. They talk a great deal about her virtue and how she is storm-tossed. I have never seen a seduction like it, we are all to ponder her chastity while she wears her gowns cut low and her hoods pushed back. She pretends to a French accent and reads heretical books. This is a modern young woman indeed. We have become fervently chaste while dancing like whores. The queen is ill; I really don't know how she manages to get through dinner while the rich dishes go out to the young women and they lick their spoons.*

*I can hardly bear court. I would not go at all if Charles did not make me. Katherine asks you to assure her that you will do nothing to undermine the state of marriage. She has heard that you have left your son's court in order to live with your lover. I told her that this must be a lie. I know you would not do such a thing. Not for your own sake, not for ours. You would not, would you? Swear to me that you would not.*

## STIRLING CASTLE, SCOTLAND, AUTUMN 1527

I do not reply at once. I cannot give Katherine the assurance she asks for; I cannot sacrifice my own happiness to support hers. I cannot mirror my own brother's hypocrisy. I cannot claim that I am guided only by the will of God. For the first time in my life I am free of fear and out of danger. James is safe, my daughter is living happily at Tantallon, the country is quiet under the rule of Archibald, Henry and I live like a private lord and lady, running our estate and enjoying ourselves. I feel as if I have never been able to be happy and at peace in my life before. At last I am away from Archibald and free of the constant mixture of fear and desire that he inspires in me. At last I can be with the man who loves me and respond to him simply, without a shadow, without lies. This is my autumn, this is my season.

We are bringing in wood for the great fires of the winter. We are laying down salted fish and smoked meats in the great castle larders. We are riding under trees that shed their leaves in jewel colours of rubies and brass, gold and emerald, when Henry nods to our castle gateway, high above us, up on the hill, and says, 'Look! Isn't that the papal standard? Are they flying the papal standard? A messenger from the Pope must have come.'

I squint against the red sunset. 'It is,' I say, my hand to my throat. 'Oh, Henry, can it be a messenger about the divorce?'

'Could be,' he says steadily. He puts his hand over mine on the reins. 'Be calm, my love. It could be anything. The Pope freed? A new pope? The divorce or any number of a dozen things.'

'Come on!' I say, and my horse leaps forward and we ride through the woods and up the hill, round and round on the twisting track to the top, and we go into the castle at a run and find the papal messenger in the great hall with a cup of mulled ale in his hand, standing before the hearth.

He bows as I come in, and when I see the depth of his bow to Henry I know that we have won.

'The Holy Father has granted me a divorce,' I say with certainty.

The messenger bows again, to us equally, as if Henry is my husband already. 'He has,' he says.

At last. I cannot believe it. I am free of Archibald at last. This is my baptism into freedom from sin, this is my birth. This is my renewal. I could almost be a heretic and say this is my second coming. I have a chance to be happy again. I have a chance to marry again. I will be the centre of Henry's life and hold my head high in Scotland and before the world. The very thing that Katherine said could never be has come about – despite her interdict. The Pope himself and I have defied her. She said that I cannot be divorced, that I must not be divorced – and I am. This is the triumph of my will over hers and I am deeply happy.

We have a great feast that night: haunches of venison, pies of songbirds, slices of roast goose, fish in plenty, roast boar, and tray after tray of sweetmeats at the end of the dinner. Everyone knows that the papal messenger has brought good news and that I am free of Archibald and someone is certain to have slipped away to Edinburgh already to tell Archibald that he has finally lost and I am free. Margaret is not to be named as a bastard and I shall demand that she lives with me.

I laugh at the thought that I am a free woman. I can hardly believe that it is true after so many years of waiting, after so many terrible letters from England. I think that they will soon hear of this, and I think of my sister-in-law, on her knees for my soul and the soul of her husband. I think I am sorry for her, for Katherine the wife who will be left behind; and I am glad and proud of myself who will be married again, and to a young man who loves me for myself. I think I am a young woman like that slut Anne Boleyn who dares to look the old rules in the face and choose her own future. I think that Katherine, and all the old people who would keep women where they are, under the rule of men, are my enemy. The world is changing and I am in the forefront of change.

'What news of my brother, the King of England?' I ask the papal messenger as the groom of the servery pours him another glass of wine.

'The Holy Father has received an application,' the messenger says. 'He is sending a papal legate to London to hear the evidence.'

I am so surprised that I drop my spoon. 'What evidence? I thought the legate was coming to reconcile them, or to talk with the queen?'

'He is hearing evidence for an annulment,' the man replies, as if the matter is simple. 'The Holy Father is making a full inquiry.'

I should have foreseen this, but Harry's ability to say one thing and do another continues to amaze me. 'My brother has sought to annul his marriage?'

'Your Grace did not know?'

'I knew that he had doubts. I thought that the papal legate was coming to London to resolve those doubts. I did not know that there was to be an inquiry. I did not know that there was any evidence. I thought that my brother the king was opposed to the dissolution of marriage.'

A small, hidden smile suggests that the messenger has been told this too. 'It is not a question of dissolution of a valid marriage,' he says carefully. 'I understand that the king believes that a valid marriage to the queen never took place. He has produced proofs. And of course, he has no heir.'

'He has had no male heir for eighteen years,' I say tartly. 'And he has a princess. Why would he apply for an annulment now?'

'Apparently, it is not to marry another lady,' the messenger says carefully. 'It is to ensure that he is not living in a state of sin. He is not self-serving; he believes that God has not blessed the marriage as it was no marriage. It was never a marriage.'

I glance at Henry, who is seated at the head of the table of lords, not beside me, since he is not yet my husband. 'Even here in Scotland we have heard of Anne Boleyn,' I remark.

The papal messenger shakes his head slowly, enjoying the twisting diplomatic denial of the obvious. 'But not in the Vatican. The curia has not heard of the lady,' he lies beautifully. 'Her name is not mentioned in any documents. Her presence at the court in

London is not material to the evidence. Your brother is seeking the annulment of his marriage on clerical grounds, not for his personal feelings. He has doubts. He does not have desires.'

## STIRLING CASTLE, SCOTLAND, SPRING 1528

Henry and I are married in the little castle chapel at Stirling. It's one of the oldest buildings on the steep side of the castle bailey and so the stone-flagged floor slopes upwards to the altar and climbs in a series of worn stone steps. As Henry and I go hand in hand towards my confessor it is an uphill walk, and indeed, I feel that is how our shared life has been.

We have witnesses – never again will I let someone claim that I had no marriage at all but a private handfasting; the priest brings a choirboy to sing the anthem, but it is a private ceremony. Henry gives me the ring of his clan, with the pelican insignia of his family crest. He gives me a purse of gold. We go to bed that afternoon and so the marriage is made, unbreakably. At last I am married to a good man in the safety of my own castle in Scotland. As I doze in his arms and the cold spring afternoon turns dark outside, I think of Katherine and the chilly comforts of her faith. I think that she was so emphatic that she knew what was right, she knew what was God's will; but here am I, her much less clever sister-in-law, less devout, less educated, poorer and with fewer jewels, inferior in every way, yet it is I who am married to a handsome young husband with our lives before us, and that while the court dances in the great hall she is alone praying, abandoned by the king who tells her that she is the finest wife he could have, but alas, never his wife at all.

We do not have a peaceful honeymoon at Stirling. Only weeks after our marriage the guards on the castle walls sound the alarm. As soon as the tocsin rings out the animals grazing in the woods outside the castle are driven into the yard, the drawbridge is cranked up and the portcullis slams down. People outside the castle visiting friends or family in the little town at the foot of the hill are exiled, locked out until danger is over, and some of the villagers who have come in to work in the kitchens or serve in the castle are trapped inside with us. We are in a state of siege within moments and I run, from my privy chamber where I was praying, to the captain of the castle at the sentry post above the main gate. To my left I can see them rolling out the big guns on the grand battery, aiming them down the hill where any attacking army has to approach, exposed to our fire on their flanks. Behind me they are arming the palace gate, and bowmen with handguns are running across the guardroom square to line the walls that look down the only road to the castle.

'What is it?' I demand shortly. 'Is it the Douglases?'

'An advance guard. I can't see who.'

I see a herald ride up the road, two men behind him, looking as nervous as any man will be under the gaze of forty cannon. Standards ripple before and behind him.

'Stand!' bellows the captain of the castle. 'Identify yourselves!'

'A warrant of arrest.' The herald raises a piece of paper but it is too far to see if it is a forgery.

'For who?'

This is extraordinary. Who can they want?

'A known traitor, Henry Stewart, for marrying the queen regent without permission from her son, the king.'

The captain glances sideways at me and sees my aghast face. This is the very last thing that I expected. I had thought that Archibald and I were agreed that I should be free. I thought it was Harry's order. I thought Ard was satisfied with the power he had seized and the use he has had of my lands.

'Open the gate in the name of the King of Scotland,' the herald shouts.

It is an irresistible password. We cannot resist the name of the King of Scotland without being declared traitors ourselves. I bite my lip as the captain looks at me for a command.

'I have to open it,' he says.

'I know you do,' I say. 'But first send someone out to make sure that it is the royal seal.'

I am playing for time, but I have no plan for the extra ten minutes. Henry comes up behind me and watches with the captain as our master of horse goes out and examines the seal. We see his gesture to the captain to acknowledge that it is genuine, and the captain bellows at his men and the portcullis slowly creeps upwards.

'Can you ride out of one of the sally ports, as they are coming in the main gate?' Desperately I hold Henry's hands and scan his white face.

'They'd capture him on the road down to the village,' the captain advises. 'They'll have a guard waiting, and pickets all around.'

'Can we hide him?'

'Then we'd be guilty of treason too.'

'I didn't think! I never dreamed!'

'I'll demand safe conduct,' Henry says quietly. 'I'll demand a trial. If I go out publicly with some of my own people, and you write to the lords of the council, they'll try me for treason but perhaps forgive me. Nobody would blame me for marrying you. Nobody can blame you. You are legally divorced.'

'It's no worse than Charles Brandon did with Mary,' I say. 'All they got was a fine that they never paid.'

'At any rate, not even Archibald will dare execute me for it,' Henry says wryly.

'He's just trying to frighten me,' I say. My shaking hands show his success.

'I'll go,' Henry says. 'I'd rather volunteer than be captured.'

I want to pull him back, but I let him go down the stone stairs and greet the messenger in the guardroom square. Slowly I follow him as the gate to the inner castle opens and Henry orders his household and his horses to come with him to Edinburgh. He speaks to the herald and I see him repeat a question and then shake his head.

'I'll follow you,' I say to him quietly. 'And I'll get hold of Archibald. He won't refuse me if I'm there in front of him, arguing for you.'

'It's not Archibald,' he says, his face shocked. 'It's a genuine warrant from your son James himself. And he is acting on the advice of the King of England. Your brother wants me tried for treason, and your son wants me dead.'

## STIRLING CASTLE, SCOTLAND, SUMMER 1528

They all write to me: Harry, Thomas Wolsey, Katherine, Mary. They all deplore my divorce; Harry threatens me with the damnation of adulterers. Katherine begs me to think of the legitimacy of my daughter, and says that I am throwing her down as baseborn. Thomas Wolsey tells me that Harry's outraged rant is a true copy of his spoken words, and Mary tells me that gowns are being cut slightly off the shoulder.

I write to Archibald, I write to James. I write to William Dacre, the heir to Lord Thomas Dacre, I write to Mary, to Katherine, to Harry; I write to Cardinal Wolsey. If I dared I would write to Anne Boleyn as the most potent advisor at Henry's court. I try to contain my terror and I write, as calmly as I can, that my former marriage was annulled by the Pope himself on the basis of my husband's pre-contract with Lady Janet Stewart of Traquair. Since I am free, I chose to marry Henry Stewart, and although I should have asked for permission for this match, I, like my sister Mary, am asking for permission after the wedding. All I am requesting is the same treatment as my sister, Mary, who married Charles Brandon without her brother's permission. All I am asking is that I am treated justly and fairly, as Mary was. Why should I accept harsher treatment than she? Why should anyone treat me with more unkindness than Mary – who was a king's widow and married her choice during her year of mourning? What could be more disrespectful than that?

I write peaceably and soberly to Archibald. I say that I am happy that our daughter is safe in his keeping, but I remind him that she is high-born and legitimate. She keeps her good name. I expect her to visit me when I request it. I expect to see her when I want to.

I have a reply from my son James. He does not even answer my appeal for mercy for Henry Stewart. He writes of nothing personal; anything he writes to me is read by Archibald's advisors. But this letter announces that James is calling a meeting of the council to complain of lawlessness on the borders. I don't know why James should suddenly address the desolate state of the borders, nor why he should tell me, when I am begging him to release my young husband.

I am writing another round of appeals one evening when I hear the shout of one of the guards and the sudden ringing of the tocsin bell. It is three loud rings, the signal that a few men have approached the main gate, not the hammering peal that warns of an approaching army. At once, I pray that it may be Henry Stewart coming home to me, and I drop my pen, pull a cape around me and go out into the outer close. The gate to the main entrance is open and as I watch, the great gates are flung open without a command from the captain of the castle, and I can hear the sound of the soldiers cheering.

This is extraordinary. They would not be cheering Henry Stewart, and I cannot imagine who else would come after curfew. I hurry across the outer close to see what late-night visitor has found the gates thrown open to him to cheers from my guard, when I see a big warhorse and above it the gleaming smile of my son James.

'James!' is all I can say, and he pulls up his horse, jumps off, and throws the reins to his groom.

'James!'

He is dressed like a poor man in a brown wool cape with a plaid over his shoulder of grey and brown. He has a thick belt around his waist and a great knife in a cheap scabbard on his hip. But he has his own good riding boots, and his own unmistakable beam of triumph.

'I got away!' He scoops me up into his arms and kisses me, a smacking kiss on both cheeks, then he takes me by the waist and dances me around the yard as his horse snorts and backs away from us and the men cheer. 'I got away. At last. I've done it. I got away.'

'How, how did you?'

'He went off to the borders to make war on his own blackguards and I told everyone else that I would be up at dawn to go hunting. I went to bed early and so did everyone else. Jockie Hart and these two had my horse ready and a spare set of clothes and swore they would come with me. We had the horses out of the stable and were away up the North Road before dawn, before they even knew we were gone.'

'He'll come after you,' I say, with a glance towards the south as if I can see Archibald's army marching from Edinburgh.

'For sure. And he'll guess I have come to you. Let's get in and get the gates closed and post guards.'

He sweeps me in, his arm around my shoulder, and I call for lights as we go into the hall and the household wakes around us, half of them sleeping on trestles in the hall, getting to their feet and cheering the news that the king is here, the king himself, and he will never be captured again.

'We must fly the royal standard,' I order. 'Then if they come against us they are declared traitors. And you must issue a warrant to ban any of the Clan Douglas from coming near you.'

'Write it out,' James says. 'I'll sign it and seal it with my ring.'

'You brought it?'

'I always wear it. Archibald has the big seal but I have this.'

'And send out a declaration that all the lords who are loyal to James are to come here to join His Grace. We'll call a council of the lords and then a parliament in Edinburgh,' I say to my chief clerk, who is writing frantically, his writing desk slung around his neck, scattering sand on the letter to dry it. I give a little excited laugh. 'It is like a masque, starting again. But this time we have the costumes and we know the moves.'

'And write to Edinburgh Castle to order the release of Henry Stewart,' James says.

I look up.

'It is your wish?' he asks me.

'Yes, of course, but I thought you were opposed to my marriage.'

'I was opposed to the scandal, not to the marriage,' he says, pedantic as any young man. 'It was Archibald who ordered your husband's arrest in my name. He wanted to please your brother and I consented, so he would think that you and I were enemies. Of course, Henry Stewart is not my choice; but if he is yours, he can be freed and I will make him a lord. What's his estate?'

'Methven,' I say. 'He can be Lord Methven.'

'Write it down,' James says, laughing. 'These are my first acts as ruling king.'

## EDINBURGH CASTLE, SCOTLAND, SUMMER 1528

We enter Edinburgh in triumph, and it is a greater triumph than ever before. The lords meet us at the Tollbooth, the people throw flowers and scented water from the upper windows and crowd the narrow streets to see James and I together, smiling and acknowledging the cheers. James, their king, is finally the ruling king and Archibald is nowhere to be seen.

We keep the castle armed, victualled and ready for a siege because I am constantly afraid that Archibald will return with the Douglas clan at his back. James has guards on his bedroom door and sleeps with an armed man on a pallet bed beside him. My brother Harry writes to me that I will be damned for all eternity for breaking my marriage vows and living in adultery. I don't even reply. It is a terrible thing for a brother to write such words of condemnation to his sister, but a brother who is leaving his wife every day in order to pursue another woman, and is chaste only because his mistress is playing a long game, has no right to speak so to me. Never again will I think that morality is different for men.

The city buzzes with rumours of a Douglas army massed in the hills outside and preparing to set a siege. The citizens and the merchants support their young king but they are afraid of the Douglas power. Only six years ago the Douglas clan spilled blood in the streets of Edinburgh, and it is less than four years since I opened fire on them from Holyroodhouse. The people don't want to be trapped in their own city between two warring powers; there is nothing in the world worse than a civil war.

The lords agree that the Douglas clan have been treasonous. The declaration is put to the horn – the herald goes to the mercat cross and, after three blasts of the trumpet, announces the names of traitors. My former husband, Archibald, is under sentence of death. Our enmity has finally brought us to this point. I have not just divorced him, and married another man, I have ordered his death. I may have to watch him executed. This must be the end of everything between us.

'We should go to Stirling,' Henry advises. We are in James' privy chamber. I am seated on the throne as James strides up and down, looking out of the windows. Some of the older lords are with us. Most have chosen the king against his stepfather. Nearly all of them say that they were loyal all along but were bribed by English gold and afraid of Archibald.

'Back to Stirling?' James asks. 'I won't look as if I am afraid. I won't run away.'

'Stirling to regroup,' I advise. 'Archibald cannot take Stirling Castle, and if he sets a siege before it, against the royal standard, then he is a self-declared traitor and no-one should support him. Let's go there, till we know if he is going to surrender to you and hand over his castles.'

James turns to the other lords. 'Would this be your advice?' he asks with careful courtesy.

'Aye,' one of them says. 'And we need to know what Harry of England is going to do for us, now we have put his nephew on the throne and his sister is married to another lord.'

They all turn to look at me, and I am ashamed that I cannot promise that I have my brother's support.

'The King of England has always favoured the Earl of Angus,' someone says bluntly.

'He cannot do so now!'

'Over his own sister?' someone else asks.

I turn my head away so they cannot see my grimace. He might.

## EDINBURGH CASTLE, SCOTLAND, AUTUMN 1528

Parliament meets, and since Archibald did not come to the council of lords, nor swear loyalty to James, nor surrender his castles and lands as he was ordered to do, they confirm him as a traitor under sentence of death.

But even now, against the will of the Scots lords, against the rights of a king, against the wishes of a sister, my brother still supports Archibald, though he has taken arms against me and my son together. Incredibly, within weeks of James' escape, there is a letter from England written by a clerk, addressed to James as king, advising him to restore Archibald to his power and his property as the best and wisest advisor that Scotland can offer.

'He says nothing of you,' James observes.

'No,' I say. 'Perhaps he is not writing any personal letters. They are very ill in England.'

The Sweat – the terrible sickness that some people call the Tudor disease – is rife and Harry has had a terror of it ever since our grandmother swore that he and Arthur should never be near anyone who was ill. The Tudor boys were such rarities that they could not be near disease. While his subjects die in their shops, behind the counters, in the churches at prayer, in the streets on their way home, Harry takes off for a breakneck tour of England, going from one great house to another and only staying if they swear that there is no disease behind their high walls. Anne Boleyn herself is taken ill and has gone off to Hever. If Katherine's God is merciful to the queen who prays to Him with such fervour, Anne Boleyn will die there.

James defies Harry's command that he must restore Archibald, and says on the contrary he will bring his former stepfather to justice. He and a small army of loyal lords ride to Tantallon Castle and set a siege. I think of the little castle that overlooks the sea, the white-crowned rock behind it, the seas breaking at the foot of the cliffs. I am in terror for my daughter Margaret, and James offers a reward for her as Archibald holds out for weeks, and then breaks out on a lightning raid on our army, and captures our cannon. He rides through the lands that have been devastated by his orders, and sends raiding parties to burn the autumn bracken on the hills to the south of

Edinburgh so that we can smell the smoke in the streets like a threat of arson. For months he demands a pardon and a return to power, and in the meantime makes the lives of the people around his castle a misery by raiding and burning. Finally, he takes the great road south to England, settles my daughter at Norham Castle, and – amazingly enough – sets himself up in London as peacemaker: as the still small voice of calm among the whirlwind of my sin.

An adulterer, a fraudster and a traitor, he is greeted warmly by people who should be my friends, and my sisters. He refuses to reply to my demands for my daughter. I don't know how I will ever get her home again. Is she to be raised as if she had no mother? Does he think he can take her as if I were dead? I cannot make myself understand the injustice. Archibald has deserted me and my cause, taken my lands, kidnapped both my children, and made war on his own people for his own ambition, and yet he is regarded as an injured husband and an exiled hero. As night follows day a letter from my sister, Mary, follows his arrival in London, but it is obvious where her attention lies.

*Cardinal Campeggio, the papal legate, has arrived and has met with both Cardinal Wolsey and our brother the king. Harry has been persuaded to doubt the validity of his marriage (not hard to imagine who by) and no-one can deny that he is very troubled. Mademoiselle Boleyn has unluckily recovered from her illness and is now in hiding at Hever so that no-one can suggest there is any question of selfish desire.*

*Actually, I hope that Cardinal Campeggio will end this terrible uncertainty. Katherine has shown him the old letter of dispensation from Pope Julius which says that she and Harry were free to marry whether or not her marriage with Arthur was consummated, so there is no basis in law for any inquiry, and she has made it clear that she will not attend any court.*

*Oh, Maggie – I was there when the cardinal asked her would she consider retiring to a nunnery and leaving*

*Harry. She was so quiet and so dignified. She said that God had called her to the state of matrimony and that she had been a good wife. She told the cardinal to his face that she had received Harry's friends (she meant his whores, it is shameful how she has been forced to live with them) as if they were her own friends – and it is true. She says that she has never failed him, except that God saw fit to take the babies to His own. She won't retire, and Campeggio will never persuade her. I think Mademoiselle Boleyn is going to have to settle for being a mistress – she can reach no higher, there is no place higher for one like her. Katherine holds firm and everyone admires her. It is costing her health and her happiness and her beauty, but she does not flinch. She says that marriage is for life, and no-one can deny the truth of that.*

*Your husband the Earl of Angus is at court and is handsome and well. He speaks so lovingly of you and the terrible consequences of your betrayal of him. He believes that your marriage with Henry Stewart is invalid, your son is badly advised and you are in a state of sin. Margaret, I pray that you will resolve this unhappiness, and invite Archibald home. Katherine shows us how a wife should be. She told me to tell you that it is not too late. She asked me to beg you to restore the earl to his place at court. Margaret, please think about this – if you continue like this we will never see each other again. Think of that, think of Katherine, and think of your boy. Think of your daughter too, you will never see her again unless you can reconcile with your true husband. I am so unhappy for you and for Katherine, I cannot bear to see our family being torn apart, I cannot bear to see you making a fool of yourself before the world. M.*

## EDINBURGH CASTLE, SCOTLAND, WINTER 1528

For the first time, my brother writes to me as he should have done before, to tell me of his fears about his marriage. He explains that he has no other lady in mind, though I know that Anne Boleyn is occupying beautiful rooms provided by Thomas Wolsey and all the court troops to see her every day, that she writes post-scripts to my brother's letters, that even this letter may have been composed with her hanging over his shoulder and turning the smooth phrases.

Even so, I cannot help but feel for him. He is my little brother. He thinks – and God knows that he has good reason to think – that his marriage has been cursed from the first day. I think of the bitter vitriol of our lady grandmother and how she swore that Katherine should never marry Harry and I think – what if she was right? What if there was no true dispensation? What if Katherine was Harry's sister-in-law all along and never his wife? What else could explain the terrible procession of dead babies? What else in the world could explain that grief?

He writes:

*If our marriage was against God's law and clearly void, then I shall not only sorrow the departing from so good a lady and loving companion, but much more lament and bewail my unfortunate chance that I have so long lived in adultery to God's great displeasure, and have no true heir of my body to inherit this realm. These are the sores that vex my mind, these are the pangs that trouble my conscience, and for these pains I seek a remedy. Therefore, dearest Sister, I require you, as our trust and confidence is in you, to declare to our subjects and our friends, to your subjects and friends, our mind and intent, and pray with us that the very truth may be known for the discharge of our conscience and saving of our soul.*

'God bless him,' I say to my husband, Henry Stewart. 'Whatever his desire for that woman Anne Boleyn it is a truly terrible thing to happen to a man – to be married for so long and to find his marriage is invalid.'

'It is like a nightmare,' Henry says. 'But he seems to be insisting that there is no beautiful young woman in the best rooms of his palace.'

'There are always beautiful young women,' I say. 'Never before has Harry thought that his marriage was not valid. There have been beautiful young women and they have given him babies – even sons. If he says that his conscience is troubled then I believe him.'

'And d'you now think Katherine should be set aside?'

I think of the girl who came from Spain, of the sulky bride at Arthur's wedding, of the widow who leapt from such terrible poverty and humiliation to being Queen of England, and the queen militant who sent her army against my husband and wanted his body pickled as a trophy.

'She has never thought of anyone but herself,' I say coldly. 'But my brother is now thinking of the law of God.'

Mary writes me a Christmas letter, but it is nothing but an anguished list of the gifts that Harry has given to Anne. She does not ask after me, nor Henry, her new brother-in-law; she does not ask after my son as he takes his power as king. As always, Mary misses the point. She is full of the glorious rooms that Anne has usurped at Greenwich Palace, and how everyone visits her and neglects Katherine. She says that Anne is wearing borders of gold set with precious stones, and heart-shaped jewels set in headpieces like coronets. Her bracelets are the talk of the court; apparently I would be grieved to my heart if I saw her rubies. Mary says nothing about our brother's distress and worry nor the state of his soul.

*Katherine is not well served in her rooms and the Boleyn and Norfolk ladies do not even attend her now. Our brother the king does not dine with her, nor does he ever spend the night in her bed.*

I feel so impatient with Mary. Why should the king spend the night with Katherine? It's not as if he is going to get a Prince of Wales from sleeping in her barren bed. It may be that the papal legate advises that they are not husband and wife at all. Why should Katherine be served by duchesses? If she is a Dowager Princess of Wales then she is not a queen and should not have that service. Mary – a dowager queen herself – might consider that rules of the court are there to be kept. Katherine has gloried in her title and her position, she humbled the rest of us while she queened around. Perhaps now the world is changing. My world has changed a hundred times with no help from her. Now her world is changing too and I cannot find it in my heart to pity her. She ruined me once, now she is facing ruin herself.

## STIRLING CASTLE, SCOTLAND, SPRING 1529

Of course, my son James turns against any idea that he might marry his cousin, Princess Mary. If there is any chance at all that her mother is merely a dowager princess and the girl a royal bastard, then she is completely unsuitable as a wife for a king. We are completely agreed on this, and then we hear a rumour that Archibald is advising Harry in favour of the marriage and a peace with Scotland. James flares up and says that he needs neither unreliable peace nor a doubtful princess. He says that he wants to ally with France and marry a French princess.

'James, please,' I say to him. 'You can't suddenly decide things like this. Nobody knows what will happen in England.'

'I know that my uncle has never honoured you or me,' he says tersely. 'I know that he has always preferred Archibald Earl of Angus to you and to me, and he is doing so now.'

'I am sure he will honour both the peace and the betrothal,' I say.

James, a boy who looks like a man, a boy with a man's task to do, blames me, whenever it is Archibald causing trouble. 'So you say! But when has he honoured his word, to a country or to a woman? Your brother the king does exactly as he wants and then glozes it with sanctity. You wait and see what he will do with the cardinals at his court. He will get his way and then make out that it is God's will. Well, he does not gloze over me.'

## STIRLING CASTLE, SCOTLAND, SUMMER 1529

I am waiting for a letter from Mary; I know that she will want to be first to tell me of the decision of the legatine court on our brother's case. When they bring me the letter, tied both ways with ribbons and heavily sealed to prevent anyone reading it, I hardly know whether to hope that the cardinals have declared Harry's marriage void, or that they have ordered him to stay with Katherine. There is no doubt where Mary's loyalties lie:

she has always been Katherine's little follower. She has never had anything from Katherine but tenderness and support. They have been true sisters to each other. For me, Katherine has been less of a blessing. It is not disloyalty to a sister that makes me wonder if I really want her as Queen of England forever. She has made this estrangement between us, over and over again. When she was in power she was terribly destructive to me, until she started falling, and then she demanded that I help her.

*Anne Boleyn is exceeding her position in every way!*

Mary starts without a word of greeting, a criss-crossed page of indignation. I spread the sheet on my knees and I look out of the window at the loch and the hills behind it. James is out riding for the day; he will not be home until dinner. I have all the time in the world to decipher Mary's scrawl.

> *This Easter she blessed cramp rings for the poor as if she had the divine touch. She lives as high as the queen herself – far better actually, since Katherine fasts completely every Friday and every saint's day. The Boleyn woman did not dare to attend the legatine court, I think if she had done there would have been a riot in favour of the queen. The women of the City and all of England are up in arms that the Boleyn whore (as they call her!) should dream of trying to take the place of our queen. If Harry gets the decision he wants from the court I really doubt that the people will allow the woman to be crowned. It is too dreadful. I cannot even speak to him about it, he consults no-one but her and Wolsey.*
>
> *You will have heard of the proceedings of the court from the archdeacon, I suppose; but what he may not tell you is that Bishop John Fisher, who was so dear to our lady grandmother, stood up in the court and swore that he had not signed a warrant that all the churchmen had agreed. Harry said there was his seal and signature and he said it was neither his seal nor his hand. It was very dreadful, very shocking,*

*everyone could see that his consent had been forged. Harry said it didn't matter, but it did matter, Margaret. It mattered to everyone. It shows that the Boleyns will do anything.*

*Anne Boleyn herself has gone to Hever and Katherine spends all her time praying. Charles says that calling in cardinals is a waste of time and Harry would do better to bed Anne at once and hope for boredom soon. Everyone says something different except dear John Fisher, who says that Katherine's marriage was good, everyone knew it was so, and he will never say different.*

*I can't say because I was too young. You had better say nothing, whatever you think. Everyone has an opinion, everyone talks about nothing else. It has got so bad that servants in the royal livery are getting booed in London and even my household has mud thrown at their horses. I think Harry will ruin this family in order to please that woman. Worst of all, John Fisher repeated in front of everyone what Harry said to you when you started the whole divorce idea (and how sorry you must be that you did!). Do you remember? 'This marriage of the king and queen is dissolvable by no power, human or divine.' So now, once again, everyone is pointing to you and speaking of your divorce and saying that if you can divorce then so can Harry – why should he not? So it is as bad as I warned you, and people are speaking of you again and Katherine is very upset.*

I say little to James about this letter when he comes home from riding, starving hungry and shouting that dinner must be served at once, as soon as he has washed and changed his clothes. I say only that the legatine court has opened in London and that, no doubt, Archdeacon Magnus will tell us more. It is Henry who asks me, as he sits beside me at dinner: 'Do they speak of us at all?'

'No,' I say. 'Just of my divorce and how Harry was so against it.'

He nods. 'I would rather they did not speak of us.'

I shake my head. 'There is so much scandal attached to the name of Tudor now, I would rather they did not speak of any of us.'

## HOLYROODHOUSE PALACE, EDINBURGH, SCOTLAND, SUMMER 1529

We come back to Edinburgh before making a summer progress up the coast, and meet with the English ambassador.

'You have news from London?' I ask him. 'Have the cardinals decided on the king's great matter?'

'The court is adjourned,' he says. 'Cardinal Campeggio tells us now that it has to be decided in Rome, by the Pope. He says that the legatine court has no authority to rule.'

I am thunderstruck. 'Then why did he come and open it?'

'He gave us to understand that he had authority,' Thomas Magnus says weakly. 'But we think now that he came only to persuade the queen to withdraw to an abbey and take her vows. Since she refuses, he has to take the evidence back to Rome for a decision.'

'But the hearing?'

'It was partial,' he concedes. 'The queen would not be questioned.'

I cannot believe that Katherine defied the Pope's court, she has always been so determinedly obedient to Rome. 'She never refused to appear before two cardinals?'

'She came, and made a speech, and then she left.'

'A speech? She addressed the court?'

'She spoke to her supposed husband the king.'

I don't even address the weasel words of 'supposed husband'. 'Why, what did she say?'

Even James, who is listening to this with half his attention, gently pulling the ears of his deerhound, looks up at this. 'What did the queen say?'

'She knelt to the king,' Magnus says, as if it makes it better. 'She said that when they first married she was a true maid, without touch of man.'

'She said that in court?' James demands, as riveted as I.

'She said that she had been his true wife for twenty years and had never grudged a word or countenance or shown a spark of discontent.'

James is openly laughing at the thought of this ageing woman, on her knees, swearing to her long-ago virginity, but I have a strange, terrible feeling, as if I am going to cry. But why should there be anything in this to bring me to tears?

'Go on! Go on!' says James. 'This is as good as a play.'

'She said some more.' Magnus loses the thread. 'She knelt to him. She was on her knees, her head bowed.'

'Yes, so you said, but what else?'

'She said that if there be any just cause by the law that anyone could say, dishonesty or impediment, then she would go, but if there was none then she beseeched him to let her remain in her former estate and receive justice.'

'My God,' James said, stunned into admiration at last. 'She said all that? Before everyone?'

'Oh, more, and then finally she said that she would be spared the extremity of the court and that she committed her cause to God.'

'Then what?' I clear my throat to ask. My heart is hammering. I cannot think what is the matter with me.

'Then she left.'

'Walked out?'

Magnus nods, unsmiling. 'She curtseyed to the king and she walked out. The king said she should be called back into court and they shouted after her, "Katherine of Aragon, come into court," but she didn't even turn her head, she just walked out. And outside . . .'

'What outside?'

'Outside the women cried out blessings on her, and the men said that she should never have been made to attend. People shouted that it was a shame, shame on the king, that such a wife should be forced to defend herself.'

I rise up from my seat. My heart thumping so rapidly that I think I must be ill. I think of Katherine, confronting Harry the liar – he has been a little liar all his life – and facing him down, before the two cardinals, before the lords, before the men who rule our world, and then curtseying and walking away. How did she dare! What will he do?

'What will he do?' My voice is like a croak. Why can I not speak?

The ambassador looks at me gravely. 'The cardinals will take the cause to the Holy Father for a decision. The king has not advanced his case, but the queen has openly defied him and said that she does not trust his advisors or his court. She has demanded to be treated as Queen of England and said that she is without fault. I don't know what will happen next. I have no instruction, and nothing like this has ever happened in England before.'

'Where is Harry now?'

'He will be going on progress.' The ambassador looks down and clears his throat. 'He is not taking the queen.'

I understand from this that it is a breach, perhaps forever. He is taking Anne Boleyn, the mercer's great-granddaughter, and she will ride beside him in the place of the Infanta of Spain. Harry has deserted Katherine. I understand also what I am feeling in this swirl of emotions. Triumph: that Harry's words against me should be quoted back into his face: take that, you little hypocrite! And yet I am sorry, I am so, so sorry that it has come to this, that Katherine should kneel to him before all the lords of England and declare that she does not trust Harry or them. The fairy-tale marriage that caused me such agonies of jealousy is over, the beautiful princess has been abandoned, and I cannot help but be glad of it. At the same time, I cannot help a measureless grief that Katherine was my sister and now she is alone.

## HOLYROODHOUSE PALACE, EDINBURGH, SCOTLAND, WINTER 1529

Our court is as bright and as cultured as any in Europe. We bring in the greenwood tree in the old Christmas tradition and we have a piper every night and we dance the wild, fast reels of Scotland as well as the courtly dances of France. We have poetry every dinnertime from the great makars, reciting in their booming Scots, poems about freedom and the beauty of the mountains and the stormy seas of the North. We have ballads from the lowland country and love songs and troubadour poems in French and Latin. James loves music as much as his father did, and he will play on his lute for the court and dance all the night. He is a lover of women and drink – just as his father was – and I say nothing against this during the season of Christmas, for every young man goes roistering and whoring at this time of year and every young man is drunk. I did not bring him up to be a saint but to be a king, and I would rather have a son who was an open bawdy lover of women than the tortured secretive man that my brother has become.

James honours the members of his court who have served him well this year, and gives rich gifts to all his favourites. Davy Lyndsay, still in royal service, never failing in his love and loyalty to the baby that I put in his keeping, is knighted and made Lyon King of Arms – a herald of great importance. This is an especially good choice for Davy, who has spent his life studying chivalry and poetry. Who better to represent James with messages to other kings or emperors? James invests the new herald himself and embraces him in public. 'You have been a father to me,' he whispers to him. 'I will never forget it.'

The old man is greatly moved. I kiss his cheeks and find them damp with his tears. 'Our boy is going to be a great king, thanks to your training,' I tell him.

'He is a great king for he is the son of a great queen,' he tells me.

We receive gifts from England, nothing that shows the loving care that Katherine used to put into the yards of silk that she chose for me, or the embroidered shirts she would give James. These courtesy gifts from one court to another come from the master of ceremonies, as part of his duties, not from a woman who loves her sister. I wonder what sort of Christmas Katherine will have now she is still a wife but no longer beloved; still a queen, but badly served. I have a letter from Mary after the twelve days which starts with the most important thing to her. I would laugh if I did not understand that she is describing the unravelling of Harry's court. This is the end of order, the order that my lady grandmother encoded in her great book. This is the end of everything:

*He let her go before me.*

Mary writes with painful simplicity. Almost, I can see her shaking her golden head, seeing again before her Mademoiselle Anne overthrowing the sacred rules of precedence, the order of the nobles, hitching up her skirt and dancing into line before my sister, the sister of the King of England, the Dowager Queen of France.

*Maggie, she went before me. It was the ennobling of her father, a perfectly nice man, I have nothing against him; he served as*

*Cousin Margaret's steward, and he was carver for you – you will remember him. Thomas Boleyn is a good servant of the Crown, I know.*

I can hear Mary retracing her thinking, her unending puzzlement.

*Harry has made him Earl of Ormond, not only that, but also Earl of Wiltshire, which is no honour to Wiltshire I am sure. His son is to be called Viscount Rochford.*

I rest the pages so that I can think. Is this to be her price? Is Harry ennobling the father to buy his daughter's honour? If this is so, then we may be at the end of our ordeal. Her father straps on the order of a double earldom, her mother becomes a bawd and a countess in the same moment, and the brother a viscount and a pimp. Why not? If Anne Boleyn will accept these honours in return for her own much-vaunted maidenhead then we can all be happy again.

*Harry gave them a great dinner to celebrate their ennoblement. Of course the queen could not attend so I took her place and led in the ladies and the Duchess of Norfolk came behind me, and we were all about to go to our usual seats when I saw that the queen's chair was behind the table, beside Harry's, and while I paused, the master of ceremonies led me to a table beside Harry's, and Anne Boleyn (Lady Anne as she is now) walked past me, walked up the steps to the dais and sat beside Harry on his right hand, as if she were queen crowned.*

*The old Duchess of Norfolk and I looked at each other agape like peasants seeing a two-headed pig at a fair. I didn't know what to do or say. Maggie, I have never been so unhappy. I have never been so insulted. I looked across at Charles and he gestured to me to sit and eat and pretend to notice nothing. And so I sat, and SHE SENT OUT A DISH TO ME! She did.*

*She favoured me as if I should be grateful. Harry was watching, he said nothing: neither to stop her, nor to encourage her. She taunted me. I served myself and pretended to eat. I thought that I should be sick of shame. Harry must be mad to treat me so, his own sister. He has put his whore ahead of his wife, he has put her ahead of me – she was my own maid-in-waiting. I think I will die of the dishonour.*

*I wish you a happier Christmas than we will have. Katherine says that she thinks that Anne Boleyn is determined to convert Harry to the reformed religion and then he will not need to consult the Pope or the laws of the Church but only what his conscience tells him. That's all they believe in, these Lutherans. But what conscience can he have?*

## PITLOCHRY, SCOTLAND, SUMMER 1530

Just as my brother is waiting for the Vatican to rule on his application for an annulment, the Holy Father chooses this very moment to send a papal ambassador to visit us. This can be no coincidence, I tell James, as we ride through the wild country north of Scone, the ambassador's big horse labouring behind us, as his excellency admires scenery that is, he tells us, as wild as the Apennine mountains that shield Rome. The Holy Father must be wanting reassurance that whatever heretical books my brother is consulting, whatever challenges he makes to the rule of Rome, that I am, at least, the true child of our sainted grandmother Lady Margaret Beaufort, remaining obedient to papal authority. James, my son, is genuinely devout and opposes the heresies of Luther and even the milder questioning of the German and Swiss reformers. Like many children raised in difficult circumstances, he clings to the certainties of the old world. Having lost an earthly father in infancy and defied a stepfather, he's not going to deny the Pope.

We love these summers, when we ride into the Northern lands that become more rugged and more and more empty the further we travel. Sometimes at sunset the skies are filled with strange rainbows in wild colours, it does not get dark till late, and dawn comes very early. In midsummer there is hardly any night-time at all; the Northern lands are the realms of the white nights and the people revel in summertime and drink and dance and hardly sleep at all for joy in the sunshine.

James – just like his father – takes justice with him wherever we go and holds summary courts and tries and sentences offenders. He is emphatic that the king's peace must run from the lawless Lowland borders to the lawless Highlands. He brings a dream to the Northern clans of a king whose justice will go from the rough northern seas, where a gale is always blowing, to the troubled countries of the Tyne and the Eden. The papal ambassador admires him and says he had no idea of the richness and power of these Northern lands. I have to admit that until I came to Scotland I too knew little of the men and women of these remote places, but I have learned to love and respect them.

'I did not know, for instance,' the ambassador begins in his careful French – then he breaks off for we have come out of a forest and into a meadow beside a wide, deep river and before us is a complete palace of wood, planted in the meadow like a dream house. It is an extraordinary sight, three storeys high with a great turret at each corner, flags flying at each one, and even a gatehouse and a drawbridge that is a tree trunk. As we rein in our horses to exclaim, the drawbridge is lowered over the moat – a diversion of the river which runs, sparkling, all around the castle – and John Stewart the Earl of Atholl comes riding out and, on her palfrey beside him, his lady Grizel Rattray wearing a crown of flowers.

'What is this?' the ambassador asks me in bewilderment.

'This,' says James, grandly, hiding his own surprise, 'this is a summer palace that my loyal friend John Stewart has prepared for us. Please come this way.'

He greets John and the two men laugh together. James slaps him on the back and praises the extraordinary building as her ladyship greets me, and I congratulate her on the creation of such a treasure.

We dismount before the tree-trunk drawbridge, the horses are taken away to the fields and the earl and his countess show us into their pleasure house.

Inside it is more dreamlike than ever, for the ground floors are nothing but the meadow, richly planted with flowers. Upstairs there are bedrooms in each of the four corners of the palace and each bed is built into the wall and planted with camomile, like a scented bower, and thrown with furs. The great hall for dining is heated in the old way with a fire in the centre, and the floor is beaten mud swept to perfect cleanness and polished with the passage of many feet. The high table is on a platform, a few carved wooden steps leading up to it, and the interior glows green with the light of the best wax candles.

I look around me with delight. 'Come and see your room,' the countess says and guides me up the wooden stairs to the chamber that overlooks the river and the hills beyond. Every wall is hung with a tapestry of silk, and every tapestry is a woodland or meadow or riverside scene so it is as if every wall is a window to the countryside beyond. The windows themselves are wooden-framed and made of perfectly clear Venetian glass so that I can look out at the river and see my horse grazing in the water meadows, or close the shutters for warmth.

'This is a wonder!' I say to the countess.

She laughs with pleasure and tosses her head with the crown of flowers and says: 'My lord and I were so honoured that you should come to stay with us that we wanted you to have a palace as good as Holyroodhouse.'

We go down to dine. The fire is lit and the smell of woodsmoke mingles with the scent of roasted meat. They are cooking every sort of bird and three kinds of venison. As we enter the room the household stand to salute us and they raise their shining pewter cups. I sit with James on one side and the ambassador on the other, the Earl of Atholl is on James' far side and his countess at the head of the table of ladies. 'This is truly very fine,' the ambassador says to me in an undertone. 'Very unexpected. What a treasure house in the middle of nowhere. This Earl of Atholl must be very, very wealthy?'

'Yes,' I say. 'But he has not built this palace from wood to prevent James stealing it from him. We are not as they are in England. A great subject may keep his wealth and lands, however grandly he builds.'

'Ah, you mean the poor Cardinal Wolsey,' the ambassador says, shaking his head. 'He made the mistake of living more grandly than the king himself and now the king has taken everything away from him.'

'I don't think it is my brother who is jealous,' I say mildly. 'Harry always said that Wolsey should be rewarded for his work in serving the kingdom. I think you will find it is the lady who now lives in Wolsey's beautiful house of York Place who is behind his downfall.'

The ambassador nods and does not answer. 'The Holy Father is very troubled by this,' he says quietly.

'Indeed, it is the worst thing that might happen,' I reply. 'And I hear that Lady Anne is a Lutheran?'

He looks grave but is too careful to name the favourite as a heretic. 'Do you write to your sister-in-law the queen?'

'I write to my sister, Mary, but the queen has been so distressed and so troubled that I have not added to her worries.'

'She has a new ambassador come from Spain to advise her.'

'She should not need a Spanish ambassador. She is Queen of England,' I say shortly. 'She should be able to trust to English advice.'

He bows. 'Indeed. But since Spain supports her, the Holy

Father must support her too. And there is no certain evidence against her marriage with your brother. If she would only be persuaded to retire. If perhaps you could suggest to her that she might become an abbess, pursue a life of holiness . . . ? Would she listen to you?'

The musicians from the gallery, the chink of glassware, the rumble of talk all suddenly become dim to me, and the brightness of the hall, the tapestries, the carved wood, the flicker and leap of firelight, suddenly fade. I think for a moment what I would say to Katherine, if I were called to advise her. I think how pleasing it would be to me, how smug I would feel if she were to step from public life into the seclusion of an abbey and there were just Mary and me, us two dowager queens, and no Katherine dominating the court. I think how much better my life would have been if she had never leapt up so high, if she had not been Regent of England, if she had not sent the English army to Flodden with orders to take no prisoners but to kill all that they could, if she had never advised Harry against me.

And then I think again. I think of her as Princess of Wales when Arthur died and left her with nothing. I think of my lady grandmother's terrible envy and enmity towards her. I think of how she endured poverty and hardship, living on the fringe of court, turning her dresses and darning her hems, eating badly, served worse, holding onto the calling that she believed came from God – to be Queen of England.

'I would not advise her to give up her crown,' I say simply to the ambassador. 'I would advise no woman to give up anything that she has managed to win. I would advise every woman to work as she can, and gain what she can, and keep it. No woman should be made to surrender her goods or herself. A wise woman will enrich herself as if she were the equal of a man, and a good law would protect her rights, not rob her like an envious husband.'

He smiles at me, very charming, and he shakes his head. 'You would suggest a sisterhood of queens, a sisterhood of women,' he says. 'You would suggest that a woman can rise from the place where God has put her – below her husband in every way. You would overthrow the God-given order.'

'I don't believe that God wants me ill-educated and poor,' I say staunchly. 'I don't believe that God wants any woman in poverty and stupidity. I believe that God wants me in His image, thinking with the brain that He has given me, earning my fortune with the skills that He has given me, and loving with the heart that He has given me.'

The earl's chaplain says grace and we bow our heads for the long prayer.

'I won't argue with you,' the papal ambassador says diplomatically. 'For you speak with the beautiful logic of a beautiful woman, and no man can understand it.'

'And I won't argue with you, for you think that you are paying me a compliment,' I reply. 'I will hold my peace, but I know what I know.'

We stay in the palace of green trees for three days, and every day James and the earl and the ambassador go out hunting. Some days they fish; one day it is so hot that James strips down naked and he and the earl and the court go swimming in the river. I watch them from the window of my bower, terrified that James will be swept away by the water. He is the hope of Scotland, he is the future of the country – I don't like him to be in any danger at all.

On the third day we thank them and say that we have to move on. James kisses the earl and the countess and gives them a gold chain from his own neck. I give her one of my rings. It is not one of my favourites: a ruby from my inheritance.

As we ride away the papal ambassador looks back and exclaims: 'Mother of God!'

We all turn. Where the palace had been tall and turreted there are plumes of smoke from the greenwood and the crackle of fire. Little cracks of gunpowder going off under the walls tell us that the fire has been set to destroy the summer palace. James reins in so that we can watch as the yellow flames greedily run up the dried leaves and little twigs and set the bracken roof alight in moments. Then there is a great roar as the walls catch fire and a crash as the first tower collapses into the heart of the blaze.

'We should go back! We could soak it from the moat!' the papal ambassador cries. 'We could save it.'

James lifts a hand. 'No, it has been fired on purpose. It is the tradition,' he says grandly. 'It's a great sight.'

'A tradition?'

'When a Highland chief gives a great feast he builds the dining hall and when the feast is done he burns everything, tables, chairs, and hall. It will never be used again: it was a singular experience.'

'But the tapestries? The silverware?'

James shrugs, a king to his fingertips. 'All gone. That is the beauty of Highland hospitality: it is total. We were guests of a great lord; he gave us everything. You are in a wealthy kingdom, a kingdom like a fairy tale.'

I think James is going a bit far, but the ambassador crosses himself as if he has just seen a miracle. 'That was a mighty sight,' he says.

'My son is a great king,' I remind him. 'This shows you the esteem of his people.'

I don't doubt for a moment that the countess took down the tapestries and all the valuables. They probably took the windows out before they fired the wooden walls. But it is a great sight, and it has done its work. The papal ambassador will go home to Rome and tell the Pope that my son James can look higher and farther than his cousin Princess Mary. Scotland is a great country, it can ally with whom it chooses. He can tell him also that I will not side with my brother against my sister-in-law. We are fellow queens, we are sisters, that means something.

## STIRLING CASTLE, SCOTLAND, WINTER 1530

James is paying a great deal of attention to Margaret Erskine, a pretty twenty-year-old young woman, the wife of Sir Robert Douglas of Lochleven. I cannot like it. She is undoubtedly the loveliest girl at court and there is a spark about her that sets her apart from all the other young women that James dances with and rides with, and – I suppose – meets in secret for lovemaking. But certainly, she's no commoner to bed and to leave. She is the daughter of Baron Erskine and they are not a family to be trifled with.

'Who says I am trifling?' James asks me with his sideways smile.

'You cannot be doing anything else when you ride into Stirling disguised and kiss the merchants' wives and then tell them you are the king.'

James laughs. 'Oh, I don't stop at kissing.'

'You should stop at kissing, James; you should see, from England, the trouble that a king can get himself into with a woman.'

'I don't get into trouble,' he says. 'I adore Margaret, but also I have a great liking for Elizabeth.'

'Elizabeth who?'

He smiles at me, quite unrepentant. 'Several Elizabeths, actually. But I never forget that I have to marry an ally to the kingdom. And I don't think it will be my cousin Princess Mary.'

'Harry will never put Mary aside, whatever the Pope rules about Katherine. He loves Mary. And see, my marriage was set aside and yet my daughter is not named as a bastard. Margaret is known as Lady Margaret Douglas and received with every respect in London. Princess Mary could keep her title even if her mother is not queen. And her father loves her.'

'He says that he loves Katherine – that won't save her.'

I look blankly at my son. 'I can't think it. I can't imagine England without her as queen.'

'Because for so long you have thought of Queen Katherine as your rival and your model,' he says astutely. 'You have lived in her shadow, but it is all changed now.'

I am struck by my son's perception. 'It was that there were the three of us, all fated to be queens. Sisters and rivals.'

'I know, I see that. But Katherine is not the queen that she was when she sent an army to destroy Scotland. Time has beaten her when the flower of Scotland could not.'

'It's not time,' I say with sudden irritation. 'Time comes against every woman, and every man too. She has not been defeated by time but by the allure of a common rival, the selfishness of my brother, and the weakness of her family, who should have sent an armada the minute that she was exiled from court.'

'But they didn't,' James observes. 'Because she was a woman, and though she was a queen she had no power.'

'Is that all that defends a woman?' I demand. 'Power? What about chivalry? What about the law?'

'Chivalry and the law are what the powerful give to the powerless if they wish,' James replies, a king who was captive for all his childhood. 'No-one of any sense would depend on chivalry. You never did.'

'That's because my husband was my enemy,' I say.

'So is Katherine's.'

James sets me thinking about my daughter Margaret, about little Princess Mary, and about her mother Katherine, my rival, my sister, my other self. If Harry names his daughter as illegitimate then he will have sacrificed his last surviving legitimate child for the Boleyn woman's promises; he will have no legitimate direct heirs at all. I think of Katherine threatening me with hell if I let Margaret be named as illegitimate – I think once again we go hand in hand into danger together: her life is mine, her horrors are mine.

If Harry puts Katherine aside and denies their daughter then my son becomes his heir, and he could be the greatest king that has ever been: the first Tudor–Stewart monarch to rule the united kingdoms, from the westernmost point of Ireland to the northernmost point of Scotland. What a king my son will be! What a kingdom he will rule! Of course my ambition leaps at the thought of it; of course I pray that the Boleyn woman never has a legitimate son to Harry. When the messenger from England brings me a sealed letter from my sister, Mary, I don't expect good news, I don't even know what I hope to read.

*You will have heard that Thomas Wolsey has died under arrest, an example of how far she is prepared to go against a great man of the realm and Harry's former favourite. Now you see her power, can any of us be safe? She designed a masque, a dance, the most terrible thing ever seen at court, any court, I don't care what anyone says. That infamous brother of hers and his friends blacked their faces to look like Moors and danced wildly, indecently. Another player was dressed like the cardinal – poor Thomas Wolsey – and the title was 'Dragging the Cardinal Down to Hell'. It was commissioned and designed by her father and brother for the amusement of the French ambassador. Thank God that they did not perform it before me or our brother. Harry is anguished at the loss of his old friend the cardinal and I think that he has lost the one man in the kingdom who dared to tell him the truth. Certainly, nobody has ever managed the kingdom like Wolsey. There is no-one who can take his place.*

*The queen will hold Christmas at Greenwich and Anne*

*Boleyn is to be there too, with her rival court. Harry will go from one to the other and receive double gifts. It would be a nightmare except that it has gone on so long that we have become accustomed to two warring courts and now it feels normal. The kings of Europe must laugh to see us.*

*Katherine is ill with anxiety and I am sick too. I have some sort of weight in my belly which I am sure is caused by worry about Harry and what is to happen next. Charles says it is a stone and that the Boleyn woman has one where her heart should be. We hear that you are happy and your son safe on his throne. I am glad of it. Pray for us, Maggie, for nothing is good in England this year.*

## STIRLING CASTLE, SCOTLAND, SPRING 1531

I learn what happens next in England from the ambassador, though he is almost struck dumb by the circumstances he should report.

He comes to me in my privy chamber, hoping to avoid any public audience for what he has to say. He bows and says that he will speak to my son presently; he thought he would speak to me first. He almost asks me how he is to broach the subject with James. First he has to consider what he will say to me.

'I have grave news from England,' he begins.

At once, my hand goes to my mouth as I think: is Katherine dead? It is easy to think of her fasting herself to the point of starvation, her hair shirt rubbing her fine skin into infected sores, dying of a broken heart. But then I think: not her; she would never leave her daughter Mary without a protector. She will never retire to a convent or surrender to death. She will never give up on herself or her cause. Harry would have to drag her from the throne, God would have to drag her to heaven; she will never willingly go. Then I think: is Archibald safe? This is a man who has spent his life on the borders between safety and danger, Scotland and England. Where is he now, and what is he doing? These are questions I am never going to ask aloud.

'What news?' I ask levelly. The musicians choose that moment to fall silent and all my ladies, and the pages at my side, and the servants at the cupboard and the doors, wait for his answer. He has to speak out into the quiet room.

'I am sorry to say that the Holy Father has overstepped his authority and made a mistake,' he tells me.

'The Holy Father is in error?' I repeat his heresy.

'Exactly so.'

He had better not try this tack with James. The Pope is guided by God, he cannot make a mistake. But the archdeacon serves a king who says that he too hears God's voice, and that the king hears more clearly than any other; the king knows better than the Pope.

'The Holy Father has finally ruled on the matter of my brother's marriage?' I ask.

He bows. 'No ruling yet, the Holy Father is still considering; but in the meantime, before the ruling is published, he has demanded that the king take up residence with the dowager princess.'

'What? With who?'

The archdeacon all but winks at me to convey his meaning. 'The dowager princess, Katherine of Aragon.'

'The Pope calls her that? Not queen?'

'No, no, it is the king who has said that we must all call the lady by that title. I speak so in obedience to him. He himself calls her his sister.'

'She has lost her title?'

'Yes.'

I absorb this. 'So what does the Holy Father say?'

'That the king must avoid the company of a certain lady.'

'And she is?' As if I don't know.

'Lady Anne Boleyn. The Pope says that the king must renounce her and live with the qu . . . qu—' He bites off the banned word. 'The dowager princess.'

'The Pope is ordering my brother to live with Katherine, though my brother swears that she is not his wife?'

'Quite so. That is why we are considering that the Holy Father has been misinformed and made a mistake.'

'We?'

'England,' he says. 'You too, Your Grace, as an English princess. You are required to call Katherine of Aragon the dowager princess. You are required to say that the Holy Father has made a mistake.'

Levelly, I look at him, as he presumes to tell me what I am to think, what Harry wants me to say.

'His Grace the King of England has decided that the Holy Father cannot rule the Church in England,' the archdeacon goes on, his smooth voice dropping lower on this outrageous news. 'Since the king is ruler in his kingdoms there can be no other ruler. The king is therefore going to be Supreme Head of the Church of England. The Pope is understood to be a bishop, a spiritual ruler, not a worldly one: the Bishop of Rome.'

This is incomprehensible to me. I look quite blankly at him. 'Would you repeat that?'

He does.

'Harry has asked you to tell me this? He is announcing it to all the foreign courts? He is telling the Pope that the Pope does not rule the Church?'

The archdeacon nods as if words fail him too.

'And he has told the Church itself? The clergy?'

'They agree with him.'

'They can't do,' I contradict him. I think of my lady grandmother's confessor. 'Bishop Fisher will never agree. He took his oath to be obedient to the Pope. He won't change that because

Harry does not want the Pope's opinion.' I think of the great churchman, scourge of heretics, Thomas More. 'And others. The Church cannot possibly agree.'

'It is not a question of the Pope's opinion, but of his traditional right,' the archdeacon parrots at me.

'Apparently he had the right to rule when Harry asked him to send a cardinal.'

'Not now, not now,' the archdeacon says.

I look at him with horror. 'This is heresy,' I whisper. 'Worse, it is madness.'

He shakes his head. 'It is the new law,' he says. 'I am hoping to explain to your son the advantages . . .'

'Like what?'

'Tithes,' he mutters. 'The Church's fruits. Pilgrimages, the great riches of the Church. They now belong to the crown in England. If your son came to the same holy decision he too could rule his own Church, he too could be Supreme Head, and then he would receive the Church's wealth. I know the taxes of Scotland are insufficient . . .'

'You want the King of Scotland to deny the Pope too?'

'He would find it an advantage, I feel sure.'

'James is not going to steal from the Church,' I snap. 'James is devout. He's not going to set himself up as a Scottish pope.'

'The king is not setting himself up,' the archdeacon tries to correct me. 'He is restoring the traditional rights of the kings of England.'

'What next?' I demand. 'What other traditional rights? The rule over women? The subjection of Scotland?'

The flicker of his eye as the archdeacon bows in silence tells me that Harry will claim these too if he ever can. That woman has inspired him to be the spoiled boy that he was born to be. I believe she is making a terrible mistake. She is showing Harry his power. Will she also show him where he must stop?

The archdeacon is as unsuccessful with James as I knew he would be.

'He dared to suggest to me that we might reform the Church in Scotland,' my son rages. He comes storming into my privy chamber before dinner when I am alone but for a couple of ladies, one of whom I know for a fact is James' lover. She takes herself off to the window seat and out of hearing. Anything he wants her to know he will tell her later. Now he wants to talk to me.

'The Pope has been a good friend to Scotland,' he says. 'And your brother had no complaint about the rule of Rome until he wanted them to declare his marriage invalid. He is so obvious! He's so shamefully obvious! He's tearing the Church apart so that he can marry his whore.'

I can't argue with my son when he is angry like this.

'And what is going to happen to the Church? Not every clergyman will consent. What is your brother going to do to those who refuse to accept him as Supreme Head? What is going to happen to the monasteries? To the abbeys? What if they don't bow to his rule?'

I find I am trembling. 'Perhaps they will be allowed to retire,' I say. 'The archdeacon said there would be an oath. Everyone will have to take an oath. Perhaps those that don't agree will be allowed to retire.'

James looks at me. 'All of them? You know that can't happen,' he says scornfully. 'Either there's an oath or there isn't. If they won't take the oath then he'll have to call it treason, or heresy to his Church, or both. You know the punishment for treason and heresy.'

'Bishop Fisher will have to leave England,' I whisper. 'He'll have to go away. But he would never leave Katherine without a confessor, without a spiritual advisor.'

'He won't go,' James predicts grimly. 'He's a dead man.'

## SUFFOLK PLACE, LONDON, ENGLAND, SUMMER 1532

*Dear Sister,*

*The supporters of Anne Boleyn – her family who have done so well from her rise and her kinsmen the Howards – have become increasingly unbearable. She has taken up residence in the queen's rooms and she is served like a royal. You can imagine how I feel, seeing her in Katherine's chair, sleeping in Katherine's bed. Now she has ordered that Katherine's jewels be brought from the royal treasure house for her to wear on state occasions. The crown jewels – as if she were a queen crowned.*

*I said out loud what everyone thinks: that you don't make a queen by putting a silk gown on a farmhand's granddaughter. You can put a gold chain on a pig and it still makes nothing but hams. Of course, everyone in our household repeated it and there was some sort of brawl with the Howard servants – as there have been dozens of brawls. And this is not my fault because I only said what everyone says.*

*Anyway, our man Sir William Pennington was getting bested and ran from the fight and took sanctuary in Westminster Abbey, and those brutes of the House of Norfolk ran after him and killed him, killed him before the altar, with his hand on the sacred stone and his blood on the chancery steps. Charles arrested them, and threw them into gaol for breach of sanctuary and murder, but the Howards ran to tell the king that their men were defending the honour of the woman Anne – as if she had any. They have Harry's ear and his attention, they are the new favourites, and now Harry is furious with Charles and me, and I don't know what we're going to do.*

*We've had to leave court – one of our household killed before an altar but it is us who have to leave! We have to wait till it blows over but we have simply no money, we never have enough money, and if Charles is not at court with Harry giving him fees all the time I don't know how we will manage. And anyway, how can I go to court if she is taking precedence and behaving like a queen? I can't give way to her. I can hardly bear to curtsey to her. What if she demands me to attend her in her rooms? Will Harry make me her lady-in-waiting? How terrible does it have to be before he sees that he is breaking my heart and Katherine's spirit, and destroying everything we have ever achieved?*

*They tell me that Christmas was very quiet, the court was at Greenwich, and for the first time ever Katherine was not at court but alone at Wolsey's old house, the More. That's where she lives now. They have sent her away. The Anne woman showered gifts upon Harry but he sent back the gold cup that Katherine gave him. Sent it back, as if she were an enemy.*

*I don't feel well at all but I suppose it is just worry about all this. Your life, so far away from England and with a good son and a loving husband, seems better than mine. Who would have thought that I would ever envy you? Who would have thought that we would both be happier than Katherine? Pray for us, your unhappy sisters.*

*Mary*

*And . . . they say that Thomas More will have to resign as Lord Chancellor for he cannot bring himself to swear that Harry is true head of the Church. Harry is tender for Thomas's conscience and says that he can leave high office and live privately. How many of us are going to have to leave court and live privately when that woman comes in as queen?*

## JEDBURGH, SCOTLAND, AUTUMN 1532

I ride south to the borders, to join James. He is holding courts, executing sheep stealers and cattle rustlers, regardless of whether they come from the south or the north of the border, promising war with England.

'I will have peace in the borderlands,' he says tersely. 'I will not stop till I get the English out of our sheepfolds and our towers.'

'This isn't the way to do it,' I say gently. 'You cannot frighten people into peace.'

'That was the Douglas way,' he observes.

'It was.'

'Do you ever think of him?'

I smile and shake my head, as if I am deeply uninterested in Ard: 'Hardly ever.'

'You know I have to make the borders safe.'

'I do, and I think you are the king that will do it. But don't threaten Harry with war. He will only bluster back. He has more troubles in his life than he can solve. If he continues to declare against the Pope, to insult the aunt of the emperor, he will find himself named a heretic king and all the Catholic kings will be authorised to make war on him. That is when you should declare against him. Not before. And now, while he is getting a reputation so terrible that kings will shrink from him – this is the time that you should negotiate with him for whatever you want.'

'I thought you were an English princess and the Tudors would always come first,' James remarks. 'You've changed your tune.'

'I came here to bring peace between England and Scotland, but Harry has made it impossible,' I say frankly. 'Again and again I have been loyal to him, but he has not been loyal to me, nor to my sister, nor to my sister-in-law, his wife. I think he has become a man that no-one can trust.'

'That's true,' James nods.

'He has moved my sister-in-law to a little house at Bishop's Hatfield and forbidden her daughter from seeing her. He has put a whore in my mother's rooms. He has gone too far. I cannot support my brother, I have to cleave to my sisters. I cannot be on his side.'

James looks at me, measuring my intent. 'Yet when he calls for you, you'll go running to him.'

'Not this time,' I say. 'Not ever again.'

## WESTHORPE HALL, ENGLAND, AUTUMN 1532

*Harry is preparing another state visit to France and is spending a fortune on gowns and jewels, horses and jousts to impress Francis of France (ransomed home but proud as ever). I have said I am too ill to go, I cannot bear the thought of it and I have such a heaviness in my belly and my bowels that I truly am too ill to face it. I couldn't dance at such a feast, my feet would not lift. When I think of the Field of the Cloth of Gold when we were so young and so happy! I could not sail to France again with a shameless woman in the place of the true queen.*

*Harry does not think of taking Katherine, he has not even seen her this year. He sends her the coldest of messages and she has to move house again and go to Enfield, because so many people are visiting her that Harry is shamed. I write to her, but Charles says that I may not go. It would displease Harry too much and I have to show loyalty to him, my brother and king, before anyone else. I have to greet the Boleyn woman with the respect due to the greatest woman in the land. I don't dare say a word against her. I do it. I do everything that Harry and Charles ask of me, with a heart like stone, and when she sends out a dish to me I pretend to eat while my stomach turns over.*

*She is all smiles. All smiles and glitter in Katherine's jewels. She shines like poison.*

*I have not seen Katherine for ten months, not for all this year, and I used to see her almost every day. She does not write to me often, she says that there is nothing for her to say. There is this terrible gulf in my life where she used to be. It is as if she were dead, as if my brother had wiped her from the face of the earth. You will think I am exaggerating but I truly feel that Harry has killed her – as if a king could execute a queen!*

*At any rate, I shall not go to France with the woman Anne. None of us will. And I hear that none of the royal ladies of France will greet her. How can they? She is Harry's mistress and her father has a title so new that no-one can remember it and everyone still calls him Sir Thomas out of habit. The only companions she can command are those who support her ambition: her sister, her sister-in-law, and her mother – and the gossips say that Harry has had all three of them. They are hated all round England. She and Harry had to come home early from this year's progress because she was booed whenever she was seen.*

*I swear that sometimes I wake in the morning and I forget that all this has happened. I think Harry is a handsome king new-come to his throne, Katherine a beloved queen and his most trusted advisor, and I am a girl again, and for a moment I am happy, and then I remember and I am filled with such a terrible sickness that I retch up bile as green as envy. Thank God that our dear mother died before seeing this woman sitting in her place and bringing such shame on our sister, on us and on our name.*

*Mary*

## HOLYROODHOUSE PALACE, EDINBURGH, SCOTLAND, WINTER 1532

Davy Lyndsay comes to court for a poetry joust. We hold a 'flyting', when one poet laughingly abuses another in a stream of extempore insults. James is witty and he has the court roaring at his abuse of his companion, complaining of everything from his terrible snoring to outrageous claims that he gets his rhymes from a book. Davy replies with a strong complaint about James' promiscuity. I clap my hands over my ears and say that I will hear no more, but James laughs and says Davy says no worse than the truth and that he must be married or he will repopulate the barren Marches with little Jameses.

When the laughter and poetry have finished there is dancing and Davy comes to kiss my hand and watch the dancers at my side. 'He's no worse than any young man,' I say.

'I am sorry to disagree with you,' Davy says. 'But he is. Every night he rides out to visit a woman in the town or outside it, and when he doesn't go beyond the palace walls he's with one of the serving maids or even with one of the ladies. He's a coney, Your Grace.'

'He's very handsome,' I say indulgently. 'And he's a young man. I know my ladies flirt with him, how should he refuse them?'

'He should be married,' Davy says.

I nod. 'I know. It's true.'

'The Princess Mary will never do for him,' Davy says determinedly. 'I am sorry to pass a comment on your family, Your Grace, but your niece will not do. Her title cannot be relied upon. Her position is not certain.'

I cannot disagree any more. Harry did not take his own legitimate daughter with him on a state visit to France; he took his bastard boy, Henry Fitzroy, and left him there on a visit with the King of France's own children, as if he were a born prince. Nobody can be sure what title Henry Fitzroy will be given next, but Harry looks as if he is preparing him to be royal. Nobody can be sure that Princess Mary will keep her title; nobody even knows if you can take a title from a princess. No king, in the history of the world, has tried to do such a thing before.

'She was born with royal blood. Nobody can deny that.'

'Alas,' is all he says.

We are silent for a minute.

'Do you hear of your own daughter, Lady Margaret?' Davy asks gently.

'Archibald will not let her come to me. He's put her in service to Lady Anne Boleyn.' I feel my mouth twist with contempt, and I smooth out my expression. 'She is high in favour with the king her uncle. It is said to be an enviable position.'

'Young James wants to marry the French king's daughter,' Davy remarks. 'It's been considered for years, she has a handsome dowry and it is the Auld Alliance.'

'Harry won't like it,' I predict. 'He won't want France meddling in the affairs of Scotland.'

'No need for them to meddle,' Davy asserts. 'She comes to be his wife, she's not a regent. And we need the money she would bring. You won't get a dowry like hers from Scots girls like Margaret Erskine!'

'Princess Madeleine of France it is then,' I say. 'Unless we hear good news from England.'

Davy Lyndsay looks at me with a wry smile. 'You hope for good news from England?'

'Not really, not any more. I never have good news from England any more.'

## HOLYROODHOUSE PALACE, EDINBURGH, SCOTLAND, SPRING 1533

We don't have good news. Harry himself writes to me in the New Year:

> *Sister,*
>
> *It is with great pleasure that I write to tell you that I am married to the Marquess of Pembroke, Lady Anne Boleyn, a lady of unimpeachable virtue and reputation, who has consented to be my wife, as my previous alliance was no marriage – as every scholar now agrees. Queen Anne will be crowned in June. The Dowager Princess of Wales will live quietly in the country. Her daughter, Lady Mary, will be a respected lady and serve in the queen's rooms.*

## LINLITHGOW PALACE, SCOTLAND, SUMMER 1533

It is over then, I think.

It is over, all over, for Katherine. My rival and my sister, my enemy and my friend, is finished with this final blow to her pride, her name, her very being. They move her again, this time to an old, ill-kept bishop's palace, Buckden in Cambridgeshire, with a reduced household and too small an allowance to maintain her position as queen. She is poor again, just as she was when she was eating old fish. I hear that she still wears a hair shirt under her gowns, and now she patches her sleeves and turns her hems. But this time she cannot draw on her credit and her youthful courage and hope for better days. She is alone. Her confessor, Bishop Fisher, is under house arrest, her daughter kept from her. Lady Mary is not allowed to see her mother; she cannot even go to court unless she curtseys to Anne Boleyn as queen.

She is her mother's daughter.

She won't do that.

I am in a better place than both my sisters. I cling to this little joy, as stubborn as when we were girls jockeying for supremacy. I am married to a good man, I am seated in my little stone room at the top of my castle, I can see my country at peace, around me, and my son is recognised king. I wish I had said goodbye to Katherine, I did not even know that I should say goodbye to Mary until I got her letter:

*Dear Sister,*

*The pain in my belly is worse; I can feel a growth and I cannot eat, they doubt that I will see Christmas. I was spared the coronation – the wedding was held in secret because her belly was growing – and I doubt that I will see the birth of the Boleyn bastard. God forgive me but I pray that she miscarries and that the swelling of her belly is a stone like mine. I write to Katherine but they read my letters and she cannot reply, so I don't know how she is. For the first time in my life I don't know how she is and I have not seen her for nearly two years.*

*It seems to me now that we were three girls together with so much to hope for, and that it is a hard world that has brought the three of us to this. When men have authority over women, women can be brought very low – and they will be brought very low. We spent our time admiring and envying each other and we should have been guiding and protecting each other. Now I am dying, you are living with a man not your husband, your true husband is your enemy, your daughter is estranged from you, and Katherine has lost her battle against the prince she married for love. What is the point of love if it does not make us kind? What is the point of being sisters if we do not guard each other? M.*

# AUTHOR'S NOTE

As the book list shows, there are few biographies about Margaret, Dowager Queen of Scotland. Many accounts of her are frankly hostile. She suffers (as do so many women in history) from being so slightly recorded that we often don't know what she was doing and we almost never know what she was thinking. The jigsaw of history gives a picture of abrupt changes of course and loyalties, and so many historians have assumed that she must have been either incompetent or irrational. They explain this by suggesting that she was in the grip of megalomania or lust, or more simply (and traditionally) a typical changeable woman.

Of course, I reject the concept of a 'nature' of women (especially if it is said to be morally and intellectually weak), and in the case of Margaret, I think she was, without doubt, more thoughtful and strategic than the she-wolf/dolt model of female behaviour. This novel suggests that Margaret probably did the best she could in circumstances which were beyond many people – male and female. Everyone seeking power in Europe in the late medieval period changed loyalties with remarkable speed and lack of honour. For Margaret, like her male enemies and friends, the only way to survive was to change her allies, plot against her enemies, and move as swiftly and as unexpectedly as she could.

She was born in 1489 as the second-oldest child of the arranged marriage of Elizabeth of York – a Plantagenet of the former royal family – and Henry Tudor, the victor of the battle of Bosworth, and I believe that this sense of being the first generation born to a new dynasty was as powerful for her as for her better-known brother Henry VIII, giving them both a sense of self-importance and insecurity. I think she may always have had a sense of her own significance, as the oldest Tudor girl, and of inferiority: as a female and not one of the important Tudor male heirs. She was the plainer older sister to a child who was to become a famous beauty, and then a young wife to a much older husband in a marriage arranged for political gain.

I wrote her story in a fictional form, in first person present tense, because I wanted to be able to draw on this psychological explanation and show it in her character. I wanted to describe her inner experience of three marriages, of which only the outward show is recorded. There is no account of what she felt when she lost the custody of her daughter Margaret, nor how she felt leaving her son James, nor her grief at the death of Alexander. The rules of writing history mean that a historian can only speculate about her emotions; but a novelist is allowed, indeed, obliged to recreate a version of them. This is where historical fiction – the hybrid form – does something that I find profoundly interesting – takes the historical record and turns it inside out; the inner world explains the outer record.

Some scenes in this novel are history. Margaret's arrival at Stirling Castle with her husband's bastards bouncing out to greet her is directly drawn from Maria Perry's biography:

> Margaret, who must have heard stories of her husband's 'past', was taken aback to find her dower castle was used as a nursery for the King's illegitimate children. There were seven in all. (Perry p 45)

Margaret's husband's devout religious observance, sense of guilt and zestful promiscuity were reported too. It was the tragedy of her young life when he was killed at Flodden, and the theft of his body as a trophy is true, and was indeed ordered by Margaret's sister-in-law, Katherine of Aragon.

It's a tragic piece of history but completely inspiring for a novelist! Thinking of Katherine issuing an order of no prisoners – in effect, an order to murder the wounded and men trying to surrender – against her sister-in-law's husband inspired me to tell this novel as the story of three sisters: the beautiful and indulged Dowager Queen of France, the well-known Katherine of Aragon, whose reign started with such hopes and ended in sorrow, and the almost-unknown Margaret, whose life was a struggle for political power and personal happiness.

With this in mind I was struck by how their histories intertwined and reflected each other. They all three experienced arranged marriages, were widowed, and remarried the men of their choice. They all three lost children in infancy. They all three depended on the goodwill of Henry VIII, they all three fell from his favour, all three were threatened by the rise of Anne Boleyn. They were all born princesses, but experienced debt and even poverty. They met as three girls before Katherine's marriage, and then again as women who had been widowed when Margaret returned to London; they worked together when they pleaded for the apprentices.

It is an unusual Tudor woman who hoped for love in marriage. Social historians would say that elite marriages were almost all arranged contracts until the 18th century. But in Margaret and her sister Mary we see two Tudor women – indeed Tudor princesses – with powerful romantic ambitions acting independently, even defying their male guardians. Margaret was a strikingly modern woman in her desire to marry for love, to divorce an unsatisfactory husband and marry again, and still hope to retain political power and the custody of her children. That she managed to do any of this in a world where the law and the Church were designed to serve men, in a country which was violent and dangerous, at a time when neither Scotland nor England had ever had a ruling queen, is a testament not to irrationality but to determination, ability and passion.

Margaret's feelings towards her three husbands can only be a matter of speculation in the absence of any personal record. I suggest that she came to love the husband who made her queen and perhaps grieved deeply for his loss. Certainly, it is said that she never spoke of him publicly after his death. That she was deeply and disastrously in love with Archibald Douglas is demonstrated by her recorded actions – the private marriage, the attempt to promote him to the council, and their reconciliations. Their nightmare flight to England was as I describe, but why he stayed in Scotland and whether he intended to be unfaithful to her from the very beginning of their married life is something that historians don't yet know, and may never discover. We know that he called Janet Stewart his wife, and that they had a daughter who took his name; but he returned more than once to Margaret. In the novel I suggest that she was always drawn to him, despite his infidelity and disloyalty; certainly we know that she was thinking of him on her deathbed:

> I desire you . . . to beseech the King to be gracious to the Earl of Angus. I beg God for mercy that I have so offended the Earl. (Henry VIII, *Letters and Papers*, Vol. 16, October 1541, 1307)

My thanks go to the historians who have explored this wonderful character and her times; following is a list of the books that I studied in order to write this fictional portrayal of Margaret. I also visited her principal houses and I highly recommend a visit to the castles and palaces of Scotland. Ruined or restored, they are truly beautiful, a fitting backdrop to the story of such a complex and interesting woman.

# BIBLIOGRAPHY

Alexander, Michael Van Cleave, *The First of the Tudors: A Study of Henry VII and his Reign* (London, Croom Helm, 1981, first published 1937)

Anderson, William, *The Scottish Nation; or The Surnames, Families, Literature, Honours, and Biographical History of the People of Scotland: Vol. I* (Edinburgh, Fullarton, 1867)

Bacon, Francis, *The History of the Reign of King Henry VII and Selected Works* (Cambridge, Cambridge University Press, 1998)

Barrell, A. D. M., *Medieval Scotland* (Cambridge, Cambridge University Press, 2000)

Bernard, G. W., *The Tudor Nobility* (Manchester, Manchester University Press, 1992)

Besant, Walter, *London in the Time of the Tudors* (London, Adam & Charles Black, 1904)

Bingham, Caroline, *James V: King of Scots* (London, Collins, 1971)

Buchanan, Patricia Hill, *Margaret Tudor Queen of Scots* (Edinburgh, Scottish Academic Press, 1985)

Carroll, Leslie, *Inglorious Royal Marriages: A Demi-Millennium of Unholy Mismatrimony* (New York, New American Library, 2014)

Cavendish, George, and Lockyer, Roger, editor, *Thomas Wolsey, Late Cardinal: His Life and Death* (London, The Folio Society, 1962, first published 1810)

Chapman, Hester W., *The Sisters of Henry VIII* (London, Jonathan Cape, 1969)

Chrimes, S. B., *Henry VII* (London, Eyre Methuen, 1972)

Claremont, Francesca, *Catherine of Aragon* (London, Robert Hale, 1939)

Clarke, Deborah, *The Palace of Holyroodhouse: Official Souvenir Guide* (London, Royal Collection Trust, 2012)

Cooper, Charles Henry, *Memoir of Margaret: Countess of Richmond and Derby* (Cambridge, Cambridge University Press, 1874)

Cox, Adrian, *Linlithgow Palace: Official Souvenir Guide* (Edinburgh, Historic Scotland, 2010)

Cunningham, Sean, *Henry VII* (London, Routledge, 2007)

Dawson, Jane E. A., *Scotland Re-Formed 1488–1587* (Edinburgh, Edinburgh University Press, 2007)

Dixon, William Hepworth, *History of Two Queens: Volume II* (London, Hurst and Blackett, 1873)

Donaldson, Gordon, *Scotland: James V to James VII* (Edinburgh, Oliver & Boyd, 1965)

Douglas, Gavin, and Small, John, *The Poetical Works of Gavin Douglas, Bishop of Dunkeld, with Memoir, Notes and Glossary by John Small, M.A., F.S.A.Scot.: Volume First* (Edinburgh, William Paterson, 1874)

Elton, G. R., *England Under the Tudors* (London, Methuen, 1955)

Fellows, Nicholas, *Disorder and Rebellion in Tudor England* (Bath, Hodder & Stoughton Educational, 2001)

Goodwin, George, *Fatal Rivalry: Flodden 1513; Henry VIII, James IV and the Battle for Renaissance Britain* (London, Weidenfeld & Nicolson, 2013)

Gregory, Philippa, Baldwin, David, and Jones, Michael, *The Women of the Cousins' War: The Duchess, the Queen and the King's Mother* (London, Simon & Schuster, 2011)

Gunn, Steven, *Charles Brandon: Henry VIII's Closest Friend* (Stroud, Amberley, 2015)

Guy, John, *Tudor England* (Oxford, Oxford University Press, 1988)

Harris, George, *James IV: Scotland's Renaissance King* (London, Amazon, 2013)

Harvey, Nancy Lenz, *Elizabeth of York: Tudor Queen* (London, Arthur Barker, 1973)

Hay, Denys, *Europe in the Fourteenth and Fifteenth Centuries: Second Edition* (New York, Longman, 1989, first published 1966)

Hutchinson, Robert, *Young Henry: The Rise of Henry VIII* (London, Weidenfeld & Nicolson, 2011)

Innes, Arthur D., *England Under the Tudors* (London, Methuen, 1905)

Jones, Michael K., and Underwood, Malcolm G., *The King's Mother: Lady Margaret Beaufort, Countess of Richmond and Derby* (Cambridge, Cambridge University Press, 1992)

Jones, Philippa, *The Other Tudors: Henry VIII's Mistresses and Bastards* (London, New Holland, 2009)

Kesselring, K. J., *Mercy and Authority in the Tudor State* (Cambridge, Cambridge University Press, 2003)

Kramer, Kyra C., *Blood Will Tell: A Medical Explanation of the Tyranny of Henry VIII* (Indiana, Ash Wood Press, 2012)

Licence, Amy, *Elizabeth of York: The Forgotten Tudor Queen* (Stroud, Amberley, 2013)

Licence, Amy, *In Bed with the Tudors: The Sex Lives of a Dynasty from Elizabeth of York to Elizabeth I* (Stroud, Amberley, 2012)

Lindesay, Robert, *The History of Scotland: From 21 February, 1436 to March, 1565* (Edinburgh, Baskett, 1728)

Lisle, Leanda de, *Tudor: The Family Story* (London, Chatto & Windus, 2013)

Loades, David, *Henry VIII and his Queens* (Stroud, Sutton, 2000)

Loades, David, *Henry VIII: Court, Church and Conflict* (London, The National Archives, 2007)

Loades, David, *Mary Rose: Tudor Princess, Queen of France, the Extraordinary Life of Henry VIII's Sister* (Stroud, Amberley, 2012)

Macdougall, Norman, *James IV* (Edinburgh, John Donald, 1989)

Mackay, Lauren, *Inside the Tudor Court: Henry VIII and his Six Wives through the writings of the Spanish Ambassador, Eustace Chapuys* (Stroud, Amberley, 2014)

Mattingly, Garrett, *Catherine of Aragon* (London, Jonathan Cape, 1942, first published 1941)

Murphy, Beverley A., *Bastard Prince: Henry VIII's Lost Son* (Stroud, Sutton, 2001)

Newcombe, D. G., *Henry VIII and the English Reformation* (London, Routledge, 1995)

Paul, John E., *Catherine of Aragon and her Friends* (London, Burns & Oates, 1966)

Perry, Maria, *Sisters to the King: The Tumultuous Lives of Henry VIII's Sisters – Margaret of Scotland and Mary of France* (London, André Deutsch, 1998)

Plowden, Alison, *House of Tudor* (London, Weidenfeld & Nicolson, 1976)

Porter, Linda, *Crown of Thistles: The Fatal Inheritance of Mary Queen of Scots* (London, Macmillan, 2013)

Reed, Conyers, *The Tudors: Personalities & Practical Politics in 16th Century England* (Oxford, Oxford University Press, 1936)

Reese, Peter, *Flodden: A Scottish Tragedy* (Edinburgh, Birlinn, 2013)

Ridley, Jasper, *The Tudor Age* (London, Constable, 1988)

Sadler, John, and Serdiville, Rosie, *The Battle of Flodden 1513* (Stroud, The History Press, 2013)

Scarisbrick, J. J., *Henry VIII* (London, Eyre Methuen, 1968)

Searle, Mark, and Stevenson, Kenneth, *Documents of the Marriage Liturgy* (New York, Pueblo, 1992)

Seward, Desmond, *The Last White Rose: Dynasty, Rebellion and Treason* (London, Constable, 2010)

Sharpe, Kevin, *Selling the Tudor Monarchy: Authority and Image in 16th Century England* (London, Yale University Press, 2009)

Simon, Linda, *Of Virtue Rare: Margaret Beaufort, Matriarch of the House of Tudor* (Boston, Houghton Mifflin, 1982)

Simons, Eric N., *Henry VII: The First Tudor King* (New York, Muller, 1968)

Smith, Lacey Baldwin, *Treason in Tudor England: Politics & Paranoia* (London, Jonathan Cape, 1986)

Soberton, Sylvia Barbara, *The Forgotten Tudor Women: Margaret Douglas, Mary Howard & Mary Shelton* (North Charleston, CreateSpace, 2015)

Starkey, David, *Henry: Virtuous Prince* (London, HarperPress, 2008)

Starkey, David, *Six Wives: The Queens of Henry VIII* (London, Chatto & Windus, 2003)

Thomas, Paul, *Authority and Disorder in Tudor Times, 1485–1603* (Cambridge, Cambridge University Press, 1999)

Thomson, Oliver, *The Rises & Falls of the Royal Stewarts* (Stroud, The History Press, 2009)

Vergil, Polydore, and Ellis, Henry, editor, *Three Books of Polydore Vergil's English History: Comprising the Reigns of Henry VI, Edward IV and Richard III* (London, Camden Society, 1844)

Warnicke, Retha M., *The Rise and Fall of Anne Boleyn* (Cambridge, Cambridge University Press, 1989)

Weir, Alison, *Elizabeth of York: The First Tudor Queen* (London, Jonathan Cape, 2013)

Weir, Alison, *Henry VIII: King and Court* (London, Jonathan Cape, 2001)

Weir, Alison, *The Lost Tudor Princess: A Life of Margaret Douglas, Countess of Lennox* (London, Vintage, 2015)

Weir, Alison, *The Six Wives of Henry VIII* (London, Bodley Head, 1991)

White, Robert, *The Battle of Flodden, Fought 9 Sept. 1513* (Newcastle-upon-Tyne, The Society of Antiquaries of Newcastle-upon-Tyne, 1859)

Williams, Patrick, *Katharine of Aragon: The Tragic Story of Henry VIII's First Unfortunate Wife* (Stroud, Amberley, 2013)

Wilson, Derek, *In the Lion's Court: Power, Ambition and Sudden Death in the Reign of Henry VIII* (London, Hutchinson, 2001)

Yeoman, Peter, *Edinburgh Castle: Official Souvenir Guide* (Edinburgh, Historic Scotland, 2014)
Yeoman, Peter, and Owen, Kirsty, *Stirling Castle, Argyll's Lodging and Mar's Wark: Official Souvenir Guide* (Edinburgh, Historic Scotland, 2011)

## JOURNALS

Dewhurst, John, 'The Alleged Miscarriages of Catherine of Aragon and Anne Boleyn', *Medical History*, Vol. 28, Iss. 1 (1984): 49–56
Whitley, Catrina Banks, and Kramer, Kyra, 'A new explanation for the reproductive woes and midlife decline of Henry VIII', *The Historical Journal*, Vol. 53, Iss. 4 (2010): 827–848

## OTHER

Henry VIII: *Letters and Papers*, accessed online: http://www.british-history.ac.uk/search/series/letters-papers-hen8

# GARDENS FOR THE GAMBIA

Philippa Gregory visited The Gambia, one of the driest and poorest countries of sub-Saharan Africa, in 1993 and paid for a well to be hand-dug in a village primary school at Sika. Now – more than 200 wells later – she continues to raise money and commission wells in village schools, community gardens and in The Gambia's only agricultural college. She works with her representative in The Gambia, headmaster Ismaila Sisay, and their charity now funds pottery and batik classes, bee-keeping and adult literacy programmes.

GARDENS FOR THE GAMBIA is a registered charity in the UK and a registered NGO in The Gambia. Every donation, however small, goes to The Gambia without any deductions. If you would like to learn more about the work that Philippa calls 'the best thing that I do', visit her website www.PhilippaGregory.com and click on GARDENS FOR THE GAMBIA where you can make a donation and join with Philippa in this project.

*'Every well we dig provides drinking water for a school of about 600 children, and waters the gardens where they grow vegetables for the school dinners. I don't know of a more direct way to feed hungry children and teach them to farm for their future.'*

Philippa Gregory